"FORCEFUL, BRUTAL, GRITTY . . .
complex characters and unyielding tension."
—Elmer Kelton,
author of *The Wolf and the Buffalo*

"An unforgettable picture of a time and place not so distant as it seems." —*Kirkus Reviews*

"EXCITING . . . a strong novel embedded in reality . . . unrelenting as a prairie fire."
—*Fort Worth Star-Telegram*

"CONVINCING AND MEMORABLE WESTERN FICTION."
—*Amarillo News-Globe*

"VIVID . . . SPELLBINDING . . . you can't stop reading!" —*South Bend Tribune*

"EXCITING . . . WONDERFUL . . . full of adventure, courage, and convincing characters." —*Anniston Star*

"A novel about the *real* west . . . about fighting and dying for the future . . . anyone who loves true western action will thrill at this book." —*Ocala Star-Banner*

CLAY REYNOLDS

FRANKLIN'S CROSSING

SIGNET
Published by the Penguin Group
Penguin Books USA Inc., 375 Hudson Street,
New York, New York 10014, U.S.A.
Penguin Books Ltd, 27 Wrights Lane,
London W8 5TZ, England
Penguin Books Australia Ltd, Ringwood,
Victoria, Australia
Penguin Books Canada Ltd, 10 Alcorn Avenue,
Toronto, Ontario, Canada M4V 3B2
Penguin Books (N.Z.) Ltd, 182–190 Wairau Road,
Auckland 10, New Zealand

Penguin Books Ltd, Registered Offices:
Harmondsworth, Middlesex, England

Published by Signet, an imprint of New American Library,
a division of Penguin Books USA Inc. Previously appeared in a Dutton edition.

First Signet Printing, April, 1993
10 9 8 7 6 5 4 3 2 1

Printed in the United States of America

PUBLISHER'S NOTE
This is a work of fiction. Names, characters, places, and incidents either are the product of the author's imagination or are used fictitiously, and any resemblance to actual persons, living or dead, events, or locales is entirely coincidental.

For Wesley, my son, the best of all possible boys, and Virginia, my daughter, whose laughter keeps the darkness at bay, and for Judy, my wife, who helps me understand and believe in myself

—and for Ethan, who sticks by me

This is a pretty country, but you white men take it away from us. The only thing this country is good for is red ants, coyotes, and cattle men.

—QUANAH PARKER

The only good Indian I ever saw was dead.

—WILLIAM TECUMSEH SHERMAN
(attributed)

PART ONE

THE SCOUT

CHAPTER ONE

1

MOSES FRANKLIN STOPPED HIS BAY ATOP A SHORT RISE of ground along the upper edge of a deep arroyo, lifted his hat, and scratched his head as he surveyed the rolling carpet of grass that lay before him. The horizon was broken only by the odd mesa or widely spaced clump of juniper or scrub cedar in the shimmering distance. He was too far away to tell if one of the flat mesas supported a small copse of pecan trees that marked the crossing for which he searched. Under a seamless sky so blue that it appeared to be transparent, the tall grass waved beneath a gentle spring breeze. In places where the prairie rose a bit, bright blues, reds, and yellows of wildflowers broke the tan landscape in a dazzling display which would have delighted the human eye under ordinary circumstances. But to the experienced vision of the Negro scout, who now pulled a canteen from his tack and unscrewed the top for a brief sip, the flowers were foreboding. He knew they meant that spring—Comanche Spring—wasn't yet over.

Replacing his canteen on its thong, he readjusted his .55-caliber Springfield "High Hammer" across his saddle and continued to study the terrain before him for familiar signs. There were none, and his forehead wrinkled. With a late spring he didn't expect to see the usual great herds of buffalo traversing the southwestern prairies, but there should have been some deer and antelope, lots of antelope. He had seen no game at all for several days. In fact, he recalled as he stood up in his stirrups and strained to see as far as he could, he hadn't spotted much game at all since leaving Saint Jo three weeks before. That worried him, for if he was confused, he knew the Comanche, who depended on the buffalo and antelope for life itself, were also. And if, as Moses suspected, white men were somehow at the bottom of the game's—particularly the buffalo's—disappearance, then the Comanche were going to be more than confused. They were going to be plenty angry.

He removed his hat once again and placed it on the saddle's pommel while he untied a bandanna and wiped a blanket of sweat from his brow. It wasn't hot, or anything like hot, but he had been sweating consistently all morning. His skin tingled in fear of what he knew lurked beyond—or perhaps in—the buffalo grass that caressed his horse's belly. A quiet, hollow terror had taken up residence in his chest ever since the wagon train in the arroyo behind him had struggled across the Pease River two days ago. It had not eased any as he continued to guide them north and west toward the creek ford, where he knew fresh water and fish would be available to provision them for the next leg of their journey to Santa Fe.

This was his fifth excursion across the North Texas plains in as many years, his fifth attempt to guide a wagon train safely from East Texas to the next jumping-off place for points west. Normally, he tried to be across the Pease by the first of April, to be high up on the Canadian by the middle of May. But the vomiting sickness had hit this train on the banks of the Trinity, delaying them for a month, and it was late April before they even got past Saint Jo, the last real town between the cattle trails of East Texas and the Pease. Moses knew well that the tribes who ruled the hunting ground between the "Indian Line" that ran from the abandoned community of Henrietta on the Red River all the way down to Mexico would no longer be safely north in Kansas and Indian Territory. By now they would have ranged along their traditional paths south, after the herds and cattle and horses of white settlements just west of the safety of the Army's forts. Unless he could move the wagons rapidly across the Southern Plains, he knew he stood to lose everything.

Ideally and with luck, he could still have made a relatively safe trip of it. By hugging the Prairie Dog Town Fork of the Red River and camping in the arroyos and gullies that ran near the sandy river until they climbed up onto the treeless tabletop of the plains, he felt he could avoid all but small hunting parties. And if they could make the barren flatness of the eastern Llano Estacado and the banks of the Canadian by June, he believed, they could ease their way into the barren wastes of New Mexico north of Fort Sumner. Then the short run to Santa Fe could be done quickly and in relative safety.

But he had had no luck at all, and the search for fresh water and game had led them more and more south. They had moved in a kind of weird tacking motion from Saint Jo to abandoned Henrietta, across the forks of the Wichita to the Pease, a motion that ate up days and eventually placed the wagon train directly in the path of the migrating buffalo and the Comanche. Only there weren't any buffalo, and Moses upbraided himself for even thinking of undertaking such a dangerous journey so late in the season.

In his previous expeditions, aside from the odd hunting party of Wichita or Cherokee and the skulking, hostile Kiowa, he had rarely seen any Indians at all. Even when he made his way back after delivering his trains safely to Santa Fe, he rarely saw any fresh signs. By late summer, they were way over to the southwest, along the border of southern New Mexico, where the alkali flats forbade enough water and game to sustain life for long. From those inhospitable climes, he knew, the Comanche would raid towns and individual ranches. Then they would disappear up onto the flat emptiness of a wasteland that was marked by so few recognizable landmarks that even veteran travelers often became confused and lost.

This year, however, the game's disappearance was matched by the oddness of the weather. Almost every night, just as the sun dipped beyond the mesas on the horizon, great thunderheads swarmed out of the southwest and angrily bombarded the train with hail and quick, drenching rain. That made camping in depressions and arroyos dangerous, which meant that they had spent almost every night on the open prairie with the thirty wagons drawn up tight together and weary men sitting atop them with '73 Winchester .44s, Sharps .50s, and Henry sixteen-shooters across their laps, watching the dark and listening to coyote yowls in the wakes of the tremendous storms. But in spite of the rains, the land seemed to be in the grip of a terrible drought. Overall, the scout realized as he thought of the rocky creek beds they had crossed, it had been a dry spring compared to previous years, when the late-afternoon storms could leave the entire prairie awash with puddles and hidden bogs and sloughs that could mire wagons and break ox and mule legs. This year, in spite of the near-nightly storms, the prairie was tinder-dry, and the grass beneath his horse's hooves covered ground that was often stone-hard and creased with the memories of previous years' spring rains.

Now, finding the creek ford at the bottom of the mesa with the copse of pecan trees became even more important. Without it, Moses knew, they would have to veer southwest some thirty or forty miles, with no sweet water he knew of and with much rougher country between them and the high plains.

The 120 people on the wagon train that labored up a gully behind where the scout sat on his bay had been plagued by problems other than the weather. The vomiting sickness had only been a preamble to other diseases, less serious perhaps but equally debilitating, that had stalled the trek continually since the setout from Jefferson, Texas. Strange fevers struck, ran their course, and then disappeared as suddenly as they had come. Days were lost while the sick were nursed and the season deepened.

Then the Ambrose woman spent two days dying in the process of bearing twins that were too weak, and Moses had been summarily informed by the wagon master, Cleve Graham, to move. They sat by a stagnant water hole until the two babies followed their mother in death. The people ignored the black scout's advice and drank and cooked with water from the rotten hole. Almost all of them came down with an epidemic of skitters so bad that they lost another three days while folks squatted in the bushes and lay about on rugs and bedding, too weak to do much more than crawl off whenever the belly cramps became too much for them. Some of them were suffering yet, and Moses suspected that more than half the casks on the train were still at least half full of the contaminated water.

And then there had been the Wichita. They were as fierce as their neighbor tribes, but they preferred to steal what they couldn't trade for rather than try to take it by force. Years of experience in dealing with white men had taught them respect for Colt's revolver and the Winchester rifle, especially when they were in the hands of able veterans of Grant's and Lee's armies.

But some threadbare blankets and a half-dozen scrawny beeves had bought the train safe passage through Wichita country for the most part, and except for some minor pilfering—horses were well guarded every night, rope-corralled, not merely staked out; Moses had insisted on that—the Wichita had proved only a minor nuisance and partial delay as their trading parties stopped the settlers from time to time to brandish their lances and feathers and look threatening.

But Wichita were Wichita. Comanche were Comanche. Moses replaced his broad-brimmed hat on top of the graying black velvet that covered his skull and felt again the uncomfortable itch that always came whenever Indians were nearby. No man he knew understood the Comanche. Unlike their rivals and sometimes allies, the Kiowa, they were nomadic warriors, loosely organized, secretive, and no tribe could match them when it came to feral warfare. They didn't band together in large villages, and they seldom followed a main chief for long. Their medicine was primitive and followed no patterns anyone had been able to figure out. They shunned treaties and meetings with the whites, particularly the *tejanos*, whom they distinguished from the Americans with whom they had briefly and tentatively dealt before. They traditionally kept their own council and relied on no one but themselves. If they followed any code or cult, Moses thought, it was nothing more than pure evil, and if they worshiped a god, it was Satan himself. They were not "red niggers," they were "red devils." Their very name, he had learned years before, meant "enemy," or "those against us," and their sign-language symbol for themselves was a snake.

Moses rinsed his mouth carefully with the brackish water from his canteen once more and spat a glob of it onto the dusty cactus plants clinging to the edges of the arroyo. With a carelessness he didn't actually feel, he pulled makings from his pocket and rolled a cigarette. He wondered dimly how many of the men in the wagons behind him had any idea how to use the rifles they kept so bravely across their knees and under their wagon seats. Some of them, he knew, were veterans of the war, and some of them were experienced woodsmen from the forests of the North and South. But many of them were farmers and city people, helpless babies by comparison, whose experience with firearms was limited if it existed at all.

He dragged a match across a brass rivet on his pommel and lit his smoke, careful to snuff the flame with his fingers before dropping it into the powder-dry grass beneath him. Over the hazy blue smoke of the cigarette, he gazed again into the sunwashed horizon, but he still saw nothing. That worried him more than if he saw a whole war party moving in the distance. Not to see them could mean that they saw him all too clearly, and this train of sick, tired settlers would probably look like easy coup for even the smallest band of Indians, particularly if they were Comanche.

He spurred his mare and rode back down to the lead wagon, where Cleve Graham rode uneasily on the rocking driver's platform. Although he didn't look it, Graham was a hard man. Moses had learned much about him by listening to Frank Herbert, Graham's only real friend on the train. A former officer in the Union Army, Graham had lost a hand at Shiloh and a son at Gettysburg. Graham, Moses understood, blamed all colored men for causing the war that left him and the nation crippled and bitter. But the war had ended nearly ten years ago, and Moses's reputation as a quality scout with enough savvy to guide over a hundred greenhorns across Texas was strong enough that Graham had temporarily put aside his prejudices and hired him. Of course, Moses realized, it was so late in the season by the time Graham organized his train that he had little choice in the matter of scouts. Only a handful would agree to cross Indian country in the first place, especially when the goal was distant Santa Fe, and probably none but Moses would have agreed to go so late in the year. It was a foolish thing to do, and Moses had wished for a chance to take back his commitment a thousand times since leaving Jefferson.

From Santa Fe they would go on to Oregon, Moses assumed, but it was none of his business, and he had never asked Graham about it. He was hired to take them to Santa Fe, and from there they were on their own. Moses had never had any interest beyond the Texas plains. It was what he knew, and he was wise enough never to try to do more than he knew he could do safely. This was to be his last wagon train to guide across anyhow. He was planning to return to these same prairies after he delivered the Graham party to Santa Fe and carry out a particular plan that might make life a bit more worthwhile for him and some of the Negroes back in Jefferson. The plan would be in motion soon, had, in fact, started already, and by the end of June or July at the latest, he hoped it would be a reality.

As he guided his bay up to Graham's wagon, however, his dream was far from his mind. His dark eyes scanned the waving grass all around him. They had more than a few dangerous miles to cross before he could concentrate on what might be. He was worried, and the white man could see it.

"What's wrong?" Graham shouted at him. The creaking, jangling noise of the tack almost covered his voice. The heavy oxen swayed through the rutted arroyo and pulled the buckboard wagon through the muddy trail that had crusted over only a few hours before. The wagon's weight broke through the dusty cover and the wheels sank into the ruddy mire beneath. "Indians?" Graham shifted his Winchester across his lap, his finger feeling for the trigger guard.

"I didn't see none," Moses shouted back. "But I got a feelin' they's there."

Graham snorted and cast a look behind his wagon to make sure no one could hear the scout, though the roar of the wagon noise made it unlikely that even a passenger in his own wagon could understand any of their conversation.

"If you didn't see them, then I'm not goin' to worry about it," Graham shouted. He replaced the Winchester on the platform's seat.

"No," Moses said. He reined his horse up to ride parallel with Graham, then he silently added, You probably won't.

He removed his hat again and scratched furiously at his head. The itch was now chronic. He had learned long ago that what he couldn't see could very well kill him.

2

MOSES FRANKLIN WAS BORN A SLAVE IN VIRGINIA ON the plantation of Dominique Franklin, a tobacco grower who also had the special distinction to Moses of being his natural father. When the boy was sixteen, Franklin's plantation began to fail, and he tried to overcome the devastation of bad management by selling off his slaves. Moses was, therefore, sold away from his mother and two siblings to Joseph Grierson, a large, kindly man who was taking his family and his newly purchased slaves to the new community of Jefferson, which had been built along Trammel's Trace and Big Cypress Bayou in Cass County, Texas.

Moses went along with the slave's bewildered resignation. He was put to work, not farming cotton and cane in the iron-rich soil around Jefferson as he had expected, but rather as a kind of combination gun bearer and tracker and, to his surprise, companion to Mr. Grierson. The master was more interested in hunting deer and small bear than in seeing his plantation prosper, which it did anyway under the supervision of a competent overseer, Evan Carpenter.

When Texas followed South Carolina and the first six states of the Confederacy of the South into secession, Mr. Grierson's interest turned away from the game around Jefferson toward the blue-coated Yankees who made such easy targets at Manassas and Fredericksburg, but Moses was well past twenty by then, and he had learned to use the variety of hunting weapons his master owned.

Left at home while his white master fought alongside John Bell Hood, Moses worked on his art as best he could in spite of the hostile and cruel surveillance of Henry Thomas, a one-eyed, gimpy-legged overseer Mr. Grierson had left in charge of his plantation and black property when Carpenter followed Grierson and enlisted in the Confederate Army.

Thomas's attitude toward Moses was a combination of envy and distrust. No Negro was allowed to touch firearms on most plantations, let alone go hunting. But times were hard for everyone as the Union blockade tightened and New Orleans fell to Federal troops, and Moses's provision of fresh meat for everyone—even though he was now forced to go into the forest shackled with a heavy chain and guarded by a white man, a moronic giant who had the mind of a child and whom the slaves called Slobberin' Jimmy—overrode Thomas's judgment.

Henry Thomas was a cruel man. Even after laboring on the docks or unloading the big Rebel river crafts in the East Texas humidity and heat, the Negroes were often set to work in the Grierson fields until late at night, sometimes doing their planting and hoeing under lanternlight. Moses often found himself wandering out at twilight with a rifle in his hand and the knowledge in his heart that if he came back without meat, he would be beaten.

When the Union general Nathaniel P. Banks led an army up the Red River from New Orleans in an attempt to take Jefferson and seal the rest of the Confederacy off from Texas, Thomas enlisted. In spite of his infirmities, he was welcomed by the volunteers, who were gathering to meet and fight the large numbers of seasoned Union troops, who were marching up a narrow Louisiana trace toward Caddo Lake.

Moses was taken along as Thomas's personal servant—although the crippled overseer was given only the rank of sergeant—since the young slave knew more about guns than the overseer did and could make sure that Thomas had a loaded rifle handy. When the two armies clashed at Mansfield, Louisiana, Thomas was one of the first Rebel soldiers to fall. He died before he ever saw a single Union trooper, and Moses suddenly found himself scurrying to the rear, cradling Mr. Grierson's precious weapons in his arms, anxious to get them back to their comfortable racks in the Grierson plantation home before someone took them away from him.

It took him two days to make the journey back to Jefferson. There he and the other slaves continued to work in town on the docks and in the factories and industries. Slobberin' Jimmy, who was totally incapable of filling Thomas's job in every department except personal cruelty and, perhaps, greed, continued to work them hard and to skim money off their rental fees for his own filthy pockets.

Mr. Grierson returned from the war in May of 1865 with a shattered kneecap and the conviction that the Cause was lost. He never asked anyone in Moses's hearing about Thomas's fate, but he fired Slobberin' Jimmy when he learned that the boy had been making his fortune by renting out the plantation's Negroes and keeping more than half the fees for himself.

When the news of Kirby-Smith's surrender of the Trans-Mississippi Department reached the county, Grierson called all the slaves together in the plantation's dooryard and announced that they were freed and could go where they pleased. The Grierson slaves weren't sure if they should be jubilant or grieving. None of them had ever beheld such a bewildering concept as an independent future, and to find themselves suddenly thrown out into the world was more frightening than inviting.

Grierson waited a few moments for the murmuring to die down, and then he offered to let them stay on the plantation and work for him as freedmen, for pay. Initially all of them agreed to do so. But by the end of the week, many had left. By the end of the year, most of them were living in abject poverty or had wandered off from Jefferson, never to be heard from again.

Moses, however, stayed and continued to hunt with his invalided former master. He drew fair wages from Joseph Grierson, and from time to time he actually thought the old man showed him more than the polite respect he offered to the several whites who now worked for him. Sometimes, he thought, there was genuine affection between them. Although Grierson never presented him with any of the guns as his own, Moses came to feel that they shared the weapons in a kind of joint ownership. Grierson bought them and paid for them, but Moses cared for them, often fired them more than Grierson did. By the time almost two years separated the end of the war and his freedom from their regular trips, now expanded to the west, out beyond the Indian Line to hunt buffalo, antelope, bear, cougar, and other wild game, Moses's marksmanship had been complimented so much by his former master that he believed the rifles were as much his as the old man's.

When Grierson died in 1867, he left nothing to his former possession: not a pistol or even a shotgun. He did leave a good pension to the crabbed and antique elder sister of the cruel Thomas, because, Grierson had often said, Thomas "gave his life in a great victory for the preservation of Texas, Jefferson, and the Cause against the mean aggression of Federal tyranny." And he also left a nice sum to the idiot Jimmy, whom, Moses heard, he regretted turning out so abruptly, given the "boy's"—Jimmy was well over thirty when Grierson returned—"mental incapacities and unfortunate lack of common sense."

Moses, of course, was not present for the reading of the will, but Daniel, a house servant, told Moses about the phrases he overheard while he carried in sweetmeats and tea to the bereaved widow and Grierson daughters as they heard the lawyer read the old man's final testament.

The hunter and provider for the Grierson table and companion to the old master had not expected Grierson to leave him anything, at least not money. But the idea of Thomas's sister—of whom, prior to the bequeathal, no one but Grierson was aware—receiving a pension struck him as cruel and wrong, even more wrong than his leaving any sum whatsoever to the drooling monster Jimmy. Moses could name ten black families in Marion County which had at least one member who possessed a permanent reminder of the cowardly overseer's whips, brands, canes, and knives. Moses's own back was not without marks to remind him of Thomas's and Jimmy's cruelty.

He went directly from Daniel's ironic giggle as he related what he had overheard to the large French windows that opened into Grierson's study. There he waited until the family rose and went to show the lawyer out. Then he removed a Henry rifle from its mount over the fireplace and took a brace of Colt's Army revolvers from the glass case where they were stored. Thus endowed with the unintentional legacy of his former master, he slipped out through a window and left the Grierson plantation forever.

He made but one stop before he departed Marion County on his way west. In the dooryard of Slobberin' Jimmy's cabin, deep in the pine and cypress woods some five miles from the Grierson house, the former slave called out the drooling white man and used the Henry he had removed from Grierson's house to put a bullet into the cruel overseer's belly. He then stole Jimmy's horse and saddle and three dollars in paper money before setting out to find his own particular freedom.

3

MOSES WANDERED OUT TO THE INDIAN LINE FOR A while. He found that his life as a man of color among hard-handed white trackers and traders wasn't much better than his life as a slave or hired man had been until he managed to persuade a Lieutenant Colonel Samuel Sturgis to hire him as a civilian scout for the Sixth Cavalry out of Fort Griffin. There he applied what he had already learned from Grierson about the plains and added knowledge of the Indians who continued to threaten white settlements from San Antonio north to the border of the Indian Territory.

He rode with experienced Indian fighters and plainsmen who had lived with various tribes, and he met Texas Rangers, who sat around the campfires and bunkhouses and told stories about their experiences riding with Rip Ford and Ben McCullouch, about fighting with John Bell Hood and Albert Sidney Johnston, about fights with Comanche, Kiowa, Apache, and other tribes of the Southern Plains. Moses found that the Rangers and white scouts hated him for being black as much as they hated the Indians they fought. But he also found that by hunkering down in his blankets and remaining quiet and as invisible as possible, he could eavesdrop on their campfire stories and learn what they knew. By carefully separating the brag from the balance of fact that each story contained, Moses soon learned the necessary basics of dealing with Indians, whether fighting with them or parlaying with them, and, more important, he learned how to avoid them.

After almost three years with the Army, during which he scouted for elements of the U.S. Cavalry operating out of Forts Concho and Richardson, Moses guided his first group of settlers from Jacksboro, the ramshackle town that had grown up on Lost Creek near Fort Richardson, to Santa Fe. The wagon master didn't want to hire him, but Moses was the only experienced plainsman available when their previously engaged scout managed fatally to lose a knife fight.

Moses was apprehensive about the job. But he learned enough on the first expedition to decide to try it again.

For a man who was both smart and careful, he told himself, the risk was minimal.

This time, he knew he needed to go to a place where trains were being organized for western expeditions, and the best place he knew of was Jefferson. It had been three years since his murder of Jimmy, but he still worried that if he returned to Marion County, his appearance might remind someone that Moses's disappearance and the theft of Grierson's guns had all taken place at the same time that Jimmy was shot down in his doorway. No one he had met from Jefferson had so much as mentioned any search for a Negro. If the sheriff or anyone else wanted to track him down, it wouldn't have been hard, for he had made no attempt to conceal his name. He slipped back into the city one night and presented himself quietly to old friends. All welcomed him back enthusiastically, and none mentioned anything at all about the stolen guns or the idiot overseer. After a week or so, he made bolder inquiries about Jimmy and learned that the prevailing theory was that he was killed by one of the several prostitutes he kept—and sometimes beat—and that the whole matter was history.

Each trip out to the plains gave him confidence. When he returned to the civilization of Jefferson, he felt something called him back to the loneliness of the West, a place where his color seemed to matter less than his ability to use the Winchester '66 and Sharps "Big .50" he had purchased out of his earnings. He also bought a fine set of Colt's .44s, which he wore proudly around Frog Town, Jefferson's Negro community, attracting admiring looks from groups of young black women who marveled at the success and demeanor of a former slave who now called himself a "frontier scout."

He passed around the word that he would guide a train of settlers west for a reasonable fee, and he set up shop in Millie's Saloon, one of the few such Negro establishments in Jefferson. Even though he was colored, Moses found that his image, especially when enhanced with buckskins, chaps, and the new Springfield .55-caliber "High Hammer" rifle he had gotten in trade for the Sharps .50, appealed to some wagon masters. Most soon found how hard it was to locate a talented and experienced man who would work for only about half what white scouts wanted and who wouldn't steal from them and leave them lost on the Texas plains.

Moses found that the wagon masters who engaged him would be so surprised with his honesty and efficiency that they would reward him with a nice bonus when he delivered them safely and with a minimum of discomfort.

Moses didn't figure Cleve Graham for a man who would give bonuses, however. Graham had hired him only after desperate attempts to find a reliable white scout. He had approached Moses in Millie's, and had barely looked at him as he talked, glancing instead at the black faces that studied him from the saloon's shadows.

Graham was a short man in his late forties. His auburn hair was thinning and cut close. His missing left hand had been replaced by a brass-studded purse of worn leather that covered his wrist. He was obviously uncomfortable facing Moses's six feet of height, and he eyed the slender figure in buckskins who stood before him with something akin to envy. Graham made his proposition after letting Moses know that he had asked around about him and determined that he was a fair scout, but he was quick to add that he wanted no nonsense. He had 120 people in thirty wagons ready to go, and he wanted to leave soon.

"I'll give you a hundred dollars in gold," Graham drawled in his southern Ohioan's accent. "Fifty now, and—"

"I want a hundred now," Moses said evenly. He concealed his shock at the man's brazen manner. No scout, white or black, would do it for twice as much—and they usually wanted it all up front. "An' a hundred when we get there. You write it out, sign it, an' give it to me."

Graham's mouth fell wide open and his eyes bulged out as he listened to the black man, and his anger grew. "Now, listen here, boy . . ." he started.

"An' I 'spect you to buy me a extra horse," Moses went on in a polite, businesslike tone he knew was infuriating.

"A horse!"

"I normally ask for two," Moses continued. "But you said it's a short train, so I guess you got to make your profit." He waited a moment for that to sink in. " 'Sides,

I got a good bay, an' if things go good, you can buy the spare back when we get there."

"Now, look." Graham was working himself up and casting his eyes around the saloon, where faces lit up with amusement. "I ain't lettin' some colored boy tell me I have to buy him a horse!"

Moses nodded silently and then went on as if he hadn't heard him, "An' I want two hundred rounds of .55s—stored in your wagon—an' some .44s too. 'Nother two hundred'll do." He turned to his beer and sipped it, but he kept himself erect and in a position of polite deference to the white man.

"No deal!" Graham blurted out. He stood as tall as he could, resting his stumped arm on the bar's counter. He was dressed in a clawhammer coat and a bright brocade vest over a white shirt with a paisley cravat: the attire of a gambler, or a dude.

Moses wasn't certain yet how to judge Graham. There was something behind the fancy clothes that suggested that he had more experience than his wardrobe implied. Clearly, he wasn't a fool, and he required respect, but he was not going to get it just because he was white. Moses had spent too many years on the frontier to give respect where it wasn't earned.

"I hunt and get the game," Moses concluded, "but if they's no game, then I eat what you eat, an' "—he paused and leveled his eyes with the white man's—"I eat with you. That's the deal. Take it or leave it."

Graham studied his stump for a few moments. "I got a hundred and twenty folks ready to leave Sunday mornin'." His tone softened and the anger washed backward from his eyes. He sounded more weary and resigned than anything else. "An' you're the only scout available." He paused and rubbed his beard with his stump. "I don't like you, and I don't trust you. But I'll hire you. I'll have your money this evenin'."

"An' the contract for the rest," Moses added.

"An' the contract for the rest."

"Bring it to Zachariah here." Moses indicated the wizened bartender, who couldn't conceal his grin behind his white whiskers. "He reads an' writes, an' he'll keep it till I get back."

Graham turned away and started out the door, muttering under his breath. Moses stopped him.

"One more thing," the black scout said quietly but with just a tinge of menace in his voice to let Graham know he was serious. "My name's Moses. You can call me that."

Graham lowered his bullet-shaped head and accepted the final condition. The white man, Moses sensed, was not a coward, and he understood a threat when he heard one, even when it came from a Negro, and he evened his voice.

"I'll watch my mouth," he said. "I can't account for the others, though." He waited as Moses nodded, then he added, "But you'll call me 'Mister,' an' you'll stay away from the women. There's no coloreds in the train."

Moses nodded and walked over to where Graham stood with his feet slightly parted and his coat open to reveal his own revolver and stuck out a gloved hand. After a moment's hesitation, Graham took it briefly. Then he was gone.

That had been months ago, Moses mused as his horse picked its way up the buffalo path which led out of the arroyo up onto the rise. He and Graham had more or less gotten along, but there existed a tension between them that seemed to grow with every mile they rode.

4

MOSES FRANKLIN WAS USED TO THE CONTEMPT OF WHITE employers and white men in general. Most of them wouldn't take any advice from him until he had proved himself somehow, by bringing in game or avoiding disaster. But he rarely had serious trouble with them. After they put the civilization of East Texas behind them, they soon became dependent on what the black scout knew, and he tried to make it easy on them by staying to himself and dealing only with the wagon master and any colored mule skinners they employed.

He had taken this train, like so many others, by Saint Jo, Texas, a crossroads for the cattle trails from the southern part of the state, well away from the Comanche. He sat on the ground and watched Graham and his apparent sidekicks, Jack Sterling and the semi-idiot Frank Herbert, Graham's loquacious friend, go inside the Stonewall Jackson Saloon along with others, all under the hostile glare of Virgil Hollister and a handful of the settlers who apparently disapproved of such establishments.

Moses knew that ordinarily a train's scout would accompany the wagon master inside a saloon or store they might encounter along the way. He knew from things he had heard and observed that a relationship often developed between the settlers and the scout that was sometimes like a congregation and its minister or a family and its father. But he was aware that to the folks of this tiny nomadic community on the rolling prairie, he was just another nigger boy for hire. He felt lucky that they let him water his horse at the well in the center of town and sit on the grass on the square across from the saloon. He probably wouldn't have tried even that except that one of the settlers, old Anthem, had walked along with him, admiring his bay and rambling on about quality horseflesh. Then Anthem had joined Graham, and Moses was alone once more. Such exclusion should hurt, but he had felt it before and so often that he hardly thought of it as he sucked on a stem of Johnsongrass and contemplated the trail ahead.

He saw Jack Sterling stalk out of the saloon and slam his son up alongside his head as he passed him for no apparent reason other than he wanted to hit someone. As the boy reeled backward from his father's blow, Sterling headed out toward where his cattle had been left to graze. Thinking that the white man might come back and cause trouble for anyone he found, Moses raised himself, mounted up, and rode down to the river, where he bathed himself. It was best, he learned, to stay out of the way of white men like Jack Sterling when they were in a rage.

Moses had no ambitions to gain the respect of all or even some of the white men on the frontier. But he was pleased when the wagon masters for whom he had worked the past several years finally came around to giving him his fair due, some even praising him in front of other white men who had scouted or who fashioned themselves to be experienced plainsmen.

But this train was another matter, start to finish. Graham thought he knew more than Moses did about everything. He was more experienced than the average boss Moses had worked for, but he still was no plainsman, no veteran wagon master. He had discarded his fancy clothes in favor of rougher garments, had replaced his plug hat with a big, floppy head cover that kept the sun from his eyes, and he handled his team with the same rough determination with which he handled most of the people on the train. He argued with the scout about every decision, no matter how small, and when Moses was wrong, Graham brayed like a jackass. When Moses was right, Graham sulked and usually took the credit. Still, as the last white settlements on the Indian Line faded behind them and the possibility of hostile Indians steadily grew, Graham came more and more to rely on Moses's expertise, and he grudgingly admitted, even in Moses's hearing, that he was giving himself and the security of the whole train over to a colored scout whom he wouldn't even have spoken to under other circumstances.

Moses turned his mare around and leaned back in his saddle. Behind him, Graham's wagon struggled up the path to the level ground. It was a buckboard, one of several in the train, and in spite of its lighter weight, it had difficulty negotiating rougher parts of the trail. So far, so good, Moses thought. He again searched the horizon for any sign of life, animal or human, and contemplated what the best plan would be for the night ahead. Off to the south, just beyond the horizon, he knew lay what the white man called Medicine Mountain, a triangular pile of rocks that improbably rose out of the rolling prairie and was held sacred by the Comanche. It was infested with rattlesnakes, scorpions, wolves, and the occasional cougar, but the Comanche medicine men liked to go there in the spring and make magic, obtain their *puha*, which would guarantee a good hunting season or—Moses shuddered again with the old fear and a reminder of his itch—success in war.

In the past few years, the Comanche had been relatively docile. There had been the usual number of attacks on wagon trains, and some raiding parties had ventured deep into East Texas, well inside the Indian Line, to steal livestock and other goods. But the Comanche had signed no treaties, or at least the Quahidi hadn't. Moses hoped that the train was still early enough in the season to sneak across the high Texas plains and make New Mexico before the Comanche came so far south.

He had good reason to cling to such hopes. He had run across the remnants of wagon trains that had met with Indian disaster. The cherished goods so carefully packed in the backs of the big, clumsy wagons were strewn across the grass and scrub cedar, and the blackened skeletons of the forlorn settlers who defended the possessions with their lives offered a hideous account of the tortures they had suffered before they died. Some of the naked rib cages would boast a withering arrow shaft or lance, or perhaps here and there a skull would be crushed or smashed by a stone ax or flint-edged tomahawk—those were the lucky ones, the ones who had died fighting and whose worst fate was to have their hair lifted as a memorial to their courage. But others, often mere children's bones, would be cruelly tied to the wagons' sides and wheels, the burned-out carcasses of the Conestogas telling the tale of how they died in flames, with their private parts cut off and stuffed in their still-living mouths, their eyelids sliced away so gnats and mosquitoes could feed directly on the exposed eyeballs, their throats cut and abdomens eviscerated in the unique way the Comanche knew which could keep a victim alive for hours—days, even—while he slowly bled to death and watched helplessly as his friends were skinned alive, his women repeatedly raped before being killed or taken off and wived to their captors.

It was no wonder at all to Moses why the white man could mutilate an Indian corpse after viewing such devastation to his own people. Nothing a white man could do to a dead Indian could ever match what the Comanche could do to a live human being.

MOSES WATCHED YOUNG JASON Sterling driving his father's cattle up the trail behind his wagon. He strongly suspected that unlike the handful of scrawny beeves which others had tethered to their wagons when the train left Jefferson, these cattle were stolen, particularly since Sterling hadn't shown up with them until the train was well away from Jefferson and the reach of the Marion County law. But he had no proof of that. So completely did Sterling hold Moses in contempt that the white man never spoke to him at all, even indirectly, and when Moses caught Sterling eyeing him it was through steel-gray hatred. Moses's only consolation was that the wagon master seemed to hate Jack Sterling as much as Sterling hated Moses.

Stolen or not, the cattle were important. They were all that was left of the entire train's beef, and they were left mainly because Sterling had followed Moses's advice not to water them from the stagnant hole. Sterling boldly announced his plans of starting a herd with them. He had no intention of allowing them to be butchered for food, even if he and the rest of the train were starving. Experience had taught Moses that a man guarded stolen goods with greater care than he would things he had come by honestly. The last four wagons, including the one with the hogs and another that was loaded with chickens in homemade wire crates, followed Sterling's small herd.

Moses put his bay into a canter to catch up with Graham's wagon, now almost over the rim and out of sight.

5

MOSES CAUGHT UP TO GRAHAM'S WAGON AND RODE awhile beside him in silence. At this point, the prairie rolled gently, but the driver and the teams had to work constantly, holding the wagons back as they went down and straining to jerk them forward as they went up, everyone sweating and cursing all the while.

Even so, the way was much easier than it had been. Often the train would come to a gully only five or six feet across. The sides would descend sharply to a loamy bottom some ten or twelve feet below the level of the prairie. For a man on a good horse, it would have been only a short jump. Even a man on foot could leap over some of these odd gaps in the earth. But for a wagon and team they might as well have been twenty feet across and a hundred feet deep.

The result was side trips. From Saint Jo on, Moses never could remember the exact routes he had taken before. He couldn't read or write and had no idea of how to make a map that he or anyone else could follow. He relied on landmarks, and as the traceless prairie rolled on to the horizon, there were fewer and fewer of those to count on.

The rocks, in fact, seemed to get worse with each trip and worse yet with each mile this particular train traveled. Already, five of the wagons had broken down and delays caused by their repair had slowed progress. And it was because of Graham's insistence that one particular crossing was too dangerous that they had tacked north for five miles and been forced to make camp near the bad water.

They had received little relief at the falls on the Big Wichita, where a strange tarpaulin-clad family named Buntin traded a few needed articles and wagon parts while the old man sat with a shotgun on his lap atop a stinking pile of buffalo hides and eyed Moses and the train sharply. The falls themselves were running mud down their short cascade, testimony to the effects of the short, lightning quick thunderstorms that blew violently, boomed and crashed with fury but hardly refreshed the droughty prairies to the west, and no sweet water was to be had there or much of anywhere since they put the tiny settlement behind them a week ago.

At the top of the next rise, the ground leveled off, and Moses galloped up a few yards and sent his dark eyes across the golden grass of the landscape, looking for the bright feathers of a war party gathering to attack. But he really knew better. They wouldn't come at them like that, not across a naked plain in the bright morning light. They would wait until the train stopped for the night, forted up the wagons, and posted sentries. Then, maybe at sunset or dawn, they would come. They liked to wait until the whites felt secure, then hit them hard, conquer them, and maybe take several days torturing and looting and raping. It was better coup that way, bigger *puha*, more powerful medicine.

If the braves were lucky, and they often were, they would sometimes discover some whiskey in a train, and then the party could really start. In this train, the black scout knew, they would find more than *some* whiskey. It was more of a rolling saloon than a wagon train full of settlers, he told himself, even though he had not seen one man take a drink from one of the kegs strapped to almost every wagon's side. Aside from the liquor they had purchased and heartily consumed in Saint Jo, the only open drinks taken since they left Jefferson had come from bottles of rotgut they kept secreted beneath their wagon seats. It was odd, he mused, to have so many kegs of whiskey—heavy kegs too—and not to break one out, even when people were sick and in need of it. But Graham acted as if the whole train were as dry as a powder house, and given the nasty effects that so much whiskey could have on men, white or red, Moses was just as glad.

Moses wet his lips. The horizon was free of clouds. A lone hawk, or maybe an eagle, circled off in the distance against a sky so blue it hurt him to look at it, but he knew as well as he knew anything that the afternoon would bring another thunderstorm, maybe a cyclone—they had seen several in the past few days, raggedly dancing and weaving across the vast distances—and they would have to pull up for the night in the open once again.

He rode back to Graham, who was loudly cursing his oxen and still using his whip, although the team was having no real trouble pulling the wagon over the suddenly flat ground. He's nervous, too, Moses thought, but he won't admit it. He doesn't trust me worth a pile of mule shit.

"We'll keep headin' north by nor'west," he shouted to Graham, who looked at him in the middle of cursing his team. "We might make the crossin' by nightfall, if we're lucky."

He hoped to spot the mesa with the copse of trees very soon, which would mean that Blind Man's Creek was within reach. Unlike most runs and creeks in the area, it was deep enough for fish to be plentiful, and because of a spring in the mesa's base, it also provided potable water and a chance to refit and rest before reaching the high plains. It was one of the few landmarks Moses counted on completely.

He brought each of the trains he guided to it without fail and always looked forward to it as a sort of halfway point. The mesa was high but unique—no more than a mile long—and easy to spot. The copse of pecan trees just as easy. The Comanche paid little attention for the water ran too fast to attract deer, buffalo, or antelope; and Comanche, like many other Indians, wouldn't eat a fish or a frog if the alternative was starvation.

Moses looked on the creek as a blessing. The promise of fresh catfish and perch was inviting to a train that had survived on dried or salted beef for two weeks, since the game had mysteriously disappeared, and if they pushed hard, Moses believed, they could make the crossing before dark. Because of the combination of almost nightly violent storms and the especially dry season, he had no way of knowing whether the stream would be moderately full, flowing fast, or easy to traverse.

Moses pulled his left foot from his stirrup and vaulted deftly onto the wagon seat next to Graham, trailing his reins and loosely lashing them to the wagon's brake handle. The wagon master wrinkled his nose and turned his head slightly away. Moses ignored him and tried to explain his plan without having to shout over the creaking and groaning of the wagon and team that pulled it.

"Then we ain't stoppin' for dinner?" Graham asked without looking at Moses.

"If we do, we'll likely not make it 'fore dark. An' I ain't too anxious to get caught out here in the open right now."

Graham turned his bearded face toward Moses and searched for a motive other than the one stated. "Folks need to eat. Need a hot meal," he said. "This is hard work, an' they're not feelin' too good anyhow with all the sickness they've had."

Moses wanted to tell him that the most recent "sickness" was their own damned fault, but he kept his mouth shut. He and Graham had been over this all before, and the wagon master had convinced everyone on the train as well as himself that the fault of the bad water was Moses's alone. He shrugged.

"I reckon it's 'nother five miles or so 'fore we spot the mesa," he said, "an' we ain't makin' good time with these beasts. We'd be doin' better if ever'body had mules."

He had tried to tell Graham that mules made better draft animals on the rolling, arid plains of Texas, but the wagon master was too hardheaded to listen to Moses's advice. So only about half the wagons were pulled with teams of the stubborn, long-eared animals, while the others labored behind the clumsy, perpetually thirsty oxen. Graham had provided the oxen through a private contract that had, Moses figured, paid for his wagon and team as well as Moses's salary without dipping too much into the fee he likely charged each family for joining the expedition back in Jefferson.

"So you keep tellin' me," Graham said sarcastically, but then he scratched his bearded chin with his stump and thought a moment. "I suppose we could divvy up. Let them with mules stop if they're a mind to, an' the rest of us could just keep goin'."

Moses shook his head, and his eyes swept the horizon again. Gooseflesh rose on his neck at the prospect of what he felt was there but couldn't see.

"I don't think we ought to split up."

Graham braced the reins between his stump and his side while he fished a cigar out of his coat and bit off the end. Spitting the piece over the side, he watched Moses's study of the landscape. "You still worried about Indians?"

There was no reply from the scout, and Graham found a match in his shirt, struck it on the wagon seat, and applied it to the cigar. "I swear to God, boy," he said through puffs, "you see Indians behind every blade of grass." He blew out the match and tossed it overboard and pulled the rifle up closer to him. "I never was afraid of what I couldn't see. I learned that at Pea Ridge, Shiloh too. But you wouldn't know about that, would you?"

Moses didn't reply, and Graham grabbed up the reins again. Moses wanted to tell him that he would be all right if he *could* see the Comanche, but he had damned well better learn to be afraid of what he couldn't see, if he wanted to keep his hair.

"There wasn't no Indians at Pea Ridge," he said quietly.

Graham's gray eyes went hard, and he stared at the black scout. "The hell there wasn't!" Graham said too loudly. Then he seemed to realize who he was arguing with and only muttered, "How the hell would you know?"

The wagon master jerked a watch loose from his vest and snapped it open. "I reckon we'll stop for an hour or so. Boil some coffee, eat somethin', and then get goin' quick as we can." He stuffed the watch back into his pocket.

"It's your scalp," Moses said as he rose and leaped back into the mare's saddle. She shied and bucked a bit from the sudden weight, but he reined her back in time to hear Graham's final word.

"That's right," he shouted. "An' it's your ass if we get waylaid before we get to that crossin'. You do your job, an' I'll do mine, an' mine's to boss these wagons an' kick your black butt if you get out of line. Understand?"

Moses nodded and spurred his horse out ahead of Graham's wagon.

Just as he reached a point about fifty yards in front of the lumbering oxen, he thought he spotted a flurry of movement in the distance, but he blinked his eyes and it was gone. He removed his hat and rubbed his forehead and face and stared hard at the invisible spot in the grass where he thought he had seen something move.

There was nothing. He looked up. High in the deep blue of the sky a circle of buzzards hovered over something freshly killed, but there was nothing else but the breeze and the ubiquitous grass with its frequent sparkle of wildflowers. Buzzards, sky, grass. He suddenly felt slightly dizzy and wondered if maybe Graham wasn't right. Maybe a good meal would help. He knew he could use some coffee. He scanned the distance once more and tuned his ears for any sound. Except for the noisy wagons behind him there were no sounds above the hissing of the grass. Out in front of the train, it was as quiet as a graveyard and no less spooky.

After a bit, Graham whistled and the wagons began to pull up. Women descended and boys began gathering dead grass for kindling to make small fires for coffee. Soon the smells of frying bacon and beans drifted across the noonday plains, and the settlers stretched their cramped muscles jolted from the morning's trek and squatted near the fires to sip their coffee and exchange thoughts.

Graham moved through their small groups, talking quietly about the promise of fresh water and catfish up ahead, and they all showed signs of feeling better. Only a few made quick, shuffling runs into the high grass to relieve themselves, and even these returned mostly with smiles instead of the pale, sick expressions that had haunted the train these past several days. Within a half hour they were all stretched out under the wagons, smoking pipes, catching short naps, and wiping up bacon grease with stumps of unleavened campfire bread.

Moses sat in the shade of his horse about fifty yards away from the wagons and pulled at a piece of jerky he had found in his saddlebag. The smell of food was delicious, but he didn't want to ask Graham for any of his, not after protesting the stop, and except for official train business, he had yet to venture into the settlers' midst. The agreement that he would eat what Graham ate and would eat it in his company had been forgotten as soon as the train rolled out of the city limits of Jefferson, and Moses saw no profit in pressing the issue. There were a number of young girls in the party, including Frank Herbert's wild and strange daughter, who frequently stared at Moses curiously from behind a wagon canvas or pile of crates, and the last thing he needed was a confrontation with an angry father, particularly one who was apparently simple.

Almost as if his thoughts were coming to life, he suddenly heard a young female voice speak behind him.

"Mr. Franklin?"

He turned suddenly, forgetting the horizon that had been the unconscious object of intense study the whole time he chewed the jerked beef, and confronted a pretty girl who stood in her calico dress and offered him a tin cup of coffee.

"My daddy said you might want this," she said, lowering her eyes away from his intense gaze and reminding him thereby to stand up in the presence of a white woman. He did so, removing his hat and reaching out slowly for the steaming cup.

"Thankee, Ma'am," he said. "An' jus' who might your daddy be?" His drawl lengthened into pure Plantation Niggerese, and he winced with the pain of trying not to speak that way. He knew better, he told himself. Mr. Grierson had seen to that.

"Jack Sterlin'," she replied. "He said you saved his cattle by warnin' him 'bout the bad water, an' "—she hesitated—"an' we're beholden." She smiled at him, and Moses felt a warm sexual attraction. He fought it back.

This is a *white* woman, you fool! What was he thinking of? God, he couldn't fight back the thought. She was beautiful, nearly perfect. She looked like the girls in some of the paintings he had observed on the Grierson walls, young women who sat around on alabaster benches and were attended by naked winged children while their gossamer-thin garments hung open and revealed milky-white breasts and round inviting buttocks. He flushed deeply.

"That's my job, Ma'am."

She wore no bonnet, and her hair was the color of ripe corn. Her eyes seemed to reflect the dark blue purity of the sky behind her. Her hands were folded across her waist, and he found himself studying her graceful fingers as they tapered into squared-off nails that were as clean and white as rain. When she smiled at him again, her mouth creased her cheeks just slightly, not creating dimples really, but attractive vertical lines of happiness that accentuated her beauty.

"Well," Moses said. "You tell him I thank him. I'm 'bliged."

She had started to say something when a fearful voice from the wagons shouted, "Aggie! You get on back here now! I told you not to bother that man."

She started to turn away. There was something hard behind her eyes, not negative, just firm and determined. She was tall, and she looked older than she was. In spite of her age, this was a woman of experience, he acknowledged, and not all the experience had been good. That was there as well.

He suddenly doubted that Jack Sterling or his strange, ugly, quiet wife had suggested that the girl bring him out a cup of coffee at all. If there ever was a man who hated colored people—or just people in general—it was Sterling. Sterling regarded Graham's hiring a colored scout as about the most outrageous thing he ever heard of, and he wasn't shy about saying so anytime Moses came anywhere near where he might be speaking.

"Say, Miss, uh, Ma'am," Moses said as she started away, "better take this back." He handed her the nearly empty tin cup and made every effort to keep from touching her. "An' I'm truly obliged . . . to your daddy."

She blushed, took the cup in a slender hand, and then raised her skirts slightly and moved through the grass back to the wagons. Moses watched her go. His breath was short, and he was surprised to find his heart pounding in his ears.

CHAPTER TWO

1

TWO HOURS LATER THEY WERE ON THE MOVE AGAIN. The afternoon sun made Moses drowsy, and he found himself not paying the sharp attention that the situation demanded. His thoughts were dreamily clouded with the vision of Aggie Sterling's loveliness, and while he entertained no ideas of doing more than looking at her again, he found that he couldn't get her entirely off his mind. He strained to remember a Bible lesson from the lips of some old black woman who had conducted crude services in the slave quarters around the Grierson plantation. Moses had never paid much attention to the old woman's religious mutterings, and on most Sundays he was hunting with Grierson. But he remembered the phrase "forbidden fruit." It seemed remarkably applicable to the way he felt about this strange, forward white girl. In a frightening way, it reminded him of how he had once felt about another girl—a black girl—named Amy.

Distracted or not, his eyes automatically scanned the horizon. He kept the mental picture of the small copse of trees on the great mesa that would mark the crossing he sought.

There was more than Indians to worry about, he reminded himself. There were hidden sinkholes and prairie dog villages. Although they were moving slowly enough not to have to worry about the pervasive little rodents' holes trapping an animal's leg and breaking it before a rider or driver might see them, Moses had heard of villages so large that the whole prairie concealed a honeycomb of tunnels and burrows. Once, he had heard, an Army supply train had collapsed into the ground underneath it, its weight too great for the thin covering of soil remaining above an enormous underground village.

The blank, unpopulated plains of Texas had held an appeal for Moses from the first time he had seen them, before he ever considered being in charge of a train of people crossing them. At first he had been almost frightened. All he had ever known was the thick forest and lush underbrush of the South and of East Texas. It was physically intimidating to be surrounded with so much space. At first he felt like climbing down from his horse and cowering underneath it, although there was nothing threatening. It was just there, all around him, all around itself, really.

But after a few days, after he watched the spectacular panorama of a western sunset, the gentle warming glow of an eastern dawn across the sky that gradually gave up its darkness to the pale blue of day, he found himself captivated by the raw beauty of the place. But when confronted with the waving grass and vastness of an unpeopled landscape, he found himself making comparisons to the woods where he had stalked deer, wild pig, squirrel, and other game, and he sometimes found that he couldn't wait to return to East Texas and the forests surrounding Jefferson.

On balance, though, he had come to the decision that he would rather be out here among the wild animals—and even the wild Indians—than back there where every year there were fewer gators to hunt, where the black bear and deer were thinning out as people pushed farther and farther into the forest, where even squirrels had become too chary to be hunted easily. Out here he could be a man. There was no one to call him "nigger," no one to remind him that he had been born in bondage, conceived out of the forced—at least he believed and hoped that it had been forced—copulation of a white man and a piece of female property over which he had total control. Out here, his ability with a rifle, a pistol, even the Bowie knife he wore strapped to his leg beneath his boot top mattered more than what color he was or where he had come from. The sweat that formed briefly on his skin in the arid climate of the plains was no match for the drenching perspiration that even minimal labor could bring forth under the shady cypress and pines lining the swamps and bayous of Marion County. But never, not once, had he felt that sweat arise out here because of a name he was called or because he was discovered to be standing somewhere or doing something that he shouldn't. In fact, the only word that ever brought sweat to his brow out here was *Indian*—particularly *Comanche*—and that could cause the bravest of men—white or black—to sweat nickels.

The land out here seemed wicked and almost possessed of evil, Moses sometimes thought. It was overrun with things that could hurt, maim, even kill. Wildcats, scorpions, red ants, wild horses, gray wolves, javelina, cougar, black bear, coyotes, and rattlesnakes lurked in the plum thickets and arroyos and along the breaks where the juniper and scrub cedar dominated the mesquite and rare cottonwood, live oak, or hackberry trees. Horseflies, yellow jackets, hornets the size of a man's thumb buzzed in the sloughs and creek bottoms, and centipedes and scorpions lurked under rocks and along the bases of cactus clumps, their thin poison sufficient to make a man or even a horse sick enough to die. But there were also other things for men who could use a rifle to defend their homes and families against such inhospitable creatures. There were wild turkey, beaver, antelope, deer, rabbit, and bobwhite quail and gray dove; geese and ducks came down in the fall, along with a huge, long-legged bird that Grierson had brought down with a shotgun. It was a sandhill crane, he told Moses, and when the black gunbearer prepared it by stuffing it with wild onions and spitting it over an open fire, he found it tasted like roasted pork.

And there were buffalo. There would always be buffalo, Moses knew. For years beyond memory the Indians had made a way of life from the buffalo, and if Comanche could do it with their dogwood shafts and flint arrowheads, then he knew that men with good-quality firearms and sharp steel butcher knives could do it as well. In fact, he knew, men were doing it all the time.

But then, he remembered as his eyes surveyed the horizon, there were still the Indians. That was one obstacle to his dream. It was formidable, but again, men with guns could hold them at bay. He had seen it done, and he knew that given the right men, he could do it as well. Somehow, they could be moved back a bit more, beaten off, or they could be dealt with reasonably. Black men weren't white men or *tejanos*, he mentally argued with an imaginary Comanche chief. They didn't want it all, they didn't even want much. They just wanted to be left alone. Surely that could be arranged. Yes, Indians could be dealt with, or they could be killed, he assured himself. He had spent too much time in the service of the Army, listened to too many conversations around Ranger fires not to believe, as well, that unlike the buffalo, there would not always be Indians.

But now, as the fear of what he couldn't see gripped the base of his spine in a cold fist and hardened his stomach into a sour rock, he wondered if he shouldn't return to Jefferson permanently, find himself a job with the tanners or even the iron smelters and try to earn a living through his labor rather than through a cunning and expertise that he often doubted he really had. He was grimly satisfied that no one had connected him to the murder of the drooling idiot Jimmy, or the theft of Grierson's guns, which he thought of as "Grierson's legacy." And now he had almost enough money to buy himself a piece of property. If he couldn't find work to his liking, he could live on squirrel, gator meat, and catfish, and it would be his game, caught or killed by him on his land.

But then he thought of the former slaves, some of them just as chained now as they had ever been, only now shackled with poverty and the hopelessness of never being more than what they were—nigger laborers. Slavery, Moses understood, was more than a set of chains or a matter of being owned. It had to do with attitude. He had watched himself and others step off a boardwalk into ankle-deep mud just so some cracker could lumber past. He had seen his fellow blacks doff their hats whenever a white man approached them, cast their eyes down at the ground, and grovel for a kind word or compliment no more stirring than a nod of the head or a muttered " 'Day." He hated it when he saw it. He hated it worse when he himself did it.

It perplexed him, and it angered him. It was as if they had been caged animals who were now set free. But there was nowhere for them to go. Whips and brands and knotted ropes had been replaced by a confusing array of papers and debts, obligations that few of them could even name correctly, let alone understand well enough to meet. They used to fear overseers and straw bosses. Now they spoke with the same quiet terror of the laws, the landlords, the banks.

Finally, Moses understood that any idea he had of returning permanently to Jefferson was foolish. He was a Negro, and nothing would ever change his status in Jefferson or in any town that had existed before the war. The Southerners hated him for being a former slave. The Northerners hated him for being a new burden. Only on the empty plains of the unsettled West could he feel like a whole man, for here he had a chance, day by day and even hour by hour sometimes, to prove his worth to other men, white or red.

No, Moses thought while his bay climbed another rise in the prairie, if a man had to keep his ear peeled for night riders, better they be Indians coming for an honorable battle than angry white men who were still fighting a war that was over ten years ago.

2

THE HORIZON'S ALMOST FEATURELESS LANDSCAPE HAD made a subtle change, and on the distant border between yellow and blue, there was the very mesa and its identifying pecan grove. His heart seemed to grow a bit in his chest. The crossing was still a long way off. If he held his hand out at arm's length, the tip of his gloved finger could blot out the whole landmark. But it was there. It was the source of Blind Man's Creek, which was increased in its flow by an ancient abandoned beaver dam at the mesa's opposite end. At the north end of the flat-topped mountain's termination he would find the crossing.

He rode back quickly to tell Graham about it. He felt excited, relieved. He wanted to whoop, and he removed his hat and spanked the bay up to a trot. He knew they had a chance of making the crossing by nightfall now, if they didn't have to stop for anything and had no trouble with the wagons.

The wagons themselves were a big part of the problem. Other wagon masters insisted on some uniformity in the vehicles that made up the train. The wagon of choice was the traditional huge Conestoga with its larger rear wheels, bowed middle, and enormous capacity. Eight of the wagons in the train followed this pattern, although several had been modified in various ways. In addition to those and the buckboards, there were some old Studebakers. Their shorter, narrower beds made for rougher rides, although they traversed the arroyos and gullies better than the Conestogas. The other three wagons on the train, except Graham's, which was nothing more than a light buckboard that lacked even the high rigging for canvas, were of no particular type other than reworked Army castoffs. They had in common only one thing with the others. With the exception of the wagon master's lighter rig, all of them were loaded with junk. Most of them, Moses realized, had been purchased used, and every one of them was subject to breakdowns.

Because of their heavy loads, the teams were larger than usual. Six mules or four oxen pulled some of the heavier wagons. Even Graham had hitched four of the huge, smelly beasts in front of his own wagon, although aside from the whiskey kegs and water casks he carried, Moses saw little beyond fodder to add weight to the wagon master's vehicle.

Graham grunted and lashed at the backsides of his oxen with his whip when Moses yelled the news that the crossing was in sight. He looked hard at the black man and returned a steady, impassive face to the scout's offer of a grinning fever of excitement. It was a confirmation of Graham's wisdom in taking the time to stop for a meal, Moses knew, and the one-handed wagon master wanted to milk the moment for all it was worth.

Moses was undismayed by Graham's lack of enthusiasm. He tallied the wagons in the line, noting that none seemed to be wobbling or threatening breakdown, and tried to remember if there were any particularly deep arroyos or gullies to cross before they got to the crossing. He couldn't recall any that couldn't be easily traversed, and he wheeled his mare around and almost galloped out front again, fighting the temptation to doff his hat at the grim-faced Graham as he passed.

Then he stopped short, fifty yards in front of Graham's grunting, slobbering oxen, and he reined the mare in so hard she nearly fell over. Moses found himself confronted with a dozen brightly painted Comanche warriors.

They seemed to have sprung from the buffalo grass that softly brushed their ponies' bellies. They were deeply tanned, and no sweat glistened on their sleek oiled and tattooed bodies or on their painted horses. They had been there awhile, waiting on the colored scout who rode out in advance of the wagon train.

Moses stared at them wide-eyed. He couldn't move, but his mind was working rapidly. If a dozen suddenly appeared, that meant that they had been hiding in a concealed dip in the plains someplace close by, and likely a dozen or more were there now, waiting in case somebody started something foolish. They weren't attacking, not yet anyhow. They wanted to parley, find out how many white men there were, how many rifles, how much stock, how many women and how young they were. Moses prayed that the settlers behind him remembered his instructions and would hide the women deep inside the wagons under quilts and comforters, invisible to the eyes of these savages.

The scout stood up on his stirrups, prepared to raise the Springfield at the slightest indication of hostility from the band, but the large buck on the pinto pony in the group's center—a war chief, judging from the confidence he showed and the way the others glanced at him for possible signals for action—sat quietly. The scalps dangling from his lance and shield spoke eloquently for his experience in spite of his apparent youth. At his side was another young man of obvious importance. He wore a large buffalo headdress which sat down on his forehead so low it almost covered his eyes. He also had scalps dangling from his shield, and he moved his horse up next to the young chief and sat staring at Moses with a deep scowl. Finally, he raised his hand in greeting and studied the black man, who clearly mystified him.

They had seen Negroes before, but they were unused to seeing a colored man dressed in buckskins and carrying what was obviously a very large and powerful weapon in front of him. Surprised or not, the young chief wasn't giving up one inch of advantage. They had the train by surprise, and they wanted to keep their edge.

The Indians' faces were painted vermilion with black stripes on their foreheads. White and red traces descended from their eyes. The chief was even younger than he first thought, Moses realized, no more than seventeen or eighteen. He had but one long braid, but it was stiff with buffalo dung, and a single owl feather was dangling from the stub of the other. His muscular chest was covered with a breastplate of bone and buffalo sinew, and on his legs were bright blue pantaloons that had been cut away to make leggings that descended to beaded leather moccasins. A large spiral of concentric tattoos circled the scar of a bullet wound in his side. Braided into the pony's mane and tied to the young Indian's body in various places were several mirrors. He carried a *bois d'arc* bow and a quiver of dogwood arrows across his back, and the crude, flat saddle had a rawhide sheath lashed to it from which stuck the brightly decorated stock of a "Yellow Boy," a Winchester '66. In the waistband of his breechcloth was a rusty Colt's Walker .44, and a large butcher knife was lashed to his right leg. All of the band were well armed, the scout noted, and except for the chief, all were carrying lances and tomahawks in addition to an assortment of firearms of various vintages and qualities.

Moses heard the wagons creaking to a halt behind him, but he dared not look around or make any sudden movement. To his dismay, the cocking of hammers also reached his ears, and he feared Graham and the rest of the fools back there would do something stupid. He turned his body in the saddle, slowly, trying to keep one eye on the chief in front of him, and shouted as loudly as he could, hoping to reach the ears of any Indians who might understand him while they hid in the buffalo grass out of sight, "Hold your fire! They want to talk."

He sat back down in his saddle and nudged his mare forward toward the heavily muscled brave with the lance, noting that he made no motion toward any of his weapons. He lowered the Springfield across his saddle in what he hoped would seem to be a peaceful gesture. For a long moment they contemplated each other.

Finally the Comanche moved his arm up and then

pulled his hand backward in a wiggling motion across his chest.

"*Idahi,*" he said. Moses was surprised to hear a deep bass voice emerge from this boyish warrior. He knew that the Comanche were supposed to understand Shoshone and some Spanish. There were men who claimed that they could communicate with them in Cheyenne and Sioux as well, but Moses knew none of these tongues. He nodded in agreement to the Comanche's word, and then sat dumbly and waited for the Indian to make the next move.

The scout tried to look as confident as he could, but his mind raced in a whipsaw panic, recalling all the lessons he had learned by listening to the Rangers, other scouts, and anyone else who professed to have direct experience with the Comanche. Although he had been around many Indians during his service with the Army, he had never been this close to a hostile Comanche warrior, not a living one anyway, and the sight of the dark-skinned, heavily muscled man in front of him awed him and froze his tongue. After a moment he was glad it did, as he suddenly recalled that it was impolite for him to speak first. The greeting of the chief had been nothing more than a formality. It was up to this well-armed youth to initiate anything like a conversation. Technically, they were the guests of these wild men, and it was their responsibility to initiate the parley.

The brave with the buffalo headgear urged his pony out in front of the young chief's. He was wearing a light robe of deerskin over a bare chest that rippled with muscles, and his eyes were set in a glare that reminded Moses of a defiant child. He also had leggings on, only his were also made of untanned doeskin, and a rattle and tomahawk were dangling from leather thongs around his neck. He was, Moses deduced from these devices, a shaman, medicine man, but his youth belied his confidence, and he was trying hard to impress everyone with his presence. Around his waist and draping down over the lance he also carried was what Moses immediately recognized as a torn and bloody Confederate battle flag. He wondered where these Comanche had obtained the filthy rag, but he didn't have time to worry about it. The second Indian spoke quickly.

"Many white mans," the medicine man said, gesturing

briefly with his lance toward the wagons. It was Moses's turn.

"We're passin' through," he said slowly, pronouncing his words carefully and a bit too loudly, wondering just how much English the Indians spoke. "We are goin' to Santa Fe." A silence fell as the Indians looked around Graham's leading wagon toward the train behind him. "We can pay. Trade," Moses offered hopefully, and he thought he saw a softening in the chief's dark brown eyes.

"Look," the shaman said suddenly without consulting with his chief. It was half command, half statement of fact, and with only a nod from the chief, the twelve braves split into two files and began riding down the length of the train. The chief led one group, the medicine man the other, and they rode toward the white settlers, tiny bells that dangled from their horses jingling quietly in the wind.

Moses followed behind the last brave. He glanced nervously over his shoulder, trying to spot any other Indians lurking in the waving grass. He saw none, an observation that gave him small comfort, and at Graham's wagon, he stopped his horse.

"What're they doin'?" Graham demanded in a loud voice, foolishly moving his rifle up a bit. The trailing braves turned slightly on their mounts and looked at him.

"Shh!" Moses hissed at him. He gestured with his eyes for the white man to put the gun down. Graham scowled and lowered the weapon. The braves walked their ponies on.

Slowly, the band moved down the length of the train, studying each wagon and its driver carefully. No women were visible, Moses noted with relief, but he also realized that the total absence of family members would give the Comanche an overwhelming curiosity about how many were hidden behind the canvas.

As the two lines reached the last wagon, they crossed behind it bread-and-butter-fashion and started back as slowly and carefully as they had gone. Going and coming, both lines had stopped to observe Jack Sterling's small herd of cattle with interest, but they didn't seem to know what to make of the hogs who noisily rooted around in the buffalo grass every time the train pulled up. The chickens, by contrast, amused the braves and seemed to frighten them a bit as they clucked and chuckled when the Indians leaned over to peer through the wire into their crude coops. In spite of the animals' antics, the tension in the air seemed to lay the wind and become more intense with each pony's step.

Moses gently spurred his horse down toward them, whispering to each driver as he passed, "Don't do nothin'. No matter what, don't do nothin' 'less I signal you."

Except for Karl Runnels, the drivers said nothing or just nodded at the advice. But Runnels, a big German tailor with a red face and a wagonload of cloth, turned even redder when Moses whispered to him and demanded loudly, "Und vot iff you're dead? Vot kind uff zig-e-nal vill dot be?"

Moses looked up sharply to see if the Indians had heard and understood the word *signal*, which the German had almost shouted in his mispronunciation. He saw them glare at the tailor and urge their ponies into canters toward Runnels's wagon. Moses slipped his gloved finger into the Springfield's trigger housing and prepared to die.

But it wasn't the German's voice that attracted them. They had spotted the bright green and red cloth that appeared in the canvas folds in the rear of his overloaded Conestoga, and they rode their ponies right up behind it and began pulling out the bolts and stringing them out onto the dusty grass.

"Gottdamnit!" Runnels shouted, and he began scrambling down from his wagon seat to collect his goods before they were entirely ruined by the ponies' hooves. Before Moses could do anything, the burly tailor was swearing loudly and shaking his fist at them as if they were malicious schoolchildren.

By the time Runnels found his footing, a scream tore the afternoon's warmth. The German's wife, Golda, was discovered by the Indians as she tried to hang on to a piece of lacy white material that one of the bucks had pulled out of the wagon. She held frantically on to the cloth while the startled and amazed braves rode around her body and studied her thick, black-stockinged legs kicking out from under her petticoats.

So red in the face that he seemed about to explode, Runnels was swearing inarticulately as he brushed by

Moses's shying bay and started for his wife, who was now totally entangled in the fabric and was clawing at the prancing Indian ponies with her fingers. He had left his rifle up on the wagon and wore no pistol, but he pulled out a lockback jackknife and started for the ground among the horses, apparently intending to slice the lace away from his wife's clutching fists, thereby freeing and rescuing her.

Regardless of his intent, the Indians took a knife-wielding white man more seriously than a hysterical woman's screams, and their grins suddenly became fierce grimaces. The brave holding the bolt of cloth in his hand dropped the lace, and with little more than a flick of his wrist, he flung his lance directly at the charging German. The spear pierced Runnels's boot and brought forth a scream, which was cut short by the sudden arrival of three more lances that knocked him down flat and pinned him to the dirt.

Golda, seeing her husband down, pulled free of the cloth and started toward him, but the chief deftly moved his pony between her and her husband's body and cut her off. She bounced hard off the Indian's painted horse and fell backward, emiting a new shriek of terror that ended when her body struck the ground and air whooshed from her lungs. She lay there in a faint. The chief walked his horse around her, raised her skirts with the tip of his own lance, and inspected her fat legs briefly before shouting something to his comrades. They all laughed, then rode off twenty-five yards and took up a line together to wait.

3

THE INCIDENT BEHIND THE RUNNELS WAGON TOOK LESS than a minute, and Moses and the other settlers who leaned out from their own wagons to find out what was going on were frozen by the suddenness of the Indians' actions. The scout moved his horse up beside the fallen German and looked down to see if he was still alive. He was amazed to see that Runnels's eyes were open and his mouth working in a kind of silent prayer. Except for the first lance, which had pierced his boot and brought forth gouts of blood, no other spear had wounded him. They had simply nailed him to the ground by piercing his coat and holding him there. He was hurt, Moses noted, but he would live. That, and the almost playful way the Comanche had dealt with Frau Runnels, made him think that maybe they might want to trade after all. Certainly they could have killed them both had they wanted to. For the briefest moment he triumphed in his idea that the Comanche could be dealt with.

Golda groaned loudly, and Moses turned to a man named William Golden, the wagon driver behind the Runnels wagon, and ordered, "They ain't hurt much. Get 'em up an' inside, an' for God's sake, keep that knife away from him."

The driver didn't move but simply stared stupidly at Moses, and the scout wondered if he was going to have to dismount and deal with the fools on the ground himself. But before he could act, he spotted a swatch of golden hair underneath the Runnels wagon. He opened his mouth to say something, but then he recognized Aggie Sterling, and his words stopped in his throat.

She moved rapidly to Golda, applied a wet cloth to the woman's face, and helped her up. Down the line of wagons, Moses could see Jack Sterling's face staring in a great, silent rage. There was nothing he could do without inviting the Indians' attention, and, Moses assumed with relief, he knew it. Finally, Golden found his legs and climbed down and obeyed Moses's command, helping the large German free himself from the lances. He and Aggie started the couple toward their own wagon as Moses rode out to deal with the Comanche, who were talking among themselves and pointing at the beautiful yellow-haired girl who had come out from hiding to help the great fool of a white man.

The chief was not engaged in the excited reaction to Aggie's appearance. He stared at her with eyes that seemed to reflect a mixture of fascination and horror. Moses saw that he was almost transfixed, and he didn't look away from her until she disappeared into the Runnels wagon. What remained was thoughtful, Moses saw, not lustful. It perplexed the black scout, but he had no time to dwell on it.

When Moses reached them, the Indians turned their

ponies and rode back to the head of the train. Moses followed at a short distance until they were about where they had met, and then the chief regained his composure, turned, and began talking quickly to the medicine man.

Although younger, the chief carried himself with a lot more confidence. The black scout studied the markings on the savages in front of him. Each rawhide shield revealed the bearer's personal medicine. None of them was particularly scratched and torn; in fact, a number of them looked as if they had been recently constructed. There were scalps hanging from several, to be sure, but his mind quickly drifted from such idle recognitions to one that was more startling. These weren't Penaterkuh, the band of Comanche which for years had terrorized the Hill Country and central Texas and had in recent years displaced themselves to the reservation around Fort Sill. Nor were they Nocona or Yampareeku or Kutsukuh, nor any of the other Comanche bands that had sometimes dealt peacefully with whites. These were Quahidi, Antelope Eaters, the most feral of the bands that roamed Comanchería. They had never signed a treaty and sometimes made war on other Comanche bands. They regarded the white man as only slightly more tolerable than rattlesnakes and scorpions. They had ravaged forts and settlements from San Antonio to Colorado and were famous for taking hostages. Little was even known about them apart from their distinctive fierceness and the markings on their shields and ponies that distinguished them from the other bands. Moses blew softly between his teeth in an inaudible whistle. It was a miracle that Runnels and everyone else weren't already dead or being carried off across the backs of the brightly painted ponies.

Moses conversed with the shaman for a time in broken English and crude signs. The Indian's voice was guttural, and his vocabulary was sprinkled with the dialect of a man who was unpracticed in any tongue other than his own, but he managed to make himself understood well enough, even if phrases of Comanche and Shoshone mixed awkwardly from time to time with the few Spanish and English words he proudly used. The other braves and the chief sat their ponies in silence, but Moses noticed their eyes playing across the train behind him, assessing men and strength, plunder and loot, and, he added with a shudder, how many more beauties like Aggie might be secreted in the wagons. After a few minutes, he wheeled his horse around and rode back to Graham's wagon.

Frank Herbert and Jack Sterling and one or two others including Virgil Hollister had come up and were hanging on to Graham's wagon, staring out at the Indians, who patiently waited about fifty yards out.

Sterling's face contorted itself into a fierce scowl as Moses reined his horse up on the opposite side. His dark eyes danced with hatred.

"I'm fixin' to kill me a nigger if anythin' happens to my girl!" he announced, not exactly in Moses's direction but generally.

Graham waved the comment off with his stump but not before shooting Sterling a quick, hard look. "What do they want?"

"Says he wants to trade for some fresh meat an' other stuff." Moses forced his voice to be calm while dealing with the men's collective ignorance.

"Meat!" Graham sniffed. "We got no fresh meat. You know that."

Moses glanced down at the oxen, who stood switching flies away from their rumps with their stubby tails. "They see it diff'rent." He saw Graham's eyes widen. "They see these here oxes an' the cattle—"

"Them cattle's *breed* stock!" Sterling cried. "They're not for butcherin'. If they was, I'd already have—"

"Look." Moses tried to sound reasonable. "They don't care 'bout none of that. The medicine man there says they's white men up on the plains been killin' buffalo left an' right, antelope too. His people's hungry, an' he sees somethin' that looks one hell of a lot easier to butcher than buffalo draggin' these wagons, an' some prime meat on the hoof back there, an' he don't give a good goddamn 'bout no 'breed stock.' "

"Well, I'll be goddamned," Sterling said and shook his head.

Graham settled back on the wagon seat with a gesture that indicated that he understood. "Well, hell, there's only twelve of them. I reckon I could take on six right now, an' you could handle a couple yourself—or that's what I hear—an' between Jack an' Frank here—"

"You don't understand, Mr. Graham," Moses pleaded suddenly when he realized what the wagon master was contemplating. "That's *Comanche* out there. They don't mess 'round with no dozen braves. Like as not they's twenty or more has rifles pointed at us right now." Graham's eyes strayed unsteadily across the impenetrable grass. "These here is jus' a bunch come to size us up," Moses went on. "Jesus God, Mr. Graham! Why you think they didn't kill ol' Mr. Runnels back there? If he was any kind of threat to 'em, he'd be dead right now. They knew they was covered, else why would they waste their lances jus' havin' fun with him?"

Frank Herbert spoke up. "Makes sense, Cap'n," he said. "This boy jus' might know what he's talking 'bout. Least, that's what we're payin' him for." The black scout stared at Herbert in surprise. He had assumed this wide-eyed, talkative man was a near moron. He was uncertain how to regard such support, but Graham further surprised Moses by staring at Frank and nodding.

"I know my job, Mr. Graham!" Moses insisted. "They's mean sons of bitches sittin' out there. They'd jus' as soon take what they want, an' to tell you the truth, they're prob'ly fixin' to try sooner or later anyhow."

Sterling spoke up. "What's stoppin' 'em right now, then? Answer me that one." He glanced up to Graham for approval of his logic. "If there's as many as you say sneakin' up right now, what's stoppin' 'em? This ain't nothin' but nigger foolishness, Graham." Sterling spat into the grass beside the wagon. "I say we start shootin' an' see what happens." He glared at Moses. "What makes you think we'd be any worse off doin' that 'n just handin' 'em what they want?"

"Nothin'," Moses said. "Not one goddamn thing. But right now, this is how they want to play it, an' we ain't hardly ready—"

"I say let's shoot it out here an' now an' get on 'bout our business. I ain't givin' 'em one heifer."

"They're goin' to hit us anyhow," Moses argued. He pulled out his bandanna and wiped his face. Fear climbed his back like a centipede. He could feel the braves watching him.

"Then I don't see what advantage there is in tradin' anything with them," Graham said.

"Look." Moses felt patience slipping away from him as a desperate fear began to flood in and replace it. "If we give 'em what they want, we still might make the crossin' by dark. They's some caves there, an' we could fort up real good. After a while, they'll get tired an' go 'way, especially if we show 'em we can shoot straight."

Graham stroked his beard with his stump. Moses could see he was thinking it over.

"If we get caught out here," the scout pressed his argument, "we got no cover, no water. Hell, we ain't near ready. Least on the creek we got a fightin' chance."

"I just hate to give away good cattle to a scrawny bunch of half-starved hunters," Graham said, but he was swayed, and Moses breathed a bit more easily. "We'll likely need those beeves. We've already traded away our eatin' stock."

"Them's *breed* stock! Damnit!" Sterling said. "They're not for eatin'." But Graham ignored him.

"Mr. Graham, that ain't no huntin' party," Moses said definitively. "That's a war lance that shaman is carryin'. Them's scalps hangin' from their shields. That paint on their faces means death. That's *Quahidi* Comanche. That chief an' them braves may look like a bunch of young'uns, but they could take this train an' ever'body in it if they've a mind to, an' I s'pect there's a hundred more braves in shoutin' distance if he wants 'em. You don't want to mess around with this thing."

Graham still said nothing. He was, Moses surmised, lamenting the dilemma of being caught between red men and a black one and not being able to get out of the crack without having to pay. "I think we can buy some time," he said finally, more to Herbert than to Sterling. "Maybe we can save the rest of the stuff."

"An' our women," Moses added helpfully.

"They ain't *your* women!" Sterling shot back at him. "Goddamnit! An' it ain't your beef, neither. Why can't we give 'em a mule?"

"Comanche won't have nothin' to do with mules,"

Moses explained with a patience he didn't feel. "They think a mule's some kind of freak."

"That's a point I'd agree on," Graham muttered. "You're going to give up a cow, Jack." His voice was rock-hard. It left no room for argument.

"Well, I'll be plum go to hell." Sterling's face was a mask of pure contempt for the black man who was taking away his cattle. "I seen you talkin' to my girl today, an' if I catch you at it again, I'm goin' to have me some black balls for a necklace. Savvy, nigger?"

"Shut up, Sterling," Graham ordered, and again Sterling looked startled, as if he had been slapped. Graham did not look at him but continued to divide his glance between Moses and the distant Indians. "Oh, what the hell," he finally sighed. "Give them a goddamn cow."

Moses tried to calm his voice. Sterling's attack on him had been so violent that he had trouble maintaining anything like a professional tone, and his nervousness angered him and made his voice quaver a bit. "It's more'n a cow," he said. "They want three beeves, maybe a ox or two."

"*Goddamnit*, Graham!" Sterling swore, but Moses went on before he could say anything else.

"That's what makes me think there's a bunch of 'em. They're askin' for too much for any twelve braves, I don't care how hungry they are."

"No oxen," Graham said flatly. "Three of Sterling's cattle, but no oxen. We need the oxen, goddamnit."

"I need the cattle, too," Sterling said sullenly.

Moses noted that the Indians were beginning to walk their ponies around a bit and to show signs of impatience. He pressed on, "They want the cloth they took off Runnels's wagon, an' . . ." He trailed off.

"What?" Graham demanded.

"Well, they asked for some rifles an' bullets—which we ain't goin' to give 'em."

"That's the first thing you've said that makes sense, boy," Sterling said. Graham nodded in agreement.

"An'," Moses finished the list of demands, "they want some whiskey."

"Whiskey!" This time it was Virgil Hollister who shouted. "That's pissin' in the wind for sure. I'll be damned in hell 'fore I'll give whiskey to a heathen Indian. I'd sooner give 'em rifles." The man's eyes were narrowly set on either side of a huge axblade-shaped nose. "Far as I'm concerned, we can pour all that devil's brew out on the ground right now an' get on 'bout our business."

"We ain't got no whiskey," Graham said to Moses. Hollister made a braying noise with his lips.

"Mr. Graham," Moses said, again more patiently than he felt, "we got barrels an' barrels of whiskey on this train. I know it, an' you know it. Half the wagons here got least one, most two or more, includin' yours. I know you prize it, 'cause any damn fool knows that he can trade whiskey for damn near anythin' in Santa Fe or anywhere else. But them Indians ain't blind. They seen the barrels, an' they want some."

Graham studied the black man sitting on a horse before him. His hand tightened on the stock of his rifle, but he said nothing. His lips were tightly pressed together under his beard, and his eyes quiet.

"Well, we ain't givin' 'em no keg of whiskey," Sterling said with finality, breaking the tension. "I think I got me a half-bottle of rotgut someplace. I'll water it down with that damn creek water everybody drunk, an' they'll shit fire an' save matches." He chuckled at the prospect.

"I think we're better off givin' 'em a barrel or two," Moses said. He held up his hand to stave off the objections. "It'll slow 'em down, since they can't carry it, an' they sure as hell ain't fixin' to leave any of it behind."

Graham thought for a minute more. All the Indians were now walking their horses around in a slow circle. "Jack," he said, "you go back there an' cut out three beeves."

Sterling shot a hateful look at Moses. "I'll do it, but I don't like it."

"Too damn bad," Graham replied. "Frank, you cut a keg of juice off the Sterling wagon."

"Off *my* wagon!" Jack Sterling shouted. "Why not your wagon? Why mine?"

"Because you come up here an' poked your nose in where it doesn't belong," Graham replied. "An' because I wouldn't be here in the first place if it weren't for you. Now get to it, Frank."

Herbert muttered a "Yes, Cap'n," and walked off

behind Sterling, who was kicking angrily at the grass. Hollister followed behind him, glaring alternately at the Indians and at the wagon master as he stalked away.

"Three beeves," Graham said to Moses and held up three fingers as if it were the black scout and not the Indians with whom he was bargaining. "No oxen, not one. No guns, no powder, no cartridges. The whiskey, an' they can have the goddamn cloth."

Moses nodded and turned his horse to return to the waiting Comanche. He believed they might take the deal, for the moment. He had no doubt they were certain that they would own the whole train and its contents soon enough anyhow.

"Say," Graham called to him in a mocking tone, "what do we get?"

"What?" Moses turned around in the saddle.

"I say, what do we get out of this? You did say it was some kind of trade."

"Well." Moses brought a hand up and rubbed the short, stubby beard he wore on the end of his chin. "He didn't come right out an' say so, but for now, I reckon, we get to keep our hair."

CHAPTER THREE

1

THEY DIDN'T MAKE THE CROSSING BEFORE DARK. THE delay caused by the trading parley stretched out as problems began concerning exactly what the Indians would receive in at least a temporary exchange for the settlers' lives.

Jack Sterling caused trouble when he fell into an argument with one of the braves over the single bull in his herd. For some reason—probably just to devil the white man, Moses thought when he intervened—the Indian insisted that one of the three cattle to be cut out would be the yearling, which would not have made very good eating, as both the red and the white men knew. A tugging and shouting match developed over the animal, and it threatened to turn violent before Moses managed to pacify the Indians by adding a barrel of salted meat in addition to the heifers Sterling was more or less resigned to parting with.

Then there had been a problem with Runnels. Revived from his wound sufficiently to watch the Indians collect the scattered bolts of cloth, he again took to cursing them in both German and English. While the braves couldn't understand what he was calling them, his tone was clear enough, and they did not like it and began answering him in their own tongue. Moses had barely settled the matter of the bull when the shouting rose once more around the Runnels wagon, and he galloped up to the German, who sat in the back of his Conestoga with his bandaged foot propped up on the rim while he swore at the two braves who were inspecting the cloth.

"You'd best shut the hell up!" Moses yelled. "You

been lucky so far, but they ain't goin' to take much more."

"You call dis *lok*? Gottdamn your black zoul!" Runnels steamed. "I vill *not* be robbed by zese heazens. You are in cahoots mitt dem! *Dis* I know! Ach!" The strain of his yelling caused him to lift his bandaged foot, and it came down and reopened the wound, forcing him to cry out. But his face showed the utter contempt he had for the two races which, somehow, had conspired to rob him of the materials of his trade.

The most serious incident took place unexpectedly. While waiting for Herbert to cut loose a keg of whiskey from Sterling's wagon, a brave boldly lifted the canvas on the next vehicle in line and, to his delight, discovered a small boy peeking out from under a quilt. Although frightened, the boy was almost as fascinated by the brightly painted Comanche, and he didn't resist at all when the buck lifted him out of the wagon and held him up high.

The boy belonged to the Simmons clan, an older couple with six children. Bob Simmons, a gunsmith by trade, was quick to react when he saw his youngest son in the muscular hands of an Indian.

He came hauling around the back of his wagon and bellowed at the bewildered brave, doubled up his fists, and delivered a smashing blow to the confused young Indian's painted face. The brave collapsed, dropping the boy and spouting blood from a cut lip. Simmons swooped up his son and placed him back into the wagon, only then turning to finish what, to his mind, was a fairly started fistfight.

To a Comanche, however, a blow struck with a bare hand was the worst insult one man could pay to another. The outraged warrior removed a club from a thong around his waist and smashed Bob Simmons's skull as soon as the upstart white man turned to face him.

The blow was not meant to be lethal. It wasn't intended to do much more than stun the white man, but the Indian was angry and insulted, and blood rushed from Simmons's ears and nose. He collapsed at the brave's feet.

His honor satisfied, the Comanche returned to watch Frank Herbert's efforts to unload the barrel, and Hilda Simmons had to do what she could to drag her unconscious husband back inside their wagon.

The Indians drove the cattle out and ran them into

the grass, firing their flint-tipped dogwood shafts into them and chasing them as if they were buffalo. They killed the frightened and confused animals quickly and, to Sterling's loud expressions of dismay and disgust, began butchering them before the train was moving again. Moses did what he could to urge the drivers to hurry their animals as much as possible. They had lost over an hour of daylight dickering with the Indians, and his landmark was already fading into a mass of distant, dark clouds when the Indians disappeared in the buffalo grass behind them.

The scout still held forth hopes of reaching the crossing and camping there rather than in the open, but more bad luck awaited the party. The Ambrose wagon lost a wheel two hours after they pulled away from the Indians.

"We can't jus' leave it!" Kyle Ambrose said when Moses rode up to see why everyone had stopped. "I mean, it's ever'thin' we got left." Ambrose was a hard-looking man with tired yellow hair that had already started to show gray, although he wasn't yet forty. His two sons stood next to him.

Graham walked down the train from the other direction and stood beside Moses's horse. "Load what you can on other wagons," he said. "You know we can't stop out here. You're riskin' the whole train."

"I ain't leavin'!" Ambrose declared. "I'll stay right here an' fix'er, goddamnit! I ain't leavin'."

Graham shrugged. "That's your lookout, Ambrose. But I think the kids ought to go along."

"It ain't fair!" Ambrose swore and kicked the disabled wagon with a broken boot. "Goddamnit, it ain't fair at all!"

"Nobody said it was goin' to be," Graham said. He looked up at Moses and gestured. "Go see if Sterlin'll take some of this stuff, especially the whiskey. He's a shade lighter since this afternoon."

To Moses's relief Sterling only grunted an agreement when he heard that the keg of whiskey he had lost was to be replaced by two of Ambrose's load. In a while they had most of the family's things distributed among three or four other wagons. Kyle Ambrose stood in the middle of his wagon's bed when the train began moving again.

"I'm goin' to fix'er an' catch up," he announced to each driver who passed.

"C'mon, Mr. Ambrose," Moses called. "We got to move fast."

"I ain't goin'," Ambrose replied. "I'm goin' to stay right here an' try an' fix'er. My boy Tom's stayin' with me."

Moses looked around and saw the teenaged Ambrose boy coming through the tall grass toward the broken wagon. The other son, Jed, was walking beside Jason Sterling, who continued to herd the cattle.

"Them Indians'll be along here in a bit," Moses argued, glancing at the darkening horizon behind them. The western sky was now revealing enormous thunderheads that climbed rapidly skyward from behind the all-too-distant mesa.

"It don't matter," Ambrose insisted. "*Goddamnit!* This here's all we got in the world. An' no goddamn Indian's goin' to scare me into leavin' it here to rot."

Moses looked over the dross of Kyle Ambrose's life. The chest of drawers and bedstead that leaned uncertainly against the wagon's denuded frame, now stripped of canvas protection, the carpetbags and other junk. He understood that no amount of talk would move the man, so he wheeled his horse around and caught up to the moving train. He looked back and saw that two of the Ambrose oxen, left unhobbled while their master absentmindedly began working on his wagon, were following along behind the train.

Two more wagons, the Newsomes' and the Hawshaws' antique Studebakers, collapsed within a mile of where they left Ambrose. This time, however, the families were more practical. Taking only those belongings they felt they couldn't live without, they tied their draft animals up and piled onto others' loads and were on their way again in half an hour.

Moses's hopes for reaching the crossing before dark faded completely when the sunlight disappeared behind the growing thunderheads in the southwest. Lightning snaked out of the enormous black clouds and seemed to make them grow larger with each flashing explosion as they advanced on the small train. He kept an eye out for cyclones and for more Indians, but neither appeared as the train pushed its way through the trackless grass directly into the huge black maw of the storm.

The wind shifted and now hit them in the face. The air seemed alive with electricity that caused the animals to shy and balk as they drew closer to a tiny grove of scrub cedar at the bottom of a small depression between two outcroppings of red sandstone. Moses spotted a circle of buzzards floating on the updrafts above the small group of trees. They were high overhead, and in spite of the wind's growing fierceness, the birds continued to circle the depression, riding the heated air currents high and then sweeping down from time to time toward their carrion meal. Moses wondered if a buffalo had gone there to die, or maybe some mustang had broken a leg in a prairie dog hole and limped in before being torn apart by wolves or wildcats.

He spurred his bay and forced her down into the trees as soon as he reached them, thinking that they made a poor substitute for the shelter and natural defenses of the crossing. But as he entered the small grove he groaned out loud. There was almost no protection from either the Indians or the weather. The depression opened on the southern end to an expansive prairie, and the trees were too green and scrawny for firewood.

He pushed the mare down into the tiny grove and set a covey of quail scurrying away from the horse's hooves. A dozen chicks followed their fat mother out of the trees and into the covering grass. All at once the bay reared back as the wind gusted and brought the overripe stink of rotting flesh. Her reluctance to go down into the hollow had nothing to do with the storm, he realized, and he complimented the beast for having the sense to want to avoid this place. But now that he had seen what was there, he acknowledged that there was no turning away.

He reined the bay around and galloped back toward the train. Graham saw him coming and pulled up. He grabbed his rifle and took up a defensive posture on the seat.

"What now?" he called. "Indians?"

"Worse," the scout said breathlessly. He drew his horse around and let her stand. "Massacre."

"What? That's impossible."

Moses shot a hard look at Graham's scowl and fought back anger. He was sick of having to argue every point with this white man. "Well, you jus' come an' have a look-see. You tell 'em it didn't happen." He wheeled the horse and rode back down toward the grove.

Graham set his brake and climbed down. He waded through the chest-high grass toward the small grove. Behind him, a number of others followed. All carried weapons high and ready.

Moses waited until Graham reached him, then pointed down into the grove.

There were three wagons, buckboards like Graham's, several mules and two burros, and a large number of people. The carnage told the scout that much. After Graham and the others came up, they all stood and stared at the remains of a Comanche raid and tried to put together what had happened.

"They was Mescans," Moses deduced aloud. "You can tell from their clothes." Coarsely woven strips of serapes and ponchos were scattered around the area.

He couldn't guess what they had been doing alone out on the plains, this far from the Indian Line and even farther from the well-worn trail that led from Chihuahua and the Paseo del Norte up to Santa Fe. People didn't travel out here except in large numbers, and not even in large numbers in Comanche Spring, at least not normally, not without a heavily armed escort, and they were too far from any settlement to have been merely lost. But whatever their intention had been would always be a mystery, for none of them survived.

Twelve scalpless corpses were strewn about the small camp like broken dolls. Scavengers had done severe damage to the remains, and it was hard to determine from a distance which of the dead were male and which, if any, were female.

Two had been tied to wagons, and their bodies were festooned with sharp sticks and broken arrows, indicating the manner of their deaths. Another pair had been hanged upside down from the wagons' uplifted singletrees; the charred remains of their corpses and blackened circles beneath their burned skulls testified to the horror of their ends.

The settlers began to move about, and some soon discovered several female corpses in the grass nearby. The unmutilated but severely decomposed body of one woman was discovered in the brush off to one side. A single bullet hole gaped between her breasts, and her hands clutched an ancient horse pistol. She had apparently killed herself.

All of the wagons had been burned, but they had not caught properly and were mostly intact. The men poked around the charred beds and found two dead children, infants, which apparently had been the victims of the besieged Mexicans before they were overrun by the Indians.

"I can't believe they shot their own young'uns," Frank Herbert offered as they looked down on the grisly remains of a family's life.

"They reckoned the Indians'd jus' do it for 'em, an' slower," Moses said. He gagged back his stomach's revolt. The Mexican men had been methodically tortured. It was as if the Indians had cooked their victims one limb at a time.

"I thought they always took kids an' women with 'em," Frank said. His wide blue eyes were heavy with sadness as he looked at the rotting body of a young woman whose breasts were cut away and stomach slashed wide open.

"Sometimes they do," Moses said. "But war parties need to move quick an' quiet. Women an' kids're noisy." He cut the bonds on a body and stepped away when it fell from the burned wheel. The odor was overwhelming, and he found himself talking aloud to keep from heaving.

"Once, I hear, down near San Antonio, they got 'em a whole bunch of kids from some schoolhouse. Hauled 'em all away, damn near as far as Kansas. Kids kept cryin', though. Nothin' would shut 'em up. So the Comanche got to a bunch of trees, like these here, an' they jus' busted all their heads in, one at a time. Just like they was puppies or somethin'." It was a long speech for the scout, and the white men gaped at him. He turned back to his grisly chore slightly embarrassed.

Graham and Jack Sterling joined Moses in cutting the men's bodies from the wagon wheels, and Graham picked up remnants of the strewn clothing and covered the ravaged bodies on the ground. He draped the ragged cloth over the corpses with what could only be described as tenderness. Moses watched him for a moment, wondering at the peculiar activity. All of the men on the train had seen corpses before. Many of them were veterans of horrible battles where bodies were strewn about as mere parts, bloody and torn from their owners by the violence of grapeshot and Minié balls. Graham himself was a veteran. But the way in which he covered the bodies, particularly those of the slaughtered women, stirred something in Moses. There was clearly more to the wagon master than the scout had at first perceived.

"Why'd they cut off their tits?" he heard Harvey Pierce, a short, wiry carpenter, ask of no one in particular.

"I hear they make tobacco pouches out of 'em," Jack Sterling offered and then laughed. "Mescans got big tits, you know."

Moses saw Graham flinch, but none of the men said anything more. They were dumbfounded with the horror of the scene. The thoughts of each ranged back to the party that was going on around the whiskey and slaughtered cattle only a few miles behind them. They each figured that the Comanche were probably plotting an even bigger and bloodier raid as soon as they finished off their refreshments and took up the trail again.

"Ain't we goin' to bury 'em?" The voice came from the edge of the clearing, and Moses looked up, finding himself not at all surprised to see Aggie Sterling standing there. She had a handkerchief jammed against her nose, and he could see her eyes were wet.

"Course we're not!" her father answered her sharply. "They're just a bunch of stinkin' Mescans, an' we're not wastin' our time. We can't camp here, now, if that's what this nigger had in mind." He turned to Moses. "We got to get movin'. Right, boy?"

Moses stood and stared back at this scowling white man. Sterling wore a thin mustache and a scraggly, dark goatee. His cheeks sprouted a three-day growth of whiskers. Long, dirty black hair escaped from beneath a once expensive but now trail-battered hat, and his open mouth revealed bright yellow teeth that formed themselves into a sarcastic grin.

The scout wondered how anyone so ugly could have

sired such a beautiful daughter as Aggie. At the same time, he remembered how Sterling no longer swaggered with pride in his walk and stance. He was feeling the strain of all the bad luck, Moses realized, and he was looking for someone to blame.

No one liked Sterling. Graham and he didn't get along, and even Frank gave him plenty of room. He slapped his boy every time the youngster came in arm's reach, and usually when the train bedded down, Moses saw Sterling sitting off by himself, smoking or maybe pulling off a bottle.

Moses was surprised that Jack Sterling hadn't already lit out on his own. He showed all the symptoms of a man who would run at the first sign of trouble. Sterling rode the best horse in the train's remuda, a big black stallion, and he could make good time on his own. But he stayed, and he gave no indication that he was about to do anything else. There was something more than the meager pile of junk in his wagon keeping Jack Sterling along for this trip, more than the dowdy woman Moses figured was his wife, Aggie's mother, more than a handful of rapidly thinning beeves. He was a slicker, Moses told himself, and a dangerous one.

Moses had been pressing for rapid movement all day. He knew how important it was to find a reasonably safe camp before dark, and clearly, as Sterling had said and as much as he hated to agree with him, they couldn't camp here. The place reeked of death. No one in the train could stand it. But Sterling's impudent, ugly grin made the scout stiffen and shake his head. He felt defiant, and something in him made him want to please this strong, pretty girl by antagonizing her father.

"I reckon we ought to plant 'em," he heard himself say, and he stood silently while Graham gaped incredulously at him.

He saw Aggie move quickly toward a wagon. She had two long-handled shovels in her hands. Sterling exploded.

"Niggers, Mescans, an' redskins!" He threw his hat down. "I swear to God almighty in heaven, I've never seen such! First you're all for buyin' time with *my* cattle, an' then the first bunch of dead greasers we come across, you want to throw the whole thing up an' bury 'em. God almighty damn! I'm tellin' you, Graham, I ain't goin' to take this. Nossir, I'm not!"

Graham moved his gray eyes between them as if trying to decide if either was worth arguing with. There was no anger in his face, only disgust, a kind of weariness. For the second time that day, he looked to Moses like a man trapped between two untenable alternatives and hating himself because he was being forced to make a choice. He lowered his head and said nothing, but Moses felt his own anger rising all at once. The scout had had enough of Sterling. He was now determined to bury these people, not out of any sense of decency—that was a commodity on the plains that was often too expensive—but simply because he knew that Jack Sterling, an ugly, mean man, a white man, didn't want him to.

"Look, Mr. Sterling," Moses said, noting that the wind was beginning to blow harder now. "You get your cattle movin'. I'll stay here an' bury these folks. You'd want somebody to bury you, an'—"

Before he could finish, Pierce, the short, wiry man, burst forth from the grass brandishing an empty bottle. "Looky here," he shouted. "Looky here what them redskins got from them Mescans!"

Sterling snatched the bottle away from the short man, who announced to everyone around, "It's mescal. Or tequila. Or somethin'. It's liquor surer'n God. If they done this after a bottle of cheap Mescan liquor, what're they goin' to do when they finish off a whole keg of Tennessee sour mash?"

Sterling handed the bottle to Graham and walked off a step, shaking his head. "Niggers an' Mescans," he said. "I'll be damned."

"There's some more bottles out there, too," Pierce continued. "They're all busted up. We better get goin'." He raced back toward the train.

"It looks like he's right," Graham said, sniffing the bottle's neck. "We can't stay here, an' it's about to come up another frog choaker." He glanced appreciatively up to a sky that was now almost completely covered with black. "Maybe it'll wash some of this away."

"It's already rained on 'em at least twice," Moses said. "I think we're okay for a while, anyhow. If they drink that whole keg, they ain't goin' to be able to ride, much less track us. Not 'fore mornin'."

The men already had started moving back toward the wagons. Harvey Pierce was informing everyone from the top of his lungs that a massacre by drunken Indians was in the making if they didn't move pronto.

"I'm goin' to stay an' dig some graves," he said.

"The *hell* you say!" Graham burst out. He turned suddenly and dropped his hand to his Colt's. He didn't draw it, but he held its butt in a ready manner. "I've about had enough of your goddamn sass for one day. You're bein' paid to do a job, an' so far about all you've done is give away our stuff an' lead us to nowhere. For about six bits I'd just blow your head off an' leave you right here to rot."

"I got six bits," Sterling said, and Moses noted that he had moved slightly beside Graham and also rested his hand on the butt of his pistols, which were arranged in front of him in a cross-draw pattern. Behind them, also, two men who had never spoken to Moses at all stood at the ready as well. They were the men who owned the hogs, and Moses knew them to be from a deeper South than anyone else on the train. One of them wore a stained gray forage cap; the other usually covered himself against the rain with a tattered greatcoat that still bore the stripes of a Confederate sergeant. Moses had instinctively ridden around them since the journey began. Now they looked at him with slightly amused expressions.

A big chunk of silence suddenly grew up in the small grove and stood like a wall against the increasing wind. Moses figured he could take on Graham easily enough. The big man was off balance where he stood, and with one arm crippled, the chances were good that he couldn't pull a gun out that fast. The two Southerners had rifles, but they weren't cocked or aimed, and that took time. Sterling's cross-draw rig was fancy, but Moses doubted that the ugly man was any sort of gunfighter; then, neither was Moses. He wore his guns high on the back of his waist with the butts pointed out for easy reach, and knew he could hit what he shot at from this range, yet he was no quick-draw artist. For Moses, guns were tools, nothing more. The tension mounted as the storm approached, and the electricity that infected the air supercharged the conflict. Moses realized that he had to fight or back down, and neither option was inviting.

"I guess the next move's yours, nigger," Sterling hissed. "Pull out them six-shooters, an' let's just end it right here. We'll leave you to rot with your bean-eatin' friends."

Graham glanced at Sterling, and Moses saw a glint of something in his gray eyes that told him he hated being backed up by someone of Sterling's ilk. But the wagon master didn't back away.

"I reckon it's your bet, Moses," he said. "Call or fold. I say we move on. Get to this goddamn crossin' soon as we can. The livin' are what's important now."

"You won't think so if you're the one that's dead." Aggie Sterling's voice cut across the clearing like a scythe. The tension that had built up was mown away like tall grass. They all turned toward her.

She stood off to the group's left, near one of the Mexicans' wagons. She spoke to all of them, but her eyes particularly focused on Graham. In her hand was Moses's knife, the one he had used to cut down the burned corpses and left sticking in the wagon's side.

For another moment, no one said anything. Then she moved quickly over between Moses and his white adversaries. "We're goin' to bury these folks," she said. "It's the decent thing to do. I just hope that somebody has the grit to bury me when they find me."

"Get back on the wagon, girl." Jack spat out the order in a vicious tone.

"Go to hell," she said quietly.

"What did you say?" Anger swept over his face in a red blush. His hand fell and withdrew his starboard Colt's. Moses was right. He fumbled with the pistol's grip and almost dropped it before he managed to get it out of the holster. "I'll shoot you like the bitch-bastard you are! Talk back to me! I ought to lick you good. You get on that wagon!" He advanced on her. Moses's hand went to the butt of his own revolver. Graham could shoot him, but the scout couldn't—wouldn't, he determined—just stand there and let this ugly man kill his own daughter. He looked quickly at Graham and saw that the wagon master had drawn his own pistol and was turned now toward Jack.

"Put it up, Daddy," another voice called from across the clearing. Aggie's brother, Jason, stood with his feet apart, a shotgun in his hand. The hammers were drawn back, and the twin barrels were directed toward his father's middle.

"Jason, get the hell back up there with your mother!" Sterling screamed. "What the hell's goin' on here? What's got into you kids?" He turned and scanned the astounded faces of the men in the clearing. Then he wheeled on his children again. "Are you crazy? I'm your *daddy*. This is your goddamn *father* you're talkin' to."

"Put the gun up," Jason repeated. "You ain't goin' to shoot her, so put it up." Moses gaped at the boy. During the whole trip he had never seen the child talk to anyone, had never heard him utter a sound. He went about the chores of tending to Sterling's herd silently, with his head bowed down. Moses watched the boy stand there with the huge weapon pointed at his father and felt a mixture of relief and guilt at the witness he bore of a family falling apart.

Sterling stood still for a long moment. This was intolerable, Moses knew. Every man on the train was watching Sterling being backed down by his children. But what could he do? There was no mistaking the deadly seriousness in his son's black eyes. There was more than some principle of decency involved here, Moses realized. There was hatred, deep and of long standing. No one doubted that Jason would as soon kill his father as he would shoot down a coyote or wolf.

The two Southerners slowly moved away from Jason's line of fire, turning their backs on the scene and making their way through the tall waving grass toward the train. Whatever their intentions had been, they apparently now recognized this as a family matter and none of their business. One by one the rest of the men in the clearing exercised their deference to Sterling's shame by shifting their positions and looking away. Only Graham remained standing where he was, and even he reholstered his pistol.

Sterling's face was bright red under his beard's stubble. His shoulders shook with rage, and he slowly put his Colt's away. He glared at Aggie and Moses. Raw hate seethed from his eyes.

"C'mon." Aggie's voice broke the silence. "Let's get to it." She handed the knife to Moses and walked right between Graham and her father and went over by some trees where she had dropped the shovels. She tossed one of the implements onto the ground near one of the abused bodies. Her eyes were blue and sharp over the red pattern of the bandanna around her face. There was something deeper there than Moses had noticed earlier, something more determined. She's got something in her that's harder than most men have, he thought.

"We ain't buryin' 'em, Aggie," Sterling said, but his voice sounded false, strained. "Get on back to the wagon."

"I'm buryin' 'em," she said. "Me an' Mr. Franklin here, an' anybody else who's decent. The rest of you can go to hell."

The men who remained in the clearing shuffled and said nothing. They had been prepared to see Moses and Graham shoot it out with each other, and suddenly a simple girl and her younger brother had shamed all of them. Sterling finally broke the tableau and stormed off swearing toward the train. Along the way, he snatched the shotgun from his son's hands and cuffed him hard on the head. "Son of a bitch," he shouted.

Moses watched Aggie's father's back and realized that the man had lost more than his ability to control his daughter. The scout didn't understand it fully, but he felt as if something solid had broken in the confrontation. He found that however much he thought of her earlier that day and again during the incident with the Runnels, he now appreciated her even more. There never was any danger of her being shot by her father, he knew. No one in the clearing, not even the aloof Southerners, would have stood for that. She likely knew she was in no real danger, but she had played it as if Sterling were nothing more than a barking dog who challenged her. She's stronger than most of the men he'd known, white or otherwise.

"You ain't stayin' here," Graham said in a firm voice. Aside from the removal and return of his gun, he had not budged through the whole ordeal. He remained with his feet unevenly planted like a statue, his eyes cold and gray as they looked at the white girl and black man who stood uneasily before him. "Not with him."

"Then you stay with us," Aggie invited in a serious voice.

"I can't do that," he said, and he brought his hand up and wiped his eyes as if he were weeping. When he took it away, however, Moses could tell that tears had not caused the reaction. He was tired, scared, and worried. When the wagon master looked at Aggie, however, Moses saw something else, something he couldn't quite define. Whatever it was, it made the scout feel suddenly very sorry for Graham.

"I'll stay with 'em," Jason offered. He had dusted himself off and was walking over. A bright red welt had formed on his cheek.

"No," Aggie said. "Mama needs you. There's no tellin' what might happen, now. You stay with her. Promise?" The boy nodded and returned to the wagons.

"We'll be here awhile," George Newsome announced. He and Benjamin Hawshaw came into the clearing with an armload of tools. "I ain't wastin' time buryin' nobody, but we need a wagon. The animals'll play out 'fore long with all our stuff burdenin' other folks. We can put it all—most of it anyhow—on that buckboard. It ain't much, but it'll do." The men went directly to the one wagon that had not been badly charred and began crawling under it to inspect for damage.

"Don't transfer your kegs. Leave the whiskey with the train," Graham said, and he finally moved over to Moses and Aggie. A sadness flitted across his face, Moses saw, but he couldn't tell if it was born of memory or regret.

"This is all your fault," he said, but even though Graham's gray eyes were directed toward him, Moses wasn't sure whether he was speaking to him or to the girl. He decided to answer anyway.

"Can't be helped," he said. "Got to do'er." He wondered why. The whole thing contradicted every lesson he had learned on the Southern Plains. He had left other men, red and white and brown, to rot and be eaten by scavengers. Why did he feel so compelled to stay here and risk his life and the lives of everyone on the train for this bunch of unfortunate fools who had come out beyond the safety of the forts? There was no answer other than the corn-haired girl who stood beside him. She had somehow made him do it. She had forced him to go against his judgment. He didn't know if he blamed her for it or owed her for it. Right now it didn't matter.

"You keep headin' north by nor'west," he said to Graham. "I'll catch you in a hour. Cut me a horse loose." He saw Graham start to stiffen. "For her." He gestured toward Aggie, who had already started turning earth in the midst of the grove. " 'Less you want her ridin' double with me. Them folks ain't goin' to have room on that buckboard for theirselves as it is."

Graham glanced over to where the Newsome and Hawshaw families were trundling crates and bags down into the area to load onto the wagon as soon as it was ready to go. He nodded and moved away toward his wagon.

In a few minutes he was back leading a small white mare, which he wordlessly tied to one of the cedars near Moses's bay. He looked for a long moment at the black man and white woman who were preparing to dig graves for the ravaged Mexican party, but he continued in silence and turned away and left them alone. Soon the creaking of the wagons and teams sounded through the wind that continued to sweep the small grove with sudden, violent gusts, and Moses and Aggie were left alone to dig the graves. The Newsomes and Hawshaws loaded their gear onto the wagon and rigged canvas over it to protect it from the rain that would be coming soon. Moses stood watching the wagons pulling out of sight, the drivers and beasts alike bent into the southwestern wind.

"Let's get to it," Aggie said, and he turned to see her dragging one of the corpses toward the bare space she had made in the center of the clearing. None of the other people paid them any mind at all. With a shrug of his shoulders that failed to dislodge the guilt he felt, he turned and joined her.

2

THEY STARTED DIGGING A LONG TRENCH, HER SCOOPING out the soil he loosened with his shovel, and in an hour they were done. The storm was almost on top of them and great drops were falling when they lowered the remains of the Mexican party into the shallow hole and covered them. They had worked the entire time in silence except for their occasional gagging. The Newsomes and Hawshaws were having trouble arranging their things under the loose canvas, which flapped uncontrollably as the wind whipsawed this way and that in advance of the storm.

"Should of hitched them other wagons up, too," Moses shouted over the wind and rain. The two burned-out hulks would still roll, he believed, and even if they were used for nothing but wheels and axles, they might be valuable. Neither the Newsomes nor the Hawshaws paid any attention to him. It was as if he weren't there.

He saw that the settlers had finally stowed all their gear as well and were trying to settle down a mule team to get them into the traces. The long-eared beasts were frightened both by the smell of death that still permeated the hollow and by the brilliant flashes of lightning that stunned the darkening sky with explosions of heavy thunder.

Aggie asked, "Oughtn't we to say somethin'?" She prodded the fresh mound a bit with her toe. "Seems like we ought to say somethin'." Her calico skirt whipped up in the wind and showed her battered high-buttoned shoes, which were now covered with red mud. She had tied a bonnet over her head, but the wind had torn it off, and it now hung around her throat by the strings and sailed out beneath her flowing golden hair.

"I don't know what," Moses said. "I never was much good at that sort of thing."

"I'd like to put up a marker, but I guess buryin' 'em was what mattered."

The storm suddenly broke with a rush, and he braced himself against the gusts of wind and grit that swept across the hollow. He grabbed the horses from where they were milling about in the trees. She had already crawled underneath the nearest burned-out wagon, following the settlers' example. Moses started to go over to where the two families crouched under their appropriated vehicle, but he realized that they would never let him share their small dry space. He securely tied the reins of the horses to the wagon's charred wheel and tried to calm them down at the same time while he bent his hat against the pelting raindrops.

"You goin' to just stand out there an' drown?" he heard her yelling at him.

He glanced once more over toward the white settlers' wagon, but he could see only a sheet of rain. Water ran down his back and blew up under his hat. He grabbed his bedroll, crouched down, and scrambled underneath the wagon beside her.

He handed Aggie an oilskin, and she wrapped herself in it against the wind, which now contained hailstones that clattered down onto the wagon's bed. Moses moved as far away from her as he could and still stay relatively dry. He didn't want the others to see him sitting close to her. They could hear squeals of mixed terror and glee from the Hawshaw children, but the storm was so furious, he realized any fear he had of being observed near the white woman was groundless. He could barely see the outline of the trees across the small grove.

"I hope the train found some kind of shelter," Moses yelled.

"Serve 'em right if they don't!" she yelled back, and she said something else that was lost in the storm's violent noise.

Unable to hear their own voices, they fell silent. Only the muddy mound of the covered trench remained to tell of the death that had lain around the grove an hour before.

After what seemed an uncommonly short period, the front of the storm passed and left a gentle spring rain in its wake, and the light in the grove rose from blackness to a dull gray. The rain diminished to a spotty drizzle, and Moses and Aggie sloshed out from under the wagon and looked around. A field of marble-sized ice crunched under their feet as they moved, but the sight that stunned them into silence was across the grove. The wagon with the Hawshaws and Newsomes was gone. Sometime during the height of the storm, or shortly before it ended, they had moved out. Muddy tracks bore testimony to their flight. Neither Aggie nor Moses had heard them leaving.

There was nothing to say, but the scout appreciated the awkwardness of their position. No matter what happened, Moses had not been prepared to remain in the tiny grove of trees alone with Aggie. He was, he supposed, willing to remain behind and bury the dead Mexicans by himself rather than allow her to do the same, but he knew that if she and he stayed behind together, there would be more trouble than the argument over the incident had already caused. He knew that aside from the hatred it would inspire against him, the danger it would put him in as a black man who was, on the surface of things at least, compromising a white woman would make her the target of the settlers' outrage.

For her part, she seemed not to consider the situation. "I'm soaked to the skin" was her only comment.

He looked with futile hope after the wagon tracks that led out of the tiny clearing back up onto the plains. The storm had lasted only a short time, but God only knew how long Newsome and Hawshaw had been gone, or why they had left. They hadn't been in the grove when the argument heated up between Moses and Graham. They likely hadn't heard anything about the fracas, so busy had they been removing their belongings from the others' wagons and preparing to take over the abandoned Mexican rig. Chances were that they had paid small attention to any part of it. They knew why Aggie and Moses were staying behind, but they had offered no help with the funeral tasks. A hot feeling of being in trouble rashed up on the back of his neck, and his hand automatically went there to massage it away.

After only a few minutes to collect the shovels and make sure they had left nothing behind, he and Aggie mounted their horses and began to follow the wagon trails in the tall grass as they wound their way north by northwest. The Newsome-Hawshaw rig intersected with the other irregular and almost parallel lines of the wagon train about a hundred yards from the grove and then fell into their deep cuts in the grass. But they were not going to be just up ahead as Moses had hoped. Instead, their buckboard's wheels cut back to the east, back to where they had abandoned the bulk of their belongings earlier in the day. The fools had gone to collect what they could of their things before rejoining the train. The western horizon was still dark with clouds, but behind them flashes of lightning continued to lighten the sky. It was as if they had gone to chase the storm and its fury, but what they were more likely to find was Comanche.

Moses debated about going after them, trying to catch them and persuade them to turn around and chase the train's tracks through the grass. But light was fading rapidly. He and Aggie sat wordlessly on their mounts at the point where the buckboard had moved off to the east, then without anything more than a nod from the black scout, the girl reined her horse in next to his, and they made their way toward the northwest, following the train.

3

THEY HAD RIDDEN LESS THAN A MILE WHEN SUDDENLY the horizon changed, and out of the darkness of the storm clouds, a brilliant line of yellowish pink exploded across the mesa and outlined the copse of trees. The storm was passing, and the clear sky brought forth a spectacular sunset that promised a dry night if not a safe one. Once again, Moses was struck by the beauty of this frontier. He had never seen a sunset anywhere else to match the majestic array of colors that streaked across the western sky.

As the rain stopped completely, they rode along in silence and enjoyed the cool of the evening. They peered into the dusk for the lights of the train's camp. Moses was certain that Graham would not have the presence of mind to forbid fires and lanterns, not that it would make any real difference. Comanche could smell white men, he had heard.

Moses had put everyone in danger, since none of the settlers had any experience with Indians whatsoever. Now he would likely be blamed for the Hawshaws' and Newsomes' disappearance as well. He was in deep trouble, he told himself, and he tried to understand why he had done it. He glanced over at the girl who rode easily beside him, and the understanding came to him in a flash of realization that almost shamed him in its honesty.

As dusk settled more heavily around them, ground fog rose from the sodden grass, almost as if the water caught in the blades was trying to moisten the dry atmosphere that had oppressed the plains all day. The sky was fading from brilliant pink to a deep purple, and the mesa's outline was now sharp against the dying light.

There was another foolish thing involved, he admitted to himself, more dangerous than any trouble that he himself faced. Her reputation was more than harmed; it was destroyed. She was out in the dark with a Negro man, alone, and that would be enough to start rumors circulating back at the train. It could be enough to start guns cocking and hanging ropes coiling as well. She had to be aware of it, he knew, but she didn't seem to mind.

Aggie, he observed, seemed unworried about the prospect of any sort of retribution, either at the hands of her volatile father or from the actions of her fellow whites on the train. He had trouble envisioning her submitting to any sort of punishment, especially anything involving a beating. She was different from any girl—white or black—he had ever met. He wondered how much impulsiveness had to do with her behavior, or if it were not something more, something he was used to seeing in brave men, who tended to do what their hearts told them was right even when common sense contradicted them, men whose experience had hardened them more than second-growth hickory, whose actions were dictated by a higher moral principle than others could fathom. He couldn't divine her motives, though, and her face, lit as it was by the fading sunlight, told him nothing.

Suddenly Aggie broke their silent ride. "You was born a slave, wasn't you?"

Moses was startled by the question. "Yeah . . . uh, yes, Ma'am, I was." His voice was unsteady. Surely that was obvious, he thought.

"What was that like?" she asked with a bright voice. "To be a slave?"

She might as well be asking what it was like to fly, Moses thought. Even so, he contemplated the question. What *was* it like? How could he even begin to describe it for this girl whose life had, perhaps, been hard, but who had no inkling of what it was like to be owned by someone else?

"It's bad, Missy," he said after a moment. "It's worse'n anythin' you can imagine."

"I s'pect so," she said slowly.

Moses thought carefully. It wasn't a question anyone had ever asked him before. People—white and black, even freeborn Negroes—never asked what it was like to be a slave. They had just assumed they knew, or, in the case of most whites, they didn't care.

"I can't imagine it," Aggie said. "I mean, we never had nothin', nothin' at all, an' we were always beholden to somebody, it seems. But we were our own folks, owned ourselves anyway. I can't imagine ownin' somebody. Not even a nigger slave. I mean, buyin' and sellin' folks. Did that happen to you?"

"Yessum," he muttered. "It happened."

"What was your, uh . . . master like?" Aggie asked. "Was he mean? Did he, uh . . . beat you?"

"No, Ma'am, not much. My actu'l master never beat me hisself. He liked me, I think. He learned me to ride an' shoot." He also let the women alone, Moses thought with an antique anger flushing through him. Joseph Grierson—and his first overseer, Evan Carpenter—had never, so far as Moses knew, messed with any of the black girls they owned and worked.

"I didn't think slaves was s'posed to know that," she said simply.

"They ain't," Moses replied. "Not many does. But I learned. He learned me good. He was a, uh . . . he was a good man." Then he added, "For a master."

"What 'bout your mama an' daddy? Did he beat them?"

"I was sold away from my mama when I was young. Never had no daddy," he said, then he silently concluded, no daddy whom he could call such.

"Did he, your master, beat others?" Aggie persisted in her questioning. "Your friends?"

A slave has no friends, Moses wanted to tell her. "No, not much," he said. "He didn't never beat me or anybody personal. But there was other men, overseers." His jaw set. "They did."

"I hate that," Aggie said. "People who beat people who are weaker than them are lowlifes. They deserve to be shot."

Moses did not respond but only listened to the night sounds. For a moment, he thought he could smell the gunsmoke and black powder of the battle where Henry Thomas had died. With Aggie's words other odors seemed to float around him and mix with his memories. The fragrance of the dung the Comanche used on their hair made Moses's skin tingle. In a while, he thought, coyote calls would howl over the prairie, and it would seem that the whole plain was alive with voices of ghostlike creatures that could chill the blood of even the bravest men.

He glanced over his shoulder, and what he saw made his own blood freeze. The dark horizon to the east was already alight with an orange glow that indicated that the moon—the Comanche moon—was soon to rise. It was a harbinger of death all across the Southern Plains. It meant that Comanche were riding that night.

"I hate slavery," Aggie went on, not noticing that he had spotted the pending moonrise behind them. "I'm glad it's done with."

"Yessum," Moses muttered. But he thought, It ain't done with, Missy, not by a long shot.

CHAPTER FOUR

1

THE TWO RIDERS' HORSES PLODDED ALONG IN SILENCE toward the darkness. Moses felt confused and disturbed by the memories Aggie Sterling had raked up and set to flaming inside him and was glad for the chance to think without having to talk to her. She unnerved him, aroused the taboos of his youth. In the shadows that fell before their horses, he conjured old ghosts, and whenever he glanced at her blond beauty, her head slightly bowed over her horse's neck, he felt deeper stirrings that vied with the anxiety the night and threat of Indians caused. Her questions forced him to remember too much, he thought, and they also caused him to think of her in a way he knew he never should.

Although Moses had helped enough around the plantation with various husbandry chores in his youth and was generally familiar with the process of copulation and procreation, he had had little opportunity to experiment on his own. It wasn't long, however, before he found his thoughts filled by one of Grierson's new purchases, Amy. He spied her as soon as Grierson brought her out to the plantation and presented her to his wife as an anniversary present, the last celebration they would enjoy before he left for Virginia and a four-year absence. Although Amy, like Moses, had been the product of forced racial mixed breeding, her skin was almost inky against the white dresses Mrs. Grierson gave her to wear while she went about her household duties. She was young, no more than sixteen, and Mrs. Grierson kept her in one of the house's lower-floor rooms, near Moses's own small closet, where she was often summoned upstairs by a bell on a pull cord that led to the mistress's bedroom.

Moses was captivated by the shy young girl when he first saw her. She was the subject of gossip in the quarters, but even a year later when Grierson and Carpenter turned the slaves over to Thomas, only a few of the house servants had come to know her at all, and Moses had only nodded and tried to smile at her when they passed each other in the hall. She had not, so far as he knew, even been out to the quarters at all.

Following a flurry of parties and preparations for departure which kept all the slaves busy putting up bunting and preparing the grounds for guests, Joseph Grierson and Evan Carpenter rode off to war, and Henry Thomas and Slobberin' Jimmy came to the Grierson plantation.

Thomas had appropriated the more inviting rooms on the house's lower floor for him and Jimmy. It wasn't long before he began sending for the slave girls—"belly warmers," he called them—and the horror began.

At first the girls went willingly enough, expressing a kind of resigned acceptance of the lot of slave girls. But when they found that Thomas demanded other, unmentionable, and, as far as Moses was concerned, mysterious participation than mere copulation, they balked. Their simple religious understanding could accept the fact that they had no choice in being called to a white master's bed, but there were some things that they would not do, even for a man as dangerously cruel as Thomas.

If any were so brave or foolish as to refuse the overseer, their punishment was usually long and bloody, and more than one had been bedridden for a week after he was finished with her. Amy, whom Grierson had owned for less than a year before he left and for whom Moses himself had developed an eye, was not the first to be beaten, but her beating was the most severe, and it was the one that changed the way Moses regarded white men forever.

One night, Amy found herself cowering in a corner of the overseer's room while he bellowed at her and raged drunk and out of control. He cared little whether he was heard by his employer's family upstairs, for overseers were hard to come by in wartime, and he often asserted the Griersons were almost as afraid of him as the blacks were.

Frustrated by her refusal to obey whatever perverse demands he put upon her, he dragged Amy out of his room by her ankles. He kicked and beat her into the compound in front of the quarters, where he stripped her thin undergarment from her and tied her to the post with her hands behind her, her small, bare breasts lifted taut into the flickering torchlight, her face already bruised and bloody from the beating his fists had inflicted. Her legs dangled helplessly down, barely permitting her toes to touch the dirt.

He roused Jimmy, who rang the bell to assemble the rest of the slaves, and they sleepily gathered, soon becoming wide awake as they saw the overseer, dressed only in underwear waisted in by a belt that carried a Bowie knife, and muttered to themselves their reactions to poor Amy's shame and the terror they all felt for what was about to happen. He screamed at them to be silent and insisted that the women stand forward of the crowd to watch what happened to "filthy nigger bitches who don't know how to do what they're told." Then he went to work with his whip.

The first blows were light, only teasing, and Amy whimpered from the brief, stinging pain that Thomas expertly inflicted on her exposed flesh. As he worked, his rage and excitement increased, and the whip's blows became sharper, eventually extracting long tentacles of ragged flesh from the pale girl's naked stomach and thighs, which now streamed with blood from her wounds, blood that seemed to run black on her brown skin in the torchlight.

The ordeal went on for almost an hour, with Thomas taking time between blows to wipe sheets of sweat from his forehead and to drink from a dipper Jimmy would bring him from the well. All the while he would shout curses at the girl. Her voice now grew harsh with screams, and Thomas, Moses noticed, had developed an erection that protruded nakedly from his ragged union suit and forced him to walk even more awkwardly than usual.

Soon the silence of the watching slaves was broken by a quiet chorus of prayers which some of the women began to utter, beseeching both Thomas and "sweet Jesus" on Amy's behalf. Thomas glared at the crowd from time to time between the blows and curses, effectively silencing anyone who was speaking, and then he delivered a particularly savage blow with the whip.

Moses felt compelled to do something. But what? To oppose Thomas was to invite the same, probably worse, treatment for himself without shortening Amy's torture an iota. He knew that the mad overseer wasn't above killing one of them if he was angry enough, and with Mr. Grierson and Evan Carpenter gone, it seemed, forever, he would likely get away with it. He stood as helplessly as the women, his breath held with each snap of the bullwhip.

Then, as Thomas paused and caught his breath, a slave finally spoke up. "You fixin' to kill her, Marse Thomas." The voice belonged to Isaac, one of the oldest of Grierson's slaves, a man so wizened that even the white employees on the plantation paid him a certain deference.

Thomas swung on the crowd and turned his gleaming eye toward the slave. Isaac moved to the front of the younger men, who grouped together, trying to shield him. He stepped through the line of women, most of whom were on their knees by now, and set his twisted hickory cane down in front of him with a marvelous authority.

"You can beat me, if'n you want. You can kill me. It don't matter none a-tall to me. But if you kill that gal, Miz Grierson's fixin' to be powerful mad with you. An' you know it."

There was a murmur of agreement among the slaves, and for a moment, Moses thought Thomas was going to strike the old black man with the butt of the whip. But a gleam rose in Thomas's eye, and he spun and delivered one final blow to the tortured Amy.

Previously, the whip had found its target on Amy's stomach, lower abdomen, and thighs for the most part, playing only with the tops of her breasts and chest from time to time, creating little rivers of bloody tracks. But this blow was viciously different. The lead tip of the braided whip snaked out and cracked with an echoing snap that silenced the slaves' prayers. As it struck her right breast, the studded lead ball licked out and bit into her dark nipple, flicking it off as neatly as if a surgeon had used a scalpel, and for a moment the ground around Thomas and his victim fell totally silent. Blood suddenly rushed from the gaping wound in Amy's breast, and the girl's stupor disappeared. Her screams lit the area like a lightning flash. The crowd of slaves turned away in shock and horror. Even Jimmy turned his head away.

Thomas was panting, and his chest heaved. He wiped his mouth with the back of his hand, stalked over to the girl, and clamped his palm against the bloody hole to stop the flow. Her face turned up to him in an expression of ghastly terror, her mouth open with piercing screams. He reached down and pulled her dangling legs up, forcing himself between her bloody thighs. With the whip's butt, he forced her chin partly closed and suddenly and forcefully kissed her bloody, chewed lips, ramming his erection close against her torn thighs and thrusting his penis into her. Her body reared against the post, and her legs kicked out wildly. New tears streaked out of her eyes, and the muscles of her neck stood out like ropes. With a half-dozen quick jerks of his hips, Thomas discharged his semen into the helpless slave girl and stepped away, allowing her to collapse and dangle unconscious from her bonds.

The slaves had mostly covered their eyes with their arms and hands after Thomas's final, hideous blow had fallen. Now they began to look again, but they found nothing to say. Even Old Isaac was quiet as he watched the sickening spectacle before him. Stepping back from his victim's body, Thomas pulled out the Bowie knife and cut Amy's bonds. She fell forward into his arms.

The overseer lifted her, the whip dangling from under her unconscious form, and turned to the black eyes that stared disbelieving at him.

"Get back to bed," he ordered from a mouth ringed with the collapsed girl's blood. His hand pressed against the open wound on her breast, and blood flowed from between his fingers. "Tomorrow's a workin' day, an' they'll be a good whippin' for any nigger's that's draggin'." With that, he carried Amy across the dirt yard to the big house and left the crowd of slaves standing in the bloody aftermath of Amy's ordeal.

Moses remained standing in the compound long after the rest of the slaves retired. He felt hammered into the ground while emotions danced around his mind and fought for supremacy. Finally, one emerged as the strongest: hate.

He vowed there to kill Thomas. It was an oath he never repeated aloud, and one that frightened him almost as much as had Amy's torture. Harming—let alone killing—a white man was unthinkable, unimaginable. But his conviction to carry out his promise was based on an idea that sprang from deep inside him. It was, in a sense, born of philosophy, for it made a distinction he had never considered and possibly never would have except for Grierson's lectures and oral musings.

They never saw Amy again. Daniel told them later that Mrs. Grierson was furious with Thomas. But the mistress of the big house never saw Amy and had no idea of how terrible her punishment had been. She took Thomas's word for the lie that he had caught her "rollin' 'round in the hay with two young bucks, stark naked an' half drunk on sherry stolen from the pantry." The story redeemed him from his employer's displeasure, if, indeed, he ever feared it.

With the mistress's permission, Thomas sold the slave girl downriver to New Orleans, Moses heard, but he also heard that Thomas shipped her off to a friend of his in San Augustine, where she was rented out to other white men. In any case, she never came back, and the beatings, although never again that severe, continued, and the slave girls who were called to Thomas's room late at night learned to shut down their sensibilities and comply with whatever the overseer wanted them to do.

FOR A LONG TIME Moses worried daily about how he could murder Thomas, even when he stalked deer in the nearby forest, shackled as he was by chains and followed by Jimmy. The thought obsessed him, but it wouldn't form solidly, and his reveries tended to make his hunting suffer. He found that Thomas's rage was inspired when he returned with only small game for the white table, and more than once the black hunter felt the sharp blow from the overseer's cane. He knew that Thomas was just waiting for an excuse to give him a real beating, and when he returned after four days in a row with nothing at all in his game pouch, he discovered that the time had come.

That evening, Thomas rang the bell and assembled the slaves for Moses's punishment. Moses resigned himself to die strapped to the post. He knew that Thomas's hatred for him stemmed as much from his status as Joseph Grierson's particular pet as it did from the fact that Moses was a crack shot and competent tracker who had access to the study and the guns, something Grierson had forbidden the overseer. That Thomas announced that it would be Jimmy, not Thomas himself, who would handle the whip did nothing to relieve Moses's fear. Jimmy weighed twice what Thomas did, and his contempt for the young hunter was profound and obvious.

As he was led to the center of the compound, Mory, a diminutive girl who had been one of Thomas's early victims and had learned to comply with the overseer's sexual urges, stumbled and fell in front of him. Moses tripped over her and went down on one knee; she pressed his hand quickly before jumping up. As she moved away she pointed to her mouth, and Moses found that in his palm was a wine cork. He shoved it into his cheek, and when Jimmy began, he moved it over and bit down hard on it.

The first blow of the whip sent a streak of pain coursing from his left shoulder blade all the way down to his toes. The second and third blows were hotter and more painful than the first, and Moses tried to concentrate on biting the cork, on the stinging pain of the thongs that bound his wrists, on the gritty soil beneath the soles of his feet, but when the fourth and fifth and sixth blows followed, he found that his whole mind was a sunburst of hurt and dread. How could Amy or any of the slaves have borne more than this? he asked himself. Jimmy struck him twice more, and Moses felt the wetness of blood seeping down his back and into his trousers. Somewhere there was the sound of horse's hooves, the jangle of spurs, but all he could think of was the next snapping burn of the whip. It didn't come.

Jimmy's pleasure was interrupted by a man who rode up and asked to hire some slaves for work in the city of Jefferson. As the overseer and the unexpected arrival walked over to discuss the matter, Moses struggled to breathe. From the corner of his eye, he could see Jimmy anxiously coiling the whip, ready to start the punishment anew. The air seemed to burn his lacerated back, and he understood that as soon as Jimmy resumed his work, whatever pain he had endured would only be a preamble. Moses cursed the man who had interrupted the torture and given Jimmy a chance to renew his strength. But he soon found himself cut down and dumped into the same trough by which he had vowed to kill the overseer a few months before. Mory and others fished him out and hauled him back into the quarters, where his back was dressed and crudely bandaged. It took them a long time to pry his jaws open, so deeply embedded were his teeth in Mory's cork.

Moses knew that regardless of the fear of killing white men, even men who were nothing more than animals such as Thomas and Jimmy, he now had no choice. He had to slaughter them, just as he had slaughtered animals in the wild. He now only waited to pick his time.

When Thomas volunteered in the spring of 1864 to go and meet the Union invasion in Louisiana, Moses was robbed of his chance to take revenge against the overseer. Going along with the pick of Grierson's firearms collection in tow, he followed the now Sergeant Thomas along the road across the Sabine into the heavily forested countryside near Mansfield, Louisiana. There, on the first morning of the battle, almost with the first shot, Thomas was cut in two by a cannonball and Moses was relieved both of his duty to the overseer and of the burden of revenge he carried.

Soon he was back in Jefferson. Slobberin' Jimmy took Henry Thomas's place, and the slaves noticed only a small difference between their individual brands of tyranny: Jimmy left the slave girls alone. But his beatings and maimings were, if anything, more cruel and more frequent than his predecessor's had been, and his corruption was less cunning and more obvious.

To Moses, though, it was all part of a single piece. It would be years before he could exact his revenge against Jimmy, but by then he found that he had been unable to feel anything for any white man again. He also steeled himself against the obvious flirtations of available girls in Jefferson and elsewhere. The devastation he felt when he watched Amy's beating, the helplessness that bound him as certainly as she was bound, also taught him the dangers of putting his faith—or his love—too far out in front of him. From the time he was a free man, he had wasted no tender feelings on women and had visited brothels only on occasion. He had so successfully avoided the feelings, that now, in the presence of this pretty, friendly white woman, they aroused terror in him. They came to the surface of his thoughts easily and bothered him more than the danger he knew they put him in.

But he had a sense that he could not avoid them any longer. Tonight, as they rode, his emotions were connected to her, and, he figured, so was a lot of trouble when they returned to the train. This was not something he could ride around, but he was at a loss for a way to deal with it.

2

"How'd you learn about Indians?" Aggie asked, interrupting Moses's thoughts once more.

He started, concerned suddenly that he might have spoken aloud.

"I don't know much, Ma'am," he replied, relieved to be once more focused on the immediate situation. The memories around him faded away, and he fought the temptation to put their horses into a lope and hurry their return to the wagons and relative safety. "I don't know no man that does."

"You seem to know lots," she went on. "You traded with 'em back there."

"Well." He felt tempted to boast, but then he thought better of it. "You pick up some things here an' there. I listen good, an' I try to remember what I hear. Most of it's no-'count brag, you see, but ever' now an' again somebody says somethin' worth hearin'."

"You hate Indians?"

"I met some I hate. But I met some that was all right. For Indians. You can't never trust 'em. That's 'bout all I know for sure 'bout 'em. They do as they please. That's for sure. 'Specially Comanche."

"Why're they so mean? Why'd they do what they did to them folks back there? They could of just took what they wanted. Might of even killed 'em, 'specially if they'd fought over it, but why . . . why hurt 'em that way?" She paused. "I mean, even the women, an' the . . . babies."

"That's just the way Comanche is. Ever'body'll tell you that. They always been like that. Nobody ever could do a lick of good with 'em. They beat the Mescans, an' they beat the Spaniards 'fore that, an' they been beatin' the Apache for longer'n anybody can remember. The Sioux an' the Arapaho, the Kickapoo an' the Blackfoot. All of 'em hates 'em. Scared of 'em, too. Seems like the only ones not scared of 'em is the white man. Or maybe he jus' don't have the good sense to be."

"You don't seem scared of 'em. I seen you talkin' to that chief, an' you didn't look a bit scared." She smiled at him.

"Maybe I don't have good sense either." He smiled back. "Or maybe it's 'cause I ain't white." Maybe a black man *can* deal with them, he thought. Maybe a black man might be able to make them understand that they were more alike, that they had a common enemy, common fears.

She laughed at his remark, and her voice rang across the empty darkness. "How did you learn what you know?"

"I was a Army scout." It wasn't easy, he admitted to her, for a black man, a former slave, to become a scout, but he had managed to do it. He remembered how lost he had felt when he first signed up to scout for the Army. Part of the problem had been his name. He had just been Moses, nothing more. Some of the slaves had taken the Grierson name after they were freed, and Moses had used it a time or two himself when a last name seemed called for, but owing partly to the stolen guns he carried and to some sense of guilt for having taken them, he didn't feel comfortable with it.

He took the name of Franklin, his natural father, not because he had any affection for that memory either, but because it reminded him of his mother and seemed in some way to connect him to something substantial in his past.

Aggie listened to him go on about his adventures as a scout, interrupting him often to ask more questions—some about him and some about Indians themselves—until they actually found themselves laughing and talking easily.

Moses's emotional discomfort disappeared in the presence of this strong-willed, frank girl who had braved her father's wrath as well as the talk of the whole train by staying behind with him. He entertained the fantasy that it wouldn't matter ultimately. They were as innocent as any two children, exchanging small jokes and stories, commenting on the night sounds that grew around them, comparing horses and wagons and even labor. Moses was surprised to learn how much she knew about field work, about saddle and draft animals, and he went along with her assumption that as a slave he had spent most of his time tending corn and cotton instead of working rifles and pistols.

"My daddy hates you," she said flatly after a while. "He said so 'fore we left Jefferson. He said Mr. Graham's hirin' you was 'bout the dumbest thing he ever heard of."

"Don't I know that!" Moses remembered the first argument he had had with Sterling over the wisdom of trying to take even a small herd along on a wagon train. He didn't tell her that the argument had grown out of his suspicion that the cattle were stolen. "I can't say I blame him too much, though. He sure does prize them cattle."

"Oh, it's not the cattle. He likely stole them," she said as if she read his thoughts. "He hates you 'cause you're a nigger."

Moses suddenly understood that she meant no insult. It was just a word she had always heard.

"You see, we're from all over. Tennessee, Mississippi, Arkansas, Louisiana. We had farms here an' there, an' Daddy traded cattle an' horses 'fore the war. Even 'fore I was born. Anyhow, we never owned no slaves. Daddy says he never believed in it, nohow. But when the war was over, we kept gettin' put off our farms, an' a bunch of Yankees—Redlegs, I think—burned us out. Then a bunch of Rebs burned us out 'cause they thought we was foolin' with Yankees." She paused and seemed to let her thoughts range a moment. "An' Daddy said it wasn't no good tryin' to have anythin', 'cause as soon as you do, a bunch of carpetbaggers'll come along an' give it to the niggers. Just like that. We had a real nice place in Louisiana for a spell, but we lost that, too. So finally, we moved up to Arkansas, 'cause we thought Daddy'd run off for good. But it wasn't no better. It seemed like the niggers had ever'thin' locked up there, too, for a while. But then I met this fellow. Todd. An' he was fixin' to marry me, but then Daddy come back, an' Todd run off to hunt buffalo. But we're goin' to meet up in New Mexico, he said. He said he wasn't scared of Daddy." She bit her lip. "I think he was, though. A little, anyway."

The speech ended, and Moses peered through the dark at her. She was clearly not a girl given to telling her story; it was a jumble of events that hardly went together. But he did gather the important thing. She didn't care much more for Jack Sterling than he did, even if he was her father. That seemed to create a bond between them.

"I ain't scared of Daddy, neither," she went on all of a sudden. "But here we are, goin' to New Mexico with him. There wasn't nothin' left to do. I sort of had to come even if I didn't want to, not just to meet Todd, but 'cause of Mama an' Jason an' Annie. Least out in New Mexico, maybe there'll be a chance for decent white folks to get ahead. Least that's what Daddy says. So here we are." There was an edge to her voice. "But I ain't scared of him. Not even a little."

Moses coughed. "I don't think you're scared of him, Ma'am," he said. It seemed to please her.

She turned to look behind them, and in the glow of the new moonlight that now outlined them and cast long shadows on the silvery grass, he saw her mouth make a hard, thin line under her blue eyes. "I'll tell you somethin'," she said. "I made up my mind a long time ago not to be scared of no man. White or nigger."

"Ma'am, I don't much like that word." Moses hadn't meant to say it, but his mouth worked before he caught himself. His body tingled with a sense that he might have spoiled the mood that had grown up between them.

"What word?"

"We're colored, Missy. We like to be called 'colored.' " He hoped she wouldn't ask him why, for the truth was he didn't know why he—they—liked to be called "colored" instead of other things.

"Oh, God!" she said. "I'm sorry!" She lowered her head. "I knew that. How stupid of me! Colored!" she repeated.

"It's all right," he heard himself mumble.

"I'm truly dumb sometimes. But sometimes, I'm not! Daddy doesn't like me much either, I should tell you. But"—her voice carried a smile—"I think he's scared of me. A little. At least I hope so." The smile vanished into a darker tone. "At least, he better be."

Moses recalled the deadly determination he had seen in her face when she held the knife on Graham and Sterling back at the cedar grove. He remembered her telling her own father to go to hell with a conviction that suggested that she was prepared to send him personally. There was something there to be careful of, he thought, if not frightened.

"He says I'm more boy than girl." She brought the careless lilt back into her voice. "An' if he hadn't brought me forth from Mama's womb by his very own hands, he says, he'd swear Mama was tryin' to fool him by sayin' I was theirs." She was silent for a moment, and then she added in a soft voice, "That's just an excuse, though. I know that. Truth is, I ain't really his. That's why he's scared of me."

Moses wondered what she meant, but he decided it was better not to ask. He was already involved too deeply with this girl, and he tried to lighten the mood. "I think I know what he means, Ma'am." He laughed.

"Well, I don't think it's funny. I don't like bein' a girl very much. I mean, I like bein' pretty. Who wouldn't? An' I know I'm pretty. Todd told me so. Ever'body tells me so, goodness knows. But I don't like doin' girl things. You know, sewin', washin', cookin', stuff like that. An' the Lord knows I've done enough of them."

"You'll learn to like it soon enough," Moses replied. "When that boy comes for you, you'll think it's a pleasure."

"You know, what I really like is man stuff. Like ridin' this horse, or shootin' a gun. I really like that. I also like tellin' men what to do. I 'specially like that."

"Most women do, Missy," Moses said, now watching the darkness for a sign of campfire lights. They should have reached the train camp long ago, he calculated, but the steady tracks in the grass were still guiding their horses, and he was certain they hadn't passed the wagons.

"Mr. Franklin," she said, "I've shot a lot of guns, an' I'm pretty good with Daddy's shotgun, the one Jason had back there." She acknowledged her brother's armed support of her position without emotion. "I've handled a pistol, too. But I've never shot one of them big rifles before. Could you . . . uh, would you let me try it sometime?" Before he could answer, she added, "I don't mean now, tonight! Lord, we'd wake up ever' Indian for miles! But 'fore we get to Santa Fe, would you let me try it just once?"

She was right about one thing, Moses thought, she didn't talk like a girl.

"I don't think your daddy would much take to the idea, Missy. He's goin' to be mad 'nough 'bout us comin' in after dark as it is." Alone, he silently added with an uncomfortable recollection of the reality of their situation.

"That's the truth." She laughed. "I'm not even s'posed to talk to you, or no nig—colored man. In fact, you know when I brung you out that cup of coffee? Well, that wasn't my daddy's idea at all. It was mine! I felt sorry for you sittin' out there all by yourself."

"You're somethin' all right, Missy. You are."

"Oh, pooh!" she spat. "I'm just a girl who tells fibs. I wanted to see your rifle close up was all. An' *that's* the truth."

The horses moved closer together, and he thought about handing the big rifle over to her, but at that moment his eyes picked up the flicker of campfires in the black distance. The wagons had found another of the isolated cedar groves and had made camp inside it, pulling them in tight to fort up. The fires were telltale, but at least Graham had shown some sense, he thought.

"So, how 'bout it?" she persisted. "Can you show me sometime?"

"We'll see, Ma'am."

"An' one more thing," she said. "I won't call you 'nigger' if you'll stop callin' me 'Missy' an' 'Ma'am.' One makes me feel too little an' the other makes me feel too old."

"Yes, Ma'am," Moses said automatically, and then, to cover his embarrassment, he stood up in his stirrups and yelled, "Riders comin' in! Don't shoot! It's me an' the girl!"

3

EXCEPT FOR A HANDFUL OF DYING FIRES AND A POOL of coal-oil light around Graham's buckboard, the wagons were dark and quiet. Aggie dismounted and led her horse over to Graham's wagon, and without a glance in Moses's direction, she faded off into the makeshift compound's darkness.

Moses found himself so bone-tired and hungry that he could barely remove the saddles from the horses and begin the elementary grooming that was so necessary for the mounts' well-being. But as he finished brushing them down and was worrying about where he might beg a bag of oats, Graham wandered up.

"Well, I see you got back." The wagon master's words slurred, and Moses recognized that he had been drinking. It was something of a shock. He knew Graham sometimes drank, found it natural to see him tilt back a bottle he kept under his wagon seat, but he had never seen him drunk. The black scout said nothing and grabbed up a nose bag from under Graham's wagon. He started off to search for some oats. "Where's Hawshaw an' Newsome?"

"Don't know," Moses said without turning around. "They took off back toward the east. I reckon they went to pick up some of their stuff."

"An' you just let them go?"

"Didn't ask my leave," Moses said as he unfolded the bag. "They just snuck off durin' the storm. If they've still got their hair, I reckon they'll be 'long direc'ly."

"Directly," Graham said flatly and finally. There was a long silence, and Moses knew that he was going to have to finish fussing with the bag and turn around. "You get the greasers planted nice an' decent?" Graham called out to him as if he were a long way off. Moses continued walking, noting from the corner of his eye that Graham was stumbling after him.

"You have a nice time with that little gal? Nigger boy."

Graham caught up with the retreating back of the scout, and Moses wheeled suddenly and lashed out with the nose bag, catching Graham full in the face, knocking him down.

He was sick of all the tension of the day, and he shocked himself with his sudden action. He had struck white men before, but usually it was in the heat of a brawl, a fight where everyone was hitting everyone. This was personal, and he was breathlessly aware of the significance of the blow. He had started something now, and he was going to have to finish it. Graham was too drunk to let him apologize and back down even if he felt like it.

"Why, you nigger son of a—" Graham sputtered from the ground, but before he could get to his feet, Moses stepped forward and placed a kick just under the white man's chin, knocking him completely backward. Graham's revolver slipped from his holster, and Moses took the chance to kick it as well, knocking it under a wagon and out of sight.

Graham scrambled around in the trampled damp grass that looked preternaturally golden in the coal-oil lamps' glare and tried to regain his footing. He spat blood from his lip, which he had bitten in his fall backward, and he dug his stumped arm into the dirt beneath him. Moses stepped back and squared his shoulders for the fight he knew was coming.

"Hold it," Jack Sterling's voice commanded from behind the black scout. His order was punctuated by the audible click of the hammer on his Colt's .44.

Moses turned and faced Sterling, who stood with his legs spread wide and his left pistol drawn and leveled at the scout's chest. The gun was cocked and ready, and in spite of the fact that Sterling's red-rimmed black eyes betrayed the whiskey that he too had been drinking, his gun hand was steady and his jaw covered by the half-grown beard was set.

"Just twitch, nigger," he said, "an' I'll put you in hell so fast, your mama won't know you was ever gone."

Graham struggled to his feet and wiped blood away from his mouth.

"Put it away, Sterling," he said in a steady voice. Sterling looked at the wagon master with surprise and disappointment. "I said, put it away. Nobody's gettin' sent to hell tonight." Graham's voice betrayed nothing more than a heavy weariness. He sounded like a man who had just come awake after a long, drunken sleep. At least, Moses noted with relief, the brawling had sobered him.

"But, Jesus, Graham," Sterling argued, "he was *kickin'* you! I mean, you just can't let no nigger kick you an' get away with it."

"I can let him do whatever I want," Graham said. Moses saw that there was no anger left behind the wagon master's eyes, only exhaustion and worry. He's scared, Moses thought, but not of me. He's got too much on his mind to worry about me. "Put the gun away an' go tend to your daughter," Graham ordered.

"I ain't got no daughter. I give her up for dead today when she took up with a nigger. No daughter of mine would ever—"

"She didn't 'take up' with nobody," Moses said, wondering if he stood any kind of chance with this drunk, angry man. If he drew on him, Sterling would get off the first shot, that was sure. But Moses knew that men like Sterling—especially drunk men like Sterling—seldom hit what they shot at. "We jus' did a decent thing. That's all. Nothin' else. The others up an' left us. That weren't our fault."

"Decent, shit," Graham said. "You risked this whole damned train for a bunch of dead Mescans nobody even cared about enough to piss on. You know that?"

"I say let's just hang him from the first real tree we come up on an' be done with it," Sterling said. His eyes moved quickly from Moses to Graham, and the scout wondered if he could draw his pistol and kill him in the instant that he looked away. He figured he could. But again, Sterling might just get lucky. If he was hurt or wounded, Graham wouldn't even find a good piece of shade to leave him in. He would just lie where he fell and bleed to death.

"Just shut the hell up, Sterling," Graham said loudly. "You an' your cows an' your whole damn family have caused enough trouble for one day. Just get the hell away from me an' leave me alone."

Sterling held his position for another few seconds and stared at Graham. There was a conflict here, Moses saw, that went deeper than the troubles of this long day or even the weeks since they had left Jefferson. He thought once more about Sterling's storming out of the saloon in Saint Jo. Sooner or later, whatever was between them would erupt, and Moses hoped that he wouldn't be in the line of fire when it did.

Sterling lowered his gun, swore, and walked away. The scout heard him ease the hammer down as he faded off into the darkness.

"You got any oats?" Moses finally broke the quiet, picking up the nose bag from where he had dropped it near Graham's feet.

"There's some in Frank's wagon," Graham replied. "You get them an' get some sleep. If we don't make your fancy crossin' by tomorrow, we're buzzard meat, an' you know it."

Moses started to move off, but Graham stopped him. "When we get to Santa Fe, I'm goin' to kill you," he said, but there was no threat in his voice, only the deadly assurance of a man who meant exactly what he said. "If I —if *we*—didn't need you right now, you'd already be dead."

Moses didn't know what to say. He didn't fear Graham, but he knew that only his usefulness had saved him from dying or having to kill both Sterling and Graham. He also knew that had he done so, the rest of the train would have lynched him on the spot, if not for killing the two white men, then for what they imagined had happened between him and the white girl.

"Nothin' happened," he said, "Nothin'. We got caught by the storm an' waited it out. The others left while it was still rainin', an' we didn't see 'em go. They could of took her with them, but they didn't. We jus' got on our horses an' come on soon as we could. That's all."

"It don't matter," Graham said. "I don't care what some little slut does, or who she does it with. All I care about is gettin' these folks to Santa Fe without losin' all of them to a bunch of redskins because of a bunch of nigger foolishness."

"I don't see it as foolishness," Moses replied.

"I don't care *what* you see it as." Graham waved him off and turned to look for his pistol. "I've come too far, done too much to get this far, to let you, especially you, foul things up now. An' I don't much care what you think or what you do besides get me an' this train to Santa Fe." He spotted the gun butt under the wagon and went down on his knees and retrieved it. Standing erect, he holstered the Colt's and turned to face Moses. "You're on a short string, boy. And why you're not dead right now is something you'd best think on for the next few days. Don't get me wrong. I'd as soon shoot you as spit on you, and if you give me cause, I'll do both. Santa Fe be damned. But I call the shots hereout. Do you understand me?"

Moses nodded. He didn't trust himself to speak.

"See that you do," Graham said, and Moses turned away to see about the horses.

PART TWO

THE CROSSING

CHAPTER ONE

1

The wagon train made the crossing by noon the following day. Sometime in the blackness between moonset and dawn, the buckboard carrying the Newsomes and Hawshaws lumbered into hearing distance of the sleepy but anxious sentries. The half-dozen shots they fired into the night before George Newsome's shouts identified the intruders managed to do no damage other than killing one ox. The next morning, the spare draft animals were hitched to the traces, and the wagons were underway just after sunup. No other bad luck struck the train, and nothing was said about the events of the night before. The settlers pushed relentlessly forward across the rolling prairie toward the approaching mesa and its copse of pecan trees.

When the train rounded the small end of the mesa, Moses spurred his bay ahead and prepared to scout the crossing in advance of Graham's arrival. He had stayed well out in front of the wagon master's team all morning, concentrating on the horizon and trying to keep from being caught again unawares by hidden Indians. But no Comanche appeared, and he guessed that they were still well behind them, probably, he hoped, too sick from the whiskey to move.

Finally he spotted the creek, and without more than a glance up and down the free-flowing water, he directed his horse down a buffalo path into the crossing's clearing.

He and Grierson had discovered the crossing by accident during one of their excursions, but they had never been able to locate it again. It was a singular geographic phenomenon in this part of Texas, and when the first train he led across the prairie stumbled into it, again by accident, he marked it by the mesa and pecan trees. He doubted that the Indians were aware enough of its importance to have laid an ambush for them. He was confident that even if the Comanche used it, they were not likely to be waiting for the train in such an obvious trap. Apparently, he was right. The crossing was deserted.

Moses began to relax as he heard the wagons straining to crest the ridge behind him. At this point, Blind Man's Creek ran east and west. On the southern bank the ground rose steadily about a hundred feet to the top of the small end of the mesa. The rise was covered with a thick growth of scrub cedar, juniper, thickets of wild plums, and first-growth mesquite. It was almost choked by a dense undergrowth of thorny weeds and brush which forbade a southern entrance. The only access to the creek at this point, in fact, was the buffalo path Moses and now the wagons took to reach the bed of the stream. Even though the previous visitors' wagons had widened the path to nearly the size of a road, it was still a steep, twisting ordeal for horses, mules, and especially oxen to traverse.

Graham drove his oxen into the stream, where the thirsty beasts immediately began lapping up the water. Moses splashed across to survey the northern bank. It was completely different from the other side: a wide, gravelly beach eased away from the rushing waters and rose gently to a limestone butte that thrust directly up into the sky. To the east a small trail led a perpendicular course away from the creek just where it bent to the north and out of sight. The western end of the butte came to a dead end where the limestone wall interrupted the creek's bed and forced a sharp bend. No rider could navigate that side without getting wet; in order to approach from the east, riders would have to come into the crossing in single file unless they rode their horses directly into the shallow rapids which broke just beyond where the creek turned.

The butte itself was a wonder. Years of flooding and erosion had carved a honeycomb of caves in the base. Some were tiny and dark, but others were large enough to contain animals the size of oxen or cattle. A few caves were actually small rooms, opening from narrow, low entrances into interiors ranging in size from mere closets to areas deep enough to accommodate a dozen people. There were concave depressions in the base with cavernous ceilings and small shelves carved into the living rock. Above the highest openings a brief, uneven ledge had been carved out by ages of water coursing down the limestone sides, and an occasional bush or tree had found purchase in the skimpy soil along each narrow foothold. It was nearly a hundred feet of smooth rock above each ledge to the top of the butte, however. No root or branch ventured from either direction to provide the meanest of handholds.

In the noonday sun, the caves appeared to be an abandoned Pueblo village. Some were invitingly open and spacious, and others were shadowy and foreboding. Moses knew that one or two of them were ventilated, as if they were constructed that way, by water-eroded tunnels in their ceilings that led all the way up to the butte's top, so fires were possible inside them. One or two had underground springs which bubbled and drained to mysterious underground streams far beneath the mesa, so even if the Indians laid siege to the train, the settlers should be able to hold out for quite a while.

The area was just as it always was, and its familiarity warmed him. His plans for this crossing went beyond this train's mere watering stop, and he sometimes feared that it had flooded over, eroded away, or simply disappeared and taken with it all his hopes.

The remaining wagons were now lining up behind Graham, and the draft animals, anxious for the cool water, bunched up in spite of the drivers' oaths and shouts. Moses rode up and down the caved wall of the butte, inspecting each entrance as best he could from horseback, and finally he galloped over to Graham's wagon, which was emerging on the northern bank.

"Need 'bout four or five men to help me 'spect the caves," he called to Graham, who scowled back at him.

"What for?"

"This time of year, all sorts of critters go in there to sling 'em a litter." Moses dismounted and tied his horse to Graham's wagon. "Panther, catamount, coyote, wolf, even bear sometimes, an' I don't think folks wants to tangle with no mama bear." He drew his Colt's .44 and started toward the first cave, reaching down and picking up a handful of gravel.

Graham called back to the wagons behind him, "Frank, pick some men an' check out the caves."

Frank Herbert shouted to a few others, who left their wagons in the stream and splashed ashore, grinning like young boys. Here at last, it seemed, was work they could do without fear. In imitation of the scout, they drew the weapons they had started wearing since the encounter with the Indians the day before and began flinging handfuls of gravel inside the caves, waiting for a growl or noise.

A few men encountered rattlesnakes, which Moses quickly came up and dispatched with a long, stout cedar branch, but eventually they moved on to the larger caves. Although some caves had obviously been occupied by various beasts, they found nothing else larger than field mice and snakes to contend with. Within an hour, Moses was able to beckon to Graham to bring the wagons up on a line parallel with the butte.

"Unhitch the teams an' put what you can in the big caves," he said. "Then pull the wagons up tight. We need one wagon blockin' the path 'round the left side, an' the rest'll give us a kind of wall."

Graham lumbered down and began unharnessing his team without a word. He shouted to others as they pulled into line to follow his example, while Moses climbed up as high as he could on the butte's steeply sloping limestone. By making use of the uneven rock atop the caves at the center of the butte, he found he could step up onto the lowest ledge. It was grainy and crumbly, running from about two feet wide to less than six inches as it meandered its way down the butte's wall. But it did afford a good lookout point, and the sparse vegetable growth that sprang up here and there provided some decent cover for a man who knew how to crouch.

He shielded his eyes against the glare of the noonday sun and made a visual inspection of the far bank. This was a natural fort, the scout acknowledged, but it was also a natural trap. A handful of gunmen on the opposite bank could hunker down in that brush and cedar and pin down an army. But Comanche didn't fight that way, he told himself. At least, he had never heard of them fighting that way.

Shouts filtered up through the creaking and groaning

of wagons. Graham ordered Virgil Hollister to volunteer his wagon as a block for the open trail—something the preacher was reluctant to do.

The sun was warm, and soon most of the men were sweating with their labors. The oxen were secured between the wagons and the caves, and both Sterling's cattle and the remuda were safely rope-penned in concave openings in the butte's wall. Moses scanned the crossing up and down one more time and satisfied himself that they had as safe a harbor as this country could provide.

Below him, Jack Sterling and his son, Jason, fussed with their cattle, and Moses could hear the train's tiny herd of hogs grunting. He thought briefly of Ambrose, and he remarked to himself how strange it was that none of the white men had suggested either last night or since that someone might go back for the old man and his son. Then he dismissed the thoughts.

Ambrose was dead, or as good as dead. There was no point in risking good men trying to persuade the old man to do what he should and could have done in the first place. It was nothing short of a blessing that the Newsomes and Hawshaws had managed to complete their foolish errand at no greater cost than the loss of one ox.

As the men continued to draw the wagons together tongue to tailgate, small children escaped and began scouring the weeds near the creek bed, capturing grasshoppers and other small insects to take down to the creek to try their luck catching catfish and perch that swam beneath the turgid surface of the stream. Women were happily chatting and gathering laundry to haul down to wash in the water.

Moses climbed down and checked the load in both his rifle and pistol. As he remounted his bay, he made a mental note to post sentries and get them something to eat. He rode out of the wagon fort and began again to pace his horse up and down the beach, watching the ridgeline. The cedar thicket and weed-choked grass appeared to be a solid wall on the opposite bank. It was ragged and green and uninviting against the translucence of the sky, but it was as steep as it was impenetrable. He knew that no Indians, not even Comanche, could mount a headlong assault from such a tangle, and the creek's flow was too rapid in places for horsemen to maneuver smoothly. Even so he felt a prickling worry on the top of his head. Comanche, he reminded himself, were not ordinary horsemen, and a bit of fast-flowing water was hardly a barrier to determined warriors.

He was running a bluff, he finally admitted to himself. About all he could pray for was that somehow the Comanche would drink the whiskey, eat the beef, and then fade off south as they were supposed to. But he didn't really believe that they would. They had seen the white man's wealth—and his women—and they would have them or die trying to get them.

He left the cinch loose on the bay and patted her rump while he watched Graham march up and down the wagon line and insist that the whiskey casks be moved from the outside to behind the wagons where they could be secure from stray bullets and arrows should an attack come. Most of the settlers complied. Moses rolled a cigarette and watched them working with a mixture of curiosity and contempt. Who did Graham think he was fooling? he wondered. Whiskey was like wildfire out here. Once word of it escaped, it spread across the prairie faster than the wind, and men—white and red—would come to sample it, or steal it. Almost every wagon carried some, and each keg was marked with the telltale X's and a government stamp that certified good liquor, not homemade white lightning from some cracker's still.

"One thing 'bout whiskey," he recalled an old cavalry officer saying through a thick Yankee accent, "was that oncet a Injun has a taste of it, they wan' the whole hog and ever'thin' that went with her." In this case, Moses figured, "ever'thin' " meant the women, including Aggie Sterling. No, he corrected himself, especially Aggie Sterling. He was still confused and anxious about the look in that young chief's eyes when he spotted the blond girl.

Campfires had been built, and food was being prepared while less anxious stomachs awaited the fresher fruits of the creek. Some of the settlers, Moses noticed, had discovered the caves with the natural chimneys, and he saw several people with armfuls of dead branches moving toward their temporary homes. He could hear the buzz of conversations as people ate and chatted, relaxing for the first time since encountering the Indians the day before. He realized he hadn't had a decent meal in days. He hadn't had a good night's sleep, either.

Women moved back and forth between the creek bed and the wagons, hauling laundry. Several children and not a few of the younger women had removed their shoes and rolled up their trousers or tied the ends of their skirts and petticoats up in knots so they could cool their feet in the water.

It was as if this were some sort of picnic instead of a forced camp in the middle of Comanchería, and Moses felt himself becoming caught up in it. Someone broke out a Jew's harp and began twanging "Old Dan Tucker" and "Buffalo Gals." The music grew with the addition of a mouth organ and several voices.

The wagon master was fussing with his oxen, Jack Sterling was yelling at his son about their cattle, and others were carrying nose bags to their beasts. Moses leaned his rifle against Graham's wagon, unbuckled his pistol belt, and hung it next to the long arm. He decided to allow himself the luxury of another smoke, and as he rolled it, he walked down the line.

Many people he encountered spoke to him and smiled, however condescendingly, as he passed and touched the brim of his hat. Some, mostly the older folks, scowled at him and turned away, and he figured that the conflict between him and Graham had set some hard feelings more or less permanently. He noticed the North Carolinians tethering their hogs in such a way as to give them all the freedom they could. These weren't what people called "pioneers," not even to the limited extent that the settlers Moses had previously guided west had been. They were just home folks, people who wanted someplace to settle down and be comfortable.

He spotted Aggie Sterling. She and her young sister, Annie, were carrying a small chest into one of the largest caves just behind their wagon, and her mother was gathering clothing together to wash. The older Sterling girl had a quizzical expression on her face as she studied the black scout. He felt a sudden pang of emotion that was difficult to define. Part of him, he realized, had been searching Aggie out, maybe even hoping for a word or two. Part of him, too, resented her. She had caused him trouble, and he was almost as angry with himself for unconsciously seeking her out as he was delighted with her simple beauty. Even though he was frightened by the feelings she stirred in him, he found that he couldn't help indulging a secret excitement he couldn't ignore any more than he could reveal.

In spite of Mrs. Sterling's scowl when she saw him, Moses felt content, infected by the security that seemed to hang over the whole train. The spring sun now filled the crossing and wagon fort. Insects buzzed in the weeds, and the fragrance of wildflowers was borne by a spring breeze. Moses felt giddy. He thought once more of Aggie's open prettiness and wondered if he was in love with her, pushing aside the discomfort that associated itself with real possibilities of the idea. They were disturbing and dangerous, and the atmosphere around him refused to admit anything so unpleasant.

Maybe they—all of them—were safe after all, he thought. Maybe the Comanche would leave them alone, recognizing that they had made a good bargain off the frightened white man. There were treaties, Moses knew—Medicine Lodge, The Little Arkansas—which should have prevented any sort of fear. But he had spent too much time in the company of Rangers and soldiers to believe that the Comanche paid attention to treaties. The Mexican party had been testimony to that. But they *were* Mexican, and that meant they didn't count. The Comanche hated *mexicanos* more than the *tejanos*, and he respected the latter only slightly more mostly because the Texans would fight back. It was a white man's world, and the rest—red, brown, or black—needed to learn to live with it.

2

Moses saw Graham storing his gear in a cave at the far end of the train. He remembered that he needed to post lookouts and quickened his step. It was not a chore that he looked forward to, since no one was going to like having to pull boring, unpleasant duty and interrupt his rest. The scout felt a sudden discomfort in the afternoon's cheery warmth.

Virgil Hollister was pacing back and forth behind Graham, holding a battered Bible in his gnarled fingers, and he was shouting at the wagon master while William Golden and several others looked on with a mixture of interest and amusement. Hollister's scrawny neck was stretched out of a yellow collarless shirt, and a long skinny finger punctuated his remarks by tapping on the Bible almost in time to his bobbing Adam's apple. Moses hoped that by interrupting the impromptu sermon the wagon master was silently but dourly enduring, he might earn some benefit in his employer's eyes. He began to speak, but the men turned all at once and looked out between the wagons toward the creek. Moses at first thought they were making some sort of joke at his expense, and he flushed with anger. He started to state his business, but he never got the words out of his mouth.

Several of the children heard the splashing first and peered upstream to try to discern what might be causing the disruption of their fishing. Moses stopped and listened, somewhat mystified. The fear he had sensed deep in the background of the afternoon uncoiled, and he turned to join Graham and the small party in staring at the sunny creek. A dozen or so women stopped their washing and talking on the creek bank and looked back at the wagons for an explanation, but their quizzical looks turned to terror as the first Comanche ponies waded into view from both the east and west ends of the creek.

Screams drowned out the splashes of the women and children trying to extricate themselves from the creek's suddenly deadly waters. Comanche braves, over twenty of them, guided their ponies to the shallower water of the ford and began their high yip-yipping. The men at the wagons had lain their weapons by and found themselves helplessly frozen where they stood or running pell-mell into one another as they sought their rifles and pistols. From somewhere on the line, Moses heard the thin crack of a small pistol, but he was too fascinated by the scene going on in front of him to move.

"This ain't happenin'!" he said aloud. "This ain't happenin' *now*!"

The braves kicked their horses so hard that some of the ponies foundered as they came out of the knee-deep water. They began swooping up some of the women and children, piling them like grain sacks across their ponies. They loosed lances at some of the women who were making their way back to the wagons, their progress encumbered by wet skirts or bare feet. The flint-tipped spears knocked the women down and pinned them where they fell. Braves leaped from their horses and pounced upon them. They pulled dresses open at the neck or simply threw up skirts and began their rapes without fear of the white men, who, for the most part, continued to look on in rigid terror or to move around without direction or purpose. More Comanche were coming down the wagon trail, riding in crazy, lurching ways, some barely able to remain on their horses.

Some of the children who had been scooped up by the Indians were putting up a brave if ineffectual fight by pounding their captors with their fists and gouging at eyes and ears. Moses saw that some of the Indians, wounded by pokes or bites from the writhing, living loot, were angered too much, and they took a club or tomahawk and split their small captives' skulls before dumping them off. It dawned on Moses that the Comanche were still drunk, still feeling the effects of bonded whiskey. That, he realized, might be a blessing.

He ran back to Graham's wagon and retrieved his Springfield .55 "High Hammer" and his gunbelt. Laying the rifle across Graham's wagon bed, he fired the first effective shot from the white settlers' fort. A big buck found himself launched into the air and deposited in a bloody heap at the creek's edge.

The rifle's single report had a stunning effect on the Indians, who thus far had not loosed an arrow or fired a bullet. In their alcoholic daze, they suddenly stopped their cries and turned toward the wagon line where Moses was shoving a second round into the Springfield's breech.

A short, paunchy brave held one of the younger women fast by her hair and was trying to lift her up onto his horse. A second crack from the rifle sounded, and the small Indian's head vanished completely in a burst of red. The woman scrambled back toward the wagons.

Moses's actions seemed to awaken others, and suddenly sporadic rifle fire from on his right became general along the whole wagon line. The Indians wheeled and raced their ponies up and down, while their comrades continued to struggle with the women they had pinned down or the captives who kept fighting back from atop their captors' horses.

A red-haired girl was fighting the brave on top of her with a carpet beater. Moses tried to draw a bead on her attacker, but every time he thought he could manage a shot, another brave would cross between them, and he hesitated. His attention was distracted by a trio of Comanche who had pulled their horses up on the left edge of the crossing and were loosing arrows toward the train with a calm indifference to the settlers' bullets. Moses fired at them, knocking one off his pony and sending the others galloping off. When he looked back at the girl and her attacker, he saw that the Indian had the girl's skirt thrown up and her legs parted around his waist. The thrusts of his hips indicated that the rape was begun. Moses dared not fire for fear of hitting her. As he debated, a sudden hole opened in the warrior's side and his left arm split into two bloody parts. He rolled off the girl. Moses could see her body heaving with the agony of her ordeal, but soon events down the line took his attention away from her.

A group of armed men had formed up near Hollister's blocking wagon and now ran out in a line from the end of the train. They shouted and waved their pistols as they charged the melee in the center of the crossing. When they were about halfway to the chaos the men suddenly fell down, almost as if they had run into an invisible rope and were knocked off their feet. Their bodies sprouted brightly feathered shafts, leaving those who were not killed outright studying the dogwood sticks that had grown instantaneously from their chests and throats.

Drunk or not, the Indians had provided a good cover from the ridge crest, and competent archers were watching from the cedar trees and plum thickets across the creek, ready to protect the raiders' conquests.

Moses fired again, enjoying the solid recoil of the rifle as it plunged back into his shoulder, but this time he missed his target and hit instead the neck of the piebald pony the brave was riding. As the horse fell, Moses saw the red-headed woman the Indians had recaptured go down under it. He could almost feel the animal's weight as it crushed her head. The Comanche, however, jumped from the falling beast and leaped upon a different horse, suddenly loosed by another brave's death. Moses reloaded and fired; the brave sprang straight up in the air with a gaping red hole spreading across his chest.

Firing up and down the line was constant now, and Moses watched with confusion and growing alarm the lack of effect the settlers' rifles seemed to have. Aside from the two or three fallen Indians, the rest of the braves were either continuing their brutal business with the women on the ground or were pulling the captives up onto their ponies and preparing to retreat. Normally, he knew, Comanche horsemen were almost impossible to hit. They could practically paste themselves to the far side of their horses and offer no targets at all while they fired their arrows and guns from beneath their mounts' necks. But this time, partly because of the whiskey's effect and partly because of the captives and rapidity of the creek's current, most of the braves were clearly visible. It was unimaginable that all of the exposed braves weren't already dead, given the number of men who had rifles. Moses decided that the settlers were trying too hard to pick their targets, and he moved down the wagon line trying to encourage them to fire less accurately and more often.

"Them's our women out there," one man said. "We don't want to hit our women!" He turned around to resume his post, and Moses was astonished to see an arrow sticking out of his back. He didn't seem even to know about it. Had it been there before the man turned around? Moses couldn't remember.

Several of the men nearby turned to see what the scout would say. Most of them were afraid to fire at any target too close to a white woman.

"Either you shoot an' take the chance, or the Comanche'll have 'em an' you won't," Moses shouted, and he himself fired again, this time dropping a brave just as he was about to guide his horse up the wagon trail with a young girl he had captured. She fell hard and lay there for a moment, and Moses feared that somehow he had hit her too, but suddenly she scrambled down the trail into the creek. She waded across and raced past the confusion on the bank, finally making the relatively safe cover of Hollister's blocking wagon.

Moses's action seemed to take effect, and the men turned back to the awful business that faced them. A number of them now had arrows jutting from their shoulders and legs. Rifle fire increased along the line, and Moses moved again down to the end, where he kept encouraging the men and boys.

Confusion and noise were now general all about the crossing, and the Indians' yipping began to die out as they came to realize that the settlers' firepower, inaccurate though it was, was too great for the raid to continue. Those who had only been able to capture older women or who were having too great a difficulty with the children they had swooped up dispatched their unwilling charges quickly and cruelly with a slash of tomahawk or club. The younger girls and all the men who had been snatched up, though, were retained by the captors, often knocked insensible or quickly bound with rawhide lariats. The braves continued to return the settlers' fire from the excited ponies, which continued to have trouble maneuvering in the rapid waters.

Moses fired randomly, dropping a brave here and there. Suddenly he realized the value in killing the ponies when he could. Without horses, their only escape was to take the wagon trail across the creek or to float downstream. Either way, they could take no captives with them.

Even so, and in spite of the now fierce fire from the wagon line, some of the Indians were making good their retreat with their human booty. The screams of terrified women and children who passed out of sight downstream filled the settlers with a renewed determination to kill as many of the retreating raiders as possible.

Winchesters and Henrys, Sharpses and shotguns barked up and down the line, but Moses noticed that while the raiding party retreated, the fire from the other side of the creek increased. Arrows darted out to sprig the wagons' sides and bounce harmlessly off the limestone rock behind the settlers, and they were now supported by the sharp crack of carbines. Moses tried to aim the powerful Springfield toward the telltale blue smoke that often clouded out of the cedars across the creek. The bursts weren't frequent, though, and he realized the braves were conserving their ammunition, content to rely on the silent and more accurate *bois d'arc* bows.

After a few more volleys from the wagon line, the Indians were gone from sight, although covering fire from the thicket continued in a deadly volume. In their wake, corpses littered the gravel alongside the creek and floated grotesquely in the swirling waters, which now were frothing bright red where they crossed the ford. There were no Comanche bodies, Moses noted when he tried to get a count of the dead, but he also knew that most of them had fallen in the center of the water and were already washed out of sight. The rest were carried off, dead or alive, by their marauding comrades.

He began moving up the wagon line once more, encouraging the men, who were now pelting the far bank with regular volleys. He found Graham lying prone under his wagon, still firing with regularity anytime a burst of blue smoke exploded across the creek. Moses climbed down and bellied up beside him.

There was no expression on the wagon master's face at all. He didn't look at Moses, but only cocked his rifle and ejected his casings and searched the cedar thicket.

"How many dead?" he asked.

"I figger a bunch," Moses said. His job was to stop this sort of thing before it happened, and he had failed. He was prepared to take the blame for it.

"Can't you count, either?" Graham snarled.

"I figger six or seven women was killed outright," Moses tallied. "Maybe six more later on, an' least half 'gin as many carried off. Some of the hurt men, too."

"They're dead," Graham said.

Moses silently agreed.

"I think they's some still alive out there . . . women, I mean. They're pinned down an' can't move. But they's no way to get to 'em, not an' live to do nothin' when you get there." He looked at Graham for a reaction, but the big man showed none. His eyes were small gray stones rimmed with red. He continued to fire by awkwardly tucking the Winchester under his body and working the level with his remaining hand.

"I saw those damn fools runnin' out there a while ago," he said between shots. "I suppose every one's dead now."

"Them as wasn't carried off, I reckon," Moses said, pulling his Springfield up and trying to sight a target so he could join Graham in his shooting. The way the wagon master was firing into the cedars there must be more to see than Moses could make out with just the occasional glance. No Indian sign offered itself, though, and Moses decided that Graham was just keeping the Comanche snipers' heads down and, he supposed, giving himself something positive to do.

"An' they's kids. Boys mostly," Moses went on. "I didn't see how many of 'em got away, but some of 'em is dead, an' some got carried off."

"*Goddamnit!*" Graham exclaimed. "That's damned near a third of us dead or worse!" He rolled on his side and glared at the black scout. "You've killed a third of us off with your goddamn 'let's give them the whiskey an' bury the Mescans' horseshit." Almost in concert with Graham's anger, a fusillade of bullets struck the wagons and the butte's limestone wall behind them.

"I didn't kill nobody!" Moses snapped back, fighting back a wave of guilty heat. "That whiskey likely saved some lives today, if you want a truth." Graham rolled onto his stomach, but Moses went on defending himself. "If them Comanche could ride right an' shoot straight, they'd made a piece of work of this 'stead of the mess they got theirselves into. I never seen sober Indians, Comanche or nobody else, come at a bunch of armed men that way in bright daylight." He thought for a second and muttered under his breath, "I never heard tell of it, neither."

More fire from the thicket forced their heads down. The attack might be over, but the Comanche weren't about to let the whites regroup.

A few wagons down a man screamed and crawled out from under his wagon. An arrow protruded from his forehead, and he ran around in a circle, clutching at it with both hands. The shaft had not penetrated very deeply, but blood streamed from his eyes. With a start, Moses saw that it was Jack Sterling, and he instantly looked around to see if he could catch a glimpse of Aggie. He feared she would run out and try to save her father.

Jack's screams echoed off the small canyon's walls, and all shooting stopped at once. Moses watched the man's boots dig into the loose stones while his hands sought the courage and the strength to extract the barbed point from his forehead.

Graham reached behind him and extracted his Colt's .44 from its holster. "He sure hated to give up those heifers," he said with a dark chortle in his voice. "An' he's goin' to hate to lose the whiskey. But that's the way the cards fall sometimes." But whatever his tone might have betrayed was not reflected in the wagon master's eyes. His gaze was steady, and beneath his red beard, Graham's mouth was drawn in a tight line. Moses knew what he was about to do, and in spite of the blank necessity of it, he was horrified.

Graham cocked the pistol and stretched out his arm to make sure of his target. "Time to fold, Jack," he said quietly. He calmly snapped off a round and knocked Sterling to the ground dead.

"Did you have to do that?" Moses asked. His eyes involuntarily scouted the wagon line as far as he could see to find Aggie, but she was nowhere in sight. Graham had just killed her father with no more hesitation than if he had been an injured mule, and Moses expected to see her fall on the wagon master with a knife or gun of her own.

But if Graham was worried, his face did not betray it. "I ought to put one through you, too," he said. There was a quiet threat in his voice, but mostly Moses sensed something distant and painful behind it. "An' I might if you don't bust your black ass an' figure a way out of this. We still have some folks alive, an' I'd like to see them get to Santa Fe sometime this summer. An' alive." He studied the puzzled look on Moses's face, reholstered his pistol, and resumed working his rifle toward the far bank. His voice dropped to a growl. "Jack had it comin'. Long time. I know what I'm doin'," he grumbled between shots. "You tend your business. I'll tend mine."

Arrows came now occasionally, single shots bringing with them that curious sucking whistle that told their targets, but often too late, that an Indian had spotted them.

Some were finding their marks in those draft animals which had not been properly hidden in the caves or closely sheltered behind the wagon line.

Moses pulled out from under Graham's wagon and looked up the line. With casualties mounting and the death of the animals, it was likely that all of them would be stuck on this creek for a long time. His mind searched for something useful to do, but nothing appeared obvious. All they could do now was wait to see what the Comanche had in mind for the rest of the afternoon.

Moving away slightly, he inspected the butte's sides. Even if the Comanche came up behind them from the north, he recognized, they couldn't do much. There was no way to get a clear shot at the wagon line's rear from the top of the butte. It was alive with cactus and brambles, and not even the most agile brave could make his way down that steep slope to the narrow shelf over the cave openings without tumbling into their midst. No, Graham was wrong about one thing, the scout told himself. This was a good place, a defensible place. There was safety within the wagon line for the time being if not longer.

He relaxed a bit. They wouldn't wind up like the Mexican party, caught out in the open with only a small clump of trees to protect them. They weren't trapped without water and food. They were cornered but not desperate. They were, however, scared and tired and feeling panic. If they could get themselves together, they might hold out long enough for the Indians to weary of the business and go away.

He stepped back under an outcropping, removed his hat, and wiped his brow. The acrid smell of gunpowder hung in the air. Greasy smoke from the guns made his face feel as if it were covered with thick oil, and a quick inspection of his bandanna's blackness confirmed it. The firing from both sides of the creek was reduced to potshotting now, and he hoped that meant the Indians were satisfied with their captives and would go away. Then guilt struck him again, and he chastised himself for so carelessly dismissing those who had been taken. They were worse off than those bodies out on the bank, he knew. Before they died, they had a special kind of hell to live through.

Maybe Graham had been more right than even he

knew, Moses argued with himself. What could he have been thinking to leave his weapons behind and go for an afternoon stroll like a dandy in a park? He knew better than that; he had more savvy.

He shook his head and moved cautiously from wagon to wagon. What he had done was exactly what Graham and Sterling had feared he would do. Maybe if he hadn't listened to Aggie and stopped to bury the Mexicans they would have made the crossing the night before. Maybe they would have had time to fort up better, he would have had time to post guards, to caution people against going down to the creek without arms. Maybe if he hadn't been so anxious to walk past her this afternoon and grin like some puke-eating dog waiting for a pretty girl's smile, he might have had his mind on what he had been hired to do. He knew that he had to regain his position. Whether it was set down in writing or not, whether it was part of his and Graham's agreement or not, he knew that he had to figure out some way of getting the train out from under attack and get those that remained to Santa Fe.

Except for the odd thudding of arrows hitting a wagon or the occasional crack of a rifle from the line, the firing had all but stopped. From the creek bank some women moaned loudly and called for their husbands or sons to come out and help. There were maybe a half-dozen still alive out there, Moses counted as he listened to the cries. He thought of Aggie and wondered—but no, he had seen her right before the raid started as she went into a cave with her mother. Or was it her sister? Where was her brother? Where had her mother gone after Moses passed her? He couldn't remember. Maybe she had seen Graham kill her husband, or, Moses thought, maybe she had seen the two of them under Graham's wagon and thought that he had done it. The idea panicked him.

He knew that if given a chance Graham would kill him—or anyone—with the same detachment. That was what he had seen in the wagon master's eyes right after he pulled the trigger. He had misjudged the wagon master. He had thought him to be mostly bluff, a dude in rough clothing pretending to be something he wasn't. He had never before considered him capable of murder. That was wrong, Moses told himself. More than anything else, Graham was cold-blooded.

A loud row broke out two wagons down. Moses moved quickly toward the noise and discovered a giant cross-eyed man pinned against the wagon by two other men. His misshapen eyes were wild, and the others could barely hold him.

"He hears his wife out there," one of the men Moses recognized as the small carpenter, Harvey Pierce, explained. "She's one of them down by the bank. He wants to go get her." Pierce's small size was offset by the strength of his hands. He held his prisoner's bicep with a tight grip. The other arm was pinioned by a large man named Dudley Warner.

"He'll die tryin', an' she's no better off," Moses said as much to the huge, struggling man as to his guards.

"I *hear* her!" the man insisted, not turning his crossed eyes in Moses's direction. "She *needs* me! Them Indians, they—"

"I know what they done," Moses said evenly. "An' they'll kill you if you go out there."

The man seemed to relax a bit, so the men let go, allowing him to turn toward the creek and squint through a crack in the wagon's canvas toward the prostrate bodies of the women. The man's shoulders shuddered; he was sobbing.

"He's all right," Warner whispered to Moses. "They got his kid, too. Toted him off, I think."

Moses started to leave, but a quick movement behind him made him turn. Freed from his friends' arms, the big man swung clear of the wagon. Moses reached for him, only to be knocked backward against the limestone wall. The man struck him with the back of his fist before dropping down and scuttling under his wagon. He wriggled out of his friends' hands when they grabbed at his scurrying boots and disappeared under the wagon. As he made his way clear on the other side, he stood up and looked around.

"Goddamnit, Sloan, come back here!" Warner yelled.

"Give 'im some cover, damn it!" Moses yelled. He jerked his .44 from its holster and emptied it into the cedar thicket across the creek. Warner and Pierce joined him, and in seconds a fusillade of lead was pouring into the cedar breaks where now the telltale puffs of smoke resumed.

Sloan stood immobile for a few seconds, then suddenly lurched forward toward his helpless wife. Two arrow shafts immediately sprang out of his great chest, and three more hit the gravel around him. Small stones also began to jump and explode as carbine fire from Indian snipers tried to find him.

Ignoring his wounds, Sloan ran on in a clumsy, awkward gait, dipping and almost falling with every second step. His motion made him a difficult target for the Comanche. He was within ten feet of his wife's pinned form before a rifle ball took effect on his shoulder, causing his whole body to spin around as a great spout of blood shot up and away from his falling torso.

"He's dead," Pierce commented. "Damned fool's dead."

But Pierce was wrong. Sloan sat up, clamped a dirty hand over his bloody shoulder, and rose to his feet, swaying and jerking. An arrow appeared in his thigh, but he continued toward his wife. He collapsed to his knees beside her and tried to remove the lances that held her to the ground.

Moses rapidly reloaded his pistol. He knew Sloan could never make it back with her, especially when he saw the bright scarlet blade of the lance the wounded giant finally wrenched from his wife's body. But there was no way to go out and help the pair.

Sloan rose to his feet and wrestled with the second spear. He finally jerked it free, and two more flint arrowheads found home in his chest. He collapsed for good. His wife, dazed and shocked, sat up stupidly, glanced at her husband, and began a terrifying, shrill scream that silenced weapons on both sides of the creek bed.

In a crazy, wrenching fashion, she struggled to her feet, displaying a broken, dangling arm and a wound in her other shoulder that poured blood down her shirtwaist.

"Murd'rers!" she screamed. "You let him come out here by hisself!" Her hair, loosed from its bun, sprayed wildly behind her. She staggered toward the wagon line in the eerie silence that had settled over the crossing, thrusting her broken arm out like a talisman in front of her.

"After what they *done* to me!" she wailed. "You let him come out here *by hisself!* Murd'rers! Cowards!"

The men shrank back from her approaching form, although she was still thirty yards from the nearest wagon. Into the absolute quiet that punctuated her accusations, there was the by now familiar whistle and quiet thump, and she pitched forward onto the bloody gravel, a single arrow rigidly standing in the middle of her back.

After that, there was no more shooting from either side, but the women on the creek bank continued to writhe under the sharp spears and knives that held them helpless to the ground. From time to time one or more of them loosed a hoarse scream that echoed up and down the canyon.

"Maybe we ought to shoot the rest of them," a voice behind Moses suggested in a familiar, emotionless tone. He turned to see Graham standing behind him, smoking a cigar and steadying his rifle on a wagon's rim. His eyes once again reflected only a dusty hardness.

"You do, Mr. Graham, an' I'll shoot you. Fact of the matter, I'll blow you in two."

It was Aggie Sterling, and Moses turned and beheld the girl, her face once again a mask of determination, her mouth set, her long fingers gripping a shotgun that was leveled at Graham's middle.

"My mama's out there, an' likely she's dyin'. But if you kill her, you'll be the very next one to see Jesus."

Her eyes were cold, Moses thought, like skim ice on a January morning, and it made him afraid of her. Her voice was cool and even. All the gentleness he had admired in her was gone. The fond girl she had been when she chatted with him or smiled at him had evaporated.

Graham looked hard at the double barrels and turned abruptly away from the girl. The look on his face had transformed into one of sick guilt. "It was only a thought," he said to nobody in particular. "I just hate to hear 'em suffer." Bright beads of sweat collected over his eyebrows. He nervously wiped them away.

"I hate to hear it, too, Mr. Graham," Aggie said, not

yet lowering the weapon. "But hear it we will. An' the Lord'll take her in His own good time."

Graham continued to look away from her. His face glowed bright red beneath his hat, but he said nothing. He twisted his body and looked out the makeshift loop where his rifle had been and pretended to study the creek bank as if something of intense interest had developed there. Aggie lowered the shotgun at last and moved back into the cave. Another unholy scream filled the canyon, and the tension between the girl and the man was broken. Moses found that he had been holding his breath, and he let it out slowly as he leaned against the limestone butte.

3

"WHEN DO YOU RECKON THEY'LL COME BACK?" GRAHAM asked Moses. He kept his gaze on the cave's entrance and flung away the dead cigar, which Moses saw was chewed in two. Then he reached into a pocket and pulled out another. Aggie had been inside for almost fifteen minutes, and others who had been standing around them had slunk off to find shooting loops that were farther away from the embarrassing scene. Sniping from the other side had ceased, and the wagons' defenders also paused to let their rifle barrels cool.

"Soon as they can," Moses replied. The sunlight had dimmed a bit, something he had attributed to the growing lateness of the afternoon and the shade provided by the depth of the crossing. As he looked upward, however, he saw enormous clouds boiling in a green roll. In a short time, thunder and lightning would replace gunfire on the creek. "We might get lucky," he said.

Graham glanced up and noted the dark blanket that churned across the brilliant blue sky as if drawn by an unseen hand. He nodded. "We'd better check what animals we got left," he said and started to move off. Then he stopped and turned to face the black scout. "Would you have let her shoot me?"

"I reckon I would have," Moses said. "I didn't see no chance to stop her."

Graham nodded, then he turned. Before he had taken

two steps, Moses's ears heard the splashes from the creek that signaled a renewal of the Comanche attack, and the by now familiar fear in his stomach reached up and clutched at his throat. A volley of arrows fell with a clatter. The fusillade was accompanied by the splintering of limestone from carbine fire. Once more, the tiny canyon was filled with the terrified screams of whites and the war whoops of attacking Comanche.

Again, the Indians came from both directions. They were reinforced by more than a dozen braves who galloped down the path from the crest of the ridge and splashed across the ford. There were many more than Moses had imagined possible. Comanche war parties weren't supposed to number more than twenty or thirty braves, but he could easily count more than that as he swung his rifle up and blasted in the general direction of the warriors. This wasn't ordinary, and it wasn't right.

He identified the young chief and the shaman he had spoken to the day before, yowling and yipping as they encouraged their horses through the water and waved their shields. Mirrors on their mounts reflected the sparse rays that found their way into the turmoil of the crossing, and the horns of the shaman's buffalo headdress also caught the glint of the dying light as he joined his leader in urging their comrades on. Moses noted, though, that the medicine man never ventured in too close to the wagons. He preferred riding his pony up and down the bank and yelling. Occasionally he would loose an arrow toward the wagons, and then he would sally toward the line before feinting and galloping back down to the water.

The howls of the Comanche were quickly matched by the explosions of the settlers' rifles and the screams of the pinioned women who lay directly in the path of the Indians' ponies. The braves rode straight over them without thought for their pleadings and cries from beneath their horses' diving hooves. The Indians kicked their mounts onward, unmindful of the screaming humanity beneath them.

A dozen braves fell at once when the defenders' rifles fired in volley. Some clung grotesquely to their horses until their strength gave out and they fell onto the gravel, where riflemen from behind the wagons picked them off. From behind him, Moses could hear other women screaming, and some of the men around him stopped firing, as if they were awed by the fierceness of the Comanche attack.

They'll crack soon, Moses said to himself. He picked a target with his Springfield's sights and watched an Indian explode in a bloody gush. They're not professional soldiers, just green settlers, home folk, he reminded himself. They can only take so much. He figured he had severely misjudged their bravery, even so. He felt more guilty than ever.

The Comanche had sobered up considerably since their first onslaught. Once their ponies had sure footing on the bank, the braves began their famous trick riding. Fewer targets presented themselves, and Moses looked up and down the line and shouted at his fellow defenders to aim at the horses if they couldn't get an Indian in their sights.

The warriors maneuvered in a careful parry of the rifle bullets that whizzed around them. Moses knew that no shield would turn away a .50- or .55-caliber slug, but some of the Winchesters were lighter than that, and most of the men using them weren't experienced enough to shoot through the shields. They seemed to be waiting for individual braves to show themselves.

The Indians now had come completely out of the water. They weren't going to make the same mistake of being caught in the swirling tide this time. Nor were they planning to be caught off their mounts dealing with children and women on the beach. They raced their ponies as close to the wagons as they dared. They rode up and down in front of the fortified line, tempting the settlers to shoot at them and crying in derision when one white man or other would jack shell after shell into his rifle only to find the redskinned target he picked still mounted and flying past him as if the bullets passed right through him.

Moses could see that the braves were trying to form a circle, which was impossible in the cramped battleground of the crossing. Frustrated, they continued to ride back and forth, loosing arrows toward any white face that appeared as a target.

Some of the Indians worked their horses up close enough to mount the large Conestogas and awkwardly climbed over the tops, trying to achieve footholds in the billowing canvas. Moses picked off one, hitting him just as the brave's moccasined feet launched him from a wagon's top and cutting him almost in half before he bounced off the limestone wall behind the scout. He couldn't believe the Comanche's determination. They never withdrew or regrouped. They just kept coming. He jammed another cartridge into the Springfield's breech and blasted a brave who could not have been more than four feet from the end of his barrel when he galloped by. When the smoke cleared, Moses saw the same Indian right himself from the lee side of his pony and scream his defiance. They were fast, Moses admitted, faster than bullets. He doubted the settlers stood much of a chance against men who could dodge .55-caliber slugs.

More braves were now atop the wagons, and women and children who had thus far busied themselves with handling ammunition for their husbands and fathers now began to fire the guns they reloaded or carried as extras. Every time an Indian peered over the top, five or six blasts ripped through the canvas where he lay, and most of the unwelcome intruders into the white stronghold were knocked high in the air.

Moses jumped to his feet and ran down the line, checking to make sure that someone was watching the top of every wagon. He stopped before two red hands stretching out from under a wagon where they found the legs of a woman and pulled her down. Moses drew his long knife and dove, plunging the blade into the forearms of the Indian. The woman was released instantly. Blood spurted from the brave's arms. The scout jumped to his feet and grabbed his pistol and prepared to kill the brave as soon as he stood up on the other side.

Before he could act, a pair of booms exploded in Moses's ear, and he flinched and almost fell beside the woman, who was still trying to recover herself. He looked to his left to find that Aggie Sterling had emptied both barrels of her shotgun at a Comanche who had just appeared over the side of the same wagon's canvas top. The blast lifted and tore away the white drape from the wagon's ribbing. Collecting himself, the scout pulled himself to his feet and swung around, but the warrior Moses had slashed was nowhere in sight.

Aggie retreated into her cave, and Moses resumed moving back toward Graham's wagon. He looked over his shoulder and saw her come out and empty the big scattergun once more, this time directly into the face of a Comanche who was galloping by. He was still close enough to see the shock in the brave's young eyes as the double load of buckshot caught him in the face.

Everyone on both sides of the battle seemed to be screaming, and the shrieks of wounded animals joined in the din. Even the hogs and chickens added their terrified cries to the confusion. Moses's ears rang, and his eyes and mouth burned with gunpowder and smoke.

When he tried to reload, Moses discovered that his bandolier was empty of .55-caliber cartridges, and he started moving in a low crouch toward Graham's ammunition stash. His pistol was still loaded, and he snapped off several shots as he made his way slowly and carefully down the wagon line. All around him, settlers were putting up a staunch defense, and he thought—hoped—that perhaps he had underestimated them. Maybe they could beat the Comanche off once more. But then a scene of horror gripped him.

The old man known only as Anthem suddenly rushed from his cover. His white hair flowed from his nearly bald head, and he began dragging a brave down from his pinto pony. The Indian was so surprised to find this ancient man fighting so fiercely that he actually opened his mouth to laugh before Anthem pulled him onto the graveled ground and began pummeling him with the butt of his rifle. The warrior's skull broke open like a ceramic bowl, but the old man didn't stop his pounding until another Indian rode up behind him and drove a tomahawk into the white skull, splitting the wispy hair and driving the blade as far down as old Anthem's eyes. He fell looking directly at Moses, a surprised and lost look on his face.

Moses pointed his Colt's .44 and spent his last cartridge to shoot the Comanche who had ended the old man's life. It was the only sure kill he had made with the pistol, but he reloaded and determined to make another. Regardless of how he felt about Graham's killing of Sterling,

Moses recognized that if the settlers followed Anthem's example and charged the Indians, they wouldn't stand a chance. Not only were the Comanche on horseback, they also were still well covered from the opposite bank, and even if Anthem hadn't been killed by the other warrior, he would soon have been mowed down as the futile mass assault had been. Moses kept an eye on the wagon line and readied himself to use his Colt's to stop any hysterical charge from the whites as he started again for Graham's wagon and his .55s.

He scrambled down the wagon line and stopped every few feet to check behind him, but apparently Anthem's attack had been a solo affair. Moses shook his head over the brave foolishness of the old white man. Anthem had been the only man on the train who was genuinely friendly to the scout. Moses took his death as a bad omen. He noticed as he managed to crawl under the last wagon before reaching Graham's that a new noise had joined the chaos surrounding the battle, and for one hopeful moment, he believed it was the sound of cannon.

He scrambled to his feet and prepared to shout the news that somehow, some way, the cavalry had come to rescue them. He knew that there were several patrols that took small guns with them out of Forts Griffin and Richardson, and if they had positioned themselves just right, they could fire directly down the wagon line and destroy the attacking Comanche. The heavy, throaty booms sounded again, and this time he was certain he saw the muzzle flash of a field howitzer.

"Goddamn!" he yelled. "The Army's come! Hurrah! It's the cavalry!" He emptied his pistol into the milling Indians. He knelt to reload his weapon and thought of climbing up to the ledge just above the cave's openings so he could pick off the Comanche when they made their retreat.

When he looked out, however, he saw that the Indians were far from breaking off the attack. He looked again and raised his head above the wagon's tailgate, searching for the guidon that would announce the vanguard of a cavalry charge, listening for a bugle signaling the settlers' rescue. But he saw nothing.

Regret flooded through his body. There were no

troopers charging, no cavalry, and no artillery to frighten away the Indians. The sound he had heard was nothing but the storm breaking. The muzzle flashes were lightning.

Rain came down in driving globs, overwhelming the sounds of rifle and pistol fire and the yip-yipping of the Indians, who were trying to outride both the bullets and the painful hailstones that suddenly pelted them. As the tiny ice pellets hit the gravel beach, a sound like a thousand galloping horses echoed in the crossing.

It grew darker, and Moses chanced stretching up to reach inside Graham's wagon for the box of .55-caliber shells he knew was there. He found that he could barely make out the creek bank in the gloom. The carbine fire across the water reported as small, sharp sparks in the storm's artificial night, and these were matched by the settlers' own bright yellow explosions as they continued to shoot into the rainy darkness.

Flashes of lightning began to explode overhead, illuminating the grisly scene below, providing momentary targets for the settlers, who now had pulled their hats down low on their foreheads and begun to fire into the confused Comanche. In one brilliant flash, Moses spotted the young chief on his pony in the center of the creek. He was holding his horse with difficulty. The water lathered in the whipping wind and washed the mount's belly, and he had raised his lance high and was calling a loud command that sounded no different to Moses's ear from what the warriors had been screaming throughout the attack.

But it rallied the Comanche, and they began guiding their horses back into the water, turning and firing one more shot or loosing one more arrow as they retreated. They weren't as confused or as hurried as before. This time, the storm covered their retreat.

Moses drew a careful bead on where he was certain the chief had appeared last and waited for a flash of lightning to give him a clear shot. He waited and waited, afraid to breathe, and just when he felt certain that all the flashes were over, a sudden bolt cracked overhead and lit the entire area with a ghostly, silver glow that revealed the young chief still encouraging his braves to move out of range of the settlers' deadly fire.

Moses was ready, and he squeezed the trigger of the

big rifle and grunted when the recoil thumped into his shoulder. But darkness and rain obscured his vision, and he could not tell if he'd emptied the pony's back or not. By the time the rain let up and the light of sunset returned, none of the raiding Comanche were in sight except for those who had fallen and died on the stony bank beside Blind Man's Creek.

CHAPTER TWO

1

MOSES LAY UNDER GRAHAM'S WAGON FOR A LONG while after the storm passed and true darkness descended on the carnage between the wagon line and the creek. The bodies of settlers, male and female, adult and child, lay where they had fallen along the beach, some washing around in the stream's flow, unable to proceed downstream because of an occasional slain pony. Once again, the Indians had risked their lives to carry off their wounded and dead.

The courage of the Comanche braves astonished him. With an arm or leg hanging in bloody tatters, they reached down to lift fallen comrades aboard their ponies. No white man would do that. Moses had even seen healthy warriors climb down from their mounts and retrieve their fallen brothers who had been almost blasted apart by the heavy slugs from the settlers' guns. Now, in the aftermath of both storm and fight, the only red bodies in view were those which had fallen inside the wagon line and rolled down to join the dead whites on the bank.

As the sunlight faded completely from the tiny canyon, Moses contemplated the melting hailstones that mixed with the limestone gravel. His eyes burned, and his head throbbed. Even the weapon lying next to him under the wagon gave off enough of the odor of gunsmoke to make his stomach hurt. The physical drain combined with the weight of worry he carried held him down on the gravel under Graham's wagon.

He wondered where Graham was. He knew he needed to get up and make certain—this time for sure—that someone was keeping watch, although the prospect of anyone *not* watching after what they had been through that day seemed impossible. His rifle barrel was still warm, and his hand felt numb as it grasped the blued steel. There were people hurt badly, he reminded himself. Someone should be seeing to them, as well. But his numbness kept him immobile. Just contemplating movement exhausted him.

For a while, before it became full dark, he had watched the girl who had escaped from her captor in the first attack and hidden in Hollister's wagon. She was trying to make her way back to the main wagon line. He believed, but he wasn't sure, that it was Frank Herbert's daughter. She was a strange one, Moses recalled from the few times he had actually been close enough to study her. He had trouble guessing her age. Sometimes when he saw her from a distance walking along in the grass back behind Sterling's cattle with a garland of wildflowers in her dark, stringy hair, he thought she must be nothing more than a child. Other times, when Herbert would be off somewhere and she would be driving the team, he would hear her low, alto voice swearing viciously at the brutes, and he would think her much older than her looks. He had observed that she stayed off by herself and seldom talked to anyone, though before the attack he had seen her fishing with a boy her age. Moses wondered what had happened to the boy, but he couldn't remember.

Since the storm abated, the girl had made false starts to come back to the wagons, but each time something—often just a harmless night creature—on the far bank in the darkness would make a noise, and she would scramble back. It was only twenty-five yards or so, and he wished she would just come on. He knew when the moon rose soon in the now clear and starlit sky, she would make an inviting target for any watching braves. But she continued to make hesitating starts and scurrying retreats, and he believed he could hear her heavy breathing.

He started to call out to her, but then he decided against it. Even if she heard him, she likely wouldn't find any more courage than she already had, and if she answered him, she could alert any Indian who was listening that she was there. He also thought about going out to get her, but with a new pang of guilt, he admitted to himself that he wouldn't. She wasn't his responsibility any more than everyone else was. Why didn't Frank Herbert do something about her? Moses asked himself. Where the hell was Herbert, anyway?

But Frank wasn't all there, Moses reminded himself. Even if he knew his daughter was missing—and even if he didn't assume she was as dead as the others out on the bank—he might not be able to do much more than talk about it. Moses furrowed his brow and chewed his lip in agitation. Maybe she would just come in on her own. Maybe not. He couldn't worry about it any longer.

In spite of his numbing fatigue, though, when he heard her feet on the gravel once more, his fingers tightened around his Springfield. He prepared himself to force his hands and arms into action if there was even a hostile whisper from across the creek. Then he heard her retreating, and he relaxed. In a way, he argued with himself, she was probably better off than the rest of them. At least where she was, she was more or less hidden. No one was consciously trying to kill her.

Through the darkness, sounds came wafting from the wagons. No light was visible, although in the deeper caves there probably were numerous coal-oil lamps lit while people tended to their wounded. There had been a lot of blood. He had lost count of how many had died.

Moses tried to calculate how many Indians he personally had slain that afternoon. It was difficult to tell. Smoke from his rifle often obscured his target when he pulled the trigger. Sometimes he knew he had hit the brave he aimed at, but he had failed to kill him. In fact, he mused, he had probably shot more horses than men that afternoon. Still, it amazed him that any man, red or white, could get up again after even being touched by the big .55 slug. It was unimaginable that any human being could take a bullet that could knock the whole insides of a full-grown antelope out through its shattered rib cage, and then get up and flee or, in some cases, keep fighting. It could be that the brave believed so strongly in his medicine that not even that much lead could stop him, or it could be that his medicine *was* that strong. Moses wasn't entirely certain that there wasn't more to the Indians' vague religion and reliance on visions and spirits than the white man would acknowledge.

He sorted through the noises that passed up and down the crossing. He could hear crickets and other nocturnal insects calling, and somewhere he thought he heard an owl screech. Of course, it could be an Indian, he thought. But it was a long way off. Frogs sang on the creek, and another night bird called in a quick, sharp cry that startled him.

All at once a low burping roar filled the tiny canyon around the crossing. The odd sound was repeated, and he relaxed his hand, which had automatically pulled the rifle to him. Bullfrog, he said to himself, and a big one. From the opposite end of the creek another bullfrog answered, and in a few moments, the crossing filled with their throaty songs.

He looked around in the dark, but no one was near him. The frog chorus continued, and Moses found himself wishing that he could go out and gig a few. A mess of fried frog legs had been a sort of ritual with him every time he came to the crossing, where the bulls were particularly large, some growing to the size of small puppies. Their legs were fat and fine, he remembered, and they had been something he had been looking forward to. He had even brought along a small tin of cornmeal in his kit. Then he thought of the risk that a simple walk with a homemade gig along the creek bank would involve. Although the moon had not yet risen, starlight gave a faint, silvery outline to everything, even the corpses lining the gravel, and he realized that if he could see that well, a Comanche could see even better. More than any other tribe, they owned the night.

2

WITH A GREAT EFFORT, MOSES PUSHED HIMSELF BACKward and out from under the wagon master's buckboard and pulled himself erect next to it. For the first time since his "stroll" of the afternoon—which now seemed a hundred years in the past—he felt safe standing up straight. His muscles cried out from the sudden stretching he gave them. He ignored the discomfort and walked through the darkness down the wagon line and noted the defenders who had been propped up to die from their wounds or had simply fallen and been left alone in their suffering. Some were moaning softly, incoherently, and others were quiet—sleeping or dead—but most of the wounded wore crude bandages torn from sheets and even the rough canvas of the wagons.

Small knots of people gathered down on their hunkers by wagon wheels or other, more formidable barricades, and Moses took a small satisfaction that the settlers acknowledged the danger of being spied even in starlight by the watchful Comanche across the creek.

He came to his bay, still safe under the limestone outcropping, and was pleased to find her unharmed and calm, waiting for him to mount her and give her direction. The sergeant he bought her from had called her Red Flush, but Moses never used that name or any other when he referred to her. One thing he had learned was never to get too attached to a horse on the Texas plains. There was a good chance she would wind up providing him with a meal before he got back.

He went back to Graham's wagon and found some oats to fill her nose bag, which he slipped over her head. He ran his hands over her withers and patted her flanks. She chewed the oats as he spoke softly to her.

He thought again of simply jumping on her and riding off. It was a delicious temptation. Even if Graham and the survivors made it through whatever the Comanche had in mind for them, he could be far to the west of here by the time they had a chance to regroup and go hunting for him. Chances were that they would simply dismiss his desertion as something expected of a worthless nigger they never should have hired in the first place.

The thought sobered him. A sudden, powerful stream of urine exploded from beneath the mare and washed over his boots as it sought a narrow gouge in the loamy soil which carried it out down the beach toward the creek. It reminded him of his own need, and he undid his buckskins and urinated against the limestone wall while the bay munched the oats. He directed his stream to mix with hers. He couldn't desert them, he admitted, not because of the simple admiration he had discovered he felt for some of them, Aggie Sterling, for example—no, his mind corrected him and sent a warm flush through his body and caused his penis to stiffen slightly in his hands, Aggie Sterling in particular—but because he knew that it was something they would expect him to do. He forced his mind to concentrate on that, and his organ relaxed and permitted his flow to continue comfortably. He would have to find a way out of this, or he would have to die trying. Not because of a white girl who made him feel guilty even though he had done nothing to her, not even allowed himself to think about her consciously. It wasn't a question of a girl. It wasn't a question of a man either. It was a question, he supposed, of what Grierson called "honor."

"You're a man, now. A free man," Grierson had said to Moses when the former slave had accepted the planter's offer to continue hunting with him as an employee. "Least the Yankees say you are. You might find out that there's more to that than simply sayin' it. You got to learn to live like it."

And he had tried to understand that. He had heard Grierson talk about a man's honor, his word, as something more sacred even than his life.

"If you say you're fixin' to do a thing, an' it's the *right* thing," Grierson taught him, "then you got to go on an' do it. Even if it hurts. Even if it kills you. A lot of young men'll never grow up for believin' that's a truth. A lot of them died to see to it you could believe in it, too. I don't think they were right. I'm tellin' you that plain. But that's why they died. Not to keep a bunch of niggers slaves, or to set them free either. They died for something else. They died 'cause they said they would. That's honor."

At first Moses hadn't accepted that. But out on the plains, he had learned that a man's word, even a black man's, was considered important. No form of scoundrel was worse than a liar, and while it seemed a natural way of regarding the problem, it could put a man into some terrible fixes. He had to be careful who he gave his word to. Otherwise, he could wind up dying for honor instead of for something more tangible, like his own scalp.

The mare stamped her foot in impatience, and Moses was drawn back from his memories. He removed the nose bag and scratched her between the ears. For a moment he let her nuzzle him, but then he sensed what she was going to do, and he slapped her before she could nip his side.

It was a game she played, he remembered with a wry grin. He had suffered enough bruises from her bites until he learned that.

Respect and honor, Moses thought with a frown and shook his head. In the face of death and rape and the harshness of this country, they seemed to be such small things. It was easy to talk of them while he sat comfortably by a campfire or strolled along the streets of Jefferson. But in reality, they meant much more than a man's ability with a big rifle or pistol or what he could do on a horse. It was all too confusing, but at the same time, it was all clear: Regardless of what he was *supposed* to do, it came down finally to the single question of what he was going to do about it, now.

3

MOSES LEFT THE MARE AND WALKED DOWN A BIT farther, pleased to see several men, one or two every few wagons, peering from the caves and openings in the limestone butte's base out into the darkness and holding their rifles at the ready. Some had not been fortunate enough to claim the proper caves but were squatting by minuscule fires they had built in the smaller concave openings that were only deep depressions in the limestone bluff. Smoke didn't always draft as it should in the shallower depressions, and from time to time, Moses would see a woman with a blanket trying to fan the heavy blue clouds away from a knot of people inside.

He was walking almost deliberately down to the Sterling wagon. He wanted to check and see if Aggie and her siblings had succumbed to grief, or whether the girl's strange inner strength had prevailed. She might break down, Moses thought. Few people were able to take all that without some kind of reaction. He also realized, with a quick guilty qualm, that he just wanted to lay eyes on her once more, to assure himself of her presence. The uncomfortable warmth her image stirred in him started again, and he allowed his imaginings to go far enough to wonder what it would be like to take her hand, to hold her long fingers in his palm and study their gentleness. It was remarkable to him that those same slender fingers had found the triggers of a shotgun and had so easily killed a savage warrior only a few hours before. It was equally remarkable—almost unthinkable—that the same hand he admired in his mind's eye had held the same shotgun on the wagon master, and that her almost magical eyes had transformed themselves into something so hard that it resembled nothing more than azure granite, unyielding and sharp, cut through with grains of defiance and determination.

It was no surprise to Moses that Jack Sterling had maneuvered his wagon directly in front of the largest cave on the creek. The opening was almost tall enough for a man to walk into without stooping. Moses stood outside and caught a faint glimmer of light from inside. The hole tunneled into the side of the limestone for about fifteen feet and then took a slight turn to the left, and he imagined that they must have a natural chimney so they could have a bona fide fire going inside. The tiny herd of cattle was in one of the large depressions that veered off to the right just next to the cave.

The cattle were moving restlessly and lowing a bit. They wanted to graze, and they probably needed water. There hadn't been time to let them do much more than wet their tongues before the wagons had been pulled into line and they wouldn't last long where they were. But he was at a loss for any suggestion for their benefit. It would have given him a reason to call into the cave, but there was nothing he could say once they answered.

He leaned against the limestone and rolled a cigarette. He lit it and cupped his hand over the match before he blew it out. He was shielded, he knew, and not even a Comanche was so good a shot that he could see over the top of a loaded wagon—even one with the canvas ripped off—to hit a tiny light like that. There was no sound from the cave, but Moses glanced inside again and instinctively felt that she was there. He wanted her to come out, to talk to him, to reassure him. He didn't know why she should, but he still wanted her to, even though to do so would give rise to a quaking fear inside him that might send him scurrying away. She was the only one who might have a good word for him, though, and he believed it would help.

But she stayed inside. So, apparently, did her brother, Jason, and her little sister, Annie. What would become of them? he wondered. How could they survive without Jack's—then he stopped. Without Jack's what? His beating them? His cruelty? His phony dapper ways? What in the name of God could a man like Jack Sterling provide for this family that anyone—even Moses—couldn't give them? The unfairness of the situation made Moses suddenly angry. His stomach lurched against the acid that flooded into it as he thought of Jack Sterling's hateful face and mean, close-set eyes. He hated him worse then than he had when the white man was alive, but he felt no guilt for it. He only felt a pang of fear come alive once more and quell the anger swelling inside him. His mind reeled, and he shuddered. Then for a brief moment he permitted himself the luxury of wondering what it would be like to hold more than Aggie Sterling's hand, to hold her close to him, to run his fingers through her golden hair, to feel her lips touch his.

The thoughts were deliciously dangerous. He drew on the cigarette and let it burn his throat that was already sore from breathing gunsmoke and dust; cold sweat emerged from under his hatband and ran down into his face. It didn't matter what he thought, Moses argued with himself. A white girl was no different from a white man when it came to a colored man's intentions. But he forced himself to calm down and to gain a grip on his emotions. There was no point in hating Jack Sterling. He was dead. Graham had seen to that. He hated Jack more than Moses did, for reasons the scout couldn't fathom. Moses needed to let it go, let it all go. There was no point in hating a dead man any more than there was in loving a white woman. No good could come from it.

The cattle shuffled nervously again, and he jabbed the smoke out against the rough grain of the limestone. One of the cattle bawled suddenly, and he moved away quickly. He needed to check the horses.

Graham's horse and Jack's big stallion were joined by a dozen others. There had been more, but those which had not succumbed to the noxious water had pulled up lame. Most of the remaining animals were hardy, Moses noted with pleasure. Graham's gray was a particularly fine animal, and Jack Sterling's stallion had also survived and seemed fit enough. They would need water, he thought with a glance at the sentries. Some of the caves had springs that graduated to full-blown streams before they disappeared into the rock or wound their way down to disappear into the gravel, and down by Graham's wagon was another small spurt of water that released its cool flow down a rivulet and emptied into the creek.

Fetching water from those sources would be hard work, Moses thought, but it would be considerably safer than going back and forth to the creek, even in the dark.

He moved on down to the terminus of the wagon fort, where a group of boys stood vigilant behind the flanking wagon. From here Hollister's wagon was only a few yards away, and he paused and listened intently for the girl, but he heard nothing.

"She still out there?" Moses asked the shadowed figures who leaned against the wagon.

"Who?" He couldn't tell which boy had spoken.

"They's a girl out there," Moses said. "Frank Herbert's daughter, I think. I heard her awhile ago."

"I didn't hear nothin'," another, much younger voice piped up. "She's a strange'un," he added without emotion.

"Well, I did," Moses said. "Don't shoot her if she takes a mind to come in."

"We'll shoot anythin' out there that moves," the first voice said.

"Where's your daddy?"

"Dead." The reply came from the first voice. "He's got 'bout a hun'red arrows in him."

There was silence again, and Moses listened for the girl. "Don't holler at her or nothin'. Far as I know, the Indians don't know she's there. Let's keep it that way." There was no reply. "You boys had anythin' to eat?"

"We're all right," the younger voice said. "Jus' leave us alone." Moses heard the unsaid epithet as clearly as if the boy had mouthed it. He decided to leave them. If the boys didn't care about the girl, then he couldn't see why he should. He turned away.

The caves were sparser on this end, and most of the

people were making use of what shelter could be dug out of the loamy gravel under the half-dug-out impressions at the butte's base.

"Mr. Moses?" a voice behind him asked. In the dim starlight he could make out a boy's face. He was young, maybe fifteen or sixteen, and there was a dark streak across his face, but whether it was blood or dirt or something else, Moses couldn't tell.

"We'll keep a eye out for that gal," he said. "Don't pay the others no mind."

Moses reached out and violated a rule he had made long ago: Never touch a white man except in anger. He knew that most would regard even the friendliest gesture as an insult if the offering limb was black. But he swallowed his promise to himself and laid a hand on the boy's shoulder.

"Don't worry 'bout it, son," he said. "She'll get in if she can."

The boy nodded and then looked up into the sky. "You ever see so many stars?"

"You get used to it out here," Moses said. "Sometimes you can see what I guess they call 'the firmament.' "

"Guess so." The boy studied the sky a moment longer. "Mr. Moses?"

"What is it, son?"

"Are we lost?"

"Lost?"

"I mean, are we sure 'nough lost? Some of the boys say we're lost. That we run right into the whole Comanche nation 'cause you got us lost."

Moses started. It had never occurred to him that anyone would think he had somehow made a gross mistake in directing the train.

"No, son, we're not lost," he said. He started to point out the North Star, but from the narrow vantage point of the crossing's small canyon, it wasn't visible. "We run into a bunch of Indians, an' they's madder'n a jug full of red ants, but we ain't lost. I know right where we was goin', an' I know right where we're at. I know how to go on, too, soon's these Indians take a notion to leave off."

The boy nodded with what looked to be wisdom and started to turn away. Then he turned back. "Mr. Moses?"

His face was a silver mask in the starlight. "Don't call me 'son.' I ain't your son." He looked out through a makeshift rifle loop in the wagon beside them. "I ain't nobody's son."

Moses stood rigidly and watched the boy retreat into the darkness. Aggie wasn't the only orphan on this train, he realized. He wondered just how many of the children he had watched playing around the wagons on this trip had parents who had been killed. He also wondered with a sick turning of his stomach if there would be any adults left to do for them what the Mexicans had done for their own babies before the Comanche descended on them.

CHAPTER THREE

1

LOUD, ANGRY VOICES INTERRUPTED THE MURMURINGS of the settlers outside the caves, but Moses couldn't make out the words. They came from another of the large caves farther up the line, one that had so small an opening a man had to stoop to enter. Moses followed them to the cave's mouth, then stooped and entered what appeared to be a council of war.

Graham stood with his back to the large cavern's wall. A small group of men, including Frank Herbert, William Golden, Harvey Pierce, Virgil Hollister, and some others Moses recognized, were all talking at once, their forms lit brightly by flaming torches placed near one of several natural chimneys.

At first the scout couldn't understand what they were saying, but he could tell that they were anxious and worried. None of them saw him enter, as all their attention seemed to focus on Graham, who looked like a large cornered animal. His eyes moved quickly from man to man, and his single hand rested easily on his belt, not far from the butt of his pistol. As he shifted from one foot to the other, Moses noticed that he also had put on a clutch holster with what appeared to be a Colt's Navy .36 to supplement his usual sidearm. He had been expecting trouble, Moses told himself, and now he had it.

Bob Simmons lay next to several other badly wounded men who lined the far wall of the cave. His head was wrapped in a bloody bandage, and his eyes stared glassily. His wife sat next to him and held his hand, but she was apparently no more conscious of the proceedings than was her husband. Her eyes were blank and far away.

Karl Runnels was also placed against the far wall. His bandaged foot was propped up on a small chest, and his hands were formed into hard fists which he kept locked on his great belly, but his face was a boiling pot of anger and indignation.

"Shut up, you men. Shut up!" Frank Herbert ordered the crowd of angry settlers. "We ain't fixin' to get nothin' done if you all talk at once." Moses once again found himself amazed by a man more than one voice had dubbed "simple." His face was beardless and his pale blue eyes widely spaced. It wasn't exactly the countenance of a child, but rather that of a young man, a boy who had prematurely acquired the leathery skin and wrinkles of experience. Herbert was balding, but the receding hairline did nothing to age him or give him the aspect of a mature adult. Even so, his voice—a thin tenor that tended to crack when he was excited—quieted the men and turned their attention toward him. Moses didn't think he had ever heard this "simple" man speak when he didn't make sense.

"Well, I say we got to do somethin', an' Golden's idea sounds as good as any to me," Harvey Pierce, the tough little carpenter, said. Then he spotted Moses crouched down in the low entrance to the cave. "What the hell you want, nigger?"

Moses was startled. While he expected to hear ugly names from time to time, this was such a fierce assault that he found himself losing control. Pierce had never been anything more than moderately civil to him, but he had not looked at him with the bitter contempt that Moses now saw in his face. Moses also felt a kinship with Pierce after their attempt to restrain the wild man, Sloan. Apparently, the carpenter was scared and tired enough not to remember that incident, and on rapid reflection, Moses decided to let the insult pass without reaction.

Moses took another step into the room and raised up to his full stature. He was taller than most of the men in the room, and he felt better, more secure and confident.

"Listen, you kerchief-headed bastard," William Golden said. "I don't know what you want, an' I don't much care, but I'm tellin' you to get out of here, an' to take your nigger stink with you."

"I've had 'bout all the name-callin' I'm goin' to take

out of you people," Moses said slowly, feeling his tone rise in anger. His voice was about to crack, and he lowered it deliberately. "Now, you got all the words right." He spoke directly to Golden, but Pierce stood near enough to catch the scout's dark gaze for a moment before Moses let his eyes roam over the knot of men. "Let's see if you can back 'em up." He opened his buckskin coat slowly and spaced his feet while he brought his hands out to a ready position.

For a long moment no one said anything. Pierce's and Golden's eyes never left Moses's hands, which hovered out from his body, ready to draw out his holstered .44s.

"I ain't no gunfighter," Pierce muttered at last.

"No, you ain't," Moses said. "You're jus' a mouth, like the rest. 'Specially you, Golden. You can pot-shoot Indians when they's ridin' 'round an' offerin' fair targets, but when somebody stands up to you, you fill up your boots with piss an' tuck tail an' run."

The men all looked at each other. Clearly none of them had ever been spoken to in such a manner by a Negro, especially by one wearing a gun and standing alone. But none of them moved or said a word. The tension in the cave was tangible, and they all were sweating, although the air around them was cool.

"He's jus' a nigger boy," Virgil Hollister said suddenly. "Y'all goin' to let a Child of Ham talk to us that way?" Moses noted that the farmer-settler-preacher had buttoned on a frayed yellow collar and knotted a string tie under his long, scrawny neck. His Adam's apple looked trapped as it bobbed up and down when he swallowed.

The men didn't look at Hollister or at each other. Their eyes fixed on Moses, or on the cave's walls. They were all armed, and Moses knew that if even one of them jerked a gun, he was dead. He might get off a shot or two before they cut him down, but he knew he couldn't stop them from killing him. He kept his face fixed into an angry mask, but behind it he felt a queasy fear. A vision of them hanging him from one of the scraggly limbs that grew out of the ledge overhead passed in front of his eyes, and he vowed that no matter what happened, they would not take him alive.

Almost a minute passed, but no one broke the silence.

Graham's voice finally filled the cave. All of them, Moses included, found the need to relax and shift positions when the wagon master spoke.

"If y'all are tired of measurin' your peckers, maybe we can get somethin' decided," he said. The men, Moses included, turned to look at the one-handed man, who, Moses realized to his mixed terror and relief, had drawn his own pistol and was covering them. He was going to have to be more careful. Every man on this train, including Graham—especially Graham—was his enemy, now. He would have to make a point of knowing where the wagon master was from now on.

Graham glanced through the flickering light and studied the crowd's eyes. Most of the men looked away and covered shameful faces as they shifted their attention back toward the wagon master, but it was clear that they felt more relieved than abashed by his interruption of the stand-off.

Graham nodded briefly and put away his pistol. "Golden here thinks we ought to send somebody for help," he said. "I reckon that's a good idea. There's usually some men up on the plains, likely huntin', buffalo skinners I figure, an' there's that settlement back the other side of the Wichita, though I don't expect they're anybody there that'd do much for us. Then there's maybe Fort Richardson, an' there's Fort Griffin to the south. An' there's Fort Whatever-they-call-it up in the Territories across the river."

"Sill," Moses offered, but Graham ignored him.

"Though, once again, I don't think there's anybody there who'd do us any good. From what I hear, they can't come south of the Red no matter what." He looked up at Moses, who was astonished at the wagon master's knowledge of the plains.

"So, what do you think?" Graham asked him.

"If a man could get out," Moses said, careful to make it clear to the rest of the men that he was discussing this with Graham and no one else, "an' I mean *if*, then he'd do best to go to the Army or Rangers. Even the Quaker troops up at Fort Sill in the Territories. I ain't sure they's anybody up on the plains this time of year, an' if they is, they ain't likely to come runnin', least not for free, an' 'specially not if they reckon they's a hundred Comanche waitin' for 'em."

"They'd come," Golden said. "They'd *have* to come! I mean, they're *white* men, ain't they? How could they just sit up there an' let us get massacred? Jesus, Graham! Are you goin' to just *stand* there an' listen to *him*?"

"Look, Mr., uh . . . Golden?" The man nodded briefly as Moses shifted his position to look at him. "Even if they would come—an' I'm highly doubtful 'bout it—I ain't sure we ain't some better off with the Comanche. Them's hunters an' skinners up there—if they's there—an' they got no respect for folks' property." He paused to let it sink in and concluded, "Or their women."

"They ain't *your* women," Pierce said quietly.

"Never said they was," Moses replied. "But if we run up on outlaws, it ain't goin' to make no nevermind whose women they is."

The circle of men chewed on this for a moment. Moses knew they were just as likely to run into Comancheros as hunters up on the plains, and sometimes it was hard to tell the difference. Sometimes there *was* no difference. Some hunters were honest, even generous, but some would as soon slit a throat as pour a cup of coffee. He had learned long ago to ready his weapons when he saw men—even a single man—on horseback coming toward him from across the distance.

"I don't know about goin' for troops," Graham said softly.

"Why the hell not?" A man named Oliver Quigley stepped out of the crowd and spoke up. He was small and dressed in city clothes. Moses imagined that they had once been fine, but now his white shirt was stained with black powder, and his swallowtailed coat and striped trousers were covered with the fine limestone dust that surrounded the wagon fort. A tall silk hat sat askew on his round head. "I mean, it's their job, isn't it?"

"I think we all know why Mr. Graham don't want to bring no troopers in on this," Virgil Hollister chirped from well back in the crowd. The men all turned to look at him. "I think we all know how important that devil's brew in all them kegs is to you, now, Mr. Cleve Graham!"

"Shut up, Hollister," Graham growled. Once again

Moses saw the wagon master's hand fall down near his pistol.

"Oh, I'll shut up," Hollister yelled. "But you won't be satisfied till that creek bank is covered with the bodies of every livin' soul on this train! All that blood, jus' to protect your blasted whiskey! This man is the devil hisself!" Hollister's voice took on an oratorical singsong tone, and he stepped forward to confront Graham. "He's put us all in jeopardy to save hisself an' his evil cargo of demon rum." Hollister's eyes flashed in the yellow lanternlight, and Moses even stepped back slightly as the preacher waved his Bible and warmed to his text. He turned and faced the men. "He's made a pact with the Antichrist, an' the minions of Satan are lurkin' in the shadows out there, waitin' to see how many white souls they—" He swirled around on Graham and thrust a bony finger into Graham's chest. "*—he* can torture in the name of iniquity an' wicked—"

Graham's hand came up quickly. He had drawn a fist down near his waist, and he put his full weight behind the punch. Hollister went flying back into the men, who caught him and fell backward as a body.

"Hollister, I've . . . I'm tired of you. Just shut up." The men regrouped as they found their feet. Hollister leaned against a wall and said nothing.

"All right!" Graham caught his breath and looked at Moses once more. "We can't go for buffalo hunters or whoever they are."

"Well, what're we s'posed to do?" Pierce spoke up again. He eyed Graham carefully and kept his distance. "I mean, we can't just sit here while the rest of us is killed by them red savages out there."

"Well," Moses said, "I s'pose we could try to make it to a fort, Richardson or Griffin maybe. It'd take two days, maybe 'nother day to get the cavalry movin', then two or three more to get back. Soldiers don't move fast, even when they's on the run. But I reckon we could hold on that long." The men looked at each other. "We got food an' water, an' I s'pect we got more cartridges and better rifles than all them Comanche put together."

There was a general nodding and agreement at that,

and Virgil Hollister muttered something about whiskey, but none of the men let on that he heard him.

"An'," Moses went on, "if the Comanche's up an' out, then they's likely troops already up an' out, too. Maybe Texas Rangers. A man might run 'cross a patrol somewheres along the way." Right now, Moses thought, he would swap this trip's entire wages for a single Texas Ranger.

"If a man can get out," Graham offered.

"If a man can get out," Moses repeated. "An' if the Army's there, then maybe they'll come."

"Two ifs an' a maybe." Graham's eyes locked with Moses's.

The scout nodded. "That's how I reckon it."

"It's settled then." Graham stroked his beard with his stump and set his gray eyes squarely on the black scout. "I figure since it's your job an' you got the best chance of cuttin' a trail an' spottin' Rangers, an' you claim to know the Army, you ought to go."

"Him?" Golden said.

"Goddamn nigger neffer come bok!" Runnels's German accent bounced off the limestone walls. "Zend a vite man, vor de loff off Gott!"

"How'll we know you just won't ride off?" Pierce asked.

"Yeah," Virgil Hollister added and came to his feet. "How'll we know you won't just hightail it once you're free of them Indians? You got no love for us. You got no love of the Almighty." Hollister's large dark eyes gleamed again in the torchlight.

"I got a job," Moses said. He struggled to keep his voice calm. "I took it, an' I give my word to see it through. That's 'nough for me, an' it's goin' to have to do for you."

"I'm goin' with him," Graham said.

"Oh, that's just *fine*!" Golden announced. "We got a cripple *an'* a nigger goin' to save our bacon. Why not take a woman an' a kid, too? Mount each one on a wounded ox an' fill their canteens with mule piss? It won't make no diff'rence if *they* get killed. With no wagon master an' no scout, we might's well just call in them redskins an' give it up right now."

"You're runnin' a lot of mouth tonight, Golden," Graham said.

"I got a right!" Golden shot back. "I got a right to protect what's mine. We made a deal, Graham. I'm holdin' up my part of the bargain. I've dumped half my stuff just to keep haulin' them kegs. But I'm not such a fool as to let you ride off with the only other man on this train who can shoot straight." He glared at the circle of men around him, who looked surprised at the admission. "It's the goddamn *truth*! This nigger can shoot. I seen him! Most of us couldn't hit one of them goddamn Indians if they had targets painted on their chests. I know I'm lucky to be alive, an' I don't know how much longer luck's goin' to hold out for any of us. People're dead out there." He pointed out through the limestone wall. "I never killed nobody before in my life—red or white—an' today I seen an' done more killin' than I ever want to be a part of again. I killed a man with my bare hands today. Do you know what it does to a man to do that?"

Graham stared at Golden without comment. Golden looked around the group for support, but the men held their faces still and showed no expression. He went on, "Well, it's too near a thing, I can tell you. Much as I hate to admit it, this nigger boy here puts us all in the shade when it comes to a rifle. Now, you're fixin' to send him out scoutin' for help you only about half think's comin', an' you want to go with him." There still was no response from anyone, and he stepped toward Graham. "That's just *fine*! Just *fine*. I know you think you'll come back. You got a reason to come back, but once you're gone, you might find a damn good reason not to. *I* could! Wouldn't be hard, an' I got a family here, not just a bunch of kegged whiskey. You might just decide that we can call them Indians in an' have a good ol' hoedown an' it'll all be okay.

"Well, it ain't goin' to happen! You mount up like you're even thinkin' of ridin' out, Graham, an' I'll blow you to hell. Swear to God! Reckon I can use a rifle that good anyway."

"He's right," Moses agreed. Golden's voice had quavered during the speech, but he clearly meant what he said. The last thing he wanted to have to do was to shoot his way out, especially with Graham doing the shooting.

What sort of deal had Graham made with these men? What did the whiskey have to do with anything? This wasn't the ordinary bunch of sodbusters looking for a better life. It was as if they had a common purpose, a goal of some sort. But it was an uneasy alliance, Moses recognized; it couldn't bear the slightest strain. And somehow, the kegs tied to most of the wagons were key to the whole thing. Golden hadn't come near dumping half his personal cargo, but Frank and the Sterlings had divested themselves of furniture and other items that should have had considerably more value than a few gallons of whiskey. But he had little time to contemplate the dilemma now.

"You goddamn right I'm right!" Golden pulled off his hat and let a twisted knot of hair fall down his forehead. He fought for control as he repeated his argument in more reasonable tones. " 'Bout half these yahoos can't hit the ground with a rock, anyhow. An' like I say, this nigger can kill what he shoots at. You an' him is 'bout half our best shots, Graham, an' I don't think we can hold off them Comanche with a bunch of noise."

"You can't go," Moses said to Graham, "but somebody ought to." He saw several eyebrows raise, and he quickly explained, "Two's got a better chance'n one of gettin' through. If we're not damn quiet, we won't get out of sight. Them Indians out there's jus' itchin' to catch somebody makin' a run for it. But I think it might be worth a try. I say two men ought to go."

"Or *tree*, vor Gott's sake, or *vour*! Vy not haf a dozen?" Runnels boomed from his pallet. "Hell's vire! Vy don't ve *all* go?"

Graham ignored the German. "Well, if I'm not goin', who is?" He looked around the group, but most of the men found something interesting on the floor of the cave. Moses saw none in the group he would trust to ride behind him. The half of them who wouldn't rabbit were likely to shoot him just for spite. "How about you, Golden? You seem to have a lot to say about who goes an' who stays. Maybe you'd like to stretch the length of your cock an inch or two."

Golden shook his head, and, Moses had to admit, stood up well to having his bluff called. "I still got me a wife an' kids to worry 'bout," he said. "I ain't goin' to run off an' leave 'em. 'Sides, I didn't sign on with this outfit to take any more risk than I have to."

"That's good, Golden," Graham said. He spat out the end of a new cigar. "Hell, that's damn near a sermon. For the price of the bullet, I'd blow your yellow ass off."

Golden brooded but didn't reply. There was more trouble brewing there, Moses thought.

"Well, what about you, Hollister? You afraid to ride into the valley of the shadow of the Comanche?"

"I think a man of God should stay with his people," Hollister answered. "Somebody needs to be here to bury the dead. The *white* dead," he added.

"Horseshit," Graham spat. "You should've helped Moses here bury the Mescans. Might have saved us all a lot of trouble." He shot Moses a quick look. "What about you, Quigley?" .

The well-dressed little man who had spent his time since the first outburst hiding behind some of the larger men only shook his head and looked at the ground.

"Well, then." Graham looked around the group. "How about you, Pierce? You feelin' the itch to be a hero?"

Pierce shook his head and muttered something.

"What was that?"

"I can't ride no horse!" Pierce exclaimed. "I ain't no horseman, goddamnit. Like Golden says, I can't even shoot straight. I can't shoot, an' I ain't no horseman. I wouldn't make it five miles, even if we did get past them Indians." He paused and looked embarrassed as the men studied him. "I ain't no goddamn horseman," he repeated, "an' I can't shoot worth a shit. I'm a carpenter, damn good cooperer, too. An' I'm a fair hand with a whip. But I don't know nothin' 'bout guns. I don't know nothin' 'bout any of this. I couldn't even keep Sloan from gettin' his fool self killed. You can make out of that what you want."

"You said there wasn't goin' to be no Indians," Virgil Hollister piped up, aiming his remarks directly at Moses. "You said we was goin' early 'nough that there wouldn't be no Indians to worry 'bout. How 'bout that? That's what I'd like to know."

"I'm the one who told you that," Graham said. "You

got a complaint about that, you can take it up with me when this is over."

"We're late," Moses said. "We should've been in Santa Fe weeks ago. We've had bad luck. That ain't my fault." He glanced at the wagon master. "That ain't nobody's fault."

"Well," Golden said, "I'd just like to know whose fault it is, then. Jesus God, you're high-toned."

Moses started to argue, but then he swallowed his words. They wanted to lay the blame on someone they could righteously hate. They were afraid to put it all on Graham, so the scout was the most likely candidate. He resented it, but he also recognized that it wasn't a killing matter. It was just a white man's way. Blame the nigger, Moses thought. It won't make it all right, but at least it fits.

"Well." Graham looked sarcastically around the knot of men, whose anger was replaced with a quiet acknowledgment of their own limitations. "Everybody's full of good ideas, but nobody can do nothin' about it. That right?"

"I'll go, Cap'n." The voice belonged to Frank Herbert, who, Moses realized, had been silent throughout the angry discussion. "I can ride, an' I can shoot fair, an' I can make sure this boy don't run out." The men said nothing. "I got no wife, but I got me a daughter whose fixin' to have the baby of one of them fellers who's prob'ly lyin' facedown in the creek yonder. An' I guess she's carried off or somethin'. I can't find her noplace. So I might as well go. I got nothin' to lose, now."

Moses's mouth hung open for a second or two before it all made sense. The boy he had seen her with on the creek bank, he recalled in a vivid flash of memory, was Jason Sterling, Aggie's brother. Half the train must know, certainly the women. Was he killed, as Frank said? Moses tried to remember if he had seen Jason since the last attack or at all since they came to the crossing, but he couldn't. Being a pregnant and unmarried girl, especially in this nest of hypocrites, was bad, and the girl was strange-looking enough to begin with. Jason, also, was an odd, quiet boy who seemed to spend most of his time staying out of Jack

Sterling's way. But now Jack was dead. Jason also, maybe. But the girl wasn't.

He realized that Frank didn't know that his daughter's lover was the Sterling boy, and he also was unaware that she was safe, hiding out in Hollister's wagon, and Moses started to say something, but then he stopped his tongue. It wasn't the time or place. Frank wasn't that sharp, Moses remembered. He took things as they came to him, and if he thought she was waiting out there, he was likely to go running to her and get both of them killed.

Also, Moses thought, someone needed to go, and Frank was able. The scout felt suddenly dirty, sneaky, but he still kept his knowledge to himself. He was not entirely comfortable with the idea that the man who would have to protect his life was slow-witted, but Frank was a better choice than some bigot like Hollister or some hate-filled coward like Golden. He would wait and tell Graham about the Herbert girl when the time was right.

Frank shook his head. "She wasn't even married proper," he said. "If she's still alive, that baby's goin' to get borned, one way or 'nother. Way I see it, I ain't got much choice but to go. If I get killed out there or in here, it don't make no difference to me. This way, maybe I can do some good. Get her back from them redskins. Maybe not. Least I'll know I tried."

At once, Moses changed his mind about Frank. He decided that of all the men present, Frank was the best choice for a partner. He was cool while the others around him were sweating nails, and he lacked any sense of false bravery. Frank might be a little light-minded, Moses said to himself, but he could be relied on.

"It's your decision, Frank," Graham said, but Moses read in the wagon master's eyes a deeper emotion. He could tell that the decision to allow Frank to go was not an easy one, but there was no other choice. "Now the rest of you get somethin' to eat, an' then go relieve them that's been standin' watch. Whether they make it or not, we can't stand no more surprises."

Moses winced, but swallowed hard and spoke up. "I think I'm bound to tell you: Them Comanche might just get tired an' leave it off. They've been known to do it when the cost got too high to pay for what they reckoned they could get." There was silence. "There might not be a need for nobody to go at all."

"Showin' a yeller streak, boy?" Golden asked.

"No," Moses said, "I jus' don't want you to feel bad if I get killed for no good reason."

"Don't you worry your fuzzy head 'bout that, boy," Pierce said. "If you get killed, I'm liable to give ol' Graham here a bonus." He and the other men pushed past the scout and left the cave.

2

MOSES FOLLOWED THE MEN OUT AND WAS SHOCKED when the cool night air struck the perspiration that had formed on his forehead and made him shiver. His shirt was soaked, and he could smell himself. He wrinkled his nose in disgust.

He looked once more at the sky and contemplated the array of stars that covered the canyon's opening. "They the eyes of the dead," his mother had said when she pointed them out to his childish stare. "They lookin' at you an' laughin'."

Frank exited the cave and almost bumped into him. "Well, looks like we're in this together," he said. "But I'm tellin' you." He lowered his voice to a deeper pitch. "You try to skedaddle on me out there, an' I'll leave you worser off than any Indian'd do."

"Best get somethin' in you to eat," Moses said indifferently. "An' pack some grub for two or three days. Water too. I don't know what direction we'll go in, and God knows when we'll find water we can drink."

Herbert nodded slowly and moved off into the darkness. Moses went down to check his bay and then walked over to Graham's wagon, where he opened a cask of salted meat and found some canned peaches and stale bread. He made the best meal he could and was wondering how much of Graham's jerky he might take for himself when a voice behind him made him start.

"You're goin' for help?" Aggie Sterling asked.

"That's what they want, Missy," he said, embarrassed. She had stolen up on him and caught him off guard.

He tried to concentrate on the peaches he knifed into his mouth greedily. He had forgotten how hungry he was. He swallowed an entire peach and almost gagged before he caught himself and forced his teeth to chew the next bite. Even so, sticky juice ran down his chin, and he reached up and wiped it off. She was looking at him curiously, and he thought how crude the gesture looked.

In the darkness her face was only a shadow, but he could smell something about her, soap maybe, which was clean and pleasant in the night air that still stung his nostrils with gunpowder and blood. Unconsciously, he took a half-step away from her to keep himself and his own odor downwind.

"Don't you think it's a good idea?" she asked.

"Don't know. It's what they want me to do."

"If you don't think it's a good idea, why're you doin' it?"

"Don't know." He could think of other answers, but he felt himself growing irritated by this forward girl who seemed never to know her place and always to be putting him in uncomfortable, dangerous situations. At the same time, he knew that he desperately wanted her to stay beside him and talk to him.

"I got me a job to do." He softened his tone. "An' I'm goin' to do it. I guess I got no choice, an' even if I did, I'd prob'ly do it anyhow. That's jus' the kind of dumb nigger I am."

"I see." She stepped back and stiffened at his outburst. He strained his eyes through the dark and saw that she was looking down at the ground. "I thought you didn't like that word."

His shoulders sagged. "I don't. I'm sorry. I jus' got to do this, an' I'm goin' to do it the best way I can. I don't know if it's the right thing to do or not, but I don't know what else they is to do. It's what they want, Mr. Graham an' the rest, an' it's what I'm hired to do, I reckon. An' I s'pose if I get killed it'll make the rest of these folks' dyin' slide down easier."

"You won't get killed," she said, raising her head in a gesture of surety.

"I ain't no smart man, Missy." Moses could think of no other form of address. "Hell, I don't even know how to read an' can't write much more'n my own name. I'm jus' a slave who got hisself freed an' learned how to use a gun. I'm still a slave."

"No," she said suddenly and loudly, "you're not. You're a free man, an' you've got a job to do, an' you're goin' to do it. You gave your word. An' you're not goin' to get yourself killed. Promise me you won't, Mr. Franklin. Give me your word on that, too."

"Well, I'll sure as hell try not to."

She hesitated for a moment, and he thought that she was actually going to make him swear it, but all at once she laughed at the silliness of the demand. "I shouldn't be laughin'," she confessed. "My daddy, an' . . . mama—"

"I'm sorry," Moses said. He frowned down into the dark dirt and wished once more that she would go away and let him get on with his work.

"I hate it that they died, that *she* died, but, you know . . ." She moved closer to him and whispered, "But, you know, I really can't feel anythin' for him. Not anythin'. I don't even hate the Indians for killin' him. No, I don't!"

"You'll feel different, later," Moses tried to explain, feeling awkward now that she revealed that she didn't know how her father had actually perished.

"Oh, maybe," she said. "Right now, I just want to get out of here. I want the Indians to go 'way an' leave us alone. I want the killin' to stop."

"Maybe it will."

"Well, I got to go." She touched his arm lightly. It was a quick gesture, and she withdrew it rapidly, her fingers wet from his sweat-soaked buckskin. He knew she had never touched a colored man before. Unless something happened for the good in the next few days, she never would touch any man again. "Mr. Graham wants me to tend to the wounded. Nobody else'll do it 'less they're their own people. 'Sides, we got the biggest cave." She paused and looked out into the blackness over the creek. "I'm not real popular around here," she said.

He said nothing for a moment, then he swallowed. "I reckon that's on account of me."

"I reckon." She nodded. "But it ain't your fault! It ain't none of your fault. Or mine. If it's anybody's fault, it was his fault: Daddy's. It's those damn people's fault who left us all by ourselves. You'd think a body could see that."

"They's stiff-necked people. They see things their own way." He wanted to add that her late father had been the stiffest of the bunch, but he only said, "An' they's righteously scared."

"I hate them!" she burst out, and for a moment, Moses thought she was going to cry. He raised his arm slightly in what he realized for one horrible second was the start of a move to reach out and touch her, hold her, comfort her. But then he understood that he had misread her entirely. What flashed in the silvery starlight was not tears in her eyes but defiance, that same granite edge he had seen in her before. "I hate every man jack an' woman, too. Time'll come, an' soon, when Todd'll come get me, an' it'll all be over."

"Todd?"

"A boy I know," Aggie said. She looked away with sudden embarrassment and waved her hand as if to dismiss the comment as a silly fancy. "I told you 'bout him. Last night. I met him in Arkansas. He's up on the plains buffalo huntin', an' he's goin' to meet me in New Mexico." She was silent for a moment. "It don't matter," she said. "It don't matter a bit. I'm goin' to show 'em that I'm as good as they are. Better, even."

"You watch yourself."

"Don't you worry 'bout me." She moved her hand slightly out of the folds of her calico skirt, and Moses saw that she held her shotgun. She hefted it so he could see. "I'm pretty good with this, but I can use a pistol, too, like I told you."

"I don't doubt it. I s'pect you can do 'bout anythin' you please."

For a moment they stood apart in the darkness without speaking, and Moses wondered what would become of this girl. The Comanche would make much of her, he knew: rape, torture, maybe ultimately squaw to a brave, but not before she had been disfigured and disgraced to the point that no white man would ever touch her. The image of her in Comanche hands was hideous. He knew that he would put a bullet in this girl himself rather than see her become the prize of some young buck, even if it meant he might hang.

He went over to his saddlebag and searched around until he found what he was looking for.

"What's this?" she asked, hefting the heavy weight of the gift.

"Pepperbox," he said. He unwrapped the cloth-covered pistol case. She opened it and squinted into it. "You get somebody to show you how to load it."

"I can load it," she admitted simply. "But why're you givin' it to me?"

"I want you to keep it for me," Moses lied. "I won it playin' dice, an' I want you to keep it safe by. It's a .26. Ain't much for distance, but it'll do."

"I don't think—"

"You promise *me* something," Moses said. "Whatever happens, save it for yourself. Don't you let them Indians get you."

She laughed slightly. "You don't have to worry 'bout that, Mr. Franklin. An' I don't think this little ol' thing's goin' to make a difference."

"That's not what I mean," he said seriously. "What I mean is, if it looks like they's goin' to get you anyhow, you save one shot for yourself. You'll have this." He reached out and touched the box.

For a moment she said nothing but searched his face, then she nodded. "I'll keep it loaded. But you watch yourself. That's your promise to me."

Moses was struck with an idea. "Say, Missy—"

"Aggie," she corrected him.

"Miss Aggie," he responded, "you got a lookin' glass an' some sharp scissors handy?"

"Sure, why I think I do."

"You go get it for me?" He turned to go for his saddlebag to fetch another implement as she hurried away to get the things he asked for. Even though his mind was occupied with this new chore, he was unsettled by the girl. His hands were almost shaking.

As he was digging around, Graham approached and studied the bread and empty peach can Moses had discarded.

"You find everythin' you need?" he asked, lightly kicking the peach tin.

"I took some grub," Moses replied. "I didn't think you'd mind. Even a man who's fixin' to hang gets a last meal."

"No reason to get smart-mouthed with me," Graham said. "This was your idea, remember?"

Moses said nothing.

"You don't think you'll make it, do you?"

"Don't know."

"You ain't goin' to waylay ol' Frank an' run off, are you?"

"Don't know." Moses's anger returned. "It ain't likely. He's done told me that if I try'er, he'll kill me. I told him he's goin' to have to get in line."

"Look," Graham said, softening his tone from the flat indifference he had affected thus far. "Ol' Frank's about as worthless as a blind yard cat. Only reason he's goin' is 'cause somebody has to, an' maybe he can keep somebody else from gettin' killed."

"I don't think so," Moses said. "I think he's goin' 'cause he thinks you want him to."

"That might be right."

"*Might* ain't goin' to do him much good if we get caught. Is he . . ." Moses trailed off. He didn't know how to ask Graham just how simple Frank might truly be. The scout had found some confidence in the man, but he needed to know if there was a chance that Frank might break down on him.

"Oh, he can ride, an' he can shoot fair, like he says," Graham went on, answering Moses's unspoken doubts about Frank. "An' he's loyal as a goddamn dog. He'll stand by you till hell freezes over. But he ain't got much savvy, not a lick of sense. He used to, but he gets a little worse as he gets older."

"Then why're you lettin' him go?" Moses asked.

" 'Cause there wasn't another way. Except to shame him. I owe him too much for that."

"You owe him enough to get him killed?" Moses asked.

"That's why I'm tellin' you this." Graham's voice took an edge. "So you'll watch out for him as much as you can.

You can count on him to do what he's told. But you got to tell him. That's sure." Graham pulled out a cigar and bit off the end. "I don't mean he won't back you up. He will. He's a good man, an' he'd die before he'd leave you in trouble."

"Even *me*?" Moses asked.

"Especially you. Because *I'm* trustin' you. Because *I'm* takin' your word. An' that's enough for him. But he don't think so good on his own sometimes, an' you got to watch him."

"I'll remember that."

"See that you do." Graham stood quietly for a moment, and then he returned. "I'd rather you bring Rangers if you've got a choice. I'd rather not have anybody else."

Moses thought for a second. "Why?"

"I got my reasons."

"Have anything to do with these?" Moses's hand stretched out and rested atop a whiskey keg inside Graham's buckboard. "Rangers is as likely to bust 'em as anybody. Nobody out here likes the idea of tradin' whiskey to Indians."

"I'm not *tradin'* whiskey to anybody!" Graham almost shouted, then he lowered his voice. "If *anybody's* traded off any whiskey around here, it's you."

"We could try tradin' the rest of it for a way out of this," Moses offered. He sensed Graham's body stiffening.

"No. If I don't come out of this with as much as I can, there's no reason to get out. Not for me, not for them." He nodded his head in the vague direction of the wagon line.

He lit the cigar, and Moses saw in the flicker of the match beneath his cupped hand the face of a troubled man. For a moment he believed that Graham felt as trapped as he did.

"I don't have to explain that to you or anybody. Now that Sterling's dead, I might have to tell . . . his family about it, but that's it. It's nobody else's business. Especially yours." He puffed and filled the starlit night with white smoke. "Only thing you have to worry about is gettin' some help or figurin' some other way out of this. Or else . . ." He trailed off.

"Or else what?" Moses's neck prickled in anger. Graham had a way of getting beneath his skin worse than any man he had ever known.

"You just see to it that ol' Frank gets back in one piece if you do. I'll shoot you on sight if you come back without him."

"I'll keep that thought," Moses said. He could tell that Graham was wanting to say more. "What else you want to say? Might as well get it all out."

"Last night I was drunk, an' I said some things."

"So did I."

"But you weren't drunk." He puffed his cigar for a moment, careful to turn his body to shield the bright red coal from Indian eyes. "Anyway, I'm just tellin' you it doesn't matter to me about you stayin' out there with . . . with Jack's girl. I don't think anythin' happened. I don't think she'd let anythin' happen, not anythin' like that."

"I'll keep that thought as well."

"I think it's a goddamn shame that it did happen—her stayin' behind—an' I hold you on account for that: standin' against me." He held up his stump as if to ward off any words of protest Moses might have. "It doesn't make a difference now. What's done is done. But if you'd gone along with my orders an' come along, it never would've happened. Buryin' them Mescans was a damn fool thing to do. You knew it then. You know it now."

"If you say so."

"An'," Graham went on, "I want you to know that as far as I'm concerned you've fouled this all up. The Mescans, this damn trap you've led us into. The whole goddamn shootin' match. This is all your fault," Graham said flatly. "There's a lot of people dead, an' there's likely to be a lot more. I'm holdin' you on account for that, too. I just wanted you to know how I stand on that."

"That's comfortin'." Moses checked his cinch again to give his hands something to do. His teeth were clenched.

"You can keep the sass to yourself," Graham said. And for a moment, once again, the two men faced each other. There was nothing to be gained by this, Moses knew, but he wasn't going to back down. After a few moments, Graham turned slightly and looked out over the crossing.

"By the way," Moses said finally, anxious to break

the tension. "I think that Frank, uh, Mr. Herbert's girl is trapped in the Hollister wagon."

"What?"

"She's been tryin' to come in, but she's too scared to."

"Well, *goddamnit*! I thought he said she got carried off. Does Frank know about this?"

"I didn't know if I ought to tell him or not. So I didn't." Moses swallowed hard. "That feller she's hooked up with is Jason Sterlin', most likely."

"Jason Sterling?" Graham chewed on the cigar for a moment. "Why didn't you go get her?"

"Ain't my job," Moses said. "I doubt she'd of come back in with me. 'Sides, I think I been seen with one too many white women on this train already."

Graham stared through the night toward the scout. "I ought to kill you."

"You can try." Moses didn't move, but inside he felt a thrill of fear.

"I could try. An' I could do it."

"It's good to know where you stand," Moses said. He relaxed with the recognition that this was not a serious threat. There was too much at stake for Graham to take out some sort of personal vengeance against the scout. He turned and swung up into the saddle, the implement he had been searching for now securely in his pocket.

"Just don't tell Frank about it. I'll get her in some way or another. He doesn't need to be frettin' over that. He's got enough on his hands tryin' to keep your mind on what you're doin'."

"Whatever you say. I know my job."

Moses started to move the bay off a bit down the line, but Graham stopped him. He held on to the bay's bridle and looked up at the scout. Moses saw his face outlined in the starlight, and he noted that the wagon master's eyes were set in a kind of determined look that he had not shown Moses before. He seemed to be memorizing his face, struggling to place it permanently in his own mind. Finally he spoke, and his words surprised Moses.

"I got to tell you that it takes more than nigger balls to go out there an' try this."

"You was ready to do it," Moses replied, now angry

with himself for trying to sound pleased with a compliment and then making some halfhearted attempt to return it.

"Horseshit. I couldn't have done it. Not with this. The squarehead's right." Moses saw that he held up his stubbed arm. "But you went right to it, an' I admire that. I just wanted you to know that, too."

"That's white of you, Mr. Graham."

"I thought you'd think so," Graham said. "But I still am holdin' you on account. An' I still plan to kill you when we get to Santa Fe. 'Course, if you don't come back, an' come back soon, I don't suppose it matters, does it?"

"No sir, it don't."

At that moment Aggie rushed up with the mirror and scissors, and Graham stepped away. "Here," she said, handing them up to the scout. "The scissors are Mama's."

"I'll try to take care of 'em," Moses said, stuffing them in his belt, then shoving the mirror down inside his shirt.

"What the hell's that junk for?" Graham asked.

"Well . . ." Moses grinned into the darkness and spotted Frank walking his horse up to them. "I don't know if we'll make it or not. I truly reckon we got less'n half a chance. But if we don't, this is one nigger's scalp them Comanche ain't fixin' to get."

"I hear they don't like that woolly hair anyhow," Graham said, then he chuckled.

"What's so funny?" Frank asked as he mounted and prepared to follow Moses around the end of the wagon line.

"I'll tell you later," Moses said, and they rode out.

3

IT WAS NEARLY MIDNIGHT WHEN THEY LEFT THE WAGON line and rode across the bloody gravel and down into the creek. They coaxed their mounts through the swirling waters, trying to make a minimum of noise as they eased upstream.

Moses knew that the first few hundred yards would be the most dangerous. He felt terribly exposed. He couldn't imagine that the Indians in the thickets and trees on the opposite side of the stream could fail to see them, but when he looked back to the wagon fort, he realized that what little light was afforded by the stars was reflected off the stark whiteness of the butte. Even though the wagons themselves were sharply outlined against it, anything away from the limestone wall was covered neatly by darkness.

He squinted into the trees and tried to catch a glimpse of lurking Comanche snipers, but the thicket yielded no indication of human movement. Moses knew that the settlers back on the crossing were nearly spent. They could hold out for one, maybe two more assaults, especially if the Comanche held off until tomorrow after the defenders had rested, but that was about it. Moses wouldn't bet the powder held in a single .55 cartridge that they could last more than three days, and it could take that long just to get to the nearest fort.

Once around the bend in the creek, Moses reined in and dismounted and instructed Frank to move the horses back into the cedar breaks. He knelt and used Aggie's scissors to cut his hair close to his skull. He then shaved his head with the razor he had found in his saddlebags. He worked mostly by feel, but twice he stopped and struck a match and squinted into the mirror to check his progress.

"What the hell you doin'?" Frank Herbert asked.

"Keep quiet," Moses ordered. He doubted that the white man would follow his example. Still, he stood and rubbed his tender skin before replacing his hat, which now sat down around his ears and gave him a comical appearance, and then offered the scissors to Frank, who just looked at him with a perplexed frown.

"I seen men who was scalped alive," Moses said. "It ain't goin' to happen to me."

"Don't see the need," Frank whispered back. "If they want my topknot, they're goin' to have to take it. Better men'n them has tried, an' they couldn't do'er." Moses shook his head and thought of Frank's balding pate and began storing his implements in his saddlebag.

They soon remounted and rode up onto a rise across and away from the creek. They spotted an enormous golden moon rising over the prairie and brightly illuminating the entire rolling prairie.

"Christ in heaven," Herbert hissed at Moses as they

guided their horses through the waving sheen of the advancing moonlight. The grass was damp from the storm, and their boots and trouser legs were soon soaked. "I could of gone forever without that damn moon."

"Shh!" Moses ordered again. He wished he had said "Shut up," or "Keep quiet," instead of the softer command, but there was something about ordering white men about that he couldn't master. An Indian might ignore the sound of horses moving across the plains, maybe thinking they were mustangs or other animals. But men's voices would attract them, and Moses had no way of knowing exactly where the Comanche were. For all he knew, they could be riding right into them.

Still, he agreed with his companion: Comanche Moon. Comanche Moon in a Comanche Spring. It seemed that the whole damned country belonged to the Comanche. Their buffalo, their hunting grounds, their creek. They might be a bloody and fierce people, savage and barbaric in their practices and treatment of their enemies, but they had some reason, Moses thought. This was their land, their moon, their spring. The white man didn't seem natural here, he told himself. And the black man . . . the black man didn't seem natural anywhere.

AFTER THEY HAD BEEN riding for some time, Moses and Frank Herbert gained a view of the Comanche camp. The Indians had confidently laid their campsite down the side of the mesa that seemed to break off the black hump and trail off to the northeast parallel to the creek. The winking fires indicated that at least some of the Indians' number remained among the cedars along the opposite side of the ridge that faced the crossing. A larger glow emanated from the long mesa's far end and marked the Comanche's main camp. No specific fire could be discerned, though, and Moses reckoned they were in a draw of some kind. The two riders felt helpless and naked on the open prairie.

"Hellfire," Frank whispered when Moses pulled his mare up to study the Indian camp. "Look over yonder. We could of snuck off, all of us. Or we might of got up behind 'em an' hit 'em 'fore they knew it."

"They'd know it. Indians ain't stupid. Too many white men've made that mistake."

"Jus' white men?" Frank asked.

"No," Moses said.

"Well." Frank cut off a wedge of tobacco and stuffed it into his cheek. "I s'pose you're right. 'Sides, with the outfit Cap'n Graham's got together, I doubt we'd do more'n shoot ourself in the foot. Biggest bunch of whinin' crybabies I ever seen. 'Sides the Cap'n, ain't one of 'em worth a tin shit in a brick crapper."

"They're not the best bunch," Moses offered.

"Well, they're the best we got." Frank was suddenly defensive. "They'll do. They'll have to. I jus' hope they can hold out till we get back."

Moses did not reply but bent his head to avoid looking directly into the moonlight. He didn't tell this simple, coarse man that he would be better off worrying about whether he and Moses would ever see the crossing again.

CHAPTER FOUR

1

MOSES FRANKLIN AND FRANK HERBERT RODE A LONG while in silence. Ahead of them the giant moon continued to rise and change from a deep orange to a bright, golden yellow and then to a pale, cool gray light that cast their shadows on the tall grass behind them. The fragrance of prairie flowers was heavy on the night air, and the mysterious nocturnal sounds of animals and insects seemed to roar all around them. A serenade of prairie wolves echoed in the distance.

It was a big, empty land, Moses thought. Anywhere grass grew this tall and lush must be fertile. He felt sure cotton would grow here, if there was enough rain for it. It was nothing like the bottomlands around Big Cypress Bayou; there was nothing to resemble the thick forests of East Texas anywhere in sight. But it must be good land. And all that stood between its emptiness and settlement was the Comanche.

Each time he led a wagon train across the vastness between the Indian Line and Santa Fe, he thought of the possibility of the settlers just stopping and staying right there. In large enough numbers, good men with good rifles could make it too costly for even the staunchest Comanche band to attack a settlement. Then there were other ways of handling the problem. All it would take was determination—maybe desperation—to make a place out here for people who had nowhere else to go.

Moses didn't want to wind up like the blacks in Jefferson who had put up crude lean-tos and shacks out near the trash heaps on the bayou. Those who could still push a broom or drag a rake could find some work in town, but those who couldn't wandered the city's alleyways and picked through trash bins, living off the garbage of those more fortunate than themselves.

Of course it wouldn't be exactly like that for him. He had saved most of the money he had made scouting, not out of any sense of putting away funds for a time when he couldn't work, but more because his needs were simple. He owned no home, had no wife. A new set of buckskins, some stout boots, a new saddle, or some other luxury would take some of it from time to time.

A surprising revelation had come to him during the past year as well. He discovered that he was lonely. He had always been a solitary person, and he told anyone who asked—and not many did—that he enjoyed being by himself all the time. But he knew that wasn't true. He envied men like Saul Jackson and Aaron Ledbetter who had responsibilities to worry them. They never had money as he did, wore no fine clothes.

Moses had closely observed Saul and Aaron and their families whenever he returned, but he had always regarded such a life as something he could never share in. He knew them, and he often took meals with them, and when the men went off to work of a morning, he found himself feeling superior to them as he settled into a porch rocker and sipped on another cup of coffee. When they returned, sometimes dragging themselves like worn-out animals up the dirt street to their humble houses, sometimes not having enough left after paying rent and buying food even to spend on tobacco, Moses again felt that their lives were being wasted. They had never known the excitement of chasing game across the prairie, of riding free and easy across the plains. But in spite of his attempts to convince himself that their lives were filled with drudgery, he felt a gnawing jealousy of these two friends, especially when they would slump into their tiny parlors to be embraced by enthusiastic children and loving wives.

Moses was regarded as a sort of uncle by the men's children, and when he sat in their kitchens playing with one or more of their bright-eyed youngsters, he felt warm and familiar inside. From time to time when he would be camping out on the prairie, he discovered himself longing for that familial companionship. He sometimes wondered if it might not be worth it after all to stay in Jefferson and try to make a living there where he could find a girl, marry, raise children.

Even so, he knew he would soon be past the point where both options would be open to him. His hair was already graying, and at night when the weather changed, aching joints kept him awake. If he was going to make a move toward a permanent home, he lectured himself, he had to make it soon.

His dream of settling here on the prairie just off the escarpment of the trackless plains did not take shape right away. He had not thought of how anyone could make it out here. There was plenty of game, but the natural fruits of the plains were solutions for only one part of the problem. He talked about it loosely with Aaron and Saul, but neither was anxious to come out to a land they had never seen without something more definite for them to do other than hunt and fish. Would crops grow? Moses insisted they would, but it was a feeling he had, not a certainty. What about things they couldn't just pick up and make? What would they do for money? Moses had no answers, and he had not yet told them that they would also have the Comanche to deal with. The idea remained nothing more than a dream to occupy him whenever he rode his horse back from Santa Fe. But then he met Glover Wentworth.

Wentworth was an Englishman and a cattleman, "in that order," he informed Moses. He had a large ranch east of San Antonio, near Gonzales; the previous year, he had taken a small herd of Longhorns north to Kansas, where they were shipped east by rail. He wasn't the first to do so, Moses knew, but it was an uncertain business. Most cattlemen followed the traditional route east into Louisiana, from where the beef could move by boat out of New Orleans. Wentworth claimed that the water route was expensive and, as he put it, "most inexpedient." His venture through the Territories along a line east of the Wichita River had been much more profitable, he claimed. But now, he had ideas that more could be done with the right kind of planning. He had been talking to other cattlemen about taking herds on a north-central route, straight up the Llano Estacado without having to swing through the Territories.

Wentworth was referred to Moses by the post commandant at Fort Richardson when the cattleman asked for details about the country west and north of Jacksboro. Moses tried to describe landmarks and watched while Wentworth noted them down with a stubby pencil.

"You see, old boy," Wentworth said, "I have this idea that the best opportunities lie west of the so-called Indian Line." He lit a tailor-made cigarette, the first Moses had ever seen, and offered one to the scout, who took it awkwardly and ran his fingers over its smooth yellow surface. It amazed him. "You see, there is this bothersome quarantine on Texas beef. There is no point in taking them east of Hays City, so there is no point in bringing them up the eastern trails. But the absolute truth is, I'd rather not advertise what I'm doing."

"They's the Goodnight-Loving trail 'cross the Pecos and up through New Mexico Territory," Moses suggested.

"Anyone who looked at a map would think that made sense, especially since the best market right now is at Fort Sumner up on the Pecos," Wentworth said. "But that is folly in my mind. There is no water out there. Cattle can endure distance, but they cannot endure it without sweet water and good grass. Messrs. Goodnight and Loving and others are fortunate men of rugged determination. But I put little faith in fortune, and determination can carry one only so far. Others will soon deduce that the most direct route is the best route, but I would rather like to steal a march on them. I would very much like to arrive ahead of Mr. Chisum in the Colorado and eastern Kansas markets, beat him to the punch, as it were."

The key to the whole thing, Wentworth went on, was to find a West Texas route to the newly established Kansas railheads, something more direct than the old Chisholm Trail that wound its way up from the Rio Grande across the Colorado and eventually across the Red between Spanish Fort and Saint Jo. "I hear there are good crossings there. Places where the Red River is a virtual road."

Moses told him what he knew and studied the crude map Wentworth made while he spoke. He had no way of knowing whether the chart was accurate or not, for his estimations of distance were based on how far a man could ride in a day relative to how far he could see from the top of a horse, both of which depended on how good the weather was at the time.

Wentworth dropped a finger on the map, a few inches higher than the Cross Timber country, just north and a little east of Fort Griffin, just about where he had drawn a wavy line next to a scrawled cloud that represented Blind Man's Creek and the copse of pecan trees at the top of the mesa nearby.

"The bloody problem," he said, "falls there. Once we get beyond the Army's protection here"—he jabbed an X that represented Fort Griffin—"we are on our own. We will need reoutfitting before we cross into Indian country proper, a place to water the animals and to let them graze a day or so before making a run through. If the river is up and running, we will need a place to queue the herd to wait. That requires grass and lots of it. We will be needing supplies by then as well. I doubt the Army is going to sell us too much out of their stocks, and I am damned if I'm going to pay the prices they charge at the outposts up there. When they see a cattleman coming, they double their prices.

"If this water is sweet, as you say, and the grass is lush, as you say, then all we would need to make it a perfect stopover would be a store, a place like Saint Jo or Red River Station. That may be too much to hope for." He shook his head and refolded the map, and Moses realized that he had been talking to himself, reconfirming his own judgments.

He told Moses he planned to move his first herd north along that route that summer, probably in August, depending on how long it took him to build a herd of the wild cattle. Moses asked him about the Comanche, but Wentworth dismissed his question with a wave of his hand. "They will be off to the south, hunting by then," he said. "And if they are not, we will buy the buggers off."

Moses had his doubts about that and said so. But Wentworth was confident.

"I am not underestimating them," he argued lightly. "They might attack me. They might pilfer a few head, maybe a dozen or so. Maybe a hundred. But I work with good men. Mexicans. Negroes, like yourself. Good shots, every one, and scared to death of the red Indian. But they have good rifles, and they are *not* afraid to shoot at the first sign of trouble. They respect them, too. I fear that's a mistake too many white men make out here."

He reached into a vest pocket, pulled out a five-dollar gold piece, and flipped it to Moses.

"Thank you for your counsel, Mr. Franklin," he said, extending his hand. In Moses's entire life, it was the first time a white man had ever offered a hand to be shaken. The gesture was not lost on him: It showed respect, he told himself. Wentworth was smiling as he firmly grasped Moses's hand. "I hope we meet again. I admire a man of confidence, regardless of his color."

While riding into Jefferson two weeks later, Moses discovered the idea that would become a dream. He had taken wagon trains through Saint Jo for years. He had seen what a lucrative business went on in the tiny community by virtue of wagon trains and cattle herds that passed. He knew about Red River Station, and he also knew that a toothless old man named Cotton at Spanish Fort was slowly amassing a cash fortune by selling flour, coffee, lard, beans, and other staples to chuck cooks who came north with the herds. He also roped in profits peddling homemade whiskey and three ugly fat Pawnee squaws. If Wentworth's idea had merit, his could be the first of a long string of drives up the western trail to Kansas, Colorado, maybe even up into Wyoming and Montana.

Blind Man's Creek was one of the few reliable sources of sweet water north of Griffin. It was also about the last one south of the Canadian. When they reached there, the herds would need water that was fresh and flowing, not brackish and sandy such as that which sluggishly filled the Pease and the several forks of the Red. The scout knew that with a little planning, he could be in possession of such water. The most logical place for a herd to stop would be at the crossing: his crossing. It was also, Moses thought, the place for the store Wentworth wished for.

Back in Jefferson, he anxiously put the plan before Saul and Aaron. The two men, one so old and one so young, looked at each other as he finished outlining the proposition. He would put up the money, he said, buy wagons and supplies, lumber for building, food, horses, even supplies to sell to anyone who happened by. They would then come out there and build a post, a store which could sit in the middle of the best source of fresh water in fifty miles in either direction. They could sell the water to the herdsmen, or, failing that, they could sell tack and food, repair wagons, shoe horses, whatever it took to keep the herds moving north. He didn't mention whiskey and women. He doubted that the two men, who were exceptionally religious and devoted to their families, would allow it, in the first place, and he also knew that where there were wild cowboys and liquor and whores, there could also be trouble.

In a way it was an ideal plan. Even if the drovers found dealing with black merchants distasteful, the need to move their cattle north would keep them from having much choice in the matter. They could file on it through the Freedman's Bureau, claim it for their own. He doubted there would be any trouble about it. No one—no *white* one—would contest a bunch of Negroes' claim to a chunk of land in the middle of Comanchería. As he spoke to them, the idea took concrete shape. He was only vaguely aware that it was still a dream. It became a plan.

But there were problems which snagged things at the outset. First of all, there wasn't enough cash to obtain the supplies they hoped to sell to the drovers. Moses would have to go west once more to make sure they didn't go bankrupt during their first season.

Secondly, there were the Indians, but Moses played down the danger. The Kiowa had been quiet for the past year or so, remaining on their reservation under the Quaker agent's eye. And he believed that when they confronted the Comanche, they would be Penaterkuhs or one of the other bands that were bound by treaties. Quahidi had not been seen that often so far east as the crossing, and Moses personally had not run across any sign of them in all his recent expeditions. He suggested that the Indians would remain north and west of them, in the Territories or high on the plains. Once the cattle trails followed Wentworth's route with regularity, they would give up and stay away from the country around the crossing. Besides, he argued, they were Negroes, not *tejanos*. They would hunt, but only enough to provide meat. They would also be well armed; Moses would make sure of that.

So Moses took on this last train, Graham's train, and Saul and Aaron and Zachariah were preparing to load up their families and a stock of goods and lumber, tools, firearms, and ammunition into three wagons, which would trail milk cows, and hogs, and even a seed flock of laying hens and two roosters. They would move out to the crossing, where, Moses promised, he would return from Santa Fe to meet them in mid to late June. He planned to be operating a genuine store by August when Wentworth came through with his herd.

Moses's plans were on his mind a good deal during the first weeks of the train's journey. Indeed, they distracted him and kept him from noticing the many oddities of Graham's train until it was too late. He was too glad to have the work to worry about those he worked for.

But as bad luck followed bad luck, his confidence in the proposition began to erode. Now, as he moved across the plains in search of some sort of help for a trapped and well-armed bunch of white men, he felt panic rise in him like bile. He decided the whole scheme was ludicrous. There was no chance that they could survive out here, not now, not this year, not until the Comanche backed off. Now that he had seen the Quahidi Comanche up close, seen how fierce they could be, he knew he couldn't deal with them. No one could. They could only kill them, and there were far too many for a few colored men from Jefferson to handle, no matter how good their guns were.

Moses had enough experience to know that, but here he was going for help because not even a hundred people could dissuade the Comanche from their traditional hatred for anyone who challenged them. And there was no assurance that help would come, even for white settlers. How he could ever have expected, realistically, that he could just ride into a fort and demand help he would never know. The idea had not seemed ridiculous back in the comfortable warmth of Saul's parlor, nor had it seemed incredible that because so many of the troops were black, they would rush to rescue their colored brethren. But when he contemplated the actuality of it, he knew as certainly as he knew anything that it was unlikely that anyone, black or white, would ride two or three days out into the deadliest country in the West to save a bunch of niggers who had no business being there in the first place.

They'd sooner come for Mexicans, Moses thought. A whole lot sooner.

2

AS MOSES RODE BESIDE THE NOW SILENT FRANK Herbert, who kept cocking his head this way and that as each new night sound hit his ear, the scout realized that the lure of his dream had overridden his common sense, and it angered him that he had been so blind to the danger. He had gone along with his fantasy and allowed it to govern his actions.

Then a new thought occurred to him: How could he stop them? Warn them? Suddenly a division rent his sense of responsibility.

Moses was not sure what day it was, nor even what month. He knew from the position of the moonrise as it shifted on the eastern horizon that it was later than it should have been, later than he had planned for it to be. How far had they come already? Panic flooded up in him.

Sweat had broken out on his forehead during the mental ordeal, and the night air seemed fresh and cool against his face. He lowered his head once more and felt his stomach churning. Honor, he thought grimly, honor and his word had nothing to do with it. It had nothing to do with earning the white man's respect, nothing to do with Graham and the rest. It had to do with a white girl who was forbidden even to his thoughts. He felt nothing for any of the rest. But if he didn't find a way to help them back there, some of the bones would be hers, and that image kept his horse set on the trail he had pledged to follow.

He felt as if he were enduring physical pain. He envisioned Saul and Aaron packing their things, Zachariah talking himself sick trying to find someone who might buy their houses for a decent price. He saw them quitting their jobs, persuading their wives and older children that this was the road to a place where they could have more, be more. How could he face them, tell them that it was all nothing more than a nigger's dream of Nigger Heaven?

He had no idea what he could say to them that would make his betrayal of their trust hurt less than the realities they would face at the crossing.

"YOU DECIDED WHICH WAY we're headin'?" Frank asked. They were the first words either of them had spoken for nearly an hour, and Moses felt the bay shudder beneath him. He himself jumped at Frank's voice, and he started to shush him. He looked back over his shoulder and saw that the mesa and the ridge where the Comanche were camped was some miles away. They should be out of immediate danger, but there still was no cause to be careless. He kept his voice low.

"South by east." Moses eyed the moon and the North Star just to make sure of his bearings. "I reckon Richardson's a better bet than Griffin. Though, to tell you true, I've got doubts 'bout both."

What he didn't tell Frank was that between the grassy plain they now rode across and the fort down by Jacksboro was what was called "the badlands," miles of rough, red, muddy breaks that hid quicksand and rattlesnake dens, roving packs of wolves, and sometimes large cats and other dangers that might be worse than the Comanche. But their options weren't numerous. If they went south to Griffin, it could take another day, and if they tried to ride around the badlands, it could take two.

"We could go up an' see the Quaker agent at Fort Sill," Moses thought aloud. "General Sherman might be there, an' he'd come on the howl. But if he's not there, I doubt we'd get much relief without they check with him or some other. Could take a day or more. They won't move if the agent don't say so, an' he never has." He bit his lip in thought. "Hell, he don't believe that any of his Indians could do anythin' worse'n stealin' a few chickens, an' since I don't reckon these is his Indians in the first place, it ain't likely we'd get much from him."

"Won't they have to check with somebody at Richardson?"

"Likely," Moses said. He had no idea how the Army would react. He had seen people come into the forts yelling about Indians, and within an hour a troop was sometimes on the move, singing "The Girl I Left Behind Me," colors flying. But he had also seen men come in to report that Comanche or Kiowa had wiped out wagons or cabins or even a small settlement, and the officer in charge would demur, send for instructions, sometimes not act at all.

"Ought to kill ever' goddamn Indian in the country," Frank growled. "This ain't no way to be. I didn't fight a whole war just to get my hair lifted by some redskin."

Moses said nothing.

"What you think we'll get at Richardson?"

"If we're lucky, the commandant'll send out a patrol to help us out. If we're not, he won't be able to spare nobody, but we can try to get a bunch together in Jacksboro on our own."

"You think we'll be lucky?"

"I don't know." Moses sighed. "We got no reason to hope for it."

"You think them folks back there can hold out?"

Moses weighed the possibilities. "Maybe," he said. "They got food an' water, plenty of ammunition. If they keep their heads." He paused and then decided this was not a time to choose his words carefully. "If sons of bitches like Golden or that preacher man Hollister or that hothead Runnels don't cause trouble, they can hold out a long time."

"Cap'n Graham'll keep Golden in line," Frank offered. "The squarehead, too." Then he added in a soft voice, "But I worry 'bout that preacher, Hollister, myself. He ain't right in the head. He sure got religion all of a sudden. Cap'n'd best keep a eye out for him. He's the sort who'd come up on you in the dark an' cut your gizzard out an' then offer to pray over your corpse."

"Was he a captain in the Yankee Army? Mr. Graham?"

"He was. An' a good'un. We was together at Pea Ridge an' Shiloh. Vicksburg some. He don't like me to call him Cap'n, but I keep forgettin'. Seems natural, somehow."

Moses didn't know what to say. Frank was speaking evenly enough, but he didn't want to push it. At the same time, he was curious.

"What's goin' on with the whiskey?"

"What do you mean?" Frank's voice took on a suspicious edge.

"I was jus' curious," Moses said quietly. "I seen trains with whiskey barrels, but this'un's different. There's more of it, for one thing."

Frank was silent for a moment. "I don't understand it all myself," he confessed. "It's somethin' to do with Jack Sterlin' an' the whiskey he brought us. Cap'n Graham says it'll make a better life for me an' my girl." He paused and spat into the grass. "I can't see how," he said more to himself than to Moses.

"It don't make no diff'rence to me," he continued. "I'll take his word for it. Right now, I got to think of findin' Lottie. But the Cap'n'll take the knots out of that, too, if anybody can."

"You seem to think a lot of him." Moses changed the subject away from Frank's daughter.

"I *do* think a lot of him," Frank confirmed. "I think a god-awful lot of him. He's a good man. I saved his life once, nearly twice, an' he's done me a good turn or two. We go back a ways."

They fell silent again. Moses's thoughts drifted again to the expedition he knew was making its way from Jefferson, then, helplessly, effortlessly, he turned his mind to Aggie. Goddamn that girl, he thought. Ever since she had come out and brought him that goddamn cup of coffee, she had been all over his mind like a heavy quilt. He couldn't get out from under her. She was damned dangerous. Everything he had done, he thought suddenly, was dangerous. *This* was dangerous, foolish. The best thing would have been to stay right back with the others, fight it out.

He felt guilty all over again. At first he had honestly believed that going for help was riskier than staying behind, but now, safely distant from the twinkling lights of the Indian camp, he acknowledged his guilt was more over his abandonment of her than over anything else.

Once more he considered their immediate destination. They would have to be more than lucky to get help from any fort, from any commander, he lectured himself. Oh, the commandant would be excited to hear about it, and he might even decide to send a patrol back with them.

Even twenty mounted troopers would be enough to scare off the Indians, for feral as the Comanche were, it wasn't their nature to stand and fight when they could run off and sneak back and hit an enemy when he wasn't looking. But, Moses realized, he probably would have the devil getting in to see the officer, whoever he was, and then he would have the *very* devil convincing him that he knew what he was talking about.

Further, Moses argued the commander's point of view, if the Indians were behaving so oddly, raiding in a large group like that, it could mean that this was a part of something bigger. Hell, Moses thought, there could be a general uprising, one started since he left Jefferson. Hope sparked brightly in his mind. Maybe Saul or Aaron would hear of it, stop or turn back, wait until they knew it was safe. Surely if there was a big Indian war starting out past the line, word would spread.

But how would they hear it? Moses wondered to himself. They wouldn't be allowed into the saloons and stores along the way. Whatever they needed to buy would likely be handed out through a back door, wordlessly, contemptuously. Most of the settlements west of the Trinity were populated by old Rebels, men who lurched around on one leg or swung stumps instead of arms or peered from only one remaining eye. If a thousand Indians were waiting with arrows nocked just past the Indian Line to kill anyone who crossed it, these men wouldn't even wink a warning to three wagonloads of niggers.

As they rode, Moses felt himself becoming more and more depressed. He looked back over his shoulder toward the mesa, which now was only a dark hump in the moonlight. They were far enough away that not even the Indians' fires could be seen, but they weren't so distant that they couldn't ride back before dawn. He fought down the desire to tell Frank that he was sure they couldn't get help, that since they were likely among the best shots in the whole outfit, they should go back and try to do something more practical to relieve the train, but he didn't know if any of that would do any good either.

Moses's head hurt from trying to think of options. He wished desperately that they would run across a company of Rangers. They would know what to do, how to do it, and it would particularly satisfy Graham. But he also knew that the odds against stumbling over Texas Rangers out here were slim.

If the Army came, Moses knew they would confiscate Graham's whiskey. He'd likely blame Moses for that as well. But if they didn't get help, there wouldn't be any whiskey to take: None of them would be alive to worry about whether there was anyone at fault or not.

3

SUDDENLY MOSES PULLED HIS MARE UP SHARPLY, lifted his large hat, and peered into the silvery light ahead of him. He wiped his eyes and stared again. Frank also reined in and jerked up his rifle, prepared to shoot at whatever it was the black scout had spotted.

"What is it?" Frank whispered. Then he saw what had stopped Moses.

In the distance an eerie glow seemed to come right out of the grass itself. Its flicker indicated that a fire was the source of the light, but it was singular, emerging from the middle of nothing in the prairie that could be discerned from the horsemen's vantage point. Moses looked behind him, but the mesa and Comanche campfires were over the horizon, so it was no outpost of the camp. Someone had built a fire in a depression in the prairie, and the light illuminated the grass for a hundred yards around.

"Maybe it's Mr. Ambrose," he hissed at Frank, and then he dismounted and motioned for his companion to follow suit.

After hobbling their horses, they crawled through the damp grass, trying not to make any noise. Moses thought they had miscalculated and missed it when suddenly he spotted the bright yellow flicker directly ahead of him. He waited until Frank reached his position and cupped his hand around his ear.

"If it's whites," he whispered, "then they's the greatest fools in the world. If it's Comanche, we may have to run for it. You wait here, an' if you hear anythin' at all, you light out quick as you can."

Frank nodded eagerly.

Moses crept forward, closer to the light, praying with every movement that he didn't lay his hand on a sleeping rattlesnake or scorpion or other biting, stinging vermin. Suddenly he came to an open spot in the grass, and he hesitated. Directly in front of him was a large red-ant bed, characterized by a circle where grass was completely stripped away from the dirt. A hole the size of a ten-cent piece was dead center of the five-foot circle, and around it the large, mean insects were coming and going about their business, oblivious to the midnight hour. The mysterious light cast a pale yellow glow across the bed, and Moses cursed to himself, backed up, and began circumnavigating the circle.

Finally he reached the brightest light of all, and he inched forward and parted the grass. He was on the lip of a small draw. In the bottom was a bright campfire, all right, but what the black scout saw surrounding the flickering light made him suck in his breath so quickly that he almost exclaimed aloud.

In the center of the depression was a wagon, the Hawshaws' or the Newsomes' broken-down rig, from the look of it, Moses decided. It had been dragged in on a broken axle and leaned awkwardly in front of a small campfire that was blazing brightly and was fed from a stack of cedar limbs stacked in the wagon's bed. Around the fire two Comanche warriors squatted; another lay nearby in what appeared to be a sound sleep. Off to the right, totally by himself, was another Indian, but he was dressed differently, and he was familiar.

He was wrapped in a cloak of antelope hide, and beneath it was a tattered and bloody Confederate battle flag. Around his neck and painted on his arms and legs and dangling from his horned headdress were the signs and talismans of a medicine man. He was the same one who had spoken to Moses the day before and who had been present at the attack that evening. He rocked back and forth on his heels and sang in a soft, muted tone.

Aside from the Comanche around the fire, no other braves were present, and from what Moses could tell, none was standing guard.

However odd the scene which greeted the black man's eyes was, the figure which dominated his vision and caused his breath to grow short was not an Indian at all. Lashed to the wheel of the wagon, Moses could see, was a living human being.

It wasn't Ambrose or his son, as Moses feared, but the captive was white, an old man from the look of the long, silver hair that clung in wet, matted clumps to his sweating shoulders. The open wounds that tore raggedly across his back testified that he wasn't going to survive the Comanche torture for long. Moses had to fight the urge to move immediately in and untie the man, who, in spite of his serious injuries, was twisting and wriggling under the leather bonds. Soon one of the braves rose and moved over to the fire, from which he took a sharpened cedar stick. This he heated until it was a live coal, and he then, almost casually, applied the torturous instrument to the open wounds on the captive's back, just close enough to sear the skin, but not so near as to burn him fatally. It was apparent that the Comanche had been entertaining themselves in this way for some time.

Moses was amazed that the man didn't scream when the white-hot brand was applied to his back. His only reaction was an almost involuntary constriction of his muscles and clenching of his fists in a futile attempt to draw away from the painful burning. Moses couldn't see the man's face, but he wondered if the Indians had cut out his tongue.

After the brave completed his treatment of the captive's back, however, the white man turned and spat derisively onto the ground beside him. He couldn't see his tormentors, but from his mouth burst forth a loud voice that convinced Moses that the white man held his cries of anguish in with a tremendous force of will. There was no doubt that he had a good deal of life left in him.

"You goddamn chicken-shit, yeller-eyed, pecker-lickin' son of a bitch's bastards! I was more of a man than you when I was shittin' my britches an' suckin' my mama's tit!" He strained to get the eye of the brave, who had returned to his squatting position and was trying to ignore the insults. "You ain't got the balls God give a green snake! You're nothin' but a hairless goat-pricked dog-fuckin' fatherless wonder with a gut full of puke an' a mouth full of Mescan turds." The brave shifted uncomfortably. He might not understand the insults, Moses realized, but he was getting the tone of the argument well enough.

"The best part of you run down the crack of your mama's ass an' got et by a horned toad when you was borned, you piss-faced, frog-eatin' son of nine kinds of New Orleans yeller whores! I could take you on jus' as I am, without no knife an' no gun. Shitfire! Untie me an' I'd take on the whole sorry dickless bunch of you single-handed with my pecker strapped down, you bunch of gut-eatin', prick-faced, cunt-mouthed sorry excuses for horseshit. I could whip ever' sorry son of a bitch amongst you with the dried-up pecker of a cut boar hog an' have enough left of it to cornhole ever' goddamn one of you till you wasn't nothin' but the greasy pile of back-shootin', bushwhackin', prickless dog puke God meant you to be."

The medicine man began a louder chant, apparently to drown out the white man's insults. He danced slowly over to the victim, who continued his tirade until it deteriorated into a series of inarticulate sputterings and slowly died away. He was weak, Moses realized, and this was all he could muster as a final show of strength. The medicine man took advantage of the pause to ask some questions in lilting prairie song that Moses recognized as Comanche. It was an uncertain language, and Moses had never heard it spoken at any length. When sung or chanted, he thought, it was beautiful, but it was not a tongue white men mastered easily, and Moses had never met anyone but an Indian who could claim to speak it well.

That the Comanche shaman wanted something from his captive was clear. As his questions persisted he became more agitated, and the captive only replied, "Go to hell, you goat-pricked bastard," or "In a pig's asshole, you pecker-headed frog-fucker." One of the braves rose and came over beside him. He was tired of the man's tone. He pulled a cedar brand from the fire and waved it threateningly in the captive's face. Moses could not see what was in the victim's eyes, but he heard his words ringing out defiantly. "Go on, you pecker-headed son of a bitch," he cackled. Moses's skin crawled with the laugh's undertones of madness. "Hell's fire! I been hurt worse'n this by a Mescan whore, an' I had to *pay* her to do it!" At last the medicine man waved the angry young brave away and moved back and resumed his chanting position, and another brave rose to resume the torture.

"Get fucked with the diseased prick of a Chinese manwhore, you web-footed, inbred, six-fingered son of a frog-peckered coyote!" the man screamed when the heated stick punctured the scabs on his side. "I hope you shit hot cactus," he gasped. His head hung down between his lashed arms, but he gulped back tears and croaked, "I hope you piss razors an' all your wives sleep with pigs. I hope your daughters're born with horns an' hide, an' all your horses die of bloat an' fall on your sons."

As the curses continued, the scout eased away from the lip of the draw. He scrambled back quickly to where Frank waited. Every foot of the way, he tried to think of some method of rescuing this incredibly brave man.

Frank was no help at all. He offered two suggestions: They go in shooting and kill every Indian in sight, or, being vetoed on that because of the common sense that Moses didn't want to rouse the main Comanche camp, they just ride around and forget the whole thing.

"We jus' rode off an' forgot Ambrose an' his boy, didn't we? You was ready to do that right enough," Frank argued. "I don't see this as bein' that much diff'rent. That whole train's waitin' on us to get through. We ain't goin' to do nobody no good if we get our ownselves killed over some ol' man who's likely dead by now anyway." He paused for a moment, and Moses heard the same edge he had noticed before creeping into Frank's voice. "I don't see this as bein' any diff'rent'n them Mescans. Only this time, that Sterlin' girl ain't here to mess things up."

Moses found the white man's willingness to abandon one of his own kind repulsive and shocking. Ambrose stayed behind by his own foolish choice. This man was clearly not a fool. He was foul and probably stupid, but he was able to endure incredible pain silently, and Moses admired that. The scout found that he was as committed to saving the mysterious, profane white man as he was to saving the train. The big difference was that he was reasonably sure he *could* save the man. The train's salvation was another matter. This was a positive action he could —needed—to take, and he wasn't about to just ride off and leave the man to a horrible death.

He didn't feel like arguing with Frank about it. There was no way to explain it, and he didn't want to try. For a moment they sat in silence, Frank nervously plucking grass stems and chewing them.

Creeping back to the horses, Moses removed a canteen and then crawled back to Frank. He poured out a bit of water onto the dirt at the base of the grass and stirred it around until he had created a small mudhole. The storms of that and previous nights had left the ground soft, and he had no problem mixing up a rich, thick goo with the hilt of his knife. He then began stripping off his clothes.

"What the hell're you doin'?" Frank demanded in an almost audible voice.

"Hush," Moses ordered, "an' listen. I'm fixin' to try to scare them Indians off, or at the best, get in an' get 'em quiet. You cover me, but don't shoot. Not 'less it looks like it ain't workin' or they start shootin' first. I don't think they ever seen a nigger with a naked head before. Least, I'm bankin' on it. If they have, then they got me. If they get me, you get the horses an' get the hell out of here. Ride south by east, an' you'll make a settlement or Fort Richardson sooner or later. Don't stop for nothin'."

"We're stoppin' here."

"I ain't lettin' them Comanche have that poor son of a bitch," Moses hissed back. "So you cover me if you can, an' if you can't without bringin' the whole bunch down on us, then you skedaddle. An' I mean it." Moses waited a moment to see if Frank would bristle from orders from a colored man.

"Don't worry," Frank said after a moment. Something in his voice said that he would do his part. Wordlessly, the scout finished his preparations.

His plan was simple, if jumping right into the middle of a bunch of Comanche in the dark or any other time, especially half naked and without a gun to back himself up, could ever be simple. He stripped completely free of his buckskins and removed his union suit. With his knife he cut off the leg of the long, dirty fabric and made a rude breechcloth, which he strapped around his groin. He then smeared the reddish-brown dirt all over his face and body to give himself a rough look, and he applied loose strands of grass all over himself wherever the mud was thick enough to support it. Then he stood up.

Frank blew out in a soundless whistle, "You look like the devil hisself. You'd scare the piss outta me, daylight or dark."

Moses grinned and squatted down again. With his knife, he opened five .55-caliber cartridges, then poured the powder into his left palm, which he clenched tightly into a fist. He had seen similar tricks during medicine shows, but he knew the showmen used a specific kind of powder, the kind the men with cameras used to flash light on their subjects. He had no idea what would happen when raw gunpowder burned. He only hoped it would work.

"Whatever you do, don't shoot off no gun," he reminded Frank, and with his Bowie knife in one hand and the other tightly clenched, he then bent down and crawled back to the lip of the draw.

Once again, he found his path blocked by a giant ant bed, but he scurried directly across, trying to ignore the insects' painful bites. Then he found himself directly above the Indian camp. He waited and listened for a minute to his heart's pounding. The Indians were again seated, and the man was quiet, but he was still alive, breathing in long heaves.

Taking a deep breath, he stood full up on the edge of the depression and bent his knees. Then with a powerful jump and a whoop that he hoped would sound like the dead come back to life, he launched himself into the air and directly toward the bare spot next to the fire and across from the three braves.

When he landed, the first reaction he noticed was that the shaman's eyes flared with a sick recognition, as if a dreaded but expected guest had finally arrived. The sleeping brave rolled over, and the two squatting Indians scrambled to their feet, their hands reaching for Winchester carbines which lay beside them. But the only sound in the draw after Moses landed was a tearing scream from the captive white man, who turned his head just enough to catch a glimpse of Moses's naked, muddy body and bald head gleaming in the firelight. He now filled the small depression with a shriek greater than any brought forth from the Comanche torture.

Moses instantly opened his hand over the fire and dumped in the powder, and the flames jumped and sparked wildly. Gray smoke rose rapidly and filled the area, and the braves brought their hands up over their eyes to shield themselves. Moses plunged his Bowie knife directly into the breast of the nearest brave and withdrew it quickly. The blade went in and out of the Indian's chest so rapidly that Moses was stunned for a moment and squinted through the smoke to make sure that he had really stabbed him, but almost immediately the ground between them was covered with blood. He blinked, and then with a quick backward motion, he slashed at the other Indian. The knife caught him under his chin and opened his throat just as he was struggling to bring up his carbine and lever in a shell. The brave launched himself backward, bubbling and gurgling, his hands jammed against the sharp tear in his neck. Behind the scout, the captive continued to scream, and Moses turned to face the remaining Indians, but the medicine man was gone.

The other Indian, his eyes wide with fear, backed quickly away. Before Moses could catch him, he disappeared into the grass. He had taken a step to follow the brave into the darkness when a muffled thump told him that Frank had indeed covered him. But his satisfaction faded when hoofbeats in the distance also came to his ear. The medicine man had made good his escape. Moses smiled with the thought of the tale he would doubtless be bringing into the Comanche camp. Not only had he run away, he also had left the slain warriors behind him.

The white man's vocal cords finally gave out, and his screams were reduced to a whimpering cry, which Moses ignored while he checked out the camp's perimeter. No sentries were posted at all, not even the usual feists the Indians were so fond of keeping around even the smallest camps.

Moses moved quickly to him and cut him loose from the wheel. He collapsed at the scout's feet as if dead. His voice was hoarse, and he pointed down to his legs and made a slashing motion with the side of his hand. "Sons of bitches cut my leg," he said. "Can't walk. Can't run. Red bastards!" He turned a cloudy eye toward the scout. "You scared the shit outta me, boy," he said. "But it's a good thing you come when you did. I'd had to take 'em on by myself in a few minutes."

Moses hefted him up as Frank came into the firelight leading the dead Indians' horses and their own, and they hoisted the crippled man over a pony and mounted quickly.

"Which way?" Frank called, and Moses pulled up. He didn't know how badly the man was hurt, but he didn't want to ride in the wrong direction and find the medicine man's friends coming back.

"North," the man gasped. "Ought to lift these ol' boys' hair, but there ain't time. Let's go." He was slung over an Indian's horse, and his wind was restricted. "Get the hell out of here 'fore I die of bein' rescued," he wheezed. At his instructions, they turned their horses toward the North Star and rode as fast as they could away from the bloody draw.

The moon lit their way, and soon they came upon another of the small cedar groves. Here, Moses got his clothes from his saddlebags and began trying to wipe off the dried mud so he could dress while Frank did what he could to doctor the white man they had rescued.

Since leaving the draw, except for curses when his horse jostled him, the rescued man had said nothing at all. Now that Frank worked on him, he resumed his habit of swearing loudly with every move Frank made.

"Goddamn, *goddamnit*, that hurts!" he yelled at the hapless Frank, who finally was afraid to touch him in any way. "I swear to the bleedin' and crucified Christ, you boys're worse than Comanche when it comes to givin' a man pain. Hand to God, I'd rather shit a burnin' crosstie than have you keep pokin' an' proddin' at me."

Frank finally gave up, handed the man the wet cloth, and squatted near him. He tried to explain who they were, where they were going, and what they were trying to do.

Then, with Moses gesturing all the while for him to hold his voice down, the man burst out with a loud laugh.

"Richardson! Griffin! I'll be cornholed by a horned toad! You can't be meanin' it!" He looked at them through the moonlight and saw them staring back at him with open mouths. "Why, boys!" he cackled and slapped his wounded legs. "That ain't goin' to do no good. No good at all!" He laughed again. "We'll jus' have to take care of it all our ownselves! An' we will! Just let me get my wind, an' them folks'll be all right. Sure they will! They'll be jus' fine as fat, or my name ain't Carlson Colfax, an' by God, you can bet your last screamin' eagle that's what my mama called me!"

PART THREE

THE GAMBLER

CHAPTER ONE

1

AS SOON AS MOSES FRANKLIN AND FRANK HERBERT rode off and the night's silence testified that they were safely away, wagon master Cleveland Tollhouse Graham had the dead that could be safely reached moved to one of the concave openings toward the end of the wagon line. While some men attended to that, he rounded up some women and ordered them to create a makeshift infirmary to treat the wounded in another, larger cave. Not without intention, it was the Sterling cave he chose. It was the largest of the bunch, something, Graham reminded himself, that should have been expected of Jack Sterling. Even so, he selected it for the hospital because he correctly guessed that Aggie Sterling would be the least likely to object to having her temporary home invaded. Even as he did it, though, Graham realized it was a mistake. Most of the females he approached just looked at him and went on about their business, fussing with their belongings and people in the light of shielded lanterns and small, flickering torches. For all the attention they paid him, he thought, he might as well have been one of the braying mules that stood hungrily awaiting fodder between the wagons and the bluff.

The women's indifference to his authority infuriated Graham, but he truly couldn't blame them. Most of them had family members of their own who had also been wounded, although not seriously enough to be moved into the hospital. Others had taken over caring for the children of the dead women who still lay out on the creek's gravel banks. Those whose husbands and sons were hurt badly enough to be moved into Aggie's cave came willingly enough at first, but even they usually had other family to tend. As soon as their loved ones were made as comfortable as possible, they returned to their wagons or to one of the caves their remaining family had claimed.

Only Aggie Sterling and her sister, Annie, a child herself, took on the work with anything like a wholehearted spirit, Graham observed during one of his several passes by the cave. But then, he reminded himself, Aggie had no one else to look after other than her sister and her brother, who was fully grown, or near it, and whom Graham had just seen drowsing under their wagon near the cattle, a Henry rifle cradled in his arms.

The deeper reason for the women's refusal to stay in the hospital cave, Graham realized, was Aggie herself. And, he guiltily acknowledged, that was his fault as much as anyone's. She was a pariah now. She had taken up with a colored man. Even those who didn't much care who Aggie "took up" with regarded this shotgun-toting blond teenager as something of a harridan. They were aware that it had been she who defied Graham and her own father for the sake of a bunch of dead Mexicans. And it had been she, they all knew by now, who had thrown her gun down on Graham again when he proposed to shoot the injured women. For her own sake, he should have put her in her place both times, but he hadn't. He couldn't.

Whispers about her behavior had been general ever since the previous afternoon, although no one had said anything aloud to Graham's face.

Will Golden's wife was likely behind this, Graham thought as he stalked the wagon line and squinted into the darkness of the creek: she, Golda Runnels, Glorietta Fulbright, and a handful of others. He knew the shrewish woman was moving from one knot of women to the other, sowing suspicion and hate as a farmer planted corn. With fear and grief to nurture it, Graham knew, that sort of thing could take root and grow rapidly. He wanted to put an end to it, but there wasn't time. Dawn would be breaking soon, and with the sun would come the Comanche.

Since their confrontation the afternoon before, Aggie had barely spoken to Graham. When he stuck his bullet-shaped head inside the cave, she offered him a quick smile, but she said nothing and received his instructions with a quick shimmer of irony behind her eyes. He couldn't understand how she could function, having lost so much in so short a time. Most girls her age would be hysterical—as, indeed, many were, he reminded himself as he heard weeping coming from the train's new orphans up and down the line. But she was harder than most girls her age. She reminded him of soldiers he had known, men who watched as their brothers and messmates were shot down beside them and, with barely a scowl of regret, went on loading and shooting at an often invisible enemy.

On his next pass, he entered the cave and watched her organizing the hospital and gathering buckets and lighting lamps while she gave instructions to the few women who were willing to work. With the exception of Hannah Morgan—whose independence Graham admired—the women were no older than Aggie. She ordered them about in a quick, singsong voice that suggested they were canning vegetables or preparing a Sunday feast rather than setting up a crude hospital for horribly wounded men. He was shocked to find such qualities in a woman, but somehow he wasn't as surprised to find them in her. He had known she was special from the first time he met her.

That was why he was in love with her.

He had not easily admitted how he felt about Jack Sterling's yellow-haired daughter, but when he finally uttered the words to himself, silently and in such frank tones that his insides tightened, he knew they were true. It had been true ever since he first saw her in Jefferson, and its truth had been so strong even then that he had accepted Jack's insane scheme even though any rational man could see how profound the odds were against it. And it was still true. It bound him as the lashings on the wagons bound the whiskey kegs. It held him when she stood against him back in the Mexican's cedar grove, and it had never been more true than when she leveled her shotgun at his middle and told him she would kill him. It took all his willpower to keep from reaching out and touching her. The sight of her made him ache all over.

Some men had nothing more than minor scratches and punctures, and once he was satisfied that all the badly wounded were being cared for, Graham moved down the line of wagons and rousted those with lesser injuries out from wherever they had taken refuge and placed them in shooting positions. Men like Karl Runnels and Virgil Hollister who had painful but not really serious wounds were propped up behind makeshift shooting loops. Graham busied a number of the children with fortifying them with ammunition and canteens of fresh water.

Twice yesterday, he recalled with a wince, they had been surprised. They weren't prepared to defend the train against a flock of geese. When the Indians came again, they would be ready. He ordered two men to each end of the creek bank to keep a picket watch. He instructed them to drag up some fallen Indian ponies and hide behind them. As soon as they heard splashing in the water, they were to send up a whistle and then take cover behind the same dead beasts and provide an enfilading fire on the Indians when they emerged from the creek.

He also posted some men up on the narrow ledge that ran atop the cave entrances along the side of the butte. He had seen Moses climb up there the day before, and he decided it would be a great shooting stand for anyone who could hunker down behind the joint fir, scrub cedar, and prickly pear clumps that clung to the limestone. The men accepted their assignments reluctantly, but Graham refused to hear their protests. He ordered them to keep a sharp lookout, and, when the Indians came back, to maintain a more or less steady fire into the cedar thickets across the creek. He congratulated himself on his defenses, and he cursed his black scout once more for not thinking of even better ways of withstanding a Comanche attack.

The sentries departed to their various posts, and Graham cautioned them to take canteens so they wouldn't be tempted to come crawling back for water. He didn't want any slip-ups or weak-sister carelessness, he told them. Eventually the men were equipped and ready, and they began to slip off into the darkness of the crossing to their various positions.

A surprising number of the men still were using old Enfields: powerful weapons, but slow to reload. He had also seen more than a couple of new Henrys which would hold sixteen rounds each. His own '73 Winchester held fifteen rounds and gave him some comfort, but he knew that there were too few modern weapons, and too few men among the settlers who knew how to fire them. He gratefully acknowledged that most of the Indians were horrible shots, and more injuries had been caused by lance and arrow than by rifle balls. He also admitted that most of the whites couldn't hit much of what they shot at either. Pierce was right: They were too excited, too damned scared.

By the time light was appearing in the eastern sky, Graham felt he had done all he could to fortify the wagon line. He stopped by once more to check on the more seriously wounded in what everyone was now calling "the hospital cave." The Sterling cavern went back almost twenty-five yards into the limestone bluff, where it narrowed and lowered and finally terminated in a bubbling spring. The girls who had been there before, even Annie Sterling, were absent. Except for Glorietta Fulbright and a woman named Kruikshank, who sat beside their severely injured men and wept and mopped their foreheads, there were no helpers in there now. They scowled at Aggie when she passed by, as if dismayed that she was offering smiles and humming softly while moving among the wounded men.

Aggie paid Graham no more mind than she did the two women's glares. He felt queasy as his eyes scanned the dim light of the cave and the stink of blood came to him in rich, salty waves. He couldn't stomach a hospital of any sort. The other women ought to help more, he thought with a renewed rush of resentment mixed with guilt. He ought to go and make them.

Outside, he discovered Annie, Hannah, and several of the younger girls tearing bandages out of bedsheets and petticoats and wagon canvas, and the sound of the ripping cloth brought back other unpleasant memories. Graham was grateful for the chance to leave the area. His latest inspection reminded him of the lack of medicine on the train. He assessed an immediate need and reluctantly detailed some men to bring a keg of whiskey from the Sterling wagon inside. They had no other form of antiseptic or painkiller. More losses, he decided. Take another card.

2

THE COMANCHE CAME AGAIN AT DAWN, JUST AS GRAham had predicted. The wagon master had settled himself on a keg beside his wagon and was struggling to open his last can of peaches with his single hand when a whistle from one of his outposts caused him to drop the half-opened tin. A shiver of terror ran all over his skin.

He grabbed up his Winchester and swung around to meet the threat. In his ears he could hear his voice yelling the alarm, but he was so excited he was barely conscious that he was doing the shouting. Even so, long before the first Indians came into sight, he heard the reassuring clicks and snaps of hammers being cocked in readiness to meet the new assault. From across the creek, white and blue puffs of smoke began to appear, and he knew that there was no doubt that the new attack was real.

The sun wasn't risen high enough to illuminate the crossing properly when the first Comanche appeared, but the brightly painted Indians rode screaming out of the shadows around the bend from the opposite end of the creek, yip-yipping and brandishing their bows and rifles, shields and lances with a renewed fury. As they approached, Graham saw the attackers' faces were painted black. When they galloped through the stream, the entire creek seemed filled with demons whose white teeth and bright, flashing eyes penetrated the mist like horrible beacons.

For a moment, no one did anything. The settlers and their wagon master were frozen in place, overwhelmed by the feral warriors who pushed their ponies through the turgid water. Finally, Graham flopped down under his wagon and began firing. His first shot unhorsed a pudgy brave and sent him somersaulting into the creek. The action awakened others, and from up and down the line, gunfire became general.

A great blue shadow covered the crossing when the Indians came splashing from the creek, and the settlers found themselves firing steadily but uncertainly at ghostly shapes that milled around on the gravel bank and tried to form a line of attack. They seemed impervious to the settlers' bullets as they galloped back and forth, screaming and taunting the whites, whose furious volleys were having small effect on their numbers.

They sat their ponies better than they had the previous day, Graham noticed, and their covering fire seemed heavier as well. Arrows and bullets ricocheted off of the limestone butte, and one or two wagons were immediately so bristled with shafts that they looked like absurd bushes sprouting feathers instead of leaves.

The remuda near the far end of the wagon fort danced and tore at ropes, and the Indians kept feinting toward the milling horses. The remains of Jack Sterling's cattle were bawling loudly. In spite of Jason Sterling's efforts, several head bolted away and raced up past Hollister's blocking wagon to the comparative safety of the open prairie. Some of the defenders managed to spot each foray the Comanche made in the direction of the horses and beat it off. Even so, two or three of the mounts, including Graham's gray and the white mare Aggie had ridden the night before and several mules, managed to break free and to join the melee in the center of the crossing.

Graham's organization of the wagons' defenses was working. He knew a thing or two about defensive fighting, he told himself as he emptied his magazine into the boiling smoke that hung before him like a series of curtains. He had learned it at Pea Ridge and Shiloh; and at Vicksburg he had watched a forted city fall because of inadequate preparation. He didn't need some ignorant bunch of sodbusters telling him how to meet a savage enemy.

These weren't tough frontiersmen or even quickly and poorly trained recruits, Graham ruefully acknowledged as he observed shot after shot going wild and useless past the screaming Indians, but then, he also admitted, neither was he. Some of them were certainly veterans, but the war was a long time over, and few had shot anything more dangerous than a deer or squirrel since Appomattox. Now they were merchants, farmers, craftsmen, who had joined his expedition out of the promise of a better life.

He fired and ratcheted shell after shell into his rapidly heating Winchester. The Indians were unable to get close enough to threaten seriously the wagons' defenders. He might have had to kick these greenhorns into something resembling bravery or at least watchfulness, but now, as the Indians found the wagon line to be a continuous explosion of gunfire, it was clear that he knew what he was doing. More than he could say for that goddamn nigger scout, he thought as he reloaded.

The settlers were at least less shock-stricken than before, and the Indians were clearly surprised. The defenders weren't just firing blindly, nor were they rushing out in a panic to meet the savage horsemen. Instead, they remained concealed and lay down a steady if more or less inaccurate stream of lead toward the prancing Indian ponies. The bodies still littering the gravel beach were all certainly dead by now, and because there was no white person exposed enough to be captured by the attacking savages, the settlers no longer tried to hold back and pick their shots carefully.

After the attack had gone on but a few minutes, Graham squinted through the whorls of smoke and made a satisfied count of more than a dozen unhorsed red men flailing about in the creek's waters or writhing on the killing ground between the wagons and the water's edge. Graham's war experience had taught him that a virtual curtain of fire would discourage even the most stubborn attackers. Still, if more of the whites were decent marksmen, there wouldn't be a single Indian alive anywhere in sight, and they might give up and leave the train to move on in peace.

But Graham had small hope that these people could shoot straight. He had seen trained soldiers loose volley after volley into charging Rebel troops seemingly without hitting anyone or discouraging the zealous, wild charge or diminishing the terrorizing yell emerging from the collective Confederate throats. It was, he recalled, no less horrifying than the yip-yipping of the Comanche as they danced their ponies up and down the creek's bank.

The plan had gone sour, Graham concluded as he worked his rifle's lever and sought a target in the smoke that once again filled the canyon. Moses had warned him that if they continued to delay, things could go against them. But Graham wanted to believe that for once his luck would hold, that if they couldn't avoid it, at least they could shoot their way out of any trouble that came their way. He had never expected it to be as easy as he had presented it to the settlers back in Jefferson. He had only half believed it himself. He certainly never thought they could all make it all the way to New Mexico without some losses. Losses, to his mind, were like ante, like folding fair hands early in the game to see where the power lay, who was bluffing, who wasn't. But he never thought they would lose everything, and the possibility made him wince.

Well, he thought, he was in too deep to fold now. There was nothing else to do but to play out the hand and hope that the next card would give him something to bluff with.

He set the rifle aside and drew his Colt's .44 and emptied it as well. His shoulder ached from the recoil of the rifle, but he had to admit that he stood a better chance of hitting something with it. He took it up once more and reloaded it from a greasy box of cartridges that was spilled open next to him.

"Niggers, Indians, Mescans, and civilian soldiers," Graham muttered as he propped his Winchester on his stump and fed the magazine once more. "Country's goin' to hell in a handcart full of Mescans, pushed by a nigger, chased by an Indian, an' guarded by some green Dutchman who can't tell a rifle from a shovel." He fired at a brave with a single elk antler protruding from a huge headdress. He was rearing his horse and waving a brightly painted shield while he yelled encouragement to his comrades. Graham's bullet struck the shield and knocked the brave off his horse. Smoke covered him immediately, and Graham couldn't tell if he had actually wounded or killed the Indian or merely unhorsed him.

A few whites were taking arrows, and more than one fell when a bullet from across the creek found its mark, but Graham sensed from the attack's outset that the whites had the edge. In a gap between the clouds of smoke, he saw that the Indians were withdrawing into the water and pushing their way out of sight.

As the last brave carrying a wounded or dead comrade across his pony's back disappeared around the bend in the creek, Graham relaxed almost to the point of complete collapse. He shut his eyes, held his breath, and tried to squeeze reality out of his mind. He had never been a man who could deal with more than one situation at a time, especially when a crisis demanded multiple considerations. He wanted to simplify all this, boil it down to elements he could assess all at once. But when he opened his eyes again, the swirls of bitter smoke and smell of blood mixed with the cries of the wounded. Shouted taunts from delighted and unscathed defenders—many of whom were still shooting although their targets had disappeared—infected his consciousness and reminded him of the desperate nature of his situation.

Further, he thought uncomfortably, he was filthy. He was always a fastidious man, careful of his clothes, mindful of how he smelled. Grit had worked its way into every fold of skin and ground away under his eyelids. The fingernails of his hand were encrusted with filth, and between his legs, he could feel a galling irritation where his thighs met the seams of his underwear.

Although the noise and smoke of battle had not yet ended, some of Golden's chickens had escaped their cages and were pecking around the bodies between the wagon fort and the creek, seeking insects in the loose stones of the small waterway's beach. Graham watched them with unwilling fascination. One hen was perched on old Anthem's shoulder and raised her feathers in a wide fluffing motion; one claw clutched at the bloody gap in the old man's skull. Graham reminded himself to tell the two North Carolinians who had brought the pigs to keep them tied to wagon wheels. There was nothing he could do about the barnyard fowl, but he had seen what hogs would do to corpses, and the memory made him gag.

Graham's experience with Indians was limited, and with hostile Indians, nil. What he knew about Comanche he had learned over gambling tables in the flats and small towns that had grown up around the forts on the Indian Line. But he had seen what they could do, and like most men in Texas he had heard stories. Some of the tales were vivid enough to keep a man awake nights, and he gritted his teeth with particular recollections. But he couldn't remember ever hearing of a war party—even a major war party as this one seemed to be—laying siege for more than a few hours.

These Comanche were behaving contrary to common sense. They were clearly outgunned, and their losses were heavy. But they continued to assault the wagon fort. White men, even Rebels, would pull out, Graham told himself. Hell, even a bunch of niggers would have better sense than to keep coming in the face of this kind of defense.

He forced his body to action and pulled himself up. Tipping back his hat, he looked at the battered and stripped wagons, at the wounded draft animals and bloody whites who stood guard over their only earthly possessions. What could the Indians want badly enough to keep coming at them? There were several possible answers—scalps, women, guns, and, of course, the blessed whiskey. Those were the only things he and the others were desperate enough to die to defend. But was that enough for the redskins to die for?

Usually, he reminded himself, it was horses that stimulated Indians, but few of the animals in the train were of sufficient quality to merit this kind of desperate attack, even for Comanche. Only a few good saddle mounts were in the remuda anyway, and the raiders already had some of them in hand. The only horse he could lay any claim to now was Jack Sterling's big black, and that truly belonged to Aggie and her siblings. And he knew the Comanche wouldn't put this much stock into the draft animals. The oxen made poor eating—even a Comanche must choke on ox meat—and Moses was right about mules. Indians regarded mules as the most contemptible quadrupeds in the world. An animal that looked and acted so much like a horse but couldn't reproduce itself was an abomination to a race that prized equine virtues so highly, Graham knew. It was about the only point he could think of on which he shared wholehearted agreement with the Comanche.

He cogitated on the matter but shortly. The puzzle of what determined the Indians to risk their lives time and again was not really confusing at all: It *was* the whiskey, he told himself with a definite nod. The thought angered him, for it was the whiskey more than anything else that Graham was prepared to give his own life for. Without it, his future wouldn't amount to cold supper. It was the key, his hole card. Jack Sterling had dealt it, and Graham had agreed—with himself as much as anyone—to play it. He wasn't about to walk—or be driven—away from it.

Now certain that the attack was over and the retreat wasn't some sort of ruse, Graham yelled for a cease-fire up and down the line. Indian snipers in the cedar were still a problem, but for some reason they weren't shooting much. He was, Graham told himself, learning to fight Indians in a proper manner. No more whites had been carried off in this last onslaught, and that, in spite of the newly wounded and possibly dead men who lay behind the wagons' defenses, he counted as a victory. Graham liked to reduce things to basic denominations, and a victory, however temporary or qualified, was one of the few possibilities that presented itself to him in such clear terms.

He saw his pickets coming in, scrambling over the makeshift defenses with big grins on their faces. One of them was pulling a terrified black-headed teenaged girl behind him. Graham immediately recognized her as Frank Herbert's daughter, Lottie.

"She was in Hollister's wagon," the man Graham remembered to be named Pete Hightower panted. He scrambled over a singletree and jerked the girl after him. She looked wild, her hair flying around her face like so many strands of greasy string. Her eyes were dazed and her dress was torn open; she made no attempt to conceal an exposed breast. Graham looked away, but his eyes strayed back to the dark nipple that seemed to stare accusingly at him from the upturned bosom. He had forgotten about her completely in the midst of his other preparations and activities, and he was embarrassed more by her forcing that recollection on him than he was by her nakedness. He felt himself redden.

"Get her back to the hospital cave," he grunted, turning away from the half-nude youngster with consternation when he realized that his eyes were again resting on the small nude breast. "An' cover her up, for God's sake."

Hightower looked her up and down as if he just noticed her exposure. He stripped off his filthy coat and wrapped her in it, then picked her up and slung her over his shoulder and carried her away. The rest of the sentries were as excited as Hightower, but more because they were stunned to find themselves alive after the attack. Grover Hildebrandt, a huge man who always seemed to wear three or four layers of clothes regardless of the temperature, kept poking his body in various places as if he expected to discover a wound.

Graham walked away from their rapid exchanges of stories of courage and fright and quickly inspected the men who remained where they had been posted on the low ledge. They, too, had come through the attack unharmed. "Good goddamn idea," he congratulated himself.

He completed his transit of the wagon fort without checking in the hospital cave. He didn't want to face that until he had to. He sat down heavily on a wooden box, sucked on a fresh cigar, and stuck his boots out in front of him. Was he the only one on the train with any sense at all? He wasn't an Indian fighter. He wasn't any kind of fighter. That was why he had hired that colored boy in the first place. A piece of tobacco stubbornly clung to his tongue, and he picked it off with a dirty finger. Moses's main job was to prevent surprises, but he had failed. It was, Graham told himself, about what he should have expected.

Fatigue suddenly gripped him, and Graham had trouble concentrating on his body's actions sufficiently to bite off the smoke's end. He was not a man who liked surprises, not unless he was the one arranging them. He had been on the giving and receiving end of surprises most of his life, and he found that one sensation could be as exciting as the other was devastating. But as every time before, he had survived, at least so far. It was one thing he seemed always able to do.

The thought bothered him, and it had caused him more than one nightmare in his life. Why should he live when others died so horribly? Why should he be the only one to walk away from death? He had done it during the war, before and since several times, and each time seemed to increase his feeling that he was supposed to have died years ago, to have been killed along with other men he trusted and who trusted him. Each time death seemed to stalk him, always wiping out everyone around him, he had the uneasy sensation that a huge mistake had been made, that he was the one death wanted; others simply got in the way. It had made him hard, cold, and distant with everyone he met, but it hadn't stopped him from continuing to try to find a way to be happy, to feel normal. He looked down at the leather covering over the stump where his hand had been. He hadn't always been unscathed, he reminded himself. He had taken his losses, but he failed to acknowledge, even in his most private thoughts, that the real scars, the real losses, were not visible.

3

CLEVELAND TOLLHOUSE GRAHAM WAS A "HARD knocks" man who had etched out a fairly good life in Ohio before the war. He grew up in a household full of books and decided even before he could read very well that he would be a teacher, a schoolmaster. The Ohio frontier did not offer him the educational opportunities to fulfill his dream, however, and he was barely in the regular habit of scraping the auburn whiskers from his face when he met and married Emma Knight, the youngest daughter of a neighboring farmer.

He still planned to find a way to obtain the education he needed in order to teach. He spent his days plowing the tough Ohio soil and attending to chores around their twenty-five acres of wooded land, and his evenings squinting at the narrow print in the several books his father consented to lend him.

Things were rocky from the start. Shortly after his son, Jonathan, was born, Emma, barely sixteen, contracted a strange fever and lay three weeks writhing in bed, bathed in sweat and yet freezing with chills. Frightening spots developed on her face, neck, and arms, and he felt helpless bathing her thrashing body with vinegar and trying to quiet their tiny son. Finally he sent a freed Negro who leased a nearby farm to summon a doctor to come from distant Cincinnati. The black man was three days returning, by which time Emma had fallen into a deep, quiet sleep. The freedman's eyes widened and he shivered with fear when Graham told him the fever had broken.

"Doc Allways say you got to burn her if'n that happen," he quaked out. "He say it the plague fever. He say it the mos' cantagerous sickness they is, an' Doc Allways say when she sleepin' an' not wakin' up she 'bout to die.

That when she the mos' cantagerous, an' you and the baby'll get it for shore." He paused for courage before continuing. "When she die, he say, you got to burn her an' ever'thin' 'round her, ever'thin' she touch. The cabin an' the whole sheebang. Else you an' the baby'll get it then for shore. He say he comin' direc'ly, but if she go to sleep an' die, you to go on ahead an' burn her, or you an' the baby get it next."

Graham sent the old colored man away. He wasn't stupid. He had read of plagues and poxes, and he had never heard of such extreme measures except during the bubonic plague of Europe. But he also knew Dr. Allways, a harried, elderly man who had arrived two days after Jonathan's birth and pronounced him fat and fit. He seemed competent. The Negro had carried the doctor's instructions back to Graham, and he might be jeopardizing his own child by waiting any longer. He paced and held the baby and watched his wife's lifeless body in the oil lamp's light and worried.

Another day passed, and true to the Negro's report of the doctor's prognosis, Emma's sleep deepened even more; she seemed to stop breathing during the night. He put his head to her chest and heard no heartbeat; he held his fingers to her throat and felt no pulse. Jonathan wailed during the examination, and he went to pick up his infant. Suddenly remembering the Negro's words, he almost dropped the child as he quickly replaced him in the wooden cradle. He ran to the fireplace, where he thrust his fists into hot soup, scalding away any infection he might have carried from his wife to his son.

With his hands sticky and smarting, Graham stood holding Jonathan in his arms in the cabin's dooryard and wept as he looked down at the gurgling infant. He couldn't bear the thought of burning his wife's body and the cabin it had taken him nearly a year to build. But the idea that he was somehow endangering his young son and himself by not following the doctor's orders frightened him. After nearly two hours of fretting anxiety, he carried the child to the clearing's edge, then poured coal oil throughout the cabin, even on the still and blanketed body of his teenage wife. He stood looking at her covered body for a long time, and he thought he perceived her moving. But he wiped his eyes and studied her form in the dim yellow light of the lantern and knew that it was just his wishing it so that made her seem to be living still. He walked outside, paused again, and finally took a deep breath and set a burning brand to the house.

The flames were dying as morning's light guided the doctor down the forest trace to Graham's farm. Allways hobbled down from his horse and wearily limped over to where Graham stood with his baby in his arms watching the smoldering ruin of his home and his love.

"I see you followed my instructions," Allways said and lit a cigar. "Where is she?"

Graham nodded toward the ashes and char that had been his home. "In there."

"In there? Did she die?"

"You think I'd burn her alive?" Graham snapped so abruptly that Jonathan cried out and had to be rocked before he would quiet down.

"Are you sure?" The doctor took a step away from the youthful farmer.

"The nigger said that when she went to sleep and didn't wake up, she would die. And she died," Graham explained stupidly.

"She went to sleep? Quietly?" Allways's voice rose. "Before or after her fever broke?"

"After, like you said. She slept like a baby. She didn't wake up. Then she stopped breathin'." Graham's voice choked. He swallowed and tried to smile down at the squirming baby. "She looked so peaceful," he added quietly.

"And you burned her up? Why?"

"That's what you said to do." Graham looked suddenly at the doctor. "The nigger said you said it was the plague."

"No, goddamnit!" Allways swore. "I knew that black son of a bitch would get it wrong. I said the fever would spread *like* a plague if it wasn't stopped. People are coming down with it all over the county. I said that when she went to sleep that meant her fever broke and it was over—the fever was over—that you should burn the bedding, the mattress, even the cabin if you have to. But I didn't say to burn her body. Goddamnit!"

Graham stood and silently rocked on his heels for a moment. "Well, she was dead," he said flatly. "She stopped breathing."

"I sure as hell hope so," Allways replied more to himself than to Graham. "Sometimes—" Then he stopped and looked intently into the trees at the edge of the clearing.

"Sometimes what?"

Allways sighed. "I mean, I'm sure you know whether or not she was dead. People have died from this thing, whatever it is. But usually, most often, when the fever breaks and they quiet down and go to sleep, then it's over. The spots clear up. They usually get better."

Graham looked at him again. The spots, he remembered with growing horror, had vanished when he last inspected her. "She wasn't better," he said quickly. "She wasn't breathing."

"I expect she was gone, then." Allways pulled at his cigar. He kept his thoughts to himself for a moment, and then he burst out, "Sometimes a man watches his woman thrashing around with the fever for a long time, and sometimes . . . well, sometimes just sleeping quietly makes her look like she isn't breathing. Are you *sure* she stopped breathing?" Graham gaped at the medical man, and Allways reached out and grabbed him by the arm. His fingers buried themselves in Graham's flesh. "Jesus, man, are you sure? Did you put a looking glass to her nose? I never heard of anybody dying after the fever broke unless there was something else wrong. Did you put a looking glass to her nose? Are you goddamn sure she was dead?"

The cabin's ruins continued to smolder while Graham and his baby boy stood quietly next to the doctor. Something snapped inside him. He felt it. It wasn't a big thing, but thin, gossamer, like a cobweb in his mind. It broke as if strained by nothing more violent than a breath of air. "I'm sure," he said, but he made no effort to free himself from the doctor's painful grip. He just stared at the cabin.

"I hope to Christ you're right," Allways muttered. He released Graham's arm, and he limped sorely over to his horse and remounted. "I never meant for you to burn her," he said. "Or the cabin. You shouldn't have sent that nigger. Son of a bitch has probably got half the county burning cabins. You could just have buried her, burned the bedding. That was all, with only one of you sick with it. This thing's catching as it can be. It's a wonder you and the baby didn't get it." He jerked his horse's reins hard and pointed it again toward the trace. "I just hope she was dead," he said and disappeared into the trees.

"She was dead," Graham almost whispered as he rocked Jonathan softly and allowed tears to stream down his cheeks.

Graham stood for an hour longer. He then put the sleeping baby aside, went into the smoking rubble of his cabin, and wrapped the charred remains of his wife in a blanket and buried her. That afternoon, he rigged a sling for Jonathan to ride papoose-style on his back, mounted his horse, and rode to the Negro's cabin a quarter mile away.

When the black man emerged from his lean-to barn, where his mule was being treated for a chipped hoof, he spotted his neighbor, a long rifle cradled in his arm, sitting on his plow horse. He raised a weathered hand in greeting and opened a warm smile. He called out that he was genuinely glad that his fellow farmer was alive and apparently well and stepped forward with an invitation to climb down and join him in a glass of applejack. Graham calmly lifted his rifle and shot him directly through the head.

He dismounted, quieted his son, who had awakened and shrieked when the gun's explosion echoed through the woods, and dragged the corpse into the cabin. He fired the log building, and with the mule's screams lighting the forest's twilight, he rode away. The only regret he ever had about the incident was that he had killed the man with the first shot. He had planned only to injure him, tie him to his bed, and then burn him alive.

But he never thought again about whether or not Emma was alive or dead. As far as he was concerned, he had escaped the fever, and so had Jonathan, and that was enough. He didn't let himself think about what he might have seen just before he burned the cabin. He told himself he was lucky to have survived the disease. So he wrote to his and Emma's parents, and when Jonathan was old enough, he told him the same thing. He never visited his family again.

ALTHOUGH ONLY SEVENTEEN HIMSELF, and although he had never seen a deck of cards, Graham had already developed a gambler's philosophy about gains and losses. He lowered his bullet-shaped head in resignation to the unpleasant surprises of life and went to work in a tannery in the tiny community of Stout, Ohio, near Cincinnati. He hired a woman to look after his son during the day, worked hard, saved his money, and learned the trade of tanning leather. In a few years he went into partnership with a Frenchman, Claude Saban, and they founded their own tannery on the banks of the Ohio River.

They prospered at first, making a kind of pigskin leather fancied for gloves and other products, and their reputation grew. The growing enterprise led Graham up and down the Ohio and onto the Mississippi seeking hides that would meet Saban's exacting standards. It was on the riverboats as they plied the muddy waters of the rivers that Graham developed a taste for gambling, prostitutes, and whiskey. He worked, he told himself, for Jonathan, to give him chances that Graham felt he was himself cheated out of.

Even so, the idea of finding another woman to marry never occurred to him. His attitude toward the women he bedded in the brightly papered staterooms of the riverboats and riverside cathouses was that they helped him with an itch that chronically needed scratching. He sought out sexual union with a rough detachment that was unemotional and, to a great extent, void of lust. It was one of life's banalities, part of his regular habits, like bathing or changing his linen.

When Fort Sumter fell in 1861, Graham was in his mid-thirties. He had borrowed money from Saban to send Jonathan back East to obtain the schooling he himself had never had. He hoped that an education would prove valuable both to the boy and to himself. But Graham's plan was still vague, and it vanished entirely when Jonathan, barely twenty years old, wrote that he had left Harvard College and accepted a commission with the Army of the

Potomac under the colors of the state of New York. He sent home a studio picture of himself, resplendent in the uniform of a Zouave lieutenant.

At first Graham was surprised that he wasn't angry. He found that he seemed incapable of anger. Depression was all he could muster, and he became drunk for a fortnight and poured out his gall in the form of self-pitying mutterings to several women in a Cincinnati brothel who were glad for the money he paid them just to listen.

After a month or so, when no major fighting seemed to erupt along the Virginia frontier, Graham's mood improved. He decided that the war would be over quickly and that perhaps Jonathan's experience as an officer would be of value to him, to both of them, and he wrote an enthusiastic letter of support to his military son. He began to see the war as a kind of grand rumor that no one really believed would happen. There was bitter talk all along the Kentucky border, but almost everyone else he talked to agreed that to go to war over Negro slavery was inconceivable folly. Even the newspapers seemed to suggest that as soon as the South wearied of its boorish posturing and ran out of noble speeches, everyone would go home and things would return to normal.

The Affair at Blackburn's Ford changed all that for Graham and everyone else. Reports from the Kentucky papers of the Union rout, many edited by men loyal to the South, claimed a complete Confederate victory would be forthcoming before Christmas. It seemed to be a certainty. Graham agonized over continuing reports of Union disasters, of retreat after retreat, of inaction and inability to act, of incompetent but ambitious officers and paralyzed politicians.

Jonathan's letters did little to relieve Graham's worry. Now a captain, Jonathan complained that they did little more than march up and down the banks of the Potomac and occasionally retreat from inferior troops who never outnumbered them. The weather was horrible, Jonathan wrote, and the food was worse. The officers were discouraged, and most of the men wanted to go home. Some were going anyway, even if their enlistments weren't up. He complained about the lack of proper supply: uniforms, arms, horses, everything. Each letter tore Graham's heart and aroused forgotten emotions.

Finally, Graham made up his mind that he had to do something himself. Without a word to Saban, he rode into Cincinnati and joined the Army of the Ohio. Because he was one of the few men present who had business experience—and a horse—and who could read and write, he was commissioned a lieutenant, and he spent most of the winter months of 1862 gathering supplies and arranging to buy beef and corn and horseflesh for the growing Army of the Ohio. The assignment failed to please Graham, and he never ceased hoping for a chance to go east and fight alongside his son, to lend his growing experience in the Quartermaster Corps to relieve the suffering Army of the Potomac. But the new Commander in the West, George Pearson Buell, had other ideas and other orders.

One late February morning in 1862, Graham was approached by a major from Buell's staff.

"Are you the tanner?" the major asked, and Graham acknowledged that he was.

"Here are your orders. You leave tomorrow," the major said. He leaned down from his horse, handed Graham a folded paper, accepted a confused salute, and rode off. Graham was mystified. He was now assigned to an artillery company. The orders were signed by Buell himself. He sought the major, but he couldn't find him anywhere, and with a sense that a big mistake had been made, he finally took himself to the landing in Cincinnati the next morning and boarded a riverboat as he was ordered.

Captain Noah Spencer, a heavily bearded but callow boy who reminded Graham too much of Jonathan, explained the orders while the boat pulled away from the docks and made its way toward the Mississippi. The captain was assigned to take six Napoleon six-pound howitzers and attach himself temporarily to Samuel Curtis's command in southern Missouri to help him pursue and destroy Sterling Price's ragtag army of Arkansas and Texas volunteers. The severe terrain of the upper Ozarks combined with a harsh winter put a strain on the rest of the equipment, Captain Spencer explained, and together with the guns, which were loaded along the sides of the boat, they were carrying a shipment of leather harnesses, saddles, and other tack to

Curtis. He had requested an officer who knew something about working leather: hence, Graham.

Graham tried to explain that he was a tanner and knew little about repairing or working leather. Acquisition of hides had been his role in his old business, he went on, but the officer only shrugged and nodded toward a now invisible Cincinnati around a bend in the river. Graham swallowed a lump he was surprised to find in his throat at the thought of leaving what had been his home for so many years, surrendered to the logic of the military, lowered his head, and accepted his disappointment.

4

When they arrived at Curtis's command in northern Arkansas, the men who came with the cannon were nearly exhausted. After off-loading in St. Louis, they had expected wide-open roads such as they knew in Ohio to greet them. What they found instead were narrow, heavily wooded mountain traces which would barely pass for cowpaths in their experiences. The limbers and howitzers constantly stuck in the boggy lanes, which were alternately freezing over or running to mud, and it seemed to snow or sleet every day.

When they reached the Federal lines, every soldier Graham saw was freezing, hungry, discouraged. Across the newly dug battlements to the south of Sugar Creek, Graham could see the bright fires of the Confederate line. It was the closest he had been to the "enemy," a word he had difficulty applying to the Southern soldiers. Since leaving St. Louis, he had come to believe that the Northern troops—greenhorn immigrants and alley scum most of them, in Graham's opinion—lacked the collective power to stop the Southern armies. He wondered what these motley Union troopers might have in common with him or Jonathan.

The snow was heavy and wet, but it wasn't that cold, and much of it melted as soon as it struck the ground. Still, the chill made trench life miserable. Graham wearily hoisted himself up and went back to organize the men and start moving the guns into position. He had proved his uselessness as a leather worker one day out of St. Louis when he had failed to mend a broken harness effectively, and Spencer had ignored him until his regular lieutenant fell from a caisson, broke his leg, and had to be left behind. As they mounted up to continue their journey, Spencer rode up beside Graham and handed him the injured officer's cap and insignia. "You're in the artillery now," he said, laughing, "and I hope you know more about guns than you do about harnesses."

Graham confessed that he knew quite a bit less about guns, but Spencer assigned a sergeant, Desmond Malloy, to instruct the lieutenant in the fine points of cannonade, and by the time they reached the breastworks on the old Wire Road just west of Elkhorn Tavern, Graham was a well-tutored if untried expert in the art of artillery.

They moved the battery into position. Malloy set to work building a redan for the guns. In the distance Graham could hear bugles blowing Retreat as the day darkened into a ghostly, snowy twilight, and he realized he would see his first battle the next day. Except for Malloy, who had fought at Malvern Hill before being transferred west and who was the only real soldier in the outfit, none of the men had been in battle. Their confidence was not helped by the sounding of a forty-gun salute from the Confederate lines, a signal that a major general had arrived and brought more troops to the Rebel forces. Even from the distance, Graham felt the concussion of the artillery pieces.

Graham spent an anxious night, but when light grayed the pine trees atop the rocky rise of ground known as Pea Ridge, no attack came, and he was surprised by feeling let-down. Spencer went forward and strained his eyes through his glasses toward the Confederate line, and then he came running back to his guns.

"They're gone!" he announced breathlessly. "They've pulled out. Run off!" The young officer was grinning widely, and Graham was again reminded of Jonathan.

Malloy spat a glob of tobacco into the white snow and shook his head. "Never knowed Secesh to run," he said. "Not when they seen us all ready for 'em." He squinted through the snowy air toward the Union line. "I s'pect they'll be 'long direc'ly."

A half hour passed and the Federal troops roused and began moving about trying to warm themselves. A few fires were restoked and coffee and breakfast were made. Finally, Spencer ordered Graham to ride to Curtis's headquarters and find out if there were any new orders. Graham mounted his horse and rode past the seven or eight log cabins that called themselves Leesville up to the group of tents that marked the general's headquarters. There he found everyone in a complete panic.

The Rebels, it seemed, had stolen a march and were now *behind* the Union rear. The entire line had to turn to meet an impending attack. The major question was why it hadn't already started. At any moment, both Federal flanks could be rolled up and destroyed. The entire Union force had to be turned around, Graham learned. The battlements they had dug out of the frozen ground were useless; they were about to become mass graves for the defending Union troops unless a new front could be established in the former Federal rear. The only clear voice Graham could hear around the tents belonged to the German general, Osterhaus, who was demanding that they all surrender.

Graham remounted and rode hard back to Spencer's position. Couriers had already started the army's reversal, and Malloy and his crew were swinging the guns around and moving them forward and to the left to meet the anticipated Confederate attack. Spencer left Malloy and three of the guns with Graham and took the remaining trio of cannon to support the flank. Graham barely had his howitzers in their new positions when he heard the opening barrage behind him.

Soon the meadow in front of them filled with churning black smoke and bright flashes of explosions. Graham tried to steel himself against the noise and concussion of the guns, but every blast from their dark muzzles was a shock that seemed to roll the earth.

Rebel artillery answered, and Graham could hear nothing but the eruption of explosions all about him. His men worked feverishly to reload and shoot again. He still had not seen a single enemy soldier, yet the whine of Minié balls penetrated the huge cannons' booming often enough to warn him that they were targets for the unseen Rebels.

His ears were ringing and he felt helpless. Malloy's lessons fled his mind, and he stood uselessly by a cannon, his sword in one hand and his pistol in the other, while his men slaved away. He became fascinated by the crew's rhythm, mesmerized by their precision. They worked frantically, but they were somehow controlled, orderly, and, he hoped, effective.

The line of Union infantry broke all of a sudden, and Federals began streaming back toward the guns. Malloy shouted something at Graham, but he couldn't hear him. He had stepped forward between two of the huge weapons when a Rebel shell scored a direct hit on the ammunition limber parked directly behind the guns. The earth rose beneath him and flung him up into the air. He rose helplessly, higher than the smoke that covered the field, and for an instant he could see the whole battlefield beneath him: men struggling through the smoky clearings and the bright flashes of rifle fire illuminating the haze. Trees were topped raggedly in the woods as if a huge, ragged scythe had swung through them, and here and there flames had broken out in the timber. To his left, incongruously, floated a singletree from the ammunition limber. It seemed weightless until it and Graham began their descent into the smoke and fire below.

He came down hard against a broken cannon's wheel. To his immediate right was an artilleryman, half of his body gone, his handless arms folded over his chest as if he had lain down for a rest. Graham struggled to his feet and was shocked to find himself unhurt except for a numbness in his hips. He somehow still held his sword and pistol, and he spun around to squint into the unnatural morning darkness. All he could see was a handful of troops dug in behind a fence and continuing to fire. Graham wanted to shoot his weapon, but he couldn't spy a Southern soldier anywhere, and he feared hitting one of his own men if he discharged the pistol blindly into the smoke.

Malloy and a corporal who wore an infantry insignia on his cap were working the single cannon remaining in Graham's battery. The crew were scattered like rag dolls all around the redan. Remains of the shattered gun were sprinkled liberally among severed arms and battered torsos. One man's legs and buttocks lay next to another's chest and shoulders as if placed there by a giant hand trying to reassemble the mismatched, ragged edges of the terrible wounds. Aside from the impressed infantryman, Malloy was working the howitzer all by himself. Graham yearned to help, but he didn't know what to do. He looked down at his two weapons and debated which one he should put down. He was confused and anxious to act at the same time, conflicting emotions bewildered him.

The muzzle of the cannon belched out gray smoke into the choking atmosphere, but he felt rather than heard the blast, and realized to his horror that he heard nothing at all but a severe ringing in his ears. The concussion from the direct hit on the limber had rendered him totally deaf. He saw three of his former crew crawling around amid the severed limbs and broken artillery pieces. He wondered what force kept him alive, why he, the most inexperienced and incompetent man on the field, should continue to stand while other abler and braver men were being cut down all around him.

Through the occasional drift of clear air that came across the ground in front of him, Graham glimpsed the mounds of dead men and horses. Blood was everywhere, and Confederate guns ravaged the reformed line and occasionally blew men up and backward from the fence.

Graham couldn't imagine what kept them in place. From time to time one would jump away and lie in an impossible position with a raw hole in his chest or head. His comrades on the left and right sometimes glanced to see if he was still alive, if he could be helped, but they rarely broke their rhythmic firing, reloading, and firing again. If one landed facedown, Graham could sometimes see almost all the way through him. The soft lead Minié balls flattened when they struck flesh and bone, and a hole the size of a two-bit piece going in was bigger than two fists coming out. It was insane, certain death to remain in the line, but somehow the soldiers stayed in place and continued to pour lead into the surging curtain of smoke in front of them. Their mindless courage shamed him.

Then Graham saw Rebel cavalry emerge from the trees and charge the Illinois redoubt. The Federal troops held their fire, and then just as it seemed the wildly dressed Confederates would overrun the defenders, the bluecoats loosed a controlled volley supported by heavy canister from Malloy and his comrades' guns to the right and left. The charging gray cavalry churned into the muddy ground, their horses writhing to free themselves from their wounded and dead riders and the tack that bound them.

Graham's mouth hung open in awe. He felt angry for the first time in many, many years. And just as it had been before, the emotion was once again self-directed.

He was doing nothing to help the frantic sergeant and the young corporal. He strained to think of the lessons Malloy had tried to teach him, but none of it seemed to matter. In this kind of battle, a man had to rely on his instincts and his experience. Graham stood amid the wreckage of the guns and men around him and realized that he had neither.

He watched in disbelief as the Confederates formed for another charge. Whatever admiration he felt for the besieged Union line was now transferred to the Rebel horsemen. Even though hundreds of them already lay dead and wounded, their numbers appeared constant. He thought of the canister Malloy blasted in terms of dragon's teeth. For every piece of ragged shot the howitzers sent into the bloody morass before them, it seemed new enemy horsemen appeared to arise to fight like a monster. It was suicide to ride into that deadly hailstorm of fire, he thought. There was no possible way the troopers in the line could miss them. Yet the Rebels waved their swords and carbines, and he could see their teeth bared in grim optimism as they galloped into a virtual forest of shot and smoke. The men leaned into their mounts, their weapons thrust out in front of them like lances.

This time the Union men didn't wait for the "Texicans and Rakinsackers" to close with the defensive line. They opened fire at five hundred yards, and Malloy's canister joined Minié balls and shot from the batteries up and down the line to decimate and drive back the charging Rebels again. Once more, the Confederate assault crumbled.

The sight gave Graham heart, and he seemed to step outside himself. He yelled a "Hurrah," grabbed his sword, and leaped out of the makeshift redan toward the Illinois men in front of him. He drew his pistol and raced through the lines, amazing the infantry officers who remained crouched behind the fence with the men.

"Charge!" Graham yelled, although he couldn't hear his own voice. "Sound the charge, goddamnit!" He waved the sword up and down the line. "We've got the sons of bitches on the run!" He looked for his horse, but the animal had shied away from the noise of battle, broken its tether, and retreated of its own accord.

Before their officers could stop them, a number of the Illinois infantry struggled to their feet and raggedly followed Graham out onto the field. They ran blindly through the smoke toward the trees, stumbling over Confederate and Union dead, horses and weapons, and stepping on the wounded, who cried out and clutched at the legs of the charging troops. Graham was horrified as he jerked his boot away from the bloody grasp of a fallen Confederate who was either begging for help or trying to stop him. It didn't matter to Graham. He slashed at the hand with his sword and sliced away two of the man's blackened fingers before he ran on.

They were almost halfway there when Graham's path was blocked by a man on a horse. He ran into the animal's side and fell backward. A Union major scowled down at him and yelled into his face, but Graham's ears were still ringing; he heard nothing. The officer gestured with his sword toward the trees, where puffs of smoke were dotted by bright sparks of musketry, and several of the Union troops up and down the line were grabbing themselves and falling into the icy mud.

Graham was suddenly shocked at his own audacity. He gaped toward the tree line, where he saw butternut coats milling around and arranging themselves for another assault toward the now exposed Illinois line. The mounted officer rode up and down quickly, organizing a withdrawal by gesturing and cursing the troops, and Graham did what he could to move the men around him back toward the relative safety of the rail fence. Suddenly the major's blouse seemed to ripple as if several small animals were struggling beneath it. Almost at once, his neck opened and a geyser of blood shot out across the men nearest him. His horse, sensing the officer's control relax, bolted from the noise and confusion around him and galloped toward the fenceline, neatly jumping it and dumping the dead major off into the yellow grass on the other side.

Graham stood transfixed and helpless in the middle of the field. Troops raced pell-mell around him, some falling as Confederate artillery began to rake the retreating Illinois men before they reached shelter. Graham didn't know what to do, how to save himself from the overwhelming humiliation he felt. His legs wouldn't move him, and his arms hung uselessly at his side.

Suddenly he was spun around and found himself face to face with the grimy corporal who had been assisting Malloy. The youth's mouth was open and he was yelling at the officer, but Graham couldn't hear a word he was saying. Finally, the young man gave Graham an apologetic look, doubled his fist, and knocked him down. He then picked him up and hauled him over his shoulder back to the Union line, which had re-formed once more and was now beating off the Rebel counterattack.

Graham's ears continued to ring, and one of them was bleeding as the corporal and he stumbled, exhausted and out of breath, up to Malloy's redan. The last gun was silent, smashed by a Confederate ball, and Malloy's body was slumped down beside it. His head was gone, and Graham spied it some distance away, a surprised and angry expression staring at the ruined battery. The corporal, who had shed his blouse and ripped open the top of his underwear, collapsed next to the dead sergeant. Filthy black sweat streamed down his hairless chest.

Graham discovered that he could hear a little now, and he shouted at the young man who had saved his life and asked his name.

"Frank Herbert," he panted back. He was a broad-faced, wide-eyed youth, whose mouth seemed to hang open in a stupid expression of idiocy. But, Graham realized, he owed this man his life, and the thought was less than comforting.

5

GRAHAM'S RECOLLECTION OF HIS PART IN THE BATTLE of Elkhorn Tavern—or Pea Ridge, as he came to call it

—was clouded. In painful moments of embarrassment, he would remind himself of his foolish charge against the Rebel line with worn-out men who could barely stumble after him. When the settlers had stupidly run out after the charging Indians the day before, the memory had flooded back to him with biting accuracy. But he also recalled the sight of the Union canister cutting through the ranks of charging Rebels, of exploding shells all around him, of being blasted into the air and hanging there for what seemed like minutes before falling back into the hell that raged beneath him.

And he recalled the much deeper shame he felt when he was breveted captain by General Curtis himself because he was the only surviving and unwounded officer of artillery from the besieged Union Army left.

Another sight he always remembered was of Noah Spencer's scalped head. Graham's youthful commanding officer's battery had been overrun by Cherokee and other Indians pressed into service by the Confederates. The Indians fought well at first. They routed the Union infantry and claimed the artillery's position, but they became so fascinated by what they called the "shooting wagons" and the tack and jingling equipment associated with the limbers and caissons that they stopped, held a victory dance around the captured guns, and failed to consolidate their position.

By the time some Arkansas troops arrived to press their advantage, the Indians had mostly faded into the woods and were sniping at the odd Union soldier who came too close. They amused themselves by dressing up in horse collars and trace chains and prancing around with their bloody trophies. They refused to march back into battle, where numbers of them had been killed while stupidly walking directly into enemy fire, and by nightfall, the Union position was reestablished.

Still, Graham never forgave the Indians for skulking in cowardice after performing their depredations against frightened, retreating troops. Chasing down withdrawing troops and mutilating them was clear out of the way. But then to retreat to safety while brave men charged into certain death for want of their support rendered them beneath the contempt of any soldier on any side. The battle damned Indians forever in his mind. His attitude toward the red man had never changed, but in the past two days it had been tempered by a surprised and ironic respect for their ability to die bravely when they wanted something badly enough. But then, he reminded himself, these were Comanche, not tame reservation Indians pressed into service by zealous Confederate politicians.

But Comanche or otherwise, so far as Graham was concerned, Indians were Indians: no different from the black man who caused Emma's death, the cause of the war, the cause of the loss of his hand, and the cause of Jonathan's death. Now, it appeared, a black man joined with the red man to cause the ruination of the final hope, the dream of Cleveland T. Graham. He couldn't abide it, he insisted, and his determination to do something to keep himself awake moved him to his feet and started him on an inspection of the damage from the last attack.

DURING HIS MOVEMENT UP and down the wagon line, he stopped from time to time and peered out over the crossing. Clumps of wildflowers and prickly pear dotted the thicket across the creek where the Indian marksmen were yet concealed. He saw no movement, and he wondered briefly if some miracle had taken place and they had withdrawn. But he knew better.

He briefly considered giving them part of the whiskey, to try once more to buy them off. But then he set his jaw and threw the cigar butt toward some chickens which had wandered back under the wagons. No, he resolved, they wouldn't have their way. He wouldn't give in. Not this time. Not while he was alive—and he was committed to staying alive, at least long enough to get even with the goddamn nigger scout who had humiliated him and threatened his dream and ruined Aggie's reputation. The first man he ever killed had been a Negro. This time was no different, to his way of thinking. It was nothing more than nigger stupidity that had caused this, and the stupid nigger man who was responsible would pay for it.

It occurred to him that the only one who had a right to be concerned about Aggie and Moses, or even just about Aggie, was dead. Even Sterling's wife—if that's what the dour old woman truly was to him—was lying out there among the female corpses near the creek, likely scalped and likely raped. And he had killed Jack Sterling himself. That, at least, had worked out, although he took little pleasure in having done it, at least in having done it that way. He missed the satisfaction of letting Sterling know who pulled the trigger. But it was done, and that was enough.

A sudden blast from the ridge above the caves caught him by surprise, and he stared again into the cedar across the creek. No rifle smoke answered the shot—the Comanche weren't so stupid as the settlers about revealing their hidden positions—but the quick, liquid sucking noise that announced a loosed arrow came to his ears, and he instinctively ducked down behind the wagon in front of him.

Grover Hildebrandt pitched off the ledge overhead and tumbled into a wagon before rolling down behind it, jumping up, and jerking at a dogwood shaft in his shoulder. He was cursing and moving so that Graham and the other two men who ran to his aid had trouble keeping him still to inspect his wound. Incredibly, the flint point hadn't even broken the skin. Grover's extra layers of clothing had absorbed the arrow's point and held it. He would be bruised, Graham noted when they finally uncovered the filthy shoulder beneath a coat, three shirts, and two flannel union suits, and maybe next time he would think to move immediately after he fired his rifle. The fall had dazed the huge man, and Graham permitted him to take a rest before going back on watch.

Since that morning's Indian attack had been beaten off without the advice of the black scout who had led them into this mess, Graham felt confident of his abilities to lead men and to command a force against a hostile enemy, even Indians, whom he had never really fought before. But an enemy was an enemy, white, red, or black, and there would be no more surprise attacks. This time he was going to do it right, and he was going to save as many of these people as he could. What he needed to find was the nub of the problem so he could take hold of it and deal with it. He felt that his ability to see the simple solution to complex problems was some kind of gift, but in order to use it, he had to be able to find that basic denomination that would tell him how to act.

"I'd give anything for a couple of six-pounders," he mused aloud, as he studied the ridge. "By God, me an' Malloy an' Herbert'd show them red niggers a thing or two then." He shook his head slowly and grinned without humor. "By God, we would."

CHAPTER TWO

1

WILL GOLDEN SPOTTED GRAHAM AND MOVED AWAY from his assigned position to meet him. Graham took out another cigar. His memories of Pea Ridge had called forth old ghosts, and one very likely ghost, Frank Herbert, who was probably scalped and dead by now. He felt guilty about that, but he couldn't help it, he told himself.

Graham looked up and noticed that it was nearly noon. He sniffed and imagined he could smell the dead out along the creek bank. The day was heating up.

"You reckon they'll come again?" Golden asked. He eyed Graham's cigar but knew better than to ask for one. No one on the train had any illusions about Graham's generosity. He had offered each one of them a piece of a dream, and they had each bought in, but he was not prepared to give them anything more.

"I figure they'll come so long as we're here to tempt them," Graham said. He struck a match on a brass button that sealed the leather covering over the stump where his hand should have been. He had Golden pegged for a righteous coward, the kind of man who would shove someone else out in front of a fight while he stood back and took all the credit for starting it: the sort of man to raise chickens. One of the few character traits Graham felt he had a right to be proud of was that he had never run from a fight. However foolishly, he had faced Rebel cavalry, Rebel cannon, and stood his ground—even charged into their midst—and he had faced outlaws and worse men than even these Comanche could imagine and survived. Golden, he thought, couldn't stand up to a good shit pain.

"Well . . ." Golden sneaked a look between the wagons as if he expected Graham's prophecy to come true at any second. He also whispered, which angered the wagon master even more. "What you reckon we ought to do?" He asked the question as if there were some secret plan Graham was hiding from everyone.

"What do you mean?" Graham wanted to sleep, and he wanted a drink. He realized that he dared not take either in any quantity, but he also knew that without a portion of at least one, he wasn't going to last much longer. What he didn't want was a confidant, at least not one the likes of Golden.

"What can we do?" He spoke in a loud voice. "We sit an' wait an' hope that Moses an' Frank come back with somethin'." He looked casually at Golden, and masked the contempt he felt. He resented the man's assumption of a position that suggested he was the wagon master's lieutenant. Hildebrandt, or even the two hog-raising Southerners, dirty and stupid as they were, came closer to the sort of individual Graham wanted at his back.

"A nigger an' a idjet." Golden spat, or tried to. His fright was showing. There wasn't enough spit in his mouth to work up a good lather. "I swear, Graham, this thing's gone 'bout as sour as it can. It ain't too late to turn back. Maybe we can tell 'em that. Maybe we can reason with 'em. Think?"

"*Reason* with 'em?" Graham mimicked him. "Reason with Indians? You're crazy, Golden. I'd be careful who I call 'idjet' from now on."

Golden's eyes clouded with resentment. Graham had seen the type before: He had always been proud of the fact that he had never taken anything off another man that he couldn't pay back. Now, facing a situation that was a good deal more dangerous than any he had ever seen, something his mouth couldn't get him out of, he was uncomfortable. Back in central Louisiana, where he came from, he would have knocked Graham's cigar down his throat, but out here, he was vulnerable, and it infuriated him. Raise the bet, Graham thought, I dare you.

Golden stood and seethed for a moment or two longer, and finally Graham gestured with his cigar out toward the creek. "Why'd you let those damn chickens out?"

"I didn't *let* 'em out," Golden said. He cast his eyes downward, but in anger, not in embarrassment. "They just got out. I sent my boy to round 'em up when they wander back over this way."

"We might have to eat 'em 'fore this is over," Graham said flatly. "If it comes to that, let's just hope they're where we can get our hands on them."

"If it comes to that?" Golden repeated. "You think it'll come to that?" He looked out at the pecking hens. "Those hens is layers. They ain't for eatin'," he said stiffly. "I'd have to shoot anybody who started wringin' necks to fill a fryin' pan." The threat was not reinforced with any emotion, and Golden refused to meet Graham's eye when he offered it.

"Oh yeah," Graham snorted. "I remember you tellin' everybody what a tough hombre you are last night." Golden's mouth tightened and his fist clenched, and the wagon master decided he had pushed him enough. "I don't know what it'll come to," Graham admitted. "I do know that those redskins won't break it off till they get what they want or die tryin'."

"Well, we ought to do somethin'. I can't stand this waitin'. My wife an' kids—"

"Well, we're doin' all we can," Graham said, cutting him off. "You better pray that Frank an' that colored boy get to somewhere an' bring back somebody useful. Otherwise, the only *reasonin'* you're goin' to do is with your balls in your mouth an' your hair in some brave's hand. Those red devils mean business." He pointed at the creek and the thicket on the far side. "We've killed a bunch of them, an' they're just gettin' warmed up. They smell loot. An' they smell cunt." He spat a large glob that accidentally caught the toe of the taller man's boot.

The raw fear in Golden's eyes gave way to red anger. He reminded Graham of a china doll.

"They're not likely to leave any easier knowin' we might take off in another direction." Graham spoke quickly to get Golden's mind off the wet mark on his dusty boot. "Which we ain't goin' to do anyhow. We got a deal. We all knew there might be trouble, but we're not turnin' back." He turned and left Golden standing dry-mouthed where he was. The man's hands were still clenched into fists, and the wagon master sensed that coward or no, Golden was likely to find some backbone to swing at him. "Get back on watch," Graham ordered. "We can't stand to be snuck up on again."

He strolled toward the far end of the wagon line and made sure no one was sleeping on watch, but his gait, which might have looked casual to anyone he passed, was really the result of weariness compounded by worry. His mind was racing in three or four directions at once, seeking a single solution to the related yet different dilemmas he faced. He felt the settlers' eyes boring into him when he passed. They all had questions like Golden's, he knew. What they had to understand was that the answers all hinged on the return of Moses and Frank, or either of them, and that didn't make him feel any better.

He checked into the hospital cave as he passed it, and groans from the wounded flooded over him in another wave of memory it was again hard to put aside. The blood-smeared grass surrounding the huge complex of tents that had been arranged as a hospital less than a mile from Pittsburgh Landing was another vision that haunted him. He remembered the piles of arms and legs, feet and hands unimaginably piled like rubble around the surgeons' tents, how white the skin of the severed limbs looked in the early spring rain. The memory made his stubby arm ache as if his own missing hand were still there.

Aggie Sterling, her young sister, and two other young women worked among the forms stretched out on the cave's sandy floor. Some lanterns had been set up to dispel the gloom of the interior. A couple of children busied themselves sloshing buckets of water back and forth. Others rolled bandages in the back of the cave. The young women carried cups of water and whiskey to the men, some of whom still had arrow shafts sticking from various parts of their bodies. Aggie and the girls were doing what they could to ease the men, but there was no real medicine anywhere on the train. About all they could do was try to lessen the hurt. Graham wondered what strength kept them smiling as they moved from man to man giving words of encouragement and comfort.

Aggie's calico sleeves were rolled up, and she had a bloodstained apron on. Her face maintained an even smile, but the lines around her mouth were strained and tight. She looked older than she had only a few hours before, almost ugly with the burden she was carrying. Even so, Graham felt a tightening in his throat while he watched her. He admired her so much he could almost touch the sensation, but at the same time, he resented the way she churned him up inside and made his words tumble helplessly over one another. He yearned to reach out and stroke her blood-streaked hands, to caress her cheek. He found himself incredibly envious of the wounded men whose brows she soothed with her long fingers. He yearned for her so much his teeth ached.

The first and only time he had made physical contact with her was when he helped her down from Jack Sterling's wagon on Dallas Street in Jefferson. The recollection warmed him. He knew he loved her at that moment, but he had been without that emotion for too long to respond to it. There would be time for that in New Mexico, he told himself. She was not a woman to be bartered for like a colt or a calf; she would have to be won. Graham determined to win her right then.

He wondered what she thought of him. She had made him feel petty when he wanted to move on and leave the Mexicans unburied. She had angered him beyond reason when she stayed behind with Moses. What could she have been thinking? It had all been so confusing, and it was truly unlike him to behave the way he had. He could just have let Sterling grab her, pick her up, and put her back into his wagon by force. She had a knife, and her brother had a shotgun, but she wasn't going to stick him, not her own father. Graham believed that, but he had stopped Jack, and then he had left her with the black scout. Why hadn't she just gotten in the goddamn wagon and ridden on with the Newsomes? Why had she come in on horseback—riding like a man, too—with Moses?

Jack had called her a "willful child" he couldn't lick into obedience. Graham wondered if Jack had really "licked" her at all. The image of it made Graham's skin prickle in anger. But then he relaxed. Sterling's tongue had overloaded the truth so often that Graham knew better than to take anything he had said wholesale. She didn't strike Graham as the sort of girl—or woman—who would tolerate abuse. It might be a better thing than he had originally imagined that he had killed Jack, Graham thought. He couldn't stand seeing her beaten. He would have killed Jack immediately had he tried it.

Then, with a chilly feeling in his chest, he wondered if she had seen him shoot Jack or if anyone else had told her about it. That damn nigger scout had seen it, had looked shocked, too. But that couldn't be helped. It wasn't personal—at least not at the moment it wasn't—it was just the only thing to do. Graham felt no guilt over it. It was just another of life's losses. But he would profit by it. Aggie would profit by it. If no one else but Moses had seen him do it, they would profit by it in many ways.

She motioned him out of the cave to speak to him, and he tried to smile. He swallowed hard to loosen a lump that was almost choking him. He felt like a schoolboy who was infatuated with his teacher, only this one was almost thirty years younger than he. God, he thought, she was pretty in spite of the exhaustion that covered her. The fierceness that had brightened her eyes when she held the shotgun on him yesterday was now replaced by weariness and frustration. His feelings for her surged up and made him blush. Would she have killed him if he had tried to shoot the suffering women? As he looked into her eyes again he suspected that she would. She wasn't cold-blooded, but she was determined, and in that quality she reminded him of himself.

He turned slightly away from her and chewed the cigar. He knew that fear had never sent him scurrying away from danger, that he had faced death too often to think himself a coward of any sort. He had given markers he couldn't cover to raise five-hundred-dollar bets while holding nothing more than a pair of deuces. But this golden-haired, blue-eyed girl beggared any courage he thought he might have. And yet, without consciously realizing it, he had fabricated her as a part of his future. She was the centerpiece in an image of his life some two or three years hence that he had conjured a hundred times a day since the moment he met her. It never occurred to him that she might not willingly take part in its realization.

She almost touched him as she spoke. "Two more's dead." She sighed. "An' two more's about to die." She wiped away sweat from her forehead. Her hand left a streak of blood from the stains on her fingers, and Graham looked away quickly. Her eyes were so clear, so purely blue, that it was almost painful to look into them. There were slight vertical dimples on either side of her mouth that deepened when she smiled or, as they did now, when her lips drew tightly together. "We could use somethin' to give these people," she went on. It wasn't like she was speaking to Graham. He sensed that she had been rehearsing the speech in her head. "We can't get the arrowheads out without cuttin', an' I don't know how to do that."

Graham shook his head. "I don't either. They'll just have to get by or not as it falls out." He looked up into the sky. It was almost iridescent, seamless, but it paled in comparison to the girl's eyes. He remarked on the incongruity of the smell of battle, gunsmoke, blood, urine, feces from animals and man mixing together in the confines of the wagon fort. He made a mental note to send a couple of boys into one of the smaller caves to dig a latrine. He couldn't have people relieving themselves wherever they felt like it.

From somewhere down the line, amid the unpleasant odors, came the smell of coffee boiling, and Graham was surprised at how much he yearned for a cup. It surprised him by displacing his longing for a drink of whiskey. "I'll get somebody to move the dead out," he said. "Or do you want to wait until the others are gone?"

"Wait," she said. "Nobody in there's well enough off to know who's alive an' who ain't." She turned away and stooped as she reentered the cave hospital. She clearly wanted him to come inside after her and to look around, and Graham was forced to make a full inspection.

"Some of these men are fixin' to bleed to death," he remarked to her in a whisper.

"I know," Aggie said with another sigh. She was growing up through this ordeal, Graham thought. She wasn't a mere girl anymore. She never would be again. The thought saddened him. "We just don't have enough rags to sop it all up."

Graham thought for a moment and spoke through gritted teeth. "Get a brand off your wagon. A runnin' iron would be best. Jack's got one, doesn't he?" She nodded.

"Take it and get it good and hot, red-hot, white-hot if you can, and stick it on the open wounds. It'll hurt like hell, an' you'll have to get somebody to sit on them while you do it, but it'll stop the bleedin'. It might keep gangrene from settin' in."

"I don't know if I can do that." She looked at the men. "That's mean."

"It's the only thing I know to do," Graham said. He knew how well it would work, and his hand drifted to his stump when he thought about it. "Just get somebody strong to sit on them."

"If you think it'll work," Aggie said, "I'll do it."

She wiggled a finger toward her brother, who was hunkered down in a corner by a pile of dirty rags. He came up to her and received instructions to go to the wagon in search of the iron.

"You need to get some sleep," she ordered when Graham turned to leave. The smells and sounds of the cave brought involuntary tears to his eyes, and he lowered his head so his hat brim would hide his face. "An' you need to eat. How long's it been since you et?"

"Had something this mornin'," he lied.

"I doubt that," she said. She was so serious about the matter that Graham wanted to reach out and comfort her. He caught himself just as his hand started to move. "You go on, an' I'll get to you when I can," she said with a disapproving expression on her face. Jason reappeared with the running iron, which she stuck into the small fire that was only barely ventilated by a narrow opening in the top of the cave.

"What about you?" he asked. "You ain't slept either. You can't just keep on going without some sleep."

"I'm younger'n you." She smiled so brightly that Graham's heart jumped and masked the disappointment he felt deeper with her reminder of their age difference. "Besides, I can sit down an' catch a nap if I need to." She turned the brand in the fire over and over. It yellowed and then reddened with the heat from the coals. "You got to keep on your toes." For several moments she turned the running iron. She lifted it and blew on it from time to time, and then she finally looked up to Graham, who nodded.

"You want to do it?" she asked.

"I can't," Graham said quickly.

She looked at him curiously, but she seemed to accept his refusal. "Jason," she said sharply to the tow-headed youth, who continued to stand beside her. "Come over here."

She led her brother to an unoccupied corner of the cave and spoke to him in low tones. Graham watched the boy's black eyes, which were no less striking than his sister's, although in color they matched his father's. She took him by the arm firmly and spoke to him again. He nodded and followed her back to the fire, where she took the hot brand and inspected it once more. With a mimed gesture designed to receive Graham's approving nod one final time, she moved over to a man who lay bleeding profusely from a large wound in his upper arm. A pile of blood-soaked rags lay next to him, and a young girl was in the process of removing one when they came up and waved her off.

Jason sat down beside the unconscious man and placed both hands on his shoulders. Jason's forearms tightened, and Aggie applied the hot iron directly to the wound. Her face contorted almost as much as her patient's when the red-hot brand bit into the man's bloody flesh. The smell of seared skin filled the cave and drew bile to Graham's throat. Jason's head turned away from the torture, and Aggie's neck bulged with forced swallows. The man's screams rose to a crescendo. He passed out, but a nod from his tormentor confirmed that the bleeding had indeed stopped. Aggie returned the running iron to the fire, and the one or two men who were aware enough to witness the treatment lay as if frozen, their eyes fixed on the calm, lovely mistress of the makeshift hospital. Aggie hummed a tuneless melody as she turned her implement over and over in the fire once more while her brother waited patiently to assist her with the next victim.

Graham left hurriedly and leaned against the butte. He was breathing rapidly and had to force himself to calm down and gain control of his heaving, churning stomach. Once his pulse returned to normal, he stalked away from the cave's entrance. But even from a distance of four wagons, he could still hear the muffled cries as the hot iron was applied to open, bleeding bodies. His wonder and admiration for this uncommon woman soared inside him, but it was matched by a sudden fear. He could never have brought himself to cauterize the wounds, to inflict that much deliberate pain on men, even for their own good. He couldn't even help her. He certainly could not have done it with such icy, calm assurance. What other mysteries were hidden behind Aggie's eyes? he wondered. How deep did that girl go?

"God, I'd kill for a cannon," he said with another quick glance across the creek as he crossed between wagons. It was a welcome change of thought, but he realized as soon as he said it that he would kill anyway, cannon or not, just to stay alive. That, at least, was simple enough for him to feel comfortable with, confident. He just wished that the rest of the complications he was experiencing could be equally reduced to such a firm decision.

He glanced up once more into the noonday sky and wondered for the thousandth time how far Moses and Frank had made it before they were caught. That they might have gotten through was too indefinite in his mind to consider. He didn't want to allow a hope that they might make it to surface.

Suddenly a new worry sprang up in his mind. Even if they made Richardson or Griffin, he realized, they would bring back black troops, buffalo soldiers. The Negro troopers had adopted the nickname with an odd measure of pride, but it filled Graham with dread. More than two-thirds of the soldiers on the Texas plains seemed to be Negro, Graham recalled. He had seen them at Fort Concho and Fort Griffin, watched them prancing around in their uniforms and grinning widely with each military accomplishment they performed. He was almost as mystified as the Indians by their presence.

They weren't even as impressive as the green recruits Graham recalled from the war, gangling farm boys with slobber dripping down their chins, ignorant immigrants who jabbered among themselves in foreign tongues. These troopers were mostly former slaves, he knew, men who were so accustomed to servile roles that initiative was alien to them. He had no faith in them, and he couldn't imagine that even if Moses and Frank managed to reach one of the forts and return with them they would be of much use.

Of course, the mere sight of uniforms might be sufficient to scare the Comanche off. A bugle and snapping guidon could often do as much as veteran troopers, Graham believed. Normally, even the threat of soldiers in the vicinity might be enough. But this wasn't normal, and Graham feared what might happen if the soldiers Moses and Frank brought back weren't experienced Indian fighters. This could turn into a massacre. He should have insisted that Moses ride north and east, to Fort Sill. Surely the officer there would have let the white troopers come across the Red to rescue white men in trouble. But then, maybe not. Between niggers and Quakers, Graham said to himself, I suppose I'm better off with niggers.

The biggest part of his problem, he realized, was Moses himself. Indeed, he admitted as he stopped to puff his cigar and to gaze between two wagons at the hazy shrouds of smoke that continued to linger over the creek, that might be all the problem. How could he, of all people, trust a Negro, hand over himself to a man who had been a slave less than ten years ago? Thoughts of an Ohio farm thirty-five years before should have stopped him from such a foolish act in Millie's the day he hired him. But they hadn't. And Moses was nothing like that old freedman from long ago. The black scout was so proud, so full of himself, so goddamned uppity. And he had been highly recommended, yessir, Graham argued with himself. In fact, you'd have thought he was a black Jesus the way people—black and white—talked about him. But like the other Negro in Graham's experience, Moses hadn't turned out to be worth much, and now Graham had put him in charge of the train's future, of his own future. He slapped his stump against his leg in frustration.

"Stupid," he said aloud. "You'd think I'd learn."

But again the wagon master pondered what alternatives had been open to him. No white scouts—or none he could find—would venture that far west into Texas, and the Army would never have let him go all the way down the Santa Fe Trail with that much whiskey. "Whiskey an' Indians don't mix," he remembered some officer pronouncing over a hand of cards in a saloon in Jacksboro. "We 'requisition' all the whiskey we find, 'cept that part that's belongin' to licensed peddlers," he had continued with a wink toward Graham when he said "requisition." Graham had been a supply officer himself, and he well knew what the term meant when the Army applied it to civilian stores.

Although the future he counted on so heavily was but vaguely formed in his mind, the whiskey was central to them. It meant that he could complete the deal and offer a future to everyone on the train. That was his promise back in Jefferson. Most of them understood it, but many didn't. That was fine with Graham. The fewer who knew how much the amber liquid would bring the better. Otherwise, there wouldn't be anything at all in any wagon but whiskey, and he couldn't count on unloading that much.

But he had been forced to take a direct route. There was no time to go north and then down across Kansas anyway. Things had to be done before winter: houses built, stock protected, seed acquired. Otherwise, there was no point to these people going out there at all. Moses was his only alternative, and in spite of the scout's willingness to go for help to Fort Richardson—or wherever the hell he went—Graham thought little of the black man's bravery. Even if Moses was successful in finding troops—black or white—and persuading them to return with him, they would be just as likely to "requisition" the train's whiskey store as any soldiers they might have encountered in Missouri or Kansas. If they were Negro, Graham speculated, they would probably be more likely.

Of course, Moses had warned him that they couldn't delay so often, had tried to hurry them along. He had also told him not to buy oxen but to rely on mules. But the oxen would be needed to break ground, to raise roofs, to do the heavy work the men would have to do in a hurry before the first snows came on them out of the lower Rockies. And Graham felt a hatred of mules that he could only barely understand himself. But, he recalled, it had been Moses who had wanted to stop and bury the goddamn Mexicans. Or no, Graham reluctantly corrected himself, it had been Aggie. Moses had, Graham admitted, simply gone along. Someone had to stay to protect her, someone besides those useless people who ultimately abandoned her and the scout to themselves. Had she appealed, personally and directly, privately, to Graham to stay behind as well, could he have refused her? He liked to think he would have, but he honestly wondered if he would have found the strength to remain with her, especially with half the men in the train watching him, waiting for him to make an even bigger fool of himself.

The bad water had been Graham's fault, and he admitted it to himself if not to anyone else. But that was just one mistake. He was tired of being told what to do every time they stopped. It wasn't his fault the Ambrose woman had died and further delayed them, however. He couldn't just go off and leave her like that, although he had found leaving Ambrose and his kid easy enough. He threw the dead cigar butt away and swore to himself. Moses was ready enough to abandon a living white man, Graham thought, satisfied in a confirmation of the black scout's worthlessness. Leave the whites and bury the Mescans. That was the nigger way.

2

EARLY ON IN HIS LIFE, WHEN CLEVE GRAHAM FOUND himself a widower with a tiny son, he decided there was little profit in wide swings of emotion that dictated action. In a way, he decided that while burying his young wife. When he killed the freedman in his own dooryard, the act had been carried out without passion or any impulsive emotion at all. It just had to be done. It was an expiation of sorts, a way of atonement for what had happened to him, for what he had done. He had had lapses of his willful ignorance of what he felt inside—at Pea Ridge, for example—but even his son's death had eventually settled in his mind as a fitting part of a war that should never have been fought, a fitting part of life that he had no right to live. That led him to cultivate a kind of dullness that was slow to anger or to love.

Graham stumbled against an exposed root from an errant cedar tree that had somehow found purchase on the limestone bluff and worked its way down to the sandy ground. He almost fell before he caught himself against the side of a wagon. "God," he said aloud, "I'm tired." He realized that as he had walked his weary mind had allowed his memories to take him over and to allow him to daydream when he should be alert. It wasn't like him to be so careless, he thought. It's not a gambler's trait.

Just down the line the two North Carolinians were struggling with a dead ox. The beast had fallen in its traces and was now blocking the narrow opening between the wagon and the bluff. As Graham approached he could smell the carcass already decaying. This was going to mean trouble, he thought. He hadn't counted the number of dead and seriously wounded animals, but their stench was only a small part of the problem. He was unsure whether there would be enough draft animals to haul the wagons the rest of the way to New Mexico. Even if the Indians withdrew and left them alone, he doubted he could amass enough pulling power to keep from abandoning the high Conestogas, and he anticipated with an even greater weariness the arguments he would have to face if and when they were able to proceed on their journey.

He bent down to try to lend his good hand to their efforts, but it was obviously no use. They could never move the carcass without help, Graham realized. Normally, they would simply hitch up a team of mules or another ox to this one and drag it off, but normally there wouldn't be Comanche snipers sharply watching their every move.

"Ain't no use," one of the men, Titus Baker, said. He leaned breathlessly against the bluff and wiped sweat from his brow. "She ain't goin' nowhere, an' we're jus' goin' to have to learn to live with her, dead as she is."

"We can't," the other, whose name Graham remembered as Holden Potter, pleaded. He pointed into a tiny opening behind the fallen beast. "The flies is already eatin' the young'uns alive. An' the stink is terrible."

Graham recalled that like many on the train, Baker and Potter had come to Texas after the war seeking a better life than they had found in the ruin left by Grant and Sherman in the deep South. But they had found making a new life was no easier in East Texas than it had been in the mountains of North Carolina. They had relatives, they said, somewhere down in the Brazos Valley. Potter had shown Graham a greasy, hand-drawn map which indicated that they were to cut southwest from the Little Wichita along a fork called Paint Creek, from where they would make their way to join one of their brothers who had apparently settled along that small fork of the Brazos.

When Moses said that he had no idea where such a creek as the one drawn on the map might be, they had smiled and appeared not at all discouraged or surprised. Baker said they had instructions written out, and when they reached the right place to head off on their own, they would know it. Graham suspected that wherever the "right place" was, it had been passed days, maybe weeks ago. But when they left the train was none of his business. They were hauling their share of the whiskey for as long as they stayed with the group, and he wasn't anxious to double up anyone else's load until he had to.

"Why don't you move your people down the line a bit?" Graham suggested. This part of the train was far enough away from the creek as the wagon line followed the slight curve of the bluff to make its natural defense less vulnerable, and two or three competent riflemen could hold out well enough.

"Why don't you go to hell?" Potter shot at Graham. "I got pigs to tend in that li'l bitty cave over yonder." He gestured toward a concave opening so small Graham hadn't noticed it. Two trunks and a pile of furniture made a rude barrier to keep the swine penned. It must be larger inside, he thought, for the men's combined herd numbered over a dozen swine. "We can't watch pigs an' young'uns an' Injuns all at once."

"Yeah," Baker put in. His face sprouted a beard made up of loose patches of hair that stood out like threatening bristles and never seemed to come together at any point. "I seen you got your wagon in a good spot. Your oxes ain't dead. We got two dead'uns, an' that means we only got six good'uns. How in hell we fixin' to get anyplace with only six oxes 'tween us? We should of brung mules like we wanted to.

"I got me a wagon full of smithin' iron," Baker went on. "It's all them four oxes could do to pull'er. Holden here had to carry all our own stuff."

The men were angry, and Graham was in no mood for an early start to the argument over wagons and animals.

"Any sign of the nigger?" Potter changed the subject abruptly.

"What?" Graham asked. "Moses? No. Of course not. He's only been gone a few hours."

"Well, you didn't ask me," Baker said, "but I think it was one dumbass, Bluebelly thing to do to send a nigger out to do a man's job."

"I didn't ask you," Graham said, and he started to turn away. He wasn't angry, but he didn't like defending Moses. These men and their innate stupidity bored him. "I didn't see you volunteerin'. I thought you North Carolina boys ate blood an' guts for breakfast. I didn't think you were scared of nothin'. Thought you marched through hell with Stonewall Jackson."

The men looked quickly at each other to check temperatures, and it was Potter who answered quietly, "Wasn't no North Carolina boys with Jackson. Anyhow, that was all a long time ago. We seen our share of hell. An' we ain't sorry for what we done. Wasn't sorry then, ain't sorry now. But that was a long time ago. We don't want no trouble with you. We 'greed to go 'long with you this far anyhow, an' all we want is to get where we're goin' an' set up raisin' our hogs an' corn an' leavin' folks 'lone. We didn't bargain for none of this."

"Neither did I." Graham dismissed them with a wave as he moved on down the line toward the last wagon. "Move your families and let the goddamn pigs take care of themselves. But don't turn 'em loose."

"How're we supposed to feed 'em, then?" Baker called.

"That's your problem," Graham turned. "If you turn 'em loose an' I see even one of 'em gettin' at those people out there, I'll kill both of you." He went on and didn't look back. Before this is over, Graham thought, I may have to kill every son of a bitch on this train.

When he reached the terminus of the wagon fort he found four teenaged boys standing watch. Virgil Hollister's wagon stood forlornly in the noonday heat about fifty yards from where he stood. He wondered how Frank's daughter was doing. He hadn't noticed her in the hospital cave, although he knew she could just as well be in Frank's wagon. She never had been a girl to seek the company and comfort of others, aside from Jason Sterling, he reminded himself. But if Jason was in the cave, where was the girl? He shook his head. He couldn't worry about her. She was safe, and that was all there was to it. He wondered if Aggie knew that her brother had made her an aunt. Hell, Graham thought, they're just kids.

He also wondered whether or not he had really been fair in picking Virgil's wagon to block the small trail leading up to the prairie. He disliked the man not only for his suddenly rediscovered religion, but also because of his adamant refusal to participate in the whiskey deal. He would need it as much as any of them when they arrived, if they arrived.

On the other hand, he reminded himself, Virgil's canvas was still intact, and his was probably the only wagon that hadn't been chewed up by arrows and bullets. In an ironic way, he might be better off than any of them if he got out of this alive. Graham slammed his fist into the side of the wagon and startled the boys. He felt more helpless and stupid than he ever had before. He felt as he had felt at Pea Ridge and again at Pittsburgh Landing, useless and unable to act effectively. What made this worse, he thought, was that this time there was a way out. He just didn't know how to take it.

One of the boys at the end of the wagon fort smiled at Graham, and the wagon master realized with a shock that he was hardly much more than a child. Even so, he stood at the ready with a rifle in his hands.

"What's your name, son?"

"Patrizi," the boy answered, and Graham remembered the family: Italian bakers from Illinois. "This is my brother." A second dark-eyed, black-haired boy who appeared to be about ten grinned up at Graham. The youngster's rifle, a Henry, was almost twice as long as he was. He propped it up on a crate. He stood on another upended crate to be able to see between the wagon's seat and the front of the Conestoga.

"Where're your folks?" Graham asked. The other two boys paid him no attention.

"Out there." The boy gestured with his eyes. "Mama was washin' quilts an' blankets, and Papa went out when the Indians came. They got two of our sisters, but I think one of 'em's dead."

"I'm sorry," Graham muttered.

"Ain't your fault," the younger boy said quickly. "They went out there on their own. Who would of thought Indians was comin'?" His dark eyes flashed, and his olive skin deepened in tone. He was angry, but not at Graham. "They left us on their own." He lifted the rifle's barrel. "I killed me two with this here."

Graham sighed and moved away to the other end of the wagon. The elder Patrizi boy came up and touched him. "Them others reckon it *is* your fault," he said. "Least they reckon it's *somebody's* fault."

"What're their names?" Graham sighed and moved as if to approach them.

"Them's the Folsoms," he whispered, holding Graham back with his arm. "Their folks is dead out there, an' their sister, too. They seen what them Indians done to the girl, Mandy. I'd jus' leave 'em be if I was you."

There was wisdom in the boy's eyes as well as his words, and Graham nodded. "What's your Christian name?" Graham asked.

"George," he said. "Giorgio, really. Mama called me Giorgio, but Papa said I had to have an American name. I was born in Italy, but I don't remember it." He paused. "I was goin' to be a priest," he said. "But now I got Rudy to look out for, an' the young'uns. They's down the line with Miss Henderson."

"They'll be fine there." Graham remembered Myra Henderson, a small, birdlike woman who reminded Graham of everyone's idea of a maiden aunt. "Keep a sharp lookout, George," Graham said. "Giorgio." He leaned his rifle next to the wagon. "I'm goin' to try to get some rest for a minute."

"Yessir," the boy said, and he moved down and spoke softly but firmly to the others.

Graham slumped down in the sand and braced his back against the wagon's wheel. He couldn't really go to sleep, he told himself; he didn't even dare close his eyes. He could hear flies buzzing and other insects noisily going about their business in the early-afternoon heat. Somewhere off in the distance he heard a bird calling, or was it a Comanche? He didn't know, and he felt too tired to care.

"Mr. Graham," Giorgio said and squatted down close

to him. "Smell this." The boy broke open a green leaf he had found growing in one of the crevices of the limestone bluff. The unmistakable odor of skunk came wafting up to Graham's nostrils, and he turned his head away violently. "Ain't that somethin'?" Giorgio laughed. He might be growing up fast, Graham thought, but in many ways he's still a boy. "The Folsoms say it's called skunk bush. Smells like a skunk to me." His eyes brightened suddenly, and Graham felt a coldness in his heart.

"It does to me, too, son," he said. His voice choked before he could clear his throat. He returned the boy's smile, and without thinking about what he was doing, he stretched out a hand and ruffled his black hair. It was a gesture he hadn't made in nearly twenty years. He felt a ghostly familiarity about it.

The boy stared at Graham's leather stump. He cleared his throat and shot a quick look behind him to see if his companions were paying any attention to him. "Can I ask you somethin'?" He paused, then almost whispered, "How'd you lose your hand?"

For a moment Graham didn't want to answer. But something inside him spoke in spite of his reluctance. "At Pittsburgh Landing," Graham said wearily. "The Rebs called it Shiloh." He felt uncomfortable with the question and the answer. Men all over the country stumbled around on crutches and waved stubby arms in the air. The hacksaws of field surgeons had probably separated more men from their whole selves than shot and shell ever did. The mountains of severed arms and legs in the bloody meadow near the Tennessee River flashed across his mind once more. No one had ever asked him about how he lost his hand before. Its absence was often noted, usually as the tag to an insult, and Graham generally ignored the remarks. It did no good to dwell on his loss. In answering this boy's innocent question, Graham realized, he was fulfilling something in himself, but he couldn't exactly determine what.

"My daddy was there, too!" Giorgio said. "You know him? He was with Sherman."

Graham shook his head. "There were a lot of soldiers there."

He studied the leather covering over Graham's stump

with greater interest. "An' you lost it there? I bet you were brave." His voice was almost reverent. There was almost too much of the child here, Graham noted with a mixture of sadness and admiration. He hoped with all his heart that they could move on before it disappeared.

"No," he said gruffly. "I was a fool."

Giorgio stood up and resumed his watch; Graham was grateful to be left alone with his thoughts and closed his eyes.

ALL GRAHAM COULD SEE was the canvas ceiling of a tent. His hand—or his wrist—was on fire, it felt, and he tried to rise only to collapse again. He twisted his neck to try to find out where he was, but what he saw around him made his senses reel.

In a forest of blood-splattered canvas, men were stretched across stacks of ammunition crates. Some were insensible, still wearing ripped and gory uniforms. Others writhed in agony and remained on their litters only because they had been tied there with leather straps. Two or three attendants leaned heavily on some, while white-coated surgeons worked on them with saws and knives. Hoarse screams and ragged groans filled the tent, and along the muddy, bloody floor, hands and feet, whole arms and legs littered the area around the doctors' shoes. There was the smell of camphor, of vinegar, of seared and mortifying flesh. This is hell, Graham thought, his eyes shifting wildly around him. No place but hell.

He put his head back and fought to stay conscious. No, he thought, it isn't hell. It's some kind of field hospital. Pittsburgh Landing. But what was he doing here? Was he wounded? He tried once more to raise himself, but he couldn't move. His left hand and wrist continued to burn, and when he finally raised his arm high enough, all he could see was a ragged, blood-stained burlap bandage covering his forearm. When he tried to flex his fingers, he felt nothing but more pain.

His mind swam. This isn't possible, he thought. He was back in the Quartermaster Corps, Army of the Ohio, his rank confirmed, and he was supposed to be buying horses for Grant's army's pending invasion of Mississippi. It was good duty, clean and safe, away from angry Rebel charges and the haunting noise of ripping canvas that told of front-line musketry.

But then, through his pain and confusion, he saw another image of himself, this time standing in the midst of falling men, his sword raised high in his left hand, his pistol firing into charging butternut uniforms which seemed to come in waves from the Southern forest toward the tents where, only moments before, Graham and others had been cursing the rain around their quiet breakfast fires. He remembered emptying his pistol and scrambling around trying to rally the green troopers who were dying in bloody heaps before the Confederate charge.

And he remembered insisting that he would stand his ground, that he would not run, that he would prove to Jonathan and to himself that he was no coward, when the weight of the sword was snatched away, and he looked up only to see a bloody stump waving in the smoky air, the stark white and jagged end of his wrist pointing toward the sky.

But that was all he remembered, and the images were quickly banished by the sounds and smells around him.

He tried to speak, but his mouth was rasp-dry. His tongue felt like scorched bark. He writhed on the stretcher and discovered that he, too, was tightly bound to the poles. Then he saw a man in a red coat approaching him. The coat had once been white, Graham realized. The crimson dye was a result of the man's grisly work. Graham fought to remain lucid as the surgeon came up beside him and grinned.

"You got lots of shit in that wound," the sawbones told him. "I'm fixin' to have to take'er off a lot higher'n you lost it. Maybe a inch or more." He laid his finger across Graham's forearm just above the wrist. "Least it don't stink too bad yet. So that'll likely be the whole shootin' match." He gestured to another figure standing some feet away. Graham dimly realized he was looking at Frank Herbert.

"That ol' boy likely saved your life," the surgeon said. "Took a bayonet, fired it up, and cauterized the stump. Then he hauled you here on his back. Hell of a friend, I'd say."

Frank lowered his head. Graham tried to say something, but his tongue was swollen and dry. He laid his head back and looked up at the doctor, who grinned and put a damp rag in Graham's mouth to ease his parched throat.

"Can't give you nothin' to drink jus' yet," the doctor said. "You got some more pain comin', an' I don't want you crampin' up on me."

"Who are you?" Graham gasped. "You don't sound like a Federal officer."

"Mobile, Alabama," the grizzly surgeon replied. "I'm a prisoner of war!" He grinned. "Took me an' the whole sheebang two weeks ago. That scare you, Yank? Don't worry yourself none. I'm workin' up to a parole. I'm really jus' a horse doctor, but they tell me that don't matter. They're keepin' count on how many of you Bluebellies I can pull through. An' hell, this is the first chance I ever got to work on two-legged jackasses."

There was no anesthetic, not even whiskey, and Graham's screams joined those of other men whose limbs were being hacked away in the complex of tents of the crude field hospital until he passed out. When Graham regained consciousness the only image he could discern was Frank's face, drawn with worry and at the same time stupidly patient. He looked as if he were sitting beside a sick child or parent. Graham passed out again, and the next time he awoke he was aboard his supply boat, Frank quietly smoking a pipe beside him, staring calmly at the stump that would serve as an emblem and a reminder that Cleveland T. Graham was a cripple forever.

CHAPTER THREE

1

"MR. GRAHAM? MR. GRAHAM?" A VOICE INTRUDED into Graham's subconscious, and he opened his eyes and came to his feet with a start.

"What's wrong?"

Giorgio smiled sheepishly at him. "Nothin'. You was talkin' to yourself," he said. "It was spookin' the fellers." The other boys glanced away, embarrassed.

"I was asleep," Graham said. It was more an admission than an explanation. "I was havin' a bad dream." He pulled his watch from his vest pocket. "What time is it? How long did I sleep?" The watch had stopped. It was smashed.

The boy looked up into the cloudless afternoon sky. "Not long," he said. "Less than a hour, I reckon."

Graham's eyes followed the boy's. Buzzards circled low over the crossing. He climbed up on the boy's crate and peered out onto the beach. Sure enough, buzzards had alighted a short distance from the corpses and were spreading their wings boldly. He was reminded of the horror of his dream suddenly. He shouldn't have allowed himself to drift off that way, he admonished himself.

"You got a shotgun?" Graham asked.

"Yeah," the boy replied. "Uh . . . yessir. Ol' ten-gauge. Kicks like a mule."

"Get it up here an' pot-shoot some of those sons of bitches before they get to your folks," he said. "We can't keep them off forever, but maybe we can discourage them some." The boy reached under the wagon and pulled up a long, double-barreled weapon. "Don't go to hell with it," Graham said, "an' don't kill Golden's chickens. I don't need more trouble from him." The boy grinned up at him. "An' send your brother down the line to tell folks what you're doin'."

He left the boys and watched as the younger Patrizi raced ahead of him. After he had gone about twenty yards, the loud blast of the old gun sounded behind him, and he heard the outraged squawk of the carrion birds as they took flight in angry surprise. A second blast sent them high into the blue sky.

Graham stopped and pulled out a bandanna and wiped his face. His dream had been vivid. It was as if he had been right back there in the Tennessee field hospital, not out here on a godforsaken prairie where the tallest tree he had seen in weeks wouldn't throw a shadow a man could stand in. He hadn't consciously thought of that terrible ordeal in years. He had never dreamed of it before. He couldn't figure out what about this situation brought forth such a vivid subconscious recollection.

And after that, whatever heart he had had for the war and the Union cause had steadily faded into a whiskey-amber, cynical haze that eventually cost him his commission and most of his self-respect.

In fact, he remembered, it had been near Vicksburg that he had met Jack Sterling. Now returned to service with the Quartermaster Corps, he was coming up the Natchez Trace behind Grant as he encircled Vicksburg. The Union cavalry needed fresh mounts, and Graham was approached by the lanky Sterling, who willingly delivered fifty saddle-broken horses in two days. He suspected that Sterling stole horses from one side and sold them to the other with the free ease of a renegade. But Graham never asked where they came from, and he ignored another officer's accusation that Sterling and his scroungy bunch had stolen fifteen head of beef a week before, when Vicksburg was almost completely cut off and starving. There was no evidence to prove the officer's complaint, and Graham couldn't have cared less. He cheerfully paid Sterling nearly twice what the horses were worth, and they split a bottle of whiskey after the deal was done.

Nothing mattered very much anymore to Graham. He completed his duties with a grim efficiency that found what motivation it required in his recollection that he had a son serving in the same army as he. That seemed to spur him through each day. He gradually withdrew into himself and drank more than ever while he went through his routine automatically. Jonathan's letters ceased coming, and in spite of the warning of his previous experience, he took to staying drunk and allowing Frank to cover for him, constantly assuring himself that Jonathan must be too busy with the responsibilities of command to worry about his crippled father.

Graham lost his commission two days after the city fell, the result of one Major Edmund Meese's finding him drunk in his wagon when he was supposed to be seeing to the receipt of rations for Grant's army.

But he also remembered that it wasn't so much his inebriation or his dereliction of duty that outraged the major. The real cause of the officer's anger was that Graham was discovered in the naked arms of a woman Meese claimed as his own.

Charges were filed by the irate officer, and at Grant's casual order, Graham was stripped of his rank and summarily dismissed from the service of the Union.

Graham hung around occupied Vicksburg after his disgrace, not really knowing what he should do next. The city was ruined. Whole sections had been reduced to rubble by the Union bombardment. But Graham learned that no matter how bad things were, there was always money around, particularly among the sorts of men in whose company a disgraced officer easily fell. He began gambling again with those who were loyal to no side but their own and who remained in the city to pick the bones of the losers and collect favors dispensed by the victors. His arm healed slowly, but he tried to avoid the drinking binges that had led to his ruination. Then Frank Herbert found him once again and brought him the news that Jonathan had been killed at Gettysburg.

Graham tried to deal with this newest disaster in his life as best he could, even remaining sober for days at a time with the faint hope of recovering his lost rank. The need to avenge himself on the Confederates who had taken his son from him gave him a renewed zeal for the Union's fight, but Vicksburg was rapidly passing into the rhythm of occupation. Graham was soon deserted by the Army and Frank, who went with it. He resumed playing cards when he could, staying drunk night and day; he considered everyone associated with the war, particularly the Negroes, who, he decided, were the cause of it, the most contemptuous of beings.

He took a boat hauling cattle up to Memphis in the fall and shoveled manure off the side into the muddy river to earn a stake. When he arrived, he gambled and drank himself into a back-alley stupor after a few weeks and then made what he could at odd jobs and barely hung on. He felt himself sliding into complete despair.

In early 1864 he managed to stay sober long enough to find a job as a faro dealer on a riverboat. A one-handed dealer was a novelty, he learned, and although he kept the job only long enough to earn sufficient money to gamble on his own, Graham believed he had turned his life around. He was lucky, he thought; not only had he lived through two major battles, he also had survived major disgrace. But his son was dead, his hand was gone, and it would be almost a decade before he would find the courage to take charge of anyone but himself again.

GRAHAM STOPPED AGAIN AND looked back to where Giorgio struggled to load the cumbersome old shotgun. The boy looked up at him and grinned, and Graham now knew why all these old memories had come flooding into his mind. Even though they looked nothing alike, the boy's innocent grin and dark hair brought Jonathan's face into Graham's mind. They had the same black eyes and bright, even teeth, the same mischief in their young smiles. Jonathan had looked so much like his mother that Graham often hurt when he studied him. But Giorgio's voice evoked the melancholy that so infected his son's adolescent croaking. Looking into the Patrizi boy's face was like looking into the past. Graham couldn't decide whether the sensation was more pleasurable than it was painful, but he couldn't tear his eyes away from him either.

Jonathan was dead, he insisted to himself, but this boy, this Giorgio Patrizi, was still alive. Graham had walked away from his particular horror with only a wound. He had left his hand there, but he had come away with his life. It was his duty to Jonathan to do something with it. He had frittered it away so far, and this could be his last chance to reclaim something of value in it. He couldn't let death catch him before that, and he couldn't let it claim this boy either.

Although he never realized it before, he had been deliberately trying to die for years. But here, on this narrow crossing over an anonymous creek in the middle of Texas, he found that he wanted to live. Unconsciously, he was trying to knit up that broken something inside him that had snapped so easily before his burning cabin so many years ago. The fingers of his mind fumbled with the fragile material, but they were not yet successful. The effort was making a difference to him, even though he wasn't fully aware of it. It dictated his actions, and it would govern his future. He was in for the showdown this time, and he was going to stick it out. Take another card, he thought.

He bit the end off another cigar and paused briefly to light it. As he drew the smoke into his lungs and felt his stomach twitch with its insistent hunger, he clenched his teeth and looked once more toward the end of the wagon fort where the boys continued their vigil. No, he said to himself, not this time, Graham, not this time. Take another card.

2

"AMAZING GRACE" RAGGEDLY AROSE FROM THE WAGON fort as Graham moved up the wagon line. "Virgil Hollister," Graham said to remind himself of the man responsible for the impromptu Sunday meeting. Virgil Hollister saw himself as the righteous hand of God about half the time, although Graham had heard no one on the train curse his animals with more profane enthusiasm than the gangly lay preacher. Only his willingness to provide an extra fifty dollars in gold had persuaded Graham to take him along anyway. Of the 120 people who had set out from Jefferson, Graham counted seventy-three still alive, not including the two Aggie had said were dying back in the cave. He also excluded Moses Franklin and Frank Herbert, but with a wince of guilt for the latter. He found himself wishing that he could exclude Hollister as well.

He paused briefly to urinate against the side of the limestone bluff right before an empty cave—again reminding himself of the grim recollections of the past hour—and when he had finished, he stooped down to peer in. The sound of a tiny spring's bubbling came to his ears from the gloom. The opening was small and slightly elevated from the ground. People would have to step up and crouch down to get inside. But once there, Graham surmised, all but the tallest men among them could stand more or less upright.

"Giorgio," he yelled. His call was passed down the five wagons to where the young Italian boys remained on close watch. In a moment, the youngster ran up.

"I want you boys to do somethin' else for me," Graham said. "It's not very good work, but it's needed."

"Yessir," the boy said, taking a tight grip on his rifle.

"Get some shovels, an' get inside this cave. Dig a sluice from the spring along a small ditch so it'll drain some." Graham knelt and traced a design in the sand. "Make it as deep as you can. Then see if you can break up a crate or two for some seats. For the women as much as anybody."

Giorgio's face revealed his confusion.

"It's going to be a latrine," Graham said. "A privy. We need it. From what I can see, the spring opening runs from about halfway back and flows into the bluff way back there someplace. You can make a drain out of it."

"A privy?" Giorgio was obviously disappointed in his assignment. "Why can't we . . ." He gestured generally toward the bluff.

"Because we can't, Jonathan," Graham snapped, then he softened his voice. "We don't know how long we'll be here, an' we can't afford for anybody to get sick. Pissin' in our drinkin' water'll make us sick sure'n hell, Jonny boy."

Giorgio looked back toward his brother and companions. "I'll do it," he said. Clearly, he just barely failed to add that he wouldn't like it.

"Don't do it by yourself," Graham said. "Get the boys

to help you. Work in pairs, in shifts. I don't think it'll take you long. Then get some rest."

Giorgio turned to go. He was exhibiting more fatigue than he had when he came running up.

"Make sure the others keep a sharp eye out while the two of you are diggin'," Graham said. "I'm countin' on you, Jonny. You're in charge."

Giorgio's eyes brightened. "We'll take care of it, Mr. Graham." He hesitated. "My name's George, Giorgio." He turned quickly and moved off with a slight spring in his step from the newfound responsibility. Behind him, Graham stared at his retreating back with a shocked expression on his face.

He had called the boy Jonathan. Jonny. He rubbed his chin with his stump and wanted to cover his face in confusion and embarrassment. His mouth felt like old, dry leather, and his legs and arms ached. A dull pain also came from his right shoulder where the recoil of his big rifle had bruised him. "I need to get a hold on myself," he muttered.

Graham turned his steps again toward his own possessions. His rifle felt extraordinarily heavy in his hand, and the weight of his Colt's around his waist seemed to drag him down. His feet were rocks, and the sand behind his eyelids became grittier with every blink. He wanted a bath. If he didn't get some genuine rest soon, he admitted, he might not make it through the afternoon—or he'd go mad. He looked up into the buzzard-filled sky. Things were not going well at all, he thought, and privy or no privy, they wouldn't be able to hold out for long.

When he passed each wagon, he automatically inspected the whiskey kegs. He had started with forty ten-gallon kegs in Jefferson, dispersed throughout the train at four kegs per wagon, except for the five wagons whose owners refused, for one reason or another, to carry it. Most of it was still intact. He had originally figured if he could get to Santa Fe with thirty kegs, he could still get nearly seven thousand dollars for them. Five thousand was all he needed. He was pleased that he and Sterling had had the foresight to order people to move the outside kegs inside before the first attack came. Otherwise, half the load would be drained out onto the gravelly sand.

Even so, a few kegs were damaged, he noted, and he

had lost one to the Indians, thanks to Moses's trading, and another had gone to the wounded in the hospital. But he still had over twenty-five barrels left, more than five thousand dollars' worth, if he had calculated right. That was a lot of money for whiskey, but it was more than enough for his purposes, plenty to carry out his plan, the train's plan, if they ever got past these damned Indians and to Santa Fe.

He noted with pride in his management of the situation that each of the thirteen remaining wagons—twelve if he didn't count Hollister's—had been turned into a miniature fort, shored up with trunks and pieces of furniture. Dead animals had been dragged into position and piled up in gaps between the wagons to form one clumsy abatis after another. Crates and other junk were stacked in their beds high enough for a man to walk upright behind them. Most of the wagons' canvas tops were stripped for bandages. What remained of each wagon's contents had been arranged to allow at least one man—or woman or child, he reminded himself—to crawl down and find a loophole from which to fire with relative safety. It was a good thing that the Indians' vantage point across the creek was elevated, Graham thought, or they would be able to shoot under the wagons. All he needed to add to the disaster was a bunch of pilgrims with ankle and leg wounds.

The only major worry that nagged at him, apart from the hostiles, who he could almost feel watching their every move, was the dead animals. In a day or so, the stench would be unimaginable, to say nothing of the smell of the dead humans—those who had been dumped together in the cave and those who were already swelling up in the afternoon's heat out along the creek bank. By tonight, they would putrefy, if they hadn't already.

He had smelled before the odor of dead horses and mules—and men, he recalled with an involuntary gagging. He knew what happened to corpses left even two days in moderate heat. They would swell first, blow up like huge balloons, flyblown and stinking, and then they would burst. Like the stench of searing flesh under hot iron, it was not a smell he was likely to forget. Afterward, he remembered with a tightening in his throat, things could get worse. Vermin would climb inside them, eat out the eyes and the soft flesh inside the mouth. Near the field hospital at Pittsburgh

Landing he remembered seeing dead Rebels being dumped into one of the mass graves. One of them seemed to be moving, and a soldier in the thankless detail jumped away. Closer inspection revealed, however, that the man's body was so completely full of maggots that the rotting flesh seemed to take on new life. And it had been cold there, late spring, not damned near summertime as it was here.

And then there were the hogs. Freed by the chaotic battle that swept across the Tennessee farms, they raided the dead, sometimes rooting up corpses from graves and feeding on them until the beasts were too bloated to move. Graham had seen them become so wild and bold as to come right up to the hospital tents and make off with the amputated limbs stacked and awaiting burial. One had actually attacked and half eaten a wounded man while he lay on his litter in line for surgical attention.

Hogs were the worst part of the whole nightmare, he thought. He'd never eaten pork since or even worn pigskin gloves. He'd be damned, he told himself, before the North Carolinians' animals were turned loose on the train's dead.

He moved quickly past the hospital cave without looking in. He wanted to see Aggie again, talk to her, and he knew he ought to check to see if the cauterizing had worked. But he couldn't bear the sight of the wounded right then. His memories were too fresh to deal with it.

Just beyond the cave, he saw Harvey Pierce and Virgil Hollister standing around talking. The tiny service had apparently broken up. Most of the men had knotted ties around their filthy necks, some without collars. Virgil's own collar was stained black with dirt and sweat. He was apparently missing the button, and his thin necktie was all that held it. Old habits die hard, Graham thought. He hoped that it had made people feel better. He had little respect for Hollister's sudden rediscovery of zealous faith or, for that matter, for any religion, but he knew that folks felt the need. He didn't really object to Hollister's ministrations, so long as they didn't interfere with the wagon fort's defenses.

What did bother him was the way the train was forming itself into cliques. Before this there had been friendships formed, certainly. But now they were losing their definition as a group. Small knots of people were always seen together. Sometimes it was necessary, as when Myra Henderson had taken charge of children whose parents were dead or badly hurt. Sometimes it was almost natural, like the way the Potters and Baker stuck together. But what worried him was when men like Hollister suddenly became the center of a group. There was trouble there, Graham sensed, and with cowards like Pierce and Golden gravitating toward a Bible-thumper like Hollister, it wouldn't be long in coming.

"If y'all are through with your psalm-singin'," Graham said as he approached the two men, "then maybe you could see your way clear to climb up to relieve those men up there. Find a couple of others, an' get up there an' keep lookout."

"Didn't see you at the service, Mr. Graham," Virgil said.

"No," Graham replied. "Get on up there, like I told you."

"Virgil here thinks we ought to get rid of the whiskey," Pierce said quietly.

"What?" Graham was shocked. Even before the wagon master knew that Virgil fashioned himself a preacher, he knew the Georgian was a temperance man who tried to preach what Graham now understood were sermons every time they stopped for the night. He knew Virgil didn't understand that the kegs represented all there was to the train's future, but he didn't expect him to try to interfere directly.

"That demon rum is what's causin' us to lose the Almighty's favor," Hollister intoned. His voice seemed to deepen with every word. "We should pour it out onto the ground. Yea, into this bloody soil that has become a sign of our wickedness an' sin."

"Get up there on that ledge, an' shut the hell up," Graham said. "Is that what you told people at that damn meetin'?"

"I preach the Word of the Lord," Hollister said.

"You said you knew somethin' about farmin'. That you were a farmer."

"I have beaten my sword into a plowshare," Hollister said, looking to Pierce for support. "But when I'm called to render the Word, I do so."

"Render your ass up to that ledge, an' keep your mouth shut an' your eyes peeled," Graham said, still controlling his anger. "Take a rifle with you, an' see what you can do about sendin' any Comanche you see to meet his Maker."

Hollister stepped backward a half-step. It wasn't total surrender, but he wasn't prepared to defy Graham's authority completely.

"You have sent the Child of Ham to deliver us from the demons of hell," he accused, "an' now you rely on Satan's helpmate"—he pointed to a keg of whiskey strapped to the wagon next to him—"to carry you through. You are a damned soul, Cleve Graham."

"Listen, goddamnit." Graham felt his control slip and his voice rise high enough to echo off the limestone bluff. "I'm in charge of this goddamn wagon train. You agreed to that. You signed the paper sayin' you agreed to it. Now, I'm in charge, an' till I'm underground, that's the way it's goin' to be." He finished quietly, "You do as you're told. You, too, Pierce. Get up on that ledge, an' if I hear that you've wasted one drop of whiskey, I'll personally see to it that you get to hell before I do."

He stalked off without waiting for the men to reply, but he glanced around after a few yards and noticed that they were scrambling up to the ledge to relieve the lookouts. Pierce, he recalled, had taken on the whiskey without complaint, but now he wondered if the man would refuse to continue to carry it when they got out of here. *If* they got out of here, Graham corrected.

No, he reversed himself. It was going to be all right. Things had looked bad before, and he always landed on his feet. He was lucky. The trick this time was to make sure that he wasn't the only one to come out alive, or, at least, that if he did live, he could still make something out of it.

3

WHEN GRAHAM PASSED POTTER AND BAKER, THE NORTH Carolinians were still struggling with the dead ox. The rest of their team had been led down to a large opening where much of the stock from that end of the train was stabled. There was nothing for the beasts to eat, Graham realized, and he wondered if anyone was taking water to them. He hadn't fed or watered his own oxen since the night before, and he suddenly was worried about them.

"You men need to leave that one be an' take care of the rest of your stock while they're still alive," Graham said.

"You're a fair one for givin' orders," Baker snapped. His hat fell off his head when he looked up at Graham. "Why don't you do somethin' useful your own self?"

"You got hungry oxen an' mules down yonder," Graham said. "An' if you don't get them some food an' water, movin' one dead ox is goin' to be the least of your worries."

"See here," Potter said. "I'm not sure why we're here at all. We should of cut south a week ago, most likely. Our kinfolk's prob'ly worried sick 'bout us. I figger we've come far 'nough with you, an' we're headin' out."

"Out where? You think that just because you have people out here someplace those Comanche're goin' to just let you ride off?"

"I've faced worse'n that," Potter said sullenly. "But jus' 'cause we're still here don't mean we got to follow your orders. We come this far, like we said we would, an' we toted your kegs, like we said we would. Our part of the bargain is over."

"If you don't take care of your team," Graham said, "you won't be totin' anything anywhere."

Graham walked on without looking back and was directly in front of the hospital cave when a fusillade of bullets struck the limestone directly over his head. He ducked so rapidly that he fell into the dirt. The volley was not a preamble to attack, however. It was just the Indians' way of reminding the whites that they were still there. He lay there for a moment, too tired to get up, when he realized that a woman was standing beside him. He scrambled to his feet.

"Scared me, too," Hannah Morgan said, and Graham quickly brushed the gravel off himself and tried not to look sheepish. She stood straight up and totally exposed. She was as tall as any man on the train and looked no less formidable. She carried a rifle, a '73 Winchester like his own, and wore a pair of large Colt's revolvers strapped incongruously over a leather apron that was stained with mud, blood, and streaks of dirt. A large Bowie knife was thrust into her belt. Hannah was one of the few settlers Graham had liked from the moment he met her. She had borne five children and buried four husbands, or so she said. She signed on with the train in order to find a place to make yet another life for herself. She claimed that she had been burned out by outriders during the war and dispossessed by Yankees afterward, that she had fought Mexican bandits and outlaws down in the Nueces Strip below San Antonio before coming to Jefferson, where she married once more and opened a saloon. Her latest husband was knifed to death after a dispute over a light pour erupted in violence two months later. Her black hair was feathered with gray, and she wore it pulled back into a severe bun so it would fit easily under a man's hat. It gave her a fierce appearance that was hardly belied by her girth. Like many men Graham had known and liked, she kept mostly to herself, rarely spoke, and seldom interfered in anyone else's business. Mostly, Graham recalled with an internal smile, she annoyed the women on the train, especially when she swore at her animals and exchanged familiarities with the men.

"You ought to be inside," he said, trying to mask his embarrassment. "They're likely to shoot at anything they can see."

To confirm his opinion, an arrow whistled in and stuck quivering in the side of a nearby wagon. They both ducked.

"Why don't they light the arrows an' set fire to 'em?" Hannah asked. "Seems that would be the best thing."

"Don't give them any ideas," Graham said gruffly. He inspected the thicket across the creek. A light breeze moved the cedars slightly, but no signs of life were visible. " 'Sides, they'd burn up the whiskey if they did that. Moses said they want the whiskey worse than anything." He immediately regretted parroting the black scout's opinion, but he swallowed hard and looked directly into Hannah's weathered face. She returned his gaze with a steady stare. Graham tried to read her thoughts and failed.

"I come lookin' for you," she said. "That gal down there's got her hands full. I stopped by, but I ain't no use to her at all. Never was no account 'round sick folks. Them other women won't hardly talk to her—'cause of that nigger boy an' her an' all the talk, I reckon. I hold you on account for that." She gave Graham a narrow look. "You ought to start settin' that to right, if you know how. Anyhow, she's plumb wore out. All there is for help is a bunch of young'un's, an' they's wore out, too."

Graham averted his eyes and looked off toward the creek, pretending to try once again to see the hidden snipers. He thought of Aggie and felt both warmth and cold guilt at the same time. What would Aggie's eyes look like against the beauty of the mountains where they were bound? He longed to find out.

"Could we get some more whiskey?" Hannah asked.

"More?" Graham spoke loudly, then caught himself. "You used up that whole keg?"

"She used a bunch of it for washin' out wounds," she said. "That brandin' you set her to doin' caused a lot of hurtin'." Her face darkened. "Keepin' 'em drunk is the only way to keep 'em from just givin' up hope."

Graham thought of how much he himself would like a drink, of how much he had wanted one when he was hurt badly in the past, and he gave in with a nod.

"There's a boy, one of the Ambrose kids—Jed, I think—who says he knows how to cut them arrows out. Says he learned to hunt with a bow, an' he's sure he can do it without 'tearin' up the meat,' as he says it." She shivered. "I just thought we needed some more." She paused and added with a glance at the full kegs all up and down the line, "If you can spare it. He's worked on most of the men already, but I ain't sure they wasn't better off 'fore he started messin' with 'em. Most of 'em is sleepin' now, but when they wake up, they're goin' to have a powerful need of somethin'."

He nodded again. Hannah sensed the whiskey's importance to Graham. She had told him more than once on this trip that he took more care with the kegs than he did with his animals. It was good stuff, bonded bourbon, not homemade rotgut. Jack Sterling, damn him, had seen to the quality, and now it represented everything Graham had in the world. Sterling had seen to that as well. He didn't like giving whiskey away to men who were probably going to die anyway. Still, his own mouth ached for the taste of it, and he knew he wasn't the only one on the train who could use a shot.

"There's a barrel with an arrow in it down the end of the line." Graham gestured. "More'n half of it's there, I'm sure. Go ahead an' get somebody to fetch it for you." He paused. "If you need more, take a full one. If there's anybody left alive tonight, I'll ration out some for every man." He rubbed his bearded chin with his hand. "An' woman," he added, "if any want some. But only the damaged keg an' one more," he warned. "We'll need the rest." He added the last comment in a conspiratorial whisper. He wanted her to know that it wasn't simply greed that motivated his protection of the sour mash.

Hannah's eyes hardened a moment as if she understood, but then she smiled in a false, almost pretty way. "If you're sure you can spare it, Mr. Graham, we're much 'bliged, I'm sure." And she turned away to find someone to fetch the damaged barrel.

She didn't understand, Graham realized. He felt guilty about his tone and his attitude. She had a right to know the whole thing, he thought. He should tell her. He needed an ally among the settlers. He was about to go after her, to try to explain, when William Golden came up and put his hand on the wagon master's shoulder. He wore the same expression of half-coward, half-troublemaker he had earlier.

"Now, don't go off half-cocked," he said. "But there's a bunch of fellows want to go out an' bring in them dead women an' kids an' bury 'em." He stepped away from Graham as if he feared the wagon master would hit him.

"Bury them?" Graham was flabbergasted. "Bury them *where*? You think the Indians are just goin' to look the other way while y'all stroll out there on some kind of buryin' detail?"

Golden drug his square-toed boot around in the gravel. "Well, we can't just watch 'em rot. You know what happens to people who lay out in the sun like that. We thought maybe we'd put up a white flag, an'—"

"Shit." Graham pulled out another cigar and bit off the end. "You go on out there, Golden. You put your wife's drawers on a stick, an' you go on out there. That's

Comanche out there, Golden! Not soldiers, not white Christian men who have a sense of decency. They'll fill you so full of holes you'll leak out what little brains you got." Graham laughed a mirthless laugh and pushed past Golden. "Bury them!" He shook his head as he walked.

"You think we're just fixin' to sit here an' watch 'em rot an' not do nothin', you're wrong, Mister!" Golden shot at Graham's back.

The wagon master turned.

"Way most folks see it, Graham, you're not doin' nothin' but nothin'. If you think we're just goin' to sit 'round here an' let 'em come in an' take us, you're just crazy. We're fixin' to do somethin'."

"What?"

Golden hesitated. He had no answer, and his eyes showed it. "We'll do *somethin'*. You can bet on it."

"Well, you go right ahead," Graham offered. "Matter of fact, I think it'd be just fine for you to go on out there an' confab with those redskins. They just might listen to you. I mean, you can see that I'm listenin', an' hell, Golden, I don't even *like* you."

Golden looked up, but Graham could see that he was defeated. The wagon master told himself that he was right: Golden wasn't much without a mob behind him.

"But I'll tell you somethin'," Graham said. "If you go, you see to it you go alone." He walked away.

Graham sympathized with Golden in spite of himself, although he doubted that the greenhorn farmer had any idea what lay in store for the settlers if the bodies had to lie out there another day or two. But he knew that the niceties of civilized behavior would have to wait.

Of those remaining alive, he mentally tabulated, more than thirty had wounds ranging from very serious to slightly disabling, and half the healthy and able-bodied who remained in the wagon fort were women and small children. More than half, Graham recounted. He had included the dozen or so carried off by the Indians as dead also, and he made another subtraction for Ambrose and his idiot son with a frown. Fewer than seventy human beings, he re-tallied, more than a third hurt too bad to fight, more than half with nothing between their legs, not even hair.

He ground the cigar butt out under his heel and

rubbed his stump. Beneath the leather cover, he could feel the small single-shot pistol he carried there. It had saved him before, he knew, and he planned to use it on himself rather than be taken alive. There was more than one way of beating the odds against being blind lucky.

He walked up behind Karl Runnels and Oliver Quigley, who were engaged in a heated conversation. Quigley, Graham reminded himself, had been a banker in the East. He claimed that the bank went under because of bad management, but Graham had also heard that Quigley had left for Texas just ahead of a mob. The wagon master disliked the pompous little banker, who always seemed to have an idea to share about anything the train did, although he was so green to the frontier that he continued to wear patent-leather shoes and a silk hat in spite of the harshness of the climate and surroundings. Graham wrinkled his nose in disgust as he approached the argument. He remembered another reason for disliking Quigley: He was willing to attach himself to anyone who he thought was stronger, likely to survive. Quigley had a Winchester in his hands, and Graham suspected that if he had fired it at all since the first Indian attack, he had hit nothing more than thin air.

"I zay vee vight our vay out of here!" Runnels fumed and struck the wagon with a hammy fist to make his point. "I kin ride, und zo kin Golda. Vee loze our ztuff, chure, but vee keep our lifes und our hair."

The tailor was propped up with his bandaged foot resting on a flour barrel. From his seated position, he could peer through two large stacks of cloth bolts and aim a rifle. He was pale and in a lot of pain, and Graham estimated that he wouldn't make a mile on horseback.

"But I *can't* ride," Quigley whined. "Mr. Pierce can't either. Lots of folks can't ride. Especially them that has children. What about them?"

Hannah Morgan had joined them, Graham saw, and he welcomed her steady voice. "Look," she said, "I say we give Frank an' that colored boy a chance. They only been gone a little while. Come on down here an' help me with a keg."

"Mine Gott!" Runnels exploded in a fuming cascade

of spittle. "Vot kind of voman are you? You goin' to trust your life to a nigger boy und a—"

"Shut up," Graham ordered, walking up. He had even less faith in Moses and Frank's chances than the German had, but he knew better than to say so, at least at this point. "I think you men"—he glanced sideways at Hannah—"had better get back to your watches. Quigley, I want you up on the ledge over the caves. Those men need relief. Hannah here needs some help gettin' some whiskey inside to Aggie Sterling to give to the wounded."

"You are *not* a king!" Runnels sputtered. "You are my employee. You take your orders from me!"

"How are the wounded?" Quigley asked.

"You can come by an' help anytime you want," Hannah said to Quigley and shifted her rifle to her other hand. She shot a look toward Graham. "That girl's holdin' her own. I ain't no good 'round sick people. I've buried 'nough husbands to know that. But she needs a steady hand with her, an' you'd do just fine." Quigley looked away. Hannah turned to Graham. "I'd do better out here'n this little peckerwood can. You want me up there? I can hit what I shoot at." Quigley was, Graham realized, a head shorter than the large woman.

"No," Graham said, "but I don't think standin' around here listenin' to him"—he thumbed a gesture at the steaming Runnels—"is doin' anybody any good."

The group shuffled in a half-circle with Runnels at the center. Graham looked at them.

"Mr. Runnels is right, Graham," Quigley said. "I don't agree with riding out of here or anything, but damn it, you aren't the goddamn boss of my life. You run the train, when it's running, but you ain't going to tell me where to go or how to get shot." Hannah chuckled at the little man's display of outrage.

"Back off, Quigley," Graham said, feeling his anger rise with a weary familiarity. God, he thought, will I ever make it back to my own wagon where I can have some peace?

"Why don't *you* back off?" Virgil Hollister said as he walked up. He had come down from his perch already, and he saw a chance to find another audience and took it. "I didn't like your puttin' my wagon down yonder at the end, an' don't think I don't know why you picked mine an' nobody else's. It's the devil's work, sure'n shootin'. If you'd do as the Lord says an' pour out that whiskey, them Indians would likely go on 'bout their business an' leave us be."

"Yeah." Quigley jumped in on Virgil's side. "Why don't you just go on about your own business? I think we might figure out a way to handle this without getting everybody killed. Maybe they would bargain for the whiskey. Why not just give it to them?"

"Gott damn right," Runnels grumbled. "You go 'vay. Vee don't need no crippled vagon master now." He looked satisfied. "Und ve kin vind more viskey later on."

"I'm half a mind to just start right now," Virgil said, placing a hand on a nearby keg.

Graham smiled gently. He rested the barrel of his rifle on his leather stump and gripped the stock. Then with a quick, even movement he swung from his waist and stroked Virgil's jaw, sending the big preacher flying onto the sand, where he sat down and immediately spat out a tooth.

Without pausing, Graham set his rifle against the wagon. He half-turned and picked up a long piece of cedar someone had collected the previous day for firewood when campfires had seemed relaxing and inviting prospects for an evening along a gentle creek. He quickly lifted it and brought it down on Runnels's injured foot. The German yowled. Blood spouted from his wounded limb and tears streamed from his eyes. Up and down the line, hammers clicked back and eyes that were drowsy with midday heat sharpened into wakefulness.

"Listen, you square-toed son of a bitch," Graham hissed at the crying German. "*I'm* in charge of this goddamn train till we get to Santa Fe." He looked quickly around him at the eyes that were straining to see what was going on. "Or until those red savages decide to come in here an' kill every motherless bastard in it. So till one of you shows me you've got balls enough to take on both me *an'* the goddamn Comanche, I suggest you do like I tell you, an' keep your goddamn mouth shut."

He glanced at Hannah. "That goes for you, too, Hannah. I told you I needed you to help Miss Sterlin', an' that's where I expect to find you if I come lookin'." He swung around and spoke loudly enough for anyone in the immediate area to hear him. At the same time, he reached under his coat and pulled out the pistol from his clutch holster.

"If any son of a bitch has *anything* else to say about how I'm runnin' this train, I think now's about as good a time as any for him to speak his piece or throw down somethin' besides a lot of useless mouth. I'm tired, an' I'm dirty, an' I'm hungry, an' I'm itchin' to take it out on somebody right now." He swiveled to check behind him and noted with an inward smile that Hannah's stance had shifted. Her hands were resting easily on the butts of her own Colt's revolvers. Her eyes moved in an opposite direction to his, and he knew that she was accepting his authority. That was comforting, Graham thought briefly. Someone would have to watch his back with this crowd. He looked around once more, but no one met his glance, and he restored the .36 Navy to its holster.

He reached down and jerked Virgil up to face him. The preacher's jaw was red under the bristles of his whiskers, and his mouth was bleeding. "That's the second time I've had to hit you," Graham said, "an' there's not goin' to be a third. The next time, I'm goin' to put an end to your pulpit-poundin' troublemakin' for good an' all. Now, I told you to get up on the goddamn ledge an' stay there." He shoved him away and picked up his rifle again. "You keep foolin' around an' you're fixin' to get us all killed. I'd just as soon put a bullet in you myself as put up with anything you've got to say."

He wheeled on Quigley, who cringed and brought his hands up to protect his face. "Now, get this, and get it straight: The whiskey belongs to me. Those who carry it, carry it as part of a contract. I don't have to explain that to you or to nobody. Now get goin' an' give Hannah a hand, an' then get your ass up there before I kick it up there."

He picked up his rifle and held it casually in his hand, but Hollister and Quigley knew when they were past their limits, and they shuffled back a few feet. Hell, Graham thought bitterly, Moses Franklin, black and uppity as he was, was better than the citified yahoos and country preachers he was stuck with. But they were here now. And, Graham admitted to himself, they counted on him in spite of what they said. He had talked them into throwing in with him and Sterling. He had brought them here, and he had to do what he could to get them there, at least as many as he could. More, he recognized, his own fortunes were tied to theirs. He needed to get to Santa Fe with as much of this whiskey as he could, but he needed them—and their wagons—also. He should have found better men than these, but none had appeared in Jefferson, so he settled for what he could find to make the best of the bad bargain Sterling had saddled on him.

"Reckon I'll jus' stay with the Sterlin' girl," Hannah said in a voice full of concession. "Can't hurt. Somebody c'mon an' give me a hand with the whiskey." She left, and the men waited only a moment before they turned and followed her. Runnels had passed out. Graham reached over and peeled back the German's eyes. Only the whites showed, and his breath was heavy and labored.

Graham spotted a youngster with a rifle almost twice as long as he poking his head out from under a wagon. His jaw hung open at the wagon master's violent assertion of his authority. "Go get his wife," Graham said, looking at Runnels. "He's out, an' he's bleedin' again."

"I'll go get Aggie Sterlin'," the boy said, scrambling out and pulling the ancient long rifle with him.

"You go get Golda Runnels," Graham barked. "Like I said. Don't bother Aggie. She's got her hands full. Why won't anybody on this train listen to me?"

The boy came to his feet and stared at Graham. "Where is she?"

"How the hell would I know? Ask around!" Graham yelled, then he grabbed the boy's gun. It was an old Kentucky rifle. "This the best gun you got?"

"It's the only one Pa'll let me use."

"Ain't you one of the Simmonses? I thought your pa was hurt bad."

"He is, but he said to leave his rifles alone. This here is all he'll let me use. My brother's got a Enfield."

"Shit," Graham swore. He knew that Bob Simmons

had quality rifles, new Winchesters and Henrys, maybe others. He was a gunsmith and had had a shop in Little Rock before he went broke. How he had packed up the guns in his shop and stolen away in the middle of the night had been a funny story around the train's campfires a week or so before. Graham knew that the old musket was likely in top condition, but there was no reason to make this child use an old-fashioned piece. "Where's your wagon, boy?"

"Over yonder."

"Go on, get that Runnels woman, an' then go get yourself a real rifle soon as you get back. If your pa says anythin', tell him to come to me. Get!"

The boy disappeared down the line. Graham stalked to the Simmons wagon and glanced inside. No one was there, and he turned and looked into the same narrow cave where the men had met the night before. He thought briefly of Frank, then shut him from his mind. A pair of oxen blocked the entrance, and he had to squeeze through.

"Bob, Bob Simmons?" he called.

"We're over here," Hilda Simmons answered. Graham's eyes gradually focused and he spotted the shape of the woman kneeling next to her wounded husband. There was no torch or lantern lit, and Graham struck a match before he moved over next to them. Bob Simmons's head was swathed in bandages.

"He don't hardly know me," she explained.

"How many boys you got?" Graham gruffly asked. He held the match up and knelt down and pulled Simmons's bandage away to look at his face. The crazy old woman had been sitting there in the dark since the torches burned out.

"Four." Hilda blinked in the bright light of the match. "Kent's my youngest. He's right out yonder. You want somethin' done, he can do'er."

"I want you to get that boy a decent rifle," Graham said. He turned Bob Simmons's head slightly so the lantern light fell into his sightless eyes and confirmed what Graham suspected.

She shook her head mechanically. "Bob says ain't nobody, 'specially one of them young'uns, was to use his good rifles. He says that they ain't old 'nough to take care of good stuff like that. 'Sides, they's all we got to make a livin' with when we get to New Mexico."

"Bob's opinion ain't worth much," Graham said flatly. "Not anymore." He regretted his remark, for Hilda Simmons winced as if his words were lashes of a whip. Thankfully, his match burned out, and they were left in the darkness of the cave. "Bob's gone," he added softly.

"I jus' sent Julia for some water," she said, as if that would make any difference. "She's due back. That girl's a worker, but she's a dawdler, too."

"Look, Mrs. Simmons." Graham struck another match and spoke softly. "You got kids to tend to, an' we got a problem here. Ol' Bob's gone. There ain't nothin' you can do for him now. Men an' women out there are goin' to die today if we don't see to it everybody who can shoot has a good gun to do it with. Now, go break out Bob's rifles an' cartridges, an' see to it each of your boys has one. An' not those ol' muskets either."

He looked at her and could see that she was staring vacantly. She never looked down into her husband's face. He must have been dead for hours. Graham didn't know what else he could do, so he turned and walked away. He mentally subtracted Bob Simmons from his remaining charges.

Outside, he spotted Golda Runnels fussing over her twice-wounded husband, and the Simmons boy standing anxiously by the wagon where he had been before.

"Go get your daddy's Winchester an' whatever else he's got," Graham ordered. "See to it you an' your brothers have one good rifle each, an' bring the rest to my wagon."

"Pa ain't fixin' to like that."

"I don't think he's goin' to care one way or another," Graham said, biting his lip. The boy only looked at him a moment more before walking away.

He passed a couple of wagons and threaded his way past the oxen and mules which were tethered between the wagons and the limestone bluff. There was going to be another problem, he realized as his boot misstepped into a pile of fresh manure. It was one thing to have a privy for the people, but there was going to be enough ox and mule shit along this narrow passage before long to make walking up and down almost impossible. He had managed to talk the Patrizi boy into the dirty work on the other end, but he doubted that anyone was going to play stableboy. He found a leather bucket hanging from one of the wagons and started hunting for someone to give it to. With water, he calculated, the animals could make it a few days.

He looked into the eyes of the men, women, and children he passed, but he couldn't bring himself to order any of them to tend the stock as he had ordered the North Carolinians earlier. He felt entirely too used up to face another argument now. Finally, he leaned his rifle against his own wagon and searched until he found an eroded depression in the butte where a trickle of water ran. It seeped out at the entrance and curved away toward the creek, and Graham used the heel of his boot to deepen the hole enough to immerse the collapsible bucket into it.

He carried the water to the far pair of oxen, which, he realized, were standing with their flanks exposed. Somehow, no arrows had found them, and he pulled them forward, grunting and groaning, until they were reasonably covered by the end of his wagon. He held the bucket up to the near ox's mouth, shoving it almost up to the beast's eyes before he heard the sucking sound that indicated that the stupid brute was drinking. This was going to take time, he thought.

The task continued down the line of huge, stinking beasts, and Graham brushed away flies and gnats that congregated around them. He felt light-headed, and his stomach growled. He promised himself to find both food and rest when he finished. He should have used mules, he realized as the next oxen finished the bucket's contents and lowered its head trying to obtain every drop in the leather container. But mules were also part of a bad memory, mules, outlaws, and Indians, he thought, niggers, Mescans, and civilian soldiers. All that had led him to this, just as all that had led him to the Valley of the High Snows and the most beautiful place he had ever seen. In a way, he thought, it was all a matter of luck.

4

GRAHAM FINISHED HIS CHORE BY TAKING WATER TO THE detested mules. What he was about with this train had nothing to do with dreams or with luck. It was a scheme and a gamble, to be sure, but it was no pipe dream. He was going to take these people to New Mexico Territory and complete the plan. It was straight business, and he felt comfortable with it. It too had come out of a basic denomination: he had had no choice in the matter. The only problem he faced was right here in front of him, and there had to be a way out of it that would leave the rest of these people alive.

He was almost back to his wagon when someone yelled, "Watch out!" and Graham instinctively fell to the earth. A long-handled ax flew over his head and buried itself in a wagon's side. He grabbed his .44 out of his holster and rolled over prepared to kill Hollister or Golden or Quigley or whoever was now trying to assassinate him. Instead, he saw an enraged Golda Runnels charging him with a butcher knife.

He almost fired, and he probably would have, but she was upon him before he recovered from the shock of recognizing her. As she threw her body on his, he was barely able to drop the pistol and grab her wrist to keep the long blade from his chest.

"Gott damn you!" she cried. "You kilt mine huzbin! You kilt mine Karl!"

Graham drove his stumped arm into her stomach and knocked the breath from the fat German frau, then managed to twist her wrist backward and force her to loose the knife. There was nothing but rage on her red face.

He found his feet and placed his boot on her arm as firmly as he dared. Pete Hightower came running up behind him.

"I tried to stop her," he declared. "But she threatened me with a ax, an' then she col'-cocked me when I wasn't lookin'." He sported a red gash on his forehead and frowned painfully down at Golda Runnels, who was so angry that she could only sputter and claw at Graham's boot with her free hand.

"She jumped me," Graham said, and he reached down and grabbed Golda's wrist in a strong grip.

A man named Weatherby, who had jumped down from a nearby wagon, came up to lend assistance in restraining the enraged woman.

"I seen the whole damn thing," he said. "Good thing I hollered, or she'd've split your head like a apple." Weatherby was a grotesquely fat man whose belt contained so many pistols and knives that he looked like a huge weapon-stemmed bush. He wheezed a bit when he talked, but in spite of his size and the burden of his hardware, he held on tightly to Golda and sidestepped her attempts to wrestle free.

Hightower stepped between them in case she managed to escape Weatherby's grasp. Graham once again brushed dirt and gravel from his vest, and Golda continued to struggle.

"Gott damn you!" she repeated. "Mine Karl iz dead! *Kaput!* Und dey say you kilt him mit a stofe vood!"

"I didn't kill nobody," Graham said in a quick defense he resented having to make. "I hit him on the foot an' he passed out cold. It didn't kill him."

"He von't vake up!" she insisted at the top of her lungs. "You kilt him, chure."

Quigley came running up. "What's going on? Miz Runnels, your husband's asking for you. He's hurting pretty bad! He wants you."

She looked wildly at the men's faces surrounding her. "Dis iz a Gott damn trick," she insisted. "Mine Karl's dead. I zeen him dead. Dis son of a bitch kilt him."

"I didn't kill anyone." Graham turned away from her with a vision of Jack Sterling in his mind. "I hit him, but I didn't kill him. But you tell him to keep his goddamn mouth shut or I'll kill him for fair an' pronto." Graham stalked away, and behind him he heard the German woman continuing to curse him and spit on the ground in his wake. "Hightower," he called without looking back, "get somebody to look at your head before you bleed to death."

Goddamn squareheads, Graham swore to himself. When he reached his wagon, an irrational anger and despair took hold of him all at once. He hoisted himself up on the side, stepping onto a wheel spoke and glaring across the tiny creek toward the cedar thicket where the unseen Indian marksmen lurked.

"C'mon, you red bastards," he yelled. "Why don't you kill me? Here I am." As his words echoed through the tiny canyon, reason settled on his mind like a weight. He realized how foolish he must look and sound, and he lowered himself to the ground with painful slowness.

All at once the combination of fatigue and anxiety sickness swam over him and gave him a feverish chill. He felt trapped all over again. His throat tightened, and he had to swallow hard to keep from gagging aloud. It was all wrong, he thought, very wrong. This wasn't supposed to be happening, none of it. And here he was in the middle of it. This hadn't been like the silly expedition he had gone on before. That had deserved to go sour. It hadn't been planned. They hadn't been ready, and for the first time in his life, Graham had been running away. But this time he was running *toward* what he had come to regard as his last chance at anything like a life. Why was it that it felt like nothing more than the foolish charge he had tried to lead at Pea Ridge, like the stupid stand he had tried to organize at Pittsburgh Landing? Was it always to turn out this way? Was every positive action he took to wind up nothing more than an idiot's dream of glory and satisfaction?

Again he thought of Emma, of his burning of the cabin with her body inside. A cold hand seemed to close around his chest. That, too, had been a positive action. It was to save Jonathan, to save himself. But Jonathan was dead. Emma was dead. And unless a solid solution presented itself soon to the dilemma he now faced, Graham himself would soon be dead as well.

Then he shook his head violently. No, he decided. This was not the same thing. This train had been properly organized. He had seen to that. There was nothing foolhardy or impetuous about any part of it. Every detail had been planned, everything but sickness, Indians, and dead Mexicans. With a contemptible glance down the wagon fort, he frowned and added preachers, bankers, and squareheads to his list of unplanned disasters. And then he thought of Moses, and he reminded himself that he was the key to the whole thing, the single basic denomination he had overlooked from the outset. Just as a Negro had ruined him years ago, now a Negro threatened him again. If he overcame that, he told himself, he would win for once. But overcoming it could take more luck than he had ever in his life enjoyed.

PART FOUR

BORDER GIRL

CHAPTER ONE

1

Aggie Sterling awkwardly raised herself from a flimsy tin chamber pot and banged her head on a jutting shelf of limestone which signaled the last place a person of her size could move into the rear of the hospital cave. She swore under her breath and straightened her skirt and apron with one hand while she rubbed her scalp with the other. The gesture reminded her that her hair was dirty, and she vowed that if she did nothing else for herself that day, she would find a way to wash it and the rest of her body. Aside from her face, hands, and a small area beneath her throat, soap and water had not touched her in almost a week, and her own odor repulsed her.

This far back in the cave, it was dark, and her errand forbade her toting along a lantern. She groped around until her fingers found the pot, and then she carried it to a keg set off to one side. She dumped it in and wiped it with a filthy cloth before replacing it atop the keg. Earlier in the day the keg had contained whiskey, but now it contained blood, urine, feces, and soiled bandages. Its stench twisted her throat into a knot.

The wounded men were mostly asleep now, and all but two of the women had abandoned Aggie and the cave. The cauterizing had forced unconsciousness on four of them, a thankful respite from their screams. The others now remained quiet also.

She was astonished she had found the strength to follow Mr. Graham's instructions to seal the wounds with the searing heat. It was not in her nature to play nurse, especially to a bunch of men who had no particular regard for her in the first place. But Mr. Graham had called on her to do it, and somehow she had. In a way it was satisfying. She knew that she was doing a better job than anyone else would or could, and the responsibility fitted her well. It was the first time in her life that she had felt so completely in charge. She was totally independent, and she liked the sense of power associated with it. It made her feel proud. As the hours of the morning wore on, she came to regard her chores as more than an unpleasant duty. This was *her* hospital, and the wounded and mostly unconscious men who lay about doing what they could to keep from dying were *her* patients. At least all but two.

Other women had drifted in and out of the cave for a while, but none of them was related to any of the men who lay suffering on the hard floor of the natural room. They stood around for a while and wrung their hands and spoke softly to each other while casting curious, disapproving glances toward Aggie, then they left. After it became clear that all that could be done for the remaining patients had been done, almost everyone stayed away. Later, Hannah Morgan dropped by, and now she returned and sat quietly on an upturned crate at the entrance. She was truly no help at all, Aggie thought while she straightened a stack of crude bandages, but at least she was one woman on the train who didn't look at her with a condemning eye and who would speak to her with civility. Hannah respected her, Aggie sensed, and she would settle for that.

The remaining pair of women and their open hostility didn't really bother Aggie. As the daughter of Jack Sterling, she was used to being treated like white trash. She had hardly known any other attitude from people. They had moved around so often and lived in such remote places that she had never formed anything like a friendship, at least not with anyone female, and she often felt more at home with horses and cattle than with people.

She spread her skirt and sat cross-legged beside a man named Hammond Gilroy. He had a grisly hole in his side which oozed with every breath in spite of the charred black edges of his cauterized wound. An arrow also had pierced one cheek, and his face was swathed in ripped canvas bandages. Only a section of his forehead and one eye were exposed. She took a cloth from a wooden bowl and wet his skin. The water seemed to sizzle when it rolled into the creases of his forehead, and she placed the back of her hand across his brow. He was on fire. His breath labored.

Jed Ambrose worked silently on another man whose name Aggie didn't know. The boy's tongue was gripped tightly in his lips; it stuck out and pointed upward as he concentrated. He was digging at the man's leg, trying to cut out a flint arrowhead that had apparently shattered when it hit the bone. The dogwood shaft had penetrated the man's forearm and stuck itself deep inside his thigh, welding the two limbs together. They had managed to get most of it out earlier, but Jed believed a shard of flint was still inside the leg, causing pain every time the man breathed. Now he chewed away at it with a narrow boning knife. The man had a piece of wood between his teeth and was biting down on it and making mewling sounds while the boy worked. Aggie stood and turned away.

When she arose, weariness swam up from her knees and made her swoon. She put out her hand against the cave's wall to steady herself. Hannah spotted the movement and jumped up and came to her. The two other women in the cave sitting next to their wounded men looked up, but neither made a motion to help.

"You'd best get some rest, girl." Hannah forcefully took her by the elbow and guided her to her crate. "You ain't no good to nobody if you keel over from pure-dee tired."

"I'm all right," Aggie protested, but she allowed Hannah to seat her and to bring her a dipper of water.

"How long's it been since you had some sleep?"

"I had a nap a while ago." Aggie sipped the water. It was cool but hard and tasted slightly of something rocky and dusty. "I'm all right. I could use a bath, though. Have you seen Annie?"

She had sent her sister out to gather joint fir root earlier, and she should have been back by now. She worried that Annie would wander away from the wagons.

"She come by here a spell back," Hannah said. "Don't worry. She's got better sense'n to go too far." She looked at what was apparently a pile of dirty rags in the far corner of the cave. "If you ask me," Hannah sniffed, "there's where a bath's needed." The rags were the remains of tattered canvas from several wagons, material that Aggie had sent Jason and Annie to gather for use as bandages. Concealed beneath them was Frank Herbert's filthy daughter.

Aggie had had no time to look to the girl's needs when she was brought in. She wasn't bleeding or hurt in any obvious way, and the only thing Aggie could do was offer her a quick smile and wave to move her out of the cave's entrance. She wandered over and collapsed on her own. Except for a wild-eyed look in the girl's eyes that appeared when she occasionally raised her head, she had shown no sign of life at all. Aggie had forgotten about her.

"I don't think she's sleepin'," Hannah whispered. "I think she's listenin'." She scowled. "She ought to be helpin'."

Aggie sat back against the cave opening and stuck her foot out into the sudden turn in the tunnel opening where a bar of sunlight spun a bright yellow glow on the toe of her battered shoe. "Let her be," she said. "She spent all night out there by herself, an' I suppose she's wore out. I know *I'm* gettin' wore out. I could use some tea."

"Thought you wanted a bath." Hannah mimicked consternation. "Young'uns. Never know what you want. You could use some sleep. Why don't you jus' make her move over an' lay down an' rest some?"

"I will in a bit," Aggie said. "I need to get some beans on. These men need to eat to keep up their strength."

"These men're mostly dead." Hannah sniffed. "You done all you can for 'em, girl. You need to rest." She looked hard at the two women who sat and stared at them. "It's 'bout time somebody else did somethin'."

Jed Ambrose rose triumphantly and waved for Aggie to come over. Hannah followed.

"Got'er," he whispered. "Got'er good." He held up a tiny piece of flint. "It was down in the muscle, next to the bone. It splintered off, I reckon. Had to cut him up good, but I got'er. He ain't hardly bleedin' no more."

Aggie knelt beside the wounded man. He wasn't bleeding at all. She rolled his senseless face toward her and was greeted by empty eyes. His teeth were embedded in the piece of wood. "We'll let him rest some," she said, shaking her head toward Hannah, who nodded once and sharply and led the boy away and sent him on an errand.

"I don't know how much more of this we can take," Aggie said when Hannah returned.

"Reckon we'll take all we have to take, more, an' then some." Hannah sighed. She glared once more at the other two women, who hovered over their men and checked their bandages. Then she smiled. "When my second husband died, I thought I'd had all I could take. Sat right down an' cried like I'd bust. But I put two more in the ground since then. I learned a body'll take whatever comes." She looked down at the corpse. "He wasn't hurt that bad. Why'd he die?"

"I don't know," Aggie said. "He lost a lot of blood. It was runnin' all over the place when Jed cut on him the first time. Then I burned him like Mr. Graham said, an' that seemed to stifle it." She smiled a thin, mirthless line. "He yelled louder'n anybody," she said. "I got him drunk as I could, but Jed's cuttin' didn't do him no good."

"I think his wife an' young'uns was killed yesterday," Hannah said. "I think he was one of them damn fools that went chargin' out there."

"He jus' give up," Aggie said. "He jus' didn't want to live no more." She looked at him and frowned. "I wonder what his name was."

Jason came in and dropped an armload of kindling next to the fire. He glanced at the sleeping Herbert girl and then stacked the small sticks. They had let the fire burn down to coals. It was cool in the cave, but smoky. The natural chimney above was inadequate.

"That's all I can find," he said. "Go easy on it. Word is we'll have to sneak out after dark to get some more. I'm hungry." He seemed to be addressing the room at large rather than his sister. She stared at him for a moment. She couldn't recall ever hearing him speak that many words at once. He was Jack Sterling made over again in many ways. He had once had blond hair, but it was darkening as he aged, and he had Jack's almost impenetrable black eyes. He was not as tall as Aggie, but he was lanky like Jack, and he tended to slink away and hide whenever he could. Unlike his garrulous father, Jason was quiet. Sometimes Aggie never knew he was nearby until she looked around and saw him standing and watching her.

"Go get me some beans," she ordered. The boy looked at her dumbly, then shrugged. "An' while you're out there, keep a eye out for Annie. I ain't seen her in a while."

"You're hard on that boy," Hannah commented when he slouched out the door. "You better lighten up. He's the only man you got left."

"I don't need a man," she snapped. She saw Hannah's surprise, and then softened her tone. "I won't have him long." She idly took a basin full of bloody rags over to the waste keg and poured them in. "I wonder every time he goes out if he's coming back."

"Why's that?" Hannah was shocked. "He seems like a good boy."

"He's his daddy's son," Aggie said with a finality that put an end to Hannah's questions.

Aggie moved restlessly among the remaining wounded men and satisfied herself that there was nothing else she could do for them. Gilroy remained blissfully unconscious, and those who were moderately aware of what was happening around them were quiet. She couldn't tell if they suffered more from fear or pain.

She went to the back of the cave again and fetched a skillet from an open crate full of pots and pans. She peered into the darkness. The spring was visible where it entered the cave from under a wall, but beyond a foot or two of its narrow course, darkness covered it. She squinted into the blackness and thought of going for a lantern until a second spell of wooziness struck her. Better to eat first, she thought.

In a few minutes Jason came in with some bacon and beans, and she knelt beside the fire and stoked it high enough to cook on. The bacon popped and sizzled in the pan as it warmed, and she directed him to go and wash his hands. "Did you find Annie?" she asked.

"She's sleepin' under our wagon."

Hannah resumed her station at the entrance, and for the moment the cave settled into a peaceful quiet. The edge of morning sun gave way to afternoon and creased the sandy floor of the tunnel opening. Except for the warm smell of blood and lingering odor of seared flesh, the whole picture seemed homey and comfortable. It was damp in the cave in spite of the fire, and there was enough moisture trapped inside it to make breath vaporize slightly.

"Wonder how far back it goes?" Jason stared hard back to the cave's dark recess.

"Me, too, but I couldn't get very far," Aggie said. "There's a kind of stream where the spring bubbles up, but it's too dark to see."

Jason arose and picked up a lantern. He hunched down and duck-walked as far back as he could. The cave bent sharply to the right, and Aggie heard him splashing into the stream. In a few moments he returned and squatted down again. His trousers were wet up to mid-thigh.

"Water's colder'n sin," he said. "It sure 'nough goes somewhere. You get past that overhang a ways, an' you can stand up or near it. Then the water takes off back in yonder someplace. You'd have to be a muskrat to follow'er." That ended his observations, but Aggie stared at him with her mouth open. He was a fountain of words this afternoon, she said to herself. She wondered if his sudden discovery of conversation was the result of Jack's death. It was likely. She knew he had feared his father. They all had. But she doubted if he had hated Jack as much as she had.

Whether it was connected to their father or not, she sensed a major change had taken place in Jason. When he had covered Jack with the shotgun back at the grove, she knew he would have shot him, if not for her sake, then for his own. That wasn't so strange; Jason had felt Jack's hand across his face often enough to hate him enough to want to kill him. But at the same time there was a spark in his eyes she hadn't seen before. She wondered if Jason had found a way out of the cave when he went back there just now, an escape that would lead him safely away from the crossing, if he would have taken it. Man or not, right now, she needed him, and she believed that he needed her. But he reminded her too much of Jack Sterling sometimes, and with this newfound tongue of his, the resemblance made her uncomfortable.

Aggie hummed tunelessly again while she stirred the beans into the bacon. She occasionally lifted her blond head and surveyed the cave room to satisfy herself that things were as well as they could be, and then she bent to her task once more.

"Get a plate," she spoke to Jason. "One for you an' one for Hannah." She looked down. "Y'all want some, too?" She cast a quick eye toward the two women.

"You jus' go on 'bout your business," one of the hens cackled sharply. "We'll let you know when we need somethin', not that we'll be takin' anythin' from the likes of you." The one who spoke was Glorietta Fulbright. Although not yet thirty, she looked like an old woman and had already developed a slight stoop when she stood. Her four children had been killed in the first attack, and her husband had taken arrows in his chest and shoulder during the second. Aggie had seen to him before Glorietta made her way into the cave. It was a wonder that he had been alive then, and Aggie couldn't imagine what was keeping him from dying now. Both arrows had gone in deeply, but Jed had cut them out with little trouble. Still, he continued to bleed. Glorietta refused to allow Aggie to apply the red-hot brand to his seeping wounds; she also refused to do it herself. The man lay where he was, breathing raggedly, raising bubbles of pink blood on his lips.

The other, Constance Kruikshank, whose husband of only six months lay by her side, whispered loud enough for Aggie to hear the words "nigger" and "disgrace." But she sensed that the woman—who was no older than she—was acting more out of comradeship with her companion than because of any genuine animosity toward Aggie. She had instinctively gravitated to Glorietta, the eldest woman present when she came in with her man, who had a massive wound in his neck. She had not lived long enough or suffered hard enough to be as bitter as Glorietta, Aggie thought, but she was caustic enough about the prospect of trading what remained of her trousseau for widow's weeds so quickly after her wedding. The wide flint point of a Comanche lance seemed to promise her just that fate. She tried to match Glorietta's glare when she looked at Aggie, but her eyes were filled more with a strange kind of longing than the contempt that flashed from Glorietta's hawkish face.

"What 'bout her?" Jason asked with a nod toward the still figure of Frank Herbert's daughter.

"Let her be," Aggie said. "When she's hungry, she'll eat." Something crossed Jason's eyes, but she looked quickly away. She wondered if Hannah was right and the girl was faking her sleeping posture. "I don't even know her name," Aggie said.

"It's Lottie," Jason said softly. He took his plate and moved away.

When she spooned out a portion for herself and Hannah, Aggie thought of her mother. It had always given the little wrenlike woman pleasure to feed people. They had only rarely had the means to feed strangers, and when they did, there were rarely strangers to feed. But in the simple routine of setting food before her own family, even when Jack was home, Mrs. Sterling—Gertie—had always smiled and demonstrated uncommon enjoyment in the simple, homely act.

Aggie could understand how her mother felt, she thought, as she ladled beans and bacon into the tin plates. There was a piece of stale bread beside her, and she tore off portions for each of them as well. This was basic fare, but it would keep them going. It was something worthwhile to feed strangers. She often wondered, though, how her mother could bear to do it after the pain it caused her in her life. Just talking to a stranger could, Aggie well knew from her mother's teaching, bring about cruelty that few people could tolerate.

She tasted the beans and found them to be satisfactorily warmed before spooning a bite into her mouth. Hannah wolfed hers down, champing the bacon bits and reaching inside her teeth with a dirty fingernail to clear a stubborn piece of pork away. Aggie liked Hannah, useless though the older woman was as a nurse. She wished her mother had been more like that. Maybe if she had been, she wouldn't be lying out there dead on the banks of that hateful creek. But no, probably she would be anyway. Hannah was a strong woman, full of muscle, and as capable of using a rifle or pistol as any man. Had she been caught out there, she would have made her way back. Aggie sensed that. Gertie Sterling had had a different kind of strength, and it had served her differently.

Gertie used to tell her daughter that she had inherited two things. From her, Aggie inherited a sense of acceptance, a capacity for endurance. It had been Gertie's mainstay since she was a girl, something to get her through one day and into the next. Also, Gertie claimed, Aggie inherited a sense of curiosity. "One of them can kill you," Gertie had told Aggie a hundred times. "T'other can save your life. Be sure, girl, you know which one's which."

She knew which one had led her to take a cup of coffee out to Mr. Franklin two days before. She had never seen a black man quite like him. Even when they had lived in places where there were plenty of Negroes about, they had kept their distance. She was curious, and that had enraged Jack Sterling and caused even her gentle mother to give her a disapproving look. The other legacy allowed her to accept Jack Sterling's contempt when she decided to stay behind and bury the Mexicans. She understood that accepting whatever he said or did to her would be part of the price she would have to pay. But she hadn't expected there to be so much of the same thing from everyone since.

After all, she hadn't planned to ride in alone with Mr. Franklin. But even if she had seen the Newsomes and Hawshaws leaving, she wouldn't have been better off going along with them. It was dangerous to go back for a bunch of junk they probably didn't need. Aggie had learned long ago not to place much value on mere things. People didn't think she had done right, even so. They seemed to be saying it would be better to be dead than to be alone with a Negro man. That was ridiculous. There was nothing in Mr. Franklin's behavior toward her that was anything less than proper, more proper, indeed, than Jack's had ever been. She couldn't understand why the others couldn't see that. She was safer out there with him than she was right now, in fact, with all these stupid people walking around too tired to breathe, each with a loaded gun gripped in nervous fingers. She was also, she reminded herself, a lot safer with Mr. Franklin than she ever would have been with Jack Sterling.

Still, their judgments seemed to stick. This wasn't Jefferson or Memphis or even Cairo, where once she had seen a black man and white woman walking arm in arm. Who was there to care way out here? Besides, she told herself, it wasn't like that. She found that she was fond of the scout; when she was around him, she sensed his strength and his uncertainty about her, his shyness and befuddled nature. It made him short with her—she smiled at the recollection—but he also had been honest. He hadn't bragged or boasted, and he hadn't looked at her the way other men often did, as if she were a trinket up for auction. He just looked at her. As one good friend should look at another. She had tried to let him know that she admired it. She knew what the others thought, and she had heard them whispering, but she didn't care. She could endure whatever they said or thought.

There was something else in Aggie's nature, which she herself recognized but didn't fully understand. It had emerged in the grove where she had insisted on remaining behind and burying the Mexicans regardless of what anyone else said or did. It had emerged again when Mr. Graham had suggested shooting the wounded people, who were out there and crying in their pain. It had made her pick up a shotgun and threaten all of them. And she would have killed them, too. It wouldn't have been the first time she had killed a man, a white man.

She knew that people saw her as a foolish child, but she also knew that she had more grit than they gave her credit for. That was what had given her the strength to throw down both barrels on poor Mr. Graham, she thought, and she smiled with tight lips, satisfied when she recalled the stunned look on his face. That was also what had given her the strength to put that hot brand on the wounds of these suffering men. Aggie prided herself that no other woman on this train—particularly not the two who scowled at her every chance they had from across the cave—could have done that. Not even Hannah. Or so she said. Even Mr. Graham couldn't do it, couldn't even bear to watch it. Aggie hoped they all took a lesson from that. They should all know by now that she was harder than she looked, and she was capable of being a lot harder.

She looked at Hannah's stout, well-armed figure in the doorway. Her apron was leather, and she had rawhide wristbands with bright silver studs inlaid in them. She was more man than woman, Aggie thought, something Jack had said about Aggie herself for years. But he made it a complaint, something to give him an excuse to strike her.

"You think you're a man, but you're not!" he would

declare just before the flat of his hand would find her cheek and leave it with a stinging red mark. "You're just a ill-bred little bitch who's too big for her britches. One of these days I'm goin' to teach you that fair an' proper."

Hannah was different, and Aggie found much to admire in this maverick woman, although she had no ambition to be like her except, perhaps, in the way Hannah seemed to exude self-confidence. She was afraid of no one. Aggie wished again that Gertie had been more like that so she could have bequeathed her daughter more than just a sense of endurance, but then Aggie caught herself. Her mother had taught her much, and perhaps the legacy that she had offered her elder daughter would save her life. It would at least keep her going.

As for the other legacy, curiosity, she thought it might help, too. She was anxious to know all she could about everything she saw. She regarded that as a virtue, maybe the only one she truly had, except perhaps, her looks. But that one wasn't likely to do her any real good. Not now, maybe never again.

From Jack Sterling, she had received nothing of value. He might have left the cattle and wagon to her and her siblings, but that was it, unless one counted nightmares. And there was also some kind of business arrangement with Mr. Graham, something to do with the whiskey Jack had stolen in Memphis. But it was an arrangement Aggie had no understanding of and less interest in now that Jack was gone. Whatever it was, it was crooked, and it was certainly worth much less than he said it was. The only surprising thing was that a man like Mr. Graham—a gentleman, she felt—was involved in it. But even gentlemen could be taken in by Jack Sterling. It had happened many times before. What could one expect from a man like Jack? He was not her father—never that—only her tormentor, and bitterness and hatred was about all the legacy one could anticipate from a man whose life seemed dedicated to using and hurting others.

Gertie had told the story to Aggie so many times that the girl had practically memorized it long before she truly understood it. She had never told Annie or Jason, because Jack Sterling was indeed their father. Gertie Sterling taught her life to her elder daughter as a lesson. She said she wanted Aggie to avoid the same pain and shame that she herself had learned to endure. She wanted her to know the truth about men, about how evil they could be, how mean. She also told Aggie that Jack would try to do more than be Aggie's father someday, and she wanted her daughter to know that he was nothing to her, no one she had to feel anything for if she wasn't of a mind to do so. He had spent too much of his life giving Gertie pain for her to allow him—or any man, if she could help it—to do the same to her daughter. So as soon as Aggie was old enough to understand at least part of the story, she began reciting the events of her life as if they were a Gospel. Aggie heard it then, and every time Gertie, whose mind was never sharp and who became weaker as she grew older, repeated it, she made it a part of the fabric of the girl's own life. There was truth in it that Aggie felt she was only just beginning to comprehend.

2

WHEN GERTIE WAS BORN IN 1840, HER FATHER WAS OUTraged. A literate if unlettered man, he was a seventh son. Gertie was also the seventh child, but unlike the previous six babies, Gertie popped out female. Her father was further deprived of the opportunity to sire a seventh son of a seventh son when her mother died a year after delivering Gertie into the world.

The old man—he was well into his fifties by the time Gertie was born—decided to make the best of his foreshortened career as the father of a mystic and magical offspring, and he moved the six boys, an elderly slave named 'Tober for the month in which she was born, and little Gertie from southwestern Georgia to the Green River in Kentucky. There he set up a combination ferry service and log-cabin church on the banks of the murky stream that snaked its way across the state. Somewhere in his sparse and haphazard education, he had heard of a place called Holyrood, which he immediately interpreted to be as close to mysterious as he was going to get. He constructed a dogtrot house down by the river, set his eldest boys to running the two-penny-a-fare crossing, and built a huge cross out of pine, which he planted directly in front of the church house. A passing Presbyterian missionary with a greater devotion to gin than to Gospel traded a fifteen-minute ordination ceremony and a thumbworn book called *Twenty-six Favorite Sermons* for a pint of potato whiskey and a free crossing, and the new minister took a vow of temperance as a testimony and painted a large sign to stand next to the cross which read: "The Church of the Holy Rod." The name fit well with his fundamental idea of child-rearing.

Each Friday night when he was home—which, fortunately for the growing children, was infrequent—he would line them up, force them to bare their hips and thighs, and go at them with a hickory sapling. He cited no specific offenses for the punishment, but he insisted that the treatment was as good a preventive as it was a cure for wayward youth. Gertie dreaded her turns with the rest, but unlike her siblings, she never resented it. She was so young when the ritual started that she accepted its part in her life. She learned to endure. Aggie's maternal legacy was firmly rooted in these weekly whippings.

By 1850, the Green River crossing and Church of the Holy Rod had become well enough known in the region to attract neighboring settlements' attention, and the minister was much sought after as a public speaker. He cut an imposing figure in his black broadcloth suit, stovepipe hat, and long, flowing mane of white hair that he permitted to hang uncombed down his back. When he preached, he shouted the petty sayings of his memory and mixed them with scripture and eloquent enthusiasm, emphasizing his point with a hickory sapling, which he slapped against his leg with no less zeal than when he applied it to the bottoms of his children. When he was truly inspired, an evening's preaching could leave him with tattered and ripped trousers and bloody legs beneath. He was particularly popular for funerals, with the result that he was away from the Church of the Holy Rod and the ferry a good deal of the time.

Gertie's brothers were a loutish lot, lazy and cruel to the animals. None was bright enough for lessons of literacy—sporadically and inexpertly applied by their father—and when he was absent, they took turns manning the ferry while the remaining brothers would scrounge up a jug of homemade liquor, sit in the dogtrot, and drink themselves insensible.

It was thus necessary for someone to maintain a watch for their father's return. If warned in time, they could arise from their stupors and pretend to be about honest work before he rode in on his mule and began their Friday punishments. When Gertie was young, the brothers cast lots for the duty, for it meant remaining out along the trace that ran up to the crossing, staying sober and awake. Once her childhood years passed, she was always the one sent out with a pallet and a jug of water and crust of bread to maintain the vigil. When she spotted their father's mule threading its way through the trees, she took a shortcut, flew back to the house as quickly as she could, and gave the alarm.

As the boys seldom knew how long their father would be gone, Gertie was often in the woods for two or three days at a time. One quiet fall afternoon, Gertie was lying on her pallet and watching birds and squirrels in the brightly colored forest. Into the clearing rode Vernon Belcher. He was tall, and to Gertie's unpracticed eye, magically handsome. He had yellow hair that flowed in curly locks from under a wide-brimmed hat, and he rode a brilliant white horse and sat upon a silver-spangled, jingling saddle. He spotted the girl crouching beside the trail, reined in, and spoke to her through a smiling wide mouth with more white teeth than Gertie could count.

After a few minutes of pleasantries, he announced that he was a naturally inquisitive fellow who had a particular and profound curiosity about pretty young girls, and he dismounted and pulled some apples from his bag and offered to share them with her. After they disappeared and he had sung two or three melodies along with his guitar, he offered a sip from a flask of whiskey, then a kiss. And when she refused the first and resisted the other, all his charm fell away and he struck her. Then he raped her.

When he finished with her in the forest, he picked her up, threw her across his horse, and led it to the ferry, where he paid her brothers with more whiskey for the privilege of installing her in her father's bed and raping her repeatedly for two days. If she resisted, he beat her with his fists until she was unconscious, then returned and completed his rape later. In between times, he drank with her brothers and played bawdy tunes on his guitar. She told Aggie she had been certain that she would die and had no idea why she remained alive. Only 'Tober came to check on her and tried to make her eat. Finally, he was gone.

When her father returned, he found her one good dress ripped into shreds and imperfectly stuffed between the bathhouse and a pile of firewood. He couldn't deduce exactly what had happened, but he knew something evil had certainly taken place, and he was determined to find out what even if he had to beat them all to death before one came forward with the truth.

It was Timothy, the youngest boy, who finally confessed. And lied. He told his father all. He claimed that Gertie and the stranger had met in the woods, come back, and claimed that they were married. Then, before the minister returned, the stranger had expressed a curiosity about the other side of the river. Once safe on the opposite bank, he had revealed that there had been no wedding at all, that Gertie had sold herself to him for money.

The old man dragged Gertie from her bed and beat her mercilessly before he finally gave her a kick that sent her flying off the porch and into the dooryard. She lay there nearly an hour before 'Tober received permission to fetch her inside. She was unable to rise without help for a week.

WINTER CAME EARLY TO western Kentucky, and calls for the minister's services declined. He chalked it up to the unseasonably cold weather, but he also noticed that fewer and fewer local people ventured to the Church of the Holy Rod for services, and on one icy December morning, he preached to a mere half-dozen snoring worshipers. As winter deepened, the boys also began to disappear, one by one.

The minister was angry and perplexed by the evaporation of his family. When the river froze, he spent his time sitting by the fire and trying to figure out what had caused the downturn in his fortunes. Since the beating, he had said nothing at all to Gertie other than to summon her to her regular whipping. She also kept her distance from him.

One night in March when the river was thawing and ice floes roared and crackled while they rubbed against each other in the current, Gertie told Aggie, she followed her nightly custom and brought the preacher a cup of tea. She stood momentarily by the only fire he would permit in the house and warmed herself, and she started to find him staring at her.

"You're carryin' his child," he declared.

She didn't know. Her monthly bleedings, a frightening phenomenon which she had only imperfectly understood from 'Tober's explanation, had not been going on long enough for her to be anything but delighted when they abruptly ceased. She had been sick in the mornings for a spell, and she knew she was gaining weight, becoming paunchy about her stomach. She didn't seem to have the strength she used to, but she had not felt physically right since her ordeal with Vernon Belcher and certainly not since the beating. She assumed that she would just be a long time getting over the experience. The idea of a baby surprised her.

"I should kill you, same way I would an inbred bitch," the minister told her. "But I might kill *it*, and bastard or not, it's a innocent soul, an' that would be a sin." His eyes lit with the familiar fever she had seen when he warmed to a particular line in one of his sermons. "*That's* the curse on this house and my church!" he resolved. "It's your mother's ghost hauntin' me an' cursin' me for damnin' her for bringin' forth a girl child all those years ago. You're a demon, girl! Woe unto you an' unto this house! You must be cast out 'fore your devil's imp is born into it an' damns us all to hell," he cried. He threw his tea into the fire and stormed out into the cold. He stayed out most of the night, and when he returned his face wore a pacified countenance beneath a beard festooned with icicles.

"I've done prayed over it," he announced. "She-devil though you be, you are still the fruit of my loins. To cast you naked out onto the road—fittin' an' temptin' though it might be—would be a sin as foul as that which you've committed 'gainst me an' 'gainst your Maker. Jesus forgave the harlots, an' so shall I. An' I will redeem your filthy soul as well."

He pulled himself erect and pointed a long twisted finger down into her face. "You will marry," he said. "An' I shall rid my house of you in an honorable an' godly way. You will remain a bitch of Satan, but it will not be on my head. God will see what I've done, an' He will restore me. You will marry the first eligible man to walk into my church." His voice boomed with the assurance of prophecy. "You will be a curse on him, but it will be in God's hands."

Winter dragged into spring with frequent returns of cold and snow. The river thawed completely, and the ferry business continued, but the church sat cold and empty Sunday after Sunday. Someone, Gertie would later surmise, was warning people away from the crazy old man and his plan. The minister continued to prepare a sermon, to go down and open up the building every Sunday morning, but after his two remaining sons filed in behind Gertie and took their places on the front row, he would pace and stew for an hour before deciding that no one was coming and then drive them out with biblically inspired and misquoted curses ringing in their ears.

In early April, just after a violent rainstorm muddied the ground so badly that even the old man almost despaired of reaching the church, they were sitting looking at the red mulch on their shoes and trouser cuffs when the grizzled head of the preacher looked up in brilliant expectation. A young man stood in the church's doorway. He held a hickory staff much like those the minister sold, almost exactly like the one he had beaten Gertie with, and he blinked rain away from his face as he peered into the small chapel.

Gertie followed her father's gaze until she found herself staring into the dark eyes of a black-headed boy somewhat younger than herself. Mud covered his trousers as high as his thighs, and his leather vest was also spotted with the clay. He was almost handsome, Gertie recalled for her daughter. Not in the romantic, dashing way of Vernon Belcher, but rather in a quiet way. He had a dark, almost fawnlike face that was smooth-shaven and seemed to glow beneath a gentle, sloping nose that separated the darkest, quickest eyes Gertie had ever seen. He didn't look that bright, but his eyes lacked the gray dullness of her brothers', and he had a kind of helpless, almost hopeless charm about his expression.

"My horse plumb give out," he announced after the quiet stares had continued for an embarrassing length of time. "Anybody here want to sell one?" His name, he allowed as he was backslapped and gladhanded up the aisle by an enthusiastic minister and two burly men, was Jack Sterling.

3

AGGIE RAISED HERSELF AND FELT THE SAME SWIMMING sensation of weariness, only this time it was heavier and more threatening. She went to the bucket and used the last of its fresh water to clean the tin plates. The remaining beans were still warm, and she spooned small portions out and took them over to two of the wounded men. Jason stood beside her, but he offered no assistance.

Hannah stood and yawned and strolled out of the cave with an announcement that she was going to check her stock. She was a strange woman, Aggie thought again. Not at all pretty, yet handsome somehow, attractive in a way Aggie couldn't understand. Aggie had seen herself only twice in a full-length mirror—most recently in the lobby of the fancy hotel, the Excelsior House in Jefferson—and she knew nothing about her was less than feminine. Hannah, on the other hand, could pass for a man if she put on trousers and a shirt. But then there were her breasts. They were apparently huge beneath her shirtwaist.

The men in her charge were all close to death. She tried to feed one of them, whose name was Carlysle Smith, but he kept spitting out the food. Gilroy was now thrashing in his sleep. The last of the second keg of whiskey had been poured into a pot, and she decided to give what she could to Smith, since he was in pain but not feverish. She felt helpless without some medicine or some knowledge or some help. It had been very foolish of Mr. Graham not to bring a doctor of some kind on the train, she thought. But she didn't like upbraiding Graham, even mentally, so she bit off the thought. She had crossed him too often, she told herself, and she promised to do something nice for him the first chance she got.

A man stuck his head inside the cave. She recognized him as Virgil Hollister. He was a preacher of some kind, she knew, and she disliked him. Her mother's story of her grandfather's cruelty caused Aggie to have an instinctive hatred of all ministers.

"I come to pray over the sick," he said.

"I doubt that'll help much," Aggie said sharply. "What they need is medicine. A doctor."

"I bring them the healin' grace of Jesus," Hollister announced. He ignored her after that and went to kneel beside Smith. He placed his elbow on his knee and kneaded the bridge of his nose violently as he muttered a prayer. Then he went over to the two women, who surprised Aggie by reaching up and holding hands with Hollister while he prayed again.

He moved about the cave, stopping and praying by each man in turn, even the dead man whose name she didn't know, and Aggie busied herself to keep from laughing out loud at this foolish man. He had on a wrinkled black coat and a yellowed shirt beneath it. His collar was askew and flapped up comically around his jaw.

She instructed Jason to fetch more water so she could boil some tea. She suddenly wanted to lie down, to sleep, and she wished Hannah would come back. Something in her forbade doing so while Hollister was here, or even in plain sight of the two women, who now looked at Hollister with plaintive eyes.

He finished and started out. "We're havin' a memorial service for the fallen," he said. "An' to pray for our deliv'rance." He stopped and looked around the cave's interior as if something there distracted him. "I thought you might like to come, seein' as how you got loved ones 'mongst the departed." His words trailed off absently, and his eyes narrowed as he inspected every item in sight.

"They didn't depart nowhere," Aggie snapped. "They got killed. They're still layin' out there, an' they're dead. I don't see how preachin's goin' to help 'em."

"Is there whiskey in here?" he suddenly asked while

sniffing the cool air of the cave. "Are you drinkin', girl? Have you no shame at all?"

"I'm not drinkin'," Aggie sighed. "I got whiskey for the men."

"For the men?" Virgil's bushy eyebrows shot up. "You're givin' *whiskey* to these poor damned souls?"

"I'm not *givin'* it to nobody," Aggie said. "We're usin' it to clean out wounds an' such. An' to ease the pain."

"Clean out wounds?" He acted as if he wasn't hearing her correctly.

"That's right. Hannah said it would work, an' Mr. Graham—"

"Hannah Morgan is a damned woman!" Hollister pronounced. "She is in cahoots with Cleve Graham, an' they're both throwed in with the devil. It's a wonder we are not all dropped this minute into the fiery pit of hell." His voice raised to a high pitch and echoed in the small room. Several of the men stirred restlessly, and Smith began a bloody coughing fit.

"I think you'd better get out of here," Aggie ordered. Her eyes fixed themselves on Hollister. He stepped backward involuntarily. "You said somethin' 'bout prayin' over some carcasses outside, an' you'd best get to it 'fore you need a prayer for yourself."

Hollister's eyebrows popped up and down quickly. "That's not a Christian attitude, Missy. No good at all. You should have more respect for the dead, 'specially since your folks is 'mongst 'em."

"If my mama was here, preacher, she'd spit in your eye," Aggie said. Her hands were on her hips, and she had already judged the distance to the shotgun.

Virgil was nonplussed by the effrontery. "God have mercy on you," he said, and he stalked out of the cave.

Aggie was not satisfied by her outburst. It was stupid, she thought, childish and foolish. She was supposed to know better than that. Gertie had taught her. Shoot, she thought, even Jack Sterling had taught her better than that. Maybe she wasn't as much an heiress to endurance as Gertie had thought. Perhaps she was just better at holding back.

The encounter had drained her emotionally, but she found some reserve strength and went over to check on

Gilroy, who had stopped thrashing while Virgil prayed over him. He was dead. The part of his face that showed beneath his bloody bandage looked frightened and sad at the same time. She closed his exposed eye and covered him with a blanket. She would have to get Jason to haul him away along with the other man as soon as possible.

The two women observed her movements and whispered to each other. Aggie felt suddenly furious. She stood and glared at them.

"If you've got somethin' to say to me, why don't you go on an' say it?" she demanded. "I hate snivelin' whispers worse'n anythin'."

Almost as if her words were blows, the women cringed and bowed their heads over their wounded men and said nothing. There were a dozen still-living men to tend to, Aggie realized, and she needed to conserve her strength, not waste it on these fools. She went over to collect the tin plate near Carlysle Smith, who seemed to have revived a bit and was looking around.

Aggie leaned down and turned her ear toward him. He spoke through tiny bubbles of blood that frothed on his cracked lips. "How you 'spect 'em to act?" he choked out. "After you took up with that nigger?"

She jerked back from the wounded man as if he had struck her physically. She suddenly wanted him to die, and her mind cast about her, searching for a weapon of some kind to plunge into his wound. But she caught herself before she actually moved, forced down the anger, pulled herself away from him, and stood. He closed his eyes again.

How could it be, she asked herself, that anyone could be so mean? She had not "taken up" with Mr. Franklin, as they put it. She had, she thought, done a decent thing, the same thing that she would have expected any one of them to do. That was all there was to it.

She told herself all those things, but the truth was only barely concealed behind her self-righteous thoughts: She did it more to make Jack see that she would do as she wanted and owed him neither allegiance nor obedience. She was sorry for the poor people who had been so brutally massacred, and she felt that they deserved to be buried. But she also felt the need to assert herself, to let Jack know that he wasn't going to control her. It was time to do that, she knew, past time. Jack was getting harder to manage with every mile they put between themselves and civilization. Fending him off was riskier than ever. He was getting to the point where he just didn't give a damn what people thought, and only by showing him that she would not obey him blindly and completely could she buy time. It had almost worked, too, she thought, but it had cost her more than if she hadn't done it.

Her main regret about the whole thing was that she had also had to stand against Mr. Graham. There was another problem. It created trouble between Mr. Graham and Mr. Franklin. That was her fault, and she admitted it to herself, even though she knew that if she had to do it again, she would.

Even so, all she had done was talk to Mr. Franklin—to Moses—to satisfy her curiosity about him. And he had been more of a gentleman than any of the white men on the train, certainly more than her daddy.

Aggie was not stupid, nor was she naive. She knew that white men hated black men, many badly enough to kill them. Once near Corinth, Mississippi, when she was only six or seven, she had seen five Negro men hanging from telegraph poles. More than once she suspected that freedmen had been dispossessed by landowners when Jack's glib tongue promised something in exchange for letting them have a cabin that a colored family occupied. And in Arkansas they had black men working for them, but both her mother and Jack made sure that they had no contact with them. Her mother said it wasn't fitting for her to talk to them, and Jack ran them off when the work was all but done. And there was Nigger Matthew and his family that Todd Christian and his brother had trusted. But that all seemed like a dream.

When Jack had brought them to Jefferson and learned that the scout for the train was to be a Negro, he was very angry, she remembered. He called Mr. Graham a fool, but not to his face. He said that "the goddamn gambler" had done it on purpose just to devil him. She knew Negroes worked on the riverboats and on the farms they passed by. She had even seen them in uniform at the stockade in the city. All her life, one way or another, she had seen them from a distance. But she had never actually talked to one, not in any way that resembled a conversation, and she still hadn't touched one, not in the way these people said. She was shocked that anyone thought she might have.

Moses Franklin intrigued her, though, and not just because of his color. She watched the way he sat his horse, the manner with which he easily handled his big Springfield. He wore buckskins and boots and the broad hat of a plainsman. He seemed taller than he actually was, stronger than most of the white men on the train, more in control of his actions. She admired that. She likened it to her own sense of endurance. He took and took as she did, and he never gave back. But she did give back. She had a hair trigger where anger and outrage were concerned, and she didn't mind letting go when people like Virgil Hollister pushed her, even when people like Mr. Graham pushed her.

After she and Moses rode in, she heard the argument break out. She hid in the shadows and watched, afraid that Jack would shoot the black scout down without giving him a chance. She watched the scuffle between the wagon master and Mr. Franklin, and she was surprised to see how angry the scout became, but when he kicked the wagon master, she almost laughed out loud. In fact, she probably would have if she hadn't seen Jack standing with his pistol drawn and his black eyes set in hatred. She was sure he would kill Moses then, almost as sure that he would kill Mr. Graham as well.

But Jack never killed any man face to face. He was a coward, Aggie thought. He preferred beating her and Jason and Gertie. They didn't hit back—at least not *usually*—and she knew that he was not the sort of man to stand up and fight when he could get what he wanted by lying and using his charm on people.

But Mr. Franklin stood up to both of them. She knew that they were both drunk, angry, and not too sure of themselves. Still, it was dangerous. The thought of the scout standing there, his feet planted far apart, his eyes steady as he looked down the barrel of Jack's pistol, excited her. It made her proud that she had also stood up to Jack once, and it reminded her that she and this black man might have more in common than she had first thought.

As soon as it became apparent that the confrontation between Moses and the white men was all over, she went quickly to bed. Jack found her and shook her. Whiskey was strong on his breath, and she could smell his body in the close quarters of the wagon. Gertie lay like one dead, but Aggie knew she was awake. She was always awake when Jack got like this. Jason was sleeping out near the cattle, but Aggie feared Jack would awaken Annie as well, and she shushed him. She probably shouldn't have done that, for it angered him even more.

He said nasty things to her, but that was to be expected of him. He called her "a nigger's whore," too. That was the first time she believed that anything more than a good scolding would come out of staying behind with Mr. Franklin and burying the poor Mexicans. Then he spat on her, and a huge glob hit her face, and that hurt even worse. They had their differences, serious differences that she feared would lead her to having to kill him to keep him away from her, but this was something else. This was contempt, not haughty resentment, which was his usual attitude toward her, and although she hated him, it hurt. It angered her that it hurt so much. The conflict in her emotions when she thought of Jack always bothered her. He had an uncanny knack for making her feel guilty and furious and afraid all at the same time.

ONE OF THE MEN started moaning, and she rushed over. The woman nearest to him, Constance Kruikshank, heard it as well and beat Aggie to the wounded man's side.

"He's breathin' rough," she said to no one in particular. The man was wounded by rifle fire, and he had a hole in his back. He lay on his stomach and was bleeding dangerously. "You didn't burn this'un good enough." The woman turned her eyes up to Aggie.

Aggie felt sorry for her. She was there to tend to her husband. Her brother lay dead out by the creek bank, not far from Jack Sterling's body. If her husband died, she would have no man to rely on. She had nursed him carefully, and Aggie had been kept away. He had bled a lot when they first came in, but he had been asleep since.

"I could try to get some whiskey for him," Aggie said. The pot was all but empty, but she managed to fill a spoon. She gently handed it to the woman, who eased the man's head around and tried to make him swallow it. He seemed to get most of it down him before she released him.

"What's your name?" Aggie asked when the woman sat back.

"Constance. Connie. That's my Grady over there. He's not too bad. I think he'll make it." Aggie saw she was lying.

"I'm Aggie. Aggie Sterling."

"I know who you are," Constance said. The older woman stared at them hard. "It's all right, Glorietta. It won't hurt nothin'."

Aggie imagined that "it" meant talking to her.

"It was your daddy talked us into comin' along back there in Jeff'son. Grady, he thought it'd be a good deal. Go out there where the land was so pretty, maybe grow us a crop of somethin'. Talked my brother into goin' too. We was headed down to a place on the Colorado, place where they said fruit trees could grow. Now . . ." She looked down at her unconscious husband and trailed off. "I'm so tired, I can't spit. I got no idea where my brother's young'uns is. Harriet—that's his wife—got herself carried off, I reckon. Or she's dead, too." She wiped her eyes. "I don't know. I wonder where they is?" She asked the question as if Aggie might have a notion. Then she added almost apologetically, "I s'pect they's in some kind of mischief."

"You go tend to 'em," Aggie said as gently as she could. "I'll see to Grady."

"No," the woman said, but there was no malice in it. "You got more'n you can do. 'Sides, we ain't been together all that long. I can't leave him just yet. Them kids'll jus' have to look after theirselves." She moved over to her husband and wet a cloth to bathe his face. The other woman turned her face away quickly.

"You know all this ain't *your* fault," Constance said. "If we'd give 'em the bull like they wanted, they'd likely left us alone. That's what Grady said, anyhow, an' I reckon he's right. I ain't sayin' that jus' 'cause he's your daddy, but most of this is Jack Sterlin's fault."

"Yes," Aggie agreed. Most of the pain in her life had been Jack Sterling's fault.

4

THE FIRST TIME JACK CAME TO AGGIE IN THE NIGHT WAS when she was barely fourteen. He had been watching her carefully whenever he was home, which hadn't been much before the war, and at first she had taken pleasure in his attentions: the hugs, pinches, idle pats on her bottom whenever she passed. When she grew older, the playful touches became rougher, especially when he was drunk, and as she matured even more, they became outright blows that sometimes left bruises and red marks. Aggie knew the couple slept separately wherever they found themselves. And they found themselves in a number of different places all her life.

Aggie was born on a flatboat on the Mississippi. Jack, confused and naive to the point of stupidity, never quite understood that his new wife was pregnant, and he greeted the news that Gertie was about to deliver herself of a child as something out of the blue.

Their marriage took place the same day they met, or, more exactly, the same day Jack Sterling stumbled into the Church of the Holy Rod out of the Kentucky rain and asked to buy a horse. By the end of that fateful Sunday, the bewildered boy found himself in possession of not one but two horses—a middling-fair gelding and a spavined mare with a split hoof—an extra saddle with a missing stirrup, and a wife two years older than he.

Gertie's diminutive size and quiet, accepting nature, however, disposed him to make the best of the confusing situation. He had had no intention of marrying anyone for a long time—romance and love had not yet penetrated his adolescent world—but the minister, who shoved his daughter toward him and announced that his happening by and seeking succor in the church on the banks of the Green River was foreordained by God, began a marriage ceremony almost before Jack was aware of what was taking place. The preacher was no novice to the uninitiated's reluctance to accept the acts of Grace, and he possessed a quality of persuasion that the adventuresome boy found impossible to resist, especially when he discovered that he was getting two mounts—which he had not yet seen—and an apparently willing girl in the bargain. Marriage, Jack felt, was a small price to pay for such a boon. He had but five dollars to his name and no prospects whatsoever.

Jack was not entirely ignorant of procreative procedures, but he was confused about the details. He understood copulation, but the process mystified him. He accepted the miracle of pregnancy as an automatic result of marriage. Through the three and a half months they had been man and wife, he had only touched her to help her up or down from her horse. He never even knew what he should say to her and had already begun wondering vaguely how he was going to get rid of her. Gertie, for her part, remained silent and was relieved that he left her to herself. She told Aggie she was happy enough to be away from her father and brothers, and she remembered thinking of the whole thing as an adventure.

Only three dozen horses and a half-dozen wranglers occupied the flatboat. His money exhausted, Jack sold their nearly worthless mounts along with their saddles for what few dollars they would bring and took a job as an apprentice with Amos Bodine, a Tennessee horse trader from Nashville. Jack soon learned that his training amounted to nothing more educational than shoveling manure from the barge into the river. When Gertie went into labor, Amos pulled Jack aside and began cursing him loud enough for Gertie to hear.

"I let you bring that mare of yours on this trip 'cause you said you was takin' her downriver to stay. I thought she was uncommon fat for a filly her age, an' now I see she's fixin' to foal. What the hell're we s'posed to do 'bout that?"

Jack was mystified. "I didn't know she was goin' to have a baby. I mean, I knew she was goin' to have one someday, but I didn't know when."

Amos cocked an eyebrow and studied the young apprentice. "Well, I guess it ain't truly no diff'rent'n a mare havin' a colt." He rinsed his hands in a bucket of water. "Least ways it ought to be considerable less mess." Aggie was born into his rough hands four hours later. Jack, with no clue in the world that the squalling squirming infant was anyone but his own daughter, felt proud and prosperous, although he had no money and no future whatsoever.

Once Gertie was resting comfortably on a bed of empty feed bags with Aggie nursing hungrily, Amos pronounced his task done. He allowed the wranglers to come by and gawk at the miracle from which they had been banished to hold the horses while the woman yelled. He lit his pipe and walked Jack back to the stern of the flat-bottomed craft where they lay.

"That's a fine-lookin' filly," he said. "Too bad it wasn't a colt, but I reckon she's healthy 'nough to foal again." Jack nodded. "I guess you got more'n your share of worries now," Amos said, "an' I guess you'll be wantin' me to take you on as a paid han'." Jack looked into the muddy water that passed beneath them and said nothing. He hadn't entertained the thought at all. He hadn't planned much beyond what they would do when they arrived in Louisiana or Mississippi, depending on which side of the river they made land.

"Well," Amos went on, "I'll tell you what. You get off down in Mississippi, fin' a place for your woman to live, an' then hightail it down to New Orleans. I'll be down there a spell, an' if things go right, I'll take you on reg'lar. I shouldn't do'er, should jus' get me a nigger an' say to hell with it. But that's a young mare, an' you're jus' a yearlin' your own self. You're strong, an' you got a face that'd make Jesus weep. You listen to me, an' I'll teach you what I know 'bout buyin' an' tradin' stock."

"I'll do it," Jack answered simply. It sounded good to him, he told Gertie later. It was more than a job—it was a chance to learn a trade.

Amos smiled briefly. "I'll advance you twenty dollars to get you started," he said. "You see you're in New Orleans by the end of August. I'll be at the Adolphus House. Don't bring that gal an' the kid down there," he warned. "There's yeller fever down there, an' they might get sick. I don't know how long you been hitched up together, but I doubt you want to cut it short right after you become a sire."

"Thank you," Jack said, accepting the money. "We've been married since March."

"March?" Amos raised his eyebrows again. He shoved his fingers in his pockets and counted briskly. "That's only four months."

"That's right." Jack smiled. "We're sort of new. Her daddy give me two horses an' a saddle to marry her." He neglected to tell Amos that one of the animals was spavined and lame for fear he would change his mind.

Amos threw back his huge head and bellowed out a laugh that echoed off the trees on both sides of the dusky river. "Well, boy," he said through his tears, "you got yourself a bargain. Two horses, a saddle, a mare, an' somebody else's filly. You might make a horse trader yet."

Although the idea that Aggie was not his child disturbed Jack Sterling, he was not entirely sure how it had come about. He took Amos's money and his advice and put ashore below Vicksburg, Mississippi, making his way over to the Black River, where he found a farmer who had a cabin he was willing to rent to the family for the winter. He explained carefully to his young wife what his plans were with Amos Bodine, and with Gertie quietly accepting her lonely fate, he left her and the baby alone with ten silver dollars, a worn-out milk cow, and a borrowed mule in the scraggy hardwood trees near the Natchez Trace.

JACK WAS OUTRAGED WHEN he returned in April. He had been up and down the Mississippi three times with Amos, and he was learning the business. The old horse trader kept his word about teaching Jack how to judge horseflesh, and he also taught him the rudiments of buying and selling cattle, a sideline the Tennessean indulged in when equine trading fell off. Not incidentally, he showed the youngster how to "dummy up" a bill of sale. "Handy thing to know," Amos assured him. " 'Specially when John Law gets to sniffin' 'round too close." Jack took to his new profession easily, and though only sixteen, he felt that in another year or two, he would be able to branch out on his own.

Amos's friends, however, found the youngster amusing. They were even more entertained when they gave him strong drink and found that he often became melancholy.

He longed to see Gertie, and he made the mistake of expressing his loneliness out loud.

"Well, if it's gettin' your pecker greased that's botherin' you," one of the men said, "I know jus' the place."

They pulled the intoxicated Jack up and walked him through the French Quarter to La Blanca's, a cathouse on St. Ann's Street famous for its blondes. Of the working women in the establishment, the bet was that no more than one was truly yellow-haired, but in a ribald attempt to find out for sure, the horse traders made the place their regular stop whenever they were in New Orleans. Jack was dumbfounded with what he imagined to be the beauty of the seminaked women who flounced around the parlor, and he settled on a heavyset beauty with flabby breasts. She led him upstairs by the cravat.

He flew down the stairs in ten minutes, embarrassed beyond mortification. The fat prostitute followed and flung a metal pitcher down the stairs as she cursed him.

"Squirted all over me, he did," she squawked. "Couldn't even get my drawers off 'fore he squirted all over me! I'm goin' to have to take me 'nother bath!"

The stockmen were amused no end, and Jack knew he could never face them again. He was furious by the time he reached Amos's boat. The old trader was nowhere around, so Jack left him a note asking that any money due him be sent to Jackson, and he took a horse, crossed the river, and rode north.

When he burst into the cabin, it was nearly midnight. Gertie hadn't thought of him in weeks. He threw open the door and found her lying on a corn-shuck mattress, and with only a glance at the sleeping baby in the corner, he ripped open his clothes and fell on her.

It wasn't a rape, not exactly, Gertie told Aggie. Once she figured out who he was and what he wanted, she didn't resist him in the slightest way. She knew this was coming, had expected it since the day her father forced her to marry this boy. She was prepared to endure it. He pulled up her nightdress around her neck and punched and kneaded her body, but she lay quietly and allowed him to have his way.

When he arose and straightened his clothes, he lit a small cigar and sat on a stool near the fire.

"She ain't mine," he said, gesturing toward the still-sleeping Aggie. "Whose kid is she?"

Gertie sat up and pulled her dress down. Her thighs were sticky, and she desperately wanted to wash them off. "You married me," she said. "You're her daddy. That's all that matters."

"You'll be havin' 'nother," he said. She noticed that he had been trying to grow a mustache in imitation of Amos Bodine, but the old trader had a walrus-sized affair that drooped down and almost touched his chest. Jack had managed only a thin line of individual hairs that seemed to race each other from his nostrils down to his thin upper lip. She wondered how she could ever have thought him handsome. "This'un's goin' to be mine."

That settled it. He announced the next day that they were moving. He used what little money he had to buy two plow horses from a plantation on the other side of Jackson, and sold the cow, and Gertie rode one of the heavy-hooved beasts up the Natchez Trace into Tennessee behind a silent and affectionless Jack, who continued to strut along the trail in front of them on the mount he had stolen from Amos Bodine.

Jason was not conceived until early 1860. When she announced that her monthly bleeding had stopped and that she was frequently ill in the mornings and explained what such omens foretold, Jack was ecstatic. He was even more thrilled when war broke out in South Carolina. A war, even a short one, meant that the horse and beef trading business was about to boom. Government money was sound money, and soldiers didn't dicker at all. He saw the coming conflict as a prosperous plum, ready for him to pick.

Jack was gone a good deal during the first three years of the war. Jason grew into a quiet and pensive little boy who tended to cry every time Jack reappeared and announced that they had to move again. Aggie was shooting up as well. At seven she was a tall, beautiful child with striking blue eyes and long blond braids. Since neither Jack nor Gertie had enough education to appreciate learning, she was confined to reading a worn-out Bible with almost a hundred pages missing, but the words confused her so much that she usually just sat and mouthed them in wonder with no intention of understanding them. The book caught her curiosity, however, and she pored over it nightly, asking Gertie about particularly difficult words and learning quickly that her mother was even more ignorant than she.

As the war raged on, Jack kept them on the move. He would relocate north or south of the Mississippi–Tennessee line according to which army seemed to have the upper hand at the time. He was registered on no census and was not officially a resident of any particular place; hence he escaped conscription orders.

Although he was not yet twenty-five, he found that he was generally accepted as a man of experience. He was more charming than ever and had a glib tongue. His easy manner gave him an ability to convince his buyers that his stock was the "very best to be had," when often it was wormy and diseased. He perpetually wore a smile under his thin mustache, and he donned a kelly-green coat so he might be easily identified as a neutral while he moved up and down the trails and traces of the Southern forest.

Meanwhile, his visits to the ramshackle cabin in the woods in Tennessee were more frequent and of longer duration. It was during one of his protracted visits that Annie was conceived, and Gertie put aside her perpetual acceptance and endurance and insisted that the family find a decent place to live. It was the first time she ever asked him for anything, and she carefully waited until he was sober before broaching the subject.

Jack surprised her by agreeing and announcing that they would depart for Arkansas immediately. His motivation had nothing to do with paternal honor, however. He had lately returned from Corinth, Mississippi, and found that there was a manhunt ongoing for someone who had killed three freedmen, stolen the cattle they were tending, and sold the beeves to a Union major who was patrolling the area north of Vicksburg. The culprit, according to reports, wore a bright green coat. Jack knew that it wouldn't be long before the idiot major who had bought the stock would put his phony bill of sale together with other officers' paperwork and manage to name him. It was time to leave the Tennessee–Mississippi border country, and Arkansas seemed as likely a place to go as any.

5

DURING A HEAVY SLEET STORM IN JANUARY 1865, THE Sterling family loaded their meager possessions into a stolen wagon, hitched two stolen mules to it, and led a small herd of horses and cattle onto a ferry which took them across the Mississippi and into Arkansas. They traveled north toward Little Rock and up into the Ozarks, where Jack managed to sell most of the stock for enough money to purchase a lease on an abandoned farm and house nestled into a small valley.

Gertie was thrilled in spite of the cold and snow that seemed to linger well into April. Aggie enjoyed the lighter work that seemed to associate the land and house with something permanent, and she was especially happy to see her mother smiling so often. Jack finally came around to accepting her—at least openly—as his daughter sometime during one of his absences. With the birth of Annie, he felt fat and content in his Ozark retreat, safe from the law, and out of the reach of the war, which was winding down to a bloody conclusion in Virginia.

He had gone to buy seed for spring planting, deciding that they could raise either cotton or corn until he found a way to gather enough capital to start stock trading again, when a group of Redlegs rode in on them. They asked no questions about the family's loyalty, but they did notice the dim "CSA" on the wagon that had emerged through the paint Jack had only halfheartedly applied, and they took that as reason enough to burn the house and set the family out in a field. Had Gertie not had a baby in her arms, the sometime soldiers might have done worse to her, but they contented themselves with running off the remaining horses, all of which Jack had carefully branded with his own sign, and firing the house that Gertie had been so proud of.

Jack used the last of his funds to buy what he needed, and then he set out to rebuild the house. It took him most of the summer to erect the walls and raise the roof, and he was compelled to hire three freedmen—"blue-gummed niggers," he called them—who assisted Jack in his inexpert carpentry and utter ignorance of farming.

Gertie was a long time recovering from Annie's birth, and she spent the cooling fall evenings sitting by the fire and staring into the flames. Aggie took over the housewifery of the Sterling home. Gertie would work for a while here and there, but mostly she sat and stared, and except for sudden, bright periods of animation, she went about the day-to-day routine in dumb silence.

When the first snows fell in the winter, the house was completed, and Jack fell into a depression. He went back to Tennessee in December and returned with a dozen horses and five scrawny cattle and amazed Gertie with his audacity, but she was happy to have the cattle, as one of them developed into a fair milker for her new daughter.

Jack divided his time between sitting in a desultory fashion in the new house, which was little more than a large cabin, and riding into Johnstonville and sampling the wares of the single brothel in the tiny community. He came to eye Aggie more and more as she moved about the house, and he often stumbled in on her while she sat in a tub of hot water and bathed next to the hearth in the kitchen. His black eyes narrowed, and he allowed his tongue to snake out and lick his lips as he watched her try to cover her nakedness during one of his unexpected intrusions. One night, Gertie found him standing casually over the embarrassed girl, unabashedly staring at her as she squirmed in the washtub. This finally was something she could not endure.

She spoke sharply to him, and he turned, more shocked to hear a harsh word of protest from his small, quiet wife than embarrassed at being discovered. He hit her. The blow was unevenly delivered, and Gertie fell back against a rocker more in surprise than pain, but he took her stumbling as a show of weakness that fueled the indignation building inside him. He stepped into her, swinging his fists.

Behind him, Aggie was screaming, and Jason began crying and trying to climb behind a stack of firewood. Jack hit Gertie a half-dozen times and knocked out two teeth before he realized what he was doing. Then he ran out of the house.

ABOUT TWO IN THE MORNING, while Gertie finally slept after Aggie had done what she could to bathe her bruises and mend her torn lips, a heavy thud sounded against the door. Aggie feared it was Jack's return, and she peeked out through a chink and discovered a giant, bearded man with a torch on what passed for a porch in front of the rude cabin. She opened the door and confronted the Goliath—or so he appeared to her—and realized that he wore the faded gray greatcoat of a Confederate cavalryman. She was confused. He studied her and the room's interior behind her. Old snow remained on the porch, and an icy wind blew off the mountains, and she shivered.

"Yer daddy here?" the man growled. She saw that there were large tears in the cloth of his coat, and he wore rough chaps instead of the leggings she was used to seeing on soldiers. "We'uz tol' in town yer daddy'd be t'home." Aggie said nothing.

"We'uz tol' in town yer daddy's a good frien' o' the South." He looked over her head into the house. "Not t'home, huh?"

"No," she said. "An' my mama's sick."

"You come out here, then, Missy." The man stepped back and held his torch high enough for her to see into the dooryard. Old, charred timbers from the previous cabin were crudely stacked against a corral, which at the moment held no stock besides the mules and a sag-bellied plow horse that had escaped Jack's frantic attempt to sell off anything that might bring in enough money to get the family through the winter.

Aggie stepped out onto the porch and saw that six mounted men were lined up in front of the cabin. A riderless horse and two men were on one side, and two other horsemen flanked the center figure, a bareheaded man who wore no coat against the cold. He was slumped over the pommel on the saddle, and Aggie could see that his hands were tied.

"You know yer horses when you see 'em?" the large man asked. It was more of a command than a question, and she nodded, her eyes wide, as she studied the large pistols he wore around his sagging belly. "Take a look at that'un." He pointed with the torch toward the mount beneath the bound man. Aggie strained her eyes.

"I don't know," she whispered.

"What?"

"I don't know if it's one of ours or not."

"Let's hang this son of a bitch an' get on with it," one of the men grumbled. He looked down at Aggie and widened his mouth into a grotesque, toothless smile. "I'm cold, an' she looks pretty warmin'."

"Shut up," the fat man ordered. Then he turned again to Aggie. "Go look at the bran'." He gave her a not-so-gentle push down the cut logs that served for steps to the porch. She had no shoes on, and her stockings had holes in them. She felt rocks cutting into her feet when she walked between the horses and looked up for the brand on the mount's rump. The man atop the saddle lifted his head, and in the yellow torchlight, she could see that his cheek was cut open; he had bruises all over his face. The men on either side of him, she realized, were also wearing parts and tatters of Confederate uniforms, but none had complete regalia. Their hats were an odd mixture of plugs, kepis, forage caps, and top hats, and some of them wore brocade vests and other odd garments. Several wore swords, and one of them had a woolly robe draped over his shoulders. Aggie could smell them as if they were a pack of animals. Her teeth chattered more in fear than because of the freezing temperatures.

The brand on the horse's rump was unmistakably Jack's, she saw. The hooked J and S had been burned in deeply, and it was clearly visible in the flickering light. She looked at it for a long moment, trying to decide what would be best to say, and her eyes roamed again to the coatless man in the saddle. He wore filthy, torn red leggings just like the band of men who had burned them out last year. She started slightly.

"Says he bought these horses here," the huge man commented. "Says they got 'em last summer. 'Course, that's hard to swaller, yer daddy bein' such a good frien' to the South an' all."

"They stole 'em," Aggie said, turning her fierce blue

eyes on the giant. "They stole 'em an' burned us out. They near killed all of us."

The man looked briefly at his companions and then studied the cabin behind him. The door was open; Jason peeped out.

"Don't look burned out to me," he said. "Don't matter. You say it's yer horse, an' I guess you know. They was a bunch of 'em. Redlegs. Satan's own sons of bitches. An' they all said they bought 'em here." He placed one finger along the side of his nose, leaned over, and blew hard onto the icy ground. Then he looked up and sighed. "Yer daddy's a Yankee, ain't he?"

"My daddy's a horse trader," Aggie said. Not for the first time, she began to fear what these men might do. "He trades horses an' cattle."

"He trades with Yankees an' Redleg scum," the man said, and he went to his horse and mounted, smoothly shifting the torch from one hand to the other. "Maybe they burned you out, an' maybe they didn't. It don't make no nevermind to me. 'Them as lies down with dogs gets up with fleas,' my mama always said. They got horses here, an' that's all they is to it, seems to me. I reckon we got to learn you Yankee sons of bitches that Bobbie Lee an' Kirby Goddamn Smith don't talk for all of us. Shake a leg, boys."

Aggie ran into the cabin and slammed the door. She didn't know what to do. Gertie lay nearly unconscious on her mattress, and Jason stood dumbly looking at his sister. "Get me the shotgun," she said.

She put her eye to a chink in time to see the men outside slap the rump of the bound man's horse. He slid easily off the saddle, almost as if he welcomed the end of his ordeal, and dangled from a rope tied to a branch of a black walnut tree near the house. They said nothing while he danced for a moment at the end of the rope, his legs kicking out helplessly before they fell slack. Jason handed her the shotgun, and she opened the door and stood out on the porch. She cocked both hammers.

"Y'all go on, now," she yelled at the men, whose horses stood in a semicircle around the hanged man. "You done what you come for."

They looked over at her. The large man came riding

over to the porch and smiled a bit under the brilliant yellow light of the torch he still carried.

"Listen, li'l Yankee gal. You jus' put that ol' thing away. We're fixin' to learn yer daddy a lesson 'bout tradin' with these goddamn Redlegs."

"We ain't Yankees, an' the war's over," Aggie yelled at him. "Y'all jus' go on."

The man said nothing back to her. He flung the torch up onto the porch, where it landed in the remains of a stack of winter firewood. It was dry, seasoned wood, and flames licked up from it immediately. Aggie's thoughts raced to her mother, who lay helplessly inside, to her infant sister, who slept near her, to her brother, who, she knew, also depended on her for protection. She couldn't bear to see the house burned a second time, and she was terrified of this animal of a man who sat his horse and grinned at her while the fire took hold and began to spread to the timbers of the porch.

"Now, we ain't goin' to have no squabblin' over who's takin' the gal," he shouted to the others, who were walking their horses around in short circles. " 'Twas me that found'er, an' I reckon that puts'er under my rope."

He stepped his horse toward her.

"C'mon, now, li'l Yankee gal." He grinned. "Less you fuss an' carry on, easier it's goin' to be."

She shook her head violently. Her hands were moist, and she tightened her grip on the long gun's stock. Unintentionally her fingers followed the motion, and she pulled both triggers before she realized what she was doing.

The recoil sent her flying back through the open door of the cabin, but the blast from the twin barrels struck the heavy, bearded guerrilla full in the chest and knocked him up and away from his horse. His boots remained in the stirrups as the animal bucked and shied away from the sudden noise, and the huge outrider crumpled into a bloody mass in the old snow of the dooryard.

Aggie pulled herself dazed and upright from the cabin floor. She looked about dizzily for another weapon, but aside from the old shotgun, there was nothing. The other men dismounted quickly and were now on the porch and in the room. She crawled behind the door and cringed in terror.

Jason flung himself instinctively against the legs of the robed man, who ruthlessly kicked him into a corner as if he were nothing more than a pile of rags he had stumbled over. The others began ransacking the house, looking for anything they could find of value. Discovering nothing, they soon turned their attentions to Gertie.

She was awake, and her eyes sparked at the man who suddenly hovered over her. He was a big man with long, dirty blond hair and a wide mouth that showed cracked and missing teeth. He flung off his makeshift garment, stripped the bedclothes from her, and ripped her nightgown open. Her small breasts lay flaccid against her thin chest, and her legs stretched out straight. The man roughly climbed on top of her, his fingers tearing at his trousers.

Aggie scrambled about and found an iron poker, raced up behind him, and struck him in the back of the head. Blood splashed from the wound, but he recovered quickly and turned around and backhanded her hard. A fierce grin appeared in his snaggled mouth, and he looked at her as if she were an annoying dog instead of a human being. The other men grabbed her and restrained her while the man set about his work again.

"Your turn's next, li'l she-bear," the man grunted and returned to Gertie.

"Hold still!" the man who held her growled in her ear. The smell of onions and tobacco on his breath gushed over her, and she gagged.

Something was wrong, she saw. Whether it was the pain of Aggie's blow or Gertie's passive ignorance of what he was trying to do or something else, the man on top of Aggie's mother couldn't perform. He fumbled with his limp penis, pulling on it and trying to pump it hard, but it refused to obey his commands. He swore at it and at Gertie. He slapped her twice and finally landed a blow to her stomach, but she absorbed his punches and continued to stare straight at the ceiling of the cabin, which by now was smoldering and rapidly filling with smoke. Finally, he rolled off of her and onto his feet.

"Let's get out of here," he shouted at them.

"Ain't we goin' to roger nobody?" the man who held

Aggie asked. His hand dropped to her flat chest and kneaded it hard. "What's the matter with you? She kilt Jubal."

He gave Aggie a quick glance and smiled. "Shit, she's jus' a kid," the blond man said. "I seen a heifer a few miles back. If you're that hard-up. Jubal's dead, an' I'm runnin' this show. C'mon, let's go."

The man cursed once more, struck Aggie hard enough to knock her down, and let her go. The cabin was now generally on fire. The men stomped out into the dooryard to reclaim their horses. Aggie raced over and roused her apparently insensible mother. She managed to wrap her in a quilt and force her to her feet. She grabbed up Annie and put her into her mother's arms, closing them around her and breathing an audible prayer when her hands took hold of the terrified and squalling infant. Cuffing Jason hard to get him moving, she herded them out of the flames that now engulfed the cabin and into the snow of the dooryard.

The marauders had fired the rude barn by now, and the mules and the horse were running in circles as the flames reached up into the trees. With shouts echoing off the burning buildings, the men gave a ragged version of the old Rebel yell and galloped off into the darkness while Aggie cradled her family together around the roots of the same tree where the body of the hanged man twisted in the icy wind.

She was but ten years old, yet she had killed a man, saved her mother from rape, and been burned out of her home twice.

THE OLD SHOTGUN, THE one with which Aggie had killed a man when she was herself but a child, had survived the fire and now rested against the cave's wall. The day before, she had killed an Indian with it, and the day before that, Jason had pointed it at Jack and meant it. She had also nearly used it to kill Mr. Graham. It wasn't that she didn't want him to end her mother's pain, she knew, only that Gertie wouldn't have been obliged for the effort. She had never taken the easy way, and it wasn't going to be up to a wagon master or anyone else to force it on her. The very sight of the weapon brought forth such terrible memories that she had trouble looking at it.

Gertie had told Aggie many times that her capacity to endure whatever came kept her alive, kept her going from one place to the next, from one day to the next. She said she believed in God, but not the God her father had taught her about, and she believed that when her time for suffering was over, He would call her home. Aggie knew she didn't need any help from would-be Samaritans like Mr. Graham, however good his intentions were.

Her mother was dead, now. If she hadn't expired from her wounds out on the gravelly banks of the creek, she had been ridden down and stomped to death by the Indians' ponies. It made her sick to think of Gertie's going in such a way, but at the same time, Aggie took a kind of satisfaction in it. Gertie had endured such terrible things and survived, and if this time the pain and horror were too much to live through, then it was what Gertie would have wanted. Aggie didn't think herself perverse for believing that about her mother. She only accepted the way Gertie was as she would accept whole cloth which would not bear piercing.

It was less than a month after that night that Gertie began telling Aggie her story. She whispered all of it by firelight every night when Jack was away, and she told it start to finish with all she could remember of the experiences that led her to the misery that had become her life. She was convinced that the man who tried unsuccessfully to rape her that night in Arkansas was Aggie's natural father, Vernon Belcher. Aggie didn't want to believe it, was certain her mother's fear had caused her to imagine it, but Gertie insisted that she was sure. "He'll never leave me be," she said. "He's with me, always wantin' to know what I'm doin'."

Aggie finally decided that Gertie's determination to make it so was too strong to be swayed. Over and over, Gertie said she wished Aggie had killed him instead of the other man, but then she would sigh and say it probably wouldn't have mattered. "He's jus' a man," she said. "An' men bring most of the pain to the world. Livin' through your nightmares is your time in hell," Gertie counseled Aggie. "Learn to accept what comes. Sometimes things have a way of turnin' right 'round while you're watchin'. Sometimes they don't. But when they don't, it's use'ly some man's fault."

Standing there and looking down that long barrel at Graham the day before, Aggie finally understood what Gertie meant. She had stood up to him twice in as many days, not so much out of any specific purpose but more out of a sense that no man—not her father, not Jack Sterling, not Cleve Graham, not even a boy named Todd Christian—would ever dominate her life again or make her do or feel anything. She was free of all that, she told herself. She was her own person who would make her own choices in life. She wondered what Mr. Graham would think of that.

What Graham might think of her didn't occupy her mind for long. She liked him, and in a way she wished that he and not Jack Sterling had been her daddy—not her father—she continued to make that distinction—for she found in his quiet demeanor a strength she admired. She also thought of him as a strong man in spite of everything she had seen him do and heard him say. He was not as strong as Moses Franklin, at least not in the same way. His strength was different: one born out of loneliness and experience. He could be kind, if he would only let himself, she thought. He had known love, she believed, and probably sadness. It showed in his face when he didn't know anyone was looking. She hoped that he could forgive her, could understand that she had to stand against him for reasons that she couldn't ever explain. And, she thought as she called forth the image of his lined, bearded face, she hoped he would find someone to love again.

As for herself, Aggie thought with a small, self-satisfied smile, she had her own plans.

CHAPTER TWO

1

ALL THE WOUNDED MEN WERE AT LAST QUIET, AND THE situation in the hospital cave appeared to be under control. Aggie stepped out into the noonday sunshine and looked up and down the wagon train. Some faces turned away from her as they gathered for Hollister's impromptu church service, but others blatantly stared at her. In another time, another place, she would have found their stares mildly pleasing or, maybe, rude. But now, here, they were only ironically amusing. She returned each blank gaze evenly and took pleasure when a pair of eyes would turn away and seek something else to focus on.

Perhaps it helped them if they had someone to turn their wrath toward. If they refrained from condemning her, even for a moment, then they would have to look at themselves. Aggie was good at looking at herself, and she believed she knew how to be honest about it. The hypocrisy of the settlers around her made her sad. If she had the energy, she thought, it would make her angry as well.

The sun was warm. It made her sleepier than before. The boom of a weapon down on the far end of the wagon line startled her, and she instinctively ducked back inside and went for her shotgun. When it was repeated again in a few minutes, she poked her head out and received an unsolicited explanation from a man on a nearby wagon that some boys were shooting at buzzards.

She looked up and saw the huge birds circling. They looked like small black clouds in the seamless blue dome, and she shivered. She had intended to peek out beyond the wagons and see if Gertie's body was recognizable among the heaps of rags that had only yesterday been living human beings, but now, with the thought of scavengers among the dead, she changed her mind.

Annie was being sleepily dragged by her brother down the line. She had an armful of joint fir root, which Aggie intended to blend with some strong tea. She knew it had medicinal powers. She planned to brew up a big pot for anyone who wanted it. Some of the settlers had been swilling coffee all night and morning, and the tea, although bitter, might be better for them.

She went back into the cave and was surprised to see a slight grin from Constance when she knelt beside the fire and fed in some more kindling. Lottie, Frank Herbert's daughter, was now awake, sitting up and staring stupidly around. She inspected Aggie and her sister, then she let her eyes drift toward Constance and Glorietta, who pretended not to notice her. Her dress was in tatters, and she had difficulty holding up the ragged ends of cloth over her breasts. The dirty coat she had worn into the cave lay beside her, but she paid it no attention.

She had said nothing to anyone since coming in, and now she continued her mute observation of her surroundings. After a few minutes, she lay down and apparently went back to sleep. Jason went over and squatted near her.

"This was all I could get at," Annie said, her voice lilting in a high soprano. For years she had come to see Aggie as her mother. Aggie looked at her. She was a plain girl and resembled her elder sister only in incidental ways. They both were tall and blond, and both possessed proud chins and small, upturned noses, but there the similarities ended. Annie, like Jason, resembled Jack Sterling much more than Gertie. Her hair was rapidly turning nut-brown, and both of them had their father's dark, almost black eyes, which tended to dart around quickly and suspiciously and to light up when mischief was afoot. Both also would grow into handsome adults, if, Aggie reminded herself, they grew up at all.

"That'll be fine," she said. "Jason, get me the tea from my chest." He obeyed with the dull movements of a sleepwalker.

She placed a pot full of water on a rock near the fire and sat back to wait for it to boil. Automatically, she checked her patients. They all seemed to be resting, and some of them were apparently awake. Incredibly, none of them had filled a chamber pot since dawn, and she knew that sooner or later that chore would be hers as well. She couldn't even ask Jason to handle that. She wondered what the women in the train would think of her cleaning the private parts of the wounded men.

The water came to a rapid boil, and she filled a small teapot with her precious leaves. Jack had brought the tea from Texas. He also had brought the teapot and the handsomely carved chest. Even the calico dress Aggie wore—now filthy and stained with blood and grime—had come back with him from one of his trips. He did spend money on her, she admitted. He liked to, when he had it. It never seemed to occur to him when he was away that his family was sometimes near starvation, freezing in the winter, destitute and begging for the charity of strangers. Jack Sterling didn't see those things. His eyes were always on some distant, future prosperity that always eluded him.

She knew him to be demanding of others, but he seldom asked much of himself. He was a man to whose mouth a lie came easily. She had heard him fabricate intricate fiction out of summer clouds. For him it was nothing to look at a tumbledown shack and ignore its leaking roof and slanting porch and see a palace. His life was an ongoing progression of what would be happening as soon as "my deal comes together," and no dream was spun without the sincerity of total conviction holding it intact. None, though, ever came true, Aggie thought. Not even those which, by the standards of his wilder fancies, were possible.

He never bought or stole a horse he couldn't trade for a better one, never faced an accusation he couldn't slip out of. "If he'd ever had schoolin'," Gertie often said, "there's no tellin' what sort of rich man he might be. Could of been a governor." There was no doubt in Aggie's mind that if he had been present the night the raiders came—either time—Jack would have talked them out of any theft or violence whatsoever. He likely would have sold them the mules, she thought.

Maybe it is as Gertie always said, she thought. Gertie told her that she had learned enough to survive no matter what, not only in terms of endurance, but also in terms of what a starving person could eat, where she could find strength in nature, how she could protect herself and those she loved even when it seemed that all was hopeless. She learned to get by without the help of men, and even more significantly, she learned how to avoid their interference. Gertie knew none of these things when she married, but she learned, and she taught her daughter well.

2

JACK STERLING DID NOT REBUILD THEIR ARKANSAS cabin. Twice burned, he declared, was enough. Somehow, the old wagon had been spared the ravages of the marauders, and with the wind howling through the Ozarks, Jack loaded what he could salvage into it, along with his family, and headed south toward Louisiana. He entertained the idea of going up into Kansas or Nebraska, to try to farm again, but his meager experience the previous year had convinced him that he lacked both a knowledge of and a taste for the agrarian life. He had a vague idea of going into Texas, of finding a place where he might actually raise cattle or horses or both, honestly. But the idea only came forth between bouts of cursing, and it remained a cloudy dream.

Work and a home eluded the Sterlings. For the next several years they lived like gypsies. They went back into Tennessee and down into Mississippi, up into Missouri and Illinois, and back down into southern Arkansas. As soon as Jack found a place where they could stay for an indefinite period, he would take off. Sometimes he would return flush with money to renew their livestock and supplies. More usually, he returned in a terrible state, sometimes bloody from a severe beating, and twice he came in with bullet wounds festering and threatening to kill him. Once he stayed only two hours before lighting out, and his dust hardly settled in the dooryard behind his fleeing horse before a federal marshal rode up on a piebald gelding with white socks, a warrant for Jack's arrest in his hand. They never saw the marshal again, but when Jack returned two months later, he was riding the lawman's horse.

Gertie, for her part, began visibly to shrink into the

crouched figure of a haggard old woman. Although she was not past her mid-thirties, she took on the aspect of a person twice her age. A hump began developing on her back as her natural stoop became permanent. Her hair grayed, and the glint in her eyes only returned when she sat around a fire and told her elder daughter of her past. Then she would take on the character of a young girl again, and in her animation, she would reflect her former prettiness and energy. She detailed her adventures and drew lessons from them as if they were fables, adding details, embellishing and enlarging those parts of them she was forced to imagine. At times, Gertie seemed frantic to teach Aggie the facts of her life through the experiences of her mother. "I want you to *see*," she always said and grabbed her blond daughter by her shoulders and peered into her eyes. "I want you to see and understand."

At first the lessons had little real meaning, but whenever Jack was around, she studied him curiously, comparing her long, lean body to his short, thin frame, her light fairness to his darker features, and feeling more and more distant from the man she called Daddy.

Jack's visits—or so Aggie and her siblings came to regard them, instead of "homecomings," as he insisted they were—were sometimes wild and terrible affairs. He usually arrived drunk, or he became so as quickly as he could raise the price of a jug. Whatever charm he had shown as a young man disappeared within hours after his arrival. His face remained handsome, but it was lined and weather-beaten, and even when he came back with money in his pockets and optimism on his lips, his dark eyes looked worn, hollow, and disillusioned. Regardless of his financial and physical state, however, he always claimed to be on the verge of great success. He spoke of big deals he had working in Texas, or of a marvelous business opportunity he had stumbled onto in New Orleans. He had a bottomless bag of schemes and tricks to "make it big," as he put it. The family was left with the impossible task of trying to imagine where he had been and what he had actually done. Aggie had no experience to help her wonderings, and she had to content herself with Jack's inflated descriptions of important people and wealthy homes he had visited.

When Jack returned happy and confident with himself, even when he had no money, he sometimes brought gifts to the children. Aggie noticed that not once did he bring even so much as a piece of ribbon for Gertie. He brought especially fine things to Aggie, however. He brought her the chest, and he brought her the teapot and tea to go in it. He brought her lace once, and a large piece of silk, which he said with a wink he hoped would be her wedding dress. He brought Jason knives and even a pistol, and he brought dolls for Annie and toys for all of them. On one trip he brought Aggie a mare, which she loved and learned to ride, and another time he brought her a piece of bright, rough stone, an agate, he called it. It was yellow with brown streaks running through it, and he said he would have it set into a ring for her after his next trip, when he expected to be wealthy beyond their wildest expectations.

It was during that particular homecoming, however, that he first gave her an inkling of how truly evil he could be. After giving presents to his stunned family, he sat by the small fire and expansively related the details of his successful "horse buying" trip down to Texas. He held forth, and continued to drink, and finally fell into a stupor in front of the fire, and the family crept off to bed.

Because Aggie was now fourteen, Gertie had decided she needed to have a bed, if not a room, of her own. They had cleaned out the rafters of the cabin and stretched some boards across it to make a loft, and it was here that she spread a pallet while Gertie took the bedroom and Jason and Annie slept in the main room of the house. They left Jack where he was, propped up on his saddle in front of the fireplace with an empty jug of corn whiskey.

Aggie had just managed to shut out Jack's sonorous breathing and to fall asleep when she started awake with the fall of his heavy hand on her shoulder. At first she was terrified, thinking that perhaps some stranger had invaded the cabin and climbed the narrow ladder up to the loft. She kicked out automatically with her long legs and caught Jack squarely in the solar plexus, knocking the breath from him and pushing him backward. For one horrible moment he seemed to hang there, his unshaven face wide with fear as his arms sought purchase in the thin air and as his stockinged feet kicked uselessly beneath him. Then he fell with a crash onto the floor six feet below and lay there unconscious. Aggie was sure she had killed him.

Gertie was roused by the noise, as were the other children, who stared wide-eyed at the broken figure of their father where he lay amid the shambles of what had been a cane table. Jack was not dead, in spite of appearances. By the time Aggie had wrapped a blanket around herself and descended the ladder, his snores filled the small room, and his family stood mutely around him.

"What'd he do?" Gertie asked.

"Nothin'," Aggie lied. "Guess he fell down." Although she sensed that Gertie would understand, sympathize with her, she also knew that not even her mother's stoicism would tolerate such a thing as Jack had tried. Oddly, Aggie felt guilty, and she figured both her parents would be furious when he awoke the next morning. Jack's anger she could handle, she thought, but Gertie's she could not abide.

He complained of nothing besides a headache when he awoke, though, and he left that same afternoon in high spirits, his mouth full of promises about the fine life they would soon be leading. He even looked a bit dashing after a shave and a bath as he rode off, and Aggie thought she had never seen him more handsome in spite of her fear about what had taken place the night before.

When he returned in a month's time, he was in worse shape than ever. He immediately sold the mare as well as her lace and her silk cloth and Jason's pistol. Annie had soiled the dolls too much to sell, and he apparently forgot about the agate. He had never brought anything for Gertie except a slap across the face if she demanded anything of him. And now, after this particular return, his blows seemed more vicious and more frequent than ever before.

Aggie came to hate him more for that, especially when it became apparent that after each visit—almost after each blow—Gertie seemed to withdraw more into herself, to do less for the children, to accept the hardness of life without question or regret.

Jack didn't try to invade his daughter's bed again for over a year. The second time he didn't make the mistake of awakening her, but merely crawled into her bed quietly and snuggled himself against her. She awoke some time later when his heavy breathing changed itself to snoring, and again she was terrified. His left hand was cupping her breast, gently squeezing it, and his right rested on her hip. She lay there listening to his roaring, whiskey-soaked breath, and her stomach hardened into a rock.

Outside the wind howled against the drafty shack, and the room was dimly lit by the red glow of coals from the hearth. She gently extricated herself from his crude embrace and crept to her mother's pallet, where she placed herself between Gertie's small body and the cabin wall. A blast of cold air assaulted her back, but she felt much safer than she had in the warmth of her daddy's arms. Once again, he failed to mention her escape, but this time when he left them, she thought less about how dashing he looked and found a shudder of fear quaking through her at the thought of his next visit. Her hatred for him took a definite shape, and she resolved that if he ever came at her again, ever tried to touch her again, she would kill him.

3

AT SIXTEEN, AGGIE BECAME THE PRIMARY FORCE IN THE family. They moved into a farmhouse that Jack claimed to have bought for them after a particularly successful venture up into Missouri. Unlike most of the shacks and cabins in the past, this was a bona fide home. It was built of clapboard, had a gabled roof, hardwood floors, and glass windows, and rested on pillars of brick. The best part of it was that it was only twenty miles from Monroe, Louisiana, someplace where they could go and buy what they couldn't make or find. Jack left them with ten gold Mexican coins, which Aggie was stunned to find were worth five dollars each. She hid the fortune away in her chest next to the teapot and the agate.

Aggie mounted the mules bareback and took them into Monroe to buy supplies. Jack left an arsenal of firearms in the farmhouse, and she learned to shoot them. She remembered her experience with the shotgun and mastered its heavy kick, and she became more or less proficient with pistols as well. When her daddy returned and watched her proudly displaying her marksmanship, he complained about her manly interests, and he upbraided her for wearing trousers when she did her chores. He then brought her three calico dresses and a new bonnet. That Gertie perpetually wore ragged homespun dresses never drew a comment from him.

It was on that same visit, however, that he started hitting Aggie hard. He stayed for a month, an extraordinarily long period for him, and after a day or two of the usual casual touching, he began striking her more often and with obvious pleasure. He found excuses to walk up behind her and pinch her arm or neck as well, and often on the pretext of hurrying her along on some errand or another, she felt his hand slapping her backside, sometimes lingering just long enough to grasp a palm full of flesh and give it a painful squeeze. If she protested or cried out, he would laugh and tell her that she needed to learn what it meant to be "a proper gal."

One night, Aggie finally felt the full fury of Jack's anger. She was returning from her evening milking when she heard him yelling for her and Jason from the house's porch. Jason was nowhere in sight, and there was such an urgency in Jack's voice that she thought perhaps something had happened to Gertie or Annie. She left the milk pail and raced to the steps, only to be met with a sharp blow to the side of her head that sent her reeling off the porch.

Jack held up a white shirt that he had long ago discarded and that had been appropriated as a cleaning cloth.

"Just who the hell gave you permission to make a dirtrag out of my good shirt?" he demanded.

Aggie put her hand to her head and tried to focus. She was dizzy and her vision was momentarily blurred. As usual, Jack was drunk. His depleted funds had obliged him to make use of a local backwoods distiller, and he had consumed almost a whole jug of forty-rod that day.

"What shirt?" she asked weakly.

"*This* shirt, this shirt, goddamnit!" he railed, flinging aside the torn rag, which he had used to wipe off his boots only the day before. He came unsteadily down the porch and kicked her, but he was off balance, and only the side of his foot scraped her arm before she scrambled to her feet.

"That's a rag!" she yelled at him through her tears. She didn't feel as afraid of him as angry over the unwarranted and unexpected attack. He advanced a step toward her, and she backed up.

"It's a rag *now*!" he yelled. "Jason! Jason, *goddamnit*!" He strode past her a step or two. "I'm fixin' to cut me a hick'ry switch an' learn you kids to mess with my good shirts."

"It's not your good shirt, damn it!" she yelled at him, but he ignored her and raised his hand to smack her once more. She ducked out of range, and he swatted the air. "I'm fixin' to cut me a switch. You find your brother, an' when I get back, I want to see your bare backsides pointin' to the moon!"

"You're not fixin' to see nothin'!" Aggie yelled at him, hating herself for continuing to cry. "An' if you think I'm goin' to stand still for a whippin' you got another think comin'!" This last she screeched out at his drunken face, and again she was ashamed, shocked at her own behavior. She felt like a brat, like a child, and she fought for control.

"Well, I'll be damned," Jack slurred in a soft growl. He moved toward her and backed her up against the porch railing. Aggie's fists doubled up, but her eyes were blinded by tears. "I'm fixin' to learn you who's the man in this family, you little bitch," he said, and he reached out and stripped open the front of her dress.

Aggie's arms flew across her exposed breasts, and Jack put his hands on her naked shoulders.

"You're fixin' to get somethin' you deserve, you little bitch-bastard," he said, "an' you're goin' to like it."

His face approached hers, but then he stopped. Aggie had squeezed her eyes shut, but when he seemed to freeze, she opened them and was surprised to see him looking up over her head toward the door of the house. Gertie's voice came evenly across the twilight of the porch.

"You can whip her, if you're a mind to, Jack," she said. "It's your right. But that's 'nough. Go cut yourself a switch. I'll get her ready. Elsewise, I think you better leave off."

For a moment Jack stood as if stuck. His hands continued to grip Aggie's shoulders, but she felt the tension moving out of them. In the dim orange light from the sunset beyond the trees, his face looked heathen, empty of humanity. Aggie held her breath and kept her arms locked across her chest.

"I'll be back," he said finally. He released her and stalked off into the trees. He didn't return that night at all, and the next day he came home, packed, and saddled up. Gertie washed and folded the rag which had once been his shirt as carefully as if it were new and left it on his bed, but he ignored it when he packed his things. As he climbed up onto his horse, he glared at the two women, one old and one young, and spat onto the ground.

"When I come back," he said, "*if* I come back, you'd better learn yourself some goddamn manners, girl." And he rode off.

He returned in a month and demanded the balance of the money, which Gertie obsequiously handed over, receiving a hard cuff on the head in return. There were only five coins remaining of the original gift, and he fumed and fussed about it for two days. Aggie never told him that she had kept three of the coins back, hiding them beneath the remaining unstained and untorn dress in her chest. Jack was angry enough that the rest of the money had gone to buy food, make repairs on the wagon, and replace the most recent mule team, which had never been worth very much to begin with.

Jack hung around and eventually got over his pique. He sold the horses, puttered around the farm, and stayed through the summer. He talked of the big deal he thought he could pull off in San Antonio: a "business arrangement," he said, that would set them up for a "fine future." He had his eye on some good grazing land down on the border, he claimed, and he wanted to go into the cattle business. He strutted and bragged around the house while Gertie tended her garden and gathered nuts and roots from the trees.

It was one of Jack's longest stays at home, and the family sagged and moaned under the burden of his continued presence. Aggie was spreading feed around for the chickens one afternoon and wondering just how to persuade him to leave them when he came up directly behind her and grabbed her. His hands grasped both her breasts, and she felt his hot whiskey breath on her neck as he attempted to nuzzle her. His erection pushed up against her hips when he embraced her, and she suddenly felt dirty all over. She wheeled around and slapped him before she realized what she was doing.

His hand flew to his cheek. She could see the imprint of her fingers crossing the pathetic mustache's left extremity. His dark eyes flared.

"You little bitch!" he spat at her. He wasn't drunk for once, but he had been drinking enough to give him courage, and now he was angry. Her outrage gave way to fear, and she began backing away from him through the fluttering hens, which were upset that their morning feeding had been interrupted.

"I'm sorry," she sputtered out, hating herself for saying it. "You scared me. I didn't know who you was." She felt her voice cracking a bit and tears starting to well beneath her eyelids, but she somehow found the strength to stop both reactions and reverse them. For the first time, she realized that she was almost as tall as he. If he had not been wearing his high-heeled boots, in fact, she would be taller. As it was, she could look him directly in the eye, and the position gave her confidence.

"Oh, an' if I'd been some local-yokel farm boy, that might have made a diff'rence?" He moved toward her, his hands clenching in and out of fists. She continued to back away until she found herself next to the fence. A hay hook was stuck in the wood.

"Get away from me, Daddy," she warned. "I'm tellin' you to stay away from me."

"I ain't your daddy, you little ill-bred bitch," Jack sneered. "I'm goin' to learn you that good an' proper."

"I'll call Mama." Aggie's voice rose a full key. Her eyes darted to the hay hook.

"You call your *whore* mama, an' I'll call your *mama* whore." He laughed, but his eyes were set. "I never got much out of this deal," he said, "but you just might be able to make up for it."

He stepped toward her, and she dropped her apron, which she had continued to hold up in a fisted sack to contain the remaining chicken feed. The hens noisily swarmed around their feet to capture the falling grain, temporarily distracting Jack, who stumbled through their squawking pecking heads, and Aggie reached out and seized the hay hook and swung wildly toward him.

She struck him with the rounded end of the implement. She was a strong girl, but swinging backward with her left hand was awkward, and she put little force behind it. The iron semicircle caught Jack on the temple and knocked him backward and off his feet into the chickens. Aggie took advantage of the opening and danced over him through the flying feathers. She leaped toward the porch, where Jack had left his gunbelt hanging on a peg.

She jerked out the heavy Colt's .44 and cocked it and fired before she realized how sensitive the trigger was. The bullet dispatched two chickens immediately and sent the rest squawking in a hundred different directions. Jack, still befuddled from the blow to his head, stumbled to his feet and held out his hands.

"Whoa!" he yelled. "Hold it!"

She grasped the weapon in both hands and fired again, this time putting the bullet deliberately and harmlessly into the dooryard about four feet in front of Jack. He leaped back from the small explosion, no less surprised than she at her ability with the six-shooter. Behind her she sensed that Gertie and Annie had appeared. Jason came rushing around from the barn and stopped so suddenly that he skidded down on his back.

Jack held a hand up to his bruised temple and affected a look of both sorrow and scorn at the same time. "What's the matter with you, girl?" he asked as he walked toward her, keeping his right hand thrust out in front of him. "You gone loco?"

"You *ever* touch me again," Aggie said evenly, keeping the gun trained on him, "I'll blow your foreskin off." She had only the vaguest notion of what a foreskin was, but she understood from her Bible that the Philistine trophies in King David's collection were important to men and dwelled between their legs.

Jack studied her, judged that she was serious, and turned red. "Give me the gun," he said. "I'm done here."

"No," she said, and her eyes hardened suddenly into blue stone. Her mouth made a firm, thin line that caused the slight dimples on either side to form deep, tense cuts in her cheeks. She was far from the weeping girl he had backed up against the porch railing before. Jack blanched to see the look on her face. He swallowed hard and didn't move.

"Give him the gun, Aggie," Gertie said from behind her. "He's done here, like he says."

She was powerless to resist Gertie's order. It was the same tone she had used when she stopped Jack before. It contained a certainty of her superiority over her husband, and it gave Aggie confidence in her mother's judgment.

She put the pistol back in the holster and walked off the porch and toward the corral, passing Jack so closely he could have reached out and touched her. Jack watched her go without moving. Then he angrily strode up to the porch, buckled on the belt, and turned to her. The side of his head glowed. He turned and went over to a shelf on the porch where Gertie had carefully stacked her jarred vegetables and swept the glass off onto the wooden slats. Then he stomped each one in turn.

"Winter's comin'," he announced. "Let's see if you need your ol' man then."

He pounded into the house and returned with his hat and a bag in which he had deposited the remainder of the money. He spoke to no one but went out to the barn and saddled the roan stallion he had ridden in on and galloped around to the back of the house. They didn't discover until later that he had stopped in the cold cellar and cut open and urinated all over the flour and cornmeal sacks.

They didn't see him again for almost six months.

AGGIE SIPPED THE BITTER tea and immediately felt better. Some honey would be nice to sweeten it, she thought, but there was no honey, no molasses, nothing. She prepared two more cups and carried them over to Constance and her companion, who took them without a word of thanks. Constance smiled briefly before accepting the cup, Aggie noticed, but she also noticed that the woman's gesture was done quickly and without danger of her friend's noticing it.

She went back and finished her drink, and then she made a cup for Jason, but she found he had flopped down next to Lottie Herbert and was asleep. The two bundles of young life looked strange lying there, motionless except for their breathing: two mere children between two blanket-covered corpses. She had practically raised him, she thought, but she didn't know him at all. He said very little he didn't have to, and he never offered anything resembling a smile. As he grew older, he came more and more to look like Jack, but he lacked his father's charm, his glib tongue, and, she added thankfully, his short temper. She flushed a bit with guilt when she thought that she should have stopped Jack from beating him, but she had lacked the resolve to stand up to him for someone else, even Jason. Jason had stood up for her, though, and the recollection shamed her.

Annie sat on the opposite side of the cave and stared off into space as if she were asleep with her eyes open. She reminded Aggie suddenly of Gertie. Silent and pensive like her brother, Annie seldom did much other than sleep that wasn't forced on her, although she had an uncommon curiosity about things. When the Indians had stopped the train out on the prairie, Jason practically had to sit on her to keep her from jumping out and inspecting the Comanche. During the first Indian attack, Aggie had found her walking up and down the wagons, trying to glimpse the savages. Then, during the night, she had found her going through a trunk someone had stacked against the limestone butte, removing the contents haphazardly as if looking for something. Aggie had decided long ago that Annie was lazy. Given a chore or sent on an errand, she was likely to lie down and take a nap as soon as she was out of sight.

Aggie worried that Annie wasn't all right in her mind. She said what she thought from time to time, but usually she just seemed to be waiting for something to happen to her. She cried when she was hurt, and she laughed when some odd thing or another struck her as funny, but mostly she simply sat and stared until someone called her or she went to sleep. The girl had looked to Aggie as a parent for so long that Aggie felt as if Annie were her own daughter, and the responsibility frightened her as much as it made her sad for Gertie.

Carlysle Smith gestured for Aggie to come over near him, and she took him some tea. She was still smarting from his caustic accusation earlier, but he was badly hurt, and she doubted he would survive. He sipped the bitter liquid with more strength than he had exhibited earlier, although she still had to cradle his head while he drank.

"I'm sorry for what I said," he whispered. "God, that's bitter stuff."

"I'm not sure you should have any," she said. "I don't know much 'bout tendin' folks who're hurt like you are."

"I'm still sorry," he said. She allowed him to lie back. "I had no business sayin' that. I hurt so goddamn much, an' it just seems like it ought to be somebody's fault."

"You're gettin' better," she offered more brightly than she felt. "Just keep quiet an' see if you can rest."

"You know, you're a pretty girl," he said.

She didn't know what to say. It wasn't a rare compliment to her ears. She never heard it from a man's lips but that it stirred something inside her. It did so again.

"I guess I'm jus' a little jealous." He coughed lightly and lay back.

"You must be gettin' better to have so much nonsense to talk," she said with a light laugh. Glorietta Fulbright raised her head and looked over sharply.

"My wife's gone," he said suddenly.

"You rest now," she said, feeling a flush come over her. She didn't want him to say anything more, particularly in the hearing of the other two women. She moved away as he closed his eyes.

Constance brought the empty cup back to the fire and squatted beside her. "Can I have some more?" she asked. "It's bitter as rind, but it perked me up."

Aggie put the water on to boil again. She wanted conversation, but the woman sat silently and rocked slowly on her haunches as the water hissed in the pot. She, too, reminded Aggie of Gertie. She was a lot younger, of course, but the signs of age were already creeping around the edges of her face. Aggie felt sorry for her. She was plain, to begin with, Aggie noticed, thinking of Smith's compliment suddenly. Likely the man she was nursing to his death was the only chance she would ever have. She hoped that Constance would find the strength to accept whatever happened to her without withdrawing into herself the way Gertie had. Hannah, after all, had buried four husbands and survived. Few women could be more open and forthright than she.

As she poured the steeped tea out into Constance's cup she was rewarded with another smile, a broader and more genuine display than the woman had shown before. It lightened her features until she was almost pretty. This time she ignored her companion's glare. "Much 'bliged," she said.

"You're more'n welcome," Aggie said. "I jus' wish I could do more for you. Or for her." She nodded toward Glorietta Fulbright, who beamed hatred toward the two.

"You're already carryin' more than we are," Constance said. She took a sip of the scalding tea, then reached under her skirt and scratched furiously. "I'd give anythin' for a bath. A real bath," she said with a light laugh. Then she opened her mouth to say something else, but suddenly lowered her eyes.

"What is it?" Aggie asked softly. "You can ask me anythin' you want."

"Nothin'," she said quickly, and she rose to return to her duties. Aggie was sure the woman wanted to know if anything had happened between her and Moses. She wished she had framed the question, but then, she decided, it was just as well. It only would make her mad, and that wouldn't do at all.

Aggie watched her go and resettle herself silently beside her husband. Even though the smile she had received, even the comment, had been friendly, she worried that Constance Kruikshank was merely patronizing her. Toleration was something people learned pretty quickly. Aggie told herself that she would never settle for toleration. Gertie had tolerated—or merely endured—Jack Sterling for almost twenty years. All it had gotten her was killed by Indians beside a creek in the middle of a wilderness, far from anything she ever dreamed.

She'd blame that on men, Aggie thought, and she'd be right. But men didn't have to be mean, cruel. They could be loving, too. The thought warmed Aggie more than the tea. I want love, she decided quickly, I want to love a man the way Ruth did, the way Solomon's wives loved him, the way Bathsheba loved David. She smiled. But I wanted to love Todd Christian, too, she thought. She poured more water into the pot to boil, smiled a beautiful, bright smile that lit her face in spite of the dirt, blood, and weariness that almost masked her entirely. And I did, she silently avowed. In fact, I still do.

4

Two weeks after Jack rode off, a norther blew in and put an end to summer in northern Louisiana. Gertie and Aggie salvaged some of the grain and meal that Jack had tried to ruin, but the early frost took care of the meager garden, and it looked like they would be hungry again. They killed the pig, sold the ham for what they could get, and kept the rest, so there was bacon, at least, salted and stored in the cold cellar, and Aggie also splurged and bought a large tom turkey, which she hoped to save until Christmas. But one bright, crisp morning when the trees were rapidly obtaining their fall colors, she learned that Christmas dinner would be the least of their worries.

That morning the turkey was missing from the barnyard and refused to come when Aggie called her usual gobbling sound. While she moved among the chickens, she was startled to find herself observed by a man in a broadcloth suit and a garish brocade vest. He sat on a swaybacked gelding; somehow he had guided the horse right up to the barnyard without her hearing him. He studied her and made no move to dismount. A cigar smoked from his lips, and purple birthmarks swam over his pudgy, closely shaved cheeks. Aggie thought immediately of a frog as she looked up at him.

"Do you min' my askin'," he finally said in a Louisiana drawl, "jus' what in the blue-eyed worl' you think you're doin'?"

His voice was high, like a woman's, a thin alto that seemed to spread widely when it came to her ears.

"Feedin' the chickens." She glanced toward the house, but her family was not in sight.

"I can see *that*, Missy," the man said, gently nudging his horse so it stepped through the feathered ground and approached her. "What I mean is, what're you doin' *here*, on this lan'?" His eyes were hazel and flat as they surveyed the home and the wasted garden. "Looks like you've settled in here," he concluded.

"We live here."

"Hell you say." He looked around nervously. "Who's 'we'?"

"My mother an' brother an' sister." He had rounded her and the sun was now behind him, making it difficult for her to see him clearly. "An' my daddy," she added, biting her lip with a bitter recollection. If this man intended to harm them, she shouldn't have hesitated in numbering Jack among those present, she realized. On the other hand, there was nothing threatening about him. He was, if anything, comical.

"An'," the man continued, "jus' who in heaven's name said you could?"

"*Said* we could? Why, nobody said we could. Didn't have to. We own it." She finished spreading the feed absently, and worked her way around the horse so she could be between him and the house. Her eyes automatically searched the fence for the hay hook; it was nowhere in sight.

"You don't own it." His voice was matter-of-fact. "*I* own it. I've *always* owned it, or my family has. We live in Shreveport, an' we own this property. It was my Aunt Judith's place, till she died 'bout a year ago."

She found herself growing angry. "Well, my daddy, Jack Sterlin', bought it. He's got papers that says it's ours." She stepped up onto the porch. From there the shotgun was in easy reach. She heard Gertie doing something inside. "He said he paid two hundred dollars for the house an' twenty acres." Suddenly she noticed a white bundle hanging from the other side of his saddle. It was their tom. "That's our turkey," she said defiantly.

He glanced down at the dead bird but otherwise paid no attention to her claim. "Well, I'd like to have a look-see at those papers. 'Cause I'm the only one in the family who has the author'zation to sell this place, an' I know I ain't sold it to nobody. I was 'bout to, though."

She went inside and made Gertie go out the back door to round up the children. The papers were in a rusty lock-box, and Aggie pulled them out. She didn't read cursive handwriting well enough to know what they said, but she saw a flurry of illegible signatures along the bottom. Across the top of the fancy calligraphy, she saw the words *Bill of*

Sale printed. She took it out and found the man had dismounted unbidden and was standing with one foot on the step leading up to the porch. Off his horse, he looked more like a fat, squat frog—no, she corrected, a tree toad, a peeper—than ever. She handed him the paper, and he pulled out a pair of wire-rimmed spectacles and perched them on the flat bridge of his nose. The eyeglasses gave him even more of an amphibian's aspect, and she would have laughed if she had not felt so anxious.

He studied the writing and wrinkled his forehead as he held the bottom of the page up and tried to make out the signatures. His cheeks blew in and out, making the dark birthmarks swell and shrink.

"Well," he said, handing the paper back to her at last, "I don't know who skinnied who, but that paper's not worth a thing. It's a bill of sale for a house an' some lan', but it don't say where, an' it don't say what. It just says that somebody"—he squinted through his spectacles—"named Jack Sterlin' paid twenty dollars for some twenty acres, which is a pretty penny 'roun' here. It don't say who he paid it to, an' I can't make out who might of signed it. I can make out that it don't have nothin' to do with this property. I know that for a God-given fact." He stepped up another step. "You're goin' to have to get off. I got a family from back East due in here any day. I jus' come by to see what kin' of shape the ol' place was in. First I thought you was them an' had jus' moved in 'fore the deal was done. I can see you ain't, now. You're goin' to have to get off. Is that truly your turkey?"

And that was that. The man, whose name was Hannibal Tyler, said he was a feed and grain dealer from Shreveport, and he produced a title deed which confirmed, when he read it to the gathered family, that he indeed owned the property. He said he would be willing to sell it to them instead of the expected arrivals from Indiana—"bunch of godless carpetbaggers, more'n likely," he called them matter-of-factly and without contempt—but when he found that the Sterlings had no ready cash, he realized it was impossible.

For a while, they stood there in awkward silence. Jason came up and stood near the door, his hand suspiciously near the shotgun, but if Tyler noticed it, he said nothing and never let his eyes fall on Aggie's young brother. Tyler continually cleaned his spectacles with a huge white handkerchief and studied Aggie, but neither knew what to say to the other. Aggie was certain that they would have to leave—it was entirely believable that Jack had left them in such a state—but if they did, Tyler was not clear about whether they had to vacate immediately, or whether he would give them a few days to pack and, Aggie thought with a sinking feeling, figure out somewhere to go.

Finally, Gertie invited him to sit down and to have something to drink, and he surprised them all by agreeing. They sat on the porch and shared a pot of tea in a continuing, awkward silence. Aggie hopelessly debated what alternatives existed.

Finally he stood. "Well, there ain't nothin' for'er. The family wants this lan' sold, an' that means you got to get off. You seem like good folks, an' I hate to do'er, but there ain't nothin' for'er. I only have the author'zation to deal for the lan'. I ain't got control of the family. I'm sorry, but you got to get off. By tomorrow." He saw the look of shock in Aggie's eyes and looked down and puffed out his spotted cheeks. "Well, the day after anyhow. I shouldn't even let you stay the night." He rose and put his hat on, then dug into his vest pocket and flipped a silver dollar toward Jason, who, to his surprise, caught it. "I'm right sorry 'bout the bird. I potted him 'bout a mile from here. Didn't know he belonged to nobody."

"But what about us?" Aggie said. "We've worked hard keepin' this place up. We don't deserve to be just thrown out on the road. We got noplace to go." She felt panic rising and fought it down. Her eyes began to take on a hard look, but Tyler had already turned away. "We ain't goin'," she said evenly, but he ignored her.

"There ain't nothin' for'er." Tyler puffed and struggled back onto his horse. Once atop the suffering nag, he rubbed his red, closely shaven chin and his eyes brightened. "Tell you what. There's a feller up in El Dorado owes me a pot of money. You go up there an' tell him I'll discoun' his debt if he'll give you a place for the winter."

Aggie was suspicious. "Why would you do that for us?"

Tyler smiled. "Well, Missy, same reason I paid you four times what this gobbler's worth. You look like you been skinnied once too often, an' I don't think you got it in you to lie 'bout whose bird this is. I don't think you're lyin' 'bout thinkin' your daddy bought this place, neither. Maybe he thinks he did. Maybe not. You think so, that's purely clear. But like you say, you've kept the place up. You've done some fixin' on'er, too, if my eyes're any judge. I don't reckon I owe you nothin' for that, as you've had the use of'er all this time. But on the other han', you might of saved me a passel of work. So you can take that as a reason if you're needin' one.

" 'Sides, there's this feller, like I say, up in El Dorado. He's owed me for 'most ten years. I give up on ever seein' a Yankee dime of'er. This'll give me a chance to feel like I'm collectin' some of'er anyhow, an' it'll get his goat for sure. He may not do'er, either. He's a stubborn ol' coot. Says the loan was made in Confederate paper, an' that quits the debt. Like as not, he'll tell you to go to hell. But I wish you good luck with him." And with that, he laboriously turned the gelding out of the barnyard and was gone.

It took them six days to get to El Dorado. One of the mules died in its traces halfway there, and what was left of Aggie's secret savings went to buy a sag-bellied mare to replace it. The horse, it turned out, was not broken to draft, and she kept balking at the tack and slipping her traces and resisting the mule to which she was harnessed.

The man who they sought was named Holstein, but contrary to Hannibal Tyler's description, he turned out to be a friendly sort, although he was in no danger of being called generous. He said he had a sharecropping place some Negroes had moved out of a month before, leaving most of the cotton in the fields. If they would agree to finish pulling the boles, he would let them have the cabin rent-free for the winter, and he would throw in enough flour and meal to get them through.

There were forty acres of cotton on the section, a full thirty of them untouched. Aggie and Jason pulled bolls from sunup to sundown in a raw, cold wind that was sometimes laced with sleet, but by mid-November, they had salvaged what they could and had moved into the one-room cabin.

Winter passed slowly. It was the worst time in their lives. The five pounds of flour and five of cornmeal Holstein delivered didn't last through December, and Aggie found herself driving the wagon into town, begging for whatever work she could find. Jason got a job splitting firewood for a hotel, and she found that the same establishment would hire her once a week to launder linens. It was more than five miles through mud and snow to get there, but by coming in on a Thursday morning and sleeping in the wagon, they could finish their work and return home by Saturday night.

It was hot, steamy work for Aggie, and cold, wet labor for Jason, but the dollar a week kept them eating and even bought remnant cloth and thread for Gertie. One Saturday night, however, the lumbering Conestoga mired itself in a muddy rut on the way home. Jason urged the unwieldy team too enthusiastically and the axle snapped before the wagon was pulled free.

"This is the end of it," Aggie said to her brother. "We can't do the work in one day, an' there's no place for us to stay in town. We need the wagon just to keep goin'." For the first time in her life, she felt total despair. It was well after dark, and she knew her mother would be worried about them soon. They were more than four miles from the cabin. She thought about going back into town, but she had no idea what a wagon's axle might cost. The single dollar they had earned was represented by supplies in the useless wagon's bed, and it was well past time for any blacksmith to have closed.

Jason, true to his character, said nothing. He silently followed Aggie's instructions and unhitched the team and hobbled them where they could graze in the sparse winter grass alongside the narrow road. The heavy forest trees came down right next to the muddy trace, and he was reluctant to lead the animals too far through the dark trunks for fear they might be attacked by an animal or just stolen. Once he had seen to their ground stakes, he curled up next to her in the wagon bed and went to sleep.

The sound of pounding hooves awakened Aggie almost as soon as she dozed off. There was no moon, and the night was misty and impenetrable, but she heard riders coming hard. The road curved away behind a stand of trees only a few yards past where they had broken down. She knew they would soon round the curve and be on top of the mired and broken wagon. She fumbled for a lantern and matches, but before she found either, the horses were upon them. She braced herself and then heard the scream of one of the frightened animals when it collided roughly with the vehicle.

The force of the collision rocked the Conestoga and threw her backward onto Jason, and she banged hard on the bed's side. She rolled down into the mud and slogged over to a man who lay facedown; he didn't move. His companion writhed and swore on the grass nearby, and Aggie yelled for Jason to come out and to fetch the elusive lantern.

Once light was applied to the scene, Aggie was shocked. The rider who lay unconscious in her lap, covered with the red mud of the road, was really only a boy about her age. A large gash was cut in his scalp. His companion, who was somewhat younger than he, had a broken arm and leg, and he was continuing to roll around in the wet grass and curse "goddamn stupid ridgerunners" who parked in the middle of a road and left no light.

Aggie and Jason carried the senseless boy up onto the grass.

"Is his neck broke?" his companion asked through gritted teeth.

"I don't think so," Aggie said. The injured boy's eyes remained closed in the attitude of a deep and contented sleep. Jason strode over and stood like a statue, holding the lantern high over the other. A horse was still down, lying on one side and occasionally whinnying.

"Here," the injured boy ordered Jason. "Put that goddamn lantern down an' get it out of my eyes. It's too late to let people know where you are. The damage is already done." Jason followed instructions and set the lantern on the wagon's high seat. "Take my pistol." He tried to roll over a bit. "Go over an' shoot that animal. He's hurt bad, an' Todd wouldn't want him to suffer so."

Jason didn't move for a moment, but as the boy cried

out in pain again when he tried to emphasize the urgency of his instruction, he finally came over and withdrew a revolver from the man's holster and dispatched the horse with a single shot.

"Now, get his saddle off an' throw it in the wagon," the boy hissed. "An' then see if you can get me an' Todd to town 'fore we die."

Jason bent to his task wordlessly, but Aggie spoke up.

"The wagon's no good. Axle's broke. That's why we're here."

"Jesus God!" the man swore. "I'm fixin' to pass out in a minute. This hurts like hell. How's Todd? Is he dead or anythin'?"

Aggie studied the boy's face in the lantern light. He was breathing peacefully. Only the bloody gash suggested that anything might be wrong with him. "He's col'-cocked, but I think he'll live," she said.

"Well, I won't," the other said. "Can you make a travois?" The question was directed toward Jason, who only shook his head.

"A what?" Aggie was embarrassed for Jason. He was the same age as this fellow or nearly, but he was totally cowed by him.

"Never mind. Listen. There's a shack over yonder 'bout a half a mile. Through them trees there, across that ridge. You get on my horse, if you can find him, an' ride over there. Tell Nigger Matthew that the Christian boys need him an' to bring some tools or whatever he needs to fix this wagon." The instructions exhausted the youth, and he laid his head back on the wet grass and concentrated on his misery.

"Go on, Jason," Aggie said, and he responded automatically.

The black man arrived in about an hour. He brought two women and three children along with him, and Aggie was amazed by the precision they demonstrated in taking over the whole scene of the accident. One of the women lifted the boy, whom Aggie had taken to be named Todd, up off her lap and carried him in her arms to a quilt they spread on the grass. She produced a cask of water and began bathing his wound. The other woman, assisted by one of the children, went over to Todd's companion and tied his leg and broken arm securely to two stiff limbs each. They didn't move him further, but Aggie could see in the lantern's glare that he had passed out.

In the meantime, the grizzled old man crawled down into the mud under Aggie's wagon and busied himself with a jack and other tools. Jason was helping him and went back and forth between the wagons fetching tools or whatever the ancient Negro asked for.

Aggie followed Todd's body over to his new resting place, and she watched and felt helpless as his new nurse cleaned the gash. She stood well away from the black woman, who was sweating in spite of the cold dampness of the night.

His injury wasn't as bad as it had first appeared, Aggie noticed. Although it had been his horse that had struck the wagon, it seemed that his brother had received the worst harm when he fell onto the comparatively soft grass. She watched the work in front of her silently and felt guilty about the whole thing, like an interloper into another world where she did not belong. Thus far, none of the party had spoken to Aggie at all.

"We fixin' to have to get this boy in to see Doc Richards," the woman who had splinted the other boy's broken limbs called out to the old man. "He's done broke some bones. It's stickin' out a mite. He'll get the gang-green if we don't shake a leg."

"Well, you can't take the wagon," the old man said without coming out from under Aggie's Conestoga. "Not if I'm fixin' to work on this'un. I got to fire up an' do some forgin'. This here's broke. Sheared clear through. Take me most of the night."

"Ain't no room for sick folks in that wagon anyhow," the woman replied.

The two women came together and consulted briefly. They gave sharp instructions to the two youngsters, who took an ax and disappeared into the woods. In a few moments, Aggie heard chopping, and they emerged after a while with two long saplings, hastily cut and stripped. The women pulled another folded quilt from under their wagon seat and tied it to the poles, which they then fastened to one of their unhitched mules. The heavyset woman picked up the boy on the ground and gently laid him in the cradle. Checking to make sure his weight didn't drag the ground, she went to the mule, hiked up her skirt, and took a slight hop before bounding up onto the animal's back. Her companion took a position beside the unconscious patient, and together they started off.

"See to it that sore on his head don't mortify," was all the mounted black woman said as they left Aggie standing in the grass.

IT TOOK MATTHEW MORE than three hours to fix the broken axle. He worked silently with Jason and the two children by his side. His wagon, Aggie discovered, was indeed full of junk: It was actually a traveling blacksmith's shop. He had a forge ingeniously rigged to fire without having to be unloaded. There was an iron trap for the coals, and a bellows was rigged in the wagon's side. The rest of the bed was a dark, greasy jumble of tools and scrap metal.

He removed the broken axle from the Conestoga and worked on it, heating it and pounding on it atop an anvil bolted to a special platform on the wagon's tailgate. Sparks from the hot iron flew around his face, landed on his leather apron, and hissed in the wet atmosphere as his hammer rang a hollow echo through the trees. Finally, he seemed satisfied with the weld, and he squished back underneath the Conestoga and worked there.

Throughout the procedure, Aggie stood by the unconscious boy. She feared he might never wake up, that through negligence she had killed him. He was, she realized once his face had been cleared of mud and blood, uncommonly handsome. He had a sturdy, smooth-shaven chin, and his light brown hair fell in attractive locks around his ears. She self-consciously found herself touching his arms and discovered firm muscles beneath his coat, and when she loosened his cravat, her hands drifted over his shirt and discovered a powerful chest. He stirred alien and frightening feelings in her, and she was ashamed of herself for experiencing them, for taking advantage of his state.

"All done." Matthew had appeared beside her. Aggie started.

"We got no money." Jason broke his nightlong silence

and spoke up. Again, Aggie was so surprised she jumped a bit.

"Don't matter. The Major'll likely fix 'er up." He looked up the road toward town. "Should of been back by now. Doc Richards ain't there, likely."

He went to the other mule of his team and led it away from the harness. He roused the two black children, who had fallen asleep in the wet grass underneath the wagon, and he mounted the beast and pulled each one up behind him in turn.

"Where are you goin'?" Aggie called, with a glance down at her charge. Daylight was gathering, she noticed. She could see him clearly. "You can't jus' leave us here. Your wagon—"

"Be back for it direc'ly," he said, turning the mule toward the ridge that was now visible in the gray predawn light.

"What about him?"

"Don't know nothin' 'bout it," he said. "That's up to the women."

Aggie didn't know what to do. She waited until light flooded the road and prayed that someone would come along. But time passed and the sun rose, and no one appeared. Jason fell asleep in the back of the Conestoga, and the injured boy remained peacefully senseless.

What heat they had obtained from the forge soon dissipated as the fire cooled, and Aggie felt a chill coming over her. She fetched a blanket from her wagon for the boy she was attending, but she knew that they couldn't wait forever. She kept hoping that the Negroes would return, but morning brightened to noon, and no one came. The sky began to gray and cover over with what she recognized as storm clouds, and she awakened Jason and together they moved Todd to their own wagon. As her brother finished hitching the team, she took one more forlorn look down the road and called to the mule and horse to take them down the trace toward their own cabin, where, she prayed, Gertie would know what to do.

And she did. She pried open the sleeping jaws of the wounded boy before she allowed his removal from the wagon, and into them she poured a homemade concoction of berries and a root she called the "healin' tree," which forced him to gag and cough and actually to sit up and spit violently when the tart mixture touched his tongue.

He was still weak and too dizzy to stand, but by leaning on Aggie and Jason, he made it into their cabin, where they laid him by the fire and stripped off his muddy coat and shirt and bathed him as best they could. He slipped back into unconsciousness as soon as they began working on him.

"He's froze clear through," Gertie said, more to herself than to Aggie, which was just as well, for the girl's eyes strayed across his smooth chest and firm young muscles. She was unaware that her family shared in the vision. It seemed to be hers alone, and it made her hollow inside. She knew she was hungry, starving practically, but this emptiness had nothing to do with food. It ate away at her heart, made her light-headed, and forced her to look away every few seconds to hold herself upright and catch her breath.

If Gertie noticed her daughter's distraction, she didn't let on but continued to massage the cold skin of the boy who lay on the pallet before her, rubbing wet cloths over his arms and chest in an attempt to revive circulation. It wasn't that cold, she said, but he was hurt and he was weak. His eyes, gray as slate, roamed unseeingly about the room, and she feared he had lost his sight. Suddenly, they focused, and his mouth parted in a wide grin.

"Hello," he said. His gaze fixed on Aggie's face. "I'm Todd Christian. Who in God's name are you?"

CHAPTER THREE

1

AGGIE FINISHED HER TEA WITH A WINCE AND LEANED back. Thinking of Todd had weakened her even more, it seemed. She felt dirtier than before, and she once more longed for a tub of hot water, a luxury she hadn't enjoyed since leaving Jefferson, where for only the second time in her life she saw water running from a pipe, right inside a building, and bathed herself in a vessel made of something other than beaten tin. She remembered Constance's sudden, furious scratching fit, and her hands went involuntarily to her underarms. The thick dampness revolted her.

She ran her fingers up to her hair once again, wishing for a chance to clean it. The impulse was childish. She had often gone for days, even weeks, without a real bath. Since arriving at the crossing, she had made a habit of washing her hands and face, and had made herself smell as good as she could by using a lot of soap, but there was something about all the blood, all the death, that made her feel that only a good scrubbing would cleanse her. In her chest was fancy perfumed soap, taken from the Jefferson hotel along with a white fluffy towel and washcloth that Jack had insisted they remove also when they left. He said that they were part of the price of the room, and knowing no better, she had not argued. It was enough for her that this time he had paid the bill. Unlike the raggy cotton cloth that normally passed for towels in her past, this one was as soft as goose down; it drank water right off her body. She washed it carefully the first chance she got and stored it away. Now, she ached to use it and the matching cloth.

Her mind swept to the back of the cave, where the water bubbled noisily and created a small echo. Jason's wet trousers told her the water was certainly deep enough for her to bathe in, even if it was cold. She could endure it, she thought, long enough to clean herself. But one of the men moaned, and she felt guilty for harboring such a selfish whim.

She wondered suddenly what had become of Kyle Ambrose, Jed's father, and his other son they had left behind. It was a certainty that they were dead, almost as much of a certainty that Moses Franklin was dead. She remembered the forlorn look in Mr. Ambrose's face when they rode by him. It was helpless, but angry. Jack always said that an angry man could survive when there didn't seem to be any hope at all. She wondered if that was true. She hoped for Jed Ambrose's sake that it was.

Was that what had driven Gertie all those years? Anger? She didn't think so. Gertie's ability to survive was rooted too deeply in her past. Aggie remembered all her mother's stories as if they were her own. She had seen the faint scars on her legs and hips left by Aggie's grandfather's hickory sapling, had watched Jack cuff her hard, sometimes just slapping her away as he might a mosquito. It was sad, Aggie thought, that her mother could put up with that for so long, could even have found a well of strength in herself to stand up to Jack when she had to, and then could be cut down so easily by a bunch of savages who bore her no personal malice, but hated her only because she was white.

A centipede crawled along the edge of the cave wall and scurried into an almost invisible opening. Aggie felt gooseflesh when she saw its red pincers. She imagined they hurt when they stung. She had heard that they could be poisonous. She wondered if she should inspect the cave for more of them, but she felt too weary, too burdened with other thoughts, to move for the moment.

Suddenly she was certain she felt one crawling on her leg, and she leaped up with a small cry. She pulled her skirts up high and inspected the torn black stockings underneath. She slapped at her calves and knees, but no vermin of any sort appeared. She realized that she had imagined the whole thing, and she felt sheepish. It was just because she was so dirty. She resolved right then to do something about it. Hannah or no Hannah, she couldn't stand herself any longer.

Constance and her companion were staring at her wide-eyed, and Aggie realized that her leaping up and swatting at imaginary insects had looked strange. Even Carlysle Smith had raised his head enough to look at her long legs when she danced around. She dropped her skirts and said nothing to any of them.

She went to her trunk and pulled out her one good gingham dress. It had been worn and washed so often that it no longer revealed the bright blue print it had once boasted. It was now a kind of faded gray, frayed around the cuffs and collar, and the hem had been mended so often that it was nothing more than a kind of patchwork of knotted thread. But it was whole, and it was clean. She had vowed not to put it on until she saw Todd again, to save it especially to remind him of the day he had brought it to her. But mud from the Mexicans' grave, blood and dirt from the men's grimy fingers, had stained right through the apron and ruined the older calico she wore. Not even Gertie's nimble fingers could have sewn up some of the rips in her skirt.

She took the dress out and shook it, wishing for an iron to press out the wrinkles in its worn cotton fabric. She raised her skirts again and decided that her single pair of spare stockings would also have to be brought into service.

She idly hoped someone might come and relieve her so she could do this in private. She might abandon the idea entirely if someone would at least come to talk to her, but no one had appeared so far besides Mr. Graham and Hannah, and no one was likely to.

She nodded once more to herself and went over and pulled a blanket off one of the dead men. It left his face exposed, his eyes staring upward toward the blank ceiling, and she found a piece of canvas and placed it over his face.

"He won't mind," she chirped to Constance and Glorietta, who continued to stare at her with questions and suspicion in their faces.

She went to the back of the cave, where a burned-out torch was jammed into a fissure of rock, and she knotted the blanket to it and then stretched it over the narrow opening, stuffing a corner into a crevice that was narrow enough to hold it. Returning to the main area of the cave, she picked up one of the lanterns, took it behind the make-shift curtain, and placed it near the blanket so she could disrobe in light but not cast a shadow against it. Then she gathered up her clean dress and the towel, cloth, and fancy cake of soap, and slipped behind the blanket curtain.

She had to stoop quite a bit behind the blanket, but once there, Aggie found that the lantern illuminated a kind of shelf that gave way almost immediately to the flowing spring that emerged from the limestone on her right and flowed for about five feet before making an abrupt turn to the right again and disappearing into a dark tunnel no more than two feet above the surface of the bubbling water. A dark opening about the height of her waist led off to the left and another one was directly across from her, but she could see nothing beyond the yellow spill from the lantern light.

She squatted down and moved next to the flow, rolled up her sleeve, and reached down into the water. It was colder than she had expected, almost painful, then instantly numbing on her hand and forearm. The middle of the small stream was about three feet deep, and she could have stepped across had there been anywhere to put her foot on the other side.

She laid aside her things carefully, sat down and unlaced her shoes, then pulled them and her stockings off. When she thrust her feet into the spring, she was shocked. It felt even icier than it had on her hand, and she almost pulled her legs out before she set her teeth and forced herself to accept the water's cold flow. Finally, she stood up and inspected the security of the blanket curtain, and then she removed her apron, dress, and undergarments, laying them all carefully by. Clothing, even soiled and ripped clothing, she had learned long ago, was always to be handled with care until it wore itself to threads.

She regretted that she had no clean underthings, but Gertie had taken her others down to the river to wash, and now they were strewn among the weeds and cedar limbs on the creek bank. Her shoes were also torn, and the sole had come away from one of them. She wondered if she could wear Jack's boots. She would ask someone to try to fetch them for her, if she remembered and if it wasn't too risky.

Totally naked now, she eased herself down into the water, allowed her long legs to acclimate themselves to the temperature, and then found her footing on the smooth rock bed of the spring and stood up. She looked down at herself. In the yellow light of the lantern, she saw chill-bumps racing up her thighs from the water's cold, and she rubbed them to try to keep them warm. She had never seen herself as attractive, but rather as a gangly girl with knock knees and legs that were too long for the stockings she often had to wear. Her hips were thin, like a boy's, and the bones of her pelvis thrust out sharply against her pale skin. A flat stomach rose from her abdomen and barely fleshed out over her lower ribs before blossoming generously into full breasts that tapered out into small nipples that were now hard red buttons, bumpy in the cold water that swirled around her calves. Her shoulders were strong, and her neck jutted up proudly to support her handsome head and long yellow hair that looked like spun gold in the lantern's steady glow.

Taking a deep breath, Aggie lowered herself into the spring water and shivered as it flowed around her lower body. The cold was truly painful now, and she felt her heart pounding in her ears and gasped with the rush of the frigid stream. The space where the deepest water swirled was too small for her to submerge much of her body, and she was too long-waisted to do much more than scrunch down and ignore the scraping bite of the limestone edge of the tiny pool where her back rested against it. But at least now she was almost completely wet. The water bubbled against the underside of her breasts deep enough to cause them to bob in the swirl, and she splashed it up onto her shoulders and neck before rising, taking the soap and washcloth, and scrubbing herself thoroughly.

The soap wouldn't lather much, and she kept squinting at the white cloth to see if any was coming off with her rubbing. There seemed to be something wrong with the water, she thought; it tasted odd, hard and almost rocky. Small flakes of white stone had appeared in the bottom of cups and bowls, but they disappeared when she touched them. After working the soap and cloth for a while, she felt sufficiently scrubbed to rinse, and then she climbed out awkwardly and knelt beside the pool and wet her long hair.

In spite of its brilliant color, her hair had always shamed her. Unlike other girls' curly locks she had seen and envied, particularly in Jefferson, her hair was fine and straight. Even when freshly washed and curled with painful hot irons, it would hang down in long strands that almost touched her waist. After they left Arkansas, she had cut it short, like Jason's. Jack was furious. Even Gertie didn't approve, so she let it grow once again. The only advantage, she thought while she tried with modest success to make the soap lather, was that it dried quickly. She knelt down farther and dunked her head the best she could, holding her breath and allowing the natural rush of the water to rinse the soap away, and then she sat up quickly, tossing her hair behind her and splattering the blanket and lantern with drops of water that stained one with moisture and brought angry hisses from the other.

Then, climbing back down into the pool, she scooched her thin hips around once more and thrust her long legs out to where the spring disappeared, finding a position that allowed her some comfort. The spring no longer felt so cold, although her shoulders were chilled by the air around her, and her head seemed shrouded in ice. She lay back and closed her eyes. It was as if this were the first time in her life she had felt truly clean, truly free, and she wondered if her thoughts had anything to do with the bath she was enjoying, or whether she was really, finally, celebrating the death of Jack Sterling.

Present dangers, the Indians, the train, what would happen next, nagged at her as she sat and tried to milk the remainder of this stolen time for all the pleasure it offered. But in the front of her mind, she cleared away the anxiety surrounding the crossing and the watchful people outside the cave. She knew that tomorrow, or even in a few hours, she could die, that she would never see Todd Christian again, that everything she had dreamed of for the past year could become nothing more than a fancy, not even worthy of putting on a tombstone. But for the moment, she preferred to pretend that none of it mattered. All of the dangers and problems of the moment would eventually fade away, and everything would right itself. Gertie would even somehow emerge from a hiding place, safe and alive. She even imagined that she and Gertie would take the children to the faraway place Jack had promised was waiting for them, a place where they could be happy. For the moment, Aggie Sterling became the girl she had never had a chance to be.

2

THE WINTER WHEN AGGIE STERLING MET TODD CHRISTIAN had several months remaining, but for Aggie, no amount of snow or ice, no howling winds and frigid nights under thin quilts, could diminish the brightness and warmth the young man brought to her life, to all their lives.

Todd and his brother, Michael, the boy explained to Aggie and her family, were the sole survivors of their immediate families. Their mother died of cholera, and their father left them in the care of a maiden aunt, then rode off to die in the opening shots of the Battle of Chickamaugua. Their aunt, Louisa, was concerned about the welfare of the orphaned boys and especially worried because their father had left them with a considerable amount of land, livestock, and money—in gold coin, too. Staunch defender of the Confederacy that he might have been, Todd laughed, he had no faith in paper script, Union or Rebel. Accordingly, Louisa accepted the proposal of one Major Clarence Hitchcock, a one-legged veteran of the Federal Army who had been maimed not by any Rebels but by having the bad luck to be run over by a panic-stricken congressman and his wife who were fleeing their sightseeing excursion at First Manassas. Union officer or not, the Major—as he preferred to be addressed—was a native of Arkansas, and as soon as it was both prudent and possible for him to do so, he returned to El Dorado and promptly proposed to the city's most eligible spinster.

The Major expressed disappointment in the two boys now under his charge: From the time they were old enough to shave, the young hellions proved themselves to be virtually worthless. They spent little time engaged in productive activity, and only by bribing the madams of the two local bordellos had the Major managed to prevent them from falling totally into moral depravity.

The Major was a strict Baptist by formal religion and a strict moralist by personal choice. He saw no contradiction to either conviction in marrying a woman who was both the ugliest old maid in Arkansas and five years his senior, for he regarded that as a business matter and not to be confused with affairs of the heart. By the winter of 1873, he had seized control of the boys' future wealth and was managing it well enough to avoid criticism from anyone, particularly Louisa. He used the money and influence it brought him to keep the boys away not only from lascivious women but also from hard drink, gambling, and other mischief, at least in El Dorado. As a result, they spent a good deal of time in other towns where their aunt's husband—they never once had addressed him as Uncle—could not reach them. It was from just such an adventure that they were returning when they happened upon Aggie and Jason.

Aggie learned that both boys had been "drunker'n coots," as Todd had exclaimed, which perhaps accounted for the relatively minor injuries they had suffered. It certainly accounted for the length of time Todd Christian had remained unconscious. He had been literally passed out drunk, on top of being injured. He told her later that it was a wonder that he was even on top of the horse when it ran into the wagon. The boys had decided to race the last two miles into town, Todd explained, and the horses were neck and neck and in a headlong rush down a familiar road when they rounded the curve and Todd's horse smashed into the Sterling wagon.

The Major was furious when he learned of the accident. Not only had the boys once again been gallivanting all over the countryside, but they had also been racing on two thoroughbred horses he had just acquired from Kentucky. Racing them in the mud and in the dark was bad enough, but since one of the animals had had to be destroyed on the spot and the other was now skittish and difficult to manage even at a walk, the Major's outrage was formidable.

He barely inquired after Michael, who had compound

fractures in both his limbs that had partly frozen together and had to be rebroken. Instead, Major Hitchcock mounted his horse, his wooden peg leg stiffly thrust into a socket especially cut into his stirrup, and rode out to see the results of his nephews' folly for himself.

The Major followed the muddy wagon tracks to the shack where the Sterling family resided and summoned them forth with a blast from his revolver just as twilight descended and sleet started to peck away at the trees and fields. Aggie, wrapped in the same blanket she had spread over Todd, emerged from the cabin with Jason coming right behind her, the family shotgun gripped firmly in his hands. The Major squinted through the ice pellets that pounded on the cabin roof and the dooryard and raised his eyebrows in surprise.

"I thought this was a nigger cabin," he said.

"Well, it ain't," Aggie answered. She started back inside. Todd was awake, and she wanted to be near him.

"You've got my boy here," the Major called to her retreating back. It was a statement, not a question, and it froze her more thoroughly than the weather.

She turned to look at the red-faced man who confronted her. "If your boy's name is Todd, we've got him. He's been hurt bad."

"I figured he was." The Major pulled out a brier pipe and lit it slowly. "Wherever there's a sow, he's usually in the rut. I saw the horse he ruined." Aggie remained silent, and except for the sharp sound of sleet falling around them, the ground between them was quiet for a moment. "Can he ride?" She shook her head. "Then when he can *walk*, send him home. He's got somethin' to answer for," he said, and he pulled his hat down on his head to cover his steaming pipe and rode away into the sleet.

Todd stayed with the Sterlings for a week. Although his injury was hardly more than superficial and healed rapidly, he claimed he was dizzy when he stood and tried to walk, and he spent the first five days lying in the cabin. Aggie wouldn't allow Gertie or Annie to come near him; she only permitted Jason to sit with him while she slept because she felt that her brother's presence during the accident gave him some rights the others didn't have.

Todd talked to her incessantly. She learned that he

was almost as unhappy as she sometimes found herself, but for totally different reasons. He lived with his brother and aunt and the Major in a three-story farmhouse that had belonged to his father. It was, he admitted without bragging, the finest house in the county. They apparently wanted for nothing, from what Aggie could gather—except schooling, which both boys had abandoned as soon as they could—and they had five or six hired hands and black servants.

Todd took total responsibility for the accident on the road, refusing to even consider that Aggie had been blocking the right of way and had failed to light a lantern. He expressed concern that she had been hurt, and he seemed to want nothing more than to spend hours simply sitting and talking to her, holding her hand, and staring into her deep blue eyes. He listened intently as she told him of their most recent dispossession, and when she also related their other misfortunes, he seemed near tears. Aggie embellished nothing, but she held little back either. Her fascination with the boy was so genuine that she felt she had known him forever. He seemed no less enchanted with her.

TODD WAS SHOCKED BY the conditions of Aggie's life. When he left a week after he came, riding their broken-down mare with no saddle, he was gone only a few hours. He returned without the mare but brought instead a pair of matched mules pulling a new wagon loaded with food, blankets, and other supplies. Tied to the wagon was a milk cow, and propped on top were three laying hens and a rooster. He handed the reins over to Jason, and then presented Aggie with a new gingham dress, which was too small and had to be exchanged, and a pair of high-button shoes—the first she had ever owned—which did in fact fit. He brought Jason a fleece-lined coat, Annie a dress which fit, and a bolt of cloth and thread for Gertie.

In the wagon more staples, food, and gear were crammed as if he had simply pulled it up to Greer's Dry Goods and General Merchandise in El Dorado and told him to load it up. There was little he could do to replace the shack, he acknowledged, but he returned the next morning with three black men who spent the day patching the roof and chinking up the holes through which the wind blew. In the space of a week, the young man who had nearly killed himself running into Aggie's parked wagon turned their meager existence into something resembling a prosperous life. The Sterlings had lived like gypsies for much of their lives, so they felt no embarrassment at Todd's largess. Gertie confided to Aggie that wonderful as it seemed at the moment, she was certain something bad would happen, for nothing in her life had ever been both good *and* permanent. Although she had not done so for months, she now began to watch the woods every day, waiting for Jack to return.

Todd visited daily over the next month. He told Aggie the Major was still furious, not only over the dead horse and his maimed brother—who it appeared would always walk with a limp and never be able to raise his arm higher than his head—but also and mostly over his continuing dalliance with what he termed "white trash that're no better than a bunch of niggers." Todd made light of his uncle's anger. Aggie worried aloud that he was giving too much to them, that the Major would only come and take it all back, and Todd's face darkened.

"It's my money, mine an' Michael's," he said in a low voice, dropping his hand to the small ivory-gripped revolver he carried. "It's my money—our money. That Yankee son of a bitch's got no hold on me or what I do. All he wants is to get rid of us an' Aunt Louisa so he can run us off an' get a hold on it for himself. It's all he's ever wanted. He can't tell me what to do, though, so long as I'm here an' healthy."

Later, he confessed to Aggie that what he said wasn't precisely true. Major Hitchcock did have a very strong hold over Todd and Michael's money while the boys were still young. But, Todd assured her, his uncle knew better than to let it out that he was denying them reasonable access to their father's inheritance, even if it went out to feed and clothe "white trash."

January gave way to February, and winter abated in southern Arkansas. Todd gave Aggie a chestnut gelding so they could ride together, and he found her equestrian ability almost equal to his own; it amazed him no less than her proficiency with firearms. She was, he told her, a marvel, and she felt certain that as soon as he could appease the Major some way, Todd would ask her to marry him. He had never shown a specific romantic interest in her, she acknowledged, never even tried to kiss her. She threw her arms around him and hugged him when he handed her the reins to the gelding, and he blushed a deep crimson and pulled away awkwardly. She sensed that he had more experience with women than he displayed, and she took his shy behavior toward her as a compliment.

One frosty morning, Gertie's forecast about good things never lasting came true. Holstein visited and told them that as far as he could see, his debt to Hannibal Tyler was acquitted. What he could actually see, Aggie figured, was that the tumbledown shack they had moved into with its lean-to shed for animals and collapsing corral fence had been transformed into a prosperous-looking farm that might attract permanent—and white—tenants. He wanted them out by planting time so he could move in a family with a man at its head and get more profitable use out of the cabin than the Sterlings could likely provide. Aggie's claim that they could handle any work he had for them failed to persuade him to let them stay; they had to vacate by the end of the week.

She planned to appeal to Todd for assistance, hoping maybe that the Major would relent and offer them a place, but she never had a chance. Todd had just arrived for his afternoon visit, and they were walking out to the barn for a ride, when Jack Sterling rode a snorting black stallion into the dooryard and dismounted.

Jack hated Todd at first sight, that much was clear to Aggie and anyone else who cared to look at him. He took a quick look at the state of things and called to her to join him on the porch.

They followed Jack up to the house, and he stopped and stared hard at Todd. He examined him all over, from his handmade riding boots to his hat, from his silk cravat to his ivory-handled revolver, from his light brown curls flowing handsomely down onto his shoulders to his bright gray eyes that seemed always to dance with laughter. Aggie was embarrassed for Todd while Jack studied him. For a long moment, no one said anything.

For once, Jack cut a dashing figure himself. His natural good looks seemed to have magically returned along with a renewed self-confidence. His face was deeply tanned, and his thin mustache even seemed fuller and was matched by neatly barbered sideburns that swept down from his thinning but heavily oiled hair and gapped precisely on either side of a small goatee. He wore an expensive black suit and had what appeared to be a diamond stickpin in his cravat. His hatband was made of hammered silver coins, and his boots were highly polished and glistened even under a covering of road dust. He wore a new brace of pistols high on his waist, cross-rigged like a gunfighter's, and the gunbelt buckle was silver with gold inlay in the design of a horse's head. His gloves were of soft leather, and his saddle was decorated with Spanish conchos. For the first time in Aggie's memory, Jack Sterling looked successful.

When Aggie finally broke the silence and introduced Todd and briefly explained the circumstances surrounding his presence there, Jack maintained a cool politeness that warmed only slightly when Todd awkwardly excused himself and took his leave. Aggie stood out on the porch and watched him ride off, wanting to saddle the gelding and go with him. She could face his uncle's anger, she thought. Anything, she thought, would be preferable to remaining there with Jack.

Jack, however, cheered the moment Todd was out of sight. He was in one of his expansive moods, and he went out to his saddlebags and produced a Mexican doll for Annie. He presented Jason with a Bowie knife and scabbard, and for Aggie he brought a set of Spanish combs for her hair. As usual, he brought nothing for Gertie, and the last item he pulled out was a bottle of White Mule bourbon, with which he settled himself in front of the hearth as if he had been away but a week and deserved the honor. He said nothing of the fact that they were more than a few miles and a whole state north of where they had been when he last saw them. When Jason had the temerity to mention something about how hard things had been, Jack knocked him against the cabin wall.

"Looks to me like you been doin' all right," he said. He then offered a lecherous wink in Aggie's direction. "That young pup been sniffin' 'round much?" No one answered him, and he stabbed a hard look at Aggie. "I could smell you five miles away," he said. "It's a wonder ever' hard lick in Arkansas ain't pissin' all over your skirts. When you're wearin' skirts." He frowned at the trousers she had donned for the planned ride with Todd, then he turned his attention to Jason. "Get on out an' tend to that horse. He's mean an' he bites, so watch him." Jason slunk out the door. Jack uncorked his bottle, drank deeply from it, and propped his feet on the hearth and spoke directly to Gertie for the first time. "Time I stayed home an' took these young'uns in hand," he said. "As usual, you been lettin' 'em carry on any way they want to."

He had a grand opportunity this time, he continued. He had met a man in San Antonio who owed him for saving his life, and they had struck a deal. No chance this could go wrong, he said with a gulp of the whiskey. It was straight business. "And," he shouted with glee in his amber voice, "you're all goin' with me."

The announcement stunned them. They had been used to following him around from place to place after one of his failures, but this was the first time he had ever included them in his plans for success. For years he had talked randomly about their moving to Texas after he had struck it rich, but he always rode off and apparently had forgotten about his dream by the time he returned. The thought of having to follow him and witness one of his disasters frightened them.

Aggie looked around and met Gertie's eyes. They had the same blank look they always took on when they were about to move. In the past few weeks, she had been more like her old self than Aggie had seen her in recent memory. But now, with Jack going on about how this "sure thing" was going to put them on top for good, how they were going to live in the mountains and raise horses, "live on the best goddamn land in the world," Gertie retreated into her mantle of endurance. Aggie hated Jack more at that moment than she ever had before. Finally, what he was saying penetrated her thoughts.

"Mountains?" she said. "I didn't know Texas had mountains. I thought it was all desert."

"Desert!" Jack laughed. "Texas is anythin' but desert. Hell, I been all over Texas, an' I never seen enough sand to put in a hourglass. Hell, no. Texas is pretty. Cottonwoods an' live oak down in the middle, pine forest an' palmetto in the east. Prairies full of grass in between. Texas is God's country."

"Where's the mountains?" Annie asked from a cowering crouch she usually assumed after Jack hit someone.

"New Mexico." Jack smiled. "We're all goin' to New Mexico."

"I don't want to go to Mexico," Aggie said. "I don't think we'd get along in Mexico."

"Not Mexico, you idiot," Jack growled at her. "*New* Mexico. New Mexico Territory. Santa Fe, or damn near it. I'm not sure 'xactly where the place is at." He waved his hand casually as if it didn't matter. "It's called the Valley of Snow or some damn thing. It's in the Tres Ritos country, I think, near a place called Taos or somethin' like that. Prettier'n hell I hear tell." He took a long draw and stared at the fire, then he turned his head and glared at her. In the firelight his face was redder than usual and his handsomeness disappeared. He looked like evil itself. His eyes appeared to be sunken above his jutting cheekbones, and she noticed that his hair was disappearing from his forehead. "Make no mistake 'bout it, girlie," he snarled at her, "you're goin'."

TODD RETURNED THE NEXT day, but Jack ran him off. He informed him the Sterlings didn't need "Yankee charity from some goddamn Bluebelly coward." Aggie followed Todd when Jack went back inside, and he told her that Jack had been in El Dorado most of the previous week. In fact, the presents he claimed were from Texas he had bought at the last minute from a traveling drummer who had set up his wagon on the town's main street. He had expressed no inkling and less concern about where his family was located, and only the local saloon had provided him with enough gossip about Todd Christian and the strange "white trash" he had taken up with to lead him home again. He hung around to learn all he could about the Major, to figure out that the boy was skylarking with Aggie for reasons that, Jack told everyone, were clear to the born blind, and he announced that if anyone was going to get between her legs in exchange for a few bobbles and bows, it was going to be Jack Sterling himself. He told no one that she was his daughter.

Aggie received this news with no particular surprise, which caused Todd to look at her in a strange way.

"Well," he said after a moment, "is he your daddy or not?"

"Not enough that you could tell it." Aggie cast her eyes down. She had no idea how to begin explaining Jack to this young man. She felt too ashamed to meet his eyes.

At that moment, Jack called for her, and for once she was grateful. "Come see me," she called to Todd as she raced back toward the house. "We got to leave here, but you come."

Todd stood confused in the shadows of the trees alongside the cotton patch and watched her go. He shook his head and then left.

FOR THE NEXT SEVERAL days Jack played a wide variation of roles where Aggie was concerned. From time to time he was the doting parent, checking on her whenever she was about her chores, advising her on various matters he imagined her to be curious about, and inquiring of her about the general health and well-being of every animal and person on the place as if she were the mistress and Gertie nothing more than a Negro servant. He praised the progress they had made in acquiring possessions and keeping their things in good repair, dismissing Todd Christian's contributions with a casual wave of his hand. Aggie's chief gratitude was that he didn't hit her anymore. He kept his hands to himself in other ways, as well.

Other times, he played suitor, bringing her flowers he found growing in a nearby meadow, suggesting that he take her into town to have the agate he gave her so long ago set into a gold ring, and even offering to teach her to dance, a suggestion that quickly died when it became apparent that there was no music to be had anywhere around. He complimented her on everything she did. But beneath all the cloying sweetness that he lay down between them was an undercurrent of tension she couldn't quite identify. She slept with the towel-wrapped butcher knife every night, but Jack kept his distance.

In between, he became his old mean self, especially

after he had downed most of a bottle of whiskey. He slapped Gertie whenever she came near him or was too slow or clumsy about doing anything, and even booted Jason or struck him when he said anything at all, telling him if he ran off he would ride him down and shoot him like a runaway mongrel. He left Annie pretty much alone, and she stayed away from him, even carrying her blanket and bedding out to the lean-to and sleeping in the hay.

The most shocking role Aggie found in Jack's repertoire, however, was that of confidant. He took her aside one morning, and she reluctantly followed him into the lean-to, where he dropped his galluses and began to pull his shirttail out of his trousers. She backed away, but he begged her to stay with an assurance that he meant her no harm and a wide-eyed, innocent look that excited her curiosity. He opened his shirt and revealed a money belt beneath. She was shocked to see it bulging with greenbacks.

"There's 'most a thousan' dollars there," he whispered, then he brought a finger to his lips. "I'm tellin' you so in case anythin' happens to me, you won't let 'em bury me without you gettin' it." He winked, and then stuffed the belt back into his shirt and buttoned up.

The money, he explained, was mostly his. The rest had come from the man he met in San Antonio. They had ridden together, he said, fighting Indians and trading horses to the Army, and they finally made their way to Jefferson, Texas. There they pooled their cash, and the man had commissioned Jack to go to Kentucky or Tennessee, whichever he preferred, and to buy horses to take to New Mexico. The man had a whole valley, he said, and he was going to sell the horses, or some of them anyway, and then settle in the valley and raise the rest. They were partners. Jack would get half of everything when they arrived; all he had to do was buy the horses and help the man drive them west.

Aggie acknowledged that it sounded real enough—at least as real as any of Jack's other plans—and she wondered why anyone would trust him to handle that much money, even if more than half of it was his. But then, she realized, few people knew him as she and her family did. He still could manage an innocent smile, a winning attitude. He could charm the skirts off a preacher's wife. And, she thoughtfully added, he did know horses.

None of it made any difference, she thought. She wasn't going to Texas or to New Mexico, no matter what Jack said or how much she might believe him. She was going to stay. She made up her mind. She was through with Jack Sterling. Gertie and the children could go along with him if they wanted to, but she wasn't. She didn't know yet how it was going to happen, but this one good thing that had come into her life, Todd Christian, was not going to slip away from her, was not going to end.

3

WHILE JACK STRUTTED AROUND HIS HOUSE AND demanded that his family pack everything into the new wagon, Todd found problems of his own. His brother, Michael, hobbling around and trying to accustom himself to crutches, fell down the stairs at home and cracked open his skull. He was dead before his Aunt Louisa, who had watched in horror as her nephew tumbled over and over down two flights to her feet, knelt and touched him. She fainted and struck her own head on the banister and fell unconscious, where she remained while the Major fumed at Todd.

The Major's delight at having half the impediment to his total control of the boys' estate removed was tempered. If his wife died while the remaining boy lived, then the entire legacy, according to the terms of his deceased brother-in-law's will, would pass "into trust" until Todd reached his majority. *Trust* meant a banker would control the vast holdings the Major himself had administered for years, and it also meant virtual penury for him, unless Todd was munificent enough to provide for him, which wasn't likely. His only recourse was to remove Todd as completely as he could short of murdering him—something, Todd felt, that was a particular possibility while Louisa continued to breathe. But if he could run Todd out of the country, the Major might be able to have him declared missing or dead in a few years—even months, if money could change hands and rumors could be turned into legally deposed facts. He summoned Todd, berated him caustically for causing his unfortunate brother's death, and banished him.

"If I even hear of you riding through one corner of this county," the Major announced, "I'll get my rifle an' shoot you on sight."

He didn't send the reluctant prodigal off empty-handed, however, for fear he might return too soon. He provided Todd with a good horse, five hundred dollars in greenbacks, and any personal belongings he could pack in a saddlebag in fifteen minutes' time, and escorted him to the gate of what had been the Christian home.

"Get out," the Major said. "If you return while I'm living, I'll kill you."

Todd knew that he would inherit his father's fortune in a few years, but he also knew that the Major had tied up most of the money and would control all of the land until then. He could have appealed to a lawyer, he supposed, but there were only two attorneys in El Dorado, and his uncle owned both of them right down to their garters.

He rode his fine horse into town and chewed on his dilemma. As he guided his mount down Main Street, his eye drifted toward the gunsmith's, and he immediately brightened. He decided that he was old enough for an adventure, and there was likely no time ever to be better than the present. He went into the store and bought a Sharps .50, and a brace of Colt's Army .44s to go with his ivory-gripped revolver. In another hour, he had purchased heavy-duty trousers, a broad-brimmed plainsman's hat, food and supplies for a two-week journey. He loaded everything onto a packhorse that was a better animal than two-thirds of the riders in the county owned and rode down to the Sterling place, where he waited among the trees until after dark before calling to Aggie as she came out for her evening chores.

"But why must you go?" she asked Todd after he whistled to her and pulled her into the lean-to shed. He explained the complications of the legacy, his uncle's anger and greed, and even his desire for a personal adventure of his own. Her blue eyes swam with tears, and she searched his face for something like compassion. It was unbelievable that he was abandoning her. Too much courage had gone into her decision to run away from Jack, and everything depended on Todd's taking her in. She felt a sudden hollow pain in her chest, as if something had died.

He patiently repeated everything the Major had said. He felt rotten deserting her, he said, but he didn't see that there was much he could do about it. He had thought of trying to find a way to marry her, he confessed. In fact, he had thought of little else since the moment his vision cleared and he first looked into her face. And to tell the truth, he went on, had Jack not shown up when he did, he would have asked her out to meet the Major and his aunt. He planned to buy her a fine silk gown and some jewelry, to have her hair coiffured in town beforehand, so they could see that far from being white trash, she was nothing less than an unpolished diamond; only a little application of some of life's nicer blandishments would reveal her true value. But things had taken a rotten turn, he explained. He had no choice but to go.

Aggie wasn't interested in either his plans or his regrets. She suspected that the prospect of adventure in the West drew him strongly. He was so proud of his new clothes and firearms that he reminded her of a small child. She saw his yearning to be off and away from Arkansas as a rival which she must combat or she would be lost. A cold panic swelled in her chest.

"Let me go with you," she pleaded. "I'm tough! You know I am. I can endure anything. Let me go with you!" She fell to her knees, and he jerked her up roughly. He was mortified. Her desperation was way out of bounds. She babbled out the truth about Jack's nature, about his designs on her. But he seemed not to believe it or to accept the seriousness of her frantic plea.

"I'm goin' up into Kansas," he explained. "Maybe Nebraska. I'm fixin' to hunt buffalo. They're makin' a fortune on the hides. I'll find a way to get along until I'm twenty-one, then I'll come back."

"But I won't be here!" Aggie cried. "We're leavin'. He's takin' us away. Let me go. You can use a woman with you. I can hunt buffalo. I can shoot as good as you. I can cook and keep a camp. I can ride. You've seen me ride!" Her words tumbled over each other as her eyes raced across his face, seeking any hope he might offer her.

"There ain't no women up there," he said, startled by her suggestion. " 'Cept whores an' Indians, there ain't no women up there. You'd be all alone."

"I won't be alone. I'll have you! We'll have each other." Suddenly she dropped the pail she had been holding and threw her long arms around his neck and kissed him. It was Aggie's first time to kiss anyone aside from her siblings or her mother. She had intended simply to hold him, hug him to her in an effort to keep him near her, but his face butted against hers awkwardly, and his own experience led his mouth to hers. She instinctively followed his motions and took the lead.

They collapsed into the hay, gripping each other, their mouths locked together. His pistols' butts jutted painfully into her stomach; his fine new hat fell off and crumpled under their bodies as they rolled around and maneuvered for more comfortable positions. She pressed her body into his even more tightly, entwining her long legs around the high boots on his calves, her mouth seeking to devour his lips, her teeth opening suddenly to receive his tongue and allow it to explore her own with hard, searching thrusts. She felt his arms grasping her back, his shoulders tense as his muscles flexed beneath the deerskin coat and new plaid shirt he wore.

Suddenly his hand was beneath her skirt, and she felt his fingers running all over her narrow hips and thighs, seeking tender spots and bringing forth involuntary moans from her when they expertly and lovingly caressed her. His other hand pulled open the bodice of her dress and worked its way down quickly to cup first one breast and then the other. Her body surged under his touch, and she felt her heart beating wildly. His fingers fondled her nipples, making them almost painfully hard, and she almost cried out as she gripped him harder and lightly chewed the fabric of his lips while their tongues fenced and their breath filled each other's ears.

She felt his penis thrusting toward her through his denim trousers, and she did not resist as he guided her hand down between his legs, where she gripped its outline and massaged it with tender but firm strokes that made him thrash about more violently and press himself even more closely to her.

"I want you," he whispered hoarsely into her ear. "My God, I want you, now!"

"Take me with you," she answered breathlessly into his ear. "You can have me. I'll make you happy. I'll help you. You know I can. Please, Todd, take me with you! I love you!"

He didn't answer but kept caressing her, seeking to love her, striving for some measure of satisfaction through their clothed bodies as they rolled and tossed on the hay. He freed one hand and sought his trouser buttons, rolling slightly away from her to help himself. In seconds he was back, his legs entangled in his pants. He pulled her skirt up in a bunch around her waist and worked his body between her thighs.

Aggie pushed her hips up toward him, seeking instinctively to join her body with his. Through the chaos that filled her mind, she heard Gertie's warnings about men, about sex, about how much it hurt and how many nightmares were born out of it. But she couldn't help herself. There was nothing in this experience remotely similar to the horrors of sexual union Gertie had described, nothing of the hideous violence she had observed that awful night in Arkansas. What she felt was beyond any experience she could have imagined. She wanted Todd to love her, to make her a part of him. She felt a hot wetness streaming down her inner thigh, and when Todd's hands again found her breasts and his mouth once more covered hers, she lunged toward him and gripped the backs of his legs with her feet once more.

Then he was inside her, and her mind seemed to explode with emotions she didn't think she could endure. She gasped, and her hips rose again. Their bodies struggled in the jumble of clothes to find a comfortable rhythm while their mouths groped toward each other and their hands sought tight purchase on one another's backs. It was wonderful, Aggie shouted silently to herself. Todd was wonderful, she thought over and over. He thrust deeply into her, and she tried to match his movements and gripped him even more tightly. Their breathing matched its pace, and she felt as if they were one person, moving in a single motion. In the distance of her imagination, she believed she could perceive a rainbow, an eruption of color that, once she reached it, she would be able to feel. But while she yearned for it, she also wanted to forestall it, to postpone what she somehow sensed would be the end of this wonderful union. Her eyes were closed, and their bodies rocked and moaned together. She wanted the movement to continue forever.

A voice stopped them both.

"Daddy's lookin' for you," Jason said. The boy stood with his mouth agape and his eyes wide. He held the shotgun loosely in his hand, but now he brought it up slightly. "He's been yellin' for you." His mouth slanted oddly down. "He hurtin' you, Aggie?"

Aggie's emotional journey ended abruptly. She felt like a broken water bag, half full, then suddenly emptied, spilled. She rolled quickly away from Todd, who turned over and tried to refasten his trousers. She stood awkwardly, pulled the loose folds of her dress together, and smoothed down her skirts at the same time. She was panting, dizzy, and her knees almost buckled. She put out a hand against the building's wall to steady herself. Jason's eyes followed the move, and she withdrew it, took a deep breath, and stood up straight.

"Tell him I'll be there direc'ly." She was still quivering, fighting for a composure she didn't want. Her heart was banging against her chest, and her hands were shaking. She thrust them behind her. Jason didn't move but simply stared down at Todd. "He ain't hurtin' me," she said. "Now go on, 'fore he comes out here."

Jason left as quietly as he had come, and she knelt down in the hay and covered her face with her hands. Todd stood off to one side and repaired his clothes, slapping his ruined hat against his legs to loose the hayseeds that had collected in it. Finally, Aggie rebuttoned her dress and struggled to her feet as well. Neither spoke, but even in the dark, Aggie could see that he was red with embarrassment and anger.

"I got to go," he finally said.

"Take me with you, Todd."

"I can't, Aggie. I just can't. But I'll come back for you."

"I won't be here." She felt tears coming. They seemed to be all that was left. "He's takin' us away."

"I can't take you with me."

"Was this"—her eyes fell to the hay at their feet—"all you wanted? Was that the only reason you come out here?" Her voice tried to be hard and cold, but the tears were now falling freely from her eyes. She refused to let herself sob, but she couldn't stop weeping. "If that's what it'll take, you can have it. I'll give it to you. You don't even have to marry me. Just take me with you."

"Oh, Aggie!" Todd exclaimed, and he moved to take her hand, but she pulled it away. She was immediately sorry, for he hung his head, and she realized that he did feel something for her. It wasn't love, but it was far from what she knew Jack felt, and it was much, much more endurable. "Aggie," he said, "I think I love you, but I know I got to go. I can't take you with me." He slapped his thigh with his hat. "Jesus, I can't explain it! I just got to go, that's all."

After a few more quiet tears, Aggie stood up straight to her full height. She surprised herself by being taller than he. She had never noticed it before, and it embarrassed her, but it also gave her strength. She drew on her mother's legacy and steeled herself to accept this horrible twist in her fortunes.

"We're goin' someplace called Tres Ritos," she said in a flat voice. "It's in New Mexico. Not Mexico, but *New* Mexico. It's a territory of some kind."

"I know where it is," Todd said without certainty. He silently repeated the name five or six times. "I'll find you. I'll come for you. I'll come next fall. By then, I'll be a rich man in my own right, an' we'll come back here an' rub the Major's nose in it," he added in a low, tough voice. "I'll come for you, Aggie. Then we'll come back here. I'll kill him if I have to. Then we'll have the biggest goddamn wedding El Dorado's ever seen. You just wait an' see."

Aggie knew then she would never see Todd again, but she resolved not to believe it, and she pushed the dread from her mind. She needed to hold on to the hope of seeing this wonderful boy—this handsome man—again, in order to endure whatever Jack had in mind for them.

In a way, she felt relieved. She would have felt guilty abandoning Gertie on the eve of this crazy trip and leaving her completely in Jack's hands. She doubted they would ever arrive in New Mexico. If Jack ran true to form, she thought, they likely would never see Texas. Unless things were really going to go differently this time, they'd be lucky to get out of Arkansas.

They stood silently when there was no more to say. Jack's voice came from the cabin and called for her into the darkness, which was alive with crickets and the distant sounds of frogs. Todd hefted his new rifle. Jack called again, this time with a mixture of anger and concern in his voice. Todd didn't move. He was afraid of Jack, she knew, but he was ashamed to let her know it.

At once, she threw her arms around him and kissed him hard on the lips. She was still inexperienced in the matter, but he overcame his shock and joined her with enthusiasm, and they held each other so tightly she feared he might hurt her. This time, their embrace was void of the sexual heat they had felt before. But her heart beat rapidly, and she could feel his own chest pounding, once more in rhythm to hers, and her throat closed with the grief of their separation. Jack's third call, now all anger, broke them apart, and Aggie turned with a heavy, choking sigh, picked up her pail, and started toward the cabin.

After two steps, she turned. It was a moonless night, just like the one on which they had met. She could not see his face, but his odor was in her nostrils, his taste in her mouth. All she could feel, though, was a hard, blind hatred for herself, a loathing for the circumstances that had brought her into the world to endure so much heartache. She felt frozen inside, and something in her hardened. Gertie was right, she thought. There were nightmares there, worse than Aggie had ever realized. She loved him, she thought. She would trust him to find her, to fulfill his promise. But deeper in her heart, behind those empty assurances, was the knowledge that she would never be the same again. She resolved that somehow she would find a way to live her own life without putting any faith at all in the promises of men.

4

AGGIE PULLED HER CLEAN DRESS ON, ALTHOUGH HER body was only partly dry. It was impossible for her to stand erect enough to use the towel efficiently, so she gave up and dressed with parts of her skin still beaded with the chilly water. Her hair hung loose and wet around her shoulders, and after she swept back the blanket and left the confining area of the impromptu bathroom, she pulled it back and pinned it up so it might dry without sousing her shoulders.

Annie awoke and looked at her sister curiously.

"Go out to the wagon an' get a clean dress," Aggie ordered. She went over and folded her soiled clothing and stacked it on the chest, then inspected her own fresh clothes. The new dress will be totally ruined, she thought sadly. Well, she thought, Todd bought it for her when she had nothing better than the old thing she had taken off. In fact, she remembered that the last time he saw her, this was the very dress she had been wearing.

"I don't see what good it'll do," Annie said from where she continued to sit and stare at her sister. "The Indians'll just get us anyway. They don't care if we're dirty or not."

"I care," Aggie said. "Now, get." Annie arose languidly and moved out of the cave. Aggie saw that Constance and her companion were still staring hard at her. "You're welcome to the soap," she said. "Soon as Annie's done. The water's cold as ice, but it's good to be clean."

"I wouldn't let anythin' that's touched you near my body," Glorietta snapped.

"Well, I would." Constance stood and approached Aggie with a smile.

"It's a sin," Glorietta spoke sharply to Constance. "That girl's a walkin' talkin' sin! She's got nigger sweat on her, mark my words. You take that soap from her, you're as bad as she is, an' you'll get it right on you. I swear it."

"Oh, I don't know," Constance said without turning. "They say cleanliness is next to godliness, Glorietta, an' to tell the truth, I been sittin' next to you near all day, an' you smell worse'n any nigger I ever run up on. 'Sides, if we're all fixin' to die, I think I'd just as soon do it feelin' clean. You watch Grady for me." She glanced down at her insensible husband. "I'm doin' it more for him'n anybody." She stepped over to where Aggie sat with a nervous smile on her face.

Aggie became impatient waiting for Annie to return, and she gave the soap to Constance, who soon secreted herself behind the blanket. Constance explained that her brother's wife had taken all the clothing she wasn't wearing down to the creek to wash. But she welcomed the opportunity to bathe, even if she couldn't change clothes, and she seemed genuinely grateful for the loan of the soap and even the damp towel Aggie offered to share with her.

Aggie checked the wounded men again and noted with a glimmer of remorse that two more had died peacefully. She approached a feverish man who continued to thrash and struggle with his wounds. She did what she could to comfort him, then stepped outside to find Annie, who was nowhere to be seen. From a distance she saw Mr. Graham in an argument with a group of men and Hannah Morgan, but she didn't want to know what it was about. For the moment, she felt fresh and clean for the first time in days, and she didn't want to spoil her renewal with the bitterness that seemed to infect everyone on the train.

She wished Mr. Graham would come by and talk to her again, but she sensed he didn't want to come inside and confront her or the wounded men. She knew he felt responsible for the men who had been hurt or were dead, and she also knew that he was looking for something—or someone—to blame it all on. She figured that it would be Moses Franklin. She didn't exactly fault Mr. Graham for that. That was the way of things. But she also knew that Moses Franklin wasn't any more to blame than anyone else, and she felt sorry for him.

It puzzled her that Frank Herbert had been the only one to volunteer to go with Mr. Franklin to get help. It also puzzled her that Mr. Graham had let him. She had watched Herbert closely since leaving Jefferson, and like most people on the train, she assumed that he was not right in his mind. He looked at things in a broad, unassuming way, but his widely spaced eyes and boyish grin confused her.

She thought again of Frank's daughter, who continued to lie inside the cave beside Jason. When she emerged from her bath and spoke to Annie, Aggie had spotted her open eyes staring up at nothing in particular, but when she stepped in that direction, they snapped shut and she pretended to sleep again. Jason remained beside her. His sleep was more genuine, his breathing heavy and unrestrained by nervousness. The girl was dark and had long, untamed black hair that trailed elusively down the back of her homespun dress. Aggie had seen her braiding some wildflowers in it once, and she had tried to speak to her on several occasions, to make friends with her, but she ran away and hid in Herbert's wagon. Just for a moment, Aggie had wondered if she was part Indian, but she doubted it. She certainly would have heard about that, she knew.

Lately, she had begun wondering about the girl and a boy who seemed to always be near her. She saw them together often, always at a distance or off in the shadows, when there were shadows. They kept away from everyone, back in the rear of the train behind the cattle where she couldn't view them clearly. But the girl was unmistakable with her startling black hair and odd way of seeming to be by herself no matter who stood or walked near her. It made her think of Todd, but rather than finding something to envy in their strange relationship, she found it amusing and had quietly given it her blessing, even remembered them in her prayers.

She hadn't recognized the boy, and she had paid him little attention, although she kept meaning to ask Jason about them when she could. She wondered where the boy was now, if he was alive. For a moment she felt a disturbing curiosity about Jason's choice of a resting place beside the girl, of his remembering her name. Then she shook her head. Still, the thought wouldn't go away. He was lying there, comfortable beside her, not touching her, but at the same time closer than he had to be. Then she frowned and shook her head once more. The boy with the Herbert girl had been taller, older. Aggie was sure of it.

Her thoughts trailed again toward Cleve Graham as she gave up looking for her sister and went back inside the cave. She was not ignorant of the way he looked at her the first time he saw her, but she was still new enough to being around men who found her attractive that she did not know if his deep, appreciative gazes carried more meaning than she at first understood.

But she was not completely naive. She knew he was fond of her. She knew that when he spoke to her he had trouble expressing himself. She thought of him as she might of a father—a real father—a man who would care for her and protect her. She had never felt that way about Jack Sterling. But in the course of the past few weeks, she had come to think of Cleve Graham in that way. His hand was creased and hard, but she also watched him pet the nose of his horse and gently roll a cigar around on his fingers. She knew that he was capable of delicacy as well. Once, when they were waiting to cross a deep draw while Moses scouted for a place that might be easier, she watched him using only his fingers to twist and braid a piece of rawhide into a small quirt, which she later saw the Herbert girl carrying around. He could, it seemed, do more with one hand than many men could do with two. She thought it a great pity that he had lost his other limb, that some of the children in the train called him "Ol' Crip" behind his back, but she considered his handicap as nothing more than a minor flaw in a man she believed to be a bona fide gentleman.

He had never approached her about anything personal. They had never really had a conversation before they came to this crossing and had been forced to discuss the care of the wounded men. Indeed, when she stood him and Jack off in the grove where the Mexicans were found, she came closer to speaking intimately with him than at any other time. There was something in his face then, and she saw it again when she confronted him over his notion of shooting the wounded women. It was something she couldn't quite identify. It wasn't pain, exactly, although she sensed instinctively that she was hurting him. But she assumed that the hurt was because she was defying his authority. She had seen genuine pain when he had to tell her that none of the other women would come in to help her unless it was their own men who needed tending. And she had seen his fear when he instructed her to cauterize the wounds. She had also sensed his relief when she took on the job without complaint. Somehow she had managed to hurt him those two times in some deeper way that mystified her, and in spite of the fact that she was firm in her conviction that what she had done in both cases was right, she felt she owed him a debt of obligation, something more than she had done by taking over the hospital or seeing to the wounded men.

There had been moments when she had hated him, and, she acknowledged, she would have killed him just as she killed the outrider years ago. But she realized that it was not Graham she hated, but the things he was forced to do. He needed someone to show him the right of things, she decided with a physical nod of her head. Even though he was stubborn, he wasn't mean. He wasn't like Jack. He backed down when he realized that nothing would stop her. He saw that her will was as strong as his, and he admitted that she was right and he was wrong. At least that was what it meant to her.

A SERIES OF SHOUTS interrupted her thoughts, and she started toward the cave door. She heard a man cry out in pain loudly, and she reached for the little gunbox Moses had left with her. Hannah had told her that if there was another attack, the Indians might well get into the cave, and no one might realize it until it was too late. She removed the pistol and loaded it, but the commotion, whatever it was, ended with the man's wail. For a moment, she waited inside the cave's entrance, tense and almost frantic in her ignorance. She wanted to run out and see what it was, but her duty, as she saw it, was here. If the Comanche were coming back, she would have to defend these helpless men from whatever horrors the Indians might inflict on them.

She wasn't prepared to use the little gun—or any other—on herself, but she was ready to use it to protect Annie or Jason and the girl who lay next to him, or the men who lay helpless in the cave, even to protect Constance and Glorietta if it came to that. She only had the small pistol and two barrels of the shotgun handy, but Jason had also stacked her daddy's rifle, a Winchester, in one corner, and when she looked around, she was proud to see that he had jumped up and had it at the ready, covering the cave's turning entrance in the event that any redskin should show himself. Lottie Herbert, also wide awake and defiant, was coiled at his feet. One dirty hand bunched her torn dress together across her bosom, and in the other she held Jason's sharp knife.

Aggie smiled at them to show that she was glad they were there. She knew that lackadaisical though he might appear about life, Jason would use the rifle if he had to, not only against Indians, but also against anyone who attacked her personally. He might look like Jack, and he might act like him sometimes as well, but he was her brother, and he loved her.

As quiet returned to the wagon fort outside the cave, she replaced the weapons and returned to the fire to clean up her tea things. She hoped that all was well, but with no shots fired, she had to assume that whatever ruckus had taken place was minor. Hannah Morgan appeared in the cave again and walked over by the wall and sat down heavily.

"That Cleve Graham's at the end of his tether," she said. Her voice was husky with anger.

"What happened?" Aggie noticed that Glorietta lifted her head when Hannah came in. Otherwise she had not reacted to the outside noise. Aggie deduced that she had been asleep. If so, it was the first time she had closed her eyes since her husband was brought in after the first attack.

Hannah noticed the attention she was receiving, and she lowered her voice and spoke nonchalantly. "There was jus' a fight over the whiskey," she said. "That preacher's gone loco over it. Wants to pour it out, an' I think Graham wants to kill him." She laughed mirthlessly. "We got any left?" She roused herself. "I need a drink."

"None," Aggie said. "I was hopin' you could get back so I could go ask Mr. Graham for another keg. Did he hurt Mr. Hollister?"

"Not so you could tell it." Hannah inspected the cave floor. "He hit him a good'un up 'side the jaw. That's twice I know of, but he didn't hurt him none. I'll 'low he'll be seein' stars long 'fore it's night, though. Chewin' on one side, as well." She smiled. "He walloped that Dutchman a good'un, too. The man's a little hair-triggered, if you ask me. Somebody's goin' to have to watch his back, an' the way he's col'-cockin' people 'round here, he's runnin' out of friends in a hurry." She picked up the shotgun. "I'm goin' to borrow this a spell. If there's trouble, a scatter-gun'll gener'ly put a stop to it."

"You think it'll come to that?" Aggie was shocked.

"Girl, let me tell you. I've seen it come from less. Down 'round Bastrop, once, there was this sawed-off little peckerwood of a dep'ty marshal name of Grimes. He took it on hisself to run some cattle rustlers out of the country. Trouble was, the major part of the rustlin' was bein' done by some real rich folks, or people who worked for 'em. He pushed an' shoved his way 'round down there for a while, stepped on some toes, and throwed a couple of important folks in the jailhouse. They come after some of 'em one night. Big ol' bunch of 'em. Well, this feller Grimes goes out all by hisself with a scattergun jus' like this'un, an' he tells 'em to break it up an' go on home."

"An' they went?"

"Hell no." Hannah laughed. "They stewed 'round a while an' drank up some Dutch courage, an' then they come at him all at once, all in a bunch."

"Did he back down?"

Hannah's eyes took on a faraway look. "He let 'em have both barrels. Killed three outright, an' two more died later. Bunch of others went home with buckshot inside 'em." She looked down. "He was a good man, an' he broke it up. They never got them ol' boys out of the jailhouse, an' two of 'em swung for it, right there in Bastrop."

"If you think there'll be trouble," Aggie said quickly, "you might take the rifle."

"Naw! Ol' Grimes taught me that a scattergun'll do the trick. Makes a bigger boom. Come to think on it, makes a bigger mess, too. Nothin' like a mess to take the fight out of folks." She checked the caps on the old weapon.

"There's some men bringin' in another keg, so don't fret yourself," Hannah said. "Graham thinks it's holy water or some such. I never seen a man get so worked up over a keg of rotgut. Maybe we should try to get on 'thout it." She saw Aggie frown as she glanced at some of the men. "Don't worry 'bout it," Hannah went on. "But if you're plannin' to get any more from Graham after this keg that's comin's gone, I think you better plan again." She walked casually over to where Aggie stood and whispered so the others couldn't hear. "That man's plumb gone. It's a even bet who's crazier, him or Hollister. He's hittin' folks, cussin' like a preacher in a cathouse, an' if he's not careful, he's fixin' to get hisself killed. That's why we need to keep a eye on him. Ol' Grimes taught me that, too."

"How?"

" 'Bout two weeks after they hung them ol' boys, after ever'body thought the fuss was over, they snuck up on him an' backshot him. Man who faces down trouble ain't never shed of it. I know that for a fact."

"You seem to know an awful lot." Glorietta Fulbright could contain herself no longer. "You seem to have a lot of tall tales to tell, but I, for one, don't believe any of it."

"I really don't give a damn what you believe," Hannah said.

"You're tellin' us all these things just to scare us. How do you know so much about it, anyhow? How do you know what happened? Was you there?" She looked Hannah's figure up and down. "You prob'ly were. In the mob, too, I s'pect."

"No," Hannah said evenly.

"Then how do you know?"

"Well"—Hannah winked at Aggie—"ol' Grimes was my husban', an' he was free with his experience."

Glorietta glared at Hannah and refused to admit to a gaffe. Hannah only smiled at her and checked the old shotgun again. "You can learn from other folks as good as you can from your ownself," she said. "So, if you don't mind, I think I'll keep a eye on Graham's back."

"I think I'll take him somethin' to eat," Aggie said with a cheeriness she hardly felt. She put the remainder of the bacon into the pan and set it on the stove. As an afterthought, she started more tea water to boiling. She knew that his nerves had to be worn thin. She also suddenly felt terribly guilty for defying him so brazenly, for standing up to him. She wondered if she couldn't have handled it better, tried harder not to embarrass or hurt him.

"You're fixin' to feed *him*!" Glorietta came to her feet and stalked over to the fire. "After what he done. He dumps all this on us, an' then goes off an' picks fights." She put both hands on her hips. "I heard what you was sayin'," she spat out. "I ain't deaf. I ain't no fool, neither. We didn't sign on with this outfit to get ourselves killed, an' that's all he's tried to do since we got started. He's jus' not worth it, an' we ain't beholden to him for nothin'. Let him come get his own vittles."

"I reckon we owe him a lot." Aggie poured beans into the bacon and stirred them. The water boiled and she poured it over the tea. She had put in an extra-large portion of joint root in hopes that it might make him relax. She figured him for a man who, like Jack, had a short temper that could cause trouble which might be better avoided. If he could get some rest, maybe he could hold them all together long enough to get them out of this.

"Oh, you *owe* him all right," the woman screeched. "You owe him for lettin' you go off with that nigger buck, an' . . ." Her hands swept the cave's interior and indicated the wounded and the dead men. "You owe him for makin' you feel like God Almighty Hisself." Her hair had come loose from its bun and was straying around her face wildly. She, also, was near the end of endurance, Aggie realized, and she backed away from the wild woman, who now formed her hands into claws and stepped toward her. Behind her, Aggie saw Jason come to his feet and bring the rifle to bear, and she shook her head. Glorietta misread the gesture as a token of disagreement and yelled all the louder, "You're nothin' but a nigger's whore, an' I'll be damned 'fore I'll let you touch me or my husband!"

Hannah's large hand reached out and struck Glorietta on the side of the head. The blow was not hard, but the woman collapsed and crawled back to her position near her unconscious husband. She wept audibly.

The remark had hurt Aggie, and she turned, her eyes suddenly full of tears, but she fought them back and saw Jason still standing, Jack's Winchester at the ready. The hammer was cocked; he would have killed Glorietta had she touched her. Annie, who had come into the cave with her usual catlike silence, crept to his side, next to Frank Herbert's daughter, who was kneeling there with Jason's large knife still in her hands. Aggie was shocked, and with her hands she gestured, palms downward, and they lowered their weapons and in a few moments had resumed their former positions of repose.

"Soon's that lady's through," she ordered her sister and nodded toward the blanket curtain, "you get back there an' take a bath." Then she turned around. Hannah remained where she had been, her hands on her hips, looking unhappy with herself.

"You truly goin' to make that girl take a bath back there?" she asked, but her voice did not carry the lightness of tone that the remark seemed to demand.

"Why not? I did. Constance, Connie, is back there right now." She turned and focused her blue eyes on the Herbert girl, fixing her as hard as she could with a no-nonsense gaze. "An' you're next." Hannah chuckled behind her. "You could do with a bath yourself," Aggie said, smiling at the woman who, it seemed, was her only friend.

Hannah lifted her eyes toward the blanket and nodded. "Well, it'll be a cold day in hell 'fore I get naked in some damn cave just to wash some dust off. 'Sides, I never take a bath till I'm carryin' 'round enough acreage to raise a fair crop of corn. It ain't healthy to wash too often. Gives you the fantods." She stalked indignantly back to her crate and sat down. A knife appeared along with a piece of the firewood Jason brought in, and she set herself to whittling and humming as if she were particularly irritated.

Aggie sat down by the fire again to check the tea. Her hands were still shaking from Glorietta's attack, but she tried to force herself to regain her calm. "Sometimes it's more than dust," she said quietly, amused that she had thought of a way to get in the last word, even if it was spoken softly.

Clearing her throat, Aggie scooped the beans and bacon out into a tin plate and added the remaining crust of bread. She picked up the teapot and without a look started out the door.

"I do find it sort of strange myself that you feel so kindly to a man you try to kill ever'time he breaks wind," Hannah remarked as she passed her.

"I think we've all been too hard on him," Aggie said. "He's got a tough job, an' a lot on his mind. A lot of folks've died. 'Sides, you said yourself he needed some rest. Somethin' in his stomach won't hurt either. We all got to look out for him."

"He killed your daddy," Glorietta hissed. The statement darted across the cave with the surety of a Comanche arrow, and Aggie stopped dead. "I seen him," the woman went on in a more confident voice. "Shot him dead as a stump." Constance had just emerged from behind the blanket, and she also froze, her eyes shooting warnings at Glorietta, who was ignoring them. Jason and Annie sat like stones, their faces fixed, as they stared at their sister to see what she would say.

"Shut up," Hannah said, but there was no conviction in her voice. She looked at Aggie with helplessness in her eyes.

"It's true," Glorietta whispered. "I seen Graham do it. He shot him down like a dog."

"Well," Aggie said without turning around, hoping that Jason and Annie could hear and understand, "that's one more thing I owe him for."

5

When Aggie returned from taking food to Graham, she heard yelling from inside the cave before she reached its narrow opening. She dropped the teapot and rushed inside to see a free-for-all going on. Annie and Hannah were rolling around on the ground with Frank Herbert's daughter. They were kicking and screaming at each other, and Jason stood over them, his sheathed knife inverted for service as a club. Constance and Glorietta were pressed against the walls of the cave near their wounded men, trying to shield them from the violent display that now rolled dangerously near the banked coals of the fire and then threatened to tumble itself over to where Carlysle Smith cringed and moaned beneath the shouting.

"What's going on here?" Aggie yelled. Jason straightened up immediately and stared at her, but the three women on the floor of the cave continued their fight. A bare foot kicked out and caught Hannah in the stomach, knocking her breathlessly backward.

"Stop it!" Aggie shouted as loudly as she could, but

Annie and the Herbert girl continued to wrestle. Aggie saw her sister's hand full of the other girl's black hair. Annie's face was a mask of anger and determination, but the Herbert girl was bigger, older, and stronger than her opponent, and she rolled her over and finally managed to straddle her and grasp her throat with her hands. Her dress flapped open, and her breasts dangled ridiculously over Annie's face.

"Stop it!" Aggie yelled again. She rushed up and stabbed her knee hard against the dark girl, who rolled away and came up with a defiant look in her black eyes, her hands up and clawed in a half-clench. Aggie was reminded of a wounded animal run to ground, and she stepped back and almost put her skirts into the coals before she glanced back and altered her course.

"What in the world has got into y'all?" she demanded. "You, Jason! Put up that knife! Hannah, I'm 'shamed of you. What's the matter?"

"Lord, if I know." The older woman pulled herself up and brushed at her skirts. "I was about half 'sleep, when all of a sudden them two was goin' at it like a couple of catamounts. I tried to break it up, but it was like puttin' your hand in a hornet's nest." She looked with a mixture of anger and grudging admiration at the two girls. "I got sucked in 'fore I knew what was happenin'."

"They're imps of the devil, both of them!" Glorietta shrieked from her position up against the wall.

"Shut up, Glorietta," Constance hissed. She eased herself down next to her husband and peered into his face.

"You *said* for us to take a bath," Annie said in a choked voice. She stood and rubbed her neck. Her fresh clothing was soiled from the fight, and her adversary's hands had left dark red marks on her pale skin. "We was jus' tryin' to make her."

"*You* was tryin' to make her," Jason said. "She said she didn't want no bath, an' you was tryin' to make her."

"I *don't* want no bath," the girl announced. "An' I can talk for my own self." She stood up and pulled her torn dress closed over her naked chest. "Don't need nobody tellin' me to take no bath. Don't need nobody talkin' for me."

Aggie relaxed all at once. Her head spun, but she

fought to get control over herself. "Annie, go outside and fetch the pot." Her sister stood defiantly for a moment, and then she finally moved. "Jason, you go out an' tend the cattle an' mules. They likely need lookin' after."

"There ain't nothin' I can do for 'em," he said. His eyes flashed with a petulance that reminded Aggie uncomfortably of Jack, but she had no time for his nonsense.

"I said go on." She raised her voice and fixed a hard stare on him. He glanced at the girl with something in his eye Aggie couldn't immediately define, and then he moved out with a shrug of his shoulders. Before he made the twisting exit to the cave, she stopped him. "Which one were you tryin' to hit?"

He looked at her, and a wrinkle of worry creased his young forehead. "Don't rightly know. I guess I was fixin' to whomp whichever one come up for air first." He lowered his eyelids quickly, turned, and left.

Aggie turned to Hannah, who was back on her crate, her face turned away. The strain of the whole situation was telling on all of them. She faced the girl.

"What's your name?"

"None of your damn business." The girl squatted where she was, like an Indian, Aggie thought with a quick shudder.

"I don't need sassy talk from you," Aggie said firmly. "You're causin' a lot of trouble 'round here, an' I don't need no more."

"*I* don't need people tellin' me what to do."

Annie came in with the plate and pot and set them near the fire.

"Do you have 'nother dress?" Aggie asked the girl.

"That's none of your business neither," she said.

"If you're in here, you're my business. Mr. Graham said I was to look after you, an' that's what I'm fixin' to do."

"Mr. Graham can go to hell," the girl said. "He sent my daddy out there where them Indians is, an' I don't give a damn 'bout him. I don't give a damn 'bout my daddy either. He run off an' left me out there in that wagon. Ever'body left me out there." She shot a mean look at the cave entrance through which Jason had just passed.

Aggie didn't know what to say. Had Frank Herbert

known his daughter was trapped out in Hollister's wagon by herself? It didn't seem likely he would just ride off if he did. But then, she reminded herself as she mentally conjured his wide, simple face, he wasn't like other people. Maybe he didn't think anything of it.

"Get back there an' take off that dress. You smell worse'n an Indian," Aggie ordered her, hoping that her tone would change the subject.

"Go to hell," she spat.

Aggie sighed deeply. "Hannah, you want to give me a hand?"

"Not me," Hannah said, inspecting a finger. "Once bit, twice shy. That's a she-wolf there. That child's got a good set of teeth."

Aggie was buffaloed. She didn't want to let the girl get away with this. But then, the girl wasn't really her responsibility. Graham's instructions had been to look after her, not to mother her. Clearly, she wasn't interested in either proposition.

"Look," Aggie said, stepping forward. The girl rose and crept backward the same distance, raising her fists again. "I don't want to hurt you. You don't have to take a whole bath. But you can't go 'round in that rag. It's tore wide open. You need to clean up, get somethin' to eat in you, an' then you can put on a clean dress an' do as you please. You're old enough."

The girl said nothing for a moment longer, and Aggie figured it was going to be a stand-off. Then a voice from behind her caused her to start.

"Go on, Lottie." Jason spoke from the cave's entrance. "It won't hurt nothin'. I'll help you."

Aggie's mouth hung open as her brother moved past her and gently led the girl away from her defensive position toward the blanket. Now, in the smoky gray light of the cave, she saw him differently. He was taller than she remembered seeing him only a few moments before. His figure was no longer that of a child. The glimpse of the man emerging from his gangly appearance she had caught two days before in the cedar grove again emerged. There was no longer any doubt in her mind that the dusty, shadowy figure she had observed walking with this strange, dark girl beside the small cattle herd had been Jason. She wondered that she hadn't seen it before, but in her mind he was still a quiet, almost frightened little boy. Now she saw him as a man, and the vision disturbed her.

They moved slowly together, Jason holding the crook of the girl's arm as if she were an invalid. Finally they stopped and whispered, and Jason turned to his sister.

"She says she wants some soap, an' she'd be 'bliged for some help," he said as if the girl were speaking a foreign tongue that only he could translate. Before Aggie could react, the girl slipped behind the blanket curtain, and Jason moved past Aggie and left the cave. In astonishment, she turned to watch him go. Hannah also was staring at his back when it disappeared.

"I'll be absolutely gone to hell," the big woman said, shaking her head.

Aggie went to her chest, where Annie had left the soap and damp towel and cloth on top, picked them up, and went back to see what she could do to help the girl.

She slipped past the blanket and found Lottie squatting beside the spring. The limestone side was wet from the three previous bathers, and Aggie feared that she would slip if she was startled.

"I won't make you take a bath if you don't want to," she said. "But you got to do somethin' 'bout that dress. It's ruined."

"Big Indian got hold of me." Her face turned red with the recollection. "He throwed me down on the ground, an' I thought he had me sure, but I kicked him one good one in the *cojones*, an' he left me alone." Aggie looked puzzled. "My mama"—Lottie crossed herself suddenly and with such unconsciousness that Aggie stared at her—"told me anytime a boy's after you, kick him in the *cojones*. Right in the fork if you can do'er." She smiled a tiny, thin smile, and Aggie returned it. "She said, 'Put some toe in it if you're goin' to do'er.' "

"Here," Aggie said. She tugged gently at the rag that passed for a dress on the girl, and it almost fell away in her hands. It was homemade, that much was clear, and the seams had not been properly sewn. The girl wore no underclothes at all, and when Aggie pulled the remains of the cloth from her, she stood unabashedly naked in front of her.

She was just a child, Aggie realized as she tried not to stare. Her hips were slim, her legs muscular and well formed. Her breasts were soft, olive-stained mounds with large, dark nipples that rapidly hardened as gooseflesh formed.

Lottie's stomach pooched out slightly beneath her ribs, and Aggie frowned. There was nothing else about the girl's anatomy to suggest that she was pudgy or fat. In fact, she was nail-thin, but she had an almost unnatural belly on her, the sort of tummy small children often had. Aggie had seen older children, particularly just after the war, whose diets had consisted solely of fried dough and green fruit. Their stomachs had also displayed this sort of swelling, and she worried about Lottie's health suddenly. She remembered that the girl had done little but sleep since coming into the cave.

"Have you been eatin' anythin'?" Aggie asked. She knelt down and wet the cloth and soap cake. She squeezed the water out on Lottie's shoulders. It ran down across her breasts and onto her swollen midsection, trailing mud from the dirt she had collected.

"I et what ever'body eats," she said with a flat voice. She shivered when Aggie's hands began scrubbing with the soap and cloth. The water was cold and uncomfortable.

"Have you had the skitters or anythin'?" Aggie asked. She worked her pattern of scrubbing down to the girl's small breasts and then on down over the slight swell of her stomach, which was not flabby, but firm, solid.

"No more'n anybody else," she said. "I was sick for a while, but I reckon that's nat'ral."

"There's nothin' natural about bein' sick."

"My daddy said it was," Lottie argued petulantly. "He said that happened ever'time he knowed anythin' 'bout it." Aggie's hands had reached the area just above Lottie's pubic hair, and suddenly the girl took the soap and rag and began cleaning herself.

Aggie tried to stand up straight, but she bumped her head.

"Ouch," she said. "Damn, I wish I could stand up back here."

Lottie, whose shorter stature permitted her to remain almost completely erect, rewarded Aggie's complaint with a broad smile. Aggie was stunned by the straight whiteness of the girl's teeth against her dark skin. Her hair strung down on her wet shoulders in greasy ropes.

"Jason! Annie?" Aggie called through the blanket. "Fetch me a dress back here for Lottie. Hurry up 'bout it. It's cold."

Lottie sat on the side of the spring and wet her legs up to her knees. She finished the soaping, and she allowed Aggie to wring out the cloth and rinse her upper body.

"My teeth's chatterin' so much I can't stand it."

"If you'd go ahead on an' get down in the water, it'd feel warmer," Aggie said, but the girl didn't move. Aggie could clearly observe the bulge of her stomach with her seated, naked as she was. She silently compared Lottie's figure to her own. Aggie was slender, but this girl was much leaner than she. There was no spare flesh anywhere on her body. This was more than sickness, she realized with a sudden recollection of Gertie: This girl was pregnant. She wasn't far along, but there was no doubt that she was going to have a baby. No wonder she had been sick. No wonder she didn't want to be bathed by Jason. They might be sweethearts, they might even have made love, made some kind of commitment, but this wasn't something any woman wanted to show to a man. Aggie flushed with embarrassment.

"How long?" she asked, pointing to the girl's stomach.

"Don't know, rightly," she said. "Can't tell. Not long."

"Is Jason the daddy?"

"I s'pect so," she said. "Least, he is now."

"Does your daddy know?"

She nodded. "I had to tell him why I was sick all the time in the mornin's." Her black eyes suddenly widened. "Didn't tell him Jason's the daddy, though. He ain't sure who is. Truth is, I ain't either." She saw the shock in Aggie's face, and then hardened her brown eyes. "It ain't what you think. I ain't no loose woman. But Jason ain't the first, you may as well know that. Daddy don't. Jason does, an' he says it don't matter. Sometimes people jus' do what they have to do. What they want to do. Ain't you never?"

Aggie shook her head slightly, then nodded once, briefly. Her thoughts ranged far away from Jason and this dark girl. She thought once more of Todd, of a night in a barn in Arkansas when she gave herself freely, even anxiously, to him. She wasn't sure if what they had done was anything like what Lottie was talking about. It wasn't the same thing, she argued with herself. "Yes," she said quietly. "I did once." But it was different, she thought. She imagined she once more felt Todd inside her, then she shook her head and offered a warm smile.

"Daddy don't like your daddy, an' I ain't ready for him to find out 'bout me an' Jason. We been . . . we been friendly since we was in that Jefferson town. In that big ol' hotel we was in. We're goin' to get married first chance we get."

Aggie's eyes narrowed in thought. It was hard to imagine the youngster she had practically raised being a father, let alone being married and responsible for this wild girl who looked more like a creature from the woods than a woman. But there it was. If he was old enough for this, she decided, he was old enough for anything. Besides, if things didn't look up soon, it wasn't going to matter one way or another to any of them.

"I love him," the girl said quickly. "If it makes any diff'rence."

"It makes a difference." Aggie once more saw a picture of Todd's face in her mind, imagined she could smell his odor about her. "It can make all the difference in the world." If it's real, she added silently.

"It won't to Daddy." The girl frowned. "Your daddy an' mine jus' don't get on."

"I reckon it don't matter much." Aggie's voice was flat. "My daddy's dead, an' yours, well, we'll just have to see."

"Daddy's not dead," she said suddenly, and a flicker of anger crossed her face. "I wish he was, sometimes. He shouldn't of run off an' left me like that."

"Maybe he didn't know you were out there."

She thought about that. "Maybe not," she admitted. "Jason swears he didn't. But that don't make it no easier. I was plenty scared out there." She cast her eyes down into the spring. "Least, he says he'd come an' got me if he'd knowed."

"I s'pect he would of," Aggie said. She was seeing Jason altogether differently all of a sudden. Did he know? She couldn't say. Would he have gone? Again, the answer eluded her. One thing she did know was that Jack wouldn't have gone to save Gertie. He wouldn't even have gone to save Aggie.

The blanket opened slightly, and Annie handed in a dress.

"Jason got it from somebody's wagon. I don't know whose. She didn't have none other," she said simply. "I'll heat some beans." And she was gone.

"You want to get into the water?" Aggie asked Lottie. The girl looked at the dark swirl that came up to her calves and shook her head.

"It's too cold."

"Well, it ain't the Hotel Beaumont," Aggie said. "But it'll have to do. Get up on your knees an' bend over."

"Why?"

"If you're goin' to be clean, then you're goin' the whole hog. I'm fixin' to wash your hair."

6

THE HOTEL BEAUMONT WAS THE ESTABLISHMENT IN Memphis where Jack Sterling installed his family while he went about his preparations. He told them five or six times a day that once he had found them a place to stay, he was going out to find the horses he had been commissioned to buy, and then they would be off for Texas and, ultimately, New Mexico. For Gertie, Aggie, Jason, and Annie, the shabby hotel on the southern edge of downtown Memphis was a wonder. They regarded its gray clapboard facade as palatial, and the tobacco-stained carpets of the front lobby seemed suitable for royalty.

Jack led them all upstairs behind a boy who wore an ill-fitting jacket with brass buttons up and down the front and a small cap with a string wrapped tightly under his pimply chin. They climbed three flights of stairs and were finally admitted to a pair of interlocking rooms which offered the first spring mattresses any of them had ever seen. The carpet on the floor was faded and frayed, but none of them either noticed or minded, especially when the bellhop led them from the room down a hallway and opened another door.

"This here's where you take a bath," the bellboy addressed the family in a pedantic tone. None of them had ever dreamed of such a facility. Jack stood off to one side and watched, his eyes gleaming with satiric pleasure while they stared at the claw-footed cast-iron tub in the center of the room. Two pipes jutted out of the wall over its end; a set of levers was placed just over it. "If you want hot water," the boy said, "you press down on this handle like this." He pumped the lever a half-dozen times and opened the valve on one of the pipes. A trickle of rusty water leaked out after a few moments, and he then pumped it again. Finally the rust disappeared, and a gush of clear water came from the pipe.

"It takes a while for it to get hot," he explained, letting his hand drift under the water. "An' sometimes, this time of year, it don't. The cold side comes down faster. If you want, you can send down for hot water, an' the nigger'll carry it up. It's two bits a gallon. Fresh towels're a nickel apiece.

"This here's the privy." He led them down the hallway, opened another closet, and revealed a flush toilet. Without verbal explanation he stepped over and pulled the chain and allowed water to rush down from the overhead tank. "My mama says this here's a sin," he muttered. After waiting fruitlessly for a moment or two while Jack ignored his outthrust palm, he turned and left them alone. The Sterling family stood in the murky shadows of the hotel's third floor and wordlessly examined the modern conveniences displayed for their benefit.

"Who's first?" Jack finally broke the silence. When none of them moved, he began ripping at his cravat and collar. "Well, I'm not shy," he boomed, and he went into one of the rooms to remove his outer clothes. When he finished, he found them sitting silently in the other room and staring at the worn furnishings, afraid to move or talk.

"You can sit here all day if you're a mind to," he said with a slight growl in his voice. "I've got business to do.

Send down for anythin' you want. You can eat downstairs, too. Jus' sign for it." He finished dressing and left.

When Jack returned three days later, he was in a foul temper and scowled at them as he marched up to their table in the dining room and sat in a chair he turned backward at the table.

"I see you're all livin' the high life," he said. He picked up a stick of bread and bit down on it. The waiter approached them, but Jack waved him away. "I hope to hell I can pay the bill."

His mood caused all of them to lay aside forks and spoons and simply stare at their food.

"Hell," he said. "I rode damn near to Nashville, but I didn't find anythin' I'd let a nigger sling a leg over. What I did find that was decent wasn't for sale. 'Bout all I *can* find is people who want me to tend to their business for them. Goddamn town's full of lazy Yankee Jews who want to make money off somebody else's sweat."

He led them up to their rooms and sprawled on a bed. He talked of the bad luck he had had trying to buy horses in western Tennessee, and he wondered whether they should go up into the bluegrass country, or whether there was time for such an errand. He had always speculated aloud about his plans, but almost always his brags or complaints carried with them the surety of confidence—either he had been done in by people more unscrupulous than he, or he was certain of his ability to take in someone less bright. This was different. He was, Aggie dimly realized, dealing honestly for the first time in his life, and the complications and frustrations of upright business stymied him. He was so unsure of himself that even Gertie listened with concern in her eyes and assured him in a small voice that they would go along with whatever he decided. Her consolation seemed to annoy him, and he ignored her handwringing and started pacing and outlining his problems over and over again. The more he talked the angrier he became. He fished a pair of greenbacks out of his trousers and handed them to Jason.

"There's a saloon 'round the corner. Go get me a bottle of good whiskey. No goddamn rotgut either. These people know how to make good liquor. Make 'em get something from under the counter. An' don't hang 'round oglin' the saloon girls. They'll bite your pecker off." Jason hesitated for a long moment, swallowed hard, and disappeared, and Aggie and Gertie sat on straight-back chairs in silence while Jack continued to speculate aloud on his options.

"I've got less than five hundred left," he moaned sadly when Jason returned with the bottle. "Where the hell does it all go?" He stacked the money into piles while the family watched him silently. "It's goin' to cost me near a hundred to get the wagon an' animals out of livery and pay us out of this damn hotel. Graham never thought of expenses at all. It's all real fine for him to be sittin' there in Jefferson soppin' up good food an' good whiskey while I do his dirty work for him. Goddamn one-handed Yankee gambler, anyway! How does he think I can buy quality stock for this piddlin' little bit?"

Aggie had heard the tone before, and she relaxed. It usually emerged when he returned from one of his trips with failure dogging his steps. He would drink a bit, then sit in front of the fire and tell them how he had come so close to success but had been done in at the last minute by a partner's incompetence or simple bad fortune. The project seemed to have fizzled out earlier than usual this time, and she felt relief.

"Does this mean we ain't goin' to New Mexico?" she asked. She wanted him to come to terms with his latest disaster while he still had cash to spend. She was certain that if they could get back to Arkansas, or even Louisiana, they could find a place with the remaining money, make a good life for themselves. Her thoughts ran quickly to an image of her waving goodbye to Gertie and the children, riding away on the chestnut gelding, finding a way to make an independent life—with Todd Christian or without him. She had no idea what she might do, but somehow the futures she manufactured always ended with her finding Todd—or him finding her—and their living together forever.

"Hell no," he said loudly. He stood and scooped up the greenbacks and began stuffing them into his pockets. "I ain't done yet. It just means that I've got to get more money." He jumped up and swept past her and started out the door. Then he stopped and returned. "Where's that agate I give you?" She went to a dresser and found it. It was the only truly personal item she owned, but she handed it over. It was, after all, his.

"Take you a good bath," he said, dropping the stone in his pocket. "Keep a clean dress handy. I might need you later." And he left the hotel by the back stairs.

Aggie did take a bath, but not because of his instructions. She found the luxury of a real tub and cake soap irresistible. She washed her hair in the tepid, rusty water from the tub's pipes. She had just climbed into bed beside Gertie and Annie when the door opened and the yellow light from the hallway lamp cut a bar across the floor.

Jack stumbled in. He sat in a chair awhile and smoked in the dark. He lit a lamp and moved to the desk. Through a cracked eye, she watched him counting his remaining money. The stacks were considerably smaller than they had been that afternoon, and there were fewer of them. Wherever he had been that night, he had lost much of his remaining fortune. He rubbed his face hard, stared at the money as if merely looking at it might make it grow, and then he turned out the light and sat smoking in the dark. Finally, she heard him undressing, and he went to the other room and she heard Jason's bed creak as he got in beside him. Things had taken an even worse turn. She wondered what would happen next.

When they arose the next morning, Jack put up a front of being his confident old self, but Aggie saw that there was a nervousness behind his eyes. He said he had to see a man he had heard of who needed someone of Jack's talents. He left while they went down to eat breakfast, and then, just before noon, he returned. He seemed happy and excited, and he ordered Aggie to do up her hair and fix herself up to follow him downstairs. His manner was brisk, excited, and he clearly was not in a mood to wait or deal with any arguments. Gertie's eyes begged her not to agitate him, so Aggie put on the best dress Todd had given her and went. Halfway down, on the first-floor landing, Jack stopped and looked at her in a strange, appraising way. She felt herself blush.

"You're a damn pretty girl, Aggie," he said in a deep voice. "An' I'm fixin' to make you proud." She lowered her eyes, but she kept herself ready to jump away if he reached for her. Instead, he fished into his coat pocket and brought out the agate. It was now suspended on a delicate gold chain. "I been meanin' to do this for you for a long time," he said. "I wanted to make a ring of it, but the man said it was too heavy for a finger bauble. You can wear it 'round your neck."

She stared at the golden stone suspended by its chain from his fingers.

"It's beautiful," she said. "I didn't, uh . . ."

"You thought I'd sell it?" he said, his dark eyes showing shock. "You think I'd take away somethin' my girl loved?" He smiled and opened the clasp, and she allowed him to enclose her neck with the chain. Her body was tense as his arms went around her neck, but he made no false move. Once the agate hung down on her chest, he stepped back and admired it.

"You're a *damn* pretty girl," he repeated. "You'd do any man proud."

She blushed in spite of herself, swallowed, and looked up at him. "Thank you, Daddy."

"You call me Jack from now on," he said. "I like that better. I think you will, too." Her blood seemed to shift direction in her veins as he looked at her with his dark eyes that seemed to show no bottom, no soul behind them. "Now, let's go. See to it you behave down here," he said.

A man waited for Jack in the lobby, where she was introduced merely as Aggie Sterling and escorted into the dining room on Jack's arm. There he seated her at the table across from the man, whose name was Joshua Marconi, an exporter, Jack explained.

Marconi, Jack announced as he lit cigars for both of them, was one of Memphis's leading businessmen. He had contracted Jack to take a boatload of bonded whiskey downriver to New Orleans, where it would be reloaded onto a larger boat for shipment to Mexico. Aggie smiled and said nothing. She had learned long ago that Jack's chief talent was an ability to change plans almost with the weather, but a boat trip to Mexico was something totally unexpected, and she had difficulty concealing her surprise and concern. In spite of her contempt for Jack, she admired his audacity. He spoke smoothly about his experience, as if such contracts were commonplace to him. She formed a mask of polite disinterest while he made up names of men in St. Louis and Cincinnati for whom he had completed similar errands. She didn't know what he might be up to, but she had to admit that between her fright and anxiety, it was fascinating to watch him manipulate Marconi into a position where the businessman expressed his complete confidence in Jack's background. He even said that it would not be necessary to delay the trip for two or three days until Jack's letters of reference from the companies upriver could be forwarded to Memphis. She resolved that it was in the family's best interest to play along. To expose him would gain her nothing except possibly a beating, and it could earn worse punishments for Gertie.

Jack kept speaking to Marconi about Aggie as if she weren't there. He called her his "little woman" and said nothing of his wife upstairs. She almost called him Daddy once or twice, but his invitation to call him Jack on the stairs was fresh in her ears, and while she had no intention of doing so, she was careful not to expose his ruse to Marconi, at least until she saw where he was really going with it. She sat and allowed her eyes to remain downcast as the waiter put a plate of oysters in front of her.

"Eat up, my dear," Jack said. "This is a special treat you'll find more of where we're going." He winked at Marconi, who returned a smile over his own plate. "The last time I was down in Vera Cruz, I ate myself sick on 'em. Them Mescans know how to do up oysters, yessir."

Marconi was an acerbic little man with pockmarks decorating both his thin cheeks. His eyes were brown, but the whites were stained blue, and deep red lines ran through them. He had long, pointed fingers with sharp, clawlike nails on each one, and a small, beaklike nose, giving him the total aspect of a bird. He took another oyster, and Aggie swallowed hard and imitated his movements as she lifted another of the gray delicacies away from its shell and guided it to her mouth. The taste revolted her, and she almost spit it out. She held her breath and swallowed it, but then she put the tiny fork down and folded her hands in her lap. Her stomach churned, and her throat fought a gagging sensation. Jack ate all of his up quickly, chewing them hard and then fishing around for some piece of something in his mouth with his finger.

The waiter took away the appetizers and brought soup and then the main course. Jack and Marconi talked general business concerns while they ate, and wine was brought and poured by a black waiter. Aggie had never tasted wine before, and the first sip, which Jack insisted she take to toast the pending business arrangement, surprised her. Unlike the bitter, burning whiskey she had sometimes sneaked a taste of when Jack had it on hand, the wine was fruity, sweet, and pleasant. It gave her a warm sensation and calmed her turgid stomach. The men ate and talked and finished the bottle, but Marconi declined Jack's offer to buy another. "Middle of the day," he mumbled.

Finally, the men stood and shook hands, and Marconi smiled at her once more. "I hope you and Mr. Sterling have a pleasant voyage downriver and on to Mexico," he said. "I understand that Vera Cruz can be a special place for young couples." He smiled at her again and winked at Jack. "When you return, I insist that you come to take supper with me and my wife. She's about your same age, and I'm sure you would find much in common." With that he bowed quickly and took his leave.

Aggie was confused, but she kept a smile fixed on her face until he was out of sight. He walked with a fragile, almost paperlike frailty that raised bumps on her skin. Jack came back with a big smile, lit another cigar, ordered another bottle of wine, and filled their glasses.

"You handled that just fine," he said. "Now, you go upstairs, get whatever you want together, an' come on down. I'm goin' on ahead to see to the boat. I've already ordered the wagon sent aboard, but I'm goin' to have to sell that goddamn chestnut." Aggie started. Her mouth opened. The horse was more important to her than anything. It was a physical tie with Todd, something that reminded her of what he stood for in her life.

"I love that—" she started.

"Don't say nothin'," he growled. "You got no business ridin' it anyhow, not without a sidesaddle. If you want another, I'll get you one. Right now, we got to get this whiskey to Texas, an' that's that."

"I thought we were taking it to Mexico."

"Don't get smart-mouthed with me," he warned.

"You know damn well I ain't goin' to Mexico. You keep your mouth shut an' do as you're told."

"But Mr. Marconi—"

"Marconi's a Jew carpetbagger an' a damn fool to boot," Jack snapped. "He stole a distillery from honest Southerners who couldn't pay the taxes on their own whiskey, an' now he's runnin' it with a bunch of niggers an' makin' money hand over fist. Anybody who'd turn over that much whiskey to a total stranger to watch out for an' pay him for the pleasure deserves whatever happens to him."

"How come he did that?"

" 'Cause I told him what a great Union sympathizer I was durin' the war," Jack snapped. "Shut up, or I'll be leavin' you here to rot. You want to go with me, or you want to stay here an' figure things out for yourself?"

"I'll tell Mother to get ready," she said, rising, but he reached out and grabbed her wrist. His face was filled with an ugly warning.

"You don't say nothin' to your mother 'bout it," he hissed through clenched teeth. "Or to the brats neither. This is you an' me." He released her wrist and sat back and refilled his glass. "This is your chance, girl. Don't ruin it, or you'll be left without nothin'. I'm goin' to Texas. You can come along, or you can stay here an' go to hell. This is your chance to stop bein' a hayseed an' to go along on somethin' that's goin' to make us rich an' happy." He paused and crushed out his cigar. "Your mother an' me're through. Don't look so surprised. You know the only reason I come back was for you." He looked at her hard, and she tried to keep the panic she felt from rising to the surface.

"The boat leaves"—he consulted his watch—"in two hours. It's the *Oregon Marie*. Be there, or get left holdin' the bag. Gertie's had this comin' a long time. It goes back 'fore you was born. But what happens to you is up to you." He drained his glass and poured another. "Here's a dollar to pay a hack to take you out. Don't take nothin' you don't need. It's a long way 'cross Texas, an' that whiskey's goin' to carry some weight."

"I thought you were supposed to buy horses," she said through a thin smile that unsuccessfully hid the queasiness in her stomach. She could hardly believe what he was saying. "You told that man in Texas you was goin' to bring him horses."

"Whiskey'll do just fine," he said. "Least, it better do just fine. Graham can like it or he can ride it out. Or he can go to hell. It don't matter to me. Either way, I've got the whiskey." He finished the glass of wine, rose, and left.

She sat where she was and sipped her own glass of wine. She wanted to cry, but tears wouldn't come. She wasn't sure what Jack had planned, but one thing was clear: He didn't plan to take Gertie and the children with him. Another thing was also clear: He wasn't planning to take Mr. Marconi's whiskey to Mexico. Rather, he planned to take it to *New* Mexico, and that would have to do. Aggie didn't know exactly how Jack was going to do it, and if past experience was any teacher, he would likely make as big a mess of this as he had of everything else. But she knew that this plan was the only one he now had in mind, and nothing she or anyone else could say would stop him.

She passed out of the dining room and into the shabby lobby in a daze. A thought struck her. She went over to the desk and smiled her sweetest smile at the clerk.

"I was just wonderin'," she said to the young man, who found himself slightly overwhelmed by this beautiful girl who beamed at him. "Has Mr. Sterlin' settled his bill yet?"

The boy was befuddled, but he shuffled through his files, then shook his head. "No, Ma'am," he said. "As of today, it comes to just under a hundred dollars. Ninety-two fifty, to be exact. Countin' the livery, the café, an' other charges."

In spite of herself, she started. "That seems like an awful lot."

"Well . . ." The boy consulted the papers in front of him. "Says here he had the mules an' horses shod, and the wagon wheels reworked, an' he charged some rifles an' cartridges to the hotel as well. Is there a problem?" He swallowed hard after the question.

"Oh, no," she said. "Thank you. I was just wonderin'

if he'd settled up yet. I'm sure he'll be by direc'ly to speak with you about it."

As she climbed the stairs her head swam with the problem at hand. Jack intended to leave Gertie and the children, and Aggie too, if she failed to show up at the boat, with the hotel charges. She had no idea what they would do to her family when they were discovered to be without funds. She glanced down at the mounted agate hanging from her neck. She might sell it, but she doubted if it would come close to paying the bill. Besides, even if they could get out of the hotel, where would they go? What would they do? Jack had the wagon, the animals, and all their household goods, and he had the whiskey. He never traveled with much more than a saddlebag for his personal belongings, and that was likely on his big black horse, which was also probably on board the *Oregon Marie*. Once he was gone, they were lost.

Hopelessness surrounded her like a swarm of summer gnats. She wondered if the Memphis police would arrest them for failing to pay. Regardless, the hotel would definitely put them out on the street. She had seen that before, in El Dorado, and the memory panicked her. She thought of calling the sheriff, or a marshal or someone, telling them that Jack planned to steal Marconi's whiskey, then take the wagon and leave him locked up in the local jail. But what proof did she have? He and Marconi had spoken of their "contract," and Jack had even said something about putting up a bond or insurance of some kind. She had no idea what that might be, but she did know that Marconi was utterly convinced of Jack's honesty. Going to him, if she could locate him, and telling him that Jack's references were nothing but fraud, or even revealing that she was Jack's daughter, not his wife, might not sway him against Jack's glib assurances. He might assume this was nothing more than a marital spat. She was all too familiar with how smooth Jack's tongue could be, and the look in his eyes during their last conversation convinced her that he would manage to save himself and leave them with no more thought than if he had run off and left a bitch dog and her litter of pups.

She was confused, and her head was spinning from the wine as much as from the problem at hand. She still didn't know what she would do as she reached the third floor, but she knew she wasn't about to abandon Gertie and the children and go away with Jack. There had to be another answer.

She tried to explain to Gertie what the dilemma was, but the older woman grew frenzied when Aggie laid out the problem. Immediately, Aggie realized that her mother was going to be no help at all.

"What'll we do, Aggie?" she beseeched her daughter. "Where'll we go? We've got to catch him. He's got all our stuff. Ever'thing! He's got the wagon. Where is he? How'll we get along without him?"

Aggie wanted to point out that they had gotten along for years without Jack, but there was no time to think through other solutions. She had no choice but to bundle up the family and follow their father aboard the riverboat. Gertie's horror was palpable, and, Aggie admitted, Gertie was right: It wasn't Jack they needed to follow so much as the wagonload of junk that represented everything they had aside from the few clothes stuffed into frayed carpet-bags. They sat forlornly in the room and waited for Aggie to make a decision, but there was really no choice. They had to catch Jack and tie their fortunes to his, or else they would have nothing at all.

They packed and fled the hotel by the back stairs. It was the middle of the afternoon, and the streets were full of people. Aggie used the money Jack had given her to hire a hack, and they loaded in and were driven to the river quays, where they located the boat and started aboard. A burly man in a dark coat stopped them at the gangplank.

"We're Jack Sterlin's family," Aggie explained. Gertie looked terrified.

"He told me he was expectin' his wife." The man looked down at a flat board with papers clipped to it. "He didn't say nothin' 'bout a whole family."

"This is his wife," Aggie said hurriedly, pushing Gertie forward. She hoped that Jack wouldn't appear. The thought of shoving Gertie aboard and then taking Jason and Annie and disappearing into the crowd along the pier appealed to her suddenly. She had no more idea where they would go or what they would do than she had had before, but the thought of being with Jack another day, even another minute, gave her a sick feeling. Gertie might not be able to face life alone, but Aggie could save the children.

For a brief, hideous moment she found herself hating her mother as much as she did Jack. Then she looked down at Gertie's bewildered expression and realized that she couldn't abandon her either. Gertie was more of a child than Annie was. Jack would likely kick her overboard the first chance he got. It was all of them or none, and for the moment, at least, it looked like all.

The man admitted them aboard with the note that there was no vacant room for unexpected family, and they would have to share the cramped quarters for two that Jack had reserved. Aggie spotted their wagon lashed to the aft deck of the boat, and she said they, at least she, Annie, and Jason, would sleep there. They shuffled down the side of the boat, and Jack appeared.

On the surface, he appeared to be glad to see them, even complimenting Aggie on getting them all there and on board with a full half hour to spare, but Aggie spotted the anger just beneath his exuberant exterior. He spoke to all of them together or he didn't speak at all. He didn't even address her directly, but twice he found a reason to strike Jason hard on the back of the head for no apparent reason. Finally, he left them alone.

That evening they saw him taking a turn on the deck with a brightly painted woman in a pink dress. He smoked a big cigar and spoke loudly enough to attract their attention. When he was sure they were looking, he grabbed his companion and kissed her and placed his hand on her hips and pulled her to him so violently that she cried out and then laughed and slapped him playfully. Gertie saw all of it but made no comment. She only lowered her head into her bonnet and pretended to stare at the muddy water passing by the boat.

The next morning he pulled Aggie aside and smiled brightly at other passengers as he whispered in her ear in a mean hiss, "You think you got away with somethin', don't you, you little bitch-bastard?" She didn't answer but tried to pull away from him. His fingers bit deeply into her arm. "Well, you ain't saved nobody from nothin'. I'm gettin' tired of you standin' 'gainst me, girl. One of these days, you're goin' to go too far. This ain't over yet, not by a sight it ain't. You got you a lesson comin', an' by God, you're fixin' to get it." With that he released her, tipped his hat to a group of men who were staring at the strange sight, and then strolled away humming to himself.

Aggie didn't sleep well until they had transferred themselves, their wagon and team, and their cargo to the *Bayou Belle* at Morganza, Louisiana, and were heading up the Red River. But by the time they reached Jefferson, Jack was outwardly in good spirits. He had gotten away with stealing the whiskey, and for once he had plenty of cash to spread around.

After he introduced them to Mr. Graham and announced the organization of the train, all his talk among them was of the great plans he had for when they reached New Mexico, and the only time she found herself shuddering was when she caught him looking at her from a distance, studying her over a cigar as if she were a prize animal he had set his heart on owning but just had not figured out how to steal.

AGGIE OPENED THE BLANKET curtain proudly and exposed a freshly scrubbed and newly dressed Lottie Herbert to the open air of the hospital cave. Hannah and even Constance stared with bright smiles as they beheld the girl's transformation. She had gone back there a virtual urchin in a torn dress, dirty streaks running down her face, her hair a tangle of greasy strands. Now she stood with her hair freshly washed and pulled back into a tight black ponytail. Her dark skin shone from the scrubbing, and the dress, oversized, plain, and gray as it was, hung demurely from her high collarbones and conveniently hid the early testimony of her condition. Her eyes seemed to shine in the smoky light of the cave, and although barefoot and still shy to the point of trying to hide in plain sight, she was unquestionably beautiful.

Aggie went over to her trunk, opened it, and removed the gold chain and agate from the nearly empty chest. She brought it back and put it around Lottie's neck. The girl's eyes sparkled as she looked down at the yellow stone and up to Aggie's soft gaze.

"I can't take nothin' like this," she said. "Pa'd skin me if I did."

"It's a present," Aggie said. "For you an' Jason. Think of it as a legacy. It's all we got. I hope it brings you more luck than it has me."

Lottie nodded quietly and handled the stone with her fingers. Her nails were broken but clean, and the wonder in her face made Aggie's heart ache with a longing to feel the simple pleasure the girl apparently found in looking at the mounted stone.

Annie completed cleaning the dishes from the meals, and Aggie reheated some beans, which she brought over to Lottie who accepted them and scooped them up with a crust of bread. Jason had not returned, but Aggie was satisfied that he would be pleased with the results of his sister's work. She also knew that they had to have a talk about what he planned to do with her. It was more than possible that Frank Herbert might not return, and Aggie wasn't certain that Jack's death would leave him feeling any more kindly toward the Sterlings than he seemed to in the first place.

She went over to the fire and almost collapsed when she tried to squat by the bucket to stack the plates. Hannah rushed to her, picked her up, and moved her over to a blanket, where she forced her down and ordered her to rest. Whatever reserves of strength she had were exhausted, and her body seemed to want to quit on her all at once.

"It's that damn tea," Hannah said. "You told me it would keep folks awake, but I seen you drink at least two cups of it, an' you can't hold your head up."

Aggie tried again to rise, but Hannah's heavy hand held her down.

"That Runnels woman's lost her mind," Aggie said, realizing that her thoughts were wandering, that she was babbling. "I was goin' to tell you, an' with all the commotion, I forgot. She tried to kill Mr. Graham with a ax. He's all right. I got him to sleep. But I was goin' to tell you. Somebody needs to watch over him. You said you would, Hannah, an' you didn't. You said you'd watch his back. He needs somebody to watch out for him. He's the only chance we got, now." She was mumbling, completely relaxing for the first time in almost three days. "I need to feed an' water the stock. Daddy's horse needs tendin'. He'll be wantin' supper soon. Don't want to rile him. That horse needs tendin'."

"Girl, you're not makin' any sense. You're wore out. I'll watch out for Cleve Graham. You worry 'bout your own self. I'll see to them that needs it. It may wind up bein' up to you an' me to pull the kinks out of this thing yet, an' I can't do it all by my lonesome. You sleep a little bit," Hannah said. "I'll call you if I need you. You ain't no guardian angel." She chuckled to herself. "An' neither am I. But I'll watch you an' Graham both. Don't you worry. Ain't nobody 'round here a angel."

There was once a boy who thought I was, Aggie thought as her thoughts relaxed and swam into a calm darkness. He had worn his big plainsman's hat and the new pistols when she last saw him. He was so handsome, so self-confident, that all the bitterness she felt toward him for abandoning her vanished. Her heart ached for him. But now there was nothing she could do but wait.

After a bit, Hannah rose and motioned to Jason to help her, and they began hauling the dead bodies out of the cave. Aggie awakened slightly and saw what they were doing, but she made no motion to help or hinder them, and she soon closed her eyes and only fretted a bit at the noise they made as they went about the chore. Soon enough it was done, and the remaining wounded continued to rest quietly. The afternoon began as the morning had, and as the fire sputtered a bit in the cave, Aggie finally fell back on what she hoped was a bottomless well of endurance, but she was quickly whisked away into a deep, dreamless sleep which lasted until the blast of a pistol and angry cries awakened her.

PART FIVE

THE TEXIAN

CHAPTER ONE

1

WHILE AGGIE STERLING PREPARED HER NOONDAY MEAL and tended to wounded men back on the crossing, Moses Franklin lay on his belly on the edge of a huge buffalo wallow and contemplated life from a distinctly sour point of view. The sun was now midday high, and the warmth of its late-spring rays beat down on his buckskin jacket. The sweat running down into his eyes from beneath his hat was not all being caused by the heat, any more than the summer sun was responsible for the itching on his newly shaved head. It was a torture so exquisite that it was all he could do to keep from scratching the exposed skin raw as his dark eyes swept the grassy horizon and he longed for more elevation so he could see farther.

Below him, some ten or so feet beneath the surface level of the prairie at the center of the wallow, Frank Herbert and Carlson Colfax sat cross-legged and engaged in conversation. Their horses—Moses's, Frank's, and the three Indian ponies they had captured from the medicine camp the night before—were ground-staked near them. They seemed oblivious to the sun.

Colfax himself had recovered sufficiently from his wounds to ride. Moses was astonished at the old man's physical strength. His body was a mass of scabs and his face wrinkled with pain every time he moved, but he never complained. On the contrary, he upbraided Frank and Moses continually for "draggin' behind" while they rode through the night, and he finally led them to this buffalo wallow. The wallow was a circle of ground almost fifty yards in diameter in the middle of the prairie's emptiness where for centuries thousands of buffalo had rolled and wallowed to create a bare depression in the grass. Only a few green milkweed and the odd clump of dandelion bravely claimed the dusty bottom of the wallow. The red sandy soil boiled in the wind that raked across it and reflected the sun's rays and made the natural warmth of the day even hotter.

They had been there since daybreak. Only the barest chance caused them to stop to rest the horses and allow Colfax to dismount so Frank could tend to his wounds again just before Moses spotted a dozen Comanche braves galloping in their direction. The Indians skirted the wallow by no more than a hundred yards, and Moses, Frank, and Colfax spent a few breathless moments holding their hands over their mounts' noses while the Indians passed on in the direction of the medicine camp from which Colfax had been rescued. The shaman Moses had frightened so badly the night before was with them. He was gesturing wildly with his hands and pointing at the grass and the sky as the braves rode. Their tiny bells jingled across the prairie long after they passed from view.

That had been hours ago, and Moses wanted to move on. If the Indians returned, they could be caught in the open. On the other hand, he argued with himself, he couldn't see that it mattered much one way or another. In spite of Colfax's assurances that he would put things right today or tomorrow at the latest, Moses couldn't help but feel that he had too much faith in the man's declarations of knowledge about the train and the Indians that besieged it. He seemed not to know or even to care how many people were trapped down on the crossing. His insistence that as soon as he "got his wind," as he put it, he could put a plan to work that would drive the Indians off or at least distract them long enough for the whites to escape was based, it seemed, on nothing more than his astounding self-confidence. Moses felt that they should be doing something besides sitting around and wasting time, but he didn't know what. Colfax claimed to be a former Texas Ranger, and Moses had previously longed for just such a source of salvation, but the longer he was around the foul-mouthed old plainsman, the more he began to doubt the wisdom of that wish. For the moment, he had placed himself in Colfax's gnarled hands, and he wasn't quite sure how to extricate himself.

The alternatives to doing nothing at all were neither clear nor inviting to the black scout. Colfax claimed he was leading them to a safe place where they could wait until dark. It was all vague, but he mentioned that he had "a boy" there—"the Cottonwood Kid," he called him—as well as arms and clothes for himself, and Moses allowed that to go to a stronghold of some sort was probably preferable to sitting out the day in a plum thicket or buffalo wallow or trying to get back to the train. He and Frank, and probably the old man as well, all needed sleep and something to eat. Their water was running low, since Frank had emptied two canteens bathing Colfax's wounds.

The prospect of returning to the train filled Moses with dread. He was supposed to be going for help, but here he sat, idly watching the day burn away. Colfax insisted that there was nothing to be gained by trying to reach a fort. Moses wondered if he would have the same luck trying to convince Cleveland Graham of that. He thought of the wagon master's threat to kill him, and now Moses knew he couldn't put up a single moral argument against the prospect. He felt as much as anyone that he deserved to be killed. All he had to show for a night and morning's work was a crippled-up, foul-mouthed old plainsman and three Indian ponies.

The scout glanced over his shoulder again at the two men and was relieved to see Frank Herbert stand up and start moving toward him. Moses gripped his rifle a bit tighter and scanned the horizon from his low vantage point, but there was no sign of the Indians' return. From time to time during the day they had heard the distant muffled booms of gunfire from the direction of the crossing, but since dawn, when the sounds of a fierce battle drifted on the wind to their ears as a series of thumps and dull snaps, there had been only a sporadic noise, indicating that at least some of the whites were still alive and resisting. Now he could see large circles of birds, buzzards and crows, circling off to the northwest, but other than that, the prairie was apparently devoid of life. There was an eerie quiet beneath the constant soughing of the wind in the grass.

When Frank got closer to the upper edge of the wallow, he crouched down and finally belly-crawled up beside Moses. He held out their remaining canteen, which the black scout gratefully accepted. It was a gesture Moses hadn't expected, but Frank apparently attached no importance to it.

"He says we ought to be movin' out," Frank said.

"*He* says." Moses almost spit out the tepid water after soaking his parched mouth. "I been sittin' up here for most of the day waitin' on him. It's 'bout time he got ready to do somethin'."

Frank shrugged. "Anyhow, he says it's time to go. He says he wants to check on some horses or somethin'."

"Horses?"

"That's what he says. Says he's got animals that need tendin' penned up not far from here. Says he needs a good'un for hisself, and he wants me to take one, too. He don't think much of them we got from them Indians." Frank looked down and then added, "He's partial to your bay, but I told him you'd not likely trade her."

Moses studied Frank's simple face. They had been down there talking horseflesh while he was up here sweating and watching for Indians to come riding up and scalp them. "You think he's crazy?" He was struck with the irony of asking that question of Frank, but Frank's wrinkled brow told the black scout that he was worried about it more than a saner man might be.

"I don't know. I never knowed nobody like him. He's a wild man, an' to hear him tell it, he ain't scared of nothin'."

"Well, let's go," Moses said, and he stood up straight and looked across the waving sea of grass all around him. The mesa was purple in the distance. Dust devils rose from the wind on the horizon, but above the blond expanse before him, the sky was a blue vault, unencumbered by clouds. It was about three miles back to the crossing, Moses reckoned. He had been gone from the train, from Graham—from Aggie Sterling—since midnight, and he hadn't covered but three miles. But that was the fault of Carlson Colfax, who first had delayed them and then had led them back north in the direction of the besieged wagon fort.

The scout turned and walked down to his mare. "Let's

go," Moses said. He felt the need to take charge again, but an ingrained deference to a white man, especially one such as Colfax, overcame him; he found that he was making suggestions rather than giving orders. It galled him that Colfax had immediately credited Frank with the effort to save him from the Comanche. Even when Frank blushed and told the old plainsman that it was the black scout and not he who had concocted the plan, Colfax merely grunted in Moses's direction and gingerly tapped one of the crude bandages he had made of a piece of torn shirt.

"Wonder if it would of broke your heart to come a few minutes sooner," he said.

Colfax allowed Frank to provide him with support as he hauled himself up onto his one good leg. The other was badly injured. The Comanche had cut into the hamstring behind the knee, and every time he tried to support himself on it, it folded underneath him like a broken hinge. Frank reported to both of them that the cut was imperfectly made, and that the leg would probably heal. Right now, it was painful, and it tended to bleed whenever Colfax tested it. The old plainsman was still nearly naked—his shirt went to bind his wounds, and his trousers and underwear had been ripped and burned away by his torturers—but he managed to make a crude breechcloth from the remnants, and his feet were encased in torn moccasins. The wounds left by the Indian tortures raced raggedly across his back and up and down his scrawny thighs. His hair was wild and white and hung down on his shoulders in a greasy mane, and his face was a wasteland of wrinkles, skin cancers, and old scars, all of which were belied by brilliant white teeth.

"Where we goin', boy?" the old man asked with a broad grin. "You know someplace 'round here with liquor an' women where we can lay up in the shade an' act like we're workin'?"

"Frank said you had somethin' in mind."

"That's good." Colfax laughed. "That's real good, by God. Let's go." He hobbled on one leg over to the Indian pony and pulled himself aboard with difficulty. He was not a man who relied on anyone's help for long, the scout said to himself.

"I need to check on my horses," Colfax announced.

"Get me a good'un. This shaggy plug's no-'count. Prob'ly stole him off them damn poor Mescans. 'Sides, there's the Kid an' stuff to look in on. You might say I got me a whole goddamn family worryin' 'bout my hide." He winked at Frank, who seemed not to notice.

"I still think we should ride for troops, get to a fort," Moses said, climbing atop his bay. Frank waited to see that Colfax was firmly seated on the Indian horse, then he also mounted.

"I told you las' night." Colfax pulled his horse's nose around to the south and lightly kicked his flanks. "That ain't no goddamn good at all. There ain't no troops at Richardson, or at Griffin neither. Least none that can leave. They likely ain't got but a dozen horses an' sorry-assed mules 'mongst 'em, an' they can't ride worth a Chinaman's fart. Half the time they can't protect the poor sons of bitches that live right up under the forts theirselves. Nothin' there anyhow but a bunch of goddamn uppity niggers, half of which is on sick call an' the other half of which ain't worth Mescan breakfast. 'Sides, the local Yankee commandant, Mackenzie—ol' Bad Hand, as the Comanch' call him—is up an' out on the plains up yonder chasin' shadows an' rumors an' collectin' buffalo shit for fires."

Colfax's face wrinkled in mock sympathy, and his voice whined, "He says he's 'on campaign.' Shit bricks! He's got 'bout as much chance findin' hostiles as he does findin' his ass with both hands. The best part of him run down his mama's ass. Comanch' done made a bigger fool of him'n his daddy done. They stole all his horses once, an' they'll likely take his hair if he ain't careful." He looked out to the west as if he could see the troops he was speaking of and shook his head. "Bad Hand my ol' lady's ass! Bad *Head*'s more like it. Worse'n the goddamn war."

He glanced cannily at Moses, anticipated the scout's next suggestion, and shook his head in a strong negative. "You can't pry troops loose from Sill, neither. Not with that goddamn peckerless Quaker in charge up there. Back when Lawrie Tatum was runnin' the show, you could get some help when you needed it. He'd get a hard-on an' send 'em on the howl." He shook his head. "But he's done been give his walkin' papers, an' they got 'em a new feller, named Hayworth or Haworth or some damn thing, an' he's teachin' 'em Sunday-school stories an' keepin' the Army tied up like a fat man's dog. So that leaves your ass in a crack where yellow-legged Bluebellies is concerned. Half of 'em's no damn good, an' the other half's confounded. It *ain't* no different'n the war, if you ask me."

"They's bound to be some help somewhere," Frank asserted quietly, but Colfax laughed and shook his head.

"They's some sodbusters an' clodhoppers an' such trash at Jacksboro or in the Flat, or Sudsville down to Griffin, but the half of 'em that's not drunk or scared shitless would as soon cut your throat as piss on you. No." He squinted off in the distance. "The nearest troops is at Concho or Fort Dodge or up on the Llano, an' either one's too far to get to an' get back in time. 'Sides, I ain't sure they'd come if they was there. I never seen a Yankee soldier worth his weight in dog farts. Half of 'em's of your persuasion anyhow"—he spat purposefully—"an' all you got to do is holler 'Comanch'!' at 'em an' their eyes roll back an' they lay down an' start yellin' for Jesus."

He bit off a plug of tobacco he'd caged off Frank. "Nossir, boy. You jus' put yourself in my hands. Them folks down on the crik'll be all right. If they sit right where they are an' don't do nothin' stupid an' wait till I get my pecker hard again. Things'll get right by an' by. You can count on it, or my name ain't Carlson Colfax, an' by God, you can bet your last screamin' eagle, that's what my mama called me!"

With that, he guided his mount up and out of the wallow and generally in a southern direction. Moses hesitated only a moment before following. He tried to ignore the questioning look on Frank's broad face and bent his hat brim against the sun. He wasn't sure where they were going, and he didn't trust Colfax. But the scout believed him when he said that every trooper—black or white—was out chasing Comanche raiding parties. If the Indians holding the wagons under siege down on the crossing were any indication, it made sense.

"So, there's an uprisin'," Moses asked Colfax's back.

"They's big doin's up on the Canadian," Colfax explained without turning around. "I'm not sure what's goin' on, but they's Comanch' of ever' stripe, goddamn Kiowa, and even them peckerless wonders the Cheyenne. They got 'em a big medicine man, named Coyote Shit or Wolf's Butt or some damn thing, an' he's tellin' 'em they got some kind of magic that's fixin' to make their peckers hard. Get the white man off the plains an' bring back the buffalo all at the same time."

"Where *are* the buffalo?" Moses asked him. "I was through here last year, an' they was ever'where."

"They still is a bunch of 'em." Colfax looked narrowly at Moses as if to test the veracity of his claim. "But they's mostly up north of the Canadian, an' out west of here, of course. They been hunted out down here for the most part, least for this season, maybe for good."

"Hunted out?" Moses exclaimed. "By who? There's never been that many hunters out here. They's a treaty—"

Colfax spat derisively. "That treaty's not worth a pitcher of warm mule piss. They's some poor sons of bitches up on the plains, place called the 'Dobe Walls or some such horseshit. Got 'em a reg'lar goddamn store an' ginmill. They're rangin' as far down as the Palo Duro country, all 'long the headwaters of the Red, haulin' in hides by the goddamn wagonload. Makin' a pretty penny for 'em up in Fort Dodge, too. That's Indian country out there. You don't go out there 'less you want to tangle with the Comanch' an' the Army to boot. 'Course it never stopped me, none." He paused and turned in the saddle. "But this year, they got 'em a Yankee general, Sheridan, up there, an' he's all het up to run the Indians off the south plains."

"So what?"

"So, I hear when the hunters went to him to ask what he thought 'bout them breakin' the Medicine Lodge treaty an' comin' down into Texas to raise hell an' hunt buff, he tells 'em to go ahead on, by God."

"I don't believe it," Frank said suddenly. "That's not right. No general'd say that, 'specially not Sheridan. Not if there's a treaty."

"Spoke like a goddamn Bluebelly." Colfax chuckled. "What outfit was you with?"

"Thirty-seventh Illinois," Frank muttered. "But I never fought much with 'em. I was at Pea Ridge an' was caught up in the Peach Orchard at Shiloh." He said the latter so softly he was almost whispering. Then he lifted his head and spoke with a high, defiant voice. "An' we kicked your ass all the way back to the South both times," he said with a firm nod.

"Yeah, well, what the hell." Colfax chuckled good-naturedly. "I wasn't at Pea Ridge nor Shiloh neither. Cornholes both of 'em. But I was at by God Antietam Creek, an' your goddamn Peach Orchard was a stroll in the garden compared to that goddamn bridge. Burnside!" he shook his head. "Now there was a man to make his mama proud. I never in my life seen the waste of so many good men. That fat, stupid, sorry-assed son of a poor man's whore."

"Sherman an' Sheridan wasn't Burnside," Frank said defensively.

"They wasn't McClellan, neither. Nor Meade. Only general you ever had that was worth a rat's ass was Meade, or maybe Reynolds—cut that poor son of a bitch in two at Gettysburg. Pope wasn't nothin', nor McClellan, nor Hooker—*Hooker*, goddamn! There was a pig's asshole if there ever was one." He grinned and spat. "Hell, if it wasn't for Grant you Bluebellies would of lost the whole shootin' match, an' Grant wasn't no general. He was just a son of a bitch."

Moses remained quiet through the almost good-humored exchange. It was an argument he had heard often. It seemed that every white man he met wanted to refight the war. It didn't matter which side they had been on, even if they had been on the same side; two or more men who had been in the war would sooner or later get down to debating whose generals were better, whose troops braver. It made him tired to hear it.

"I don't care," Frank said. "Neither Sheridan nor Sherman never said to break no treaty."

"Well, damnit, he didn't come right out an' say it like that." Colfax grinned. "What I heard was that he said, 'If I was fixin' to hunt buffalo, I reckon I'd go where the buffalo was.' Anyhow, it 'mounts to the same thing. I talked to some ol' boys who heard it direct from the god-damn horse's mouth. They're up to the 'Dobe Walls right now, an' I'll bet you a Saturday night in San Antone none of 'em knows that half the Indians on the plains is 'bout to come right down on 'em." He laughed.

"How come you know so much 'bout it?" Moses demanded.

Colfax looked injured by Moses's challenge. "You want to keep your hair out here, boy, you'd best make it your business to know all they is to know."

Moses flinched at the rebuke, and Colfax softened his tone and explained with a grumble, "I run 'cross some hunters up on the Prairie Dog Town Fork three days ago," he said. "Poor sons of bitches was all dead. Not just dead, they was *bad* dead. Kilt the hell out of 'em, goddamnit! I ain't seen Indians do nothin' like that in years, not since the war, truth to tell, not this close to the goddamn reservations. Anyhow, that's how I got caught. We buried them poor damned souls, me an' the Kid, an' then when I sent him back I come upon that bunch of stupid Mescans. They was havin' a field day with 'em, too. Goddamn Mexes kilt their own young'uns! I was tryin' to reckon some way of helpin' 'em out—not that I got no love for the chili-eatin' sons of bitches. What they was doin' out here God only knows. Anyhow, I got caught. Plumb snuck up on me, an' that ain't easy to do. I guess I'm gettin' old. The red bastards got my pistols an' my Winchester, but thank Jesus I give my Sharps to the Kid."

"Why didn't they kill you?" Frank asked. "Like the others?"

"That's damn near a myst'ry." Colfax rubbed his beard. "I savvy enough Comanch' to know what they was talkin' 'bout, though. This here bunch"—he waved his hand toward the mesa's northern terminus—"is what the Mescans call *retragrados*. They're young an' out to pull their peckers much as they can, but they're slow to start. For some reason or 'nother, they've had a fallin' out with the main bunch of goat-fuckers, but sooner or later they're goin' north to join up with Mo-way an' Parra-o-coom an' the rest of them Comanch' shit-heels. Quanah's up there, too, an' from what I hear, they got a mess of Comanch' an' Kiowa, maybe Lone Wolf, runnin' right 'long 'side them. You put this bunch of young'uns with 'em, you got the biggest goddamn war party the plains has ever seen."

"What's holdin' 'em back?" Frank asked.

"Their leader," Colfax said. "He's jus' a pup, but he got his tit in a ringer a month or so ago, an' he's been runnin' 'round tryin' to get it out ever' since. He's raised hell down 'round the Double Mountain country an' all 'long the Brazos, an' he ain't the onliest one, either. Whole country's on the warpath, which is why Mackenzie an' half the stupid sons of bitches in Texas's out there chasin' their tail 'round right now. This bunch'd be easy to round up if Mackenzie could find his pecker when he wants to piss."

"What happened?"

"Near as I can figure, they're stymied. Got 'em a run of bad luck. The trail chief lost his medicine bag, for one thing." Colfax laughed again. "Damn near lost somethin' else."

"What?" Moses couldn't understand.

"He lost his medicine bag," Colfax repeated slowly, pronouncing the words as if Moses was an idiot.

"I don't understand," Frank put in. "What's that got to do with anythin'?"

"You'll see." Colfax chuckled. "Things got goddamn confounded in a hurry after that, anyhow. They likely would of gone north anyhow, but one of 'em cooked a skunk an' got caught by ol' Coyote Turd, or whatever his name is. Pitched a fit, I s'pect. I hear tell he's a stickler for keepin' the medicine pure. Wanted to kill the poor son of a bitch, likely."

"A skunk?"

"That's what I said. Don't you know nothin' 'bout Comanch', boy?"

Moses shook his head. He'd thought he knew enough. "I'm learnin' all the time."

"Out here they's only two kinds of men," Colfax said gravely. "Them that knows the Comanch', an' dead'uns. The first kind's mostly still back behind the Line, which is where you sound like you belong, 'less you want to be the next kind." He looked up into the rising sun. "Killin' a skunk is bad luck, damn near as bad as losin' your medicine bag. When you add a little bit more bad news here an' there, you got yourself the makin's of some goddamn bad medicine." He paused and judged the sun's position. "Anyhow, that's why they didn't kill me right off. But they damn near wore me out."

Colfax volunteered no further information about his capture and why the Indians had allowed him to remain alive. But they were moving, and Moses felt a little more secure than he had before. He liked the idea that they were going someplace, even if he didn't know where. They came atop a short rise of ground and then dipped down into an arroyo, which soon gave way to a series of breaks that were ripe with juniper and scrub cedar in their blood-red soil. Deer bounded suddenly off to their left, causing Moses to lift his rifle. It was the first game he had seen since crossing the Wichita.

"Whoa there, boy!" Colfax cautioned. "We don't want no shootin'."

"My name's Moses," the scout said in a low voice. "Moses Franklin. That's my name." He lowered the Springfield and stared hard at Colfax.

Colfax's bushy eyebrows shot up. "Well, now, knock my pecker in the dirt! Ain't you somethin'!" He studied Moses a moment. "Can you use that six-shooter an' that rifle, or did you jus' steal 'em?"

"I can use 'em if I have to," Moses said evenly. "But right now, I want to know where we're goin'."

Colfax pulled up and stared at Moses. "Well, I tell you." He gestured off to the southwest slightly. "There's a river down yonder, an' we're fixin' to ride right up to her, or goddamn near it. Then we're goin' to cut west for 'bout a mile or so where I got some animals that need tendin'. That all right with you, *Mister* Moses?" The scout nodded. "You say you been out here before."

"I have, but only passin' through. Or with the Army."

"Well, sure as there's preachin' on Sunday, the god-damn Army don't know nothin'. Which means you don't neither. But I know somethin', an' by God, that's 'nough. That is, if it's all right with you, *Mister* Moses Franklin."

He wheeled his horse around and started riding out far ahead. He tried to appear tough, Moses knew, but he could tell from the way his body twitched when the horse stumbled over a rock or shifted its weight too rapidly underneath him that he was in considerable pain. There were no stirrups on the Indians' rawhide saddles, and Colfax's injured leg flapped out awkwardly.

"Thinks he's smart," Frank whispered apologetically

when he steered his mount up beside Moses's. Since the rescue the night before, Frank had paid Moses an unusual deference.

"If he's so smart," Moses grumbled, "how'd he get caught by them Indians?"

"Said they snuck up on him," Frank said. "Said they got him while he was drawin' a bead on one of 'em."

"I still wonder why they didn't jus' go ahead an' kill him," Moses thought out loud.

"Said they wanted him to tell 'em 'bout somethin'," Frank replied. "He didn't say what. Said we'd find out, an' we'd be surprised, or his name wasn't Carlson Colfax an' we could bet our last screamin' eagle—"

"I know, I know." Moses cut Frank off. "But I don't trust him. Not yet. An' I don't care what his mama called him."

2

THE THREE RIDERS STEERED THEIR ANIMALS DOWN INTO a steep arroyo alongside brilliant blue and red wildflowers intermingled with cactus and juniper. Feather plume, yellow gourd, and devil's claw clutched at their horses' hocks and hooves whenever the vegetable growth covered the narrow trail, and occasional frantic lines of bobwhite scurried away from their approach. They rode single-file for a hundred yards through the deepening ditch until they finally emerged into a series of breaks that ran in rocky iron-and-copper-rich soil down to a yellow riverbed below them. The river's sandy bottom was lined with pools of water and narrow streams that barely flowed in the early-afternoon sun.

"Is that the Pease?" Moses asked as Colfax reined up to take his bearings now that the river was in sight. The scout knew they had crossed a similar river some days before back to the east, and he was confused.

"That's her."

"The Pease?" Frank said. "Why in hell didn't we just turn an' follow'er when we crossed'er? Looks to me like it would of been considerable easier than fightin' that prairie. Safer, too."

Moses was about to explain, but Colfax laughed.

"Well, if you mean 'safer' 'cause the Comanch' might of missed you, you might be right. 'Cept for makin' a camp, they tend to stay off the rivers. But on the other hand, I doubt you'd of got very far. She might look like a goddamn sleepy road, but I guess you'd have to ride far an' wide to run 'cross a meaner son of a bitch than that riverbed."

Frank blinked his wide eyes and looked down.

"Water's no good," Moses put in. "It's salty, but the animals would of drunk it anyhow. Then they'd of died."

"That's right." Colfax eyed Moses narrowly and with marginal respect. " 'Sides, that river's hell for quicksand. I seen whole buffalo bulls go down in five minutes out there. They's also flash flood, dens of rattlers hidin' in the breaks, cottonmouth in the sloughs, an' with these goddamn cyclones blowin' up ever' night, they's better than a fair chance you'd been blowed to Kingdom Come if you'd of made it through the loblollies. Which you wouldn't of."

Frank nodded and lowered his head, and Colfax turned his mount's nose to the west and dipping ridges of the breaks. It was rough going, and the men said little while their horses picked their way around the scrub cedar and cactus as they rode across the cuts that finally grew into proper canyons, causing the horses to stumble. They slid hock deep into the loam when they descended and struggled to keep their footing as they climbed to the top of the next narrow peak. At last, Colfax reined his shaggy pony in, looked into a canyon with a deep interest, and guided his mount back into it toward the north.

The animals were breathing hard, and Moses could feel his bay trying to collect its remaining energy as they rode up a slight incline that twisted as the canyon gave way to a shallow arroyo. When they came around a final bend, the ravine deepened again, and Moses almost groaned aloud. It was a dead end. A mountain of tumbleweeds and dead cedar blocked their way, and the sides of the ditch were too steep to climb. He was about to speak out and suggest that maybe it was time he took charge of the group when Colfax slid down from his horse and hopped on his good leg over to the side of the arroyo. He stuck his hand behind the twisted trunk of a mesquite tree that grew at a slant from the sharp bank of the ditch and came up with a rawhide rope.

"Come over here, goddamnit," he said to Frank. "I can't do this with this leg." Frank eased his horse over near where Colfax stood. The crippled plainsman handed the rope up and told him to loop it over his pommel. "Now back away easy, damnit," he said. "This won't work if you jerk it." Frank backed his mount away, and both he and Moses gasped aloud when they saw the line dig itself out of the loamy side of the arroyo. It grew taut and revealed itself to be strung to a small pulley block in a hackberry tree up on the edge of the bank. The other end disappeared into the deadfall of juniper and tumbleweeds before the three men. Slowly, and with only the slightest rustling noise as the tumbleweeds and dead branches moved, the massive brushpile lifted itself like a gate. The base of the structure was made of tightly bound pickets to which the dry weeds and tree limbs had been lashed to resemble a brushpile on the outer side.

Behind the gate were four horses, two mules, and a burro, all tethered lightly to a rough wagon on which rested several saddles and other tack. The bed of the wagon was piled high with buffalo hides, from which a cloud of flies arose. The sour stink of the hides mixed with odors of manure and horse urine. It was a natural and exceedingly well hidden corral, and Moses and Frank stared openly at it.

"Don't jus' stand there, damnit," Colfax ordered. "Tie'er off." Frank did what he was told, then dismounted and followed Moses and Colfax inside the enclosure. Colfax was now leaning against the black scout and huffing and puffing in obvious pain. He hobbled over to a large limestone rock and sat down.

"When there ain't no Comanch' roamin' 'round, I let 'em out to graze," Colfax wheezed. "Here lately, since the uprisin', I've had to tote water an' feed to 'em, an' I ain't got no more feed. I'll need some help doin' the water this time. They ain't had none in two days." He lifted himself and half hobbled, half hopped over to the wagon, where he pulled out two collapsible leather buckets and threw them down at Moses's feet. "I'd be 'bliged if you could see your way clear," he said with a tone in his voice that indicated that he had no expectation of a denial. "There's a li'l ol' spring back down the arroyo 'bout a hundred paces. You'll have to lift up a big red rock to see it. It's hid pretty good, I guess. You may as well take these plugs with you while you're 'bout it."

Moses resented being given the chore and started to assign it to Frank. But then he noticed that Colfax's bandages were blackening with new bloodstains. He instructed Frank, who was wandering around the natural enclosure, to check the old man's wounds, and he took the reins of their mounts and led them to the spring.

With difficulty, he filled the buckets, then left their three mounts tethered by the spring, where they began noisily slurping the mossy water from the pool, and walked back. Each of the animals in the corral had a light piece of cheesecloth tied over its snout to keep it from nickering in greeting to any approaching mounts, and when the black scout removed the dusty rags, each of them whinnied loudly in protest at the restraint and the delay in their watering schedule.

The black scout lifted the buckets to the penned animals' noses, and they greedily snorted up the water. Colfax lay on his stomach and allowed Frank to mop the wounds on his back that had reopened during their ride. His cut leg was also bleeding, but there was nothing to make bandages from. Frank poured water on the wound and then retied it with the same ripped shirt he had used before, stiff as it was with dried blood.

In an hour's time, they were rested, the animals watered, and Moses stood next to his bay, smoking a cigarette and waiting on Colfax to suggest the next course of action. Although the hidden corral was safe from the view of anyone who didn't ride right up to the lip of the arroyo, it was a box canyon, a trap if they were detected. He couldn't see the sun from the bottom of the deep ditch, and he knew it was getting late.

"You goin' to be able to ride?" Moses asked Colfax.

"I'll ride your ass to hell," the plainsman shot back suddenly. Then he muttered, "It'll take more than a bunch of frog-fuckin' Indians to keep me off a horse."

"What did that Indian, the medicine man, want with you?" Moses asked suddenly.

Colfax grinned. "I was wonderin' when you'd get 'round to that." He sighed. "You ain't goin' to believe it, though."

"Try me," Moses said quickly. "I think I earned the right to know."

"I s'pect you did, boy." Colfax grinned again. "Well sir, here it is. 'Bout two months ago when all this mess was just heatin' up, this same bunch of red bastards you run into—same outfit that killed the Mescans—raided a settlement down on Paint Crick, near the Brazos."

Moses smelled a lie. "They ain't no settlements down on Paint Creek. Not anymore. Not since the war. Not that far west."

Colfax frowned meanly. "Well, I'll be plumb gone to hell! That jus' shows what you know, boy. Bunch of goddamn nesters come out here last year, right when the weather turned cold, an' set 'em up a dugout. I knowed 'em. They was good ol' boys for the most part. Wanted to grow some pigs an' corn an' the like. Anyway, I tol' 'em they was 'bout the biggest goddamn fools I ever seen. They tol' me they'd fought Grant an' Sherman, an' they'd be goddamned if a bunch of redskins was fixin' to run 'em off. I told 'em I'd faced Yankees my own self, but they ain't seen nothin' till they seen Comanch'. But they wouldn't listen. Bunch of cracker hard-dicks, don't you know."

Suddenly Moses remembered the two wagons with the hogs. Graham had told him that they would be leaving the train and heading down on the Brazos somewhere, that they had family out there with a settlement. The thought bothered him, but he shook his head. No one would be crazy enough to try to settle that far west, not that far from the forts.

"What happened to 'em?" Frank asked. He seated himself on the ground and listened to Colfax in the manner that a small child listens to an old man spin yarns.

"Kilt 'em," Colfax said, spitting expertly to one side and striking a grasshopper which had crawled up on a limestone rock. "Kilt the hell out of 'em. Ever' man jack of 'em got killed. Women an' kids, too. Mostly, that is. I have to say, they put up a fight. Took out a half-dozen

Comanch' 'fore they got wiped out. Time I got there, they was most all used up."

"Time you got there!" Moses repeated suddenly. "You mean you were there an' got out alive?" Or did you just watch? he silently added.

Carlson frowned at the black scout. "I heard the shootin' from a ways off. I was huntin'. Truth to tell, I was on my way to 'Dobe Walls with that load of hides we took away from them poor dead sons-of-bitchin' skinners we buried. I swung down south tryin' to see if I could pick up some more, but I kept runnin' into Comanch' or soldiers or some other worthless bastards all over the Double Mountain country, an' the pickin's was gettin' slim, so I hightailed it back. I reckoned to hole up an' wait out the storm. Anyhow, we heard the commotion from a ways off, an' time I got my gun an' rode down to where they was, they was mostly used up. I took out a couple, but there wasn't much else I could do."

He looked hard at Moses and said in a level voice that was suddenly void of brag, "I done what I could, but I didn't live this long by actin' the fool. I had the Kid with me, though, an' we done what we could." He smiled slyly as he finished and fell into silence for a moment.

"Anyhow, they figgered I had somethin' they wanted."

"What?" Moses asked.

"The medicine bag," Frank guessed happily.

"You wouldn't be far off the truth," Colfax said. "That medicine man was the one who snuck up on me. He had a notion if he could get me to choke up that missin' bag, he could hand it over to the trail chief. Then he'd be a big hero with 'em all. Then you run up on him an' spoilt their fun."

Carlson looked sad for a moment. "They're all het up over this business. One thing 'bout Comanch', medicine's got a lot to do with ever'thin' he does. An' you an' your bunch jus' rode right into it an' added fuel to the fire." He winked, and Moses wondered if he knew about the whiskey. He seemed to know everything else about them.

"Hadn't we ought to be goin'?" Moses asked all at

once. Colfax looked at him quickly, and Moses saw a flash of pain run across his eyes before he nodded.

"I hate to do it, damn it, but I got to turn these animals out," Colfax said. "I got nothin' for 'em to eat, an' we ain't got time to graze 'em, even if the whole damn prairie wasn't crawlin' with goddamn Comanch'. One thing 'bout Comanch'. They can smell a horse to steal a mile away, an' they'll do'er too, if he ain't well hid, that is." He looked at Moses's and Frank's mounts with a studied eye. "I s'pect you want to keep that bay. She's a good'un. But Frank, you need a better animal 'neath you. Take that buckskin. He's got a fair to middlin' topline an' good lungs, an' he'll ride you to hell on mesquite beans an' goatheads. I'll ask you to saddle the roan for me. Get my rig out of the wagon."

Frank began the chore, and Moses unsaddled the horses and removed the blankets. "Keep the pinto an' the gray," Colfax ordered. "We'll need 'em. Saddle 'em, if you please. Hell, saddle 'em if you don't please." He sniffed and bit off another plug of tobacco. Moses showed him nothing of his face as he completed the work.

"How long you had this place?" Frank asked, eyeing the McClellan saddle he found in the wagon. It was an unusual seat for any plainsman to have, particularly one who had fought for the South.

"Oh, couple of seasons. But I've had others like it. It don't do no good to keep 'em in one place for too long," Colfax said around a mouthful of tobacco. "It's the onliest goddamn way I know of to keep horses in Indian country. You can't hide 'em too good. As it is, I've had too many stole from hideouts better'n this'un. Goddamn Comanch'll cut right through a chain if you give 'em a chance. Horses is pure gold to a Comanch'. I know of one ol' chief whose got more'n a thousand head in his caviard. I asked that ol' son of a bitch one time, 'Why is it you need so many horses? You don't sell 'em, an' you're too old to ride 'em. An' you'd sooner starve'n eat 'em.' He looked at me like I was a idjet an' said, 'Comanch' got horses. Comanch' always got horses.' An' that was a end to it. Comanch'd rather have a horse than a woman. Sometimes he'll trade that way. Rather fight than fuck. That's what's mostly wrong with 'em." He looked over at the animals. "I'll likely save the wagon, but I hate to give up these animals. It's a goddamn bitch is what it is."

"Where do we go from here?" Moses asked, leading the roan over and helping Colfax up into the strange saddle. "It's gettin' late. We need to do somethin' 'bout the train."

Colfax winced as the black scout fitted the foot at the end of his injured leg into a stirrup. "I s'pect we got plenty of time, Mr. Moses," he said. "From what you say, ain't nobody down there goin' noplace, an' we got to get to Mosely's Hole so I can get fixed up decent." He winked at Frank. "No offense." He kicked his mount out of the corral and rode over to where it was tied off. Frank and Moses followed him and stopped as he untied the gate and allowed it to fall after the animals they led out. The mules bucked slightly and raced down the arroyo and out of sight.

"Son of a bitch! I'm goin' to miss them mules," Colfax declared. "Sometimes I think a good mule is 'bout all there is in this goddamn life you can count on."

"I know a man who'd give you an argument on that point," Frank Herbert offered.

"Well, he's prob'ly a Yankee," Colfax grumbled.

"Yeah, an' a good one."

"No," Colfax said solemnly, "all the good ones is dead." He turned around and led them away, past the tiny spring and back toward the breaks and Mosely's Hole.

3

THEY ARRIVED AT MOSELY'S HOLE BEFORE EITHER Moses or Frank knew that they were anyplace different from where they had been. The seemingly endless series of arroyos and tiny canyons they rode up and down became a tedious, sweating monotony for the weary men. Only the stumbling of their horses in the loamy soil kept the men from falling asleep in the saddle. Moses was amazed by Carlson Colfax's determination. In spite of his wounds, he never once complained while his body slipped and slid from one side of his McClellan saddle to the other. If anything, he seemed to gain strength from the ordeal. The plainsman cursed "Comanch'," "weak-minded, slew-footed" horses, "Mescans," and "ign'ert sodbusters" who came out to Indian country and expected to find a "Sunday picnic," but he kept his comments directed toward general targets, and he failed to arouse either Moses or Frank, who were by now nearing total exhaustion.

For more than an hour their mounts threaded around high sharp outcroppings of limestone and cedar thickets until, at last, Colfax led them up a narrow path next to a large pile of rocks that had seemingly been dumped by some giant's hand to block the trail. He reined up and stepped painfully from his horse.

"Mosely's Hole," Colfax said matter-of-factly. He hopped on his good leg over to a blasted hackberry tree that grew crookedly out of the rocks and lowered himself down to his belly. At first, Moses thought he was going to lie down for a rest; instead, the old frontiersman scrambled under a low shelf of limestone, kicking the fine dust out in a powder behind him with his good leg. He disappeared beneath it.

"Where'd he go?" Frank wondered.

Moses didn't respond but climbed down from his bay and walked over to where Colfax had disappeared. He knelt in the yellow dust, but he couldn't see much besides darkness beneath the outcropping. From his half-crouched position it appeared that there was hardly enough room for an opossum to crawl under there, yet Colfax was completely gone from sight. The scout was more annoyed than curious about where the old man went, and he removed his hat and shook his head. Frank continued to sit atop his horse and stared down at Moses with quiet patience.

Suddenly, a square of sod atop the limestone shelf moved slightly, and Frank brought his rifle up in alarm. Moses scrambled to his feet and drew his Colt's .44.

"You bastards fixin' to stan' 'round out there all day with your thumb up your ass?" Colfax demanded from beneath a dusty covering of lime that showered down from an ingenious trapdoor that was revealed at the top of the shelf's border. His head was slightly above the two men in the low arroyo, and if Moses hadn't seen it emerge from under the trap, it would have appeared to be disembodied and simply lying on the side of the deep ditch. "Tie off them horses an' come on in. It's time you met the family."

With that, he lowered the trap and was gone. Moses and Frank looked at each other in astonishment.

Once the animals were secured with ground stakes, Moses hesitated more out of weariness than anything else before flopping down onto his stomach. He inched forward, stuck his head under the low shelf, and discovered that the opening immediately widened and grew deeper as the depression slanted into the darkness. By wriggling and pushing his Springfield and pistol belt in front of him, he was able to crawl beneath the jagged edges of the rock and push himself into what appeared to be utter blackness under the outcropping. After shoving through the bitter dust for ten or twelve feet, he looked down and saw yellow light spilling out onto the ground in front of him, and he squirmed forward rapidly. Finally, he was staring at the dirty bare feet of Carlson Colfax, who was comfortably seated on a three-legged stool and grinning down at him.

"Where're your manners, boy?" Colfax roared with laughter. The atmosphere inside the cave was cool enough for his breath to vaporize, and gusts of smoke shot from his open mouth. "Don't you know 'nough to stand up when you come into folks' houses?"

Moses pulled himself upright. His eyes adjusted to the bright lantern light quickly enough, and his mouth hung open in wonder at what he beheld. He felt rather than saw Frank rise to stand near him, quiet, but no less astonished than he.

Directly in front of the scout and his white companion was a large room no less than six feet tall. Four lanterns spilled bright yellow light onto the limestone walls, which were festooned with stalactites and stalagmites behind which shadows appeared to conceal a hundred different openings and doorways. A crude ladder was propped against the far wall; Moses observed that it led up into darkness, presumably up to the trapdoor. In addition to the three-legged stool, a rough-hewn table with a gray clay jug sat in the middle of the room, and a crude gun rack rested against one wall. It held two Sharps rifles, two Winchesters, and a half-dozen gunbelts.

"I told you it was a goddamn good hideout," Colfax declared. "I wouldn't think of tryin' to come up here 'thout it, not if I planned to live to tell 'bout it." He reached over and tilted the jug high and allowed his scrawny Adam's apple to pump some of the liquid down into his stomach. When he finished he set the vessel down hard, and Moses noted that his eyes were glistening.

"Have a drink," he offered more to Frank than to Moses. "It's made a new son of a bitch out of me, I can tell you. Nothin' like it to wash down the piss-sour taste of Comanch' an' make your pecker hard again."

Frank stepped forward and took the jug and sipped slightly on some of the liquid, then he hesitated only a moment before passing it to Moses. The scout wiped the muzzle of the crude clay vessel briefly and tilted it back. What came into his mouth was pure fire. He choked immediately and spat violently into the dust.

Colfax exploded with laughter. "Never did see a nigger who could hold his liquor," he declared through tears. He relieved the jug from the table where Moses had shakily deposited it and took a second helping. "Mescal," he said. " 'Pache medicine, damn tootin'. What it won't cure, it'll sure'n hell kill. I use it to drink or to start fires with. It don't matter. Better'n coal oil, an' it won't kill you near as quick." He proved his strength with one more swig, and then rose, steadying himself on the table as his bad leg threatened to give under him again.

"Y'all sit down, an' make yourself to home. I'll be back direc'ly, an' I'll bring the family. I done told 'em 'bout you, an' they're jus' chompin' at the bit to see the men who saved my hide." With that, he plucked a lantern from the wall and hobbled back into the shadows between the jagged limestone points.

For a moment, Moses and Frank stood silently and stared at the now black hole through which Colfax had disappeared. Once the light from his lantern faded from view, the opening looked identical to a dozen or so others that were too dark to invite exploration. Moses walked over and peered up the ladder toward the trap. Huge boulders enclosed the opening and would permit nothing more than a man's head after a certain point. Muffled noises came from somewhere in the cave, and Moses suspected that others—"the family," as Colfax had described them—were in a distant room.

"Where you think he went to?" Frank whispered.

"An' who's he talkin' 'bout? You reckon he's got folks down here, for sure?"

"I don't know," Moses replied. He was angry with himself for being buffaloed by this mysterious old coot. He now regretted not just riding around the light they had spotted on the prairie the night before, leaving Colfax to his fate and keeping themselves ignorant. He was uncomfortable and anxious all at the same time. The excitement he felt upon entering the strange cave was now receding, and his weary body was demanding that he sit down. The mescal burned his throat, and he longed for a cool drink of sweet water.

"Is this the goddamnedest thing you ever seen or what?" Frank spoke louder. "Wonder how he found it?"

Moses stepped around the room and examined his surroundings more closely. He discovered that what he had mistaken for dirt on the cave's floor was actually something else, and by taking one of the lanterns and holding it up high, he discovered what. Bats were resting, asleep, in their normal upside-down condition, in the crevices and nooks that formed the cave's ceiling. Underfoot was their feces, dried to a fine powder that dusted up every time one of the men moved. The walls were marked with black streaks from candle flames, and several symbols and letters had been burned into the yellowish stone. Pegs were driven into the living rock here and there, and a second, but empty, gun rack rested behind some of the jagged limestone points that surrounded them.

"Wonder if they's any snakes in here?" He spotted a long, narrow trail in the guano, but the temperature was cool, almost chilly, inside the cave.

"Where'd he get off to, anyhow?" Frank asked again, scowling into one of the numerous dark closets that surrounded the room.

"Your guess is good as mine," Moses replied. The room, which was no less than ten feet in diameter inside the jagged limestone teeth that walled it, was circled by tunnels and passageways that ranged in size from a few feet in height to large openings a man on a small horse could have navigated. He held up his lantern to try to illuminate first one, then another, but all he peered into led to dead ends or veered sharply away to the right or left, and he feared venturing into them. He no longer remembered which one Carlson Colfax had disappeared into.

Frank went over to the stool and sat down. His hat, which remained in his hands, turned unconsciously beneath his fingers, and he frowned down at the floor.

"I don't like this," he said with a slight whine creeping into his reedy voice. "He said he was fixin' to help us out, but all I can see is he's led us to some hole in the ground an' run off an' left us. He seemed like a nice enough feller, for a Johnny Reb, but I'm beginnin' not to trust him." His face twisted into the aspect of a small boy who was facing monstrous disappointment. "What're we goin' to do?"

Moses turned to face him. He wasn't sure what course of action to take. One thing was clear: They had been gone from the wagon fort for almost a whole day, and they hadn't come any closer to relieving the train of its siege.

"I think he said for us to wait here," he stated dumbly.

"I don't see as we got any choice," Frank responded, and Moses sat down in the dusty guano next to the white man and waited.

4

The heavy sounds of people shuffling along together startled Moses into consciousness. The scout leaped to his feet, shocked to discover that he had been sound asleep. He had been dreaming as well, and in the dream he had lain by a long river which insisted on roaring, although when he rose to look at it, it was placid and green. When his eyes fluttered open, he was bewildered, and he instinctively grabbed for his pistols. His mind then registered that the roaring had been Frank's sonorous breathing; his snores were echoing off the limestone walls. Moses reminded himself that it had been days since either of them had had a proper rest. They were dangerously close to exhaustion and apt to be careless, something they could not afford to be, especially now.

Feeling angry with himself and no less foolish and self-conscious, Moses shook Frank awake, and both men stood and backed up as light emerged from directly across the room. Carlson Colfax entered after a few moments. He was carrying a torch that he stuck in a nook in the limestone wall. Moses didn't recognize him at first. The old plainsman was now clad in buckskins that were more worn but better made than the scout's own. His long gray hair appeared to have been washed and oiled and was pulled tightly back in a single braid that fell down to the middle of his back. Across his scarred forehead, a bright bandanna was tightly bound. Although he still limped, he no longer bounced around, and Moses saw through a slit in the buckskin's trouser leg that rawhide bindings had been tightly wrapped around his hamstring to reinforce the injured limb.

"Still can't walk worth a pitcher of mule slobber," Colfax grumbled when he jerked over to the stool. He reached for the jug and sat down and took another long sip all in one motion. "Give me some more of that chaw, an' I'll have us some grub fixed up here direc'ly." Colfax stuck out his hand and accepted Frank's plug, from which he sliced a large portion with a long knife he kept strapped to his belt. "One thing I truly miss out here is a good chaw. I ain't had one in near a month."

"Don't you think we ought to get started?" Moses finally asked.

"Jus' where the blue-eyed hell you think you're goin' to go?" Colfax chuckled softly. "You jus' simmer down, Mr. Moses. I already told you I admire your grit, but we can't do nothin' 'fore dark anyhow. Not an' keep our hair, though I see you still ain't growed none of yours back."

"Don't you think you ought to tell us what you're fixin' to do?" Moses asked. "I mean, don't you think we ought to have some kind of plan?" Frustration welled up in the black scout. "I mean, *what* are we goin' to do?"

Colfax's face narrowed and darkened beneath its whiskers and scars, and his eyes sharpened in the yellowing lamplight. "Listen here, boy. I been in sharper scrapes'n this. You're talkin' to by-God Carlson Colfax here, not some goddamn shavetail with a bunch of chicken feathers where his balls ought to be.

"Your sodbusters got theirselves into a fix down on the crick, an' it ain't none of my goddamn business. But you saved my hair, an' I got to admit you done it with flash, blacker'n Satan though you are. I admire any man with that kind of hair 'tween his legs: nigger, Mex, or white. I'll take care of things down on the crick, don't you worry. While you was nappin' like a couple of sweethearts in here, I was thinkin' on'er an' gettin' stuff together. But 'thout some grub in our bellies, we ain't fixin' to do no good at all. Hungry an' tired, we're jus' goin' to piss all over ourselves. If you had the sense God give a Mescan, you'd see that."

Before Moses or Frank could reply, another light appeared from the same opening from which Colfax had emerged previously. The lanterns had begun to burn low, and the sudden appearance of a second torch brightened the room considerably. Moses and Frank stepped back and stared as a young man dressed like Colfax moved into the room. He carried a sack and a long stick onto which were stuck three small birds—prairie chickens, Moses guessed—done to a turn and filling the cave with their delicious, greasy aroma.

"Quail," Colfax said with a smile. "Bobwhites. There's some sody crackers in that sack, too. Got 'em up at the 'Dobe Walls on my last trip. Had me a bottle of gin, too, but it got broke. Have some more of this 'Pache fire." He shoved the clay jug toward Moses, and then pulled one of the birds off the stick and extended it to Frank, who took it and immediately brought it up to his lips to bite off a large chunk of the small bird's breast. The smell of the roasted fowl filled the small cave and caused their stomachs to growl in anticipation.

Moses took his bird from the boy, who had a long shock of blond hair falling down across his forehead. The youth kept his eyes cast down as if there was something wrong with his neck, but there was vigor in his movements, and Moses felt rather than saw that there was something seriously wrong with him.

"Where're *my* goddamn manners?" Colfax demanded of himself suddenly around a mouthful of roasted bird. "Kid, this here's Mr. Frank Herbert, an' *Mister*, by God, Moses Franklin, one of the goddamnedest hobgoblins you ever seen. Careful how you talk to him. He's a partic'lar son of a bitch 'bout what you call him." Colfax's eyes danced. "Gentlemen," he intoned with mock civility, "meet the Cottonwood Kid."

The boy stood up as straight as he could under the cave's ceiling and presented himself for inspection. His gesture reminded Moses of Aaron's and Saul's children, who so frequently were subjected to formal introductions and behaved in the same way.

The Cottonwood Kid appeared to be about eighteen, nearly six feet tall, and had clear blue eyes, Moses saw in the torch's flickering light. He wore a light beard, but it was not a full growth, not a deliberate attempt to imitate Colfax's own luxurious facial forest. Under his buckskin jacket, he wore a well-made leather shirt that had wooden pegs for buttons, and across his narrow waist were buckled two Army Colt's revolvers. A skinning knife was strapped to his leg, and he stood during the satiric ceremony of the introductions with childish pride as Colfax munched his chicken and wiped his greasy mouth with the back of his hand.

The boy was handsome, Moses could see, and he looked strong and fit. But there was something about him, something in his face, that didn't register. Then Moses saw that around the Kid's neck was a scar, a rope wound; the boy had been hanged or dragged by his neck: not enough to kill him, just enough to torture him. The scar cut deep into his white flesh and had browned with age, but it was still there, still visible above the collar of his leather shirt.

"He ain't much for talkin'," Colfax said in an apologetic but serious tone, "but he's hell for doin' what he's told. An' he's a fair shot, 'specially when they's a Comanch' on the other end of his bead. I never was much for comp'ny, but he's been a good man to have 'round. He don't wear you out palaverin', for one thing." He bit off the final sliver of meat from the small bird's carcass. "If you ain't fixin' to eat that, I'd be 'bliged," he said to Moses, who suddenly came to and bit into his own bird.

"Get the gal," Colfax barked to the Kid, who turned without expression and disappeared into the cave.

"Been with me four months, or damn near it." Colfax sighed as if impatient. "Saved his young ass from a rope, an' he's beholden. Good man. But don't mess with him. I learned him a few things, an' he's like as not to fly off the handle. Got him a temper, an' you reach for him, you're likely to jerk back a stub. I've gotten sort of fond of the li'l son of a bitch, though I'd have to 'low that he was a pain in the ass at the start."

Moses and Frank stared after the disappearing light from the youngster's torch. Colfax watched their eyes, then sighed and explained.

"He found me when I was up in Kansas last winter. Took a shine to me, I reckon. Said he wanted to be a gunfighter or a buffalo hunter, weren't particular, an' he'd heard I was good at both." Colfax winked. "I got me somethin' of a reputation, you know. Anyhow, he said he wanted me to learn him 'tricks of the trade.'

"I told him to go to hell, that I wasn't no schoolmarm an' didn't want no young pup followin' me 'round, suckin' my horse's hin' tit. I always been a loner. But he followed me anyhow. Couldn't get shed of him. Ever' time I'd look 'hind me, there he'd be, doggin' my trail like a lost yearlin'. Wouldn't ride on in, mind you. Just sat back, made his camp close 'nough to keep my smoke in sight, an' far 'nough away I couldn't yell at him nor run him off."

Colfax winked. "It's a free country, or so I hear tell, anyhow."

"So what happened?" Frank asked, settling down in the dust of the cave's floor and crossing his legs. His pale eyes were wide and his mouth hung open.

"Well, I could see I wasn't goin' to get rid of him that away, an' I was 'bout to give it up as a cornhole, invite him on in, then take his horse an' leave him afoot in walkin' distance to somewhere. You know, hornswoggle him."

Frank nodded, and Moses frowned. It was just the sort of thing he would expect a man like Carlson Colfax to do.

Carlson's brow furrowed. "But one mornin', I got up on my horse an' took a look-see, an' he was gone."

"Gone?" Frank asked.

"Wasn't sure at first," Carlson went on. "It was snowin' like hell. Hard to see more'n few hun'red yards. I rode off a ways, then I got to thinkin' maybe he was hurt or somethin'. Lost, you know. Easy thing to do. Happened to better men'n me up on them godless Kansas plains. Ain't a tree or a hill noplace you can see half the time. So

I doubled back, an' after a bit, I run up on some tracks an' followed 'em down to this little ol' crick. They was a goodly stan' of cottonwood there, an' there I found him, trussed up like Christmas turkey an' ready for hangin' by one of them goat-dicked Kansas lawmen."

"He was an outlaw," Frank guessed.

"None of it," Carlson exclaimed, and his eyes almost twinkled in the firelight. "You see, it was me the ol' boy was after, but he sort of got mixed up. He wasn't sure, really, hisself. An' when I come up on him, he was puzzlin' over it an' tryin' to make up his mind."

Moses sat down next to Frank and rubbed his chin. He felt anxiety growing with every passing minute, but he also knew that Colfax was one of those men who proceeded in his own way in his own time. He wouldn't be hurried.

Carlson took a swig from his jug. "You see, I was sort of wanted up there in Kansas. Got into a little ruckus up near Hays City a while back. Had to kill me a feller. Two fellers, matter of fact. An' there was a flier out on me. Picture an' all. Wasn't a good likeness, though. An' that's where all the trouble come in.

"All I knowed when I rode up was that he was the man in charge of the whole shootin' match," Carlson told Moses and Frank. "An' I knowed I better watch him, or I'd be in worse trouble than the Kid."

Carlson smiled. "Well, turns out he was a federal marshal out of some goddamn place up in Nebraska. He claimed he'd been trackin' me, or who he thought was me, all this time, an' he figgered he'd fin'lly run Carlson Colfax to ground. He had me all mixed up with the Kid there. I had to shoot him to get him to see the right of things."

"But he was a lawman!" Frank interrupted Carlson's story, a look of shock on his simple face. "A marshal."

"Out here that don't make no nevermind," Carlson snapped back at Frank. "That don't make no diff'rence at all. Don't you boys know nothin'?" He winked quickly. " 'Sides, *I* didn't kill him. Jus' winged him couple of times to keep him quiet."

Frank shrugged, and Moses looked away. The scout knew about lawmen. He knew that often it was impossible to tell one from the outlaws he chased. There was no other way out here. They couldn't stay alive otherwise.

"See, he was righteously put out with the Kid. Who he thought was me. Seems he rode up on the Kid an' tried to take him quiet, but the Kid wouldn't have none of it. They got into a ruckus, an' he had to pistol-whip him some." Carlson drew a set of bony fingers across his forehead to trace the kid's scar. "Must've hit him a good lick. 'Nough to col'-cock him, 'nough so he was too woozy to tell this yahoo that he wasn't me. 'Nough that he ain't right in the head now, not all the time. Not that it'd made no diff'rence anyhow to Mr. By-God John Law. He was hell-bent to hang him, he was. Goddamn goat-dicked Bluebelly marshals. Think they're the goddamn Second Comin'."

Frank's face looked pained, and Carlson's expression softened. "Look, it wasn't my fault, an' it wasn't this ol' boy's fault neither. He carried justice coiled on his saddle horn. His business is runnin' men down: Find 'em, hang 'em. Saves time. But that don't mean he's got the sense God give a goat. Hell, he's more deadly'n a rattler. Has to be to make it from one meal to the next. It was either shoot him or let him hang the Kid, an' seein' as how the Kid was in this mess sort of 'cause of me, I couldn't see no other goddamn way out of it."

Colfax flexed his injured leg and massaged the wound. "It wasn't easy, though. I shot him twice, but he wouldn't die, jus' lay there tryin' to crawl 'round where he could find some kind of stick or somethin' to wallop me with after I pitched his gun away. I didn't have a notion to kill him, see?"

"So what happened to the Kid? To his neck?" Moses asked suddenly. "Did he hang him anyway?" Or did you? he added silently.

"Well, when the shootin' started, his horse shied up an' took off. Left him danglin' like a turd on a string. Why it didn't bust his neck I can't tell you. I seen men tougher'n him by a sight jus' snap when they hit the end of their ropes. Anyhow, time I got to him an' cut him down, he was damn near strangled to death. I didn't think he had it in him."

"What?" Moses asked.

Colfax took a deep breath. "He got hisself up on his own hin' feet, wheezin' an' coughin', walked over to where that marshal was floppin' 'round in the bloody snow, took up his pistol, an' shot him right 'tween the eyes."

For a moment the men were silent.

"Boy's got grit," Frank said in a low voice.

"Shit." Colfax spat. "Nothin' of the kind. After that, he throwed up, passed clean out, an' I had to toss him over his own saddle an' tote him home. There's more to killin' a man than jus' puttin' a bullet in him," Colfax said. "It ain't hard durin' a war when ever'body's shootin' ever'body. But when you face down a man an' drop a hammer on a cap, you best know what you're 'bout. I reckon that boy learned that up in Kansas. I reckon he knows it now good as I do. But case he takes a notion to forget it, I call him 'the Cottonwood Kid' to remind him jus' how close he come to goin' south for once an' all."

Colfax stretched his arms over his head and yawned. "Anyhow, took me damn near a month to nurse him back to health. An' he still can't talk hardly 'bove a whisper. An', like I say, I don't know how straight he's thinkin'. But he's loyal as a goddamn dog. An' I prize that in a man, 'specially one who knows what it's like to be on the workin' end of a Colt's.

"Since we got back," he went on, "we done some huntin'. But I'm stayin' clear of Kansas. I might of talked my way out of that other business, but I sure'n hell shot that marshal, even if the Kid did send him to meet his Maker. So I s'pose folks is still lookin' for me up there. Here too. Rangers an' the like. Wouldn't be the first time. Won't be the last."

"Maybe that's why you ain't so het up on goin' for soldiers," Moses suggested.

"Maybe." Carlson's eyes narrowed slightly. "But I never lied to you 'bout it. Half them soldier boys is out chasin' their peckers, an' the other half's not worth a Chinaman's fart. No, if you want them folks saved, you're goin' to have to rely on me and do it our ownselves."

"I don't see why you should risk your hair for a bunch of people you don't even know," Moses said. "What's in it for you?"

"I told you, Mr. Moses." Colfax winked. "I admire the way you work. You saved my skin, so I'm returnin' the favor."

"Where'd he go, anyway?" Frank asked. He had been working his quail with relish and now stood with the greasy bones in his dirty fingers, afraid to lay them on the table and uncertain about flinging them down into the dust below them to join Colfax's meal's remains.

"He'll be back direc'ly," Colfax said. He pointed around the room. "They's thirty-two passages leading out of this room. Thirty-one'll take you noplace. A dozen of 'em'll lead you 'round in circles till you can't tell your ass from your elbow. Some of 'em's marked. Some ain't. But one of 'em'll take you right on back there. You could get lost in here so God Almighty can't find you Hisself." He waited for the effect to sink in. "This is the best goddamn hideout in Texas."

Before the scout or Frank could question him further, a shuffling noise and torchlight announced that the Kid was returning. He entered the room with the same blank expression and silent movements as before, but when he came near Carlson, he turned and allowed his torch to light the way behind him. From the shadows between the crags, a girl emerged.

Like Carlson and the Kid, she was wearing the rough clothing of the frontier, a loose leather shirt tucked into a broadly cut skirt that hung down to mid-calf, where it met the tops of roughly made moccasins, and at first Moses thought she was a squaw. But her hair belied such a lineage. It was blond, golden yellow, and her size and fair complexion also banished his first assumption. She came in with her face lowered and fumbled through the bright light over next to the Kid, who put a protective arm around her. Moses's breath drew in sharply. He heard Frank do the same.

"She was down on the Paint Crick with them crackers when the Comanch' hit," Carlson explained. "Like I said, I come up on 'em too late to do much more'n save her, an' I ain't yet sure if I done the right thing. But one thing's sure'n God made Injuns ugly, she's the cause of most of the trouble 'round here since."

She looked up sharply into the faces of the two strangers, and Moses's legs almost gave way. He took an unsteady, involuntary step backward as her striking blue eyes lifted toward him. His heart started pounding. It couldn't be, he told himself. It wasn't possible. But there she was, and there was no explanation for it.

"I'd introduce you proper," Colfax went on, unaware that anything was wrong with his rescuers, "but I don't know her name. She ain't said word one to me, not even 'thankee' or 'howdydo.' But the Kid here's right partial to her. Won't hardly let me near her, an' won't leave her 'lone for twenty dollars gold." He shook his head and looked at the effect she was having on the two men who stood astonished into silence before him.

Both Moses and Frank stood transfixed and stared into the face of the girl who appeared in the flickering torchlight to be no one other than Aggie Sterling.

CHAPTER TWO

1

MOSES AND FRANK STOOD IN DUMB SILENCE FOR NEARLY a full minute before Colfax ordered the Kid and the girl to go outside and see to the horses.

Silently, almost automatically, the pair dropped to their knees and crawled out through the cave's narrow opening. Frank and Moses exchanged bewildered looks, and Colfax stood himself and took a final pull on the jug before limping over to the rifles and removing them from the racks.

"Looks like I'm jus' goddamn surrounded with the deaf an' dumb," he said, laughing, while he stacked the weapons on the narrow table. "Guess that beats bein' throwed in with the blind an' helpless, but when you add in the simpleminded an' a nigger, I can't see how I'm much better off."

"Where did she come from?" Moses choked out. He was surprised that his voice failed him utterly. He had to swallow hard to consume the shock he felt at seeing the girl.

"I told you. Don't you listen to nothin'?" Colfax shouted. He addressed Moses as if he were a small child, pronouncing each word separately. "She's the onliest single survivor of 'the Massacre at Paint Crick.' Or that's what them jack-legged newspaper sons of bitches'll call it when they get wind of it. If they do. An' they likely won't."

Colfax delighted in telling how he and the Kid had heard the shooting while they were out hunting. He was aware of the settlers' place on Paint Creek, had, in fact, scorned it when he discovered it the first time, but he and the Kid came on the run when they realized that the white men were under attack. He gave the Kid his Sharps and placed him on a knoll, while the old man rode in and rescued the girl.

"Snatched her right from the jaws of death." The old man grinned. "Buck naked an' spittin' fire. She never seen me. Jerked her right up on my horse an' rode out with her hittin' me with one hand an' tryin' to cut out my gizzard with the other till she got a good look at me. Left them redskins standin' there with their peckers hard an' nothin' to do but whip their meat." He winked. "Kid had me covered, don't you know." He took thought. "Sharps goes a long way toward givin' a Comanch' a case of limp pecker."

Moses stood in silence while Colfax spoke. Through the cave opening he heard the boy's voice, but the words were lost. He could only hope that the horses were still standing in the arroyo outside the cave. The shock of seeing the girl was wearing off, and now, he insisted to himself, he didn't trust Colfax at all. The old man was too fond of surprises, kept too much a secret for too long. The scout's frustration was becoming intolerable. He had wasted almost a whole day fooling around with Colfax, but there didn't appear to be another choice. He felt angry and confused, and he wasn't sure what he could do to extricate himself from Colfax's company.

"She was in bad shape," Colfax remarked while he strapped a bandolier of cartridges across his chest. His voice softened. "I tried, but I jus' couldn't get there quick enough. At least one or two of them goat-dicked sons of bitches had their way with her, an' she wouldn't talk for more'n a week. Can't say as I blame her. Outside of the Kid there, she won't have nothin' to do with nobody. Least, she won't have nothin' to do with me, an' it was me who risked his skinny ass savin' her. Him, too. I'm gettin' soft-hearted or soft-headed in my ol' age. I don't know which."

Colfax turned away and limped again to the rack, where he fussed with a small bag. Frank, who had been silent up to this point, whispered to Moses that the girl looked enough like Aggie Sterling to be her sister. But Moses put a finger to his lips and moved his eyes sharply toward Colfax's buckskinned back. Frank's eyes widened in response, then he dropped his eyes and studied his boot tops in the flickering light.

It was true, though, Moses thought. Only this girl was plainer, bigger-boned than Aggie but not as tall, and she looked older as well. She also seemed weaker, and she had leaned on the Kid's arm the whole time she was in their presence and stared at them, and with one hand she had held on to something she wore around her neck.

"What was that around her neck?" Moses asked. "She had something on a string."

"That's what all the fuss is over, mostly," Colfax said, turning.

He winked at Frank, and Moses wondered if he had heard the remark. He also wondered, not for the first time, just how much the old man knew that he wasn't telling.

"When that young trail chief jumped her, she come back at him with a skinnin' knife. Took a good swipe at him, up close if you know what I mean, an' she got that young buck's medicine bag. I don't know how. They'd rather you took their pecker, balls an' all, than to get that bag. From what the Kid here says he seen, she damn near did that, too." He grabbed his crotch and hefted it. "They wear 'em strapped tight right there. By the time I got to her, she had it, an' she ain't 'bout to let go of it."

Suddenly something began to make sense to Moses. The young Indian leader's interest in Aggie hadn't been born merely out of a desire for the yellow-haired beauty, as he had thought. The chief confused Aggie with this girl. It wasn't booty they were after or whiskey or even the women. They were after vengeance, and they were after Aggie. The bad luck that had haunted the Comanche, Colfax had noted, was likely connected to the loss of that bag as well, and the whites back at the crossing were in deeper trouble than they could imagine.

In a way, Moses was relieved. For the first time he stopped blaming himself for the tragedy of the crossing. It had nothing to do with him or with the time of year or with anything that anyone could have foreseen. He had stumbled into something that was beyond anyone's control. Now, the problem was what to do about it.

"Let me ask you somethin'," the scout said.

"Questions is cheap." Colfax grinned. "It's the answers that get costly. What you want to know?"

"I jus' don't see why you'd be riskin' your hair for a bunch of people you don't even know. What's in it for you?"

Colfax stood for a moment with a sour, pained expression on his face. When Moses's steady gaze didn't waver, the old man's frown disappeared and he winked. "I told you, Mr. Moses," he said. "I admire the way you work. You saved my skin, an' I'm jus' returnin' the favor same as I would for a white man. I always been proud of my democratic leanin's."

"Hadn't we ought to be goin'?" Moses asked. He didn't know what else to say. He couldn't read Colfax at all.

"It ought to be sundown, direc'ly." Carlson scrambled up the makeshift ladder to the trap and stood with his good leg on one rung while he spoke to the Kid or the girl. He then climbed down. Dirt covered his face, but he didn't seem to notice. "It's time," he said. "Let's go."

They knelt down and crawled out through the low opening and back to the outside. The sky was indeed darkening, although a bright sunset forced an extended twilight in the arroyo. Their mounts were where they had left them, Moses noticed to his relief. Frank checked them, and Moses saw that the Kid and the girl were also preparing to climb aboard the two spare horses Colfax had brought with him.

"So what do we do?" Frank asked.

"Well." Carlson rubbed his chin. He had limped more and more during the afternoon, but once aboard his horse, Moses admitted that he looked stronger and more confident than the scout would have expected after the old man's ordeal of the night before. "First we got to find their camp, an' then we'll see."

"That's jus' fine," Frank said without irony. "We jus' goin' to ride in on 'em an' kill 'em all?"

"Not quite." Colfax smiled into the gathering darkness. "Least, not right off. But if that's what it takes, I'll do'er or my name ain't Carlson Colfax, an', by God, you can bet your last screamin' eagle, that's what my mama called me!"

2

ONCE THE STRANGE QUINTET RODE UP OUT OF THE breaks along the river, they discovered that it was not as close to nightfall as they had imagined. The sun hung as a low, red ball on the dusty horizon, and red and pink clouds, like streamers, fled its heat across the sky. The prairie rolled away all around them, and in the eastern distance, the purple hump called Medicine Mountain stood sentinel over a gathering dusk.

"No rain tonight," Colfax mumbled. "Guess we're back to drought."

They rode while the sun fell lower and became redder and redder until it seemed to explode in color from behind the southern end of the landmark mesa with its tiny pecan grove, a sight that made Moses all the more uncomfortable. He continually strained his ears toward the feature's northern end, where, they hoped, the wagon train continued to hold out against a Comanche siege.

Carlson Colfax led the group, still cursing softly under his breath every time his mount's hoof fell on uneven ground and caused him to jolt slightly in the saddle. He was still in a good deal of pain, Moses realized, but he continued to push the horses at a fast walk through the buffalo grass and multicolored wildflowers toward the northwest, often letting the roan jog a bit when the prairie leveled out and afforded a good view of what was ahead.

"I'm gettin' old, goddamnit," he said to no one in particular one time when Moses found himself drawing up parallel to the plainsman. "I can't believe I let a bunch of young frog-fuckers like that sneak up on me an' steal my rifle an' my horse. Would of got this goddamn saddle, too, if I hadn't of let the Kid use the roan that mornin'. I had this Yankee ball-buster since the war. Never thought I'd come to like it, but I guess you can get used to anythin'."

"Why're you doin' this?" Moses asked him again suddenly, and Carlson shot him a narrow, impatient look. "I mean, why're you helpin' me? You got no use for them people down on that creek." Moses paused and chose his words carefully. "I ain't callin' you a liar, but I ain't nobody you'd help. What is it you're after?"

For a moment Colfax didn't speak. "I got to say it, boy, you said a mouthful, an' that's a fact. I spent a good part of my life killin' men better'n you'll ever be, even if you was white. An' I'll say that six days out of seven I wouldn't of gone out of my way for that poor son of a bitch back there." He nodded toward Frank. "Though I'll 'low that he's a good 'nough ol' boy, simple though I think he is." Moses nodded slightly. "An' I ain't fixin' to tell you it's 'cause you saved my skin or nothin'. I can see you're too goddamn smart to keep buyin' that load of horseshit. Anyhow, them goat-dicks wasn't 'bout to kill me. They got bigger snakes to kill'n me. I'm jus' a sore on their peckers right now. Hell, when you come in, I had 'em on the run."

Moses laughed, but his smile was more inward than in agreement with the plainsman. "If I'd of had 'nother minute or two to get my pecker hard, I'd of whipped all of 'em whether you showed up or not."

All at once his voice dropped in tone and turned serious. "Don't get me wrong. I'm 'bliged to you. More beholden'n I been to any son of a bitch, black or white, for more years'n you been alive. But that ain't why I'm goin' out of my way to do more'n give you a full belly an' point you an' that bunch of green jackasses toward Richardson an' say the hell with it." He spat and stared at the fading sunlight.

"The fact of the matter is that you got you a load of whiskey on that train, an' I'm aimin' to save some of it for me. For us. Me an' the Kid, an' the gal too, I reckon."

The statement stunned Moses.

"I can't really say 'xactly why I'm doin'er," Colfax went on. "It's the goddamnedest thing, actu'ly. I'm jus' gettin' old, I guess. Jus' gettin' so nothin' much seems to make me give a damn." He glanced over his shoulder at the Kid and the girl, who were bringing up the rear of the odd processional.

"The Kid back there's jus' a pup. He come out here full of coyote piss 'bout 'the frontier.' I could see he wasn't hell-bent to stay out here for any longer'n he had to, but now he's found that gal, I s'pose that's all she wrote." He shook his head and chuckled. "I don't know what gets into some poor bastard like that when he'd let a female turn his head an' strike him blinder'n a bat. Thinkin' with his pecker, if you ask me." He gauged Moses's reaction and quickly added, "But that's what happened, an' it wouldn't be the first time. Hell's fire, you'd think we was in a preacher's paradise out here, not in the big middle of the emptiest, hottest, coldest, deadliest, goddamnedest country west of the Trinity."

He shook his head, and something soft crossed his eyes. "But that ain't the way the Comanch' see it. They spend most of their time runnin' the goddamn 'Pache off it. They see it as bein' as much theirs as anybody's." He turned slightly and painfully in the saddle, forcing weight down on his injured leg. He squinted hard at Moses. "The truth is, they like it down there for livin' an' here for havin', an' they're scared shitless somebody with lily-white skin an' a Bible is fixin' to come out here an' take it away from 'em so they can't even visit on it. An' they're right."

Colfax leaned forward on his pommel and stared hard at the black scout. "Tell you the truth, boy, I'm inclined to fight with 'em 'stead of 'gainst 'em. 'Cept for one or two ol' boys sittin' on porches an' droolin' in their mush down in San Antone, I don't know that many livin' souls I'd piss on if they was standin' tinder-dry in the middle of a prairie fire."

"So why?" Moses repeated, pressing the point. "Why not jus' ride off an' tell me an' the train to go to hell?"

Colfax reflected for a moment. His horse slowed to a walk. "In a way," he said, "it reminds me of that goddamn bridge back at Antietam Crick an' all them goddamn Bluebellies. We killed 'em an' killed 'em, but they kept on comin'. An' even though we kept right on killin' 'em—kind of like shootin' buff from a stand—kept on pilin' up Yankees one on top of 'nother like cordwood, they jus' kept on till they took that son of a bitch. Bein' dead didn't bother 'em as much as not havin' it. I guess them folks down on Paint Crick an' a thousand more like 'em is the same. This country might not look like much to the Comanch' or nobody else, but if enough folks want it, they'll goddamn take it. An' no Indian—Comanch' or elsewise—is goin' to be able to stop 'em."

He turned again and glared at Moses. "Way I see it, this here's part of the same thing. World don't belong to old farts like me no more. This land—" he swept his arms across the blackness that now completely surrounded them—"this good-for-nothin' land don't belong to me, neither. An' she don't belong to no Comanch', not no more. Way I see it, she belongs to the toughest son of a bitch that can take her an' hold on to her. The Comanch' may have her, but they ain't got a Chinaman's chance in a whorehouse of holdin' on to her, no more'n me an' them poor sons of bitches back there at Antietam could hold that bridge, no more'n me an' Rip Ford an' Sam Walker could hold on to somethin' else out here that we thought was worth a tin shit."

He took another deep breath and stared hard into the inky blackness that enveloped the riders so completely they could barely see one another. "It's jus' like them goddamn soldier boys down to Richardson or Griffin or anywheres else. White or nigger, it don't matter. They're all green. An' their goddamn officers is green. Jus' like that kid back there's green, an' jus' like you're green."

"I've been out here before," Moses said, defending himself.

"Oh, I can *see* that! I can see by the guns you wear an' the way you sit your saddle you *been* out here. I can see you *think* you know what you're goddamn doin'. I can see all of that. But you're greener'n you are black, boy. An' if you wasn't, you wouldn't be in such need of help from an' ol' half-dead son of a bitch like me."

"Maybe I don't," Moses grumbled. "Maybe we'd get on 'thout you."

"An' maybe your black balls'd be hangin' from a Comanch's lance by mornin', too," Carlson declared. "Listen here," he said in a low tone. "I ain't jus' tuggin' at my pecker. I don't know why them Comanch' is after y'all so hot an' heavy. It ain't ord'nary, an' it wasn't counted on, but this ain't a ord'nary country. I'm fixin' to help you 'cause I said I would. An' I'm fixin' to do what I can to bring you through this. I may be old an' half dead, but I know a trick or two yet. An' I suggest you stop countin' the teeth in the mouth of this ol' horse. Jus' take it an' be obliged."

"What 'bout the whiskey?" Moses asked. "I don't think Mr. Graham's goin' to part with none of it."

"Well, I don't know no *Mister* Graham, whoever the hell he is." Colfax spat. "But the way I see it, he don't got no goddamn choice. He can sit on it till it dries up for all I care. Way I see it, he can part with the bug juice or he can part with his hair. It don't make no nevermind to me. Either way, it's a better deal than he'd of got out of them two ol' boys I run up on the other day."

"The hunters?"

"Hunters my ass!" Colfax spat. "Don't you know when somebody's pissin' on your boots? They *looked* like hunters, an' they *smelled* like hunters, an' they even had 'em 'bout half a load of hides to prove it, but they *wasn't* no hunters."

"I don't understand."

"They was hired guns. Comancheros. I knowed one of 'em from the old days down in the Pecos country. I run up on 'im a week or so ago, an' he tried to give me some horseshit 'bout turnin' honest an' doin' some hidin'. But hell, boy, that sorry-assed son of a bitch never used a knife on nothin' bigger'n a man. You can count on it! I s'pect they killed some ol' boys an' stole the hides jus' in case they run into troops or Rangers or somebody who might wonder what they was about. I knowed he was lyin' right off, an' he knowed I knowed. An' that's when he told me they was hired by some rich ol' boy out to Santa Fe. Said a whole goddamn train full of greenhorn sodbusters with a load of high-quality bug juice was comin' 'cross the prairie bound for New Mexico. They was plannin' to take it, kill who they had to, make it look like Indians done it, an' then bring it on in theirselves. I can tell you, they was mean 'nough to do it, too.

"But I got me a idea that the Kid an' me can make good use out of that much kegged Pine Top our ownselves. Hell, them ol' boys up to the 'Dobe Walls'd pay a han'some price for it if nobody else would. Maybe it'd set us up so we could get the hell out of this country, maybe go out to California or someplace where we could make us a good home out of the way of the goddamn sodbusters, Comanch', an' ever'body else who's got a stake in fuckin' up this country." He spat once more and grinned through tobacco-stained teeth.

"I reckoned to throw in with my ol' buddy. Like I

say, the Kid there's a pretty fair hand with a Sharps, an' if we had to kill 'em to make 'em see the right of it, well, the world be better off 'thout couple of prickless cutthroats such as they was.

"Trouble was, time I got down to the Hole to fetch the Kid an' got back to 'em, they was already dead. Kiowa, from the looks of things. Scalped 'em an' skinned 'em. I took their buffalo hides an' wagon an' stored 'em. You seen 'em, seen their wagon, too. An' I was on my way to find you folks my ownself when I run up on them poor Mescans an' got myself caught." He laughed again. "The nub of it, boy, is that I got 'bout as much int'rest as anybody in gettin' rid of them redskins. So y'all got my help whether you want it or not. An' the best you can do is to do what I say, an' maybe I'll jus' leave you be once I get rid of the Comanch' for you an' take what I can haul out of the drinkin' stock. I owe you that much, but don't push it."

With that, Colfax spurred his horse ahead and left Moses riding behind him in the dark, following more by the sound of the roan's footfalls than by sight.

3

THE MOON ROSE AND ILLUMINATED THE PRAIRIE ONCE more with its silvery light, and Moses was astonished that the old frontiersman could find his way through the maze of arroyos, depressions, and cedar groves as he guided them toward the mesa, which now was clearly outlined not only by the moonlight but also by the yellow glow from the Comanche camp.

"How many you reckon they are?" Moses rode up beside Colfax and whispered the question.

"I counted damn near fifty braves, maybe more," he responded. "Likely more, in fact. But they got women with 'em, young'uns too. It's a whole goddamn family, a full band, an' they's likely some Kiowa with 'em now. If what I seen then was right, they was headed this way, too. Like as not, if they hadn't et that skunk, they'd all of pulled out by now. Should of pulled out anyhow. Somethin's keepin' 'em here, though. They're young, like I said, but that jus' makes 'em more dangerous, harder to kill. How many redskins you reckon you killed down there?"

"Hard to tell. I know I dropped eight or ten for sure, but they carry 'em off, or they washed away. We never did get a good count."

"An' how many whites is dead?"

"Thirty, maybe more by now."

"Carried off?"

"I counted 'em as dead."

" 'At's right," Colfax agreed. "I seen 'em kill one of 'em yesterday. Woman. Made me watch it. Did it to scare me, I reckon. Cut her up good, too, goddamnit." Moses shuddered. "They told me they had a bunch, though I let on like I didn't savvy what they was sayin'."

"Well, I jus' hope they're dead by now," Moses said.

"You best hope they ain't," Colfax said sharply. "I'm countin' on 'em hangin' on a mite longer." He reined his horse up and waited until the rest of the entourage closed up.

"What's wrong?" Frank asked as he came close to Moses. His loyalties were obviously torn. By rights, Moses knew, he owed allegiance to the scout and his reluctant partner in the rescue. But he also acknowledged that Carlson Colfax was, in spite of his age and infirmities, in charge of the expedition. The Cottonwood Kid and the girl guided their horses around to Colfax's other side, and as soon as they were all close enough, the plainsman spoke to them in a hoarse whisper.

"Look over yonder." He pointed through the moonlit night toward the mesa. The bright glow Moses and Frank had seen the night before was perceptible from the southern end, indicating a large bonfire.

"From here on," Colfax rasped, "we don't talk. Keep your horses at a walk, an' check your tack so it don't jangle. Since last night, I reckon they're spooked, an' they're goin' to be hard to sneak up on again. Leave your hammers down. I don't want no goddamn shootin' if we can help it. Get your knife ready." The girl immediately unsheathed a large skinning knife and held it up so the moon's light could reflect from the blade.

"You ain't goin' in there," he said to the girl, who looked at him with a blank expression that was just barely visible in the darkness around them. "I know you're itchin' to get that Arkansas toothpick into one of them red bastards, but you're goin' to bide your time." He spoke sharply to her, and Frank stepped between them.

"I think you ought to watch how you talk to her," he said in his simple voice that betrayed no threat or emotion at all.

"I told you to keep your goddamn voice down," Carlson hissed.

"I ain't been talkin'," Frank protested but more quietly now. "You an' him here been carryin' on like a bunch of ol' women."

"We ain't talkin' from here on," Carlson repeated. "Nobody is that wants to keep his hair. You let on you're anywheres nearer'n San Antone, an' the rest of us'll jus' ride off an' leave your sorry ass." He turned to the girl. "When we get up there a ways, you hold the horses. The rest of you stay back of me an' keep your goddamn yaps shut."

He turned his roan around and rode off into the night with the rest following in silent single file.

THE MOON CLIMBED HIGHER in the sky, and Moses judged it to be near midnight when Colfax silently drew his horse up and waited until the four riders who followed him clustered near enough for him to speak to them.

"We walk from here," he whispered in a tone so soft that Moses wasn't sure he had actually heard it.

Colfax climbed down and pulled the bandanna from his head to wrap across his horse's nose. Moses dug around in his bay's saddlebag and did the same, and the others followed suit. Just over the plainsman's shoulder the glow from clustered Comanche fires illuminated the night sky. Bull bats and night birds chasing insects swooped down into the golden light that quickly dissipated in the moon's silver, softer glow. A sharp rise of ground prevented them from actually seeing the Indian fires, but they could hear shouts and cries coming from the near campsite.

Once the horses' noses were muffled, Colfax gathered the reins and handed them to the girl without a word. She accepted them, then squatted in the tall grass. The plainsman was armed only with his pistols and a knife and a small leather bag, which he checked quickly before moving off through the grass and causing Moses and Frank and the Kid to have to hurry to follow him, lest the tall strands close behind him and hide his trail.

Just as they came to a point where the rise crested, Colfax dropped down on one knee and pulled a flask out of his bag. He opened the top and sprinkled something on his shoulders and feet, then he handed it to the Kid, who did the same. Frank followed in turn, and Moses accepted the small tin bottle from him and sniffed it. Whatever it was stank with a pungent, sour aroma, worse than skunk, worse than a privy. He touched Colfax on the shoulder lightly to get his attention and raised his eyebrows in a question.

"Horse piss," the old Ranger hissed at him after pressing his bearded face to Moses's ear. "Dogs won't smell us that way. Won't chase us, neither." He then moved away, not standing now, but duck-walking through the grass, two awkward steps at a time for almost fifty yards. The plainsman's injured leg was thrust out awkwardly to prevent it from bending, and he moved through the deep grass silently.

Once again he stopped, and the four men bunched up once more, and Colfax put a finger to his mustache, which was now visible in the reflected light from the Comanche fires.

After checking to make sure they were all with him, Colfax crawled away on his belly. Using his arms and hands, he slithered through the grass stems like a snake, careful not to disturb them any more than he had to as his body made its way to the crest of the rise some distance away. Moses followed, and behind him he felt rather than heard Frank and the Kid bringing up the rear.

When Colfax finally stopped and lay still, Moses crawled up next to him, with Frank flanking him on the other side. The Kid remained slightly behind them, silent as ever, propped up on his elbows with his rifle at the ready as he watched their rear. As quietly and with as little motion as he could manage, Colfax parted the grass in front of them and peered down into the steep decline of ground that concaved away from them all the way up to the base of the large mesa.

The Indians' camp itself was laid out in a triangular fashion, with the widest side up against the base of the mesa and anchored by twin teepees. A third buffalo-hide tent marked the apex of the campsite and was only about a hundred yards from the men who secretly viewed it. Other, smaller teepees were erected with no discernible pattern throughout the camp, and a large remuda of horses—the band's caviard—was staked off to one side, guarded by several young Indians on their own mounts.

It was the center of the camp, however, which caught their attention and held it in horrible fascination. Small fires burned everywhere, but a giant bonfire was snapping and crackling from its cedar fuel in the middle of the triangular layout. Encircling it were a dozen human figures. They were naked and their arms and legs were pinned to the ground by stakes that were crusted with their dried blood.

Indian women moved about the spread-eagled captives and paid little attention to them. The victims themselves lay still. At first Moses assumed they were dead, but as he watched one or another would move slightly, raise a head, and attract the notice of a squaw, who would come over and strike all of them with a stick or arrow.

Moses was transfixed by the sight. Frank, also, was staring through the parted grass with a glazed expression of terror on his face. He was almost shaking, and Moses suddenly remembered that Frank still believed his daughter was down there.

The Kid apparently was watching Frank as well. As the simple man gathered his knees under him, the boy reached out and put a hand in the small of his back and pressed down hard. Frank responded to the staying gesture, and he lowered his face into his grimy hands and remained still, although Moses could tell that he was shaking and almost out of control.

An Indian emerged from one of the near teepees and stood for a moment before throwing a buffalo robe over his shoulder and striding over toward the large fire. Even though he was not wearing his headdress, the bright stripes on his cheek and the mirror he wore around his neck identified him as the shaman Moses had confronted the night before. The medicine man stood for a moment and studied each victim lying on the ground, but he made no particular motion toward any of them.

The shaman continued his rounds. Finally he stopped next to what Moses had assumed was a pile of buffalo robes and animal pelts and reached into it. From the distance between the observers and the camp below them, it seemed that the Indian did indeed possess magical powers. He thrust his arm into the pile of hides, which suddenly began writhing and moving of its own accord, and when he withdrew his hand, he was holding on to a short, black-haired woman who appeared to have come to life and was now pulling hard against the Comanche's strength.

She wore an underdress of dull gray, but it was torn and ripped. She had no shoes and dug her bare heels into the dusty ground of the camp when the Comanche dragged her away from the pile, which Moses now realized had other human figures in it as well. Her mouth was open, but no cry came from her while she was pulled across the campsite. Suddenly, the scout recognized her as one of the Autrey girls. Their father had been cut down in the stupid, fatal charge that the white men had mounted against the first attack, and her mother and sister, Moses remembered, were among the dead women who lay on the banks of the crossing.

The medicine man held but one of her wrists, and her other hand grasped his and tried to pry his fingers away. Behind her in the pile, four or five women were now discernible as they huddled together and watched the girl being taken away. Their heads were well up, and Moses counted each and silently named those he recognized. He knew there were more, and children as well, and he searched the campsite for signs of them, but he saw nothing.

"Where're the rest?" he whispered softly into Colfax's hairy, wrinkled ear, but the plainsman only shook his head.

The girl's cries were now audible to them as the medicine man drew her closer to the teepee from which he had come. She kicked and screamed at him, and from time to time, Moses saw, she tried to draw his grasping hand close enough to her mouth to bite him, but he cuffed her hard when she began to struggle too violently. Finally, he dragged her to the tent and thrust her inside.

Another brave came out from another teepee and looked around. Moses strained his eyes to see better, but the figures below, well lighted as they were, were often covered with smoke from the greenwood fire, and he had trouble discerning the hideous extent of their injuries.

The second Indian also went to the women, who had once again huddled down into a tight pile, and made a selection. He came up with a redheaded girl of the Hill family. Moses recollected that she was no more than twelve or thirteen, truly a child, and his stomach tightened as he watched the brave swing her high in his arms as he wrenched her away from the hands of the other females, who had tried to shield her.

Under other circumstances, the scene would have looked playful, a man—really only a teenager—swinging a young child high in the air and causing her to squeal with delight. But the sounds which came up the rise to the ears of the watching men were anything but those of play. Terror filled the camp as the girl's shrieks were joined by cries of the remaining women, who alternately cursed and pleaded with the Comanche to release her. Squaws quickly rallied themselves, however, and with stout cedar sticks and clubs they beat the protesting women until they fell silent. The brave walked away with his struggling, crying prize and in the same manner as his comrade flung her inside his tent.

Moses felt his muscles tightening, and only by forcing himself and digging his fingers into the loamy soil beneath him could he remain still. He glanced at Colfax, who had not moved a muscle but continued studying the scene with cold detachment.

Moses wondered if this was what the plainsman meant by hoping that the captives were still alive, still hanging on. Once more his doubts about Colfax's sanity arose, and he glanced at Frank, who still had his face covered and had not moved. He wanted to act, but before he could decide what he might do, Colfax looked at the black scout and scowled. He motioned for Moses to look once more on the grisly horror that was being acted out in the depression below the men.

The Autrey girl, now naked, burst from the teepee and fell forward to the ground. It was hard to tell whether she had been trying to run away or if she had been thrown out by her Indian captor. It was also hard to see if she was alive; she lay absolutely still. Two squaws moved over to her and began pushing at her with sticks, but she refused to react, and they struck her with greater intensity until she rolled over and tried to protect herself from their blows. One Indian woman reached out and grabbed her by her long black hair and dragged her along the ground. Her screams lit the entire camp. For a moment, Moses feared the squaw was going to scalp her alive, and he knew he couldn't bear to watch it without trying to help her. He braced himself to rise and shoot and hoped that Colfax or Frank would do the same, but before he could tear his eyes away from what he was sure was about to happen, a nudge brought his attention back to his companions. Colfax pointed at the circle of bodies once more.

The two nearest victims were men, Moses saw, and his groin tightened automatically when he saw the bloody stains that appeared between their legs. The rest, however, were female. The blood on their chests, he realized, was from where the Indians had cut away their breasts, and two of them were also bleeding from other cuts and defacements.

He once more sought the Autrey girl. She was now bound tightly and hauled over to the fire, where other Indian women poked at her with sharp sticks that were coal-red on the ends from having been heated in the fire. A hackberry tree stood at one end of the camp, and after a few moments of torture, she was dragged to it and hauled up by her wrists. Only her toes touched the ground. The women stabbed her and pelted her with rocks.

A new scream tore the air around the camp, and Moses's glance dropped once more to the circle of figures around the fire. One of the men was writhing and rolling in spite of the bloody stakes that kept him in a mock crucifixion near the spitting blaze. Two women had brought live coals and were placing them on his exposed stomach, manipulating them with sharpened mesquite sticks. His shrieks echoed across the camp and brought the attention of everyone except the gray huddle of women, who continued to cling to each other as if their mutual touching would postpone their fates.

Moses had seen enough, and he motioned to Colfax that they should go. The Kid, impassive as ever, continued to rest with one hand on Frank's back. Frank had recovered himself and was staring at the scene below him. Colfax nodded, and without uttering a sound, he turned and crawled with the same, slow, slithering motion he had used on his approach back toward where they had left the horses.

4

"MY GREAT BLEEDIN' JESUS GOD, THAT'S WORSE'N anythin' I ever seen!" Frank's voice rose as soon as they had recovered the horses and ridden in silence a mile or so away from the camp.

"*Whisper*, goddamnit," Colfax barked in a hoarse hiss. "You want to join 'em?"

"Well, they're fixin' to notice soon 'nough," Frank said. He pulled out his pistol and checked the load, something he had done often since leaving the rise behind them in the darkness.

"Not till we're ready," Colfax said evenly.

"You mean we're jus' fixin' to ride off an' leave 'em down there?"

"Them people is dead already," Colfax said.

"The hell they are!" Frank cried, forgetting again to lower his voice. "Can't you hear that? My Lottie's down there, goddamnit." His simple face in the narrow light was wide with distress.

"No, she's not," Moses interrupted. "She's back at the train."

Frank spun on Moses. His voice fell to a menacing whisper. "What kind of damn fool you take me for, nigger? Don't you try to put one over on me. I ain't as sharp as Cap'n Graham, but I'll kill you sure 'nough."

"You ain't fixin' to kill nobody," Colfax said gruffly, then he turned and walked away, taking the Kid by his arm and leading in turn the girl with him off out of earshot.

"It's a fact," Moses said. "She was trapped in the Hollister wagon. I seen her go there durin' the last raid, an' I heard her there 'fore we left."

"An' you left her there? Why didn't you tell me?"

"Mr. Graham didn't want me to," Moses said. "He said he'd take care of it when we was gone."

Frank was silent for a moment. "You best be tellin' me the truth," he said. "I swear to God Almighty, I'll skin you alive if I could of helped that girl an' went ridin' off with you instead."

Before Moses could say anything else, Colfax moved back to them. "You simmered down?" he asked Frank. Frank didn't reply, and the plainsman turned to Moses and said loud enough for Frank to hear, "We can't do them people no good at all. But if I got it reckoned right, they can still help us out. Least they can help you out."

"I don't know if we can do that," Frank said, too loudly again, and then quickly lowered his voice. "I can't jus' ride off an' leave 'em like that. They're better off dead."

"Ain't no arguin' 'bout that," Colfax hissed. "But they done 'bout all the killin' they're goin' to do on them poor sons of bitches." He spat into the darkness. "You goddamn greenhorns give me the bellyache. Look. They done killed them men, or damn near it. Wouldn't live nohow. They're not goin' to kill them women any more'n they have to. They're jus' softenin' the young'uns up. Make slaves out of 'em, or wives, or they'll trade 'em off, them that don't up an' die on 'em. If they raise too much hell, they'll stake 'em out or hang 'em up. In a way, you could say them sorry bastards're luckier'n most. I seen men skinned an' roasted alive over a slow fire. This ain't half as bad as that."

"You got a peculiar notion of things," Frank said and turned away.

"Maybe I do," Colfax agreed, "but I can tell you one goddamn thing, we're better off'n I thought we was."

"How's that?" Moses whispered.

"Well, they's Comanch' an' Kiowa down there, all right. An' that's not good. But they's mostly young pups, like I said. They ain't likely but 'bout half sure what they're 'bout. Hell, most of 'em's only heard tell 'bout this sort of thing. Likely the squaws know more 'bout it than the bucks do. It's a good bet they're scared shitless an' can't even talk 'bout it 'mongst theirselves for fear of lettin' on."

"I still don't like leavin' 'em down there." Frank was brooding off a few paces and only muttered his comment. His voice carried, however, and all of them were reminded of how close the Indians were.

Colfax turned to Frank. "You jus' go hellin' on down in there an' see how far you get. You might even knock off one or two 'fore they get a rawhide rope 'round you an' have you dressed up like a Sunday roaster. Now, I don't care one way or 'nother. But you ain't goin' to do them poor sons of bitches no good, an' you'll get your own tit in a ringer sure 'nough." He waited a beat or two before going on. "I got me a plan, an' if it works, ever'thin'll be jus' like I told you, or my name ain't Carlson Colfax!"

"What's the plan?" Moses said, to cut him off. He was no happier than Frank was about leaving the women down there at the mercy of the Comanche. He had, like Frank, believed that Colfax was planning to lead them right down into the camp while the Indians were vulnerable and preoccupied. But in thinking it over, he decided Colfax was right. They wouldn't get five feet.

Colfax stared at him for a moment. "I got a look at the lay of the land, seen the odds. Now, we got to get to the crick," he said. "I got to see if they's anybody left down there who can use a gun. An' they's one or two other things I need to look over." He paused, and Moses imagined that he winked at him, but in the darkness he couldn't be sure. "It jus' comes down to whether them people want to live or not their ownselves. Once I see that, I'll let you know."

"I think we have a right to know now," Moses insisted.

"You can think till you turn white," Colfax growled. "I'll tell you in my own goddamn good time. I don't like to chew my cabbage more'n once. For now, you can do as I tell you an' damn well like it or not. It's all one to me."

With that he lay down right where he'd been standing and looped his horse's reins around his wrist. He pulled his hat off and placed it under his head and studied the heavens. The moon was shrouded inside a misty ring. "I was wrong 'bout the drought. Mark me, it's goin' to come a turd floater tomorrow. If it comes early, that'll be to the good." He lay back and tucked his hat beneath his head. "Y'all wake me 'fore moonset," he said. "Right now, I'm fixin' to get some shut-eye. By an' by there's goin' to be some killin' called for, an' I'm a ol' man. I need my rest."

PART SIX

THE VALLEY OF THE HIGH SNOWS

CHAPTER ONE

1

AFTER HIS SURPRISE ENCOUNTER WITH GOLDA Runnels, Graham was unable to stop shaking. He wasn't sure whether the reaction was simply nerves or something more serious was wrong with him.

He spotted four children struggling toward him. Two of them—boys—were heavily laden with rifles and gun-belts, and the other two, the girls, were dragging a huge crate. For a moment Graham was confused, and then he remembered: the Simmons clan.

The boys were breathless when they struggled up to him, and the girls all but gave out and finally just sat atop the heavy crate, allowing the rope handles to droop.

"Here's Pa's guns," the older boy said. "I took me a Winchester, an' Bud here got a Henry, a sixteen-shooter." Bud hardly looked big enough to heft the huge rifle. "All of us has somethin', even the girls. You want the powder guns too?"

"Not now," he said. "But keep them loaded and handy. They might be needed."

Graham reached out and relieved the boy of a Sharps. It had been a while since he had hefted one of the big .50s, and he wondered that he had ever thought he could handle such a weapon.

Hilda Simmons appeared from around the slight turn in the bluff and strode deliberately toward the small group. Graham braced himself for trouble.

She came past the girls with barely a look at them and then walked right up to Graham. In her hands was a brace of shiny .44s, top-strap cartridge revolvers in a fancy black holster with silver inlay. They looked brand-new.

"These here's Bob's pride an' joy," she said, staring directly into Graham's eyes. "He said for you to give 'em to somebody who felt good enough to shoot 'em. But he said for you to look to 'em. He wants 'em back." She giggled slightly and covered her snuff-stained front teeth with a gnarled hand. "Sometimes I think that man's crazier 'bout them guns than he is 'bout his young'uns."

Graham nodded and tried to meet her gaze. The woman had lost her mind. Her pale blue eyes seemed washed empty in the yellow sunlight. He was familiar with that look, the vacuity of the helplessly mindless. It was different from the mad rage he had seen in Golda Runnels's eyes, and it was different from the shock and fear that drove men crazy and sent them scurrying pell-mell from battle and a charging enemy. This was hopeless insanity.

"I was tellin' your children to go find a place to shoot from," Graham said flatly, then added with a thought of the family's loss, "An' to keep their heads down."

"They's good kids," she said. "You want somethin' done, they'll do'er." She looked back at the girls, who had recovered their wind and were again struggling with the huge crate. "I got to get back to Bob, case he wakes up an' needs tendin'." She whirled around and popped the younger boy gently on the head. "Toby," she said, "get to doin' what Mr. Graham says." And she trudged off, the weight of her madness almost visible on her stooped shoulders.

The crate, Graham found after he had loaded the rifles and stored them in his wagon, contained powder and shot as well as rimfire cartridges of varying calibers. There was a loading press, and a box of brass sleeves as well. He sent the Simmons children back to their posts with a caution to get some rest and mostly to stay out of sight of the opposite bank of the creek, then he squatted and began sorting the ammunition.

The grinding sound of footsteps forced Graham to look up to face whatever new problem was approaching. But it was Aggie Sterling coming toward him, and in her left hand was the welcome sight of a teapot. Her right hand carried a plate with a tin cup on it. She looked startlingly different to him, and he frowned and tried to figure out what about her had changed.

"Here," she said. "Jus' stay down there an' rest. You can't keep goin' without somethin' to eat an' some sleep. There's tea in here. I found some joint fir growing along here, an' I crushed some berries an' put those in as well for sweetenin', but they make it more bitter, like as not. Mama used to say joint fir'd make a owl sleep through the night." She smiled at him, and Graham surrendered and squatted back into the sandy gravel beside the wagon.

There was an odor about her, something wonderful and clean, and all at once he realized she had bathed. Her hair was still wet and pulled back behind her head. Her skin shone from scrubbing, and the pleasant perfume of soap seemed to rise from her in perceptible waves of freshness. She had discarded the other torn and bloody dress.

"I heard 'bout what you done up there to Mr. Runnels," she said. "It scared me." She gestured with her shoulder behind her. "I reckon it scared them more'n anybody. You're the only one knows what to do." She poured the tea into the tin cup and continued in the same flat voice, "Least you're the only one 'sides Mr. Franklin, an' he's gone. You got to be careful, or somebody's goin' to sneak up on you."

Graham hid his discomfort behind the cup and began scooping up food and shoveling it into his mouth. He was terribly hungry, he discovered. The plate rested comfortably on his stump, and he noticed her watching him and slowed his chewing. "I doubt that Mrs. Runnels shares your sentiment," he said around a mouthful of beans. "She came at me with an ax."

"It wouldn't do for you to go an' get yourself killed over some foolishness," Aggie said.

"How is the Runnels woman?" Graham managed to ask around another full mouth. "I hit her pretty hard."

"She's down there nursin' Mr. Runnels, so I reckon she'll be all right. He will, too," she continued, "if you'll quit hittin' him with stovewood." She lowered her face to hide a laugh, Graham thought, but when she looked up at him, there was nothing but seriousness in her face.

"Should've killed him," Graham said, more to himself

than to Aggie. "What about the two, uh . . . wounded men? The ones you said were the worst?"

"They died," she said. "Two more besides. But there's a boy—Hilda found him—Jed Ambrose, he's worked wonders on them arrowheads. I think he got most all of 'em out. It'll help, if it don't kill 'em."

"You had to, uh . . . cauterize any more?"

She shook her head. "Won't do any of the rest any good. More've died than I thought would."

He groped for a way to change the subject. "How in hell did you manage to clean yourself up?"

"I took a bath!" She grinned. In Graham's eyes, the sunlight was dimmed by her smile. "I'll get my sister cleaned up, an' the Herbert girl, too. Mrs. Kruikshank's goin' to as well."

"It could be dangerous," Graham muttered. "What if the Indians come back?"

"Then we'll die clean."

"You look more than clean," he muttered to her, embarrassed by having begun a compliment he would now have to finish. "You look . . . damn near radiant."

"You do flatter a girl, Mr. Graham," she said, laughing. "But you might work on your manners." He blushed deeply, and she laughed again. "It's all right. I ain't used to manners anyhow. I just couldn't stand myself, an' my dress was too tore up an' bloody to keep on. We had the spring. Couldn't see any harm could come from usin' it."

Graham nodded and set the plate by. He sipped the tea, which had cooled sufficiently to allow him to drink. The food and warm narcotic in the drink were already working on his body. He felt himself physically relaxing for the first time since they had encountered the Indians two days before.

"We sure could use a doctor," she said. "Men are dyin' that might not if they had a doctor. I can't help but feel that all I'm doin' is helpin' them men die."

"You need some rest yourself," Graham said. "You look like you're about to fall down." He shouldn't have put it that way, he thought as soon as he said it. "I told that Quigley fellow to come in an' give you a hand. Hannah, too."

"Oh, I lay down now an' then." She forced a smile

that struck his heart like a knife blade. "Hannah Morgan did come in to help me. She's not much account. She won't hardly touch a bloody rag to save her life. But I had one or two others in there before. I guess they felt sorry for me. Mr. Quigley ain't shown up yet. I'd just as soon he didn't. I got all I can handle with Mrs. Fulbright. Hannah said they'd bring in some of your whiskey, though. We're beholden."

Graham imagined that they felt anything but sorry for Aggie Sterling, and he was reminded that the whiskey was as much hers as his. At least she was heiress to half of it. But he said nothing.

"The main thing," she said, "is for you to watch yourself. There's people on this train that wouldn't mind if you *was* dead, an' I'm not just talkin' 'bout Mrs. Runnels."

"I'm not too worried."

"All the same." Aggie's brow furrowed. "You watch out. Hannah said she'd watch your back, but she's lookin' out for me, too. She don't say so, but I know she is. She can't be two places at once."

"I'll be all right," Graham insisted. "You do what you can for the wounded, an' I'll handle the train." He resented the lecture on his personal safety from the girl, and he especially hated the idea that Hannah had taken on the role of protector. But in spite of his wounded pride, he also appreciated it. "Don't worry about me," he added softly.

"I don't." Aggie smiled brightly once more, and then she straightened her lips into a serious expression. "I got my own to worry about."

She refilled his cup and rose to go. "You go on an' finish that, an' I'll be back for the cup direc'ly."

He didn't want her to go, and he stopped her with a question. "How old are you, Aggie?"

She turned and gave him a disapproving smile. "Now, ain't you the familiar one? I don't remember you askin' if you could call me by my given name."

Graham knew he should have felt embarrassed, but he desperately wanted her to stay by him, and he fought down abashment and tried to bluff the game out. "I just wanted to know if you were old enough for me to start callin' you Miss Sterlin'." He tried to smile over the steaming cup.

"Well, *Mister* Graham," she said and knelt down beside him, "I'm eighteen, an' I got me a beau back in Arkansas who says he's goin' to come out an' marry me soon's he can." She smiled again, but there was a faraway look in her eyes that made Graham wonder. "So you better get used to callin' me *Missus* pretty soon." She looked away, and he couldn't read her expression.

Graham felt disappointment sliding down on him, but he tried to hide it. "Well, *Miss* Sterlin'," he said through a half-grin, "I just wanted to know."

"How old are *you*, Mr. Graham?" she asked, still teasing.

"Nearly fifty, forty-eight anyway," he said. "Old enough to be your daddy." The last was an admission he had been making to himself since the first time he set eyes on her. More reluctantly he acknowledged he was almost old enough to be her *grand*daddy.

"You was in the war, wasn't you?" she asked, spreading her skirt and settling down on her bottom and holding the teapot loosely in one hand. The tea was working hard on Graham now, and he felt himself relaxing. "You fought with the Yankees."

"Yeah," he said, going flush. "That's how I met your daddy the first time."

"He wasn't no soldier."

"No." Graham shook his head, thinking of Sterling again. "He never was."

"He was a horse thief." This was offered without inflection. "Some folks said he was worse'n that."

"If he was, I didn't know about it." He was lying, and he knew that she knew it. They both looked away and were silent.

"It ain't your fault," she answered him. "I'm sorry I pointed that shotgun at you when you wanted to put them folks out of their misery. I know you was right, but I just couldn't let you do that."

He hesitated and swallowed hard. "Aggie," he said, deliberately using her first name, "there's somethin' you need to know."

"I already know." She stood. "I said it ain't your fault, an' I meant it."

"I don't think you know all of it." He swallowed again and pretended to inspect his cigar. "I killed your daddy. I shot him. I had to. He was hurt bad, an' it would've been awful." There, he thought, he'd played the card. It was said, or most of it anyway.

"I know," she said, but there was nothing in her eyes to tell him what she was thinking. They had turned again into the cold blue mirrors that seemed to defy the world's hurt. "They told me about it," she said. "Hannah knew 'bout it, too."

"I just shot him," Graham said. He felt like crying suddenly and fought back the emotional wave. What was wrong with him? He wondered if it was the strange tea. He felt like just shutting his eyes and drifting away. "I'd want somebody to do the same for me," he admitted softly. "But that's not all of it. I shot him because he—"

"Look, Mr. Graham; uh . . . Cleve," she said, and she lowered her eyes in embarrassment. "My daddy wasn't a very good man. He beat Mama an' me, an' he beat Jason a lot." She blushed. "Beatin's not all he wanted to do, not all he done." She turned even redder and looked away in shame, then her color gave way to a blush that grew out of anger. "He *was* a horse thief, an' a coward, an' worse. An' he was a liar an' a cheat. Likely he deserved hangin'. I know it. You likely know it. Most everybody who had any dealin's with him would find it out sooner or later. Mama hated him. She was scared of him, an' he beat her for that, too. But she's dead now. So's he. An' you shot him. If you hadn't, somebody else would have. I might have. Jason might have. Somebody would have. Or they'd hung him sooner or later. He was a bad man, and by an' by, it had to catch up to him."

She had hardened her eyes, and Graham saw a fiery wrath behind them. "I don't mean no disrespect. I mean, he's just lying right out there, an' it don't do to talk bad of the dead. But when you shot him, you made my life easier. Jason's too. An' Annie's. It means Todd might— it means—" Her eyes flared with the same hardness Graham had seen before. "It means more than I can really say."

"Where is, uh . . . this Todd?"

"He's out on the plains somewhere, I think," Aggie said, her eyes again taking on a distant, doubtful look. "He had some trouble with his uncle, an' my daddy, Jack, run him off, too. He's rich."

"Rich," Graham repeated dumbly.

"Well, he will be. He's huntin' buffalo for a while, but he said he'd come to New Mexico an' get me."

"Do you think he will?" Graham wasn't pleased with the question, and he dreaded the answer. What man in his right mind would fail to go to the edge of the earth to find this girl? "I mean, do you think he can find us?"

"I don't know." She was suddenly serious. "He's just a boy, an' he's hardheaded. If he hears that Jack's dead, he might. He was some scared of him, I think." She paused. "Then, he might meet somebody else."

Graham fell silent. The cigar, unlit and forgotten, dangled in his fingers. Killing Jack might have given him more problems than he at first thought. He could handle Jack Sterling alive. He wondered if he could handle Aggie with Jack dead and this Todd always on the horizon. "I still feel bad about it," he said. "An' about your mama."

"Can't be helped," she said. Then she wrinkled her forehead and looked at him seriously. "You need to get some sleep," she said. "I'll come back direc'ly an' check on you."

Graham started to protest, but he felt too weak, too tired, to do much more than shake his head. Before he could find words, she started away, and then she turned back, knelt quickly, and kissed him on the cheek. "You know, Cleve Graham," she whispered again, "I don't think you're near as mean as you want folks to think you are." She held his bearded face in her hands and showered him with a smile. "Now I got nobody to look after me. No mama, no daddy. Neither does Annie an' Jason. I guess you took us on when you shot my daddy. An' that's fine with me. Now, you get some sleep. There's more than a bunch of orphaned young'uns lookin' to you to get us out of this." She beamed at him, and his heart grew, opened, reached out for her. Then her expression changed. Her forehead wrinkled. "If you can, after it gets dark, could you see if you can crawl out to Daddy's body?"

"Why?"

"I sure could use his boots," she said. "It sounds awful, but these shoes is wore out, an' I ain't got no others." She held up her skirt and exposed the battered toe. The leather was worn completely through; he could see two of her toes.

He nodded, and she smiled again. "You call me if you need me," she said.

Then she was gone. He found himself as helpless as a rag doll, staring at the toes of his own dusty boots and holding the cigar in his lap. His cheek burned from where her lips had quickly bussed his whiskers, and he could feel her hands on his face. He was warm inside, and he fought to capture the sensation and hold on to it permanently. Try as he might, though, he couldn't keep feelings of guilt from creeping around, spoiling it for him.

He had told her most of the truth, he thought, about why he had shot Jack. But he hadn't told her that he had enjoyed it, that he hoped the bullet would also free her for him. But she didn't look upon him that way, he realized. Her kiss told him that much. She was fond of him, surely, but she kissed him the way a girl kisses a favorite uncle or grandfather. She only saw him as some kind of substitute for Jack, someone to watch over her until some beardless ridgerunner from Arkansas found her and carried her off. He wondered if he could put up with that, and he understood that he probably had very little choice. What was more confusing, he thought, was that she seemed actually relieved, even pleased, that he had shot her father. That couldn't be right, he thought, but then what had she meant when she said that beating her wasn't *all* Jack wanted to do?

It's all been for nothing, he told himself with a wince, and then he forced the thought away as he continued to drift under the tea's narcotic and, mentally, to avoid the specter of Jack Sterling's dark, laughing face. Then he let his mind wander back to his first trip west, to Santa Fe, and to what lay before him.

"I'm a gambler," he muttered as he eased into a heavy sleep and thoughts took over where whispered words died out. And I'm lucky. All I need is one more hand to pay out.

He made a halfhearted effort to move over to where he could see Jack Sterling's corpse from beneath the wagon, but the maneuver required too much, and he gave it up. He wanted to sleep, that was all. Finally, he gave up and let himself go.

2

CLEVELAND GRAHAM'S SUCCESS AS A GAMBLER WAS truly never so much a matter of luck as the result of supreme indifference. Whether he won or lost was as immaterial to him as was which of the several whores who flounced around the boats' parlors he took to bed after a night's gaming was over. Most people who knew him believed he was capable of tremendous control, that he had a priceless poker face that could display disinterest regardless of what cards he was holding. Little did anyone imagine that Graham's lack of expression grew less out of a true impassivity than out of an internal despair. He had come to believe that he was one of the luckiest men alive, that his walking around while so many men lay dead in his wake was some sort of huge cosmic accident.

The waning days of the war had seen every conceivable kind of river trash and scalawag boarding the huge side-wheelers up and down the Mississippi, Ohio, and Missouri rivers, and Graham's opponents across the tables were sometimes desperate, vicious men who had little to lose and less patience to spend on anyone who won it from them. He wore his pistols prominently and constantly and carried a small sleeve gun as well.

He stayed with stud poker in spite of the social stigma it carried. Keno and faro were risky games, too attractive to tinhorns and cheats. Poker was a game he could control, and it fit his inward passivity perfectly. It was also a one-handed man's game, and the rubes and greenhorns suddenly pouring into the defeated South with money stuffed into carpetbags were easy marks for seasoned gamblers on the waterways of the far Midwest.

Eventually, Graham came to regard Jefferson, Texas, as home. Although he would take riverboat trips down the

Red River and up and down the Mississippi from time to time, he learned that establishing himself as a tough opponent in Jefferson was a profitable and reasonably safe venture. He came and went for months at a time, but when anyone asked where he was from, that was the city he named.

It was in Jefferson, though, that his life took another of the unexpected turns he had come to believe were unique to him. One evening, he had been playing for hours in a small saloon in Blood Alley along the waterfront. He had been winning a little and losing most of it back when a large ugly man with the aura of the frontier about him sat down across the table and entered the game. After several hands he became aware that Graham was bluffing his way into most of the money. He was a gangly old man whose brown teeth looked more like fangs, and whose bulbous nose had a large red scar running down its length. He stank of horses and was already drunk when he sat down. His beard was long, white, and unkempt, and after a few more losing hands, Graham noticed that his apparently unconscious stroking of his facial hair was a not-so-subtle way of concealing key cards which he could then extract when he needed them.

Graham tolerated the sloppy cheating for a hand or two, and then he calmly announced that he was retiring.

"You can't quit," the old man raged suddenly. "You got most of their money an' all of mine." He gestured around the table. The other players looked embarrassed. Experience told them that it was more than bad form to challenge Cleve Graham. It could also be dangerous.

"Look, friend," Graham said, "I've had enough. I'm going to find a lady and then go up to my room and to bed. You can stay down here an' sharp these fellows if they're of a mind to keep playin' with a light deck, but I'll say good night."

"Are you callin' *me* a cheat? I don't s'pose you're wantin' me to believe that all that pile in front of you is honestly come by?"

Graham kept his eyes on the man's hand, which was kneading the bunched whiskers. He pulled his cash toward him and stacked it. "Good night, gentlemen," he said.

"You ain't quittin'," the old man said matter-of-factly. "You can't jus' sit there an' call a man a cheat an' then jus' sashay off like you didn't do nothin' more'n break wind or nothin'."

"I said good night," Graham said firmly. He kept his eyes on the old man's continual beard stroking. All at once he saw the gnarled fingers reaching inside the white mane deeply enough to find a weapon, and Graham calmly placed his hand on his .36-caliber Colt's Navy.

The man saw the move and pulled his hand from inside his whiskers quickly. Gripped in it was a huge skinning knife that caused a gasp of surprise from around the table.

The man slashed backhanded at Graham, aiming for his throat, but Graham lowered his chin rapidly and felt a quick, cool sensation cross his face. He glanced down and was more surprised than alarmed to see blood gushing onto his brocade vest and spilling onto the green felt of the table. It doused his money and glistened in the light as it pooled on the worn cloth.

The other two players scrambled to their feet, but the old frontiersman was faster than they reckoned. He used the knife Indian-style and slashed both of them open before they could escape his arm's range.

Graham's hand tightened on his Colt's, and he pulled it, cocked it, and fired twice directly into the old man's chest, knocking him backward and sending one ball directly through him, wounding the bartender.

When the old man's body was searched, a small revolver was found concealed in a breast pocket along with several face cards. Graham had a bad cut on his chin that ran in a sharp line across his lower left cheek, but a drunken doctor appeared on the scene, and after bathing the wound with raw alcohol, he stitched it up right there in the room. The other two players the old man had ripped were dying and had to be carried out on doors that were taken down and used as litters. Trails of blood led across the floor and traced the sheriff's way to where Graham sat next to the ruined table.

Witnesses told the sheriff they weren't certain who had started the fight, and the sheriff, alarmed by the degree of violence and weary of Graham's seemingly incessant attraction for trouble, was anxious for an arrest. But just when the sheriff was preparing to march Graham off to the Calaboose, a man stepped forward and claimed that he had seen the whole thing. Graham had done all he could to avoid the fight, he averred, and he wasn't guilty of anything more than defending his own life.

Graham squinted at the man, who busied himself by collecting the bloody bills and coins from the upturned table and handing them carefully to Graham. He was young, and he cut a dashing figure in spite of a thin mustache and small, dark eyes that seemed constantly to search the room behind whoever he was talking to. Graham knew he had seen him before, but he didn't know where. The stranger's testimony was reluctantly accepted, and Graham wasn't charged with any crime. Because it was Graham's second problem over a card table in Jefferson in less than two years, the sheriff suggested that he take to the river trade again, which he did on the next boat.

It wasn't until Jefferson disappeared around a bend on the Big Cypress that he remembered the name of the stranger who had helped him. It was the same man who had sold him horses on the Natchez Trace during the war almost ten years before: Jack Sterling. He stopped downriver at Natchitoches and sent back a wire in care of the brothel, thanking Sterling for his unsolicited help. Although he owed the man a considerable debt, he wasn't anxious to make a friend of him. There was something about Sterling's easy manner that excited mistrust in the gambler.

Graham grew a beard to hide the knife's scar and stayed on the rivers for another three months, but another shoot-out occurred on a boat near Shreveport. After being unceremoniously put ashore in a mosquito-infested swamp, he hiked into town and gave his situation a good deal of thought. He realized that his was a bad life, and he sought some basic denomination, some simple solution that would change it.

He took a boat again and steamed up into Arkansas as far as Kansas, and then came down again. He traveled up the Missouri River, and down the Mississippi to New Orleans, and along the way he would play, winning or losing and not caring much one way or another. During the next year, he had to shoot three more men. Two died, and Graham was developing a reputation.

Graham finally realized that what had been a "gentleman's occupation" was rapidly becoming a bog of suckers and scoundrels. Every time he sat down, he was risking an eruption of violence. He adopted the habit of always sitting with his back to a wall, careful never to allow anyone to stand behind him. He always kept his weapons loaded. But he reminded himself constantly that however lucky a man was, there was a limit to how often he could walk away.

One morning in Glasgow, Missouri, he stood idly watching a group of people outfitting themselves for the long journey across the prairie, and like thousands of others who found the postwar middle border unbearable, Cleve Graham put his old life behind him and took the ultimate gamble: He headed west.

3

WAGON MASTER CLEVE GRAHAM STIRRED TO SEMICONsciousness but kept his head down, his eyes shut. He heard the soft murmur of the wind disturbing the grass on the prairie up over the bluff behind him. It reminded him of the journey he had taken two years before, when, outfitted in the rough clothes of a frontiersman, he had traded his fancy pistols for a Sharps .50 and trudged across Kansas behind a small group of mule-drawn wagons bound for the silver mines of Nevada. He never made it. That trip, too, he recollected with dread, encountered disaster: They became lost in the snows of an early winter storm. Their mules, unreliable and, as far as Graham was concerned, unridable, ran off, and then they were attacked by a roving band of outlaws and left for dead. That had been a near thing, he recalled in his doze. But once again, his luck had prevailed.

"Take another card," he mumbled.

Somewhere, the Jew's harp he had heard the previous afternoon—or a different one—sounded again, and a mouth organ was added to it. "From Greenland's Icy

Banks," a favorite hymn of several of the party, was unevenly intoned by a few ragged voices, and Graham wondered if someone else had died and there was another funeral going on. No, he remembered, keeping his grainy eyes shut tightly and deliberately trying to drift. Virgil Hollister was doubtless holding another service.

The hymn rose and fell sporadically while the singers searched for the proper words. Graham frowned and consciously kept his eyes closed. Virgil's rasping baritone sounded louder than all the others combined. He needed to jerk Hollister back, he told himself. The would-be preacher was becoming more than an annoyance. He was becoming dangerous. But the effort of rising was too great, and although he now felt himself wide awake, Graham didn't want to move. His limbs refused to stir of their own accord; commanding them took too much concentration. The gentle relaxation he found after eating the food and drinking the tea and taking the nap was too delicious to abandon. The hymn swung into a second clumsy verse, and he allowed himself to continue to sit as the music stumbled along to a ragged finish.

Virgil Hollister's voice suddenly rang out from down the wagon line, and Graham struggled to his feet. The preacher's tone was angry, and a chorus of agreement chimed in every time he paused. The wagon master could put off dealing with Hollister no longer, he knew. He didn't look forward to it. These people were desperate, and whatever Hollister was offering them probably sounded better than merely waiting this thing out and taking their chances.

"I just can't believe I let some goddamn nigger scout lead me into this mess," he said aloud as he checked the loads in his pistols. But the words did not put to rest the burden he felt. "We got to get out of here," he said to the crossing. "I've got business to tend to, an' this ain't part of it."

He almost walked off before he remembered something, and he turned, knelt down, and picked up the tin cup and plate. He might as well take them back to Aggie, he thought. She had enough to do without fetching and carrying for him, and, besides, it would give him another chance to see her. Thrusting the dishes under his bad arm, he strode toward the sound of Hollister's hoarse sermon.

4

GRAHAM WALKED DOWN THE WAGON LINE TOWARD THE sound of increasingly angry voices. Aggie Sterling's cup and plate were under his stumped arm and twin Colt's Peacemakers were tied down on his thighs. He found a tight knot of people gathered near the entrance to the hospital cave. They had ceased singing and now bobbed their heads in agreement to the harangue of a single voice. On a keg of whiskey he had removed from a wagon, Hollister stood and berated the group, which included mostly women and children and only a few men: Pierce, Golden, and Quigley. They saw Graham and shifted their weight nervously, but none turned away.

"I tell you people," Hollister shouted in a hoarse voice, "it's this demon's elixir that's keepin' us penned up here like sheep ready for the slaughter. Them red devils want the rotgut, an' I say we give it to 'em an' hightail it out of here."

Hollister eyed Graham briefly and continued, "Better yet, I say we jus' hole ever' keg of this swill on the train, an' then throw 'em out there an' let 'em see that it's gone. They'll go 'bout their own bloody business elsewhere, then."

A murmur of agreement and a chorus of nodding heads greeted this idea, but Graham could see that the crowd was caught up more in the spirit of assent than in any hard commitment to Hollister's idea. They weren't a mob, not yet, but they were exhausted, frightened, and dangerously close to turning mean if this man was allowed to continue.

"I tell you," Virgil went on, "the Bible forbids it. 'Do not take strong drink thou!' That's from the Leviticus book, an' here we are tryin' to take the milk from the calf of Baal right into a promised land most of us'll never see 'less we dump this evil liquor out onto the ground in front of the minions of Satan." Virgil paused and wiped the spittle from his stubby chin.

Graham pushed his way past several people. "Get down off that keg an' shut up," he ordered.

"Get thee behind me, Satan!" Hollister began to work

himself up to a good roar. "I'll *not* obey the voice of Pharaoh!" Hollister screamed to the people. "Pour out this whiskey, an' let my people go!" He raised the hatchet and waved it in a circle over his head. "I'm the hand of God Jehovah, a paraclete for salvation, an' I'm fixin' to strike a blow for righteousness!"

He brought the hatchet down hard and struck the keg. Whiskey jetted out of the split in the staves and began running an amber downhill stream beneath the feet of the gathered women, who pulled up their skirts and shouted their approval in the form of amens. Graham set his jaw, pulled a pistol out, and fired.

It was not Graham's intention to kill Hollister or even to wound him. He mentally placed his shot just behind the gangly man's head, hoping that the impact of the slug on the limestone bluff would be sufficient to cool the preacher's ardor. But Bob Simmons had filed the new gun's trigger for a quick draw, and the weapon went off before it was elevated properly. The bullet struck Hollister in the calf of his leg and spun him around. Graham automatically recocked it, but a woman next to him pushed his hand down, and the weapon discharged a second blast harmlessly into the gravel.

"Goddamnit, let go of me," he hissed at the woman he recognized as Clarissa Golden. She kept her hand on his, and he pounded at it with his stump. Aggie's tinware was still firmly gripped under his arm and hampered his actions. He never thought to drop it. She dug her nails into the fleshy skin between his thumb and forefinger, and a sudden numbness fled up his arm. He released his grip on the nickel-plated revolver and allowed it to fall into the dirt. Someone kicked it away.

Hollister had been knocked backward with the shot to his leg, but he braced himself against the limestone wall behind him and pushed his body back up on top of the rapidly emptying keg.

"I tell you, this is a blow for the God Jehovah!" he yelled, and he reached down and extracted the hatchet. Blood gushed from his trousers where Graham's bullet had passed through, but the minister was caught up in the fire of his passion, and he waved the implement over his head once more. "Bring me 'nother barrel!" he shouted. "We'll run this damnable creek brown with the sinful squeezin's of man's folly!"

He brought the blade down again and smashed the keg completely open, almost losing his balance. Graham finally freed his hand from Clarissa Golden's grip and knocked her backward with a backhanded slap. He quickly clenched his fist several times to restore circulation and then reached around for his other revolver. It was missing from the holster.

William Golden pushed his way through the tight knot of people now dancing around Virgil. Golden didn't stop his stride but drew back a fist and struck the wagon master in the mouth.

Graham had been hit in scuffles before. He knew what it felt like, but this was different. He saw Golden's knuckles rushing toward his mouth, and before he could even blink, he felt a sharp blow on his front teeth. At the same time, a bell went off in his ears, its tone clear and distinct. His eyes crossed, and his head spun. The tone of the bell faded off, and he felt a sharp point of pain on his inner lips where his teeth had creased their tender skin. Graham spun, fell, and caught himself on one knee.

Before the wagon master could collect himself, Golden knocked off Graham's hat, grabbed him by a fistful of hair, and jerked his head back and hit him again and again, until the wagon master was down on the ground, his stumped hand trying to cover his face from Golden's boots as they kicked at his head. Finally the blows stopped when Golden's chiseled boot toe made contact with Graham's temple and sent the wagon master's senses reeling. A starburst of brilliant colors flooded across his vision.

Golden was heaving deeply. He pulled out a pistol and leveled it at the wagon master.

Graham looked up and tried to focus, but his eyesight blurred. He saw a swimming vision of Hollister's hatchet poised for a blow into the second keg, which Quigley and Pierce were holding up high over their heads, and the hazy image of Golden's angry face shimmered before him.

"No!" he tried to shout, but words failed him. Golden's mouth was a thin scar of hate, and Graham's head was spinning.

People around Golden grabbed at him, but he waved

his revolver dangerously and warned them off. Clarissa Golden was unhurt and said so over and over again, but her husband didn't look at her. He cocked the revolver and bit down hard on his lower lip. Graham's vision continued to blur, and black circles danced before his eyes. Seems like everybody on this train wants to kick me, he thought. The area around him began to close in darkness.

"Shoot him," someone yelled. "Shoot him an' be done with it."

The boom of a shotgun lit the small area, and Golden's chest exploded. He sprawled onto the people behind him, who screamed and moved away from his bleeding body as if it were a burning rag that had been tossed among them. Clarissa's scream surrounded the whole group, and Virgil was frozen, his hatchet raised for the blow he was about to deliver to the keg Quigley and Pierce continued to hold aloft for destruction. Golden's blasted body twisted and jumped in a death spasm on the whiskey-soaked ground beneath their feet.

Hannah Morgan stepped forward into the group, Aggie's smoking shotgun held at the level of Virgil Hollister's stomach.

"Jus' stand easy an' put it down," she said evenly. "They's already one idjet dead, an' I got me 'nother barrel here for anybody who wants it."

The women and children in the group scrambled back from her. Her eyes were fierce in their determination. Everyone took a step backward to enlarge the semicircle around Virgil, who remained in his former attitude. The keg was suspended between Quigley and Pierce, still in Virgil's reach, and his eyes drifted toward it with greedy glee.

"You killed him!" Clarissa Golden shrieked and fell on her husband. She came up to her knees, her fingers soused with his blood. "You jus' killed him!"

"Saved us from hangin' him," Hannah said evenly. "Back off, now, or I'll give you the same. Jus' 'cause you're a female don't cut no soap with me."

The fire was gone from the crowd. Hannah was formidable. Behind her the girl, Aggie, now justified their earlier opinion of her by standing just inside the entrance to the hospital cave with a rifle, backing up the older woman. Aggie held the rifle easily, but the expression on her face told them that she would use it. One or two of the group began to drift off from the edges. Quigley and his companion also began to step away.

"Don't you move!" Virgil ordered his two accomplices. "I'm fixin' to pour out this whiskey." He waved the hatchet again, although the zeal was gone from his eyes. "Bring it closer. The Lord God hath ordained it." Quigley and Pierce obeyed, although they kept their eyes warily on Hannah's shotgun. Virgil raised himself up to his full height. The shattered keg beneath him rocked dangerously. The top of his head reached the ledge of limestone. "In the name of God, I cast this evil liquor—"

The slick whistle of an arrow cut him off. A dogwood shaft appeared in his throat just below his Adam's apple, the bright red flint point jutting out and stapling him to the limestone wall. It was as if it had been inside him and quickly sprouted from both sides of his neck. Quigley and Pierce dropped the keg they had been holding up for sacrifice and caught him in their arms as his body weight tore him loose and he fell.

"Get him into the cave," Hannah ordered. Virgil's arms were swinging akimbo, and he gurgled inarticulately at the two men who held him. "Some of you help Graham inside, too. If anybody tries to mess with him or me, I'll kill you, so help me."

Pierce and Quigley hesitated a moment and then stumbled past her and hauled Virgil into the hospital cave, but the rest of the group were too stunned to move.

"Help him in," Aggie said. Graham was trying to sit up and rub his eyes.

"I think you ought to do as she says." Hannah waved the shotgun menacingly toward the diminishing knot of people. "I don't care what you think 'bout what happened or 'bout what's goin' on. He's the only one that matters. Now help him."

Slowly, Baker and Potter pushed through and pulled Graham to his feet. A large red spot was forming on his temple, and blood trickled from one eye.

"I can't see," he said. "What's happenin'?" His eyes were crossed, and he was about to pass out.

Aggie backed up and allowed the two North Carolinians to haul Graham into the cave. "Watch 'em, Hannah," she said and followed them in. As they wandered off, some of the group peeled Clarissa Golden from her dead husband and hefted his body up to take down to the cave where the dead were being kept. Her sobs could be heard even inside the hospital cave.

"What happened?" Glorietta demanded of the sudden mob of people who had invaded the makeshift hospital.

"There was some trouble. 'Bout the whiskey," Pierce started, but a quick wave of Hannah's shotgun shut him up, and he pushed Quigley out of the cave ahead of him. They had dumped Virgil onto a pallet, and Constance was attending to him as best she could. Blood gushed from his neck and his leg, and his eyes were glazed over.

"Whiskey's the main trouble here," Glorietta pronounced, but Aggie's frown silenced her. She looked again down to her husband, who lay still with his eyes open and dead.

Graham felt weak and stupid. He couldn't focus on anything at all no matter how hard he tried. His left eye was burning as well. When the two men dumped him roughly onto the floor of the cave, the pain shot from it and into his brain with a hot jolt.

"Jesus Christ! I'm blind!"

"You'll live." Aggie's voice came to him, but he couldn't see her. "Just lay quiet an' let me tend to this over here."

Graham tried to push himself up on one arm, but he felt weaker and weaker, and he lay back. In a bit, he felt someone raising his head, and the hot taste of liquor passed his tongue. He tried to focus again, but his head rebelled and agony throbbed from the damaged eye.

"Who—is that you?" he asked stupidly. "Goddamnit, I'm blind."

"You ain't blind," Aggie's voice came to him. "But you're hurt, an' hurt bad. You got to rest that eye, or you'll lose it. You may lose it anyhow." She gave him more whiskey, a large swallow, and he lay back. The liquor burned in his stomach, and he felt himself swimming in a hazy gray cloud.

"I got to see to things," he said. "The whiskey. Those folks're—"

"You got to rest a bit," Aggie said, and he could hear the worry behind her voice.

"Who shot Golden?" Graham asked.

"I did," Hannah said simply. "He was fixin' to kill you, an' I can't have that. I said you needed watchin'."

Aggie gave him more whiskey, and he tried to fathom her shape. All he could see was a wavy blur. The fresh smell of soap was still about her, and he could feel the softness of her hands as they touched his face. His mind raced around, but the whiskey began to take hold. Once again he felt trapped, and he wondered just how lucky he was after all.

"Lay back," Aggie ordered, and she put a cold cloth over his eyes. The coolness soothed them, but his temple throbbed, and his head rang with a hot hum.

"I'd rather be deaf than blind," he said.

"How d'you feel 'bout dead?" Hannah chuckled mirthlessly. She had stationed herself at the cave's entrance. She reloaded the used barrel of the shotgun and laid it across her thighs. Outside, a loud hubbub of muttering could be heard.

"We can't let 'em smash the whiskey." Graham almost rose up before Aggie firmly pushed him back. "It's the only thing we've got."

"You just lay back an' let me see to Mr. Hollister," Aggie said.

"But you don't understand," Graham pleaded. "If we lose the whiskey we lose everything."

"If we lose you," Aggie said, "we don't have much of a chance anyhow. You're the only one knows where we're headin'."

Graham drank more whiskey and lay back. Pain roamed from his left eye all the way down into his neck. Golden had kicked him good, he thought, and he'd died for it. Hannah had shot him deader than a rock right in front of all those people. My God, he thought, what's happening? A sense of helplessness swam over him. He wanted to give up, to just roll over and go to sleep. He had had enough.

The liquor warmed him and forced him to count his

troubles. Panic subsided as the heated murmurs outside the cave began to quiet. Maybe Aggie was right, he reasoned. He couldn't do much if he couldn't see. His thoughts ran to the distant Valley of the High Snows, to the dream he had nourished for this train from the beginning of the trip. He knew that deep down he really didn't care about these people, but they were still his responsibility, and in a way he had come to regard them as something like a last chance to redeem himself for a life that had been largely wasted. He had to get back on top of things. He couldn't just let them fall apart.

Hannah came over and lifted his head and gave him another sip of the whiskey. He wasn't sure if it helped his headache or not, but he welcomed the sweet burn of it on his tongue. It was good whiskey—that much he would give to Jack Sterling. He had bought quality liquor—and it again reminded him of Santa Fe and the first time he had seen the Valley of the High Snows.

"Just rest a bit," Hannah said to him. He nodded gratefully and lay back.

"What happened to Hollister? Is he dead? Who's watchin' him? Aggie said somethin' . . ."

"He's alive." Hannah patted him roughly. "Arrow got him in the throat, an' you shot him up pretty good, too."

"They should've killed him," Graham muttered. "Should've been him an' not Golden. Golden was a good man."

"Golden damn near kicked your head in," she said. "An' he would of shot you if I'd let him."

"Did you have to kill him?"

"Look, Cleve," Hannah sighed, "I've fought Mescans an' Apache, outlaws of ever' kind there is. I've seen men killed most all my life. Some of 'em was my own. There's a look a man gets when he's 'bout to kill 'nother man. He had that look. So I shot him. I ain't glad I did it, but I'd do'er again. 'Sides, if I'd let him kill you, I'd had to hang him. An' that gets ugly."

"They'll hang you," Graham said.

"Not so long as you're drawin' breath," she said with mock confidence in her voice. "I saved your life, so now you're bound to stay healthy to bear witness for me."

"Let me know if they try to come get you," he said. He blinked his eyes and tried to see, but it was no use. One eye refused to focus and the other remained blind.

"They ain't fixin' to try nothin'," Hannah said. "They're mad an' bewildered, but they ain't goin' to do nothin' now." She gave him more whiskey, almost too much, but he gulped it down and then lay back and reveled in the dizziness it caused. He was numb, but he also felt the need to do something. For the moment, however, there was nothing to do but lie there and hope that he would be able to see in a little while. He had felt that way before, but he had been alone then. Now, there was Hannah—and Aggie—watching out for him, and the comfort he took in that helped him rest.

CHAPTER TWO

1

GRAHAM EVENTUALLY WENT NO FARTHER WEST THAN Santa Fe. After the bushwhacking that left his companions dead and himself badly wounded and abandoned for dead, he was found, he was told, by Indian hunters. They brought him for barter to a mountain man, a virtual hermit, named Jock McFee, whose Pueblo wife nursed the gambler back to health. The next spring, they took him down out of the mountains. They rode as far as Taos before leaving him with a burro, his own twenty dollars in gold, and directions to the city that had come to be known as the Capital of the West.

"I'm grateful," Graham said when he realized that McFee was leaving him alone in the middle of a beautiful valley between purple mountains. "I guess I owe you my life."

"Owe it to the bloody, rotten Blackfoot, goddamn their wretched souls," McFee said. "I'll not ha'e the obligation." McFee's r's rolled heavily, and spittle sprayed.

Graham said nothing. He had asked several times why his hair wasn't hanging from a Blackfoot's lodgepole.

"You're to go south an' west." McFee now turned and pointed vaguely off to the snowcapped mountains around them. "You're to come to a river, the Rio Bravo, the Mescans call it. Whites, the Rio Grande. Same river. It's in a grand great gorge. You canno' miss it. Follow it south an' you'll reach Santa Fe in two days, maybe three. D'you think you can make it?"

Graham nodded. He realized he had no choice.

"Who owns this valley?" Graham asked, trying to prolong the conversation. McFee clearly wanted to be on his way. He seemed uncomfortable every time he spoke to Graham.

McFee looked around, then pulled out a pipe and lit it. The wind from the mountains was chilled, but the sun warmed Graham. All around him the swaying grass of the valley moved in stark contrast to the quiet snowy peaks. For some reason he couldn't fathom, he felt more content than he ever imagined he could.

"Owns it?" McFee spat out smoke. "No one owns it. Pueblo and Navajo ha'e claimed it. So ha'e Comanche and the Mexicans, Blackfoot, Cheyenne, Ute. The bloody Spanish say they found it. But no one *owns* it." Graham's question angered the mountain man, and he stared off toward the distance. "The Almighty dinna' hand out deeds of property when He made it. Whoever is on it owns it, it seems to me." For a moment he was silent, then he sighed and spoke in a softer voice tinged with disgust. "There's talk a wee man named Jigger Tuttle lays claim to it. He's in Santa Fe, but I ha'e never heard of him coming up here. He's no right to it, but he says it's his own an' has a paper to show for it."

"What's it called?" Graham asked.

"The Indians call it the Valley of the High Snows," McFee said. "But I dunno' know if there's another name. That one fits. I dunno' know of any other place in these parts where the snow falls lighter in a hard winter." He went on to describe the valley. There were two small rivers which flowed out of the mountains and crisscrossed it, and there were numbers of berry thickets. The whole area was alive with antelope in the spring, McFee concluded. "There were buff here years ago, but they've all been hunted out or driven off. I dunno' think they ever left, winter or summer." He knocked out his pipe and spat.

With that, he was off, and Graham pushed the burro southwest, alone and feeling his usual luck guiding him.

When Graham arrived in Santa Fe, he roamed around and tried to get into small-stakes poker games with the money he had left and what he raised from selling the burro, but he found that his attitude toward the game had changed. His luck also deserted him, and while his skill and ability to manipulate cards to his favor kept him from losing everything he had, he rarely dared try to make much money from any of the lowlifes he played with. The dirty clapboard bars and back-alley brothels his reduced means forced him to gamble in brought him into the company of dangerous and usually well-armed, heavy-handed men. Twice in his first two weeks he saw men casually accused of cheating and gutted where they sat, their bodies tossed out into the alleys behind the buildings, where dogs could sometimes be heard snarling over them.

He didn't know what to do. He couldn't return to the riverboats; he was too old for that life, he told himself. He had seen enough of death for two or three lifetimes, and he had no desire to seek it any more than he seemed to find it in these scurrilous surroundings. He also began to lose interest in prostitutes, most of whom were dark-skinned Mestizos, Negroes, or mixed-breed Navajo and Pueblo Indians.

He thought often of the pretty little valley, and he wondered what it would take to go back there and live. The valley had seemed so peaceful and remote from the filth and squalor of Santa Fe, from the danger and loneliness of the plains or the mountains. He longed for it. More than once he asked his fellow players if they knew of a man named Tuttle, but none did. Given the class of individuals with whom he played, Graham wasn't surprised.

One night, as a treat to himself, he entered a fashionable hotel to have his boots blacked and fell into conversation with a well-dressed man who discovered that Graham was game and invited him to play. The men with him were cattlemen, they said. The game was private, and the stakes were high. Graham knew better than to bet into heavy pots, and he was careful to keep his play aboveboard. His mind kept drifting away from the cards, however, and he discovered that his contributions to the conversation, which had centered on the relative quality of grazing of one locale to another, had vocalized his musings over the Valley of the High Snows.

The men were politely amused at the gambler's conversation, and more than one spoke up to say that the valley was too remote.

"It's safe enough," one responded to Graham's comments. "We just ain't needed it yet. We're saving it for when Texas runs out of good grazing, about a hundred years from now." They all laughed.

The game continued, and Graham sadly watched his funds depleting. He couldn't afford to call the bets the ranchers were casually making. His play indicated that he was obviously lacking money, and they diplomatically called a recess in the game and adjourned to the adjacent restaurant, suggesting that Graham could find some other amusement in the meantime.

Graham overheard their mirth at his expense and felt himself flush with embarrassment and anger. He went over to the bar and ordered a whiskey. The dirty brown liquid that was poured in front of him tasted like coal oil. He sipped it and let it sit.

"Is this the best stuff you have?" he asked the bartender, a large mustached Mexican who only shrugged and nodded before walking away.

"It's what we can get," a voice next to Graham said. He turned and found himself facing a man in a high silk hat and cutaway coat. He had a young, clear face and evenly spaced dark eyes that showed intelligence. "Whiskey comes at a premium here." He smiled. "Let me buy you a tequila."

"Don't care for the stuff," Graham said and smiled to show that he wasn't being impolite. "Tequila is just mescal with a beard." The man grinned back an agreement to the jibe. "How about a beer?" Graham offered before he mentally tabulated just how badly he had lost that evening. His hand reached into his pocket and fingered the five cartwheels he had remaining. "At a nickel a glass, it's better than this."

"Most of the whiskey is locally distilled," the man said, gesturing for the bartender to draw two beers. "They sell it for two dollars a bottle, but I daresay it doesn't cost half that to produce."

The man nodded and toasted Graham's health with his beer mug. "Most of the rye and bourbon we can get overland arrives as damaged goods," the man said. "Or contraband. We can't obtain gin with any regularity either. Finer liquors are simply idle dreams." He watched Graham through chocolate-dark eyes for a moment over his glass.

"Tell you what, you come with me, and we'll have a real drink."

Graham followed the man to a back room of the saloon, where he was seated in a comfortable office. He was once again embarrassed as he realized that the man was apparently the owner of the establishment.

"Didn't mean to be criticizin' your stock."

The man walked over to a wooden cabinet and extracted a dusty bottle. "Think nothing of it," he said as he poured out a small glass of amber liquid for each of them. "I don't drink that stuff myself, and I say a little prayer for anyone who has no choice."

Graham tasted his glass's contents and sat back approvingly. "That's the best whiskey I've ever had." He held the glass up to the fireplace and examined the color. It had a deep, smoky flavor and flowed down his throat so smoothly he scarcely knew he had swallowed it.

"It's imported." The man sipped from his own glass. "I've three bottles of it left of the single case I received a year ago. I usually don't give it away, but I hate to drink it alone. It was meant to be shared. If I had a case of it, I could sell it for twenty dollars a bottle. There's a place on the south side of the square that had some Tennessee sour mash in here last year, and they sold it for four bits a shot. Could have gotten twice that. Whiskey, as I told you, *good* whiskey, is a premium."

"Here's to good company. My name's Cleveland Graham."

"Jigger Tuttle. A pleasure to meet a man of good taste."

Graham's breath stopped. "Are you the man who owns the valley up in the mountains? The one the Indians call the Valley of the High Snows?"

"Guilty," Tuttle answered. "Although I haven't heard anyone use that name for the place in years. I heard you've been looking for me." Graham looked surprised. "Mr. Graham, these are dangerous times in Santa Fe. A man such as myself is well paid to have good information about anything that might concern him." He shrugged lightly. "I have my spies, and more than once it's kept me from getting a knife in my ribs. Why are you interested in a worthless piece of property I was sharped into buying when

I came out here?" The question was put suddenly, and Tuttle's dark eyes brightened as he awaited Graham's reaction.

"I thought it was a nice place," Graham muttered. He felt stung, used, tricked again. "I had an idea I'd like to live up there."

"I doubt you'd survive," Tuttle said, laughing.

"Why's that?"

"Indians, mountain lions, bears, wolves, snows so deep in the two passes a man can't get in or out three-quarters of the year. Loneliness. A party of hunters went up there last October, became lost, and then were snowed in by an early blizzard. They wandered around for six months before the passes opened and let a search party in. Two of them died, and the one who came out was nearly insane. He was well fed, though. Speculation was that he ate his partners, although I don't give the story much credence. There is plenty of game up there. I suspect he went mad talking to himself." He poured another brief round of the whiskey. "Aside from the passes, the only way out is up through the mountains, and no one I know aside from the mountain men would try that route."

"That's the way I found it."

"If that's so, then you know I'm telling the truth." Tuttle sipped his whiskey. "It's worthless to me now."

He poured them another drink and recorked the bottle, which announced the end of the good stuff for that evening. Graham was disappointed. The whiskey was smooth and gentle, almost seductive. He had tasted nothing like it. It was in no way comparable to the rye and bourbon he had enjoyed on riverboats and saloons up and down the Mississippi.

"I want to buy it," Graham said, although he knew he didn't have the money to purchase a square foot of it. "I think I could run horses on it."

"Do you know anything about horses?"

"Not much," Graham admitted. "I was a buyer for the Army during the war. I don't know." He paused and then surprised himself with an outpouring of words. The whiskey relaxed him, and he felt weary of the ordeal his life had become. Tuttle's friendly, open nature served as an invitation to speak freely, and Graham obliged him. "I just know that I want to live up there, make a life up there. I don't know why. I just know I've had enough of back-room poker games and smoky saloons." He sipped the last of his drink. "And whores. I need to find something steady. It was nice up there. Seemed like a place a man could find some peace."

Tuttle studied Graham; his face revealed nothing of what he was thinking. He uncorked the bottle again and poured another dollop of whiskey into their glasses. Finally he rubbed his chin and spoke. "I'll make you a proposition, Mr. Graham," he said. "It's a gambler's chance, but it might make us some money, and it might fulfill your passion. Wait here."

He left the room and returned with a rolled parchment map, which he spread on the desk between them.

"This is the so-called Valley of the High Snows. It's really the westernmost stretch of what is often called the Cimarron Territory. It's part of a Spanish land grant that goes back over a hundred years. In fact, the man we bought it from claimed that his grandfather was the original owner, although that's doubtful." He glanced narrowly at Graham. "Don't worry. It's legal. My deed is clear."

He leaned back and sipped his whiskey. "You say you want to buy it? Fine. I'll sell it to you. I paid nearly ten thousand for it. I'll let you have half for five."

"Why would you do that?"

"I don't have a use for it, at least not all of it, at least not now," Tuttle said, moving forward and studying the map a moment. "I do have a use for money. I also have a passion for horses." He looked into Graham's eyes. "Here's the proposition: You either give me the cash or fifty head of decent breeding stock, and half the valley's yours. You can have everything but the grassland here in the south, near the river. I'll need that for the horses."

"Money or horses," Graham repeated.

"Money or horses. I should tell you that I know a man in Lexington who could acquire the horseflesh I want. I'm not interested in wild mustangs or in substandard stock. They don't have to be thoroughbreds, but I would want quality. Good cow ponies are going to be at a premium in this country in the next few years, and I could corner the market if I could produce the stock."

"What makes you think so?"

"The railroad."

"You said it was stalled."

"It is, for now. But I've seen the plans, and I know that when they swing south and make for Santa Fe, they're going to run right through that valley. From the eastern to the southwestern pass. They don't have any choice unless they cut through solid rock."

"I still don't see." Graham wrinkled his brow.

"When the railroad comes through, the cattle business here is going to become very important. Texas herds are already coming up to Fort Sumner, and we're well west of the quarantine in Kansas. They can ship from here, and they know it. A railhead up in that valley with good grazing and good horses would mean a major terminal, especially if the western pass was closed by snow, and particularly if a handful of stockmen filled the valley with premium beef ready for shipment. I want to be there when the track is laid, and if you're there as well with people and a bona fide town, then we can pull it off. To do it, I need money or horses." His eyes were wide as they waited for Graham's answer.

"A town?" he said.

"A town, Mr. Graham. A large settlement at the least. If we bring in people, set up a real settlement, build farms, and so forth, then our stock business will flourish. We'll have a proper town, and there's not one damn thing anyone can do about it."

"What about the Indians?"

"All the more reason for a large settlement. The Indians won't raid a fortified town. There's too much risk involved. We're not dealing with Comanche or Sioux up there anyway. Just Blackfoot and Ute, maybe some worn-out Cheyenne. There's miles of heavy mountains between that valley and any large tribes. It was Navajo country for the longest time. They're scared of their shadows. Besides, if enough people move in up there, the Army will have to take notice of it and make sure they're protected."

"A town." Graham shook his head.

"That's good grazing land," Tuttle said quietly. "Texas ranchers have had their eye on it for years. I've had a couple of offers, but I've held on to it. But no plan will work without cash and lots of it. Right now, cash means horses. At least, to me it does."

"I'm really not much of a horse trader," Graham said.

"Then get the money. I can send for the horses once the railroad's in, if I have the capital. Right now, I don't. In fact, I could likely get good horses from California, or even from Texas or Mexico if I had ready money. But hard cash is harder to come by here than good whiskey, and it tends to evaporate more rapidly. The truth is, I could do as much with whiskey as I could with money, provided it was good sour mash and not the red-eye swill I'm obliged to pour."

He drained his glass and leaned forward and studied the floor for a moment before looking up sharply at Graham. The liquor made his face red, and his eyes glistened in the lamplight.

"I will tell you this much. This is good country. But it needs people. Not a bunch of land-grabbing hooligans with hired guns behind them. I can profit by it, certainly. There's nothing wrong with profit. I have the land, but I need horseflesh on that grass to do me any good. With it, I stand a chance to make a modest fortune. Without it, I can stay here and be the proprietor of a ginmill until I retire or someone kills me. Money or horses, Mr. Graham. One's as good as the other to me."

"I don't have that kind of money," Graham said. "I shouldn't even be thinking about it."

Tuttle began rolling up the map. "I like you, Mr. Graham. You're a man of passion. You're also a man who likes good liquor and knows enough to tell the difference. I'll tell you what. You come back here with five thousand dollars' worth of anything—horses, cattle, even whiskey—and I'll still make the deal. The valley's not going anywhere, and unless someone comes along who is a bigger fool than you—or I—it's not likely to be sold anytime soon."

"I'd take your deal, Mr. Tuttle, but I've got nothing to deal with. No stake, no ante."

"The deal stands as offered, Mr. Graham." He opened the bottle once again to seal their tentative agreement. "There's no risk unless you choose to take it. Horses or cattle, whiskey or cash. Hell, if you brought back five

New Orleans yellow prostitutes, it might just work as well. Otherwise, I'll trust my judgment, and bid you empty your glass and have another round to honest men."

"Honest but poor," Graham muttered.

"Honest but poor." Tuttle extended his glass in a toast. After one more round of the excellent whiskey, Graham returned to the saloon. He felt worse than he ever had before. The valley appeared before his eyes like a prize to be won. It held a promise, something he thought he had been searching for for years. It wasn't just his idea, his idle dream. It was something other men wanted, powerful men, big men with money behind them. With nothing but emptiness in his pockets, he wasn't likely to win it in the near future. He had never in his life had that much money in cash, and as he passed through the saloon and waved halfheartedly to the others who had resumed the poker game in his absence, he doubted he ever would.

2

WINTER WAS HARD UPON SANTA FE, AND STAYING IN the town depressed Graham too much to bear. He returned to the small-stakes games for the next several weeks and finally sharped his way into enough money to buy a horse and saddle and to replace his familiar .36 Colt's. He decided to return to the East, to Jefferson if he could, where he knew the people and the game and where he was also well enough known to borrow his way into a sufficient stake to give him a chance to renew his prosperity.

As he rode off from Santa Fe up the famous trail back toward Emporia, Kansas, where he caught the AT&SF back to the East, his mind stayed back in New Mexico. It obsessed him, as he made his way back to the riverboats and down again into Texas, and pushed ahead of his interest in poker. Often while holding a hand that required intense concentration and a well-acted bluff, his mind wandered in the little valley Jock McFee had led him through, and his desire to find a way to raise an impossible sum overrode his immediate need to win a hand. There was a sense of urgency underlying his thoughts, a need to find a way to buy a decent string of horses and return to Tuttle's saloon in Santa Fe. He dreamed about it, and sometimes his dreams took place when he should have been reading the cards in his hand and figuring the odds against a decent draw on the next deal. More than once on his return journey to Texas, he felt he should quit playing for good. He had become an easy mark, and he wasn't comfortable in the role. He arrived back in Jefferson more than a year after he left, financially broke and spiritually bankrupt.

After a few months in Jefferson, Graham left East Texas and traveled south to St. Augustine and then down the Old Royal Highway to San Antonio. He was trying to find something to displace the vision of New Mexico in his mind and to fill a hollowness inside him that refused to go away no matter how much he drank or where he went. An unnatural anxiety seemed to surround him all the time like a heavy coat, and the only relief he found from it was when his thoughts rambled back to Tuttle and his offer.

He had been in San Antonio a month when he gave in and paid a dollar for a bottle and a woman. Her name was Dolores, and Graham estimated that she couldn't have been more than fourteen or fifteen. Her long, dark hair hung to her tiny waist, and her skin glistened with sweat after he rolled off her and lay there sipping strong tequila and examining her smooth, almost hairless body.

He stayed with Dolores every night for a week, paying generously for her favors, buying her dresses and jewelry and delighting in her surprise and gratitude when she opened the packages. Her youth made him feel more like her father than her lover—or customer—and he was almost embarrassed to walk along the *paseo* with her on his arm. After the week had passed, they moved into a cheap hotel, the Pasada de la Rosa, on Market Street and set up regular housekeeping.

He stayed in San Antonio through the summer and was thinking of remaining there permanently when he encountered Frank Herbert. The meeting was a surprise for Graham. He had not realized how hungry he was to encounter a familiar face, and he found himself a little flustered by how eagerly he welcomed a reunion with his old comrade.

Frank was in bad shape. He had drifted to San Antonio from Galveston, where he had been working on the docks. His mental slowness worked against him in numerous ways, not the least of which was the advantage cruel employers took of him: He often worked a week or longer only to have his wages cut or not paid at all and then found himself kicked out of a foreman's office with a threat and laughter ringing in his ears. Frank came to take such abuse philosophically.

When Graham ran into him on a street near the main square of San Antonio, he felt expansive enough to set him up to a meal and a suit of clothes, then rented him a room in the hotel. He introduced Frank to Dolores, who, in turn, introduced Frank to a friend of hers, Ursula, a girl of only thirteen, who delighted Frank almost as much as he seemed to please her. When they were together, they reminded Graham of a couple of children playing at being adult, although Frank was nearly forty and balding.

Frank often surprised Graham by coming up with manly, mature observations and comments in his thin tenor voice, and Graham found his company was undemanding and pleasant. For his part, Frank seemed content to allow Graham to care for him, and when the gambler suggested that he find some kind of work, Frank went out to the stockyards and broke some horses; he returned so worn out and bruised that Graham felt guilty for putting him through the ordeal.

Summer gave way to the curious wet fall that comes to central Texas. Graham's luck didn't change, and while he was never without funds, he seldom had more than a couple of hundred dollars of gambling money in his pocket. Such circumstances kept him out of the high-stakes games that went on in the hotels and confined him to the cantinas of La Villita and the back streets of the city. Even so, he was clean and well dressed, and the two girls and Frank were happy. He almost forgot about Jigger Tuttle and the Valley of the High Snows.

One night in a cantina-cathouse named Mama Fuego's he sat down at a table and was surprised to see a familiar face across the green felt.

"I think I know you," Graham said as he shook hands with the other four men and came around to the black-hatted, dark-eyed man across from him. "I'm Cleve Graham."

"Jack Sterling." The man smiled and widened a thin mustache. " 'Less I'm mistaken, I saved you from a noose in Jefferson a few years back."

Graham was embarrassed, but he acknowledged the truth of the statement and made brief explanations all around as the game continued. Sterling looked pretty much the same as he had in Jefferson. His mustache was still a pathetic dark smear across his upper lip, but he had grown some fairly impressive muttonchop sideburns and had tried to sprout chin whiskers. His dark eyes were friendly, however, and he seemed to want to attach himself to the gambler. Afterward, Graham escorted Sterling to the bar for a drink.

"This stuff's bad as anythin' I ever pissed on a fire," Sterling said, frowning into his tequila glass. "It gets you drunk, but it takes its toll the next mornin'."

Graham agreed. "The whiskey's better, but you have to go to a hotel saloon to get it. Nothing's as bad as the rotgut I had in Santa Fe, though."

Graham found Sterling to be an open man who invited confidences such as he rarely shared himself. Graham drifted into a discussion of what Santa Fe was like, how it was surrounded by beautiful country that seemed to invite a man to come there to stay. But then, he admitted, it was a town that was still remote from civilized comforts. He pointed out the trouble people had getting whiskey in Santa Fe, about how a keg of sour mash might go for as much as six hundred dollars. He almost told him about the proposed deal Tuttle had made him before Sterling interrupted.

"Say," Sterling said, "I come down here on a business deal, but it fell through. Now, I'm headin' out to the Indian Line. I found me a string of horses I'm fixin' to sell to the Army."

"Same way you 'found' those you sold me back in Mississippi?" Graham asked with a smile.

"Careful how you say that," Sterling warned, and Graham was aware that the man's hand had casually drifted down near the fancy Colt's he wore in a black holster. It was an unnecessary gesture, Graham thought. It had been a casual jibe. Who cared what had happened all those years ago? But he could see that Sterling took it seriously. "They're bought an' paid for. Got me a bill of sale. It don't much matter where they come from." He seemed to sense that he had overreacted and shifted back to a more nonchalant tone. "They're plugs anyhow. Unbroke mustangs for the most part. Most of the soldiers out there is niggers anyway. Be happier on a mule. Or behind one." He gave a smile, and Graham returned it without comment.

"Anyhow," Sterling went on, "I thought you might like to tag along."

Graham was startled. "Me? What would I do out there?"

"Well . . ." Sterling accepted a cigar from Graham. "I'm goin' to Fort Concho, Griffin, an' Richardson, 'less I sell ever'thin' 'fore I get that far. I got forty head. Hayburners an' jugheads mostly, but the shavetails they got runnin' them outfits wouldn't know a good horse from a dead steer. Half the time they don't have enough mounts for more'n a quarter of the men to saddle. It's a wonder to me the damn redskins ain't campin' in the middle of the Menger Hotel lobby. Anyhow, ever' one of them Army forts has a flat or a town nearby—sudsvilles an' shantytowns most of 'em—but the soldiers come in there an' fill up with gin an' cheap whiskey an' spend their money. You're a fair poker player, an' I thought you might find 'em easy pickin's."

"You play poker," Graham said guardedly. Even though he felt a bit of gratitude toward this apparently open young man who smiled so broadly, he had been around too many gambling rooms and back-alley saloons to trust him completely. He had already told him too much, and he remembered the ease with which Sterling's attitude had shifted from affable to deadly serious when Graham stepped outside invisible boundaries and trod on what the horse trader clearly believed was his own personal business.

"I play *at* poker," Sterling said. "You do it for a livin'. An' you're handy with that." He pointed toward Graham's pistol and winked. "You come along with me, you could make some real money." His eyes deepened in an inward thought that took him away from Graham for a moment. Then he brightened and flashed a bright smile. "You just might put together enough money to get you back to Santa Fe. You could prob'ly make a killin' out there 'mongst them nigger troops. They don't know how to throw cards for spit, an' you could clean 'em out."

Graham felt himself flush with the proposition. He hadn't realized that his thoughts of Santa Fe had been that close to the surface of everything they said. Even so, he mulled the idea over. Frank Herbert appeared, and introductions were made. Frank invited the horse trader to join them for dinner, an offer which Sterling accepted enthusiastically.

They sat around a table at the Cattleman's Café, and Frank introduced Dolores and Ursula to Sterling, who, Graham noticed, was enchanted by both women. Ursula spoke more English than her elder friend, but the girls pretended not to know anything about what the men said. The evening ended after they went to a cantina and danced a bit, and while they said good night to Jack, Frank pulled Graham aside and spoke rapidly to him.

"He says he wants me to break some of his stock for him," Frank said eagerly. "Says he'll pay me a dollar a head. That's twice the goin' rate, an' I can do five or six tomorrow."

Graham was skeptical of the man's munificence. He had a sense that Sterling was trying to work his way into Graham's life. Even if he did owe Jack a debt for standing up for him in Jefferson, he already knew too much about Graham and his hopes and dreams. Graham made a further vow to watch what he said from that point on.

"I'd watch him, if I were you, Frank," Graham warned, but Herbert took no notice of his friend's advice. The next day he went to the stockyards and broke four of Jack's horses and one of his own legs.

It wasn't a bad fracture, but Frank was off his feet for a while. Sterling became a regular dinner companion of Graham, Dolores, and Ursula, chatting amiably about the money he hoped to make out on the Indian Line by bilking the greenhorn officers. Graham decided that his first impression of Jack Sterling had been accurate when he realized the dark young man was courting Ursula while Frank lay up in his room with his leg splinted. Each evening when he and Dolores would retire to their room, Ursula said her good nights and then, Graham suspected, slipped off to meet Sterling. He had no proof, and he had no right to confront Sterling with his suspicions—after all, he argued with himself, she *was* a whore—but he felt he was reading the situation right and he resented Sterling's behavior.

Graham's luck began to turn sour again. Without the few dollars Frank could bring in from his occasional employment, Graham's funds were being strained by keeping the two rooms at the hotel and feeding four people and usually five. Sterling never offered to pay for one of their nightly meals, Graham noticed, and most often it was Graham who plunked down a silver dollar to buy drinks for them when they bellied up to a bar.

Jack grabbed on to the notion that whiskey was something that might have a high market value in New Mexico. He was fascinated by the idea of taking some out to Santa Fe and selling it and becoming rich. He spoke to Graham of New Mexico as if he knew it well. He averred that whiskey would travel easily, and the profits they stood to make selling it would set them up for life.

"Why, if a man could get out there with twenty barrels of good White Mule or even Pine Top," he proposed one night, "he could sell it for over a thousan' dollars."

"More," Graham agreed reluctantly. "A lot more. Rotgut goes for a dollar an' four bits a bottle now, and it's not worth a nickel. Good stuff, really good stuff, sour mash with some age on it, would bring up to five dollars a bottle, maybe more."

"Hell, a keg holds ten gallons." Sterling strained his forehead in mathematical concentration. "An' that's forty quarts. At five dollars a quart, that's two hundred a keg!" The realization made his black eyes shine. "Is there hard money there?"

"Money's tight," Graham said, thinking of what Tuttle had told him. "Cash dries up pretty quick for most folks, but it can be found for whiskey and, uh . . . other things." He almost said "women," but he caught sight of Dolores and altered his statement. "The Army's there, an' the place is full of miners down from the mountains with pokes full of gold and silver, ranchers, cowboys, even outlaws who have enough money to spend on good whiskey."

Jack's eyes glazed over with the prospects as Graham outlined them. Finally, Graham gave in to his inclination to think out loud. "Soon there'll be railroad workers there, too. Irishmen, most of them. They can drink, an' they like their whiskey."

"A man could make a lot of money haulin' bug juice out there."

"A man could get killed haulin' anything out there," Graham said flatly. "I came back through Kansas, an' stuck by the railroad an' trail. You have to be where the Army patrols, or you're buzzard meat. There's five kinds of Indians out there. Comancheros, outlaws, every kind of damn thing that can kill you. You'd have a hell of a time takin' a wagonload of somethin' like whiskey across Kansas. Besides, the Army won't tolerate large wagon shipments of whiskey. They've been known to confiscate even a single keg."

Sterling dropped the matter, and Graham returned to the game he had interrupted to have a drink with this newfound friend who, he thought, was becoming something of a pest. When he arose from the table, however, he was down to less than a hundred dollars. The cards just wouldn't fall right for him.

Returning to the hotel, he saw Frank's light still on, knocked, and entered the room. Ursula was absent, and Frank brightened when he saw him.

"I been thinkin' 'bout leavin' town." The announcement surprised Frank no less than it had Graham. He opened his mouth and out the statement came. It seemed like a pronouncement of hidden intentions.

"Where you goin', Cap'n?" In spite of Graham's repeated requests that Frank call him Cleve, the former enlisted man insisted on addressing Graham by his lost rank.

"Out on the Indian Line, I guess. I need a change of scenery, change of luck."

"That's risky out there, Cap'n," Frank commented, but he made no further remark.

"I'll be back by Christmas," Graham said. "Then we'll see."

Frank nodded and asked Graham to send Ursula to him if he saw her. He said she hadn't been around all evening. Graham had a drink in the cantina, but he never spotted her, and he went to bed. Dolores said she hadn't seen her friend either.

The next morning, Graham found Sterling out by the stockyards inspecting his remuda. They were shaggy, small beasts, and he only glanced at the bill of sale Sterling ostentatiously flashed in front of him.

"I'd hoped to have more of 'em broke by now," Sterling said. "But I hired two Mescan boys to come along an' wrangle for me, an' they claim they can get the job done. I'm 'bout ready to go if you are."

A thought struck Graham. "Say, could you get your hands on some good stock? Quality horseflesh?"

"Sure." Jack smiled. "But it costs. These here cost twenty a head, an' they're not worth nigger stew meat. They're half wild an' hard to work with."

"What about good stock? Blood stock?"

Sterling rubbed his tiny goatee. "I could prob'ly lay hands on blood stock for seventy-five a head, maybe fifty if I bought a bunch. But, truth is, I don't think anybody's got more'n two or three. You'd spend half a year ridin' from one ranch to another tryin' to round up that high a quality." He tipped his hat back. "Why? You thinkin' of goin' into the business?"

Graham balked and looked away. "No. I was just curious. You'd think with all the cattle around here, there'd be better horses."

"Oh, there are! Hell, half the ranches in the state got good stock on 'em. Damn cowboys're particular 'bout their horses."

"So where do they get them?" Graham asked. "If there's so few places where you can buy them?"

"Mexico." Sterling smiled. "Steal 'em from Mexico, mostly."

"Risky," Graham muttered.

"Damn right. Why you think I'm foolin' 'round with these here plugs? If you want good horses 'thout stealin' 'em, you got to go to Tennessee or Kentucky. Elsewise, you're payin' for 'em."

"Horses an' whiskey, both seem to come from the same place," Graham said, more to himself than to Sterling.

"That's right. Hell, I ain't seen nothin' or met nobody

in this goddamn state that was worth a damn that didn't come from someplace else. Ever'thing else is either nigger or Mescan."

Graham returned to the hotel and said goodbye to Dolores. He was sorry for her. Few future customers would be as kind as he had been, but he already felt foolish for the time he had spent with her. He gave her twenty dollars and left twenty more for Frank with the hotel's manager. That would take care of room and food for more than a month, Graham knew, and by then Frank should be able to get around on a crutch. Graham had no idea what he would do for money when that was gone, but he hoped that his luck would improve with the soldiers and he might be able to send a few dollars back. He also hoped Ursula would look after Frank after he mended, and he sent Dolores looking for her, but she had disappeared. By noon, he and Jack Sterling were well on their way toward Fort Concho.

At the second day's camp, Graham poured some coffee for himself and joined Sterling, who was cleaning a pistol.

"We're about out of the season for snakes," Sterling said, "but it don't pay to get careless. There's all sorts of critters out here that can hurt you, an' some of 'em are two-legged." He smiled at Graham.

"How far is it to the Concho?"

"I figure we should make it in a week or ten days, if we don't have bad weather or no trouble. We've come damn near thirty miles already, but the country's rough."

"You've been out here before?"

"Nope," he cheerfully admitted, "but I know people who have."

"Where're you from, Jack?"

"Arkansas, Louisiana, Mississippi, all over."

"You have any family?"

"None to speak of. You?"

Graham shook his head.

"I'm likely to, though." Jack smiled a wide toothy grin. "You remember that little Mescan gal, Ursula?"

Graham nodded. A tingling sensation crept all over his body.

"Well, I up an' married her."

Graham's mind reeled with the announcement. The whole idea was ludicrous! She was just a child and a prostitute. He *married* her? What would Frank say? Graham rallied his thoughts and fought to hold his poker face steady. "You married her?"

"That's right." Jack smiled shyly and reloaded his pistol. "She's a feisty li'l thing. Reg'lar hot pepper! Said she wouldn't have it no other way. We rustled us up a padre last night an' tied the knot."

"But she was, uh . . ." Graham stopped himself. He had almost said "whore."

"I know what you're thinkin'. She was sort of took with ol' Frank, but I tell you, Graham, there never was nothin' to that. Ol' Frank's a little slow in the brainpan department, if you know what I mean." His expression was serious, and his tone was paternal and thick with false concern. Graham looked away. He was angry, but it was Frank's problem, and he didn't know what to say.

"I told her she needed to go by an' look in on him now an' again." He winked. "But no foolishness, mind you. She wasn't none too happy 'bout my takin' off yesterday, but I told her once I sold these horses, we'd have money for a real weddin' trip, maybe over to Galveston or someplace. Hell, we might just tag along with you an' go on up to Santa Fe. What do you say to that?"

Graham said nothing. He made a slow show of lighting a cigar and nodding noncommittally.

If Jack noticed, he didn't let on. He changed directions and went on about plans to continue to trade horses until he got enough money together for a place of their own down on the border near Brownsville. Graham only half listened. One of Jack's schemes sounded about like the next: Each ended with Jack Sterling sitting pretty while someone else did his work for him.

Graham found himself regarding Jack more warily than ever. He was repulsive in his unbridled enthusiasm for whatever he was "fixin' to do," as he put it, and he was dangerous, Graham decided, if he got too close to something he wanted, regardless of whether it was available or not.

The next several days Graham tried to ride alone, but

every time Jack had an opportunity to leave his horses and ride up to travel alongside Graham, he would speak fondly of his new love in San Antonio or pump Graham for more information about Santa Fe. Graham had never been naturally talkative or given to speaking freely about anything, except in rare spurts, but Jack Sterling had a way about him that charmed the gambler out of himself. He found that he wanted to tell the younger man things about his background that he had told no one else. Sterling was not particularly likable or inspiring of trust, but somehow he managed to ask the right questions in the right way.

To keep the topic of conversation away from Ursula, Graham finally weakened and began telling Sterling about the Valley of the High Snows, about Tuttle's offer to sell it for a mere five thousand dollars, more than a hundred times the money Graham had buttoned in his leather stump for safekeeping and about which Sterling was ignorant. His companion warmed to the subject, and Graham discovered that he, too, liked talking about the proposition as if it were a possibility. So interested did Sterling become that Graham almost gave away Tuttle's name and located the valley for Jack. He bit his tongue to keep from saying too much, although he told himself that it made no difference. There was no way he could ever have the money anyway. The way his luck had been running lately, he'd be lucky to get back to San Antonio with enough for a stake. Even so, he felt he was showing Sterling his hole card, and all he was getting in return was a load of manure about plans Jack had, plans that even Sterling himself seemed to know were nothing more than pipe dreams.

3

STERLING AND THE MEXICAN BOYS MANAGED TO KEEP the remuda together, and they arrived in Fort Concho—or, more properly, San Angelo, a dismal collection of wood picket, adobe, and fieldstone buildings across the dirty little river that ran near the fort—only twelve days after they left San Antonio. Jack Sterling took his horses across the river to dicker with the quartermaster, and Graham took up residence in a filthy single-story hotel that boasted only a dozen rooms, none of which was larger than a cell or possessed any luxury beyond a grass-filled mattress and a cracked washbasin.

The cantina next door, however, did have several rickety poker tables, and Graham set up shop over a piece of torn greenfelt at the Arc Light Saloon, the most likely-looking watering hole in San Angelo.

There were few takers. The enlisted men—who were, as Jack Sterling had predicted, mostly black soldiers—expressed little interest in poker playing, preferring to gather in the back alleys of the flat in small groups where they lost their meager earnings on rolls of dice. Graham wasn't too disappointed to miss their business. He had never sat down with Negroes to play cards even in the worst ginmills and brothels, and he wasn't sure how to act toward these former slaves, many of whom seemed arrogant when they strutted in their uniforms back and forth in the muddy streets of San Angelo.

Graham managed to organize only three real games during the first two days, and he quickly cleaned out the civilians who came to his table and spent more time pumping him for news from San Antonio than they did paying attention to their cards. By the third afternoon, he tired of dealing solitaire to himself, and he was relieved when Sterling showed up and announced that they were leaving and taking the horses with them.

"Yankee son of a bitch won't pay but ten dollars a head," Sterling complained. "He don't want but five head to boot, an' he wants 'em broke to that heavy military hardware." He spat into the dirt. "Hell with him. Let's try our luck up the Line."

Graham's luck at cards was no better in the Flat, a shantytown near Fort Griffin. Neither was Jack's. Cursing the government and its agents roundly, he set out for Phantom Hill, a temporary outpost located where an old camp had been. Graham stayed behind.

Graham was strangely relieved when Sterling left. He joined a supply train for Fort Richardson near the developing community of Jacksboro. He had not realized what a burden Jack's company had been to him, and he hoped

that at last he would be able to concen
when he reached the post. He was rewa
luck finally improved.

Graham found the officers and the
eager to sit down over a hand or two, an
liberated more than six hundred dollars fro ockets
inside a week.

His old skills began to return to him, and his powers of concentration came back as well. The cards continued to run against him more often than not, but as he played, his confidence was building. He wished they had more money to wager so the pots could grow to a respectable size.

"I wonder why more people don't go out to Santa Fe," Graham said one night across the table. He casually passed the buck and waited for the man on his left to deal another hand. "There's plenty of land, an' there's clearly money to be made from the buffalo."

"Comanch', Cheyenne, Sioux, Blackfoot, Kiowa," the man responded. "Them's reason enough. Redskins don't take kindly to people killin' off their meat an' taters."

"Sodbusters, nesters, an' squatters," another man said, and spat. "Whole goddamn plain's fillin' up with 'em. I can remember a time when a man could ride from the Trinity all the way up to Colorado an' not see a single white man. Now you stumble 'cross one ever' time you turn 'roun'. Can't throw a rock 'thout hittin' a wagonload of snot-nosed kids jabberin' on in some lingo you never heard the like of. I come out here to get away from that, but hell's fire, li'l ol' bitty towns that wasn't even there two years ago is more crowded'n Chicago or St. Louis. Same goddamn thing's fixin' to happen to Texas. You jus' hide an' watch."

"Indians'll keep 'em out," the first man repeated.

"Army'll keep the Indians out," the other put in.

"The Army?" The second man held one finger against a nostril and emptied the other with a loud snort, "Tit on a boar hog! Useless bunch of pecker-headed niggers ridin' 'roun' followin' some green kid with a yellow patch on his shoulder, thumb up his ass, an' a sword in his belt, shoutin'

‐rs like some kind of preacher savin' souls. Spend half ıeir time chasin' each other. Hell, they've killed more mules ridin' 'round in circles than they'll ever kill redskins. Army! In a pig's asshole!"

"Nobody can survive crossin' West Texas," a third man put in. "Can't be did 'less it's a man who knows where he's goin' an' how to get there. There's five hun'erd ways to die out yonder, an' only a hun'erd or so has to do with Indians. Soon's I get myself a stake, I'm goin' back to Mississippi an' raise pigs. It ain't fixin' to make me rich, but it'll surer'n hell keep me alive. Nobody I know has went out there by hisself an' come back alive."

It was then that one old man told the story of a black man who was scouting for settlers going west across Texas. The old man's name was simply Dutchman, he said, and he bragged in broken English that this scout was making a name for himself across the lower plains.

"Dey zay he's zavvy," Dutchman insisted. "Zay he don' act like no darkie at all. Zay he's gute mit a rifle, an' he knowed his vay. I don't know. I never zeed a nigger who vouldn't get lost 'tween de barn an' de privy, but dat's vat dey zay."

"What's his name?" the first gambler asked.

"Calls hizself Moses," Dutchman said with an ironic chuckle. "Moses Franklin. Maybe he's a Yid. A nigger Yid." He lit a pipe and then said reflectively, "But I hear he's damn gute. If dot's true, don't matter vat color he is. Not vere de Comanch' is concerned."

"Where Comanch' is concerned," the first man concluded, "bein' 'good' just means bein' alive."

"I'm tellin' you," Dutchman said as he inspected his holdings and found them too wanting to continue in the game, "de only vay a man who don't know de vay kin croz Texas an' lif to tell 'bout it is mit a gude zcout und a lot off guns. Odervize, he ought to ztay home. Come to tink of it, if he's got a lick of zense, he'll ztay home anyvay. Dot's vere I'm goin' zoon as I get me a ztake, boy. You kin count on it. I vant to die in my bed mit my chil'ren 'round me. I don't vant my hair hangin' vrum no Comanch' zchielt, boy."

Graham noted with slight disgust that Dutchman was

as bald as a rock, and he excused himself and retired from the rough company for the night.

The next morning, Graham rose early and counted his holdings. He owned a decent horse, over thirteen hundred dollars in greenbacks and gold, two pistols, and a handsome saddle a cowboy had lost to him. He didn't know what was to be the next trail in his life, but he realized that he was better off than he had been in years.

Jack Sterling showed up that same afternoon in time to pass dinner with the gambler. His luck had not been so good. A Kiowa raiding party, he claimed, had stolen the fourteen horses he had been unable to sell and killed both *charros* in the process. The whole story as he related it was vague, and Graham doubted it from the start. His doubts grew stronger when Sterling refused to report the depredation to the post commandant, claiming, "It won't do no good. Shit, they'll just send out a bunch of these poor nigger bucks to get theirselves killed."

More than likely, Graham told himself, the two Mexican boys got fed up with Sterling's bossing them around and rode off with whatever horses he had left. Or, Graham thought, it was just as likely that Sterling had sold all the horses and killed the boys to keep from having to pay them.

Jack claimed that he had fewer than two hundred dollars left from the sale, and after he bought a round of drinks with two wrinkled bills, he seemed more down and prone to get drunk than Graham had ever seen him. Graham sensed an opportunity and bought a bottle, which they drank while the gambler searched for a tactful way to tell Sterling that he was thinking of heading out on his own. He was rambling through his options in general terms, holding firm in his commitment to part from this odd, perplexing man forever, when Jack brought up the subject of New Mexico again.

"How much you reckon it would take to start a horse ranch up there?"

"I don't know," Graham said, truthfully. "I know to buy the land I want, it would take five thousand dollars or fifty head of blooded breed stock. That wouldn't buy me in completely. It would only get the land, or half of it."

"Fifty head?"

"That's what the man out there wants. Money or horses."

"Why hell, fifty head's nothin'." Jack sat back and studied the coal-oil lamp on the table between them. "Hell, I can raise fifty head of horses for a fart an' a song!"

"*Good* horses," Graham said, wondering just how much horse*shit* Sterling could raise. "Not a bunch of sag-bellied plugs or wild mustangs. Breed stock. The man wants near-thoroughbred quality, and he wants them from Kentucky or Tennessee. That would take more money than I've got."

"Have you got a thousan' dollars?" Jack Sterling asked. His black eyes narrowed, and he seemed to sober instantly as he leaned forward. "For a thousan' dollars I can get you your valley. Where we go from there is up to you."

Graham was intrigued, but he also was instantly on his guard. He felt the money hidden on his person was like a part of his body. He wasn't willing to let Sterling know that he had that kind of cash. He didn't want to lie, and he struggled against revealing too much; but at the same time, Sterling's proposition opened a warm sense of possibility inside him. The dreams of the past months came flooding into his consciousness with a cozy familiarity. He evaded the question.

"The man wants people out there. He has an idea that the railroad might come through. Horses, people, good land. It's kind of an idea he has. It might work. It might not."

Sterling slapped the table with the flat of his hand. "Goddamn right it'll work! We'll be partners in the biggest deal you ever seen."

"I don't know," Graham muttered. "It's nice to think about."

"It's better to do," Sterling said. "I can do'er. You come up with the money, I'll get you your valley. The rest, like I say, is purely up to you."

"Come up with the money," Graham repeated. "That's what the man said. Money or horses." Then he added, heedless of a warning voice inside him, "Or even good whiskey, or anything that represents cash. I don't know."

"Well, *I* know." Sterling's eyes gleamed from behind his alcoholic enthusiasm. "I know an opportunity when I see one. It's sort of my trademark."

"I'll have to think about it," Graham said guardedly, but in his heart, he was committed. It seemed that everything that had ever happened to him had led him to this point. It was a basic denomination. He was going to do it, risk everything on one hand. It was an inside straight, he told himself as he looked at Jack's smiling, almost comically greedy expression, but sometimes a man has to gamble, trust to luck, and just hope the hell that he gets away with it. Sometimes it just comes down to taking another card and then betting the pot.

"I'M ALL RIGHT," GRAHAM insisted, while Aggie Sterling and Hannah Morgan tried to hold him down. "Let me go, damnit!" He wrenched his stubbed arm free from Aggie's grasp harder than he meant to, and immediately he turned to try to focus to see if he had harmed her.

His right eye was fine. The effects of the blow to his head had finally left him with nothing more than a throbbing headache—which could also be the result of the large drinks of whiskey he had taken. But his left eye was clouded and blurred. He could focus with it closed, but it still smarted and tended to make him dizzy.

"I need some kind of patch," he said, stumbling away from Hannah. He closed the eye painfully and tried to get his bearings. The cave stopped spinning as it had done the first three times he attempted to stand. Hannah reached out to steady him. "I'm all right," he insisted again, but he stumbled and sat down hard.

Near them Virgil Hollister sat upright. A new bandage brightly stained with blood was wound around his neck, and the calf of his leg was also wrapped in a crude canvas rag that had a big red splotch in its middle. He said nothing and offered no particular expression. He just stared at Graham with a quiet but seething contempt.

"He'll be all right," Aggie said to Graham. "He's

weak, but he's too mean to die. I just thank the Lord that he's quiet for a change."

Hannah handed Graham the twin nickel-plated revolvers, and he awkwardly reholstered them. "Fancy guns," she said with a mixture of admiration and contempt. "Did you have your rifle?" she asked. Graham shook his head. "Shouldn't go 'bout without your rifle. I can't be ever'where at once."

Aggie ripped a strip of canvas and tied it around Graham's head to cover his injured eye. "It looks some better," she said, "but it's still seepin' blood. That fellow Golden kicked you for fair."

"Is he dead?" Graham tried to remember, but the sight of Golden's angry face was all he could conjure.

"I reckon so." She lowered her head and rested it on her hands. "I hated to see it," she said. "He went out of his way for me. But it was him or you, I reckon. An' Hannah did what she had to."

"I guess I owe you my life." Graham squinted at Hannah. He was getting to the point where he owed his life to half the people he met, he thought.

"You don't owe me nothin'." She looked away. "I jus' know with that colored boy gone, Sterlin' dead, an' nobody else on this train but me an' this gal with a lick of sense, there ain't much choice but to keep people from killin' you. You're the onliest one can get us to New Mexico, if that's where we're goin'."

"That's where we're goin'," Graham said. The bandage helped. He looked around the dim cave and learned that with the patch over his left eye, his right focused well enough. Jason and Lottie Herbert sat off to one side, holding each other. Glorietta Fulbright was gone, but Constance Kruikshank remained next to her husband. "But I'm a hell of a leader," he said. "One-handed and one-eyed. If I lose a leg, then I'll be done on that side."

"You keep talkin' like that an' I'll cut it off myself." Aggie looked up with a stern expression.

"I'm sorry you had to kill him," Graham said to Hannah. He looked toward the bright sunlight that streamed through the cave's entrance. "We have enough trouble without that. They're not goin' to let you get away with it."

"I can live with it. I've lived with worse," she said. "An' they ain't got enough backbone to hang a woman." She grinned soberly. "Nor enough grit to hang me. It's been tried, or worse has, an' there ain't nobody 'roun' to tell about it." She rose and moved over to the whiskey keg. Jason stood and pulled Lottie up with him, then they joined Annie and went out of the cave. They didn't take their eyes off Graham until they cleared the entrance.

Hannah poured another dollop of whiskey into the cup. "I killed a man when I was fourteen," she said. "I killed 'nother when I was eighteen, an' I would of killed me 'nother'un a year later, but he run off 'fore I got the chance." She took a sip from the cup and handed it to him. "I've taken on one or two others since. I've handled Mescan bandits an' thievin' Indians an' Yankee looters. In uniform an' out. An' I've stood my groun' ever' time. I doubt serious that a bunch of busted hoe-hands like that's goin' to get me. If they do, then I got too high a opinion of myself."

He accepted the cup from her and drank off the whiskey in one swallow. It burned his throat again, but he found he was getting used to it. His head rang and hurt.

"I got to get out there an' talk to those folks," Graham said. He saw that she started to protest, but she thought better of it and helped him to his feet. He grimaced with the pain of moving. "I wish I could call them all together an' talk to them, explain what's happenin'. I got to make 'em see that fightin' amongst ourselves won't solve anything."

Although he said nothing, Hollister's glare seemed to increase, and Graham thought he could feel it. He turned and looked at the injured preacher.

"You're lucky it's not you that's dead," Graham said. "It ought to be." Hollister did not signify that he heard. Aggie and Hannah also remained silent. Graham turned to them. "Y'all try to get some rest. Things could get hot when it gets dark. They might hit us at sunset like they did last night. We can't count on a storm every time."

Graham stiffened his posture as best he could in the low cave and moved out into the sunshine. Those settlers nearby turned their heads and studied him as he adjusted his hat against the afternoon blaze, and he looked at them as evenly as he could from his good eye.

"Good luck," he heard Aggie whisper behind him. Her voice was full of sincerity, and he felt his heart growing warm inside his chest. He nodded and started down the wagon line to try to reassert his authority.

CHAPTER THREE

1

"PRIVVY," THE SIGN OVER THE LATRINE CAVE SAID IN crude lettering.

"Ain't nobody used it yet," Giorgio Patrizi said to Graham while he inspected the boys' work.

"Well, if you get away from here for a bit, maybe they will," Graham said.

His walk up the wagon line had been more rapid than his previous inspections. The afternoon's air, although much warmer than the cave's, had awakened his senses, and while his head still throbbed with a dull ache, he found that it was tolerable and that his vision was mostly clear in his exposed eye.

The people he passed on his quick stroll past their wagons shot him deep, furtive looks. He was no longer observed as the source of an answer to impossible questions. Rather, he found that he had joined Aggie as an outcast, but with a difference. They had put their trust in him, and because of him—now directly because of him—another man was dead. He stopped and tried to talk to several of them, but they stared right past him as if he were nothing more than a barking dog to be ignored until he went away. Finally, he gave up and stalked past them without pausing.

He stood in front of the makeshift privy and removed his broad-brimmed leather hat and wiped his injured eye. It was more than he could bear. He owed these people nothing, he told himself, not one goddamn thing. He had told them it would be risky, admonished them to be certain to arm themselves, cautioned them that some wouldn't make it. But he had known even when he said such things that each individual was confident of his ability to get across the prairie alive. It would be someone else who would be hurt, sick, or killed.

He turned and headed himself back toward his wagon. It was now gloomy late afternoon in the crossing's tiny valley, and Graham's disposition was only somewhat better. He collected his rifle from where he had left it and made another inspection. He saw Pierce and Quigley up on the ledge, in position. Maybe something good had come out of Golden's killing after all, he thought. At least the rest of them seemed to be doing as they were told. He approached two sleeping men and instructed them to go up and replace the lookouts. They did so without comment or back talk, and Graham felt better.

When he passed the hospital cave, he stopped and peered inside. In the gathering shadows of the afternoon, the interior seemed black to his single eye, and he strained it and felt pain from his injured temple shoot down once again into his neck. He spotted Aggie lying on a pallet near the small spring that bubbled in the back. Hannah Morgan saw Graham peering in and put a finger to her lips. Graham backed out of the opening and slumped down next to the Sterling wagon. His head ached and his eye burned. Hannah came out just as he was thinking of trying to get someone to unwrap it and take another look.

"I jus' got her to lay down again," Hannah whispered. "She's wore to a nub, an' for good reason. I don't know what got into me. That girl's carried the whole weight of this thing on her shoulders." She shook her head. "I jus' jumped in an' made things worse."

In spite of his agreement with Hannah, Graham resented her accusing tone. "She's not the only one under a strain," he said.

"Yeah?" Hannah said sharply. "Well, don't go all God Almighty on me, Cleve Graham. You ain't lost your mama an' daddy all in one day an' then had to sit all by yourself an' nurse men who had no chance of livin'. 'Cept for that Smith fellow, not one of them hombres has a prayer, an' I seen bogged heifers two days in the mud that had better chances than he's got. Ever'one of 'em's good as dead." Graham dropped the number of survivors to fifty-eight with the automatic calculation of a veteran gambler. "Now she's got to watch out for you, too, or so she says. I swear, Graham, you got to get this thing back on the road. We might get run down an' killed out there"—she gestured vaguely to the trail leading west out of the crossing—"but here we're goin' to wind up jus' as dead."

Graham looked away. Hannah was a hard woman. She was also a strong woman, but he knew that she had a breaking point as well. She was coming as close as she dared in showing him that right now, and he needed to find the right thing to say.

"Them Sterlin' girls are a wonder," she said. "It's more of a miracle, knowin' their daddy."

"Well, he's dead."

"I know he is. An' I know how," Hannah said. "We all know how." Graham stared at her. "Don't worry none 'bout it," she said. "We seen what you done an' why you done it. Ain't nobody blamin' you. But I'll tell you this." She glanced once more to see if anyone was listening to her whispered conversation. "Ain't nobody fixin' to get in your way if they're hurt like that, an' you best see to it that you don't get hurt your own self." She pressed her cracked lips one more time with a crooked finger. "I ain't the only one they'd like to see danglin' from a hackberry branch. You think that colored boy'll be back tomorrow?"

"I don't know," Graham said. He felt as if he had uttered those words a thousand times that day. "Frank'll do what he can. But I don't know." He rubbed his face with his hand. His beard felt greasy. "I don't trust him."

"Is that right?" She shook her head. "Then why didn't you go your ownself? What's the matter with you, Graham? You hire a nigger boy an' give him a man's job. Now you're having doubts. If you didn't think you could trust him, why'd you take him on?"

"It was a mistake," Graham said. "Not just because he's colored. That's not all the reason." Graham scooted up a bit from his slumped position and tried to see beyond Hannah's head. He didn't want to be jumped while he stood and talked. His temple ached, and he had to concentrate hard to keep himself alert. "It doesn't matter whether he's colored or not. I don't think he's doin' his job, an' I think this is all his fault. He led us into this trap."

"I don't think so," she said quickly. "I know you was

mad at him for stayin' behind to bury them greasers back there. But I think there's more to it'n that. More to it'n him bein' colored, too."

"It was a foolish thing to do," Graham muttered. The woman's assessment of the situation made him feel small. He studied his boot tops and tried not to look Hannah in the eye. "The point is that I gave him an order an' he ignored it. I'm the boss of these wagons."

"You sure it don't have more to do with *her* stayin' behind with him?" Hannah's eyes drifted toward the cave's entrance. "Ain't that's what's sourin' your well?"

"I told him to come on an' forget about it. I told her, too. She's not my responsibility. He is. Maybe if we'd just come on, got settled in here a day earlier, we wouldn't have been caught so easy. Just maybe there wouldn't be damn near fifty people dead. Maybe they wouldn't be gettin' ready to string us both up." He was suddenly weary of the argument. "It was a damn fool thing to do."

"Aggie thought it was the right thing to do," Hannah said with a low voice. "An' if doin' it caused all this"—she waved a hand in the vague direction of the creek—"then it caused her mama an' daddy to die, too. But I don't hear her whinin' over it. Not one bit." She sighed. "They'd of caught up with us anyhow. They's too many of 'em for one little ol' barrel of whiskey an' a couple of skinny cows to satisfy for long."

"It was still foolish."

"It ain't none of my business, Cleve, but then maybe it is, since it's my hair as much as it is anybody's, an' since it's led to my havin' to shoot a man who never done me no harm. But I think you're actin' like a damn fool. I think you've got somethin' in your craw you can't spit out. I don't know what it is, but I hope to Jesus you get it out 'fore long. Elsewise, it's fixin' to get more'n fifty folks killed. It's fixin' to be the end of this train an' ever'body left in it." She paused. "I've lived through a lot, Cleve. I've seen what can happen when men go just a little bit crazy over a woman. I've lived through it before, an' I've killed because of it. In a way, I think I killed Golden for it. I sure hate to die for it, 'cause it's a lot of goddamn foolishness." She stopped again and looked hard at Graham. "She's a wonder, Graham, but she ain't worth gettin' ever'body killed over. I sure hope you can come to see that 'fore it's too late."

"I don't know what you're talkin' about," Graham growled and turned away.

Hannah flapped her hands against her skirts in a hopeless gesture. "Yeah, well, my first husband said the same thing when I told him to leave well 'nough alone. I buried him, an' I jus' hope to God somebody comes along an' buries me when this is over."

Graham flushed red under his beard. He felt his emotions showing, and he tucked his chin into his chest to try to hide his face beneath the brim of his hat. "Let's hope all the killin's done. Let's hope that they get back here with some kind of help, an' we can . . . bury the dead an' just go on. I've already killed one man, an' caused you to kill another." He held up his hand to stop her from protesting. "It isn't because of . . . of what you think. There's more at stake here than that. I haven't lost my mind. But I don't want to have to kill another man." White man, he mentally amended his statement. "An' it's likely I'll have to do just that.

"But I'll tell you one thing! Without that whiskey, there's no point in goin' on for any of us. An' if that nigger boy don't get back soon, the whole thing's just gone belly-up an' there ain't nothing neither one of us can do about it." He looked out over the creek suddenly. "They'll likely hang us no matter what."

"I ain't scared of 'em," Hannah said. "I did what I had to do, an' I'd do it again."

"I would too," Graham admitted.

Hannah glanced inside the cave and checked to make sure Aggie was still asleep. "What I want to know is if it'd been Frank Herbert bad hurt like her daddy was, or me, or somebody else, would you of shot him, too?"

Graham reddened and thought about the question. It was not something that had occurred to him before. "Yeah," he said finally. "I would have."

"So why do you feel so guilty?" She smiled at him and her eyes flashed. "You're sparkin' that gal, ain't you? Or tryin' to. That's it, ain't it?" Her smile broadened to a grin that forced a deep blush underneath Graham's beard. "I s'pose that's natural. She's a pretty li'l thing an' hard as nails."

"I don't know what you're talkin' about," Graham said quickly, finding himself unable to look Hannah in the eye.

"Oh, you know, all right. I thought it was somethin' like that. You're what the Mescans call *loco para corazón*. Hell, I should've seen it all along. You're worse'n any lovesick bull I ever seen. Harder to get 'long with, too."

"That's not it."

"Oh, yeah." Hannah smirked. "Don't worry. I ain't accusin' you of nothin'. But I tell you a truth." She looked quickly around and then leaned forward and whispered, "You better make damn sure I'm hurtin' that bad 'fore you try to put a bullet in me."

Graham remained quiet, his chin down, his eyes averted. "I'll make sure, but if you need a bullet, I'll give it to you."

He walked away and forced thoughts of the blond girl out of his mind. If it was that obvious to Hannah, then it was to everyone, he thought. Was it obvious to Aggie as well? Part of him wanted it to be, and another more fearful part of him hoped that it was not. Above all, he feared appearing to be a fool. When he reached his wagon, he checked the loads on all his weapons. He squinted through his good eye up and down the train.

I don't know anything about this, he confessed to himself and almost spoke the words aloud. I'm not a wagon master. I'm a gambler. I'm a dude, not even man enough to fight my own fights. A woman had to save me. He mentally pictured Hannah. She's a formidable woman, he admitted, and a sharp one, but a woman nevertheless.

Aggie treated him like a baby, made him lie down and take his medicine. She fawned over him like a hurt puppy, and in spite of the pain and embarrassment, he let her, and he loved it. Hannah saw what he felt for the girl plainly, and she was amused by it. He felt like an idiot.

"Goddamnit, goddamnit!" he swore. Newsome looked up from his position nearby, and Graham turned away and continued his self-chastisement silently. I was a fool to think I could lead a bunch of people out into the wilderness to some kind of promised land, he thought. How in the hell did I get trapped into this?

As he agonized over the question, he glanced out onto the gravel and spotted Jack Sterling's foot stretched out at an odd angle only a dead man could achieve, and he knew.

2

THE ENTIRE ADVENTURE EVENTUALLY BECAME JACK Sterling's own. During the days they rode east from Fort Richardson through Fort Worth and the young community of Dallas on the Trinity, they talked the plan to death. Jack was fascinated. He would take Graham's cash, over a thousand dollars, go to Tennessee, buy the horses—he was sure he could get them for twenty dollars a head or less, horses of no lesser quality than the big black he himself was riding—and return to Jefferson and meet Graham by late winter. They could hire a wrangler or two, and then they could make Santa Fe with the stock before midsummer. With luck, more than one mare would be ready to foal, and Tuttle—Graham had by now laid out the whole deal, including the valley owner's name—might sweeten the pie.

Graham was afraid to believe in the plan too wholeheartedly. But on Sterling's tongue, it took hard shape. When they reached Jefferson, Graham set up in the Excelsior House and found himself a comfortable table in the Red River Saloon on Soda Street. He demurred for a week, and he wired a hundred dollars to Frank with a letter advising him to collect Dolores and to come on. He worried about Frank's reaction to Jack and Ursula being married, but there wasn't much he could do about it.

The end of January came, and he played carefully and won more money to add to his stash, all the while fending off Sterling, who dogged his tracks and constantly urged him to turn over the cash so they could set things rolling. Finally, Graham gave in and handed Jack the bills. He watched the wily horse trader open a money belt and stuff the notes into it. Graham wondered if he would ever see any of it again.

"There's more than a thousand dollars there," Graham said in an even, serious tone. "You lose it or don't come back, I'll find you an' kill you."

Jack grinned away the insult. "You don't have to worry, Cleve," he said. "I'll be back in a month with the prettiest goddamn horses you ever seen. I know just where to get 'em. You just hire us the wranglers an' let me handle the rest."

As he watched Sterling climb onto his fancy saddle and guide his horse away from the hotel, Graham felt his stomach churn with misgivings. Only the strongest force of will kept him from running after the retreating black and pulling Sterling down and forcing him to return the money.

February dragged by slowly, and March finally began. Graham played poker less and less as the days warmed and the trees and flowers budded. Frank failed to show up or return word, and he was beginning to worry about him as well. He went for an hour or two every day to the road north to watch for Jack's prancing black to come down the street, and each time he cursed himself for his impatience. He told no one of his plan, but he did consult with the local Army headquarters about the situation west of the Indian Line.

"I wouldn't go out there," a smooth-shaven major advised him with a shake of his head. "It just ain't smart. Hostiles're more nervous this spring than ordinary. We're gettin' reports of raids as close as Denton County."

The news distressed Graham, but he continued to wait for Jack to return. Maybe they could head the herd north, take them up through Arkansas and Missouri, and then join the Santa Fe Trail and follow it all the way. It was a possibility. But any hope Graham had for following through with alternatives to crossing Indian country in Texas were negated when Jack Sterling finally showed up, not with fifty head of prime horseflesh, but with forty kegs of Tennessee whiskey.

"You spent the *whole roll* on whiskey?" Graham shook with rage.

"Wasn't no horses to be had." Sterling opened his palms in a helpless gesture. "I mean, I could of bought maybe twenty head of the quality you wanted for the money you gave me, but you said he wanted near fifty, an' fifty couldn't be had for twice the price."

"Twenty head! For more'n a *thousand dollars*! What'd they have? Wings? You said you knew men an' you knew horses. You said you knew right where to get them!"

"I said what I said, but it's been a long time. Things have changed back there. Jew carpetbaggers got hold of ever'thing. I could of bought hay-burners with split hooves an' the mad staggers for ten dollars a head, but prime stock, good stock like you want, costs a lot more money." His eyes narrowed in a show of shrewd bargaining. "I got the whiskey for twenty dollars a barrel. An' it's quality stuff. Bonded. Stamped an' ever'thing. From what you said, we can sell it for more'n a hundred. That's damn close to five thousand dollars, close enough I'd say."

Graham stalked up and down in front of the landing and pondered what he should do. In Jefferson the whiskey wouldn't bring much more than Jack had paid for it, and he had no plan for getting it to New Mexico at all. It would take two or three wagons and teams—that is, if he could find men to drive them across hostile territory where their hair would be at risk the whole time. By the time he added the men and their equipment, deducted what it all would cost, they'd be lucky to clear the nearly eleven hundred dollars Jack had sunk into the proposition.

He watched the black dockworkers sweating as they rolled the heavy kegs down a plank and stacked them on the dock. "This is no damn good, Jack," he said, trying to control his anger and disappointment. "You've put me between a rock an' a hard place on this deal. I'd allow that the whole thing's off."

"Off!" Sterling's face darkened, and Graham stepped back. Once again, the horse trader's easy, glad-handing manner evaporated, and Graham found himself facing a different man altogether. This was a purer strain of evil than Graham had believed him capable of concealing. "It *ain't* off! Ain't *nothin'* off. We don't got horses, an' I'm sorry 'bout that. But we got somethin' just as good. There's more'n five thousan' dollars' worth of high-powered bug juice in them kegs, an' if you won't take it out there, I will." Sterling turned on his heel and back aboard the boat, presumably to see to the off-loading of his horse. "You said the man said money or horses," he called over his shoulder. "An' from what else you said, whiskey's just as good. So I'm goin'. You do what you want."

Graham went back to the hotel. He had been defrauded. He felt defeated. The money was only part of it. The rest evaporated like the dream. He had been gutted, played for a fool, he told himself, and he should have known better. It was the same old song all over again.

Along his way back to the Excelsior House he passed lines of wagons, settlers mostly, queued up on side streets awaiting a chance to join a train to head west. Like him the year before, most of them had only a vague idea of where they were bound for. They were running away more often than not, from poverty, hopelessness, bad land, bad luck. Most of them were what were called "good people," though. Only a few had the look of fleeing the law or other, more serious trouble. A thriving business in draft animals was taking place at neighboring ranches and farms. Mules were hard to come by, and Graham had noticed in the *Jimplecute* that numbers of oxen were coming up for sale. He wished he were also preparing for such a simple journey to a new life. He didn't want to be involved in quick deals and gambling chances anymore.

He was surprised when he returned to his room to find Frank Herbert sitting on the side of the bed, waiting for him. In a chair was a pretty, dark girl whose long, stringy hair hung down and almost covered her face. Her dress was homespun, and she wore canvas shoes with holes that showed her toes.

"This here's my li'l girl," Frank said. "Lottie, say hello to Cap'n Graham."

"*Mister*," Graham said as he stepped forward and took the girl's limp hand. He was shocked and surprised. "I didn't know you had a daughter, Frank."

"Her mama died a couple of months ago," Frank said. "I didn't have no way to go fetch her till your money come. She's been over in Louisiana ever since, down 'round Jefferson Parish. Her mama's a Cajun. They lived in the swamps. I think she's a li'l bit wild." He looked at her approvingly in spite of the dirty dress and long, greasy hair. "I sure 'nough loved her though."

Graham gestured, and they stepped outside and strolled down into the hotel's lobby.

Graham smoked a cigar and thought about it for a moment. "Did you talk to Dolores 'bout comin' up here?"

"She run off," Frank said. "I don't know where she went." Graham felt as if he had been slapped. He hadn't realized how much he felt for the girl until that moment, and disappointment came over him unexpectedly. Frank went on, "I heard Mexico, but I also heard New Orleans. I was laid up with my leg till near Christmas, when they throwed me out of the hotel, an' she'd skedaddled it by then."

"What about Ursula?" Graham was reluctant to have to break the news to Frank. But he apparently already knew, for his face darkened and he looked down at the braided rug on the lobby's floor. But when he spoke, Graham almost dropped his cigar in surprise.

"She's dead, Cap'n," he said. "They found her right after you an' Jack took off. Somebody got her up in a hotel room over on St. Mary's Street an' beat her to death with a full tequila bottle. Didn't break it or nothin'. He jus' walloped her again an' again, they said. I figured that's why Dolores run off, too. They don't know who done it, but I was sure sorry. I really liked that li'l gal."

Graham felt fear crawling up his back like a column of ants. His body tingled.

"When did you say they found her?" Graham asked through clenched teeth.

"Right after you left. I heard 'bout it from that Mex porter in the hotel. Said she must of been killed that night. That was the same night you come by to say adios."

Graham shivered. For the second time in an hour he felt the desire to murder Sterling, but again he fought it. There were other things to worry about, and killing Jack right in the middle of Jefferson would only complicate matters. It could also, he reminded himself, get him hanged.

The two men stood silently in the hotel corridor. A couple walked past them and stared. Graham puffed angrily on his cigar, and Frank stood stock-still and silent before his former officer. He didn't seem at all uncomfortable with Graham's silent contemplation. Graham tried to quiet the storm he felt raging inside him.

Married her! Graham's inner voice screamed in an ironic tone. The son of a bitch had said he'd married her. And Graham had believed him. He hadn't even thought that much about it. Hell, she was only a child—barely had breasts. But then, maybe Jack did marry her. Maybe he went out and found some Mexican priest, and maybe they went through some sort of ceremony. Then he took her to a hotel, and when he got what he could have had just as easily for two greenbacks, he took a bottle and killed her.

Graham thought about going to the sheriff. He could get rid of Jack that way, have him arrested, then he could see if he could sell the whiskey for what he could get and then clear out.

And go where? he asked himself. Off in the distance he heard a riverboat's steam whistle from the downtown area, and he shook his head. No, he told himself, he couldn't go back to that either. There was only one place he wanted to go, and that was now out of reach as well. He was boxed in. He was in league with a thorough scoundrel—a murderer and likely a thief, Graham thought with a memory of the horses and the scrappy bill of sale Jack had insisted on showing him. But the sheriff of Jefferson was out of the way also. Even if he believed Graham—and there was no reason why he should—why should he care if some Mexican whore was beaten to death almost six months ago? Hell, Graham thought, they probably wouldn't even arrest Jack for that down in San Antonio.

"I felt real bad 'bout it." Frank finally broke the long silence. "She was a sweet li'l thing." Graham continued to smoke and cogitate. "You know, Cap'n, we never, uh . . . did nothin', you know?"

Graham looked up and stared at Frank.

"I mean, it'd been too much like bein' with my own li'l gal, Lottie." His eyes pointed to their room's door. "I never went in for no whores anyhow. Jus' never saw no profit in it."

"There rarely is," Graham said. "Most of them are just lookin' for a soft place to fall."

"Ain't we all, Cap'n." Frank stared at his feet and shook his head. "Ain't we all."

Graham left the hotel and started back down the street, but Jack met him and pulled him into a saloon.

"Look," he said when he had ordered a round of drinks and expansively paid for both, "I know you're mad, an' you got a right to be. But if you think on it, we're better off. Horses can be a lot of bother. They get hurt, they get sick, they run off, an' out there"—he looked through the west wall of the saloon as if he could see the distant, Indian-laden prairie—"they get stole. Men get killed tryin' to protect a herd of horses. Look what happened to me last winter, an' them horses wasn't worth cuttin' up for a Chinaman's breakfast."

"Men get worse than killed tryin' to haul five or six wagonloads of whiskey out there," Graham said.

"Not if there's a lot of men." Sterling winked and signaled for another round. " 'Sides, we're not fixin' to give any whiskey to any damn Indians, not that stuff anyhow. That's bonded," he repeated. "It's got the seal right on the keg. You ain't tasted nothin' so good this side of Vicksburg. It's mother's milk, pure as rainwater." The barkeeper brought their drinks. Graham sipped his and winced more than was necessary. "You said that money an' horses was what this fellow Tuttle wanted, but you also said that he told you that if you bring him anythin' that would add up to the right amount, then he'd go on an' make the deal. Well, I been thinkin' on it, an' I think I got it figured out."

He laid out his idea, and when he finished, Graham acknowledged that it was the only option open to him. They, he and Graham, would form a wagon train, a collection of well-armed settlers who would provide both the protection and the vehicles to carry the whiskey from East Texas to New Mexico.

"Hell, this town's crawlin' with suckers lookin' for a way west. We'll give it to 'em," he said with a quick glance around. "We can charge 'em to join up, sell 'em their animals, to boot. We might come out with a healthier profit than you reckoned."

At first Graham was doubtful. He had no experience heading up a wagon train, but Sterling continued to argue and appeal to Graham's sense of desperation to get back to Santa Fe. The elusive dream began to take shape again.

"You was an officer," Sterling stated. "A supply officer. You know how to equip an outfit. You know as well as I do, all Indians is interested in is horses an' buffalo hunters. We won't have neither." He claimed he was confident that Graham could boss a train—especially with Jack standing right behind him—and he sweetened his argument by suggesting that Graham and he could sell parcels of the valley to the settlers when they got there, taking deposits in advance, allowing them to swap room on their wagons on which the whiskey could be loaded in exchange for a hundred acres when they arrived. If they wanted, Sterling concluded, they could purchase more land with hard cash, which would give Graham—and, Graham assumed, Sterling as well—money to start their own ranches with once they arrived.

"Hell, it's a sweet deal," he exclaimed. "If these idiots want to farm, then fine. Let 'em. You can just sit in the shade an' watch 'em. 'Sides, what good does an empty valley do you?" Sterling demanded. "You got to have stock to run on it, an' if your man out there has all the horses for the price of half the land, that don't leave you much."

Graham left Sterling still talking and walked alone up and down the streets of Jefferson and considered the idea. Much as Graham hated to admit it, Sterling seemed to have a point. Once again, the wily horse trader had wormed his way into Graham's confidence, set him thinking along lines the gambler would not have considered even moments before.

Graham couldn't forget Ursula, though, and with a sudden return of horrible suspicion down deep inside him, he wondered if Dolores's disappearance hadn't been too convenient as well. Frank said he hadn't seen her, hadn't been able to find her before she disappeared. But he fought down the questions. He didn't need to know. He didn't want to know. He detested Sterling, had enough reason to kill him right now, but like it or not, his fate was linked to Jack's, and the chain led inexorably toward the warehouse down by the landing where he had stored the forty barrels of Tennessee whiskey.

Graham walked the streets and smoked and weighed possibilities. He could see that as spring waned, the settlers were trying to organize themselves. Scouts had posted handbills advertising their services way back in January, and one or two wagon masters had also put up notices that they had room for more people on their trains. Most of them had already pulled out, and the handbills posted to the sides of buildings and lampposts were faded and torn. Some outfits were still about, however. Graham sought out one of them. It was headed by a rough man named Wilson, who was assembling his train near the Bluebonnet Farm, a plantation south of town.

"They's only three thin's you got to worry 'bout," Wilson said as he shared a cigar with Graham near his huge Conestoga. "But all three'll get you kilt." Graham waited, but the man took his time continuing.

"One's Indians. Never sell 'em short. Many a man's hair's hangin' from a Comanche shield 'cause he thought he was stronger or smarter'n Indians. They's out there, an' they'll likely fin' you if they're a min' to. If you see 'em, shoot 'em quick. That's the onliest way of discouragin' 'em. Onliest good Indian's a dead'un. Onliest dead white men's them that don't think so." He sucked on the cigar. "Can't talk to 'em nohow," he concluded. "Onliest lingo a Indian can savvy comes with a lead slug pushin' it." He smiled with the thought.

"Nex' thin' is gettin' lost. Once you pass the Little Wichita, you're pretty much on your own. Some fellers been takin' cattle up that way from down 'roun' San Antone, but they've got more balls'n brains, if you ask me. They's grasshoppers the size of cats out there can run a team right off a bluff when they get in their ears an' eyes. They's rattlesnakes ten foot long, pizenous lizards, wildcats an' wolves the size of a small horse. But the biggest worry is gettin' just plain lost. I've heard of people gettin' turned 'roun' in a cyclone an' wanderin' for days 'fore they fin'ly just give'er up an' come on back. Or died. Sweet water's hard to come by, too. You need a good scout."

"Do you know where I can hire one?" Graham asked.

"You can hire one damn near anywheres." Wilson blew smoke out through his nose and studied Graham. "But *findin'* one, well, that's 'nother matter. Most good'uns is a'ready took. Rest is all drunks or jus' so full of theirselves you can't trust 'em. Like as not, they'll haul you out somewheres, stick you up for whatever you got they want, then hightail it, an' leave you with your pecker in your han' an' Comanche sneakin' up ever' night."

He looked around a bit to see if any of his party were nearby listening. "You can't never tell 'bout 'em. I was takin' a bunch down to 'roun' Austin two years ago, an' the son of a bitch come up on me, stove my head in, an' lit out with my horse an' damn near five hun'erd dollars in gold. Lucky for me some Rangers come up on him—thought he looked like a thief an' hung him on the spot. When I got there, they give me back my horse, anyhow. Lost the money." He plucked a piece of tobacco from his tongue. "Never had much use for Rangers ever since. Anyhow, it's hard to make sure you're gettin' a good man. I like to never foun' one myself, but I fin'ly got me a good'un, I think. Least he don't drink. Much. But it really don't matter. I'm jus' goin' as far as the Brazos. Down 'roun' Waco. Then I'm headin' south to the Llano River. These folks already got their lan' picked out, an' this time I ain't carryin' no gold."

Graham pondered the problem. He knew well what getting lost could mean. When he had crossed the high plains before, they had simply pointed their wagons away from the sunrise each morning and headed west. Often, he recalled, they found that a cloudy day would cause them to veer off to the north or south, but they had no specific destination, just the mountains and the silver mines beyond them, and they encountered settlements often enough to ask directions if they felt they were wandering too far off course.

"It's late in the year," he commented. "Most scouts are taken." A memory took shape in his mind. "You ever hear of a colored man who scouts for trains?"

Wilson looked sympathetically at Graham and rubbed his chin. "Nigger boy," he said slowly. "Yeah, I've heard of him. I hear he's took four or five an' got 'em through. Right 'cross Comanche country. Says he knows somethin' 'bout Indians, least how to stay clear of 'em, an' says that he knows the country. If it's true, he's got hair on his balls, nigger or no. Personally, I wouldn't try her with a *white* man whether he'd done'er before or not."

"What's he called?"

"Franklin." Wilson rubbed his whiskered chin in thought. "Somethin' Franklin. Hangs out in a nigger saloon called Millie's or somethin' like that up in Frog Town. Don't post no bills. Folks who want him gen'rally fin' him right along. I don't know much 'cept he totes a six-shooter like he knows how to use it."

"Millie's?"

"Yep," Wilson said. "Never'd hire him myself. Don't hol' with puttin' folkses' lives in the han's of the igner'nt. But then, some has, and I guess they come through it all right. Least, talk says they did. 'Course, it's a long way to Santa Fe, an' if they didn't make it, I don't know how anybody's goin' to hear 'bout it." He saw Graham frown and look down. "Listen, I don't know. That's all I'm sayin'. Them Bluebellies over to the stockade's high on him, I hear. Say he did some scoutin' for the Army out on the Line, an' if that's a fact, then he's likely to know what he's 'bout. Sure'n shit stinks, a lot of these yahoos runnin' 'roun' here with buckskin britches an' high-topped boots never been west of the Trinity."

Graham asked Wilson more questions and thanked him for the advice. Then he asked, "You said there were three things to worry about. What was the third?"

"The people you take with you," Wilson said. He turned and pulled his shirt up from his trousers, exposing a deep slashing wound. "I took a bunch of Frenchies up on the Trinity from Galveston a few years back. This was my thanks."

Graham stared at the ugly red scar. "What did they do?"

"One of the li'l gals took a shine to me," Wilson said. He stuffed his shirt back into the waist of his dirty pants. "Least I thought she did. Pretty li'l thin'." Wilson winked at Graham. "Her daddy saw thin's differ'nt. Took a auger to me. Thought he'd kilt me when I shot him."

Graham bade Wilson good luck and accepted the same before returning to Jefferson. Once again, he felt he was walking into a trap. His head swam with the complexity of the problem. His life seemed to be nothing more than a puff of cotton, blown first this way and then that, but now that he stood on the sidewalks of Jefferson and watched people shuffling back and forth and searching for a way to their future in the West, he desperately hoped that this might indeed be a final move on his part, something that might take him to a place where he could light for a while. To make it work, he had to act deliberately, keep an eye on the basic denomination, run the game and control the pot. Check the bet. Take another card, he said to himself.

As he walked down Dallas Street, he discovered Jack standing by a large wagon on which sat the most beautiful girl Graham had ever seen in his life. Later, on a blood-soaked creek bank some three hundred miles west of Jefferson, he would recall that first sight of Aggie Sterling, and he would know that from that moment on, he was committed to a partnership with her father.

3

"THIS IS MY FAMILY," JACK STERLING ANNOUNCED proudly as Graham walked up. "Aggie, Jason, an' Annie," he named the children, who were perched up on the wagon seat behind a gray woman whose head was bowed and who didn't look up. "I brung 'em along on the boat." He winked at Graham. "Y'all, this here's Mr. Cleveland Graham, the business 'ssociate I was tellin' you 'bout."

"I thought you didn't have any family." Graham spoke out of anger before he thought.

"No, I never said that." Jack smiled and helped Annie down from the seat. Graham recalled that he spoke truly. Jack's answer had been "none to speak of," and he hadn't spoken of them at all. Jack did not introduce or acknowledge the woman up on the wagon seat. She was so much older-looking than the dapper horse trader that Graham wondered if she was his mother or some sort of family servant. Her eyes were cast down toward the rumps of the mules in front of her. Jason dropped down next to his younger sister, and the blond girl, Aggie, started down on her own. Graham automatically extended a hand to her to help her, and when their fingers met, he looked into her eyes and felt an electric jolt run throughout his body. Her touch was light, and her long fingers grasped his palm with the softness of owl feathers. Once she released his grip, he could still feel the gentle pressure of her hand on his.

"I wasn't sure where they was," Jack prattled on. "They was run off our farm in Louisiana, an' they sort of got misplaced. I found 'em up in Arkansas. That's what took me so long gettin' back."

"With the whiskey," Graham muttered. The girl reached the sidewalk and stepped away to her brother and sister. She wore a faded gingham dress, and her hair was pulled back behind her head in a manner that allowed its golden length to spill freely onto her shoulders. She shot a look at Sterling that Graham was surprised to see was filled with a mixture of hatred and fear. No, he corrected himself immediately, not fear: What he saw was utter contempt.

"With the whiskey," Jack repeated. "I told 'em 'bout goin' out to New Mexico, an' wouldn't you know they was all het up 'bout it. I was plannin' to wait till we got settled an' then to send for 'em, but nothin'd do but for 'em to come 'long right now. So I loaded the whole kit an' caboodle, wagon, mules, an' the whole thing, on the boat an' brung 'em 'long with me."

Aggie stared at Graham so intensely that he turned away. She wasn't listening to Jack any more than if his words had been the annoying buzz of a mosquito. She was studying Graham, he realized, and he wanted to return her gaze, to memorize her beauty. Her direct look confounded him, and he shifted his eyes toward the other children. He kept her in view, however. He couldn't help it. She was delicate in some ways, he saw from a narrow side glance, but there also was something hard there. Jack went over and put his arm around her, and Graham fought an impulse to step forward and push him away. It was a profanation for him to touch her, Graham thought all at once, and he was shocked at how strongly he reacted. He caught himself before he made an impromptu move, however, and settled for a hope that she would reject Jack's embrace on her own.

She didn't resist him, but instead stood stiffly, and

Graham thought that Jack might have his arm around a lamppost. Graham sensed her skin tighten around her, seeming to shrink from her father's touch. Small vertical lines at the corner of her mouth fixed themselves in a firm attitude, and he sensed that her teeth were clenched. Her eyes stared straight ahead, cold as frost.

" 'Sides," Sterling said, winking at Graham, "this girl of mine's gettin' all growed up, an' I didn't want ever' houn' dog in Arkansas sniffin' 'round after her when I was gone." He leaned over and planted a wet kiss on Aggie's cheek, and Graham felt as if he had been struck hard in the chest. He jammed a cigar into his mouth to prevent himself from speaking.

She moved her head away from Jack's lips quickly, and her blue eyes flared momentarily, but otherwise she stared straight ahead. He might be nothing more than an offending tree branch that brushed her face. Graham turned his back and stepped away to light the cigar. He was surprised to feel feverish. She was having a prodigious effect on him. His palms were sweating. He was overwhelmed with the emotion, but he played with the lighted match at the end of the cigar and tried to compose himself.

Just as suddenly as the confusing feeling had swept over him, it disappeared. Anger replaced it, and the reddening of his face remained constant. His hand was shaking, and he thrust it into his pocket to keep it out of sight.

It all became very clear to him suddenly. Jack Sterling had manipulated him all along and very well. It had started back in San Antonio. Graham cursed himself for being so stupid. He was supposed to be a professional, to see things like this coming and avoid them. Sterling had sharped the gambler worse than anyone had ever done over a hand of cards.

Sterling had never intended to buy any horses at all, Graham decided. It was never a part of the plan. He intended to go back, collect these people, and move them west. He probably had had the whiskey stashed somewhere all along. Or he had stolen it somehow. He would bet that if he ripped open the dark man's shirt and found that money belt, he would discover most of his cash still intact. Graham and his money were the ticket for Sterling's future. God only knew what other skulduggery was behind his plastic smile. The chances were damned good, Graham told himself, that somebody was after Jack, somebody who had a hanging rope already dangling.

"You done anythin' 'bout gettin' us organized yet?" Sterling came up beside him and slapped him on the back. If he saw how upset Graham was, he didn't show it. "I hear if we don't get shed of this place by spring, we might as well not go."

"Maybe we won't go," Graham muttered angrily. He shook off the hand that continued to rest on his shoulder and turned to face Jack squarely. "Look, Sterlin', I'm not happy about any of this. I think you took me, an' I think you're playin' me for a fool." Graham fought to control himself. He didn't want to push Sterling into a fight, not right out here in public. But at the same time, he wanted to accuse the man of murdering the girl in San Antonio right here and now, right in front of his children. Jack Sterling, Graham told himself, was a tin-plated son of a bitch. Graham wanted to hurt him, to make him miserable, but his glance strayed helplessly toward Aggie once more, and he managed to calm himself and back off. To make such a charge, to do anything which pushed Sterling too far, would also mean hurting this beautiful girl, who stared at the two of them with an impassive, almost uninterested expression on her face. It was as if she had seen all this before, expected it even. If anything, Graham thought, she looked bored.

Even so, Graham had almost said too much already. Sterling's dark eyes narrowed, and Graham prepared himself for an outburst. But what he saw in Jack's face was hurt rather than anger. For a brief moment, Graham thought Sterling was going to cry.

"I'm disappointed you feel that way, Cleve," Sterling said in a whining voice. "I done the best I could. I told you I tried, but I just couldn't buy no stock with that little bit of money we had. I tried, an' I spent a lot of it runnin' 'round Tennessee just tryin' to *find* horses. I really did my best. You can ask Aggie here. Ain't that right, girl?" She just looked at him with eyes as hard as granite. They said nothing in her father's favor. "Well, I *did* try. We just didn't have as much money as I figured."

"Jesus God," Graham growled a throaty whisper,

"you had more'n a thousand dollars. I don't suppose you have any left?"

"Here." Jack reached into his coat and extracted a leather wallet. He fingered out a small sheaf of bills and a folded paper. "That's eighty dollars, all that's left of the money, yours *an'* mine. That's the bill of sale for the whiskey. You can see what I paid for it. I held out for travelin' expenses. You'd of done the same, I reckon. You got the whiskey. You do what you want. We'll jus' go our own way."

Graham accepted the folded bills and paper. For a moment he stood still and held the wad in his hand. This wasn't the way it was supposed to work out. Was it absolutely impossible for him to read this man at all? Here he stood, debating the wisdom of raising him, and Sterling upped the ante and did him one better. Now it was he who felt like a son of a bitch. Sterling had shamed him, made him look like a piker right in front of his whole family, right in front of this girl whose steady stare continued to fascinate Graham. He barely glanced at the paper, but he split the bills in half and handed forty dollars back to Sterling. Once again, the man's affectation of sincerity worked on him, and even though he suspected—no, he told himself, he was sure—that it was bogus, that the bill of sale he now stuffed into a coat pocket was as phony as Jack Sterling's smile, he also knew that no useful purpose could be served in starting a fight over something that was done.

"I'm gettin' old," he said. "An' I'll admit to bein' scared. An' I'm madder'n hell 'bout the whiskey. But we got it now, an' I don't see that there's much we can do but go ahead on an' try to get it out there if we can. I'll send word to my man out there an' see if he wants to buy it. It may take a while to get an answer, but I'm not takin' it out to the middle of nowhere unless we've some guarantee that there's still a market for this stuff." Jack smiled even more broadly. Graham sighed. "I guess we better get on with gettin' organized if that's what we're goin' to do."

Sterling pocketed the money sheepishly, and turned to join his children, who continued to stand together on the sidewalk next to the big wagon. "Jason, get up there an' move this wagon down to the bayou where I showed you. We're goin' to need her. Get the axle greased, an' see to the mules an' my horse." Sterling's tone of voice took on an unnecessary harshness. He might as well be ordering a nigger boy around, Graham thought.

Jack continued his instructions, and Graham took a final look at Aggie and walked off toward the telegraph office. Through the entire conversation Jack Sterling never once acknowledged the existence of the bonneted woman on the wagon's bench, and she had failed to utter a word.

THERE WAS NO DIRECT telegraph line between Jefferson and Santa Fe, and Graham had almost despaired of hearing from Tuttle at all when an answer came through. He said he would take the whiskey, all forty ten-gallon kegs, for five thousand acres of the land plus twenty-five hundred in cash. That was better than four dollars a quart for the bonded sour mash, more than twice what the homemade rotgut served in Santa Fe was selling for, almost three times what a decent bottle would go for right there in Jefferson.

Tuttle's response to the idea of Graham's bringing out settlers for the valley was also enthusiastic.

"Settler idea perfect," his wire said. "Pick useful people. Site surveyed when you arrive." Graham knew what Tuttle meant by "useful." Likely, Graham thought, he wanted people who could shoot straight and who didn't scare easily. As the future wagon master looked over the hopeless collection of pilgrims who fussed over their wagons and loads on the side streets and down by the bayou, however, he doubted that many of them could do much more than follow a mule in a plowed furrow. Most of them looked worn out, used up. The heartier folk had already departed, and those remaining seemed to be reluctant to take the final step toward a commitment to a new life in the West.

Tuttle's final line aroused Graham's curiosity as well. "Wire word of your exact—repeat, exact—route of travel soon as possible." What difference did it make? Graham wondered. But he shrugged off the questions and went to seek his partner.

Looking for Sterling, the gambler went down by the bayou and found that only Jason had been left to guard the wagon and mules and the big black horse. The others, the boy explained, had been put up at the Excelsior House, and Graham was struck with a mixture of disappointment and relief that the girl, Aggie, was not there at the bayou. He dreaded seeing her and he looked forward to it. While his thoughts leaped to possibilities of encountering her back at the hotel, he also began quietly plotting how to move in and out of the building without accidentally meeting her. The conflict in his emotions bothered him so much that he only idly searched for Jack for the next hour.

Finally, a barkeeper at the Rosebud Saloon said that Jack had announced he would be at Booker's, a brothel down on the far side of the turning basin. Graham was only mildly shocked to discover his partner's whereabouts as he waded through the mud up to the dilapidated building's front door and entered. Nothing where Jack Sterling was concerned could surprise him anymore.

"Is it a deal?" Sterling drunkenly asked Graham when he walked up to him. He was sitting next to a naked prostitute who was curling his thin hair around a finger and blowing on his neck.

"I'm puttin' a train together startin' tomorrow," Graham said gruffly. "I ordered some handbills." He felt like an old man. Jack Sterling behaved like a green kid, and the gambler was disgusted. "Maybe you can pass 'em out 'round town. I've got to see to hirin' a scout."

"Good damn deal. You collect the sodbusters. I'll see what I can do 'bout makin' us rich," Sterling slurred, and he gave the whore a sloppy lick on the ear and received a giggling, playful push in return. Graham had had enough.

"You listen to me." He reached down and grabbed Jack by his lapel and pulled him erect. "I think you're a third-rate, half-loco son of a bitch, an' I ought to gut you and leave you right here." Sterling's eyes focused and cleared. They were fixed on Graham's, but the gambler saw no fear or even anger in their black pools. Perhaps he was too drunk, Graham thought, or maybe he thinks I'm just a fool.

"We're goin' ahead with this deal because you stuck me with it, an' because I got no choice but to just ride out an' let you have it all. I thought about it. But that'd be too damn easy. I'll see the last card. But I'm tellin' you, you cross me one more time, you just think 'bout it, an'

I'll kill you. If the chance comes, I'll kill you anyway." He released Sterling and dumped him into the ample lap of the prostitute, who continued to giggle drunkenly.

Sterling lay where Graham had dropped him. He made no effort to move, and just continued to stare at the gambler as he nestled his head into the whore's crotch. "I might kill you first," he said.

"You might. But if I see you comin', you'd better bring an army."

4

Jack Sterling had brought no army, Graham acknowledged as he stared at the horse trader's twisted body, but he had put Graham and everyone else on the train at the mercy of the Comanche, and that was worse. In a strange, faraway sense of things, the wagon master knew that he had suspected all along that things would turn out this way.

The wagon master put his hand over his right eye and tried to focus with his damaged left. For a moment things were still hazy, but he found if he squinted and ignored the pain—which came more from the socket than from the eye itself—he could make things out clearly enough.

He found some jerky in the wagon and chewed on it, and after a bit, his whiskey headache left him. He climbed up to scan the creek bed once more, but all was quiet. The shadow of the bluff now completely covered the crossing, and the creek gurgled happily by as if the lumps of dead people on its gravelly banks were nothing more than discarded baggage.

Arranging for the train had been incredibly easy. It was late enough in the season that most settlers with hard cash had already departed for points west—or really southwest, as few were foolish enough to cross Indian country—and what he found coming to his hotel room to sign on for the adventure were the dregs: people who found themselves almost hopeless if not destitute, and whose few measly dollars had to be reserved to outfit their wagons and teams.

Most were anxious to join a train that included as a part of the bargain virgin land in the mountainous region north of Santa Fe. By arranging a deal on oxen with a man near Marshall, Texas, he also managed to sell them draft animals and to talk them out of the ever-popular long-eared mules, beasts Graham had learned to detest on the plains of Kansas the previous year.

And then there had been the matter of the scout. Moses Franklin had been the only one available, and Graham found himself without any choice in the matter at all. Wilson's guarded recommendation had been repeated by several in Jefferson, including the local Army commandant, who had knowledge of the black man's previous military connections, and Graham was only mildly surprised to learn that Moses was the same man he had heard of the previous winter. Moses apparently was the only Negro in the vicinity who followed that occupation.

Their first meeting had not endeared the former slave to the new wagon master at all. Graham's dislike for Moses was instantaneous and increased with every passing minute of their acquaintance. But there had been no other choice. There was no way the gambler was going to traverse the Texas plains without someone who had at least been across them once, and while there was no shortage of men in Jefferson who laid claim to the adventure, there was none left in town who would do it again for any price. Moses, at least, had been recommended by people who were supposed to know, and that would have to do.

By the time he concluded the oxen deal, bought two wagons—one for himself and one for Frank Herbert and his daughter—and outfitted both with supplies he imagined they would need in New Mexico, he was nearly out of cash. So when they set out from Jefferson, nearly two months before they reached the crossing, Graham had just over twenty dollars in his pocket and only the promise of New Mexico to keep him going. He received a rough idea of their route from Moses and wired it to Tuttle, as requested. Everything seemed to be falling into place in spite of Graham's continued suspicions of Jack Sterling.

Sterling, though, remained affable. He absented himself from any plans concerning the train and apparently found—or had held back—some cash, which he spent liberally in the saloons and whorehouses of Jefferson. He also outfitted his rig and had the axles replaced. He sold his old animals to Quigley and bought a new team of mules—disdaining to accept oxen from Graham even for his cost per animal—and then was nowhere to be seen when the train lumbered away from Marion County. For a while, Graham enthusiastically entertained the notion that the horse trader had run out and left his children and the strange woman to their own devices.

But Sterling, herding his cattle before him, rejoined his family in Daingerfield. He claimed he got them "for a fart an' a song" from a man near a place called Mount Pleasant, but Graham suspected different. The dried red mud on the cattle's flanks suggested that he had driven them across the river out of the Territories; if he stole them from Indians, Graham thought, trouble was likely following them already.

He could have called the whole thing off in Saint Jo, he remembered. It was still early enough in the expedition for people to turn back. Saint Jo had become a regular crossroads anyway. But he was distracted from the welfare of the train. Since Saint Jo, he hadn't thought of much more than killing Jack Sterling at the first opportunity.

He was standing in the dusty gloom of the Stonewall Jackson Saloon, tipping back the first taste of real whiskey he had sipped since leaving. The kegs were to remain inviolate, he told Jack—and everyone else—and promised himself as well, and the cheap swill they had stocked in bottles beneath their wagon seats was pure fire to swallow and gave Graham stomach cramps. The grizzled old man who played barkeeper behind the narrow slab of oak had poured out two small glasses of amber liquid as soon as they entered. Jack even paid, scooting Graham and their drinks down the bar to make way for Quigley and Pierce and the others who suddenly crowded into the small room and began demanding refreshment.

The men on the train had changed perceptibly since leaving Jefferson, Graham noticed. At that point, they had faced no real danger, and they had managed to drive the stupid oxen far enough to make themselves feel like frontiersmen. They were hot, dirty, and tired when they hit town, and while the women and children went to a nearby creek to wash themselves and their clothes, the men paused to slake their thirsts.

The conversation was convivial after a second round of drinks, and Graham passed Sterling a cigar. The trip had begun to settle into a routine at this point, and he felt confident. He might just bring this off. He tried not to think of Moses's warning that they were still a long way from the Indian Line and an even longer way from the mountains of New Mexico.

The noise in the saloon grew, and then Sterling's arm was taken by Jason's hand. The boy pushed his way through the crowd and was yelling at Jack.

"Ma says the black might of pulled up lame," he yelled over the din.

Jack frowned. "Take him over to the farrier an' have him take a look at him. I think he's 'bout to throw a shoe is all."

There was some discussion about money, and Jack slapped Jason in a good-natured but firm manner on his head as he reluctantly handed him a dollar and turned back to Graham. What he saw caused him to blanch, his dark eyes widening in surprise. Graham was staring at him incredulously, a stricken expression on his face.

"What's wrong?"

Graham stared a moment longer, his mouth working. He was having difficulty finding words.

"I thought you said you . . ." he started, but he trailed off and started again. "Do you mean to tell me that that woman out there is . . . is your wife?"

"Well, hell yes." Sterling winked at Grover Hildebrandt, who was in a heated debate with several others over whether he should bathe or not. Grover couldn't hear him and only scowled back at Sterling. "She ain't much to look at, but she's mine. What'd you think?"

"I thought she was—" Graham started. "I thought she was some kind of hired help."

"Well, for all the good she does, she might as well be." Jack poured another round for both men. "You look like you need a drink."

"What about Ursula?"

"Ursula?" Sterling turned the glass in his fingers and

studied the whiskey. A small insect floated in it, and he frowned down. "Oh, that little Mex? What 'bout her?"

"You *said* you *married* her."

"What if I did?" Sterling yelled down the bar, "Hey, old-timer. There's a bug in my glass. What kind of place is this?"

Graham reached out and pulled him around and forced him to face him. "You said you married her. You're already married."

"Well, so what?" Jack asked. "She wasn't nothin' but a Mex."

"She was a child."

"Not any diff'rent from the little wench you was samplin'." Jack shrugged Graham's hand away. "Hey, old-timer. Get your bony ass down here, an' get me a fresh glass an' 'nother bottle, pronto!"

Graham stared for a moment longer. "You killed her, didn't you?"

"Killed who?"

"Ursula, goddamnit! You killed her the night before we left. You beat her to death."

Sterling stepped gingerly away from the bar, his hands drifting down to his sides. The old barkeeper shuffled down with a fresh bottle and a glass.

"I'm shore sorry 'bout that." The old man peered at them through spectacles so covered with crusty dirt it was a wonder he could see at all. "We had some of them buffalo hunters in here two days ago, an' they had too many fleas. Got into ever'thin'." He poured a fresh drink and left the bottle next to it. He chuckled. "Hell, I got fleas on my pecker."

"You killed her," Graham repeated steadily. The din in the bar continued unabated. "You beat her to death. What kind of man are you?"

"I don't know what you're talkin' 'bout."

"You told me you married her."

"I told you what I did. I married her. We got a padre an' got married. I married her, bedded her, an' left her."

"You're already married."

"So what? You never went to bed with a woman you had to lie to? So what? I ain't Cath'lic, so it didn't count. An' she didn't speak 'nough English to know what I was sayin' nohow. What the hell diff'rence does it make? I didn't kill nobody."

"You weren't surprised when I said it."

"No, I wasn't. She was a Mex, an' a whore," Sterling said. "You think 'bout it, Graham. Why would I want to kill her?"

"I don't know. I just know you did."

"You're crazy, or drunk, or both. Sober up, an' we'll talk this thing out sometime. I got me a horse to see to." Jack drank off the poured glass without taking his black eyes off the wagon master, then turned and pushed his way out of the saloon.

Graham stood still. His head was buzzing from the whiskey, and he wondered if he *was* crazy. Maybe he had imagined the whole thing. Maybe there had never been an Ursula, or a Dolores, or a San Antonio. Maybe it wasn't worth it.

Then he turned and sipped his drink, and in the bar's mirror he saw the astounded expression on the face of Frank Herbert. He had been standing off to one side, slightly behind the giant Hildebrandt. He had heard everything.

Frank walked up behind Graham and looked at his reflection in the fly-specked mirror. "Guess I'll have to kill him," Frank said. "I hate to do'er, but I don't see nothin' else for it." He might be talking about having merely to speak to Jack about some business matter or other.

"He needs killin' anyhow," Frank went on as quietly as he could in the noise of the bar. "I knew that the first time I seen him, I reckon. An' I guess direc'ly I'll go an' do it."

"You'll have to wait behind me," Graham said, and he poured for both of them. Frank nodded and sipped his drink.

BUT NOW, JACK STERLING was dead, and Frank Herbert was out somewhere with the goddamn nigger scout and probably dead himself, and the rest of those who had so boisterously enjoyed the party in the Stonewall Jackson Saloon were either dead, dying, or sitting behind crates and wagons and waiting to die.

Graham's mouth was dry, and he pulled a canteen

from his wagon. The water was not fresh; it tasted splintery and sour on his tongue. He rinsed his mouth and spat.

There was a division in his mind, and it wouldn't resolve. Part of him envisioned the two of them in the Valley of the High Snows, tending to a cabin, stock, living and even having children of their own. It wasn't too late for him, he tried to insist when he thought of that picture. He wasn't that ancient. And she was older than her years. She was like him, he decided—a loner, a woman who made decisions and stuck by them, stubborn—and when he looked at her or even thought of her, his whole body seemed to yearn for her touch to rekindle the sensation he had experienced when they first met.

Another part of him, however, rejected the whole idea. She said she was waiting on someone else, some kid, no doubt, with a headful of hair and two good hands to hold her with. He *was* too old, he argued. He was a gambler, a man with no future. He sometimes thought that when they reached Santa Fe and sold the whiskey, he would just collect the money, tell Tuttle to go to hell, and take off on his own: go to Nevada or California as he had thought of doing before. He felt the need to put the whole ordeal behind him, and the prospect of doing just that made him feel guilty for once more rejecting responsibility even for his own life and just trying to fold and walk away with his stake intact.

But no matter how often practicality invaded his mind, it was always routed by Aggie herself. Since Emma, he had not felt the way she made him feel. And when he thought deeply about it, as he often had while his wagon lurched and rattled its way across the prairie, he found himself disturbed that he couldn't really recall how he felt about Emma at all. Her face, her presence in his life, had become a vague shadow belonging to a man who had died years before.

He lit the cigar and started to make another circuit of the train. He needed once again to talk to some of the people, to let them know that he was doing everything he could to help them. "Three things to worry 'bout," he recalled Wilson's words as he touched his sore eye. "Well, at least we ain't lost."

5

THE SETTLERS WERE RESTLESS AND PAID HIM LITTLE attention as he passed. They knew that night would be falling soon, and that meant the possibility of another attack. That was not a pleasant thing to contemplate, and he spoke to them only to make sure their loads were right, that they were alert. There was no need to try to explain things. Those who acknowledged him and paid him respect would do so on any account. The others never would.

A sudden shout came from the narrow ridge above, and Graham stopped, ducked slightly, and turned his eyes anxiously toward the near end of the creek. He brought his rifle up and searched for a target. Even with his damaged eye squeezed tight, he found his vision wasn't clear. Everything from the end of his rifle's barrel on was a shimmering blur. Graham hoped against reason that it might be Moses and Frank returning.

Instead, he squinted hard and spotted six braves splashing slowly down the creek, walking their ponies through the water and allowing the flow to dampen their ankles before turning the horses and guiding them almost gently up onto the gravel. They acted as if the whites were not even there. The clicking of rifle hammers up and down the line announced that every pair of eyes in the train was waiting for the moment when the Indians were clearly in view before firing. They were waiting for someone to give the order to fire, and the wagon master's finger tightened on the trigger as he brought the lead rider's body atop the sight of his Winchester. But Graham suddenly had a thought and relaxed his grip on the gun. Maybe they want to parley, he desperately told himself. Maybe Wilson was wrong: Maybe he could talk his way out of this yet.

"Hold your fire," he shouted as loudly as he could. His voice was hoarse, and he was surprised to find his throat dry, his tongue raspy as it tried desperately to moisten his cracked lips. He dispatched one of the boys to run down the line and pass the order along. "Hold your fire," Graham yelled again. The order was echoed up and down the wagon line, and the Indians came to the center of the beach.

There they stopped, seemingly ignorant of the array of corpses that littered the beach around them and of the firearms aimed at them, and they waited. Across the backs of two of the ponies were two naked bodies. The warrior in the center urged his spotted pony forward a few steps and sat quietly in the sun. Sweat glistened on his muscular body, and the late-afternoon light was caught and reflected from the mirrors that dangled from his horse.

The other five warriors waited as patiently as their leader, and Graham pondered his next move. With chagrin, he wished for Moses to advise him. Should he go out and talk to them? He didn't speak Comanche, had never even heard it spoken. He knew that some of these redskins spoke Spanish, but his Spanish was limited to café lingo. How was he to know what they were saying? It was hard to tell what to do, but the whole train was waiting for him to act. They might hate him, they might be ready to hang him, but he was once again important to them.

"What you think they want, Mr. Graham?" Giorgio Patrizi whispered. "Think they want more whiskey?" He sighted down his rifle's barrel. "I could pick one of 'em off."

"Hold your fire," Graham growled. "Let's think on this a spell."

Minutes ticked by, and finally the suspense became too much for Graham. He imagined that it was infecting all the settlers, as a quiet murmur had arisen from the train, and he could hear it. He walked out finally, alone, but carrying his rifle easily where he could bring it up with his stumped arm. Sweat ran from under his hat and swam into his eyes, causing the injured one to sting worse than ever.

He went out halfway to where the brave sat astride his pony and waited. Behind him he heard the gravel crunching, and with a slight turn of his head he was shocked to see the North Carolinians, Baker and Potter, coming up behind him.

"Couldn't leave you out here on your lonesome," Potter whispered.

"Even a asshole-stupid Yankee like you deserves all the help he can get." Baker joined Graham on his left.

The Indians offered little obvious reaction to the white

men's approach, although their eyes followed every tiny movement Graham and his two companions made. Graham had never been so close to hostile warriors, and he tried to take in everything about them at once. At close range, the Comanche looked even more formidable than they appeared from a distance.

Their faces and bodies were painted black, with ocher, red, and yellow stripes crisscrossing and descending from their foreheads and necks. Their faces also showed tiny streaks of white and gray and red running away from their eyes. The leader's body was heavily tattooed. All but one, who wore a huge headdress made from the skin and horns of a buffalo's scalp, were bareheaded, although two of them had small feathers trailing in their tight braids, and all of them wore necklaces of bear and panther and elk teeth. Bells and other trinkets were sewn into the sparse fabric across their bodies and woven into their horses' manes. The ponies' tails were tied up, and all of the warriors had a piece of cloth wound around their waists. Each wore a quiver filled with arrows, and each carried a bow and a rifle. The leader had a large revolver shoved into the waist of his breechcloth, and all of them had knives and tomahawks. Except for their breechcloths and leggings, they were naked; their unpainted and exposed skin was a deep muscular bronze, almost truly red, as it rippled in the low sun. They stared at the upper half of the bluff where the sentries remained more or less hidden from view.

By far the most shocking revelation Graham had was that they were only boys, children who wore the fierce masks of men as if in absurd imitation of their elders. The Patrizi boys, he realized, were older than two or three of this party. But he did not allow this information to lull him into a false sense of confidence. They might be young, but they were still Comanche warriors, and the scalps dangling from their shields told a more accurate story of their experience than the youth in their faces.

The leader finally deigned to look down at the trio of white men in front of him and smiled and spoke a greeting. Graham was reminded of the smile of a drummer or tinhorn. The Comanche's teeth were perfect. Graham felt his heart pounding hard beneath his vest, and almost without thinking, he shifted the rifle to the crook of his arm and reached inside his coat ever so slowly and brought forth five cigars, all he had on him.

He handed one each to Potter and Baker, then boldly stepped forward and stretched out an arm to the head-dressed brave, who hesitated only a second before accepting them and passing one to the youngster next to him. Potter came up with a match and lit the Indians' cigars, lighting a second stick to fire his and Graham's smoke, and finally lighting Baker's.

"Good smoke," said the Indian with the buffalo headdress, whose pony stood to the left of the leader's. He blew out a blue cloud over his pony's head. Graham let out an almost audible sigh of relief. At least this one spoke some English. The brave gestured with the cigar toward the wagons. "Mebbe more?"

"I've got more," Graham said evenly. "Potter, go to my wagon and get the box under the seat."

Potter moved away quickly, and when he returned he passed the cigars out among the braves. Graham noticed that the Southerner's hands brushed one of the corpses briefly, and he jumped away so fast that the Indian's pony shied a bit. Be calm, Graham thought, be calm. If the Indians suddenly opened fire on them, he figured he could take two, maybe three before they got him, but the North Carolinian was a goner. Potter composed himself and finished distributing the tobacco before he came back and handed Graham the remaining smokes. Graham removed three, stuck them into his pocket, and handed the half-dozen remaining stogies to the Indian in front of him. Through the whole process, the Comanche remained impassively smoking and studying the train, his eyes flicking left and right and up to the ridge, where the sentries could now be clearly seen sighting down on him.

"You fight pretty damn good," the Indian who had spoken before said as he dropped the six cigars into a beaded pouch he wore around his waist. He looked at the bodies of women and children lying around them. Some were covered with flies, and others were swollen from the day's heat. "You got young'uns fight pretty damn good. Women fight pretty damn good. Where black man?"

"We want them back," Graham said. "We want those you took."

The Indian shook his head slowly. "No," he said. "Was white man, now Comanche." When he said "Comanche" he moved his hand in a waving motion backward across his chest. His voice was deep, throaty. There was nothing childish about him, Graham thought. The apparent leader, whose horse stood slightly forward of the others, continued to stare at them and say nothing.

"We want them back," Graham repeated with a more definite tone in his voice. "We'll buy them back."

The Indian looked at him suddenly and smiled. "Mebbe trade?"

Graham thought wildly. What did they have that the Indians wanted? "Horses," he said. "Horses, and the rest of the cattle. All of it for the women and children you carried off."

"Whiskey," the Indian said steadily. "Big two for one womans." He held up two fingers on one hand and one on the other and studied them to confirm the equation.

"Whiskey," Graham repeated dumbly and shook his head. "No whiskey. Horses and cattle. Mules, too. No whiskey."

"Jesus Christ! Give him the goddamn whiskey, Graham," Potter hissed through his teeth. "Are you plumb crazy?"

The headdressed brave smiled in a friendly fashion at the scowling, serious face of the wagon master, and leaned down slightly. "You give whiskey, mebbe we give back two womens. No goddamn good anyhow."

When he leaned forward, Graham heard Baker's breath hiss out loudly. The cloth wrapped around the brave's waist, which Graham had mistaken for some sort of filthy rag, was clearly a Rebel battle flag. It was torn and ripped and stained so badly that the dim stars and bars were hard to make out, but its original design was unmistakable. Potter also spotted the flag, and he made a small noise in his throat. For a brief, terrible instant, Graham thought the men would open fire.

"One keg," Graham said. He was giving in, and he wanted his voice to sound like it. "That's it. You bring *all* the women and children, and we'll give you one keg." He held up a single finger, and the Comanche studied it with the same intensity as he had regarded his own digits a moment before.

After a moment, the Indian sat up straight and continued to smile. With a barely perceptible movement of his hand, the brave gestured to the braves behind him, and they unceremoniously dumped the two corpses onto the gravel. The bodies landed with a wet thump. One rolled over, and Graham was horrified to see that the eye sockets were empty, bloody holes. The nose and ears were also gone, and a cascade of raw, seared flesh raced down the chest to the groin, where only a bloody wound remained between the man's naked legs. He heard a short, quaking noise from Baker.

"Goddamn buffalo hunter mans," the Comanche pronounced. "Mebbe kill much buffalos. Dead now, goddamn." He sat up and spat. His spittle hit one of the corpses on the forehead.

"We're not buffalo hunters," Graham said, fighting to keep his voice steady. "We're settlers. We don't even want to stay here. We just want to go in peace."

The Indian flung the cigar down onto the ground.

"You go," he said simply. "Go."

"How much? How much do you want?" Graham demanded.

The Indians stared hard at the train for a moment, then they visibly stiffened on their horses. The leader pointed beyond Graham, who swung around to look. At first his injured eye wouldn't permit him to focus clearly on the wagon fort, but then he pressed his hand over it and squinted with the other, and he spied Aggie Sterling standing up and holding her shotgun on the braves before Graham. Behind him the leader spoke hurriedly and argumentatively to the spokesman. Graham turned and saw that the braves looked unnerved.

The leader said something to Graham suddenly, speaking for the first time, but in his own language. Even so, his eyes told what he meant.

"No!" Graham said firmly. "We don't trade women. We don't trade people."

The leader repeated his demand, but he could read Graham's resistance in the wagon master's face. His own eyes were steel-hard, and Graham could see hatred behind them. There was more on his mind than rape, he knew. Something about Aggie had almost transfixed him.

"That woman bad, goddamn," the headdressed brave said quietly, almost as if he were speaking to the chief.

"She stays where she is," Graham said with greater heat than he meant to, but the Indian didn't seem to notice. They looked at each other and communicated wordlessly.

"Mebbe come back," the Indian said finally, and he looked into the late-afternoon sky toward the east as if he could perceive the moon's rise. With that, he turned his pony and guided it back into the creek. The others followed him, and in a few moments they were gone.

Graham and the two men next to him suddenly realized that they were completely exposed, but the Comanche snipers across the creek continued to honor the temporary truce and held their fire while the white men hurried back toward the wagon. Graham hesitated for a moment and looked down at the two bodies lying on the gravel in front of him. Something made him want to reach down and pull them up and drag them back, but he knew that it was stupid to even think about it. He owed more to the others who had died out here than to these two. Suddenly he looked up and realized that Potter and Baker had already gone, and he hurried after them. Graham followed them across a singletree, and Baker turned and spoke in a loud whisper.

"I don't know. Might be fair," he said. "Her for the rest of us."

"No," Graham hissed at the North Carolinian. He grabbed the man's dirty shirt and pulled him so they were face to face. "That's *not* a deal. It won't happen. Believe me, it won't."

"They's a lot of folks dead on your 'count already. I can't see one more's goin' to matter. 'Specially her. What's a Indian buck to her?" Baker asked.

"They'll be back tonight," Potter put in, physically pulling his companion away from Graham's grasp. "That was Olin's flag, I swear to God."

"You don't know that," Baker hissed. Then he turned to Graham and argued, "They'll come back. He said they would. They'll be back tonight. I say we give 'em that gal an' be done with it. If they come wantin' to trade, I'll by God trade."

"Not while I'm alive," Graham said. "If they come, we'll be ready for them." He tried to sound confident. "You keep your mouth shut. I'm not above puttin' a bullet in either of you if you say anythin' to anybody—*anybody*, you hear me?—about tradin' her, about tradin' *people* off. What kind of men are you, anyway?"

The two Southerners stood still for a moment. Finally, Baker lowered his head. "I wasn't thinkin'," he said suddenly. "We ain't for tradin' people. Not even her."

"You're goddamn right we're not," Graham said. He turned and stalked back toward his wagon. He felt inside his coat for the few remaining cigars. Gave away a whole damn box, he thought. Voices asked questions about what the Indians had said, but he ignored them. They would know soon enough, he thought, and Aggie's life was now in greater danger than before. If these people thought they could get away clean by sacrificing her, they would. What was one more life, one more woman? Especially one no one wanted?

He reached his wagon and took up a watch on the creek. Afternoon was now over. Evening was beginning and the sky in the east was beginning to purple with night. "Mebbe come back," the Comanche had said. Evening meant moonrise, and moonrise meant they could come back at their leisure, to trade or to fight. They might all be dead by morning. Even so, he hoped that the Indians wouldn't attack for a while, maybe not until dawn, at least long enough for him to sleep some more, to try to think things out.

They needed another day to wait at least, he told himself, wait for Moses and Frank to return, wait for something to happen to end all of this, to expose a basic denomination he could grasp and hold onto. All there was to do was to wait and see if they could get out of this or die trying, but mostly, just to wait. Of all the things he had to endure in his life, waiting seemed always to be the hardest.

PART SEVEN

THE SETTLE-MENT

CHAPTER ONE

1

DAWN WAS STILL HOURS AWAY WHEN CLEVELAND GRAHAM's restless sleep was interrupted by several shots from the ridge over the limestone caves. Cries of "Here they come ag'in!" wrenched him awkwardly to his feet and sent his hand groping for his Winchester. It had been a hard night, and Graham's first reaction to having his sleep interrupted was anger.

Since sometime around midnight, shortly after moonrise, the horrible cries of the Indians' victims had come echoing down the tiny canyon of the crossing and seemed to hang in the air over the creek like palpable spirits. At first, the settlers were shocked into silent horror when the tearing, hideous cries of the whites in Comanche hands flew through the moonlight. This quickly gave way to outrage, then to anguished endurance as each man, woman, and child in the wagon fort settled down and tried to ignore the pitiful shrieks. No one spoke of it after the anger passed, but Graham could sense the agony of those who believed that each cry of pain and unimaginable atrocity came from someone they knew or loved. He also shared their guilty relief when they realized that the Comanche were otherwise occupied and would not come back in the night.

The hideous echos ended sometime before the moonset, and he and the others were finally able to doze a bit and to try to put out of their consciousnesses the images that the cries had brought to mind.

When the alarm awakened him, he squinted hard out through his rifle loop, but no gunfire was yet coming from the Indian snipers, and there was none of the high pitched yip-yipping that had accompanied earlier Comanche attacks. His left eye was caked with sticky gum, and he realized when he looked up into the starlit sky that his vision was still cloudy. But it was so dark over the creek that he could have seen nothing even if he had two good eyes.

Sometime during the night while the pathetic screams of the captives continued to send thrills of horror and guilt through every human being on the crossing, Graham had belly-crawled out from under his wagon and retrieved Jack Sterling's boots for Aggie. It was dangerous, he knew, in the moonlight, probably the most foolish thing he had ever done. But he felt he had to do something to counteract the helplessness that had infected him since the sounds of Indian torture had begun with the moonrise. The boots came off the dead man's feet easily enough, but the small noises the wagon master had been obliged to make seemed to fill the crossing and left him breathless and shaking. Sleep had come slow after that, and now he felt more exhausted than ever.

Graham set his ears and watched the empty blackness of the crossing and waited for the Indians to appear. Soon he realized that he was holding his breath. But no Indian shapes emerged. Instead, the shadow of three riders emerged in dim outline against the black water. They pushed their horses through the turgid creek and galloped hard for the wagon fort. Two shots boomed out prematurely from the wagons; the brilliant muzzle flashes reminded everyone just how dark it was. Then the defenders heard the welcome sound of Frank Herbert's voice calling, "Riders comin' in! Hol' your fire, goddamnit!"

Several men raced to shove aside the makeshift abatis between two wagons to admit the three horses, which came in at such a speed that they almost trampled the defenders and ran blindly into the limestone bluff. The effort of plowing through the creek had worn the animals out, and they and their riders were dripping wet and heaving from the effort.

From overhead along the ledge, the lookouts posted several more shots for good measure at the cedar grove. There was no return fire, and they soon ceased and called out demands to know what was happening.

Graham made his way hurriedly to the men, who were calming their mounts and ignoring numerous excited questions. Although there was occasional light from a shielded lantern or cave's entrance, it was too dark to see much, and he pushed through the knot of people who milled around the sodden horses and men and started yelling for them to get inside a cave. They made their way into a low opening, where they squatted around a small dying fire.

Moses's face was still covered in streaks of red mud, and he made a frightening sight, particularly when he removed his hat and revealed his shaven pate. For a brief moment, Graham thought he had been scalped, but then he saw that the cuts across the black scout's skull were the result of clumsy razor work, not a Comanche knife. Frank was dirtier and wearier than usual, but his eyes danced with the thrill of the adventure they had just been through. The third man in their party, an incredible figure in greasy buckskins and bristling with weapons, his bright eyes taking in all he saw around him in the firelight, captured all attention as the three continued to ignore questions and waited to report to Graham.

"This here's Mr. Carlson Colfax," Moses said. The scout still had not caught his breath completely, and he only gestured weakly between the two men.

Colfax grinned like a sly idiot at the wagon master. The long white beard and braided gray hair surrounding a sunbaked and wrinkled face impressed Graham as the marks of a frontiersman of confidence and experience in spite of his advanced age and cunning smile. He knew what he was about, and he wasn't afraid to press. Colfax thrust out a gnarled hand.

"By God, you can bet your last screamin' eagle, that's what my mama called me!"

Graham frowned in return and took the man's hand. The grip surprised the wagon master. It was firm and spoke of muscle concealed in the buckskin sleeves.

"You must be the Bluebelly this'un here calls Cap'n." Colfax pumped Graham's hand briefly and resumed his squatting position. "Hear him tell it, you whipped Bobbie Lee all on your lonesome with your pecker tied down an' one hand behind you." Unlike his two companions, Colfax had recovered almost completely from the hectic arrival.

If anything, he looked to be spoiling for more action. His eyes glistened in the dying fire's light, and his teeth sparkled. He cannily studied the faces that peered at him and nodded to each in turn. Most turned away, embarrassed to have been caught staring.

"I'm Cleve Graham, boss of these wagons." There was an almost imperceptible snort from the men who stood and stooped around him. "Where'd you come from?"

"'Round here." Colfax shot Moses a wink. "You might say I live hereabouts. I hear you got your ass in a crack over some Indian troubles." Graham said nothing. He kept inspecting this strange frontier apparition as if it were a ghost. "Well, don't worry yourself none. We got us a job of work to do, but once she's done, you can go on an' take your whiskey to wherever the hell you're goin'. Or most of it, anyhow." He winked again.

Graham started. "How do you know about . . . about us? Who the hell are you?" He glared at Moses.

"Oh hell, Yank." The plainsman chuckled. "Ever'-body knows 'bout you. Ever since you come through Saint Jo word's been out that a trainload of Pine Top was headin' west. I been keepin' up with you pretty close since you crossed the Wichita. Reckoned you'd run into this bunch of red pups an' get your tit in a ringer."

"They knew about the . . . the whiskey, too?"

"Hell, they ain't nobody west of Jack County who *don't* know 'bout it, 'cept maybe the dead an' buried." He winked at Moses once more. "Got me a notion some of them knowed 'bout it, too."

"Well." Graham took a moment to absorb the news that his and Jack's secret was never a secret at all. At last, his gaze fixed on the black scout. "I guess you got some reason for comin' back empty-handed."

Moses looked up from a dipper of water someone had passed around. He was still wet from the creek's splashing water, and his eyes looked red and tired. He studied the wagon master with a pitying glance that made Graham furious. Before he could say anything, Frank spoke up.

"You should of saw it, Cap'n," he said. Gasping up huge chunks of air between phrases, he slid down and folded his legs under him in the gravelly dirt next to the fire. "I swear, they're killin' them folks by inches. I ain't seen nothin' like it in my life." A nervous murmur buzzed through the men in the small opening. "I'm s'prised you couldn't hear 'em."

"Where's the troops?" Graham ignored Frank and continued to direct his attention toward Moses. "I sent you for the goddamn Army. Or Rangers. Or *somebody*, goddamnit!"

"I'm not makin' it up," Frank insisted. "We was close 'nough to touch 'em, to smell 'em for certain. It was somethin'. They was screamin' an' carryin' on." His wide-spaced eyes opened to an even greater degree. "All I could do to sit still. They got 'em a bunch of our people down—"

"Shut up, Frank," Graham shot. He stared hard at Moses. "I said, where the hell's the goddamn Army?" Graham repeated. "Don't make me ask you again." He glanced briefly at the men who stood around and stared at the trio before them. He wanted it clear that he had the situation in hand. "Where've you been? What's goin' on? Who in hell is this?" He looked over at Colfax, who had received a dipper of his own and was casting an amused look toward Graham as he drank. "I need some answers, an' I need them now."

"Take'er easy, Yank," the old plainsman said. "You keep that up, you're fixin' to bust somethin'." There was a spate of nervous laughter from the other men who had squeezed into the cave.

Graham tried to stand upright and found the cave's ceiling too short. He spoke in a low, serious voice. "I want some answers, an' by God I want them now! Where's the troops? You were sent to bring back help."

"They ain't no Army," Moses said. He gestured toward Colfax. "An' this is all the help they is."

"We can see that!" A voice from the circle spoke up. It was Harvey Pierce, his face contorted with anxiety and disappointment. "I told you not to send a nigger out there, Graham. I swear, you're tryin' to get us kilt quicker'n them Indians."

"Shut up, Pierce," Graham said to the small carpenter. "You had your chance to go."

"They ain't goin' to be no Army." Moses drained the

dipper and drew attention back to himself. "Least none we can get to an' get back with."

"What are you talkin' about?" Graham gagged a bit. The small cave was reeking with the smell of sweat, urine, and dirty air. His vision continued to cloud, and he also believed he could still smell on himself the rotting odor of Jack's body. He felt claustrophobic. His throat was tight. He wanted a drink or a cigar—both.

"I tell you, Cap'n," Frank piped up again, "it was the worst thing I ever seen. It was worse'n Pea Ridge. I swear it was. They got them people, them women—"

"Shut the hell *up*, Frank!" Graham ordered. Frank winced and dropped his eyes into the fire and said nothing further. "We heard it," Graham stated. "We heard everything. Now, everybody shut up. I'm tryin' to find out what the hell's goin' on around here, an' all I'm gettin' is horseshit." He looked at Moses again. "You better start talkin', an' you better start now. I'm out of patience."

"I'm goin' out an' see to things," Colfax said. He pulled himself up and started out of the cave. "When you get things straight in here, come an' get me. There ain't much time. The moon's down, an' we got to ride 'fore daylight. We're leavin' soon as the horses blow an' the Kid comes in. If they's any grub, you might put some in your belly."

"Ride?" Graham asked. "Just where the hell do you think you're goin' to ride to?" He felt panic rising. "I want to know what's goin' on here, an' I want to know *now*! I'm still in charge here, goddamnit. Moses, where's the Army?"

Colfax shrugged and grinned briefly at Moses. "Ol' Frank was right 'bout one thing, he's a feisty son of a bitch." He turned to Graham. "Tell them trigger-happy yahoos not to shoot when the Kid comes in. I got him out scoutin' 'round. There'll be hell to pay if somebody shoots him or the girl." He winked again at Moses before going out of the tiny cave.

Graham glared at Moses, who sighed and looked back evenly.

"Things is gone plumb to hell," the scout said. "They ain't no Army. They're up on the Llano chasin' Indians." Graham rubbed his bad eye with his hand. It started throbbing suddenly. "We're right in the middle of a uprisin'. Mr. Colfax out there says it's the biggest Indian war ever seen in this part of Texas, an' we're right in the smack-dab middle of it." Moses reached into his pocket and pulled out tobacco and started rolling a cigarette.

"There's no Army," Graham said more to himself than to Moses. He hadn't realized just how much he had believed that there would be troops or at least Rangers coming to rescue them. He had not let himself consciously admit that it was a viable possibility, but in the back of his mind, he had kept the hope alive. Apparently he had not been alone. The other men around the fire began again to mumble among themselves; there was more despair than anger in their whispered voices.

"None we can get to," Moses said. "An' if what he says 'bout a uprisin' is true, I doubt they'd come if we could. They got their own folks to worry 'bout." Moses rubbed his eyes briefly. "I don't know if he's tellin' the truth. I been tryin' to figure him out for most of a whole day. I don't know nothin' from nothin' no more. I'm jus' tired."

Frank nodded enthusiastically. "Ol' Moses here saved Colfax all by hisself. Jumped right in the big middle of a bunch of Comanch' an' jus' killed all but two. With a knife. Pretty as you please. I got one, an' one got away. Mr. Colfax says we got to get out on our own," he said. "Says we can't count on the Army. Says—"

"On our own?" Graham blinked and cut off Frank's report. "What the hell you think we're *tryin'* to do? Half of us—or damn near it—are dead tryin' to get things done on our own!" He turned but found no place to go in the small space, then wheeled again on the scout. The sudden movement made his head ache and his vision blur even worse than before. He felt dizzy and gasped for air. "Who *is* he?" He looked toward the cave opening through which Colfax had disappeared. "Where'd you find him? Christ, why didn't you come back with a banjo an' a fiddle an' we'd have a jamboree?"

"He saved his bacon is where he found him," Frank said. "I swear, Cap'n. You never seen a man hurt that bad an' still be up an' walkin' 'round. They burned him with hot sticks an' cut up his leg, an' he can still ride any man I ever seen in the dirt."

Graham stared at Frank and tried to gather in his emotions. He was shaking with rage and frustration, but he looked around at the others and lowered his voice once more. He struggled for a mental grip. Things were close to out of control. "Frank, why don't you go see to your girl?" he said softly.

"Oh yeah. Think I'll do'er." Frank grinned and pulled himself to his feet. "I can't believe she's all right! Whole time I was watchin' them Indians, I reckoned they had her. Damn near went down to get her! I couldn't see her, though, 'count of she wasn't there. Where is she?"

"She's in the hospital cave," Graham said, quickly holding up his stumped hand when Frank's eyes widened. "She's all right. She's, uh . . . with the Sterlin' boy. That's their cave."

"*Their* cave? The Sterlin' boy?" Frank asked, a look of wonder in his eyes. "Jack's boy?" His eyes narrowed slightly. "I'll be damned. Never had much use for ol' Jack. You sure 'bout that? Jack's boy?"

"That's right. Now go on." Graham forced himself to be calm until his old friend left. Frank rubbed his chin and rose. He was muttering as he lumbered out of the small cave's entrance and disappeared.

Graham turned his attention once more to Moses, who sat and stared into the empty fire and said nothing. His hands still fiddled with the cigarette makings; his fingers couldn't seem to work right.

"You want to tell me what's goin' on?"

Moses related the events of the night before. He admitted he had doubts about Colfax, about his motives, his abilities, but he also pointed out that they didn't seem to have any other choice except to sit right where they were and wait out the Indians.

"They might jus' ride off," the scout concluded. "They had their fun." His eyes lowered. "For tonight anyhow. We might be able to wait 'em out. But they ain't actin' right. It ain't normal. An' I don't think it's the whiskey they're after, either. He thinks maybe it's 'cause they're jus' a bunch of young'uns." He hesitated. "But maybe it's somethin' else. Maybe it's got to do with their religion . . . with . . . medicine. I don't know." He looked away, and Graham suspected that he did know more. "But I don't got no other ideas neither," Moses continued. "I think we ought to listen to what he has to say. I can't see we got much choice."

"No Army, no Rangers, nobody," Graham repeated again. Some of the men had drifted off to spread the disappointing news, and now only two or three still squatted in the circle around the dying fire. It was too dark for him to discern faces with his impaired vision. His hand kept wiping his injured eye, which now was watering profusely and throbbing.

"You mean to tell me that you stopped an' risked everything to save this old man?" Graham fairly whispered, but his voice was filled with hate. "You're either crazy or stupid. Right now, I don't care which. I just ought to shoot you and be done with it."

"I got to tend to my horse," Moses said angrily, flinging away the abused tobacco pouch. "Once they've blowed, I think we're goin' back out." He turned and stared out of the opening.

"I swear to God in heaven!" Graham shouted at him. "Don't you walk away from me like that." He stumbled across the ashes of the fire and grabbed Moses by the shoulder and wheeled him around just outside the door in the blackness. The men around him stepped away in confusion. Frustration and anger welled up in Graham and forced his hand into a fist. He threw a punch toward the black scout's face.

Moses swung up his arm to fend off the wagon master's attack. He caught Graham on the right side of his face and knocked him backward into the limestone wall. Graham bounced hard off the rock; the desire to fight left him when he observed Moses's stance. The scout had his gloved fists up and ready to defend himself. But he wasn't advancing. Graham picked up his hat, and after a moment, the scout turned and walked away.

Graham felt weakness flood in to drown all his anger. "Come back here," he said. Then he followed.

Moses said nothing but moved on down the line toward his horse. Graham moved into the narrow opening between the wagons and the bluff. Up and down the line people were now fully awake, watchful, apprehensive. More lanterns had been lit. There was the smell of coffee in the air. Graham came up behind the scout and stood silently while Moses loosened his cinch and eased the saddle up on the bay. She was still sweating hard, and the scout dug around in a nearby wagon until he came up with a curry and brush and began working her.

The wagon master swallowed and forced calm into his voice. "Let me see if I got this right. You were on your way to get troops. Two days' ride, maybe more."

"Likely more."

"But you stop along the way to save some crazy old man an' put the whole goddamn train at risk. That about it?"

"That's it. 'Cept you left out the part where I come back. Seems to me the train was already 'at risk' when I rode out of here."

Graham waited half a beat before hissing, "You got any reason why I don't just shoot you down right here?" Moses said nothing. "You got any reason in the goddamn world why I don't make a necklace out of your balls an' trade it to the goddamn Indians for safe passage?"

"I got no reason, Mr. Graham," Moses said, turning around. "But I think you better get on with it if you're a mind to do'er. I'm wore out with you threatenin' me. I'm tired of you always tryin' to hit me or make me hit you. Either jerk your gun an' let's get it over with, or put it out of the way. I don't 'tend to go 'round watchin' my back all the time."

"You nigger son of a bitch." Graham's breath shortened. All the anger and blame he had attached to the black scout returned and crested in his voice, and his hand fell to his pistol. "I don't have to backshoot you. I—"

"Look, Mr. Graham." Moses spoke quickly and in a voice heavy with a weary, even tone. "This ain't gettin' us nowhere." Graham stood where he was. Both men were shaking with anger. "If you're of a mind to shoot me, jus' go on ahead an' get it over with. Tell you a truth, I'm too goddamn tired an' too goddamn scared to care one way or 'nother. I won't try an' stop you. Fact is, I think I could use the rest." He waited a moment, but when Graham didn't move, he turned and resumed working the horse.

"Why didn't you go on for troops?" Graham's voice calmed, but there was still anger behind it.

" 'Cause like I told you, Mr. Colfax says they ain't no troops. Not at the forts, not any that's likely to come, even if they could an' wanted to, which he didn't reckon they would. An' even if they was willin' an' able, he don't think they would of come right now." He added quickly, "He may look too crazy to wipe his own ass, but I'm tellin' you he knows more 'bout Indians'n any man I ever met. Least he claims to, an' last night he went a long way toward convincin' me. Mr. Herbert, too."

"Frank!" Graham's voice communicated his outrage. "Frank don't know—"

"Frank's a lot smarter'n you think," Moses said hurriedly. "But that don't make no diff'rence. Whether that ol' man knows anythin' 'bout Indians or not don't matter. What he says 'bout the troops makes sense." He looked out into the darkened crossing. "This ain't ord'nary. He says it's a goddamn big war. A uprisin'. I think he knows what he's talkin' 'bout. Even if he don't, you can see for yourself that they's a mess of Indians out there. More's comin' all the time, if he knows anythin' about it. We done killed a bunch of 'em an' they ain't goin' away, an' I can tell you that ain't ord'nary from my own 'xperience."

"Your experience," snorted Graham.

"My 'xperience," Moses insisted. "Listen to me, Mr. Graham. I been out here most of my life. I never seen or heard tell of this many Indians in one place at one time. But what I seen before don't matter. What does matter is that them Indians is here, an' we're in trouble. Chances are we're not the onliest ones that's noticed 'em, an' if that's a truth, then the Army's likely out on patrol, jus' like he says."

"But—"

"Ain't no buts 'bout it," Moses went on. "I've rode with the Army, an' I've rode with Texas Rangers, an' I can tell you that if they's Indians out here an' they don't want to be found out, they won't be. That's for sure. I could of went on for troops like you told me, but I didn't see how that would help if they ain't no troops to come. This way, we might have a fightin' chance. Least that's why I come back. I didn't have to."

He paused to let Graham have his say, but the wagon master remained silent in the darkness. He could think of nothing else to use as an argument. He knew that recrimination against the black scout was getting him nowhere, but he couldn't think of anything else to do.

"I'll say this," Moses went on. "*If* he's right 'bout the Indians here, an' *if* he's right 'bout the Army, then maybe he's right that the whole plains is in a uprisin'. If that's so, what we got to do is find a way out of here an' hightail it back to the Wichita—or further—an' wait this thing out."

"Two ifs an' a maybe," Graham said aloud in a soft tone. "I think I've heard that before."

2

MOSES LED HIS HORSE DOWN TO THE NARROW SPRING from which the wagon master had watered the oxen earlier. A small shielded lantern lighted the area, and Moses allowed the animal to lower its nose and slurp water from the shallow run. Graham's ears sharpened to try to pick out any human cries in the night, but aside from the frogs and crickets, there was no sound.

The wagon master felt strange, suddenly liberated by the audacious tone of a man he had held in contempt from the first moment they met. As Moses leaned down to adjust his stirrup, Graham felt his head swimming again. His tussle with the scout had taken most of what energy he had out of him. He was now so tired that he couldn't imagine feeling any other way. He felt nothing but a buzzing exhaustion ringing about his head like a swarm of angry gnats.

Niggers, Indians, Mexicans, and now a crazy old man, he calculated. He was trying to stop up something that was leaking everywhere he looked. There was no clean way out, no ready solution, just a hope that Carlson Colfax knew what to do. It was a slim hope.

Finally the silence became uncomfortable. Someone needed to speak, and Moses took the lead. "How're we fixed? Many more dead?"

"There's fifty-eight left alive," Graham responded

numbly, then he quickly amended it: "Sixty, with you an' Frank."

Moses turned to him. "Already counted us as dead?"

"Figurin' the odds," Graham responded. "An' you just may be anyway." He put that in quickly and then asked quietly, "What do we do now?"

"He—Mr. Colfax—says they's only after one thing," Moses said. "Won't tell me too much 'bout it, but it ain't got nothin' to do with us, or with the whiskey, least not 'specially. He's got this partner, a kid, that he left out there." Moses looked through the darkness toward the southwest. "Says it's not nothin' we done. That's the whole thing right there." He shook his head. "I don't know. I think you'd best let him tell it." Moses paused, then he said, "They's somethin' else."

Before he could go on, there was the sound of someone approaching, and both men stiffened. From the darkness between the wagons and the bluff the silhouette of a woman appeared. Aggie's voice came between the wagon master and the scout.

"Here." She handed Moses a tin plate full of beans. "There ain't no sidemeat left, least none I can get to. I split up what was left of the beans for the three of you."

"Smells good," Moses responded, taking the plate and squatting as he scooped up the beans with a spoon. "I'm 'bliged."

"Least I could do," she said. "I would of brought you some," she said to Graham, "but that's all there is, an' that's Hannah's. Other folks won't give me none. Mr. Colfax et two platefuls already, an' I thought he'd eat this 'fore I could get away." She paused for a moment. "He's peculiar."

"He's nothin' if he ain't that," Moses said through a mouthful of beans.

"He took one look at me an' kind of danced a jig." She lowered her voice into a conspiratorial whisper. "Then he starts singin' 'I Seen the Light,' or some such nonsense."

Neither of the two men responded. There was a long silence as the sound of Moses's spoon scraping the tin plate seemed to echo quietly in the night air.

Finally she said, "Well, I thought it was peculiar. But

he just kept lookin' at me an' laughin'. It was kind of spooky."

"I think I know why," Moses started, then hesitated. Aggie squatted down next to him, hunkering in close. Graham's shadow moved away in the darkness. He walked off several yards until he couldn't see them anymore. Their voices came to him across the night clearly enough. He held his head in his hand and tried to rub away his headache.

"They's a gal looks a lot like you out there," Moses said.

Graham felt himself go cold inside.

"For a minute, I thought she was you, matter of fact," Moses continued.

"Like me? Out there?" Aggie's head turned, and Moses could see that she was peering out into the night. "What's she doin' out there? Who is she? You're funnin' me."

Moses chewed between words. "She's out there all right. She don't say much. She—" He paused and scooped up the final spoonful. "She had a run-in with the Comanche."

"An' he left her out there?" Graham reinserted himself into their conversation. "Just run off an' left her?"

"She's with a man," Moses quickly added. "The kid I told you about. They'll be in direc'ly. He'll tell you 'bout it. I reckon he wants to."

"He's crazy," Graham said.

"I kind of like him," Aggie put in. Then she giggled. "He's sort of like one of them dwarfs that travels 'round with the medicine shows. I seen one in Corinth once. 'Cept he's too tall to be a dwarf."

"He's tall enough to get us all killed," Graham growled. "I can't believe you come back with nothin' more than that. I can't believe you didn't go for somebody with some savvy. I should just shove you out there an' let you have at it on your own. I ought to just—"

"Don't you think there's been enough of that kind of talk, Mr. Graham?" Aggie said sharply.

Graham's form visibly stiffened. His shoulders snapped back as if he had been slapped. She stood up and faced him.

"All I've heard out of you is how you're fixin' to kill somebody. I know you don't like Mr. Franklin here. I know it's 'cause he's a—'cause he's colored an' all. But it seems to me like he's doin' the best he can. Seems to me like that's all any of us is doin'."

Her tone turned cold, and Graham held himself still. He could sense a growing indignation inside him. How dare she speak to him that way? She was just a girl. Jack's girl. She shouldn't talk to him like that. She had no right at all!

"So far, all you've done is whine an' carry on," she continued in a voice building in intensity. "I never seen the like! All you've done is make things worse. People are dyin' here! You may be hurt some, but you ain't dyin'. Not yet, you ain't. It wouldn't hurt you none to show some respect for them that's doin' the best they can. Sometimes you make me so mad I could just shoot you just to keep you quiet. Why don't you shut up, an' let them that knows how things are take charge?"

Graham stood rigid. He could feel the smarting sting of her words physically falling on his face. Since being cashiered from the Army, he had never been spoken to in this manner by anyone. He was usually quick to assert himself, to take action. This time all he could think to do was to turn and stalk off. He walked five large paces away and wheeled. Aggie and Moses were only dark forms against the limestone bluff.

She turned to Moses, who stood up instantly. Graham smiled. He figured it was the scout's turn to feel her wrath.

Instead, the words that she spoke altered their tone completely, and Graham felt a pain in his heart as real as if he had been struck by a Comanche arrow.

"I'm sorry for the way he—the way everybody treats you," she said to Moses. "It's my fault as much as anybody's, but I want you to know I don't feel that way. I admire you. I'd rather have you standin' with me than a dozen men like that." Graham couldn't see her gesture, but he knew she had nodded her head down the line toward him.

"I'm 'bliged for the say-so," Moses muttered and lowered his head. Graham's stomach turned over. His face burned.

"I mean it," she insisted. "You don't just talk—you do." Her voice raised itself, but the tenderness in her tone was still there. "An' I ain't 'shamed of what we done," she continued. Graham saw her head turn toward him to make sure he was near enough to hear. "Which wasn't *nothin'*." The remark was elevated in volume, designed to reach Graham's ears. He felt small, petty, foolish. "It was a decent thing, an' you did me a kindness by stayin' an' protectin' me while I did it. While we did it. I trust you," she said at last. "You do what you can, an' that's a lot more'n half the men on this train."

She reached out and took the tin plate from Moses's hand and started away from him.

"I want you to—" Graham mumbled as she passed him, but she didn't hear him. She kept moving. He reached out and grabbed her shoulder, and she stopped. He couldn't tell what she was feeling, but her body was suddenly stiff. Inside him alarms were going off in a deafening clatter. You're *touching* her! he screamed at himself. What could he be thinking? He could smell a mixture of smoke and sweat and soap emanating from her. Her shoulder felt firm but somehow electrifying and feminine beneath the thin fabric of her dress. He wanted to grab her to him, pull her tightly to him and kiss her. The urge was overwhelming, and it took everything he could muster inside himself to fight it off.

"What?" she asked, and her voice trembled. "Just what do you want now?" They stood there for a moment, frozen, yet touching. Beneath his fingertips he could feel her pulse racing, and his own heart, he realized, was pounding even faster. His breath was short, and his forehead was alive with cold perspiration. He hadn't felt this way ever before, he told himself. He was touching something totally forbidden, had put his hand where he had promised himself he couldn't without fear of losing it as certainly as his other was gone. But it remained where it was, and Graham allowed himself to indulge in the exquisite misery of having what he had dreamed of under his touch but being unable to do more than that to make it his own.

He suddenly remembered that the scout was only a few yards away. He mentally begged her to move—away from him, closer to him—just to move so he would know what to do. She remained where she was, still, her breath coming in deep but even intervals, and then, almost unconsciously, he allowed his hand to drift away from her, fall to his side.

"I'm sorry," he said. "I don't know what I was thinkin'."

"No, Mr. Graham," she said in a cold, flat voice. "You never seem to know what you're thinkin'. Maybe that's why we're in this mess."

"I . . ." Graham could think of nothing to say, and after a beat, she stepped away from him.

"I want to thank you for the grub," Moses called softly to her. Graham felt a swell of hatred rise and fall inside him as she turned to face his voice. He hadn't seen the gesture, but it didn't matter. He was there. It seemed he was always there, always between him and this girl. "If it wasn't for you, nobody'd feed me, likely," the scout concluded.

"Well, you're more'n welcome," she chirped, but the tone was forced, strained. She stepped not toward Moses so much as away from the wagon master. Graham felt his insides constrict as if he had received a hard blow in the stomach. "Like I said, I'm just sorry there ain't more."

"Here," Graham said gruffly and all of a sudden. He moved quickly past her and went over to the side of his wagon, where he reached down into the darkness. When he stood up, he thrust out Jack Sterling's boots. "I snuck out an' got these earlier." He felt more foolish than ever. God, he thought, he despised himself, and, he suddenly realized, he despised her as well.

Aggie stood between the two men and said nothing. She accepted the boots and hefted them. "I'm obliged, Mr. Graham," she said at last. "I truly am." There was apology in her voice, but there was also distance, wariness.

"An' there's food in my wagon. Beans. Maybe some salted meat."

"We're beholden," she said. Then, at last, compassion rose behind her words. "How's your eye?"

"I'll know more when the sun comes up," he said flatly. His heart was racing, but inside he felt hollow. What did she feel for him now? Pity? God, he thought, how he hated her.

Moses turned to fuss over his horse, and for a moment the only sound was the noise his brush made against the bay's coat.

"How many times they come since I left?" the scout finally asked. "I heard shootin'."

"They've been back a couple of times." Graham stepped away from Aggie and allowed a measure of pride to come into his voice. He didn't want this goddamn nigger scout to think that they were helpless, but even that spasm of emotional reaction came too automatically for him to be entirely aware of it. He spoke mechanically, repeating words his mind told him to say, but he found that they sounded alien to his ears, coming from his mouth, but seemingly spoken by someone else. His tongue felt like pasteboard. He could hear his voice, but it was as if someone else were speaking. He couldn't find himself anywhere inside him.

"We took care of them." He realized that his voice clearly was directed as much toward Aggie as anyone. But there was no emotion at all behind his words. He spoke as if he were reading from a script. He wanted to talk to her, but he couldn't with Moses standing there. Maybe, he admitted to himself, he couldn't even if they were alone. "They come to parley once," he forced himself to continue.

"Parley?" There was surprise in the scout's voice. "What'd they want?"

Graham related the conversation he had had with the medicine man briefly and concisely. He omitted any reference to the chief's reaction to Aggie but focused instead on the dead hunters. Otherwise, he hardly realized what he was saying. His mind was racing, but he knew it was going nowhere.

"Hunters?" Moses asked.

" 'Buffalo mans.' " Graham repeated the Indian's words. "That's what they called them."

"They look like hunters to you?"

"They didn't look like much of anything," Graham snapped.

Moses said nothing, and Graham completed his story.

"Whiskey for the women?" Moses shook his head. He paused. "Did you know the dead men?"

"No. I told you, they were hunters or somethin'. I didn't study on them." He gestured with his stumped arm. "They're right out there. Go look for yourself. They're bad."

"The women won't be any better," Moses said bitterly, and then he seemed to remember that Aggie was still standing right there in the dark.

Graham had also forgotten her for the moment. He wanted to reach out to her again, but he controlled his hand this time. It was surprisingly easy to do so, he found. The rush of desire he had felt before had passed; all he felt now was emptiness that covered a deep, throbbing ache.

"I'm sorry," Moses said quietly. "I shouldn't take on 'bout it. What I seen—"

"She doesn't need to know what you've seen." Graham spoke sharply as the throbbing deep inside him surged, and he stepped toward Aggie. The move was automatic, a sudden impulse to protect her. He wanted to undo something, reclaim something. Then he realized how obvious and stupid it must look, how unwanted it must be, and he stopped himself and stepped around her, putting himself between her and the scout.

"We all heard what you seen. The *hearin'* of it was enough," he said. There was a glimmer of emotion in his voice now, but he was having to force it. He tried to find something in the situation that, once more, would make him angry, would make him care. There was nothing.

"The ones that come in here was no older'n Jason," Aggie said softly. "How could boys like that be so mean? The one I shot was no older than Jed Ambrose."

"Comanche don't have no boys," Moses responded. "They got braves an' they got women. An' what I know 'bout it is that the day they're borned, they'd as soon kill you as look at you. They're all young'uns from the look of 'em, even the chief an' the medicine man. But I seen what they can do. An' I reckon you heard it. It don't make 'em any less mean to be young."

Hannah Morgan came up quickly and joined them. "That man Colfax wants to talk to you, Graham. Said for us all to start packin' up." She waited a moment, but no one said anything. Graham was silent, and Moses waited like a statue. Aggie's form remained dark and silent.

"He's fond of givin' orders." Hannah's exasperated tone suggested she might as well be addressing the oxen. "An' he's righteously proud of his name." More silence followed, and finally she slapped her hands against her skirts and turned and walked off. "Hand to God!" she muttered. "Ain't seen nothin' like it from a bunch of Mescans." Aggie waited a moment longer, but when neither Moses nor Graham said anything, she followed Hannah.

Graham felt his shoulders sag and his heart sink. It was a feeling he hadn't had away from a gaming table, something that usually came when he folded a winning hand and didn't realize his advantage until it was too late. He felt older than ever, more worthless. But he didn't know what he could do about any of the feeling he now tried to banish deep within himself once more.

"An' you don't know a thing about what's goin' on?" Graham asked Moses once more. He wanted things to return to normal, to be as they had been before Aggie came up and reduced him to the role of a naughty boy. But his voice sounded flat and uninterested in his ears. "You said there was somethin' else. A kid. A girl."

"I tried to tell you 'while ago," he said softly. "This gal out yonder belongs to a bunch of folks down on Paint Crick that got theirselves massacred."

"Paint Creek?" Graham thought immediately of Baker and Potter and their insistence that the flag draped around the waist of the warrior belonged to someone they knew named Olin.

"From what Mr. Colfax says, she's the onliest one to get away. An' . . ." He paused and looked through the darkness toward where Aggie had vanished. "She didn't get away clean. Anyway, I got it figured out that them Comanche think Miss Sterling is that other girl. It's the damnedest thing."

Graham remembered how the young chief's eyes had lit up when he spotted Aggie Sterling, and suddenly things were beginning to make sense. "I thought they were after the whiskey. They wouldn't go to all this bother for a girl, even a . . . a pretty girl."

"It has to do with a medicine bag," Moses said, replacing the saddle on his horse and tightening the cinch. "He don't think they'll leave off till they get that, or the girl, or both. They put a powerful store in them bags."

"You mean to tell me this is all about a bag full of bones an' chicken feathers?" Graham was incredulous. But then, he thought, nothing could surprise him anymore. "An' all we got to save us is that old man down there?"

"All I know is that his name is Carlson Colfax, an' he's 'bout the toughest ol' coot I ever seen." Moses sighed. "He knows the country, an' he seems to know a hell of a lot 'bout Indians. He says he can get us out of this, 'thout losing more'n we have to. An' maybe he can." Moses paused. "Right now, I don't see as we got no choice in it. I say we got to go 'long with him, whatever his price is."

"All this over a girl." Graham chuckled mirthlessly and shook his head. Yes, he answered himself: all of this over a girl. The irony of it settled on him and made him weaker than ever. He wanted to laugh. "You mean, if we just give them the girl, they'd ride out." Give them the girl, he thought. As if she was his or anyone else's to give.

"Prob'ly," Moses said. "But it ain't that simple. An' it ain't likely to happen."

"You know, nigger boy . . ." Graham's voice had no malice in it. He felt nothing, and his voice now seemed to come from far away. The response was automatic, plastic, but he made it anyway. "That's the first thing you've said that makes sense."

3

"We need to be ready to hit 'em come false dawn," Colfax assured Graham around a fire in the same cave where the men had met the night before. Now Moses stood off to one side and felt helpless. The train was well represented: Karl Runnels and even Virgil Hollister had been brought in, although the latter's wound was serious enough to prevent him from doing much more than staring harshly at everyone, and Runnels's foot was still bleeding through a huge bandage that someone had wrapped around it.

None of the men looked happy, and their stormy

countenances matched the general mood in the cave, except for Colfax. He was almost jolly as he described what was required of the settlers to save themselves from the hostile barbarians who surrounded them.

Pierce, Quigley, and several others were present, and added to the group from the previous night's council were Potter and Baker, who slouched in the cave's opening, insensible that their silhouettes could be seen from the cedar thicket across the creek. Colfax assured them that the Comanche had tired of trying to pick off the settlers one by one from hidden and uncomfortable positions across the crossing, that their visit the previous afternoon had signaled a new tactic.

"Them red bastards got 'em a thing 'bout first light." The plainsman spoke as if he were teaching children the fundamentals of a game. "If they're not killin' some poor son of a bitch, they think the spirits're runnin' 'round, an' they find their holes an' wait till sunup. 'Course, that ain't definite. One thing 'bout Comanch': Ain't nothin' definite. Thanks to Mr. Moses here"—he nodded toward the scout—"they got 'em a goddamn good reason to believe this place is full of haints of one kind or 'nother. Comanch' don't gen'rally use pickets. But they won't be runnin' 'round at false dawn. We got the drop on 'em if they hang on to that."

Moses looked down at the loamy soil in which Colfax had traced a line that stood for the mesa that rose away from the crossing. A large X was marked to indicate the Indian camp, a line showed the ridge that bordered it to the east, and a circle to the north indicated the crossing itself. The camp was less than a mile from the crossing, but the ridge rose up and created a barrier in between. The easiest and most direct route between them ran directly across the mesa, down the ridge to the cedar thicket across from the train. It was like a long canyon, he realized, and there was no wonder that the settlers could hear the echoing screams of the victims being tortured to death. The Indians knew that, of course, and they clearly had planned the night's events to frighten the settlers into senseless behavior.

"They hit us at dawn yesterday," Graham said. "Then they came to parley near sundown."

"Well." Colfax bit off a chew from a plug and lavishly worked it around in his jaw. "I doubt they'll come again till mornin'. They likely only come down last evenin' to get a gander as to how you're doin' close up." He grinned. "'Pears to me you've got yourself set up pretty goddamn nice." Moses leaned uncomfortably against the cave wall and said nothing. He had learned that Colfax would have his joke no matter what.

"You got a reg'lar li'l ol' homestead right here on the crick," Colfax went on. "But I tell you what: If I was a Comanch', I'd figure you was easy pickin's. Pretty soon, you'll get comfortable an' let down your guard. Hell, you got whiskey, women, an' goose-down pillows. You could run you a reg'lar goddamn whorehouse right here. They's prob'ly jus' riled 'cause you didn't ask 'em in."

Eyes shot across the group.

"Zis is vot you brung back to safe uz?" Runnels shouted from his recumbent position against the cave wall. "You zend a nigger out, you brung a madman back. Ach! Graham, if I could ztand up, I vould kill you myzelf."

Virgil Hollister glanced approvingly at Runnels. Harvey Pierce and one or two others nodded quickly.

Graham ignored them. "What's your point?"

"Well." Carlson squatted. "You showed 'em diff'rent. Least you beat 'em off. More'n once. An' they spent most of tonight gettin' their peckers hard so they can come at you again an' finish you off." He paused. "One thing 'bout Comanch': He may be a sorry, hardheaded son of a bitch, but he ain't yeller. They ain't nothin' out here he's 'fraid of, least of all a bunch of goddamn feather-dicks such as the likes of this." He waved his hand around contemptuously. "He'll come when he's good an' ready, an' from what I seen 'round here, y'all don't have a Chinaman's chance in a Mescan whorehouse of standin' 'em off again."

"I think we're doin' fair to middlin'." It was Harvey Pierce who spoke up. He was scrunched down next to the fire as if he were one of the most important people on the train. He glanced quickly at Graham, then looked down into the flames and spoke bravely. "We've done sent a bunch of 'em to hell, an' we can hold out if we have to."

"Horseshit." Colfax spat into the coals. "You been lucky so far. These here's a bunch of pups. They ain't got a fix on how to do it right yet, an' they's hung up. But they will. You can kill 'em here an' there, but that's all right. They jus' get madder when you do that. Stronger, too. Makes it a bigger notion when they get one of you. They need you for their medicine so they can join up with their *compadres* on the high plains. They got some makin' up to do, an' you got stuff that'd do jus' fine for it—whiskey bein' one of 'em, scalps an' women bein' 'nother. One woman in partic'lar," he added with another wink at Moses, who shifted his eyes downward as if he didn't notice. Baker and Potter exchanged looks, but they said nothing.

"If you had a bunch of horses, likely you'd all be dead by now," Colfax continued. "One thing 'bout Comanch': He'll fight like a panther for women an' whiskey an' such, but he'll die for horses. This bunch'll die for somethin' else 'fore they'll let you go." He continued to fix his eyes on Moses.

The scout knew what Aggie's position was. He wasn't certain just how desperate people would have to be to throw her out as some kind of offering to the Indians. If they knew about the other girl and the stolen medicine bag, he had little doubt that she would survive.

"So you don't think we could just wait here and stand them off?" Quigley spoke up from the side of the cave. His voice was strained. "I don't know about going out there without protection of some kind."

"Look." Colfax turned to spot the shabby little banker in the battered silk hat, who shied away from the plainsman's eyes. "You got water an' some grub. Though I'd have to 'low that what I just et wasn't worth a good goddamn. But you also got animals that need grazin'. In a week they'll be dead. Hell, in two days the goddamn stink of them that's already dead'll drive you out. If it comes a flood—an' dry as it's been, it might take a notion to—this whole creek bank can fill up like a poor man's privy. You're by God trapped here, an' the Comanch' know it."

"It's not of our choosing," Quigley whined. "We want to move on."

"Sure you do." Colfax laughed. "That's clear. But you ain't goin' nowhere with them Indians out yonder."

"That's about right." Graham spread his feet a bit for

leverage. He tilted his head slightly toward whomever he addressed and kept squinting and blinking in the flickering lantern light inside the cave. "I sent Frank an' this boy for troops or Rangers or somebody. But all they came back with is you. I don't see that we're any better off tonight than we were yesterday. Two men, one of which I ain't even seen yet, wasn't exactly what we had in mind."

Graham sounded like a man giving a speech, Moses thought. There was nothing personal in his voice at all. He spoke as if he were half asleep.

"Well, we'll see if that ain't enough." Colfax worked his tobacco. "Them horses rested an' watered?" Moses nodded. "As I see it," he went on, "you're holed up here, an' for the time bein' it's a good place to be. But it ain't goin' to last forever. I reckon they's 'tween thirty an' fifty braves, maybe more, still out there with plenty of fight in 'em. An' they ain't fixin' to go 'way jus' 'cause you want 'em to."

"There's more'n that," Pierce said. "Hell, they've had the ridge covered with sharpshooters who was pickin' us off."

"Hell, that was likely nothin' but women an' young'uns. Might be a brave or two over there if one's hurt too bad to ride. But I can tell you: Comanch' fights on a horse. Hell, he does ever'thing he does on a goddamn horse. He'll even wet his pecker on a horse if he can. Ain't no full-growed braves over yonder. This time of night, ain't nobody over yonder." He squatted again and glanced over his drawing. "They's somethin' else," he said ominously.

"We went up yonder an' took a gander at 'em, like I tol' you. An' what we seen wasn't pretty." Colfax looked up at Moses and then studied his drawing. "That ain't jus' Comanch' out there. Most of what I seen is, but they's Kiowa, too. Some anyhow. That's bad. Real bad."

No one said anything for a moment, and finally Frank spoke up. "What diff'rence does it make? Indian's a Indian."

"I tol' you they was big doin's up on the high plains," Colfax went on. "Tol' you 'bout them hunters we found." He shot Moses a warning look. "That's them they brung in, I s'pect. Poor bastards. Anyhow, that could mean the goddamn Kiowa is hooked up some way or 'nother with the Comanch'. Ain't no tellin'. Hell, they might have somebody else throwed in with 'em. Cheyenne, likely. In any case, it's big medicine, goddamn big medicine."

"So what?"

"So what is that them dog-fuckin' Kiowa is carryin' on 'bout some kind of big medicine that'll keep 'em from gettin' kilt. Say they got 'em somethin' that'll make bullets jus' fall right out of a rifle on the groun'. It's only a rumor, an' it'll never be a fact. You know it, an' I know it. But it's been floatin' 'round for a while, near a year. But if they's anythin' to it, goddamn Kiowa'll believe it. An' if they've convinced the Comanch', then no white man's hair is safe. Any way it goes, we need to hit 'em an' get you the hell out of here 'fore it starts." Colfax looked around the circle.

"There ain't no answer for it. Nossir, if you want to save your hair, you got to move. You're wore down to a goddamn nub as it is, an' squabblin' 'mongst yourselves like a bunch of nigger sudswomen." His eyes shot toward Moses quickly, and then he continued, "If I can see it, they can see it. One thing 'bout Comanch', Kiowa too: They may be goat-pricked dog-fuckers, but they ain't blind, an' they ain't stupid."

Colfax stood, and the men backed away to give him room.

"Moses says you have a plan," Graham said, and the scout stood up straight. Graham was just playing along, Moses thought, as if he didn't care anymore. He was growing weary of the discussion, and time was running out. He calculated that it would be light in the east soon, and the Indians would likely hit them that morning. Moses knew that Colfax was correct about one thing: These people here couldn't take much more. They surely couldn't stand another day on the crossing. But if he was wrong that they'd be wiser to move out, why didn't Graham see it? Why didn't he challenge him?

"Well, now." Colfax grinned, his former good humor restored suddenly. "That's a possible. But first, somebody get me a swig or two of bug juice an' somethin' to chaw on. Then I'll get down to savin' your bacon whether you want me to or not."

4

"HOW MANY WAGONS YOU GOT READY TO ROLL?" Colfax asked. He had a tin cup of whiskey in his hand and a plug of tobacco in his cheek. He was asking questions about the train's makeup as if he were taking an inventory. Graham had answered each query in a soft, quick voice that showed no emotion whatsoever.

"Most of them are all right. It's the teams that are a problem. I count a dozen possible matches," Graham replied in the same monotone. "Includin' the mules. We picked up that buckboard out there. I don't know if it's any good." Neither the Hawshaws nor the Newsomes were present in the cave, Moses noted. Several others were also absent.

"Animals I seen look peaked." Colfax looked at Moses. "You can't pull all of 'em."

"If they were lightened an' if we used the horses—"

"We'll need the horses," Colfax grumbled. "How many saddle mounts you got?"

"They was twelve at last count, but some of 'em's took arrows." It was Grover Hildebrandt, who had entered the cave and spoke from the rear. He had a small pot in his hand, and he stepped forward and replenished Colfax's cup. The aroma of the liquor filled the cave. "I fixed one or two up, but I doubt they'd get very far. We got maybe eight that can ride, maybe nine head."

"An' mules?" Colfax asked.

"They're counted in with the haulin' stock. The oxen have a lot of wounds," Graham admitted flatly. "An' they're slow."

"Well." Colfax rubbed his beard a moment. "Hitch up eight wagons, if you can, no more'n four animals to a team. Load ever'body into 'em an' get ready to skedaddle."

"Leave?" Graham spoke as if he had suddenly been awakened by the old plainsman's order. "Just leave? Just like that?"

"Not 'xactly. When the time is right, though, jus' pull out."

"When will the time be right?" Graham asked.

"First light. When the fun starts other side of the mesa. You sure you got 'nough stock to pull eight of them wagons with four to a team?" He addressed the question generally, ignoring Graham's authority. Several men looked doubtful, but none said anything. "Well, then get as many hitched up as you can. Do it while it's still dark. Them Comanch' may not be watchin' you all night, but they'll sure'n hell know when you're gettin' ready."

"What 'bout the wounded men?" This time it was a woman's voice, Hannah Morgan's, which spoke up. She came into the cave among the men and squatted down next to Colfax. "Some of 'em can't be moved 'thout killin' 'em."

"It's move 'em an' kill 'em, or leave 'em for the Comanch'," Colfax said evenly. "They'll kill 'em slower, 'cause they'll be madder'n a nest of rattlers if they slip 'round us an' find out that y'all vamoosed. They'll die hard. Harder'n that bunch died over yonder. You got to make up your mind."

Several of the men mumbled, but Hannah nodded. "I ain't the one you're goin' to have to convince of that."

"Gott damn, Graham. Vill you not be zatisfiet till ve are all kilt? Zchoot dis zon off a bitch und hang him out dere mit der nigger und dis murderin' bitch. Zen ve kin vigger out vot to do. Vot der hell are ve payin' you vor? Vy der hell are ve, any off uz, lizenin' to you?"

"Who's the sausage-eater?" Colfax jerked a thumb toward the injured tailor. "Never had much use for goddamn Dutchmen. Bunch of chicken-shit, square-toed pigfuckers, if you ask me."

"Nobody asked you," Harvey Pierce said.

Colfax turned to Graham. "I ain't got a lot of goddamn time for palaverin' with a bunch of peckerless greenhorns. You interested in keepin' your hair or not?"

"Which way do we go?" Moses asked. "If we go west, 'cordin' to you, we're ridin' right into a uprisin'."

"If you follow the Red out a ways, two days, maybe three"—Colfax looked at the western wall of the cave as if he could see through it—"you'll hit a supply camp the Army's set up. It's at a place called Duck Creek. They ain't many troopers there ord'narily, maybe none. But I never heard tell of Comanch' raidin' it. Might be a place to wait this thing out."

"I say we head back east," Pierce said. "I done told you, Graham, I ain't no Indian fighter. I say we hightail it back to where we can be safe an' then decide what to do."

"You signed on for the whole trip," Graham responded in a low quiet voice that grew in intensity as he spoke. "You agreed to go on when we started. I'm tired of your mouth an' your whining. You, too, Runnels, goddamnit. I'm still runnin' this show, an' if we go, an' I mean *if*"—he shot a look at Moses—"then we're goin' west like we planned." There was a moment of silence, and he added in an apparent afterthought, "There ain't nothin' to go back for."

"But that was before all this!" Pierce's voice took on confidence as several men around him nodded their heads in agreement. "We didn't bargain for none of this. Goddamn, Graham, we're shot to hell! It's a bust."

"Well, I ain't leavin' Aggie." Hannah spoke up again. "That girl's carried too much of this on her own, an' I got a feelin' she ain't fixin' to leave them men, an' I ain't leavin' her."

"I'm tired of hearin' 'bout what Aggie Sterlin' wants," Graham said with a deep sigh. His stumped hand brushed quickly against his trousers, and he stared at his feet. "I'm tired of hearin' what any of you want. It ain't up to you. It ain't up to me. It ain't up to nobody."

" 'Pears to me," Pierce said quietly, "that somebody's losin' his grip, somebody who never had much grip in the first place." He looked around and took courage. "I say we take a vote on what to do."

Colfax turned on Pierce, who immediately stepped back. "*Vote* on it! Did you say 'vote on it'? You sawed-off little pissant! I ain't heard of nothin' that asshole-stupid in all my days! You think the goddamn Comanch're goin' to vote on it? Or was you fixin' to *give* the redskins a vote?" Pierce's eyes were overlarge, and his mouth was working, although he said nothing. Colfax's body seemed to grow in size as he backed the small carpenter up against a wall. "Well, I'll tell you one thing sure'n God give balls to a rabbit, you better goddamn *well* give 'em a vote, 'cause they're sure'n hell fixin' to have a *say* in it whether you want 'em to or not!"

Pierce slipped around Colfax and moved over by Runnels.

"This is the biggest bunch of sorry-assed sons of bitches I ever heard of!" Colfax railed. "I swear, *Mister* Moses, if I was you, I'd light out an' leave 'em to the Comanch'. There's not a one of 'em worth a bottle of Mescan slobber. I swear to God Almighty! I never would of hooked up with such a bunch of sodbustin' shitheels if I'd of knowed what I was doin'."

"I jus' don't know who's runnin' the show, that's all," Pierce muttered.

"The *Comanch'* is runnin' the show!" Colfax snarled. "The Comanch' an' the Kiowa an' anybody else out there who's with 'em." He hitched his belt up and squatted again by the fire. "You ain't got nothin' to *vote* about, Mister. The onliest one 'round here who's got sense 'nough to piss on a rock is me. You better reach down into the shit in your britches an' find 'nough backbone to do what I tell you, or some redskin squaw'll be wearin' your balls for bells by noon tomorrow. You're headin' out, an' you're headin' west, or you ain't headin' at all. Get that through your skull. You go east, you're dead, sure'n sunrise."

"You people start loadin' wagons," Graham ordered. "Get the wounded men on first." He looked at Hannah. "Make them as easy as you can. You tell Aggie—Miss Sterlin'—to do as she's told. If she don't want to, get somebody else." He paused. "Goddamnit, tie her up if you have to! She ain't a special case. Get the whiskey on board, too. Pull the kegs inside—"

"You can't carry nothin' like that." Colfax's laughter interrupted the wagon master's instructions. "That's goddamn dead weight. Heavier'n hell. You're goin' to have to make good time, maybe even run for it a ways. You'll be doin' good to get away jus' carryin' all these chicken-dicked greenhorns." He spat once more. " 'Sides, you take that forty-rod out to the Army, you might as well piss it out on the ground." He stood up suddenly and faced Graham. "Best thing to do is pass 'round a stiff drink to all concerned. It ain't goin' to do nothin' but get you killed elsewise."

Graham looked as if he had been slapped. Moses felt the wagon master's depth of shock from across the cave. This, at last, was the showdown, and he braced himself for the explosion.

Suddenly Colfax stood. His comic demeanor dropped away, and the people in the cave found themselves facing a deadly-serious frontiersman as he stood and hefted his gunbelt. "I ain't got to help you," he said. "I ain't got to do one goddamn thing but ride off an' leave you here to rot. I'm more'n half a mind to do jus' that. I never seen the like! You people can't even decide which way to go or who's the strawboss."

He squinted at Graham. "This nigger here said you was the honcho, an' ol' Frank yonder thinks your sorry ass is worth savin'. But damn me if I can see why. Ol' Frank thinks you're Jesus Goddamn Christ. But you look more like a Judas goat to me. Get hold of your own pecker, man! What is it you want to do? Save the whiskey or your own goddamn hair?"

"Frank's got some curious ideas," Graham muttered and looked at his friend, who was staring back at the wagon master. Hope filled his eyes. Graham averted his. "He's—"

"Way I see it," Colfax snapped, "Frank's the onliest friend you got. He's countin' on you for some reason, an', tell you the truth, he deserves better. You ain't got no more idea what you're doin' than a blind whore at a Baptist funeral. You best get a hold of these people an' one on your own self while you're at it. You best make up your goddamn mind whether you want to live or die. It don't make me no diff'rence at all. I was doin' jus' fine till you come 'long an' spoilt my supper."

He surveyed the group, who shuffled and looked down at the fire. "Bunch of goddamn sodbustin' shit-heel greenhorns! I should of knowed better than to mess 'round with horseshit like this. Like as not, it'll be *my* goddamn topknot danglin' from a Comanch's shield come sundown tomorrow."

For a moment, Moses thought Colfax was just going to turn and walk away. The black scout decided that if it happened, he was going with him. Then, all at once, Moses realized that the old man was not about to abandon them.

It was all an act. Colfax wanted the whiskey. He had no more intention of riding off without it than he had of letting Graham take it with him. He was playing his part well, and, Moses sensed, he was going to win. But act or not, the scout had to admire the plainsman's nerve. He was out for himself, and he was apparently willing to risk quite a bit to get the load of whiskey. What was more, Moses understood, he was right: If they were going to make a run for it, they couldn't haul dead weight.

"Look." Graham glanced at the group of frightened men and then addressed Colfax. For a moment, Moses thought he heard a tremble in the wagon master's voice, but Graham quickly cleared his throat and spoke clearly. "I don't know if you know what you're doin' or not. I don't know you at all. I do know we can't stay here forever. If you're right about the Indians keepin' on at us till they break us down, then you're likely right 'bout gettin' out while it's dark. An' about goin' west." He paused, and then he spoke quietly but steadily. "But the whiskey has to go. It's part of the deal."

"There ain't no deal," Moses said quietly.

"What?" Graham wheeled on the scout in a slow, deliberate motion.

"Tell him." The scout looked at Colfax.

"I don't know nothin'." Colfax looked sheepish.

"Tell me what?"

"Them men the Comanche brought in," Moses said quickly. "They wasn't no hunters. They was Comancheros. They was sent by somebody to steal the whiskey. They'd of killed us all for it. Ain't that right?"

Graham followed Moses's eyes to the plainsman, who shrugged.

"Might of. Hard to tell. Neither one of 'em was worth a dog fart with a gun, 'less they was backshootin' some ol' boy from 'bout three feet off. Reputations exceeded 'em, you might say."

"What the hell are you talkin' about?" Graham demanded. "Who were they? Who sent them? From where?"

"I don't know what's goin' on, Mr. Graham," Moses said, opening his hands. "But he told me two men was sent to steal the whiskey. They come from New Mexico, he said. They was hired guns, he said. He was goin' to kill 'em an' take the job off their hands, but the Indians got to 'em first." He looked at Colfax. "Tell him!"

Graham looked back and forth between the two men. "Does this boy know what he's sayin'?" he asked Colfax.

Colfax shrugged. "Might. Hard to tell with niggers."

"An' you were just goin' to kill us all an' steal it?"

"No!" Colfax's eyes sharpened, and he glared at Moses. "*Mister* Moses here let the cat out of the bag 'fore I was ready, but I wasn't plannin' to kill nobody. 'Cept maybe them two ol' boys. That was all. I never said I was goin' to kill nobody other. Did I?" Moses shook his head. "An' it don't make no goddamn diff'rence now one way or 'nother, does it? Seems to me like you got bigger troubles than a bunch of kegged Pine Top to worry you. Goddamn Indians seen to that."

"How do you know they were goin' to steal it?"

Colfax sighed and opened his hands in a gesture of confession. " 'Cause like the boy here says, I knowed 'em. They was good 'nough ol' boys one time or 'nother, but they'd fell on hard times. Said some rich son of a bitch hired 'em out of Santa Fe to head off the bug juice an' haul it in their ownselves. If somebody got kilt in the bargain, it wasn't no skin off their ass. They was playin' like they was hunters. Even had 'em some hides. They was worried they'd missed you already when I run up on 'em, but I knowed diff'rent."

"You planned to take it yourself?"

"I was," Colfax admitted. "That's a fact. Not all of it, but some. An' I'll tell you a truth, I still do."

"The whiskey goes," Graham said. "If I still have it, the deal's still on."

"You can't carry it," Colfax insisted. "It'll slow you down. You got to leave it an' run for it."

"I'll see you in hell first."

"You try an' carry it, you likely will."

"He's right, Graham," Pierce said weakly. "That stuff's heavy, an' the Army'll just take it anyhow."

"I have a contract," Graham insisted. "I have a deal."

"I'd 'low your deal's been done." Colfax grinned. " 'Pears to me you been cornholed."

"You haul the devil's water, an' you'll wind up in the devil's fire." A rasping, choking voice caused all heads to turn toward Virgil Hollister. Like a great wounded hawk, he leaned against the cave wall and glared at the men around him. His voice was weak, and his throat wound had impaired its tone, but he found the ability to speak and he now struggled to stand and point at Graham.

" 'Thou shalt not *kill*,' " he wheezed. "You are leadin' these people down the road to hell. Their blood'll be on your hands, Cleve Graham." He wasn't finished, but weakness struck him, and he collapsed back to a semi-seated position and continued to frown at the group in the cave. "No whiskey," he croaked.

"The whiskey goes." Graham put a final point on his voice to end the discussion. "If it don't, we got no reason to go at all. I don't know what's goin' on, but I'll be goddamned if I'm just goin' to ride off an' leave it for this crazy ol' coot, just on his say-so. I have a deal, a *contract*. Can't you understand that?" No one said anything, and Moses was surprised to see the wagon master's authority questioned so completely. Much had happened since he and Frank rode out the night before. Where, the scout suddenly asked himself as he surveyed the people in the cave, was Golden? He was usually right behind Pierce in any argument.

"If we don't haul the kegs, there's just no reason to go," Graham repeated. His voice lacked confidence, Moses observed. He was scared, and he was losing.

"I'd say hair on your head's a pretty goddamn good reason all by its goddamn self," Colfax put in.

"I'd say he's right 'bout that," Potter shouted over the din inside the small room. "I seen them two them Indians brung in, an' I can tell you, it ain't pretty. We all heard them screams all night long. I ain't riskin' my family for no whiskey." The hubbub died out all at once, and the men turned to look at the Southerners.

"I s'pect they's a lot of stuff we can't take," Baker added as he stepped forward to face Graham.

"You can't take *nothin*'!" Colfax turned his eyes on the North Carolinians. "You can't take one goddamn thing but guns an' shot. You can take your skin, for what that's worth, an' you can take grub an' water. But don't try nothin' else. You got to move fast, an' you got to move now. Daylight's fixin' to be burnin' soon, an' we got to get ready to go."

Graham continued to stand still, like a statue. Moses saw that his gray eyes weren't focusing on anything in particular. Only the slight movement beneath his vest suggested that he hadn't died where he stood.

"Very well," he said almost in a whisper. "I fold. Leave the whiskey. I don't give a good goddamn."

"What I want to know," Pierce asked, pushing through the group and eyeing Colfax, "is what makes you think we can get away? Why do you think we'd stand a better chance out in the open than holed up here?"

Colfax grinned and let his eyes play on the group for a moment. "Well," he said slowly, "I reckon to keep 'em busy awhile to take their minds off this here. An' since you mention it, I'm goin' to need men who know what they're 'bout 'long with me. If it all falls out right, we'll buy enough time so Mr. Yankee Wagon Boss here can get y'all away."

"I'm not goin' with them," Graham said evenly. "I'm goin' with you."

"Mr. Graham." Moses spoke up suddenly. He felt flushed as his voice carried across the gathered group. "You got to stay with the wagons. You're the boss. If you—"

"Shut up." Graham spoke in a strange, dead voice Moses had never heard him use before. "I've been told what to do all night, an' I'm goddamn tired of it. I don't need some nigger buck tellin' me what I 'got' to do." He spoke generally to the men assembled in the tiny cave. "I have nothin' to go for. If we can kill the goddamn Indians, then I might have somethin' to come back here for. But if we don't, then it doesn't matter. I'm goin' with you. Deal me in."

"Cap'n . . ." Frank started to speak, but he fell silent.

"It's all right, Frank," Graham said. "It doesn't matter."

For a moment the men stood silently, and then Pete Hightower asked, "If you don't stay with the wagons, who'll be in charge?"

"Pierce seems to be doin' a good enough job," Graham said. "He's got the mouth for it. But I reckon Hannah

Morgan'll run the show if anybody needs to. Or somebody will. You'll probably get tired of Pierce's whinin' in two miles. Probably shoot him. I hate to miss that."

Pierce stood shuffling his feet, glaring at Graham, saying nothing.

Graham grunted, and Moses frowned deeply. An hour later, the Kid and the girl came in, and Colfax formed them up. Silently they followed the old man out into the water of Blind Man's Creek and up onto the prairie beyond. One thing each of them would have agreed on, Moses figured as his bay slipped into the cool creek water: All of them had seen enough of Moses Franklin's crossing.

CHAPTER TWO

1

DAWN BROKE OVER THE HORIZON ON WHAT PROMISED to be the first really hot day of a north-central Texas summer. Although another thirty minutes or more would pass before the sun actually split the eastern sky and sent the high, thin clouds away, an alert man would notice that he had actually been able to make out the gray outline of shapes around him for a good while. It was as if the terrain gave off a light of its own, a ghostly glow that would burn off with the morning dew when the fiery sun rose and dominated the June sky over the rolling prairie.

Off to the northeast, the ugly purple hump of Medicine Mountain rose incongruously from the prairie. Aside from the slight wind that had come up suddenly and now rippled through the buffalo grass, the only sound consistently discernible along the crest of a slight ridge on the prairie was the heavy breathing of animals and the occasional grunt of a man as he shifted his weight in the saddle and brought forth a squeak of protesting leather. The plain was so quiet that the sudden coo of a mourning dove or caw of a crow off in the distance turned the heads of the riders to make sure that the noises emanated from a bird and not from a painted Comanche warrior.

Along a line to the left and right of Moses Franklin waited a dozen horsemen. They were unlikely warriors at best. Weariness and fear sat on their shoulders like weights, pulling them into unnatural stoops while they leaned on their pommels and occasionally gave their mounts nervous pats of halfhearted assurance. At the center of the thin line, Carlson Colfax sat on his old roan stallion. In spite of his awful wounds and a lack of sleep that at least matched that of any man on the line, he looked alert, energetic, almost resplendent. Beneath his white beard, his cheek bulged out over a plug of tobacco, distorting his face and giving him a comical aspect. Only the big Sharps .50 across his saddle suggested that he was anything more than foolish. But Moses imagined that what he took for a mischievous twinkle in the old man's eye was more likely to be the glint of anticipation.

Next to the plainsman was Cleve Graham, his black's reins held in the same hand which wrapped its fingers around the stock of a '73 Winchester. His head was down, his gray eyes hidden beneath the brim of his hat. Down the line from Graham was Frank Herbert, who also had a Winchester at the ready. Apart from Colfax, he was the only rider whose physical attitude seemed to communicate excitement rather than weariness and fear. On Moses's other side were others—Titus Baker and Holden Potter, Grover Hildebrandt, Pete Hightower, a man named Weatherby who was so festooned with tomahawks, knives, and other implements of combat Moses wondered how the small dun gelding he rode could support all the weight. And there were three more volunteers: Dudley Warner, and two men named Gilbert and Harrison, all riding mules.

Four other men, boys really, should have by now secreted themselves in the dense weeds and patchy juniper that decorated the eastern side of the long mesa. Led there by circuitous route, they had followed Colfax's youthful partner and were supposedly preparing to offer the Comanche and Kiowa below a taste of their own sniping medicine. It was, Colfax assured Graham and Moses the night before, their only chance to catch the Indians in a crossfire, confuse them and kill them or, at least, drive them away. "Beard the red bastards in their own den," the old man chortled.

It probably won't work, Moses thought, but he had nothing else to suggest. This was the only alternative Carlson Colfax gave them.

Moses squinted into the growing light's illumination of the ridge and toward the Indian camp's location just over the rise of ground that crested and then, he recalled, descended to the base of the mesa a mile away from the line of men. White smoke rose from the camp in irregular clouds, and he heard one of the Indians' feists barking suddenly and angrily from the same direction. The dog sounded as if it were far away, and the smoke came over the ridge only in erratic puffs that quickly dissipated in the morning air.

A cough startled Moses Franklin from his reverie, and he realized that he had been very nearly asleep in the saddle. The warmth of the now fully risen sun had lulled him into a comfortable near-doze, and he blinked his eyes rapidly to dispel invisible cobwebs that clung to their lids.

Colfax turned completely around and squinted toward the eastern sky. The sun's glow had turned golden, and now the yellow ball itself was perceptible. Colfax swung down from the saddle and undid his trousers. He glanced at the men, who watched his every move.

"Few more minutes," he said in a soft voice that was almost inaudible over the flow of urine that spilled into the grass. Finished, he fussed with his britches. "If you got to squeeze your lizard, do it now." He grinned at them. "They say if you get hit by one of them goddamn tommyhawks, you'll piss yourself sure'n the Almighty can make a flood."

Moses felt his stomach tighten. He wasn't about to give any of these men a show by being the only one to climb down and follow Colfax's suggestion. He shifted in the saddle and put his mind on other things. None of the others took advantage of the moment, either. Colfax grinned again as if he knew what they were thinking, spat, and remounted, then he sat and studied the sky as if waiting on some special signal to start the day's bloody business.

Moses let his gloved hand fall on the stock of his Springfield and wished the old man would hurry and give the order. Waiting was harder than anything else.

Colfax finally spoke once more in the same soft voice. "It's time. Keep the sun at your back, an' kill anythin' with black hair an' braids you see. Women, children, don't make no goddamn diff'rence. You can count on it that they'll sure'n hell kill you if they get the chance."

He kicked his horse forward. "Once you get started, don't stop," he ordered without looking behind him. "It's hell for breakfast, boys, an' the fat's in the fire."

The line of horsemen glanced nervously at each other.

Then they moved out in a loose V formation behind the old plainsman. Graham hung back a moment, Moses noticed, but then he urged his big black forward. His head was tilted at an odd angle, and he reached into his vest and brought a cigar out. It was broken in two, but he put it between his teeth and kept riding at an even pace with the rest of the horsemen.

The deep, rich sounds of the horses' hooves clomping in the buffalo grass seemed preternaturally loud in the morning air, and Moses felt a need to dismount and take cover. The sounds of the moving horses seemed to grow louder, and Moses felt danger in the air. His head itched horribly, and he had to fight to keep himself from pulling off his hat and clawing at his roughly shaved pate.

Colfax didn't even look around to see if his reluctant army was following him. He kept his Sharps up and at the ready, and Moses saw him draw an extra pistol from a saddle holster and shove it into the belt that gathered his buckskin jacket. He seemed to grow more youthful and to sit taller in the saddle as they climbed the ridge.

Without warning, Colfax spurred his roan and picked up the pace a bit; the horses were jogging when they topped the ridge. A heavier breeze hit their faces high on the grassy crest. Moses spied their shadows as the new sun cast them against the jagged red stone of the mesa beyond, and his eyes scanned the scraggly cedar that covered the formation, searching for the boys who were to provide covering fire.

The horses were loping now, and then running, crossing the grassy ridge and plunging the men into the depression where the Comanche teepees were standing a quiet watch around the dying, smoking fire, still ringed with the bodies of the Indians' victims. None was moving, and the scout knew they were dead. Moses spotted the Autrey girl hanging limp from the tree where the Indian women had left her the night before, but there was no sign of the other women. He dug his spurs into the bay and felt a thrill of excitement flow through his body. He raised his rifle to port.

For a full minute, the only sound in the tiny valley was that of galloping horses. Moses glanced over to where the Indian caviard had been the night before and was momentarily distracted by the vacant area—the horses are gone, he said to himself, where to?—but the sudden blast of Colfax's Sharps drew his eyes back to the camp. A hole appeared in the near teepee, and the old plainsman cast aside his big rifle. He grabbed the reins of his roan mount in his teeth, drew his starboard pistol, and urged the horse on through the belly-high grass toward the camp's perimeter. Baker and Potter raised a ragged yell, which several others joined, and Colfax waved his pistol and lowered his broad hat against the wind as he charged.

Moses searched for a target, but none presented itself. Except for the blackened corpses staked to the ground and the suspended girl, he saw no humanity in the camp at all. He realized suddenly that the Indians were gone, and he was about to shout to Colfax when clumps of bushes and piles of debris from the abandoned beaver dam erupted with puffs of blue smoke. Colfax whooped, and he was joined again by Baker and Potter and even Hildebrandt and Hightower and the others as they lowered themselves over their mounts' necks and pushed them toward the teepees. All were now firing generally toward the camp and waving their weapons wildly in the air. Even Graham, Moses saw, was imitating the plainsman by guiding his horse inexpertly with his legs while he tried to manage his Winchester and sight over his stumped arm.

They were less than thirty yards from the near teepee when Potter leaped backward from his mule as if he had suddenly discovered it was hot and was trying to get away from it as quickly as he could. At the same moment, Pete Hightower's mount collapsed and flung the huge man and his many layers of clothing off in front of it before rolling over on top of him. The well-clad giant spun in the dirt for a moment and climbed to his feet and staggered forward after the charging horses. He was still hanging on to his rifle and firing it one-handed.

Moses had not fired his weapon or seen a single Indian. His eyes swept the camp and searched for a target from behind the rough ambuscade that concealed snipers and archers who now seemed to be all around them. Just as he spied a knot of black hair over by the ruined beaver dam, a spotted dog suddenly ran barking and snarling from a clump of juniper toward his horse. The bay shied, stumbled, struggled for balance, then went down and threw the scout off to one side, where he lay stunned and sore in a patch of prickly pear.

Gunfire was now general, coming from all directions at once, even behind them. Moses extricated himself from the cactus spines and saw that Colfax and Graham and the vanguard of the white attackers had reached the camp's center. They were milling about in a swirl of dust and gunsmoke. Hightower limped toward them, pausing only to ratchet off a round or two from his Winchester in one direction or another. He had to hold the rifle's stock under his arm to cock it, and his left arm was twisted out away from his body. He was hurt badly, but he continued to stumble toward his comrades, shooting and screaming all the while.

Moses crawled around in the dirt and found his rifle, shouldered it, and sought a target, but in the confusion amid the teepees, he could find nothing. From the ground, he couldn't see the dam any longer, and the rocks, cedar, and other cover around the area concealed the Indian snipers from view. He swung the weapon back and forth, felt the unnatural coolness of the stock's wood against his unshaven cheek, and fought the temptation to lie down, to find a piece of cool shade away from the whining bullets and whistling arrows that seemed to come from everywhere and nowhere all at once. Sweat danced on his forehead and dribbled down to bathe his eyes. He blinked it away and continued to search for a Comanche to shoot.

A black flash of braided hair appeared quickly from a makeshift battlement behind one teepee, and Moses fired. He couldn't tell if he hit the Indian or not, for another puff of white smoke came almost immediately from the same spot. He was astonished that so many Indians could hide so effectively in the sparse cover. Now Grover Hildebrandt was down and rolling on the ground, an arrow jaggedly protruding from his chest. Baker was turning his mule around and around, firing his pistol indiscriminately into the swirl of dust that rose about the camp's center. Gilbert took an arrow in his side and pitched off his mount. He tried to stand up, but before he could, three Indian squaws raced from behind a small cedar clump and fell on him with tomahawks.

From where he knelt, Moses saw the bright red blood on the crude ax blades as they bit into Gilbert's body. They rose and fell around his hands, which lifted themselves in helpless defense. Suddenly, one of the squaws raised a dark swatch of bloody hair high in her hand, a scarlet-bladed knife in the other. Her white teeth caught the early-morning sun in a broad grin as she triumphantly waved her trophy over the heads of her two comrades. She turned and started to make her way back to cover behind her sisters, but Moses's sights landed on her. He squeezed the trigger, and she fell with a large hole in the back of her buckskin dress. One of the other women was cut down by Warner and Harrison, who finally had seen what was happening and were spurring toward the fallen man.

Baker then rode his mule around and blocked the flight of the third girl. She was the youngest of the trio, no more than twelve or thirteen, Moses guessed, and she ran blindly into the side of the beast and fell backward, stunned. The North Carolinian leaped to the ground and tackled her before she could recover or lift the bloody tomahawk she still clutched in one hand. He rolled her over and pinned her arms to the ground while he gathered his breath. She squirmed underneath him, and her teeth flashed in her effort to stretch her neck over far enough to bite him. He held her hands down over her head for another moment, and then, gathering her smaller hands in one of his larger fists, he drew a butcher knife and stabbed it through her chest. She let out no sound Moses could hear but continued to kick out and wriggle under him, but his size and bulk kept her down, her arms still tightly held over her head.

Moses looked away quickly. He knew Baker was doing nothing less than the Comanche had done, and he himself had just shot down a girl no older than the one struggling under the Southerner. But the sight repulsed him, and he didn't want to watch Baker toy with her.

There was more to the Southerners' anger than principle, Moses acknowledged, and their loss was much more immediate than any set of antique ghosts. The girl the Kid had brought back in, Moses learned only a few minutes before the horsemen lined up to await the dawn, was niece to Holden Potter, part of the settlement on Paint Creek he and Baker had been on their way to join. And she was apparently betrothed to Baker. So unnerved was she that she hadn't recognized her uncle or any member of his family. In fact, when the Potters determined who she was, they went down to the hospital cave to "fetch her back home."

In a few minutes they returned. She not only refused to recognize them, she rejected them. "Thought I was a ghost," Moses heard Potter say. "Wouldn't let me touch her! Don't that beat the band? All's she can do is hang on to that young'un an' stare at us like we was spooks! Don't that beat all?" Both Baker and Potter referred to her as "Ol' Bess," and spoke of her as if she were dead.

Moses glanced again at Baker. He was beating the girl with his pistol butt.

"Go on an' kill her," Moses muttered and looked away again. "Go on an' be done with it."

Moses put another cartridge into the breech and moved his rifle barrel backward and forward across the confusion in front of him. For a moment, he thought the two men who had tried to save Gilbert would come for him, but they quickly wheeled their animals and galloped toward the melee that continued around Colfax and Graham in the center of the camp.

The Comanche were clearly waiting for their attackers, Moses realized; they were ready for them, and there was nothing they could do now but stand and fight. In the back of his mind, the scout felt another itch. Something wasn't right even in all the wrong that had destroyed Colfax's plan. He couldn't figure out what it was, but it had to do with the missing horses.

He looked back up toward the ridge. The sun had crested it now, and blinding yellow light spilled over it and bathed the dusty, smoky scene below. More rifle fire came to the scout's ears. He saw blue-gray puffs of smoke coming from high up on the mesa's side, and he realized that the Kid and his young companions were in position and finding targets below. But there was something else: All at once he realized what about the whole affair was so wrong. There were no men, no braves concealed about the camp. Comanche women and children were defending the camp with deadly effect, but where were the warriors? No Comanche brave would hunker down and shoot from cover. Where were they?

In answer to his question, a red bandanna tied to a stick was waving from the cedar cover, directing their attention off to their left. He turned and looked, and what he saw made him want to sink into the ground. A line of mounted Indian warriors was riding around the mesa's near end, lances and rifles waving in the air, their high yip-yipping coming to his ears even over the gunfire in the camp. The buffalo headdress of the medicine man was visible in the lead, next to the young trail chief on his pinto. The situation became immediately clear to the scout. The Comanche had let them attack, the women and children left in the camp just to keep them off balance and confused. Now they were being attacked themselves, flanked by mounted, fresh warriors, and none of the white men at the center of the ambush was aware of it.

He took a deep breath to steady himself, dropped to one knee, aimed, and fired. The buffalo headdress toppled backward from the warrior who wore it, but the shaman and his companions continued to charge. They were less than a hundred yards away, and they were coming hard. There was nothing left to do but run.

Moses reloaded as he raced for his horse, but he no more than had one foot in the stirrup when he saw that gore leaked from beneath her cinch in huge red-and-white globs. She had been shot through the lungs, cut nearly in two, and was barely able to stand. His weight in the saddle caused her to stumble around and drop to her knees. He stepped off the bay just before she fell over. The whining buzz of a bullet passed by his head, and he realized incongruously that he had somewhere lost his hat. He had almost turned to look for it when the first arrows from the charging Indians began to fall around him.

Potter stumbled up from where he had fallen, holding a shattered arm with the other hand, and reached Moses's side just as a shaft hit the top of his bare head and split his skull. The flint point jutted out at an absurd angle just over his left eye with bits of brain and bone sticking to it. He reached out for Moses and brushed the scout's arm, then dropped backward with a stunned look on his face, both eyes trying to look up at the brutal point sticking out of his forehead.

Moses turned and stumbled toward the white attackers, who had by now discovered the charging braves and were dismounting and trying to form a line near a collapsed teepee.

Moses looked behind him for Potter's companion. Baker had completed his work with the Indian girl, and he was again up on his feet. He had a pistol in his hands and fired blindly in all directions until he emptied it. He retrieved his rifle and made his way to the men at the center of the camp.

Shouts and screams dominated the tiny valley. Gunfire and the thundering of charging horses clashed together. Warner kept up a steady stream of fire, and Frank Herbert spelled him whenever his magazine was empty. Graham snapped shot after shot in the direction of the charging Indians, but the harassment from the camp's perimeter had not lessened. Dirt kicked up, and ricochets whined around them. For a brief moment, Colfax turned in Moses's direction and grinned a wide, toothy smile at him. He said something, but Moses couldn't hear his voice across the distance. The scout knelt, fired, and rose to scramble toward his comrades once more.

Dust and smoke rose in tremendous clouds as the Indians closed with the white attackers-turned-defenders, who continued to lay down a murderous fire toward the Indians. A dozen braves were unhorsed when the men on the ground combined and concentrated their aim with the five guns on the mesa, and for the moment the Comanche charge was broken. The warriors' horses stumbled in among the fallen braves and milled about in dusty confusion.

Moses stopped once more in his scramble for the center of the camp and knelt to try to kill the concealed Indians who continued to provide a blistering enfilading fire. He pulled his trigger and reloaded quickly, not stopping to pick his shots or tell their effects, but rising after each blast and running two or three steps while his fingers fumbled with another cartridge. Then kneeling, firing, and rising and running once more, he stumbled on. His lungs were seared from smoke and heat, and his pulse hammered against his temples. Two out of three of his shots told, he could see, as more than one exposed black head exploded in a gush of blood, but confusion was general, and he continued to push his feet forward, wondering if each step would be his last.

He was no more than twenty-five yards from Graham. The wagon master was also in a kneeling position, holding his Winchester across his leather stump and firing carefully toward the attacking Indians. Moses felt his right arm go numb all at once, as if he had run into an invisible tree. He glanced down and saw the Springfield lying in the red dirt and felt himself awkwardly conscious of the fact that there was a clump of mud just beneath the trigger guard.

"Got to watch that, black boy," he said aloud in a voice that sounded to his ears identical to old Mr. Grierson's. "That'll ruin a good rifle, sure 'nough. If you don't want this job, I can find me some other nigger to do it." He felt his mind go suddenly light, and his thoughts raced around the impromptu battlefield. Everything took on a sudden unreal aspect, as if there had been a change in the sunshine making it brighter and more intense. He could smell blood, manure, gunsmoke, and dust all around him in a new burst of sensitivity. A wetness made itself known to him, and he realized with a mixture of shame and relief that he had lost control, urinated all over himself. His buckskins were soaked from the crotch all the way down through the leather saddle pads inside the legs.

"*Goddamn*, nigger," he swore at himself in a voice giddy and uncontrolled. His head swam and his tongue felt thick and hot. Something faraway seemed to hurt, but he couldn't locate it exactly, and he tried to ignore it and obey his own woozy commands.

Although he had stopped fully and commanded his hand to reach down for the weapon, he found his arm wouldn't obey. He could see the limb well enough, but he couldn't make his gloved hand open and close. When he looked again and saw a gaping hole in his yellow buckskins, a tear filled with a ragged, open wound that laid open the pulsing, bleeding tension of a lacerated bicep and exposed the splintered and incredibly white bone of his arm, he knew why. His arm was torn nearly off.

"I'm dead," he said aloud. "Oh, Mama, I'm dead."

His vision blurred, and he grew dizzy and weak. His knees swayed, and sweat broke out anew on his bald head and drenched down into his eyes, washing them in salty agony. A tiny pain from a blister on the bottom of his foot became unbearable all at once. He was conscious of a bird singing somewhere and wondered how its song could possibly penetrate the din of battle surrounding him. He swallowed hard and found his tongue was dry as a rasp, and then he discovered that he was fighting for consciousness, not caring at all that he was standing up and fully exposed. He could see through eyes hazy with sweat and shock that the Indians had collected themselves and were now riding in a wide circle around the camp, and with a sudden, violent shake of his head he came to himself.

"We're done," he shouted, wondering that his voice sounded so distant and small. "Let's jus' give'er up. We're done."

Moses knew that any moment horrible pain was going to come, that his arm would scream with a thousand voices in protest at the wound that had laid it open. But with his left hand, he reached down for his Colt's .44. He saw Graham and Colfax trying to hold their bolting horses, but other animals were down, and Frank, Warner, and Harrison seemed to be behind them, using them as breastworks. More than one of them was sprouting arrows from his shoulder or back.

Moses took a tentative, staggering step forward and snapped off a quick shot at a fleeting, ghostly figure, and then he stepped again, only to find himself suddenly pinioned, roped by a rawhide lariat that encircled his torso and pulled his wounded arm tightly to his chest and sent a cascade of pain flowing from his right side throughout his whole body. Bile rose to his throat, and he felt as if his eyes were bleeding in the pain's intensity. He screamed out. It was as if boiling water had been forced through his blood vessels. His eyes met Graham's across the narrow distance between them, but the wagon master only squinted back at him as if he were looking right through him. There was a sneer on his employer's face, and he wished with all his heart that Graham would make good his threat and shoot him now, before the incredible hurt searing through his body drove him mad.

Graham jerked his rifle up and fired, Moses thought, directly at him. He fired again, but the black scout felt nothing. Graham had missed.

"White man never could hit what he shoots at," Moses said, but the words were choked. His throat was dry fire, and he struggled against the bands of hurt across his body and twisted against the plaited rope that held him until he was pulled off his feet and dragged backward through the red dust and cactus behind a yipping, screaming, wildly triumphant Comanche shaman.

2

BY THE TIME GRAHAM SAW MOSES GO DOWN, ROPED BY a shrieking warrior, the battle was almost over. The surprise arrival of the mounted Indians had thrown all of them into momentary confusion, and each had been too occupied with fighting for his own life to worry about another.

"It's a goddamn cornhole!" Colfax had shouted into the din and pointed up toward the waving bandanna from the side of the mesa and then out to where the charging warriors screamed at them. A satisfied grin spread across his bearded face while he paused in his defense against the almost invisible snipers and stared with a twinkle in his eye toward the oncoming Indians. "Goddamn! Goddamn! We're flanked sure'n a pig's asshole. They seen us comin' an' they was ready. One thing 'bout Comanch': You can't never tell what they might do. Give 'em hell, boys! Them goat-pricked frog-fuckers mean business!"

In spite of being outnumbered and badly wounded by the hidden Indians, the whites' heavier rifles and enfilading help from the four guns on the ridge served to blunt the Indians' surprise attack. Graham personally killed five or six warriors, and he passively congratulated himself on remaining cool under the pressure of battle. He felt no panic, no fear, no return of the helplessness he distantly recalled from Pea Ridge and Shiloh. The men to his right and left knew what they were doing, and so did he. His only responsibility was to himself, and whatever fear he had felt before was replaced by a casual acceptance of the notion that he could die at any moment.

Graham's eye was, if anything, worse than ever. He had to turn his head slightly to see what was in front of him. By closing his left tightly, he could see fairly well with his right, but the effort it took to keep the injured orb shut cramped his facial muscles and added to a throbbing headache he had felt since Golden's first well-placed kick. He should have wrapped a bandage around his head again, blocked it off with a patch of something, he told himself. He kept thinking it would be better after a while, suddenly clear itself of its own accord. But when he squinted, one-eyed, at anything too far away, he felt dizzy; when he opened both eyes and tried to focus, a cloud seemed to whiten a circle around any object. It was like looking through a fuzzy white tunnel, and it seemed to become more narrow and to make his head ache even more.

In a way, though, his physical discomfort helped offset the coldness that had seized him. Since Moses had come in with the old man—the old thief—since he had been so sharply put into his place by Aggie, since he had lost control of everything, nothing had seemed to matter anymore. And then, of course, there was the whiskey. And the valley.

The thought of Tuttle sitting smugly in his saloon in Santa Fe forced Graham to retreat even more into the numbness he felt. He should have seen it. The man was too smooth, too easy, too openly trusting to begin with. Why would he offer to share half of something so apparently valuable in exchange for whiskey—or even horses—with a man so obviously desperate as Cleve Graham? Tuttle was a sharper, not even a good one. But he had deceived Graham from the start of things, drawn him in, and suckered him into thinking that it was possible to win. How many others had he made the same offer to? How many men had gone away from Santa Fe, collected horses or whatever else the saloon owner wanted, only to find themselves waylaid on the route back, killed and left to the buzzards and prairie wolves while Tuttle enriched himself? Even had Graham shown up with hard cash, the wagon master reasoned, Tuttle would likely have had him robbed and killed.

"It probably doesn't matter," Graham muttered to himself. "I'm already blind. I might as well be dead."

But the white tunnel of his vision served his aim, somehow, and his sense of being at once outside himself and at the same time so deeply cocooned inside his body that he could feel nothing seemed to aid him as well. His indifference to the chaos raging in the camp gave him a sense of amused detachment. He exposed himself foolishly, but the arrows and bullets that tore through the other whites and their mounts and kicked up dust all around them missed him completely.

When Moses reached his horse and tried to ride the dying animal, Graham found himself grinning. Shows you what it's like to bet on a sure thing only to find it's a bust, he silently advised the scout.

He saw Potter take an arrow in the head and was instantly reminded of Jack and started to shoot him down, but the Southerner collapsed immediately. Then Moses fell, and Grover Hildebrandt was shot down. Graham spied Indian women and even small children shooting arrows and rifles toward them from behind hastily constructed, crude breastworks thrown up around the dam, but there was none of the confusion he had felt during the earlier attacks, none of the self-doubt or fear. He felt as if he were acting independently of himself, more interested in the play of the hand than the outcome. No Indian arrow or bullet would touch him, he was confident. He was impervious to frivolous death.

He grinned widely at Baker when the Southerner scrambled into the crude perimeter and fell breathlessly down on the ground. "Ain't much like Shiloh," Graham yelled at Baker, who rolled over on his back and gulped air. He didn't know why he would say such a thing to such a man. He suddenly felt magnanimous and wanted a friend, someone with whom to share the unexpected euphoria that grasped him.

"Wouldn't know," Baker gasped back. He rolled back over and took up a position and started firing. "Wasn't there."

Graham suddenly realized that Frank lay on the ground with a bubbling, frothing wound covering his chest. His wide-spaced eyes were glazed, but he looked up from time to time and kept a sure grip on a Colt's pistol. The wagon master was prepared to kill him rather than let him fall captive to the cruel warriors who rode around in a dusty semicircle and continued to harass the whites from a reasonable distance, but he could see that Frank's mind was still clear. There was pain in his face, but he kept a wary surveillance of the dusty world around the defenders. For a moment the shadow of a deep emotion penetrated Graham's numbness and crossed his heart. He channeled the feeling into determination, and turned and fired again, this time unseating a stocky brave with a direct hit to his chest.

He reloaded and watched Grover Hildebrandt continue to ignore his wounds and roll backward and forward, firing and reloading his weapon from a stash of cartridges in a pouch he wore around his neck and fighting no less vigorously for the arrows stuck in his body. Pete Hightower, cradling a shattered arm, also staggered up to join the men, and he, too, continued to ratchet shell after shell into his chamber with his one good limb. A jutting white bone stuck from beneath his shirt and threatened his chin with its jagged point.

Two of the attackers lay dead at Colfax's feet, and Weatherby charged around the tiny imaginary perimeter the whites had formed and dragged down any warrior who came too near, then dispatched him with one of the weapons he wore all over his body. Every time his hand came up to hammer down on some pinioned brave, a different knife or hatchet was revealed. He went from Indian to Indian in a businesslike manner, completing his battery on one before turning to find another. The huge man's hands enfolded the youthful Indians' arms and broke them like twigs. Baker moved swiftly around as well, firing rapidly. But their targets were now their own horses and mules, which they shot and pulled down to form cover around the ruined teepee. Four mounts fell before they stopped and turned their attention to the circling braves once again.

"Kiowa," Colfax yelled over the din, and Graham realized he was shouting at Moses and pointing toward two braves who wore heavily feathered warbonnets. "Told you they was here." The old plainsman took aim and fired at a brave who screamed by. The warrior jumped off his horse and hit the ground in an explosion of feathers at such a speed that he skidded into a teepee and knocked it over, revealing two young snipers with bows, who were immediately dispatched by Warner and Harrison. Both men now had arrows sticking out of their backs and shoulders. Harrison, Graham saw, also had a cruel gash in his neck and another wound in his side, but he continued to aim and fire at any target which presented itself. Warner was in bad shape, too; his face formed a tortured mask as he fired and reloaded and fought to remain on his feet.

Baker took an arrow in his shoulder, and another struck him in the back almost immediately. He collapsed briefly, but then he raised himself and knelt and shot from behind Frank's fallen horse. Then, almost as if whatever drove him to go on was used up all at once, he stopped and looked down at the feathered shaft sticking from his shoulder. He stared at it as if it were some sort of abnormal growth. "Goddamnit," he said, "I never seen the like." He collapsed like an empty sack. Warner fell on top of him moments later, his eyes wide in death, his mouth still forming the toothy grimace Graham had seen before.

Graham used his new pistols from time to time, but he found the accuracy and power of the rifle made it a better choice. His impaired vision wouldn't serve him as well without the long barrel of the rifle to sight down. He couldn't bring himself to kill the big black, which continued to rear and struggle against the reins that held it to Graham's stumped forearm, and apparently the Indians also respected Jack Sterling's choice of horseflesh, for they refused to shoot at him while the animal danced and swayed around the wagon master and provided him with more aggravation than cover.

Now that Graham had settled into the routine of the fight, the cloudiness was worse. He squinted through his right orb, seeking target after target down his unique white tunnel and finding that his vision was becoming more and more restricted as the battle raged. The whoops and high yip-yipping of the Comanche seemed to aggravate it, to penetrate his skull and pierce the throbbing headache that now spread over his left temple. His physical discomfort became intense, and the brief euphoria he had felt disappeared; numbness returned, and he went about the business of the fight with quiet seriousness.

He turned his good eye toward Moses and squinted. The scout was struggling in the dusty near distance to make it over to where they were. Moses's hat was gone, and he was having trouble making progress against the swirling attackers' circle.

"That boy's got more balls than most white men I ever seen," Colfax confided as he moved over near Graham and reloaded his pistols. His Sharps was still out where he had dropped it. Graham watched him empty an entire cylinder of the Army Colt's. He stood upright and calmly reloaded from a powder flask and cartridge box with no more concern for the carnage around him than if he had been shooting targets on a Sunday afternoon in the park. An arrow's dogwood shaft stuck bloody and broken out of his upper arm, but he paid it no attention. He was also bleeding from his calf, where a bullet had opened the buckskin in a ragged, bloody tear. He leaned against one of the ruined teepee's lodgepoles and continued to work his sidearms with casual precision.

"I got that roan 'gainst your black says he don't make it," he yelled. He emptied one of his weapons again at three braves who rode past together. Two arrows sang past Graham's ear at the same time; had he not turned to hear Colfax, both would have lodged in his head.

"You'll lose," Graham yelled back. "He's like a boil on your pecker: Turns up sore no matter what."

Graham imitated Colfax and emptied his magazine all at once and believed he brought down at least two braves. He admired Colfax in spite of everything. Insane or not, the man understood the value of concentrated shooting. He glanced up on the side of the mesa and realized that, truly, the only thing keeping the circling Indians at bay was the fire from the boys up there. They had time to pause and pick their targets, and they were also safely out of bow range. He shoved more shells into his rifle and sighted again, but he missed an unusually tall brave who slanted over beside his pony when he raced past and loosed an arrow that struck Harrison squarely in the chest with a wet, hollow sound.

"Question is, are *we* goin' to make it?" Graham yelled

as he squinted down and decided that Harrison was dead where he fell.

"Us?" Colfax's eyes danced, and he raised himself high and smiled widely at Moses, who continued his kneeling and firing dance toward the white men. "Goddamn right we'll make it! Hell, Yank, I seen fights worse'n this at a nigger weddin'." Turning about, he calmly emptied both revolvers into the circling Indians to throw back a charge that four had tried to mount on the flank. His teeth were bared in a satisfied grin, and he shook his head in self-praise.

"Guess I win the black," Colfax announced. Hightower lurched forward, his right side bleeding profusely and a gaping wound in his cheek. He pitched over Frank, who used his free hand to roll him off him. The settler continued to breathe, but he was unconscious and bleeding badly.

Graham looked up and saw that Moses had also been shot and was standing upright, still as bronze. He heard Frank say something and started to kneel down, but at that moment, the stallion, still secured to Graham's stubbed arm, screamed and reared and pulled him off his feet. He dropped his rifle and scrambled up only to feel a searing pain tear through his thigh. He fell next to his old friend and grabbed at his bleeding leg.

"They got you good, Cap'n," Frank croaked out. He aimed and fired directly into the face of a feathered brave who had ventured in too close.

The horse struggled against Graham's arm. His leg was on fire, but no bone was broken. He staggered to his feet and moved over and retrieved his rifle. He wanted, suddenly, to be the one to kill Moses Franklin. It was the same sort of thing he remembered feeling when he shot Jack, but it was also something he believed he had to do to save himself. Sudden panic swelled within him.

Graham lifted his Winchester and looked out toward Moses. An Indian Graham recognized roped the scout. It was one of the Comanche who had come in the afternoon before, the spokesman. Moses looked at Graham, and for a moment their eyes met. Graham squinted hard and raised his rifle to shoot the black scout where he strained against the thin rope, but before he could fire, he was distracted.

Two Indians raced toward the struggling scout, one carrying a war lance that was poised for Moses's back. Graham fired and knocked the brave off his horse, and he jacked in another shell and killed the other Indian's pony before he could reach Moses. Then he turned his rifle once more on the scout, but he was surprised to see Moses being hauled away behind the Comanche brave, who galloped off out of Graham's injured line of sight. Graham squinted and swirled his barrel in a narrow circle, trying to get a bead on Moses as he bounced along the ground across a patch of cactus and disappeared in a swirl of dust behind the Indian's pony. They were soon lost in the grass that surrounded the tiny camp, and Graham lowered the weapon. He felt an awful sense of loss, as if a part of him more vital than his hand had been cut away.

The young trail chief yipped high and loudly, and suddenly, with one last blast from their rifles, the Indians began to withdraw. It seemed that in part at least, they had what they wanted.

From all around them, Indians popped up from behind cover and ran helter-skelter toward the milling ponies of the retreating warriors. Most were women and some were only children dressed in breechcloths and bareheaded, but all clutched bows or rifles in their hands. They raced toward the nearest mounted warriors and were hauled up onto the ponies and carried away. The dust seemed to grow more intense as the Indians rode around and tried to collect their dead and wounded. The shooting had all but stopped. Even the shots from the mesa side above them tapered off. Neither Colfax nor Graham fired anymore. Aside from the diminishing pounding of horses' hooves, the ruined camp became quiet. The battle was over. The noise of the yelling Indians faded off, and the whites sat on the ground and said nothing for several minutes.

Graham sank down beside the dead body of Baker. Weatherby, who was amazingly unhurt and still full of fight, waved an iron mallet over his head and cursed the retreating Indians. Finally, he pulled Frank to his feet, carried him over to a bare patch of ground, and propped him up against a fallen Indian pony. Hildebrandt was still alive but bleeding badly from his wounds, and Pete Hightower simply lay on the ground and heaved. The others were dead.

Colfax used a broken piece of lodgepole as a crutch and limped around and fussed over his horse. He steadily cursed Indians, horses, and everything else that came to mind while blood flowed freely from his several wounds. His beard and face were black with powder smoke, and his jaw still bulged with the tobacco plug. Graham noticed he never stopped grinning, even though his wounds were terrible.

The stallion jerked again, and Graham stumbled to his feet. A stream of blood ran down his leg and filled his boot, but for some reason, the burning pain in the wound had stopped, and he found he could stand. He discovered when he moved a little that the beautiful big stallion had finally taken a wound. An arrow stuck from his neck below the mane, and blood leaked down in a dark, stout flow. As the wagon master tried to inspect the injury, the horse fell and rolled over.

Graham lowered his head. He unwrapped the leather reins from his stump and stared down at the ruined animal. Tears came to his clouded eyes, and a lump formed in his throat. He found something painful inside him that wouldn't go away. The emotion defied any ability he had to define it or keep it away from his heart, and it overwhelmed him and obscured his mind as much as the white cloud had now completely blinded his left eye. He pulled the Navy Colt's from its clutch holster beneath his arm and fired a single bullet into the black's head. Then he stood up and breathed deeply.

"Got to borrow your horse," he said to Colfax, stepping over two unretrieved Comanche bodies. Both had bullet holes the size of fists in their backs. The churned earth around the makeshift battle perimeter was muddy with blood. He took the roan's reins up and swung himself up into the odd saddle.

"Where you goin'?" Colfax growled. He held his wounded arm stiff and tight to his chest. He was bleeding from the side, and his calf was nothing but exposed raw meat beneath the hole in the ragged buckskin. His face was pale beneath the beard, and Graham saw that he was having trouble remaining on his feet. "You an' him"—he glanced at Weatherby, who was sitting Frank down and daubing at his chest with a dirty rag—"is the onliest ones not shot up too goddamn bad to help. I need you. More's the point, goddamnit, I need that horse."

Graham looked off into the distance, toward the east. He squinted into the sun's glare and pulled his hat down low over his damaged eyes. "It ain't right they should kill him," he said.

"Looks to me like there wasn't no love 'tween you," Colfax said. "Let him go. He's jus' a nigger. Hell, you can find you 'nother'un."

Graham checked the loads in his pistols and in the Winchester. He felt blood squishing in his boot as he worked it into the stirrup. "I'm goin' after him."

"I'm askin' you not to go, Graham," Colfax said. "I thought we had us a deal."

"There never was a deal," Graham said evenly. "You were going to steal what you wanted an' hope I got killed in the bargain. That was the only deal."

Colfax raised his pistol and pointed it toward Graham. "I need that horse."

The click of a revolver being cocked drew their attention to Frank, who pointed his pistol directly toward the plainsman.

"You go on, Cap'n," Frank said in a weak voice. "He's a good man. Save him if you can. I'll keep a eye on things here."

"Feather-peckered Yankees," Colfax swore. "All het up to get kilt."

Graham could see that his old friend would die if he didn't get real help soon. The entire front of Frank's shirt and pants was covered with blood. His eyes were fixed on Colfax, but they were hazy and vague. Graham jerked the roan's nose toward the sun.

Colfax studied Frank for a moment and then grinned and spat out his plug. "Ain't no goddamn use arguin' with a dead man," he said. "But you take care of that horse. He's the onliest one I got left."

Graham kicked the roan into the bloody wake left by the roped and captured Moses Franklin.

3

GRAHAM HAD IMAGINED FROM THE SWEAT THAT SOAKED his shirt and ran down into his eyes during the battle that it was midday, but when he reached the rolling surface of the prairie, he was surprised to find that it was still morning. He reckoned that less than an hour had passed since the attack started. The sun had emerged in a yellow ball to crowd the blue from the sky, and overhead a circle of hawks—or buzzards, they were too high to tell—lazily drifted over the killing ground below. The wind was up as well; the grass swayed and rattled around his horse's legs, and the stiff southwesterly breeze shifted around to the north and struck his sopping wet shirt, cooling him. He now felt as if he didn't have a dry stitch on. Huge white clouds gathered from the west and began to form themselves into towering dark gray thunderheads. The wind had the smell of rain on it, and it felt good on his back, and if he had not had the stink of gunpowder and blood all over him, he might have thought that it was as fine a late-spring morning as he had ever seen.

Graham had no experience in tracking at all, and his eyesight was all but gone for anything in the practical distance. But even a blind man could follow the trail where Moses Franklin had been dragged through the buffalo grass off to the southeast away from the camp. A wide, bloody swath was open in the yellowing grass and led off into the prairie: Graham drove his horse into it and urged it on at a fast walk.

The roan was still skittish from the battle and hard to handle. Graham found the old plainsman's McClellan saddle uncomfortable, and he kept shifting his weight and inspecting his bleeding leg as the horse pushed aside the strands of grass and moved on. His head swam a bit behind the ache that continued to throb in his temple, but he bit his lower lip, lowered his head, and pushed the horse on.

After about an hour's steady, slow ride, he finally saw what he was searching for. Medicine Mountain was a huge mound of almost pure rock. It rose from the yellow buffalo grass and stood purple against the sky. Outcroppings of sandstone emerged from its base, and among the scraggly juniper and mesquite that had made an uncertain home in the formation's sparse shade were tethered three Indian ponies. Graham recognized one of them, a gray, as the same horse that had dragged Moses off.

He pulled up the roan about twenty-five yards from the Indian ponies. He now was confronted with his quarry, but he had no idea what to do. He thought that somehow he would go riding in shooting, that he would take the Indians by surprise and would kill them before they knew he was there. But he suddenly realized that even if such a wild scheme were possible—and the way the outcropping lay up against the base of the small mountain, it wasn't—he didn't stand much of a chance of executing it.

He sat on his horse and cogitated. It was still not too late to turn back, to return to Colfax and the others, or simply to ride back to the creek, reclaim his whiskey, and then find animals to pull his wagon. The oxen should still be there, he reminded himself. They could pull a wagon-load of whiskey all the way to Santa Fe, all the way to the front of Jigger Tuttle's saloon, or, he calculated, even back to Jefferson.

He reached for a cigar, but his pocket was empty. All at once things reduced themselves to a familiar, basic denomination. He was not going to turn away, and he hadn't really come this far to save Moses Franklin at all or even to kill him. He realized that he had come out here to gamble against fate once more. He had come out here to die.

It was no surprise to Cleveland Graham that he was alive, that he had suffered nothing more than a relatively minor wound. He had been convinced of his special invulnerability long ago. It would not have surprised him had all of them been killed—Colfax and the youngsters on the side of the mesa as well—and still he had ridden away. It was never his life that was in jeopardy, he understood, only his plans for it. He was not to die; only his dreams died. Take another card, he thought.

The admission that he sought death out here on his own settled on his mind like a comforting blanket. At last, he felt the numbness that had shielded him from the emotions of the past several hours fall away; when it went, the nameless pain he had discovered inside him emerged in full force. Even though his vision was still cloudy and uncertain, he felt he could see things with a new clarity. The pain gave him that. It was a hollow hurt, something he had not ever let himself feel, not when he had burned his cabin and his wife, not when Jonathan was killed, not ever. And as the wind became more fierce and howled around him in the midmorning air, he knew that what he was doing was the only thing he could do that was absolutely right.

He kicked the roan forward at a slow walk and came up behind the Indian ponies. He then walked the horse around them until he approached the three Comanche and their black captive.

Graham's eyes could barely make out the scene in front of him. Moses was seated on the ground next to a huge limestone boulder. Two of the three Indians who stood around him poked at him with arrow tips from time to time, causing an involuntary shake that indicated that he was still alive.

Graham pushed the horse forward a step or two. The wind was up higher than ever; the Indians still had not seen or heard him, and he calmly sat and studied them. For a brief moment, he thought again of riding off. If Moses wasn't yet dead, he couldn't survive, and even if he did, he would likely hate the man who saved him. But Graham had come to die, and the only problem facing him at the moment was how to set about it. He pulled the Winchester from its boot and leveled it across the roan's pommel.

"*Idahi,*" Graham said aloud, remembering the pronunciation of the word of greeting the Indians had used the night before.

4

THAT MOSES FRANKLIN WAS STILL ALIVE AMAZED NO one more than him. From the moment when he found himself being dragged behind the Comanche pony up over the ridge and out onto the prairie, every experience had been surrounded with pain. His wounded arm, cut as it was by the Comanche's rawhide lariat, was a blinding, continuing flash of agony, and the bouncing, thumping, tearing ride he took when he was towed through the prairie grass added degrees of searing hurt to every part of his body. As each yard passed beneath him, he was certain he would die. Nothing he could imagine had ever been this bad.

While rocks and thorns tore the skin from his face and limbs and his gloved hands fruitlessly tugged at the rawhide rope, he rolled over and over behind the galloping Indian pony and screamed until his throat was scarred and hoarse. Finally, blessedly, just when a quick glance over his shoulder revealed that they were making their way toward Medicine Mountain, he lost consciousness.

When he awoke, it was the result of a water skin's contents poured over his ripped and bleeding forehead. Three Indians danced around in front of him, waving various implements and loud gourd rattles in his face. They taunted him in their hateful language with derisive words and sneers, and one—the shaman, Moses recognized—raised his face to the gathering clouds overhead and sang a lilting song of triumph as he moved back and forth in front of the scout, who now discovered that he was tightly bound to a boulder.

His arm was on fire, and he looked down to find that the rawhide bonds that held him cut directly across the exposed wound, touched the whiteness of the bone, and grated with lathering blood and exquisite pain every time he moved. He blinked his eyes to force sweat and, he discovered, blood out of them. Every time he thought he had control of his reactions, every time he thought the hurt would subside to a bearable level, the Indians danced in and prodded him with sticks and weapons, forcing him to scream until his voice gave out and all he could do was open his mouth and weep inaudibly.

Moses had no idea how long his torment lasted. He bobbed in and out of consciousness constantly, and every time he permitted his eyes to focus, he was faced with a new terror. He wanted to die. But no matter how much he willed himself to give up, he could not. Every escape into insensibility was quickly interdicted by the Comanches' water bags or by painful thrusts of their knives and arrows.

Each time he awoke, he had trouble believing that what was happening to him wasn't some hideous nightmare. He would shake his head and blink his eyes, and his actions seemed to infuriate his torturers even more. After one particularly long period of blackness, he was awakened by a renewed sensation of pain. His eyes flew open and he discovered the shaman jerking the buckskin trousers away from his legs. Moses's mouth opened in protest, but before he could force words from his parched throat, the scout's mind recoiled from what his burning eyes told him was about to happen.

The shaman flung the ragged buckskins aside quickly and drew his knife. Without wasting a move, he reached down and parted the scout's thighs, forcing them open with his own legging-covered knees. As easily as if he were cutting a piece of fruit from a tree, the Indian grasped and sliced away Moses's penis and scrotum.

At first, the scout felt nothing between his legs except the icy touch of the knife's blade as it brushed against his thigh. He convinced himself that the Indians were only trying to frighten him, to make him cringe and whine in terror. Even the blood that spurted from his crotch failed to convince him that what he had witnessed had actually happened. The image of the prancing medicine man holding the bloody trophy high overhead and yipping and dancing about in the gravel in front of the imprisoned scout seemed to be some sort of ridiculous imitation of reality. Only when his eyes fell once more to his torn and bleeding crotch did the mutilation register.

A great weakness overwhelmed him, and he felt tears coming to his eyes. "How'm I goin' to piss?" he asked in a choked whisper. "Answer me that'un, you son of a bitch. How'm I goin' to piss?" His head spun, and his body began to give up to the anguish it suffered. Then the pain struck his brain, and once more, he lost consciousness.

When he awoke, he was certain that this time he was dreaming. The Indians continued to force him to keep his head up. He couldn't close his eyes completely, and he realized that they had at some point cut away the upper lids. His eyeballs burned and itched with dust that the wind now blew around the small area. He lowered his head to protect them as best he could and discovered that they had placed a pile of tumbleweeds beneath his bloody legs: They were going to burn him.

He ground his chin into his chest and tried to close his mind. The pain that coursed up and down his body was now so general that he could no longer identify any single wound or hurt. Somehow he had bitten into his tongue, and his mouth was filled with the salty taste of blood. He wasn't going to die, he decided, not before the Comanche were ready for him to, not before they finished with him.

When the Comanche greeting reached his ears over the keening wind, he was certain his mind had snapped. He raised his head and doubted what his burning, itching eyes told him. Behind the grinning, prancing warriors stood a roan horse. Across the pommel in a generally threatening attitude was a rifle, a Winchester, and astride the mount sat a white man. But not just a white man, Moses understood through the constant pain that washed over him in increasingly violent waves: The man on the horse was Cleve Graham.

All three braves jumped nearly off the ground, turned quickly in surprise, and took up defensive positions. The sudden discovery of an armed white man in their midst stunned them. The shaman, the ragged Rebel battle flag still swaddled around his waist, was the most seriously shaken of all. His mouth fell open in a gape, and he looked quickly at Moses, his black eyes wide. The tortured captive was instantly reminded of a small boy who had been caught in the middle of mischief. It was as if he expected the black scout to say or do something to save him.

The shaman wasted no more time. He reached for a slung Winchester "Yellow Boy" that dangled behind his back and began to bring it up toward Graham.

"I see you an' call you," Graham said calmly. He squeezed off one round before the Indian could react. The blast tore into the shaman's chest, exploded through his back in a bloody, ragged tear, and threw him into the rock behind him. Moses watched impassively, almost as if what he was seeing was being acted out for his amusement. It was too much like a dream to be real. Incomprehensibly, he wanted to laugh and clap his hands, but the mere thought of such actions brought a renewal of pain from his whole being.

The other two braves were frozen where they stood. Their bows were slung, and they had no other weapons at hand. The wind whipped through the outcropping, but no other sound could be heard.

Moses raised his chin and looked up at Graham. The scout's eyes burned as if they were on fire. It was too much like a dream for him to take Graham's appearance seriously. He wanted to laugh again. Graham sat calmly on his saddle and held his rifle steady to cover the remaining Comanche braves.

"You a haint, or you really here?" he choked out.

"I'm here," Graham replied.

"You're a mite late," he said in a weak voice. "Think I'm done dead."

"Saves me the trouble of killin' you." Moses could barely hear the wagon master, who was yelling back over the howling wind. The smell of rain came to his nostrils.

"Guess you're let down," Moses said, then choked and coughed. "I know you had your heart set on it."

"I'm learnin' to live with it," Graham yelled back.

The two warriors remained where they stood without moving. Moses had a clear view of their faces. They showed no fear. Moses could sense that their minds were working, looking for a way of getting an edge on the white man.

Graham suddenly lowered the rifle. "What's Comanche for 'Get the hell out of here'?"

Moses shook his head. "Don't know. Never had to use it."

Graham sat still, his head tilting to one side so far that he appeared to be looking at them upside down.

"Ain't you of a mind to kill these two young'uns?" Moses asked.

"It seems to be next play," Graham answered. Moses saw a bloody gash on the wagon master's leg. "But I was thinkin' of just lettin' 'em go."

"I reckoned you'd be the last one to want that," Moses said.

"It doesn't make any difference," Graham said. "Not anymore. The deal's over."

"Well, don't do nothin' on my account," Moses said. "I'm already dead." His strength began to leave him again, and he felt his head spinning. He wanted a drink of water worse than anything, he decided, worse even than an end to his pain.

Graham sat still for a moment and studied the pair. His gray eyes flicked back and forth between them and Moses. Finally he sighed deeply. He stood and raised his rifle. The two boys did not flinch or blink.

"I don't think they reckon I'll kill them," Graham said. "They think I'm bluffin'." He reached up and rubbed his injured eye with his stump. "It's a bad bet, but this time, maybe they're lucky." He shook his head sadly. "Go on," he said, waving the rifle toward their ponies. "Get out of here. Go on. Get!"

The Comanche shifted their weight for a moment, and their eyes narrowed as they tried to understand. Graham repeated his order, finally lowering the Winchester and pointing his stubbed arm off toward the empty prairie. The wind whipped their greasy braids around their necks. They looked briefly at each other and then moved rapidly in a zigzagging run toward their ponies. Graham turned to watch them ride off. Then he dismounted.

He limped over to Moses and knelt down and cut his bonds. The scout continued to sit upright, his legs supported by the tumbleweeds. His head was down again, and blood ran from his lips. His eyes were watering ferociously.

"You hurt bad?" the scout asked.

"Nothin' to brag about," Graham grunted as he glanced down at his own wound. He looked up and down Moses's body. "You're a different story."

"They done me up right," Moses agreed in a whisper. "Gelded me."

Graham glanced down at Moses's wound. "I've seen worse."

"I'd be 'bliged for a drink of water." Moses's tongue felt four times its normal size and throbbed from where he had bitten through it. He wondered how Graham could understand his garbled speech.

Graham moved over to the roan and brought a canteen. The water burned Moses's seared throat so badly that he shook his head quickly and spat it out.

"No," he said. "I need it. More." He drank again, and this time managed to swallow. "Funny thing," he said in a choking chuckle, "it don't even hurt no more. I guess they hurt me so much I can't feel it no more." Graham's eyes drifted down to the hideous wound between Moses's legs, then they came up again and met the scout's involuntary stare directly. "Man I used to know—Ol' Isaac—he used to tell us when we was goin' to get whipped that after a while, they break your hurtin' bone, an' it don't hurt no more. Guess that's what they done to me."

Graham nodded.

"Least they was neat about it," Moses went on. "White man makes a mess of this kind of thing."

"I'd agree on that," Graham said.

"Where's the wagons?" Moses asked through a sudden moan. A new chorus of agony rose from all over his body, and he shivered with it. His voice was alive with pain and fright. "Is ever'one, is . . . Miss Sterlin', is she—"

Graham's face stiffened. "Look," he started, but before he could finish, Moses heard the sound of hooves beating toward them. Graham rolled away and reached for one of his Colt's Peacemakers, but he moved too late. The two braves he had released charged into the narrow outcropping waving lances, which they loosed together. One struck Moses's chest and went all the way through the right side with a soggy sound and was stopped by the solid rock of the boulder behind him. The other spear glanced off Graham's arm and knocked his pistol away.

Graham rolled to the right as the Indians' horses danced through the gap between the boulders and then wheeled around for another pass. Both braves were yelling, and one waved a pistol in the air. The other had nocked an arrow and was taking aim as his horse charged. Graham rolled again and jerked his Navy Colt's from the clutch holster under his arm. Moses gripped his lower lip in his teeth against the pain, pumped his bloody legs back and forth, and managed to scramble away from the boulder. His left hand reached up and pulled the lance down, and he rolled across the gravel, breaking the shaft.

Graham completed his maneuver and fired blindly. One of the braves somersaulted backward off his pony.

The other fell smoothly over to the opposite side of his horse and guided the animal out past the boulders of the outcropping and across the prairie into the gathering thunderstorm.

The sound of hooves disappeared into the wind, and both men lay still. Moses's eyes refused to focus, but he could hear Graham's panting over the noise of the storm. The scout lay on his stomach and his breath blew small flakes of sand away from his bearded chin. His previous claim that his capacity for pain had been reached was now proved a lie: His body screamed pain from every point. He realized that there were dimensions of agony yet undiscovered.

He wanted to close his eyes, to fall again into the painless oblivion of unconsciousness, but he couldn't.

"Graham," Moses croaked, but his voice was nothing more than a raspy whisper. He licked his torn, bleeding lips. He felt himself bleeding all over. He tried to turn his head. When he did, his eyes cleared from the dirt that had blinded him, and he saw Graham standing over him, the Navy Colt's in his hand, the barrel pointed down toward Moses's own forehead.

Graham, Moses knew, was not a man to forgive small hurts or to forget hard promises. He had seen what the wagon master had done to Jack Sterling, and he knew what Graham had wanted to do to the wounded down on the creek. Moses also remembered what Graham had sworn to do to him. There was no doubt: He was going to die with a bullet from Cleve Graham's gun in his brain.

Graham squinted at him and brought his revolver directly to bear on the scout's head. Moses didn't want to live. He felt as if he had been pulled inside out, and he couldn't imagine what was keeping him alive. He couldn't bat away a gnat. All Graham had to do was pull his trigger, and Moses wished he would with all his heart. But even now, even knowing that the simplest of actions would relieve the pain that raged through him, he couldn't bring himself to ask Graham to do it. He returned Graham's look and tried to smile.

"See what happens when I mess around with you?" Graham asked in a strange quiet voice. "Goddamn nigger scout. All you've ever done is try to get me killed." Graham weaved as he tried to keep steady. Moses swallowed and tried to force some spit into his mouth.

"If you're goin' to kill me," Moses said finally, "this is as good a chance as you're fixin' to get." He was breathing hard with the exertion of speaking. He was broken inside, bleeding everywhere. His eyes were scalded by sweat and blood. He tried to swallow and found he couldn't. "Tell you a truth, I'd be 'bliged for the favor."

"I hired you to take me to Santa Fe," Graham said after a beat. He lowered his pistol and limped over to the canteen, which he brought over to Moses. He turned the scout over, rested his head on his lap, and wet his lips. He sighed. "You're as good a man as I could find, worthless as you are."

Moses looked up into Graham's eyes. The scout had almost lost his sight, but in the gloom, he saw a familiar light in the wagon master's face. Graham put more water on his lips and shook his head. "Never seen but one nigger that was worth the bullet. You ain't him."

Moses felt his body relax finally. Light was going fast, he thought, too fast. All the pain began to fade away. "I doubt you could of done it anyhow," he whispered. "Miss Sterlin'd never let you get 'way with it."

He felt Graham's grip on him tighten, and his wounds sang with new hurt. His thoughts drifted away once more to Saul and Aaron, and he struggled to say something to Graham, to ask him to go and warn them, send them back. There could never be a life out here, he now knew. The Comanche couldn't be dealt with, couldn't be treated like people. This was their land, and they would kill for it, die for it, every square inch of it. They would never share it. There was no room here for anyone but Indians.

Things became dark at last, and he could feel the wind on his face. His thoughts seemed to fly, and suddenly his vision seemed to return and he saw the whole prairie spread out before him. He saw Saul and Aaron coming, and he heard them and their families singing as their mules drew their wagons across the grass. He wanted to speak to them, but he couldn't. He could only rest, with Graham's stumped wrist beneath his head and the droplets of water sitting on his lacerated lips. There was much he wanted to say, much he wanted to do, but none of it seemed important suddenly. He contented himself by watching the men singing, laughing with their children and women. Oddly, Mr. Grierson was with them, too. So were Old Isaac and Amy. That didn't make sense, Moses argued with himself, but there they were: Grierson sitting right on top of his favorite horse, and Old Isaac walking along beside the wagons with his crooked walking stick, Amy in a bright yellow dress and huge straw hat with flowers around the brim. Moses wanted to ask why they were there, but before he could find the words or make his swollen tongue work, he saw Aggie Sterling. She sat on a small white horse and rode next to Old Isaac.

"We're going to build a town," she said. "A good town." Moses could hear her voice clearly above the song. Her smile flashed white in the sun, and her long blond hair wisped around her face as she reached up to remove an errant lock with her long fingers. Her beauty made his heart pound and overcame his pain. Then he discovered that he felt good, better than he had ever felt in his life.

"We're fixin' to build a town," he muttered to Graham. "Place of our own. Place to be free." He felt suddenly proud. Then he felt nothing at all.

5

IT TOOK GRAHAM THE REST OF THE MORNING TO FIND the strength to pick up Moses Franklin's body and strap it to the gray pony the Comanche had left standing near the outcropping. Rain broke out in a furious gale halfway through the chore. Since he was obliged to work only with the rawhide bonds that had held Moses to the boulder and to hobble around on his wounded leg, the job was poorly completed under silver strobes of lightning and a jumbled roar of thunder. At first he just lumped Moses across the pony's back, but after considering for a moment, he decided that the almost naked corpse needed—deserved—cover. The wagon master went back to the torture site and removed the tattered flag from around the young shaman. Although it was ripped and full of holes, stained with blood and now muddy as well, it covered the scout's body. The wagon master was soaked through long before he completed the job, and his leg wound continued to bleed. He no longer worried too much about his impaired vision, as the rain beat down so heavily that he couldn't see very far in any case.

The storm had blown out its initial fury by the time he rode back out onto the prairie, but a steady downpour continued to drench him as he headed toward the northwest. He found that he had trouble concentrating, and sometimes his surroundings took on a surreal aspect through the sheets of water that fell before him. He fought to remember that he had no other present intention but to get to the crossing, where, he knew, there could be a fire and some warmth. There would be nothing left there but the whiskey and some abandoned wagons, but Graham felt that he wanted a drink now more than he ever had in his entire life. A drink would clear his head, maybe his vision. It might give him some notion of what he was going to do next.

He rode for an hour until the rain let up enough for him to squint around and spy the copse of pecan trees that marked the deadly creek, and he steered the worn-out horses in that direction and was soon coming up the rise that would lead him down to his wagon.

His mouth ached for the taste of the whiskey. He vowed to open a fresh keg and drink himself into a stupor. It no longer mattered how much was left, for there was no reason to guard it. It was his, after all. His leg had stopped bleeding, but now it was hurting again as if it were on fire. He wished for a cigar and convinced himself that somewhere among his belongings he might find at least a half-smoked stub. He focused his attention on the prospect and congratulated himself on surviving once more, ironically grimacing.

He had beaten the odds again, he told himself. He had managed to come out of this more than alive. For once, he still had a stake. He had done better than break even: He still had the whiskey, thanks to that crazy old plainsman. And he had the plainsman's horse and a Comanche pony to boot. His mind began to range far ahead of the plodding hoofbeats into the seamless curtain of rain.

He saw himself facing Jigger Tuttle. He wouldn't kill him. Graham smiled. No, that wasn't the way at all. He would find a marshal, maybe a judge of some kind. He would show them Tuttle's wire, which was still in Graham's pocket, especially the part about reporting his intended route. He would explain the contract, force them to see that Tuttle had no choice but to turn over the valley to him. Then he could deal. The game was far from over, he assured himself. There were still many cards to play.

As the horse topped the ridge that overlooked the crossing, the gray balked in a sudden torrent of rain that burst anew across the prairie. Graham lost his balance in the McClellan saddle. He was dangerously dizzy. He fought to right himself atop the roan. He would rest up, he told himself, then take the horses and catch up to the train. Somehow, he would persuade them to listen to him, to hear him out about the Valley of the High Snows, about the life they could have if they would only gamble once more. They had all taken losses, but there was still a chance, a better one than before, more for everyone. He could make them see that.

The plan was still a good one, and they could make it work. Graham could convince them that going on—with him, with the whiskey—was the only chance they had. He could convince all of them except Virgil Hollister, at least, and, if he had to, he could kill him. Hell, Graham thought, I've killed better men than that. I've killed better men than Jigger Tuttle as well.

Thoughts reeled in his swimming head. They soon turned to Aggie. He decided to forgive her for her meanness toward him. He understood that when she saw him, she saw an old man, a crippled-up old man, a man who had no future. He would set that right. He couldn't be younger any more than he could grow another hand, but he could explain how he felt about her, that he just wanted a place of his own. He would tell her, he decided, that she needed to give him a chance to make her happy. He had beaten the Comanche, he argued with her shape in his mind, he had saved them from the worst Indians the plains had ever seen. They had a chance for a good life. Together. It could happen. It could be.

He thought of her reaction to the news that her black scout—her black knight—was dead, and he wondered how she would take it. He would have to convince her that he had done all he could to save him. He would tell her about his riding out to get him and bringing him back to her. Colfax would confirm it. So would Frank, if Frank was still alive. If Colfax was still alive. Even if they weren't, it would work, he assured himself. He would bury the scout right there at the crossing, and that would prove something to her, prove that he was not just a man driven blind with jealousy of a Negro's affection for a white girl, not just a ruined gambler with no compassion.

It had to work, he insisted. The basic denomination was in place. All that lay between him and Santa Fe and the Valley of the High Snows now was some rest and the reassertion of his authority over the train. He would take Hannah into his confidence, he told himself. She would back him. He would take them all in. They would all stand with him. They were going to make it.

He stopped the horse atop the ridge and squinted down toward the creek. It was raining hard again, and thunder echoed in a constant symphony of deafening cracks and rolling rumbles. Tiny white-capped waves whipped in the wind. The abandoned wagons, some still laden with the settlers' discarded possessions, remained pulled up in the old line. Many still bristled with Comanche arrows and other signs of battle. The creek was rising, Graham noticed, and he made a mental note to be careful crossing it: The roan was tired and might not be very surefooted on the gravelly bottom.

Some horses had wandered up from somewhere. The sight elated him. He didn't care where they came from. Horses were horses, and the train would benefit even more. He could give one to Jigger Tuttle as a token of his good intentions, to show there were no hard feelings, maybe as a gift to replace any shortfall caused by the used and damaged whiskey kegs.

Graham closed his bad eye and looked again. The creek bank was still littered with bodies. He was astounded. He had been automatically certain that Aggie would insist on burying them. It was incredible. He would speak harshly to her about that. She had been right about the Mexicans, he found himself admitting: There was a time to be decent, to do the right thing.

Several dead oxen were also visible out away from

the wagon line. Then through the white cloud that surrounded everything he saw and threatened to close in completely every time he tried to focus, he noticed other shapes among the dead: small, round shapes that were scattered down as far as the creek's water. For a moment he had the horrible thought that they were the hogs rooting out among the corpses, and a hot flash of anger came over him. But the shapes weren't moving. He narrowed his right eye and put his hand over his left, and then his jaw fell open in genuine horror.

Graham sat stupidly on the roan and stared with his one eye down at the rain-bathed crossing. Five, six, seven . . . he counted the broken whiskey kegs.

"Hollister!" He felt the old sense of betrayal surging up in him. "That goddamn sanctimonious son of a bitch." Then, with a quick note that several more horses could be seen behind the near wagon, he spotted a short figure in a swallowtail coat and a high silk hat moving around the abandoned vehicles.

Quigley, Graham said to himself. Another man was visible also, and Graham knew what had happened. Hollister and Quigley had stayed behind to ruin the whiskey. They let everyone else go on, and they stayed to destroy the very reason they had to go in the first place.

Graham dropped the gray's rawhide lead, lowered his bullet-shaped head against the rain, pulled a pistol from its holster, and spurred the roan forward. The horse moved down the muddy trail toward the creek just as thunder sounded once more, and the wagon master gritted his teeth and swore loudly enough to drown it out.

"Quigley, you bastard, I'm goin' to blow your pointed little head off," the gambler shouted.

The horse splashed into the creek, and the thunder roared again in a crackling ripple. The storm was renewing itself, and hailstones began pelting down on his head, forcing him and the horse beneath him to shiver and try to withdraw into their own skins. Graham spurred the roan hard, mindful but not caring that pain radiated outward from his injured thigh and that the water was so high that he was wet to the waist. Colfax's mount had trouble with the creek's storm-whipped fury, and Graham had to fight to stay on him.

The horse struggled up onto the gravel, and Graham gave him one more kick, driving him hard to the wagons. He noticed only with a quick regret that he was riding over the bodies of slain whites who covered the ground between him and the silk hat that his imperfect eyesight had picked out as a target. Jack Sterling's corpse was turned over and his hideous, eyeless face seemed to be laughing at him.

Graham wheeled out of the saddle and fell to one knee. He cried out in pain, but immediately rose and lumbered in a stumbling run toward the wagon and the man whose back was still turned to him. He hobbled up to him. The driving rain combined with his injury to blind him almost totally. But in his imagination's fury, he had already cocked the pistol and put a bullet through the little banker's head, and he was already, in his mind, moving off to find the loud-mouthed self-appointed man of God to kill him as well.

When he reached the silk-hatted form, Graham's stubbed arm shot out, glanced off the shorter man's shoulder, and knocked off the battered headpiece. Just as he had mentally rehearsed it only moments before, the wagon master cocked his pistol and prepared to raise it, but it stopped halfway up, frozen in space.

He wanted to say something, but he couldn't. The echo of his heart thumping in his ears drowned out any possible sound. He wanted to move, but he couldn't. His arms and hand felt numb, and he was but dimly aware that the Colt's had fallen from his fingers. For the first time in his life he understood what it meant to find an absolutely basic denomination. For once, he had bet into a sure thing and lost it all. For instead of looking into the cowardly aspect of the little banker, Graham stared into the rain-coursed, ebony-painted, jubilant face of the Comanche chief.

CHAPTER THREE

1

AGGIE STERLING'S EYES WERE BURNING AS IF SHE HAD been crying, but the girl had shed no tears at all, not for hours. The sense of draining pain and frustration she felt gave her all the symptoms of deep self-pity. Her heart physically ached, but she refused to give in to such weaknesses. A change had come over her. She didn't understand it, she wasn't sure she liked it, but it kept her moving, kept her from just sitting down on the ground and weeping. She felt old, older than Hannah Morgan, older than her mother, wrung out, too tired and disgusted to indulge herself in emotional release. Instead, she concentrated on the anger she felt, on the determination to endure she still believed was a part of her mother's legacy. She was in charge of her life for the first time ever, and whatever happened, whatever she faced, she was prepared to make decisions on her own.

She lashed out furiously at the exhausted mules that drew her wagon through the muddy trace in the high buffalo grass, and she swore openly and loudly at them. She imagined those who heard her over the jangling harnesses and tack were shocked, but she didn't care. Her only care in the world was to make sure that no one—particularly no man—tried to stand in her way any longer. She had had enough of men, she insisted to herself, and she slashed again at the mules to emphasize the point.

But there was still one man in her way, and for the moment, there didn't seem to be a thing she could do about it. About fifty yards in front of her, the bent, mud-splotched blue back of a fretful and frustrated United States Cavalry major leaned forward on a worn-out chestnut gelding. His hat was battered from hail that had struck the wagon train and combined with a total loss of direction to force a halt to their westward trek only a few miles from Moses Franklin's hated crossing.

Along either side of the cavalry officer straggled out twenty uniformed men who stumbled along in the whipping wet grass. Some leaned on their rifles as if they were crutches, but none looked up any higher than the heels of the man in front of him. All but seven were black troopers, and two more were Indians—Tonkawa, Aggie was told—but none was mounted. Two of the white men wore heavy chains on their arms and legs, and none walked with any energy. They plodded along the uneven ground beneath the soaked prairie grasses and kept their heads down against the light rain that splattered across their backs and seemed to drive them eastward.

Aggie's bonnet was swept back off her blond hair, which was unkempt and still damp from the drenching it had taken in the sudden morning storm. The clouds were passing, at last, and the western horizon behind her was light with a brilliant sunset that burned its way through the remnants of the thunderheads. Her hands were raw from handling the reins, and her shoulders ached with weariness. Her only goal was to find shelter for herself and those she now thought of as "her family." As for the others, the settlers, most of them children and wounded men, Aggie had no feelings at all. She was no longer a part of them nor they of her. If they wanted to follow her, fine. If they stopped where they were and rotted, that was fine, too.

It didn't matter to her that they had no choice. They were beaten, and they knew of nothing else to do but to turn and follow her. It was that or sit right where they were in the open, without animals, without shelter. That was the Army's threat. The major had made that quite clear.

She really had no idea what they would do when they got back to the crossing. That was as far as she had thought things out: Get back, dry off, find something to eat. All she knew for sure was that they were going east, back east.

The darkening horizon told her that they had little daylight left. They would be lucky to make the crossing by dark, and once there, she knew their chances of surviving for long were slim. But she feared finding herself out on the naked prairie, unprotected in spite of the weary troopers and their rifles, unable to defend herself against Indians or anyone else.

For days—years, it seemed—all they had looked for, hoped for, prayed for, was the appearance of soldiers. They had all come to believe that the blue-uniformed men would save them. But when they met them, they, too, were defeated, more useless than the spent, frightened settlers. They promised to be a greater threat to the train and its weary population than the Comanche ever were.

From her bouncing wagon seat, Aggie saw the mesa and copse of pecan trees in the near distance. The crossing was not her favorite choice of destinations; it was simply the logical one: It was the only place she knew. It seemed to satisfy the major as well. He wasn't a hard man, Aggie told herself for the thousandth time since their midday encounter. He was only frightened and angry, desperate as well. But not as desperate as she. She felt driven, although she herself had chosen the direction.

The whole day had begun a new series of horrors for Aggie that wouldn't end. Of course, no one had consulted her. Mr. Graham, Moses, the rest of them made the decision. Men again, she thought. It was men who led them out here, and it was men who were trying to kill them. Carlson Colfax was also a man—probably a crazy one. But he, she thought, along with the others, was likely dead by now. They hadn't shown up, and they weren't likely to. That many fewer men to worry about, she thought, and she snaked her whip out over the mules' ears once more.

In spite of her feelings, she found her thoughts tracing back to the feel of Mr. Graham's hand on her shoulder. It reminded her, somehow, of Todd's hand when he took hold of her. It was a firm grip, yet tender. It seemed to communicate something deep. At once, it frightened her and lulled her, and she hadn't known what to do. She sensed that he wanted to pull her to him, to hold her, and she was surprised to discover that she wouldn't have minded, not a bit, not even in front of Moses. She needed to be held. It had been a long time since anyone had held her.

Then, when his hand went away, back into the darkness and silence of the early morning, all she felt was a shivering coldness. She was stunned by it. She wanted him to touch her again, to reach out and take her in his arms. She sensed that he needed her as much as she needed him. There was no promise about it, no hope for anything like a promise. There was just a raw need, but she walked away and left it. Right then she decided to stand on her own: without a man, without anyone. She could do that, she knew. She could endure if nothing else.

She lashed out at the mules with a renewed viciousness. Things were going to be different from here on out, she promised herself. She was going to have *her* way for a change. Even Jason and she were at odds. But that would pass, she hoped. Before they pulled out he had stayed off to one side, obviously brooding. Aggie was almost relieved when he finally spoke.

"I'm goin' with the others up on the mesa," he announced to her back. She hesitated and then heaved herself aboard the wagon seat and stored her weapons. When she turned to him, she saw that he was sweating profusely in spite of the morning's gray cool. He was covered with dust.

"No, you're not. You go down there an' get the cows ready to move."

"What on?" Jason looked up and down the line. "They took all the horses, even the black, an' every mule we got is hitched up. We'll just leave 'em."

She knew he was right, but she felt she had to keep charge of her own family. It was all she had left. "Go on," she ordered. "Do what I tell you or don't. I don't care."

Jason shrugged and started away toward the end of the line. He was moving slowly but deliberately, waiting, she sensed, for her to stop him.

"You might think of Lottie." She glanced back into the wagon bed, where the dark girl sat next to Bess Potter. The world seemed to be full of strange, quiet, misplaced women, Aggie thought, each dependent on some man who would abandon her as casually as he would shoot an injured horse. "Her daddy's already out there. What's she goin' to do if you don't come back?"

Jason stood still with his back to his sister. She wondered just how much like Jack Sterling he was.

"You tellin' me to stay?"

"I need you with me, Jason," she started, then she surprised herself: "I'm tellin' you I love you."

He stood still for another moment, and then he turned. "I'll go with you, I reckon." His black eyes were filled with tears, and her heart moved. In the darkness of her brother's eyes, she saw a love for her such as she had never witnessed from anyone else. She wondered if anyone, even Gertie, had ever said that to him.

His face shifted away. Without a word, he came around the back of the wagon and tossed his rifle inside. He retrieved his stick and walked down the corpse-littered beach to start the cattle moving.

"Guess you won that one," Hannah called from the wagon in front of her as she hauled herself aboard. Aggie only nodded and blinked tears away.

She hadn't won a thing, she thought with a renewing surge of anger swimming over her. She sighed, then bit her lip hard and settled her thin buttocks on the wagon seat once more. In a sense, she envied the dead. At least for them, it was over.

The last crisis before they departed the crossing that morning concerned the whiskey. Aggie recalled it with a shake of her head: the goddamn whiskey.

If it were up to her, she said to herself, they could pour it all out. But something inside her forbade that, not for the sake of opposing Virgil Hollister and the rest, and not because she felt she had any personal claim on it at all. It was for Graham. He might not care for any of them, but for some reason he cared about the damned whiskey, and she felt, somehow, that she was the only one who cared about him.

Pierce and Quigley and several others were moving from wagon to wagon, cutting the kegs off and letting them drop, then splitting each one with a hatchet. It was steadily graying in the east by then: time to go. She tried to pay no attention to them, but she heard the splintering crack of one of the barrels being smashed, and she could contain herself no longer. She jumped down and went quickly toward them. Before she arrived, though, someone else stepped in to stop their destruction.

"You split 'nother keg, an' I'll kill you."

The choked, strained voice halted Aggie's advance. It was loaded with youth, but its whispery tone did nothing to reduce its threat. There was no question in it, no hesitation, and the men stopped where they were.

Aggie peered through the dim morning light toward the Cottonwood Kid. His tall, buckskinned figure casually held a Sharps .50 on Quigley and Pierce.

She took two faltering steps forward and squinted to see better in the gray gloom.

"Get back out of this!" he ordered hoarsely when he saw her move. "This is what Mr. Colfax said might happen. Get back, now." He stepped forward, and Pierce made a move for him. The Kid slid his body to one side, and Pierce grasped empty air and fell. The butt of the Sharps .50 caught him behind the head as he went down, then the boy brought the gun up and trained it on the others.

Quigley looked quickly at Pierce for support, but the carpenter was up on his knees and rubbing his head. "You do what you want, Preacher." Hollister had not shrunk one inch from his defiant posture. "I've got to get folks ready. We're runnin' late." He walked off.

Quigley glanced at Hollister. The boy was taller than the banker, and he clearly was not intimidated by the small man's hatchet, which Quigley continued to hold in a more or less defensive manner. For a moment it appeared that he might stand his ground against the defiant youngster before him. But the boy made a quick swipe with the barrel of his rifle and knocked Quigley's hat from his head, then stepped back to see if he would answer the challenge. But without reaching down for the crumpled headpiece, Quigley turned and followed the others. Virgil Hollister held on to his companion with a firm grip for another moment or so, and then he too retreated.

Aggie stood for a moment and studied the Cottonwood Kid's form. Finally, he decided she constituted no threat to him, and he returned to the boys he was organizing for their expedition.

The whiskey was saved, and all there was to do was leave.

2

NO MORE HAD THEY LEFT THE CROSSING BEHIND THEM than the wind rose along with the sun. Great, dark clouds formed over the southwestern horizon and turned everything an eerie greenish gray. Lightning flashed in the purple wall of swirling clouds that raced rapidly across the western sky. The air was heavy, and the distant, muffled sounds of thunder rolled across the prairie. When the storm finally broke, the mules lay back their ears and seemed to take each step more reluctantly than the last. Breaking wind and braying in protest, they kept trying to turn out of the blasting rain and hail. Only the whips and curses of the drivers kept them moving.

They tried to cover up as best they could, but there was no escape from the weather's violence. Dust swirled up and filled eyes and mouths with choking grit. It was impossible for the wagons to maintain a straight line. After a while, all six of the listing wagons seemed to be taking separate routes, each swerving off in first one direction and then another before the straining drivers could whip the mules back into the teeth of the western storm behind the swaying canvas of Virgil Hollister's Conestoga. Soon all were tacking off in separate directions and drifting out of each other's sight.

An arroyo stopped them at last, and hopelessness set in, it seemed, for good. Harvey Pierce's gun blasts, lighter and sharper than the bass of the thunder, barked out of the darkness and brought them all together along the edge of a deep, craggy ditch that traced its mesquite-torn sandstone sides down to a narrow bottom that was awash in flooding water and debris. The rain became a steady, heavy downpour, but the wind abated and the lightning stopped. The tension of the storm was broken, and the thunder was moving off to the east and behind them.

The rain continued to fall, although it had decreased except for infrequent violent outbursts that sometimes brought renewed thunder and caused man and mule alike to shudder. While everyone argued about what to do next, Aggie made up her mind that she had followed idiocy and indecision long enough. Sitting in the rain with their backs to this ugly dent in the prairie and talking about the problem wouldn't do at all. She didn't know whether they should go north or south. It depended as much on the way the mules turned as on anything else, but she knew that they had to move on.

She raised her whip, and then she saw the unmistakable blue uniforms, and she believed they were saved at last.

"Soldiers," she whispered. Like ghosts, they came out of the mist toward the stalled wagons. She shook the rain out of her eyes and blinked rapidly. It was hard to believe what she saw was not a hallucination. "Soldiers!" she then screamed and turned every head toward the southern horizon. "Thank God! We're saved!"

The settlers greeted the arrival of a patrol from the Ninth United States Cavalry with awe. They gathered around the mounted officer and blue-coated men who walked behind him as they emerged through the rain-soaked grass. Their weapons were slung over their backs, and their hats were beaten down with the water and hail, but they stepped more quickly when they saw the wagons, and their black faces lit up with wide grins and waves that soon gave way to broken ranks.

The scene quickly became pandemonium as the settlers rushed around the troopers, slapping their backs and grabbing their hands. Most all of them were buffalo soldiers, but it didn't matter to the battle-weary, frightened, and lost whites. Here at last were men in uniform, with guns, and they had come to deliver them from the Indians, to guide them to safety. That was enough. That all of them were on foot except the officer, who rode off to one side and surveyed the welcome from a distance, and that some wore bandages and limped didn't diminish the enthusiasm with which Harvey Pierce wrung the hand of a huge black sergeant as if he were kinfolk.

Aggie remained on her wagon. "Where's their horses?" she asked aloud, but no one was near enough to hear her.

"Goddamn, goddamn!" Pierce kept grinning up at the burly man, who stood as far as his arm would reach away from the small carpenter, his eyes wide with astonishment. "Goddamn, I knew we'd find you! I jus' knew it!" He surveyed the wagons with the eye of a triumphant parent. "Where you been?"

The sergeant tried to say they had heard Pierce's gunshots earlier and had begun moving through the storm toward them until they crossed the wagon tracks, then turned and followed them, but no one was listening. Disaster had turned to holiday, and everyone was dancing in the muddy, trampled grass around the soldiers and shouting at once.

It wasn't until the major allowed his horse to find its weary way into the midst of the impromptu celebration that the settlers began to see that things were not all right at all. The officer surveyed the crowd around him with sad eyes, then held up his hand for silence and began speaking, but few paid any attention to him. Two Tonkawa scouts wearing military blouses over their buckskin leggings squatted down under the Runnels wagon and dug out a pipe, lit it, and began to smoke. Most of the soldiers simply leaned against the wagons and rested while settlers yelled their tale of horror at them.

The officer was speaking softly, and Aggie couldn't hear what he was saying. One by one, though, members of the settlers' group began to make sense out of his words, and she saw their bodies stiffen and their shoulders droop. She climbed down and made her way to the circle of people standing around the mounted officer. When she heard his words, she couldn't believe them.

". . . So, that's what we're going to do," he said. "In a few days, we'll have a patrol out to help you, but for now, I must get to Fort Sill, and you people have the only serviceable mounts not in hostile hands for miles. It's my right, and it's the law. You don't have any choice."

"You can't do it," Harvey Pierce railed at him. He was hoarse from shouting. "You can't jus' leave us out here. We're shot up, an' half our stuff's gone. We got people hurt and dyin'! You can't do it."

"I've explained to you," the major said patiently. "I have no choice. I know you people have been through a bad time. But I have my orders from Colonel Mackenzie. I have to carry them out."

"Vell, you kin do vot you vant mit de udders," Runnels spluttered. "But I didn' come dis var to haff mine animals ztolen by zum gottdamned Prussian. Nozzir!" He placed a closed fist over his chest and looked around defiantly at the soldiers, who shuffled their feet and kept their heads down.

The officer, Aggie saw as she moved closer, looked too tired to sit his mount. The animal was worn out. She wondered why he didn't climb down and give the horse a rest, but she saw that his gloved hand held the rein in a tight grip, and the flap on his holster was undone as well.

"Well, I ain't fixin' to let you do it!" Pierce screamed. He flung his hat down and pushed his way through the crowd. "Nope. I won't let him have 'em. I didn't go through all this shit jus' to give up to a bunch of nigger troops. Nossiree." He stalked through the trampled grass toward his wagon.

"Sergeant," the major said heavily. The black man with three stripes on his arm whom Pierce had welcomed so enthusiastically snapped erect. No other words were needed. He nodded and moved off toward Pierce's wagon.

"You can't do it," Quigley piped up suddenly. His sparse hair was matted by the rain, and hailstones had raised red welts on his pate. "I know my rights, and you can't do it." The major turned his sad eyes on the small banker and then looked away. Quigley flapped his arms uselessly against his sides and fell silent.

"This is stealin'!" Aggie hissed at Hannah. "They can't do that. They're soldiers! These are our animals."

"Says they can," Hannah said. "Says it's the law or some such. Says he was sent out to capture them fellows." She pointed a dirty finger toward two forlorn men who stood in shackles off to one side. They were white men, and their uniforms were torn and ripped. Neither wore a hat, and their hair lay across their mud-streaked foreheads in dark wet strands. A pimply-faced white soldier with a bandage on his shoulder stood guard over them, although there was nowhere for them to run.

"Deserters," Hannah explained. "He was sent to catch 'em, an' he did, he says. But some Kiowa hit 'em sometime yesterday an' shot 'em up an' stole their horses—except that'un he's ridin'. Left 'em afoot. Now they want to ''propriate' our mules, as he says. Leave us here is what he means."

Disgust filled her voice, but Aggie thought she also could detect a slight panic in the older woman. It was the first time Hannah had seemed to lose confidence, the first time Aggie had ever seen her afraid. She looked around and noticed that several of the troopers were wearing bloody bandages, and more than one was propping himself up on his rifle. All were exhausted.

"We can't let them," Aggie said. "We'll die out here without animals."

Hannah sighed. "I don't think we can stop 'em. One thing I've learned, gal: When a Yankee soldier wants somethin', he's like as not to take it."

Aggie looked around and tried to count the animals who stood in their traces. "We only got 'bout thirty head, and mine's half dead."

"Goddamn rain," Hannah said, wiping her eyes. "Goddamn Graham, an' goddamn nigger scouts, an' goddamn rain." She spat into the muddy grass. "An' goddamn soldiers. Take ever'thing a body has, kill her man, run her off, chase her down, an' take it again." She turned and went back to her wagon, slapping her skirt with a quirt.

At that moment, Harvey Pierce burst into view from the back of his wagon. He waved a bullwhip wildly and ran toward the major, who immediately reined up his horse and pulled his pistol from his covered holster. Before the officer could find his aim, the burly sergeant grabbed Pierce. He wrestled the whip away, grabbed Pierce's left arm, and twisted it quickly to one side. The sound of the bone snapping echoed through the rain, and everyone stopped where he was.

Karl Runnels started moving. He had been leaning on his wife, but he now hopped and stumbled on his good foot over against his wagon. He reached up to the seat and grabbed his rifle, cocking it smartly as he jerked it down. The major nodded, and the two Tonkawa underneath grabbed Runnels's legs and jerked him down into the grass, causing him to cry out as his injured foot was dragged under him.

"Tie him up," the officer said, and two soldiers immediately set about the task. They used trace chains. Runnels sputtered and cursed all the while.

"If there's any more foolishness like that," the major

said in a rumbling voice, "I'll order my men to shoot you down. You people have had a hard time. I understand that. But you don't have any rights out here. You shouldn't even *be* out here. I told you that the best thing I can do for you is to get to Fort Sill and send help back."

Aggie noticed that all the troopers were now more alert and held their rifles up and ready.

"I'm going to explain this once more." The major holstered his pistol and placed both hands on the pommel of his horse in the attitude of a lecturer. "I'm under orders to get these men to Fort Sill. I need mounts for my men, because some of them are wounded. They can never make it on foot. Not in a week's time, maybe not at all. On top of everything else, there appears to be a general uprising to the northwest of here, and we need to report it as quickly as possible. The colonel is out there right now on campaign trying to find and subdue the hostiles, likely the same ones who attacked you. He's moving generally in this direction, and he's ignorant that the Kiowa are up and out as well. He needs every available man with him if he encounters Indians of any stripe."

He sighed. "I don't like it, but those are my orders, my responsibilities. There are laws covering military priorities, and I'm violating no statutes in commandeering your animals. I'm not taking all of them, only as many as I need to complete my assignment.

"I could use a wagon as well, but I'll forgo that on humane grounds. That leaves you with enough to go on —if you are foolish enough to go on—or to return to wherever you came from. Or, as I've suggested, you can remain here until help arrives. Those are, to put it simply, the only options you have." He folded his gloved hands on the saddle's pommel again and chewed his mustaches a moment. No one said anything, and he continued.

"I have no orders to provide an escort for you or anyone else. Indeed, my instructions are to the contrary. We've already been delayed, and likely more lives than yours hang in the balance. I'm sorry, but there it is."

His words hung in the wet atmosphere for a moment. Aggie looked around. Jason was sitting on their wagon seat, her old shotgun across his lap. If they tried to take any mules from the Sterling wagon, she knew, there would be bloodshed, likely Jason's, likely hers. She glanced around at the settlers. They shuffled in the wet grass and sought solace in the mud. Soldiers weren't Indians, and they weren't ready for another fight, she thought. No one was going to do a thing.

She made up her mind suddenly: They could all go to hell. She stepped forward.

"Sir," she said, and he looked up. She cleared her throat and moved through the knot of people over to where he sat his horse. He looked at her from behind a defensive mask, but she could see that behind it was insecurity. She had seen it many times before. Whenever Jack was out of bounds and knew it, he wore it. It covered fear.

"Seems to me that you've got a bigger problem here." The rest of the settlers stared at her. "Seems to me that you're in trouble, an' you know it."

"Now, see here," the major sighed. "I have explained—"

"Seems to me that you was taken by surprise an' lost your horses, an' if this colonel or whoever finds out about it, you're fixin' to be in deep water. That about the size of it?"

The major chewed his mustaches. The settlers began to mutter among themselves, and he looked quickly around. "I've told you everything I have to tell you. I've discussed it all I intend to. It's perfectly legal, as I've said. This is a martial-law situation. I am authorized by the Department of—"

"Seems to me," Aggie interrupted, now addressing the crowd but keeping her eye on the major, "that the best thing that could happen is that he could take our mules an' just ride off an' forget that he ever saw us. Sooner or later, we'd wander off on our own, or the Indians'd find us, or we'd die. Seems to me that that's what's goin' on here." Almost as a congregation listening to a welcome sermon, the settlers nodded their heads. They were now all staring at her, waiting to see what the major or Aggie would do next.

The major pulled his hat farther down on his forehead. His hand once more fell to his pistol butt. "Now, you just listen to me, young woman. I've given you my word. I'm an officer in the United—"

"I've been sold down the river by better'n you," Aggie snapped. Her voice seemed far away to her ears, as if it belonged to someone else, had a mind of its own. "I've been beat an' burned out by men who'd eat prissy little fools like you for breakfast." She swung herself around now and confronted him full on. Her feet squared and her hands were on her hips. Her eyes flashed in the rain, and every settler's face was turned toward her. "We're in trouble, an' you're in trouble. The only thing I can see to do is for us to help each other. Elsewise, somebody's likely to get hurt." She glanced over at Pierce, who sat dumbly on the ground and cradled his broken arm. "Hurt bad. But I can tell you a truth: You ain't takin' even one of our mules."

The major sat up straight. "I *can* just take them," he said. "It's my right, and I can do it. I could take *all* of them. By force if necessary." His eyes rose to observe Jason and one or two others who had moved near weapons. "What's going to stop me?"

"We're not 'bove killin' the likes of you." She perceived the people around her stiffen, and she quickly changed her tone for fear that someone would do something foolish. "You're up against it, Major, just like us. You're wore out. We're wore out. You got wounded. We got wounded. But you only got you. We got everythin' we own, an' nothin' more to lose."

She softened her face and changed her tone once more. "Most of our animals're blown. They can't take us much farther anyhow. They'll be dead 'fore nightfall if they're pushed too hard. You won't get much farther than we would. We need shelter, rest. We've been through too much. If you leave us, it's murder. Just that simple. Same as if you tell your men to shoot us down. We ain't fixin' to just stand by an' watch. Killin' you or you killin' us won't make no difference to nobody. It'll just make things quicker, that's all."

The tension between the mounted officer and the defiant girl was palpable. He blew through his mustaches and considered her.

"There's no shelter around here," he said. "There's nothing but this rill, and more of the same to the west. The ground gets rougher if anything else. Soon you'll hit the breaks, and your mules had better have wings to get up them if you don't know where the cuts are. This place is as good as any, if you're determined to stay out here and wait."

"If you take the mules, we got no choice but to wait," she said. "An' we'll die. But if any of us lives, if just one of us lives to get back an' tell the tale, you think what people will say." She looked around and discovered that they all were staring at her with expectation on their faces. It was such a different emotion from what Aggie was used to seeing in their eyes that she almost blushed.

"If *I* live," she continued with a glance at Hannah, who had moved up near her and was holding her rifle loosely in her arms, "I'll find you an' kill you." She smiled suddenly at him, her lips thin when they connected the vertical dimples in her cheeks. "I got nothin' to lose, Major. Nothin' at all." She waited and allowed him to stare at her for another moment, then she ordered him in a soft but firm voice, "You'll take us to a safe place 'fore you steal our animals. Or we can start killin' each other right here an' now. It don't matter to me."

He stiffened his back. "I am an officer in the United States Army. I think I'm a gentleman, at least I've always tried to be. I'm not trying or planning to kill anyone, and I'm not *stealing* anything." He looked at his men. "I am *not* stealing. I will pay you for your animals."

"You will take us to shelter," she repeated.

He studied her for another moment, then his shoulders sagged even more. "Where?" he asked finally. He was defeated and she knew it. It took all her energy to restrain a genuine smile of triumph. The rain picked up again suddenly and swept them hard. Every head but Aggie's bowed. She was determined not to give in even to nature. "Where do you want to go?" he asked.

The question stumped her. She had not been prepared to make that decision. She knew they couldn't go far, and the only option that came to her filled her with dread. But she knew she had to speak quickly and without hesitation or his giving in might be taken back.

"The creek." She couldn't bear to see the faces behind her and fixed her eyes on the major. "We'll go back to the crossin'."

3

It shocked Aggie that all of the settlers in the train so easily accepted her decision to return to the crossing. As she looked into the faces of the men who had become the titular leaders of the train, she saw no more anger, no more determination. No one seemed to have any hate left. It was as if they were dead inside, unable to think or decide anything for themselves any longer. But she discovered that she didn't care anymore either. They could follow her or not as they chose.

She looked up once more and saw the major's silhouette outlined against the gray blackness of the eastern sky. He had reached the ridge, and he raised himself high in the stirrups and scanned the crossing. Then his shoulders sagged, and he turned the mount and rode back to where Aggie's wagon led the line of settlers toward the almost invisible trail. The soldiers sat down in the grass as he passed them, but the two Tonkawa scouts went on over the high ground.

"I don't think you want to go down there." The major reined up and turned his horse to ride parallel to Aggie's steady course.

"I seen what's down there. We all seen it. That's our folks down there."

For a moment he looked confused and started to say something, but then he rubbed the stubble on his chin and set his jaw. "That's not what I meant," he muttered. He rode along for another moment, studying her openly.

"How old are you?" he asked at last. She looked straight ahead and ignored him. "You're old enough, I guess. You're sure a hardheaded woman, however old you are," he said. Aggie paid him no attention but concentrated on the mules.

They rode another several yards in silence. "They said there were some others. Men. That they were supposed to meet you after they distracted the Indians."

"That's right," Aggie said. "But they should of caught up by noon. Maybe they got stopped by the storm." She thought for a moment and kept her eyes steadily on the rumps of the mules. "Maybe they're dead." The shock of hearing her own conviction about the men—about Graham and Moses—voiced so clearly and definitely struck her hard. She shook her head and forced her attention to remain on keeping the mules from pulling apart. They balked and wanted to stop all of a sudden. Their final reserves of strength were running out. The mesa seemed as far away as when she first spotted it.

The major stared at her for a moment, then he spurred his horse into a weary trot, drew a saber, and called to the sergeant to form up the men. "Ready arms," he shouted.

"It don't matter how old I am," she hissed at the mules and tried to keep her level of anger high enough to sustain her energy. "Don't none of us belong out here. *Old* ain't got nothin' to do with it. Never did." The mules sensed her anxiety and pushed themselves into a fast walk up to the higher ground.

Her wagon topped the steep apex of the ridge, and the mules hesitated briefly before making their descent. She grasped the reins tightly and jerked them back, forcing a halt. The crossing appeared before her eyes all at once, and only by jamming her throat closed and clenching her teeth was she able to stifle a cry of hopeless horror at the vision.

Blind Man's Creek was up and running. The storm's washing had spilled the lazy stream out of its banks; it now climbed fifteen feet up into the cedar thicket on the opposite bank. Two or three bodies were stuck in the prickly green branches of the scrubby trees, all hanging in grotesque positions and swaying with the tide.

Most of the other bodies, the ones which had stretched up and down the beach, were gone, apparently washed downstream in the flood. Water covered most of the killing ground and lapped the wheels of the abandoned wagons. Up against the turn where the bluff cut into the creek's course, the floating carcasses of horses and oxen had jammed with pieces of oxbows, singletrees, wood, and the broken whiskey kegs in a dam that caused the turgid water to splash over it as it followed its unnatural flow.

But beyond the shock of seeing the turn of events caused by the wind and rain, it was the abandoned wagons that caught Aggie's horrified attention. All but two were in ruins. Charred planks and other evidence of fire suggested that they had been burned, at least partly. The remains of the seared vehicles were ripped apart and crushed as if a mob had descended on them and torn them to flinders. The three that were still intact sat together, pulled up tightly in front of what Aggie remembered to be her cave, and they also showed signs of careless vandalism. Two sat without wheels on one side and tilted at a precarious angle toward the shallow but rushing water. The third, Mr. Graham's buckboard, the only one that was apparently undamaged, was loaded with what she recognized as a half-dozen kegs of Cleve Graham's whiskey.

Aggie sat rigid on the wagon seat and stared. The major led his men single-file down the path to what had been the crossing and then steered his horse hock-deep into the swirling flood to allow them to make their way along the higher ground down to where the gravel rose to the old wagon park. Several of the caves were flooded, but the ground caused the water to crest unevenly and kept the center of the butte above the flood line. The only sign of life was a horse, a laden gray Indian pony, that stood forlornly on the opposite bank, out of reach and almost ghostly in the gathering darkness. Behind her she felt and heard a heavy breath, and she realized that her sister was standing up in the wagon bed and looking over her shoulder.

"What is it?" Annie asked in a whisper.

"Crossin's flooded," Aggie said. "We can't stay here."

The sounds of jangling trace chains and the oaths of drivers behind her came to her ears, and she strapped her mules down toward what had been her only idea of safe haven. The other settlers followed automatically, each pausing briefly at the crest of the ridge to view the natural destruction below before following Aggie's wagon into the flooding creek.

The major sloshed his horse over to her and allowed it to step out onto the bank.

"This is it?" he asked. "This is where you want to be?"

Aggie didn't answer him. For a long moment she sat still. Worry and weariness numbed her. The drizzle ceased, and the bright, golden light of sunset struck and yellowed the tops of the cedar trees on the opposite bank. Overhead the sky was a clear, washed purple, now deepening into darkness. The crossing was likely ten feet deep at the ford, she realized. They couldn't go back, and they couldn't go forward. This was, to answer the major's question, most definitely where they would have to be.

Soldiers invaded the ruined wagons and picked around at the contents. One came running up to the major and spoke to him, and the officer turned around to glare at Aggie.

"There's whiskey on that wagon," he said. "Kegs of it."

Aggie nodded, and the major gaped at her.

"What in the blue-eyed hell? Hauling whiskey out here! I thought you people were crazy when I first saw you. Now I'm certain of it." He turned in the saddle and shouted, "Sergeant!" The same black sergeant who had broken Harvey Pierce's arm stuck his head up from behind the whiskey wagon and shouted back. "They's a man here," he called. "He's 'live, but not much."

The major spurred his horse through the water and quickly dismounted.

Aggie froze. She reached down and pulled up her shotgun. The charges were wet. Fumbling beneath the wagon seat, she found the box Moses Franklin had given her and opened it. The pepperbox rested on a velvet bed. In an instant she checked the primer and load, then climbed down, wetting her skirts to her thighs, and waded awkwardly in Jack's oversized boots toward the wagons behind her.

"Annie, get ever'body down an' behind the wagon," she yelled. She moved quickly from wagon to wagon and pointed them toward the caves. The abused mules stumbled around each other, and they drew the wagons up in a half circle around the abandoned and ruined vehicles. Braying and sloshing vied with the settlers' curses and shouts in echoes down the flooded crossing. The soldiers continued to pick around, and the major climbed atop Graham's wagon.

"What're you doing?" he yelled.

"I'm drawin' us up," Aggie shouted over the noise of the tack and harnesses. "They might come back."

"I doubt it," the major said. "Not with us here. Besides, they took everything they wanted and"—he looked down—"left what they didn't."

Aggie waded through the water over to Graham's wagon.

"Don't—" The major leaped down and tried to restrain her, but she waved the awkward pistol in his face. He backed off quickly and almost fell. She couldn't explain what motivated her or who she expected to find behind the wagon. She shoved away hideous images and dreadful warnings that seemed to make her legs heavy and reluctant to move her forward. Her thoughts raced wildly, and she pushed the soldiers aside, then stopped and almost fell backward with the horror that confronted her.

The vehicle had been jacked up on one side with limestone rocks and cedar limbs to allow the inner wheels to turn freely. Strapped to the front wheel, bound tightly with rawhide tethers, was what was left of a man. He was naked; his head was bare, but only a close inspection revealed that he had been scalped. His skin was covered with vivid red raw streaks, and it was charred black from head to toe. In spite of her determination not to stare, her eyes instinctively ran up and down the tortured body. Her first thought was that this was a woman, but then she observed that the victim had been emasculated and deliberately burned over a slow fire. The sodden coals that remained of the Indians' burning were positioned directly beneath the wheel, which, if turned, would ingeniously allow the body to cook evenly for hours. Every movement or struggle could cause the wheel to turn, and the poor wretch had apparently struggled violently and often, for he was seared all over. Only the bright pink patches of bloody wounds emerged from the charred blackness that covered him.

"Mr. Franklin?" she asked, approaching the man, whom the soldiers had not yet cut down and released. She was filled with compassion for Moses, and anger also flirted with her thoughts as she considered that the sergeant, a black man, had left him there without cutting him down. But when she came within five paces of the hideous face in front of her, she recoiled.

Lidless ash-colored eyes looked pathetically out at

her, scanning her at first with an unknowing stare. Then, when a spark of recognition ignited in them, she tore her own eyes away and saw to her further dread that one of the victim's bound limbs, his left arm, was strapped tightly to the wagon in an unusual fashion. There was no hand to hold it beyond the knots, only a rough stump, burned black and securely bound by rawhide. "Mr. Graham," she whispered tonelessly.

"Cut him down," she tried to say, but her voice was nothing more than a whisper. She swallowed hard. "I said, cut him down! How can you leave him like that? Cut him down!"

"Ma'am." A hand touched her, and she looked into the eyes of the black sergeant. "We can't. It'd kill him worser. He's hurt too bad. You're lookin' at a dead man there."

Aggie swallowed again and moved a step or two closer to the wagon master. The stark whiteness of his exposed skull was still visible in places where the fire hadn't seared away the blood and tissue. His mouth hung open in a black gape, and she understood that the Indians had burned out his tongue.

"Are they all . . . all dead?" she asked the gray eyes that continued to plead with her, running themselves up and down. No sound came from Graham, no movement other than that his eyes continued to make. She heard the other settlers coming up behind the soldiers, peering in at the scene in front of them. It was obscene, she thought, and she wanted to shield him with her body, find a blanket or coat and throw it over him.

"It's best to let him die where he is." The major came up beside her. "Sergeant Forbes is right. He's already dead. They skinned him alive. You can see that." He nodded toward Graham's limbs, which had been stripped of outer skin and were crisp from the fire. "You say his name was Franklin?"

"No," Aggie whispered. "Graham. Cleveland Graham. Our wagon master."

The major shook his head. "If we cut him down, he may just fall apart. All that's holding him together is the rope. There's nothing we can do."

Aggie turned on the gathering crowd and ordered in

a choking voice, "Go away! How can you all just stand there an' *look* at him that way?"

A gagging sound behind her caused her to wheel and look again into the gray eyes of Cleveland T. Graham. It wasn't a voice or anything that could be described as a voice. It was a dead sound such as a wounded animal might make as a hunter's club fell on it. She looked once more into his eyes and felt her heart turn over. She couldn't say why she felt anything at all for him other than the same pity she would have felt for any human being so tortured, so wasted. But her breath continued to come in brief jerks, and behind the pain in his maimed and black-charred face, she read something of his truer feelings. He looked on her as he had never looked, and the longing she found in his eyes moved her. She felt her feet wanting to leave the muddy ground beneath her, and her arms wanting to reach out and embrace his crisp, seared skin. Yet she couldn't move. She couldn't make herself touch him. No one had ever looked at her with such feeling before, and her heart beat faster, and her breath came in shorter and shorter gasps until she feared she would faint.

His eyes continued to search hers, and then, she realized, they darted time and again to the small pistol she held forgotten in her hand. Each glance down was followed by the same searching, longing look that told her what he wanted.

Her own eyes dropped to the weapon, and then she looked once more into the face and eyes of the man who, she realized all at once, loved her. Her heart pounded even harder, and her breast heaved in spasms. The tendons of Graham's neck stood out with a sudden surge of strength, and she saw his arm muscles flex, revealing their naked sinews beneath what charred tissue still covered them as it cracked open. Again he made the inhuman, tortured cry from somewhere deep inside his seared lungs. She raised the pistol.

"You can't do it," the major said from behind her. "I can't let you do it." He grabbed her shoulders and spun her around and looked deeply into her eyes and saw the defiance in them, and his hands fell to his sides.

She gave him a long look, then turned and put the pepperbox to Graham's black and bloody forehead, her finger on the trigger. Graham's eyes seemed to lead the rest of his body in giving up a tension, to relax all at once, and his torn and burned limbs hung limp in their bonds.

"Goodbye, Mr. Graham," she said quietly. Then she whispered into the grateful, helpless stare of the wagon master, "I love you." She pulled the trigger and the small gun barked a sharp, snapping shot.

4

THE CREEK CRESTED JUST AFTER MOONRISE. THOSE WHO knew about waterways recognized that this was a flash flood, something brought on more by the rapidity of the rainfall than by any great volume. The general dryness of the season allowed the water that bottlenecked in the crossing to be quickly absorbed by the numerous arroyos that fingered off from the main body of Blind Man's Creek. By the time the silver brightness that for so many belonged more to the Comanche than to anyone came over the crossing it was well after midnight, and the water was receding.

The settlers' lanterns burned late, but except for the sentries the major posted, everyone slept deeply under the clear, cool sky. There was no sign of Indians. The Comanche were gone, following their moon toward the western horizon.

The next morning, the waters were safely inside their banks. The crossing was clean, washed brightly in the sunlight. The wagons pulled up again into their old line, and several men used mule teams to drag the remains of the ruined vehicles to the edge of the creek.

Although he was no less anxious to depart than before, the major ordered his men to retrieve the bodies that continued to dangle from the cedar bushes across the water. Only eight corpses could be added to those which had been left in the caves. The rest had washed downstream and were covered with mud and debris from the flood. The officer also detailed two men to try to catch the gray horse with the curious bundle atop it they had seen the evening before, but they returned empty-handed.

Gertie's body was not there. Jack's, however, was.

Aggie, Jason, and Annie looked down on his corpse impassively. For a moment they made a tableau in the center of the crossing.

As the morning warmed into noon, they went about the business of dragging the dead—animal and human—into one of the small concave openings down near the bend of the creek, where the remaining coal oil was poured over them and they were burned. There was no convenient place to dig that many graves, the major successfully argued, and the stench was already unbearable. No one objected except Aggie, who refused to allow anyone to touch Cleve Graham's corpse. It remained wrapped in a blanket in the old hospital cave. She even drove Jason away. "I killed him. I'll bury him," she said in her only response to reason.

The smoke from the funeral pyre rose high and black into the sky. Virgil Hollister stood mutely in his wagon while the majority of the remaining settlers gathered to sing two or three hymns outside the "funeral cave," as they had come to call it. Once more, "From Greenland's Icy Banks" and "Amazing Grace" raggedly wailed over the crossing; but this time, there was no deep emotion informing the singers' voices, merely a resigned weariness. Aggie finally left her vigil beside Graham and joined Hannah atop the Sterling wagon to watch Virgil's ceremony. After observing them from a distance for a bit, the major rode up.

His gelding was better for the night's rest, as were most of the other animals, but whereas they had been only splattered with mud the day before, now they were covered with a mixture of red and gray muck from their work around the creek. Aggie looked up at him. Somehow, he had managed to find a way to shave.

"We're pulling out right after the service," he said. Hannah turned away. "We'll cut northeast and find Cache Creek. I think we can make Fort Sill by tomorrow evening, maybe the next day, depending on whether the river is up or not." He coughed slightly. "Some of the people here—all of them, in fact—have decided to go back with us."

"How?" Aggie turned around and faced him. She shielded her eyes from the sun and tried to see him more clearly. "If you need the mules, I don't see how—"

"The wounded men can ride in that buckboard." He pointed with his eyes toward Graham's wagon. "Those who can't walk will have to ride. They're worn out. I'm worn out. None of us is likely to die, but walking all the way is still out of the question. So, to tell the truth, is riding too far. I must get back and make my report, hand over the prisoners. Return you all to civilization. I presume you'll want to go with us, too. I can't say when we'll be back. I may be sent directly to Fort Griffin or maybe straight back to the plains. I don't know."

"That's not what you said yesterday," she pointed out.

He cast his eyes down. "Yesterday you people seemed so determined to go on, I was afraid you'd try to stop us or slow us down if we tried to force you to return with us." He paused and wiped his eyes quickly. "I didn't lie, but I wasn't thinking clearly. I had my orders. I still have them. So I'm taking the wagons as well, and I'm doubling up everyone as much as I have to. We're moving out."

Aggie looked to where Jason had the cattle down by the receding creek. Lottie waded in thigh-deep water beside him. It was beautiful in the crossing.

"We'll be leaving in an hour's time," he went on. "I'd like to make the Red River by dark. The Tonks claim they know a good ford that likely won't be washed out to quicksand by the storm. You'll want to get ready. I don't think we should try to take the cattle—"

"I'm not goin'," she said. Hannah turned around and stared at her. "*We're* not goin'," she said. "My family an' me're stayin'."

"Don't be absurd," the major started. "You have to think of your people, do the right thing—"

"I ain't goin'," she interrupted him. "Yesterday you was ready to leave us all out here, an' now you're raisin' sand 'cause that's what I'm *fixin'* to do. 'The right thing,' " she sneered. "Seems to me, Major, that you have a peculiar notion of what's right an' what's not. I don't think you're 'thinkin' clear' again." She laced her fingers and folded them in front of her. "I ain't goin', an' that's a end to it."

"I told you I don't know when I might return. I can try to send someone, a patrol, but it might be some good time before anyone gets back here. The Indians might—"

"Let 'em." Aggie smiled. "Let 'em." She looked up at him. There was no threat in her voice or her manner. "Me an' mine're stayin'. I lost a mama here, an' . . . a daddy. I lost ever'thing I had here. I got no reason to go off. Anybody who wants to go can go. We got nowhere else to be. We're stayin'."

"I really must insist that you come along. I can't really say that leaving you here would be looked upon—"

"You go on an' do what you got to, Major," she said evenly. She reached out and took Hannah's hand, rough, red, and muddy as it was. "We'll make do till you get back."

The major stared at her a moment. "I must insist," he said. "I can't leave you out here by yourself. Yesterday . . . yesterday there were men with you."

"Men?" Aggie snorted. She waved her hand contemptuously up and down. Then she softened her face. "We'll get on. I think I'll get on out here better'n I ever did anywhere else."

He frowned once more and started to say something else, but instead he wheeled his horse around and started down the line. She called to him, and he reined up and swung around on his saddle.

"If you do come back," she said, looking down at her ruined gingham dress, "you could do me the favor of bringin' me somethin' decent to wear. My sister, too, an' Lottie an' the others. Jason needs boots. Call it a trade for the mules you're stealin'."

He started to smile, but the import of her words suddenly registered, and he blew through his mustaches. "I'm not *stealing* anything," he said. "I will bring your mules back to you." She looked away, and he lowered his voice. "But I'll bring you clothing as well. *If* I come back. If I *can* come back. You have my word on it. As a gentleman," he added. He waited for her to respond, but she continued to study the cedar thicket across the creek, and he turned and spurred his horse on down the line.

The service broke up and the settlers returned to their vehicles, making them ready for travel. Hannah reached over and took Aggie's hand. "I reckon I got to go, too," she said in a whisper, and Aggie stiffened. "There's been too much meanness here. I'm like you, I reckon. I got noplace else to go, but there's been too much blood spilled here for us to jus' stay here an' think on it ever' day. I always moved on after one of my men died. I didn't lose nobody here, but I got to go. I can't stay. You ought to come on yourself. Stayin' here ain't no good."

She waited for Aggie to say something, but when the silence continued, Hannah reached out and cupped the girl's face in her weathered hands. "I can't jus' ride off an' leave you out here. You're jus' a girl. You need somebody to watch over you. I can't jus' leave you here. You an' a bunch of young'uns."

"I won't leave, Hannah. I don't think I *can* go. I'm not strong enough. Where'd we go, anyway? What'd we do? I can't stay at no fort, an' sooner or later I'd have to find us somethin'. Someplace. 'Nother shack, 'nother farm. 'Nother place somebody'd come run us off of. I'm tired of movin' on. All my life I been movin' on. Here to yonder. I was born movin' on. I'm tired of it. There comes a time in a body's life when they got to stop, make a home. This ain't the place I'd choose." She looked around the crossing. "But in a way it means more to me than anyplace I ever been. It's good as any. Better'n most I been to." Their eyes were locked together.

"Stay with me, Hannah," she asked softly. "Meanness is ever'where."

Hannah broke off from her and looked at the settlers straggling back to their wagons. Her face twisted in agony, and once more Aggie saw the fear she had observed in the woman the day before.

"I can't," she whispered through tears that seemed to choke her. "I want to, an' I guess I ought to, but I can't. I'm too old to start over from scratch. There's a man I know." She glanced over the top of the cedar ridge. "He asked me to marry up with him, an' I guess I was runnin' away from him much as anything else. I reckon I'll go back to him."

"How old are you, Hannah?" Aggie asked. The sky was blue overhead. Far off, a mourning dove cooed. Everything seemed suddenly clear to Aggie.

Hannah looked startled. "How old? Lord, girl. That's no question to ask a woman my age." Then she smiled. "I'm forty-somethin', I reckon. Never did know for sure. My folks was killed by Creeks when I was jus' a sprout."

"An' you've been married a lot," Aggie went on.

"A lot." Hannah nodded. "I been married more'n most women has kids." She smiled. "I had my share of young'uns, too. They're all dead, too."

"Did you ever love any of them? The men, I mean."

"Hell, sugar." She laughed loudly. "I loved *all* of 'em. Start to finish."

"An' it hurt when you lost them?"

"Always does." She stood up and looked out over the crossing. "Sometimes it hurts so bad I can't think I'll live through 'nother'un." She made a thin line of her lips. "Guess that's why I was runnin' away this time."

"How do you get over it, bein' hurt, bein' left alone?" Aggie's eyes searched Hannah's.

"I guess you never really do," Hannah said with a slight smile. "You just remember the good times an' "—she winked—"you look for 'nother'un quick as you can." Her hand went out and smoothed down Aggie's hair. "Hell, girl, if I was young an' good-lookin' as you, I wouldn't worry. When all this mess is over, you'll be beatin' 'em off with a stick." She brushed her dirty skirt. "Me, though, I'm jus' a ol' mare with too many years in the harness for most men to look at."

"Then stay, Hannah," Aggie let herself plead. She bit her lip to prevent tears from coming. "Please."

Hannah shook her head. "I can't, girl. This is no good. I'm goin' back an' find that ol' boy. An', like I said, if he ain't found some whirlago gal or somebody ain't shot him yet, an' if he'll still have me, I'm his."

"He'll have you." Aggie smiled brightly at her and blinked away the mist in her eyes. "Any man would be proud to have you."

Hannah smiled again and blew her nose on a bandanna. She looked again at Aggie, but there was nothing more to say, and she climbed down from the wagon seat and lowered her head. "I wonder if anybody'll stay."

"Any who wants to," Aggie said. "But I'm stayin'. An' that's a fact."

ASIDE FROM JED AMBROSE, who had begun to follow Jason around like an anxious puppy, no one else outside Aggie's "family" elected to stay either. On the major's instructions and as a result of direct threats, Aggie suspected, some of the departing settlers offered to share what they had in the way of food. Even Golda Runnels came up with half a sack of flour, which she handed over with a derisive grunt. No one looked at Aggie as if she was immoral or wicked, only crazy, pitiable. She noticed that none of them mentioned Mr. Graham by name. If they spoke of him at all, he was only "that man" or "the wagon boss."

Connie Kruikshank was among the last to climb aboard a wagon. She stopped for a moment and looked at Aggie, and finally she came over to her.

"I want to thank you for all you done."

"I never done nothin' that didn't need doin'." Aggie looked beyond her. Connie looked haggard and tired, but her eyes were bright.

"I'm obliged for your kindness even so," she said. "I wish there was somethin' I could do for you."

Aggie shrugged. "Ain't nothin' to do."

"I'm still obliged," Connie said, and Aggie nodded again. The two women looked at each other for a long moment before Connie turned and fairly ran to Glorietta's outstretched hands.

As Hannah's wagon joined the others, overloaded with soldiers and children and straining as they made their way across the crossing, almost every one of the departing group followed Hannah's example and waved at Aggie. Jack, she thought, would be proud of the way she had handled things. Moses, too. She wondered if Mr. Graham would be.

Bess allowed herself to be led away by the Potters, who apparently had relented in their resentment of her and accepted her into their family. She seemed no more sensible to their ministrations than she had been to anything else that had happened, but she climbed aboard their tailgate and continued to search the horizon as their wagon fell in behind the repaired Mexican buckboard in the rear of the tiny procession.

As the wagon pulled across the creek, Bess jumped off. She ignored the cries of the Potters, who urged her to return. She waded through the stream, ran up to Aggie, and stood silently before her. For a moment, their blue eyes met and held, and then, wordlessly, Bess reached beneath her long blond braid and removed the small leather bag from around her neck. She presented it to Aggie by folding it into her fingers.

"If he comes back, give him this for me," she said. "Tell him my name is Bess Potter. If he comes back, you tell him that. Tell him to come get me." She looked quickly toward the Potter wagon. "I'm a goner with them folks. I won't last. You don't know how they look at me."

Aggie's face hardened. "I guess I know something 'bout that." She looked up into the girl's mud-streaked face. "Stay here. Wait for him here."

She shook her head. "No. If he's kilt, they's all I got. Whatever happens, they's still my kin." She looked at the bag resting in Aggie's palm, then raced away across the creek. The Potter family's arms hauled her back up into the rumbling vehicle's bed.

Only the major and his Tonkawa scouts, mounted on two mules taken from Aggie's own team, remained on the near side of the creek. As the last wagon departed, he rode up to Aggie and doffed his hat. "Last chance to change your mind."

"You got my mules." She smiled.

"I'm leaving you two." He smiled back at her. "This is too hard a country to leave anybody without an animal for long." He paused and then looked down in an attitude of shyness that surprised her. "I'd like to see you again, to tell you the truth."

She was suddenly attracted to him. He was not too old at all; she found him appealing, almost dashing in his dirty military blouse. An alien feeling struck her as she admitted to herself that she hated to see him go. "You could just stay."

"I suppose the colonel would have a thing or two to say about that." He grinned. "But I'll be back before you know it. And I won't forget what you asked me for."

"Don't forget your orders, either."

"The Army doesn't tell me everything to do," he said, laughing. Then he replaced his hat and splashed his worn chestnut across the creek and up the trail after the wagons.

5

THREE HOURS AFTER THE MAJOR AND HIS SMALL TRAIN departed, Carlson Colfax came down to the creek across a lame white mare. The horse pulled a crude travois containing the badly wounded Frank Herbert and was led by the Cottonwood Kid. In their wake were the triumphant Patrizi and Folsom boys, brandishing their arms and feeling grand, and the gray pony with another body wrapped in a Rebel battle flag and strapped across its back. The other survivors of the battle in the Indian camp—Weatherby, Hildebrandt, and Hightower—slogged heavily down the muddy trace behind them, cradling their wounded limbs and peering from behind their makeshift bandages.

When they sighted the four wagons drawn up by the caves, though, they set up a whoop and ran, stumbling headlong into the creek and crossing it, greeting the surprised children with embraces and, to Annie's embarrassment and Lottie's anger, demanding a big kiss from each girl. They were dirty and bloody, stinking and nearly starving, but elated to find themselves alive. All their miseries were forgotten as they related their various versions of the fight. By the time the excitement abated and all had settled down to eat the beans and salted meat they had been grudgingly left by the departing settlers, Aggie reckoned that they had killed, by their individual count, some several thousand Indians each.

"It took us longer'n it should of to get back here," Aggie heard Weatherby explaining. "We had no way of reckonin' where y'all was. But we knowed we couldn't catch up to you, an' this was the onliest place we knowed where we could get to. We seen your smoke, an' drawed us a bead on'er. Didn't have no horses at all 'sides that stove-up white we run up on, an' the ol' man rigged the travois hisself. We didn't want to try to drag Frank neither, but weren't nothin' for'er. He's hurt real bad," he concluded. "So's the ol' man. He's out of his head more'n not. Got him a fever. When he knows what's goin' on, though, he'd rather die'n 'low it was anythin' more'n a splinter in his butt."

For all his initial bravado when he was lugged down from the mare and made as comfortable as possible in Aggie's cave, Colfax was obviously dying. He howled with pain at the slightest movement and cursed everyone with such fiery profanity that she gave up any notion of nursing him and only fortified him with a cup of whiskey. After that, he roused himself only to demand that everyone leave him alone until Frank "healed up 'nough to get his skinny li'l butt over here an' do me some good doctorin'."

Frank Herbert's chest still oozed blood, but he seemed to know where he was and what was happening around him. Jason took charge and installed him in the hospital cave across from Graham's corpse. Lottie also tended to him, and he spoke to her in a barely audible voice and admonished her to take good care of Colfax. Soon both were asleep.

While the triumphant whites roared their exploits to all ears, the Cottonwood Kid led the loaded gray off to one side of the wagons and waited until Aggie's curiosity overcame her and she came down to him.

"It's the nigger." He nodded toward the misshapen lump strapped across the horse's back.

Aggie pushed past him and went around the other side of the horse and lifted the flag. The scout's face was down; she couldn't look at it.

"This here's his rifle," he said, holding up the Springfield. "Frank said that he said that if anything was to happen to him, you was to have it. His bay, too. But the horse got kilt." He unslung a pair of saddlebags from his shoulder. "They's cartridges in here. Money, too. Some. I don't know what happened to his pistols or the rest of his stuff, but this here's yours."

She stared at the powerful carbine and finally took it and the heavy leather bags. The Kid smiled suddenly. "You're hell on horses an' niggers," he said. "But you ain't hard to look at."

Aggie jerked back from him. "Why're you givin' this stuff to me?" she demanded angrily. "Why don't you just take what you want an' ride out? That's what you was bent on doin'. You're jus' like every man I ever seen. One hand full of gimme, an' the other full of I don't know. Ain't one woman 'nough for you? God, I hate you! I never met a man worth the shovel it'd take to bury him."

He glared at her hard and stalked off. She saw him searching into every cave. Aggie knew what he was looking for and frowned after him. "Let the son of a bitch find out for himself," she said aloud.

Aggie led the gray down by the cave where the bodies had been burned. She wanted to cut Moses's body down and put it inside the ashy opening, but she lacked a knife, and then she realized that that was only an excuse. She couldn't touch him. She went back up to her wagon to see if Jason would look after it.

When she came up to the hospital cave she saw the Cottonwood Kid continuing to search the crossing and to peer hard into everyone's face. He asked nothing of anyone, and no one said anything to him. He never once checked on Colfax. She was preparing to go into the hospital cave when the Kid emerged from behind a ruined wagon and grabbed the rawhide bag Aggie had put around her neck, snapping the string. He studied it and looked into her eyes.

"What'd you do with her? Where'd she go?"

"I didn't do nothin'," Aggie cried out of fright, and then she felt herself growing angry all over again. "She gave it to me! To *me*. She said you run off an' left her, an' she said for me to keep it. She said to tell you to forget her!" Aggie barked at him. "She said she was leavin' you to do for yourself."

"Where'd she go?"

"She said to forget her!" Aggie shouted at him. The shock of her words registered hard on his face. "What's the matter? Don't you like bein' left behind? How's it feel?"

He glared at her harshly, and then, without speaking, he flung the bag down and raced down to where Jason and Jed Ambrose were standing around the cattle.

Aggie went inside the cave, but it was too dark to see, and she thought to build a fire. Before she could set about it, however, she felt the tears coming. Her entire body racked with a sudden, intense pain, and she sat down on the ground and shook with the grief and strain that spilled out of her.

When no more tears would come, she emerged from the cave and blinked her eyes against the sting of the afternoon's light. She felt worse than ever, but she knew that her depression was not being caused only by a lack of rest. She was emotionally wrung out, and she didn't know what she would do next. She glanced down the bluff and discovered Moses's body dumped off onto the gravel. The gray pony was gone, and so, she learned when she asked Jason about it immediately, was the Cottonwood Kid and the rest of the men.

"They jus' took off," her brother admitted with a downward cast of his eyes. "He asked where that gal he come in with went, an' I told him, an' he took off. The rest of 'em followed him. Took the mules, took that stove-in white. Took ever'thin'."

"I know."

"I should of been watchin'," Jason brooded. "I should of kilt him."

"There's been enough killin'," Aggie commented and went back inside.

"He jus' run off?" Carlson said in a weaker voice than anyone had heard him use during their short acquaintance. "Jus' like that?" The brief rest had restored the old man's lucidity, but his survival, Aggie could see, was unlikely. He seemed to be bleeding from every limb. Beneath the rags his buckskin trousers had become, his injured legs were black and swollen, and his face was drawn and tight. He reeked of mortifying flesh.

"That's about it," Aggie confirmed. She was squatting next to the old frontiersman. She wondered if he knew that he was dying.

"Well, that's a goddamn pup for you!" He coughed and spat. Blood dribbled into his beard. "Never did care much for him. Only thinks of hisself. Goddamn goat-pricked yellowbelly! Don't give a good goddamn 'bout nobody else. Cornhole you an' run off! Should of let that ol' boy hang him."

Anger seemed to give him strength. "All pecker an' no brains," he cried. "Saved his goddamn ass for him, an' this is what he does! Shouldn't never of throwed in with him." Carlson's eyes were bright with fury, then he chuckled, shook his head, and spoke in a soothing tone as if Aggie were a child who needed consoling after losing a favorite toy. "Now, tell me 'bout this bunch of thimble-riggin' soldier boys. They take the whiskey, or they comin' back for it?"

"He said he'd try to come back."

"That's the goddamn Army for you," Colfax growled. "Bunch of prickless wonders runnin' 'round with their heads up their asses. Rather fuck than fight. Never did have much to say 'bout 'em that was worth a good goddamn."

He winced and shuddered, and then reached out and grabbed her hand with his gnarled fingers. "Listen, girlie, one thing's sure. You can't stay here," he hissed through his pain. "Not down here. That little turd-floater wasn't nothin'. This is a dry season. When it takes a notion to rain, this crick fills up like a redheaded whore. Hell, these caves'll run like rivers."

"I'm not goin' back," Aggie stated. "None of us is goin' back. There's nowhere to go."

"Well, then, I guess we'll have to make the best of it," Colfax gasped with a grin. "I been in worse trouble'n this." He looked at her and winked. "I swear, girl, you're a pistol. Soon's I'm up an' 'bout, I'll be pissin' on your petticoats for fair. You ain't had a real man till you've had Carlson Colfax, an' by God, you can bet your last screamin' eagle that's what my mama called me."

He gripped her hand in his, but there was no passion in his grasp, only pain. Aggie let him hold on to her until he closed his eyes and relaxed his grip. She was still there when Jason came into the cave and sat down in a cross-legged pout.

"I told you I should of kilt 'em," he said. "They took the goddamn food!" His dark eyes flashed and his face flushed with anger. "Took it all. The meat, the flour, all of it!" He gripped Jack's old rifle hard, and his face was contorted in anger. "Even took the salt an' the meal, and two more cows is missin'." His eyes were now filling with tears. "Left us here to die," he said. "Jus' like that. Left us here to die."

Aggie shook her head. "We're well shed of 'em," she muttered.

"Tit in a ringer?" Carlson rasped at her. The old frontiersman was awake and grinning up at her. His strength astonished her, but she could see it was momentary. His forehead was awash in sweat, and bleeding continued from all his wounds.

"I thought you'd be dead by now," Aggie said.

"I'm too much of a son of a bitch to die," he said. "The devil wouldn't have a place hot 'nough for me. I got to get up an' about. There's that whiskey to sell. Time's wastin'."

He coughed hard for nearly a full minute. He was weakening, she knew, but when he recovered himself he looked up and winked at Aggie and nodded over toward Graham's corpse. "Don't take no sudden notions while I'm sleepin'. I don't fancy bein' sent to hell 'fore Satan knows I'm comin'." He lay back. His face was pale beneath his beard. "They tell me he don't like unexpected comp'ny."

The others came in and sat around a small fire in silence after Colfax drifted off again. The hollow eyes of the children told Aggie that she needed to do something. She felt despair sitting on her shoulders like a heavy coat.

No one said anything as they stared into the fire. Carlson muttered in his stupor for a long while as the fire began to burn down. His rough breathing filled the room, but it was a long time before anyone realized that it had stopped.

Aggie finally stood and went outside into the early twilight. A star winked from atop the opposite side of the crossing. No one else moved. Lottie came out and met her in the gathering dusk.

"Hard to believe Indians might be out there now," the dark girl said. She folded her hands over her stomach and looked to Aggie as if she had aged years in the past several days. "My daddy's some better." She waited a beat. "When you come out, he woke up. He says . . ."

"What?" Aggie was ready to be angry again. She sought any emotion that would displace the hopelessness she felt. "What did he say?"

Lottie looked away in the fading light. Then she took a deep breath. "He says we ought to bury 'em." Aggie said nothing. "Well, that's what he said," Lottie concluded.

Aggie was stunned. It seemed that everything around her spun quickly and then fell into place. The gathering evening seemed suddenly translucent. There were the children, and now whatever happened was up to her.

It was late, and they were hungry. But she recalled a phrase she had sought strength in for days: It was the decent thing to do. It was the only thing that could be done.

"Time we made ourselves useful." She returned to the cave. "You, Jason, get Jed an' go down an' get Mr. Franklin's body. We're goin' to have us a funeral."

6

IT WAS NEARLY DARK WHEN THEY RETURNED. PULLING the travois themselves, they hauled the bodies up onto the prairie and buried them together in the swaying grass under a brilliant orange-and-yellow sunset. Jason joined with Jed Ambrose in attacking the sod with an enthusiasm born out of a need to do something steady and difficult. They put Moses in first, carefully removing him from the flag that still was wrapped around him and stretching his abused body out to form a cushion for the other two. Then, as the knot of children stood around the freshly turned earth, Aggie started reciting part of a psalm she indistinctly remembered. In a way it wasn't just for the three men, strangers, who lay beneath the prairie soil, it was also for those who had died during the previous days. It was for those who remained as well, for all their dreams. When she finished, she carefully folded the flag across her arms and turned to go.

Jason left his shovel standing upright at the head of the twin graves, and just as they walked off, back to the crossing, Aggie saw Lottie turn and hang something from the cross of the tool's handle: the agate.

"I hope you don't care that I done that," she said. "I know you said it was somethin' pretty to you, an' all. But I don't know why they brung us out here. They jus' did, an' I guess there was a reason for it." She looked at her father, whom Jason and Jed were now pulling on the travois back over the ridge and down to the crossing. She put both hands on her stomach. "Daddy told me that he thought 'most as much of Moses Franklin as he did of Cap'n Graham. He liked that Mr. Colfax, too. I'm glad they're all lyin' together, even if one is a nigger."

Aggie studied the fresh mound in the gloom for a moment. "He wasn't a nigger," she said. "He was a man. A colored man. A good man. Moses Franklin was his name. He didn't know much more 'bout this than we did, but he got us somewhere where we could be safe, an' I guess that was all he could do."

"WHAT'LL WE DO NOW?" Annie asked when they had returned to the caves. Aggie had seated herself on the abandoned whiskey kegs. There were nearly twenty left, she reckoned. Part of her wanted to break them open and dump their vile contents out into the crossing. Somehow, she understood, the bigoted, stupid men were right. The whiskey was the cause of all their troubles. Stolen as it was, it carried with it the taint of evil, not because of its value as an intoxicant or even an item for barter, not even because of its potential danger as a lure for savage Indians and bad men, but because it had to do with Jack's incessant planning and scheming. It was ill-gotten, she thought, and it should be destroyed.

But she lacked the energy to do it. She leaned wearily back against her wagon, trying to think, to plan, but thoughts wouldn't come.

"I asked, what'll we do now?" Annie repeated, and Aggie suddenly realized that her quiet, almost invisible little sister had asked the question.

"Gertie—Mama—always said we had to endure." Aggie sighed. "She always believed things would turn out, if we could just get through whatever was in front of us."

Annie looked out over the crossing. Her eyes were dark under a floppy man's hat she had put on during the rainstorm and had refused to take off.

"They's lots of bad men out here," she muttered. "I don't know if Mama knew that or not."

"I think she knew more 'bout bad men than you an' me'll ever learn," Aggie said.

Annie squinted through the darkness. "What's that?" she asked.

Out of the gloom of the gathering night, Aggie saw humps of moving figures crossing over the trail that ran down from the cedar-covered ridge.

"They've come back!" she declared. "Annie! Jason! Lottie! They've come back!"

She stumbled down to the edge of the creek and clasped her fists tightly together. Then she stopped. Instead of the familiar faces of the settlers who had abandoned them, she found herself watching three old Studebaker wagons clamoring down the gravelly trace. They were heavily loaded, she quickly noticed, bulging with barrels and boxes, and even in the darkness, she could see that several milk cows were tied to them. The two in front were drawn by mules who strained for the water just ahead, but the one in back, one that was almost empty, was pulled by a single ox. Black men drove the first two vehicles, and she spied women and small children peering through the darkness over their shoulders.

"It ain't them," Aggie said quietly. She felt a mixture of disappointment and confusion and fear churning inside her. She strained her eyes and saw sitting in the driver's seat of the ox-drawn wagon the determined, stiff, and proud figures of Kyle Ambrose and his son.

The wagons pulled up to the far edge of the creek, and the men dropped their reins and sloshed down into the water.

They knelt and drank deeply, and Jed Ambrose ran to his father and brother. The largest of the black men rose and crossed to where Aggie and the rest of the children had gathered to welcome them.

He was an old man, Aggie saw. His woolly hair was white and caught the early-evening starlight when he doffed his hat. "We're lookin' for a man of color, name of Franklin." He glanced up at Aggie's face and then stared at the ground when he reached the near bank. "Moses Franklin. S'posed to be fixin' up a town. Is this where he's at?"

"No," Aggie said, a smile forming on her pretty face, her eyes bright with tears as she shocked him by thrusting out her long fingers to grab his hand and hold it. "But you're welcome anyhow." She turned and swept her hand around behind her across the gravelly beach and limestone caves. "This here's . . . this here's Franklin's Crossing."

ABOUT THE AUTHOR

CLAY REYNOLDS, author of *The Vigil* and *Agatite*, is one of Texas' best-known writers. He is Novelist-in-Residence at the University of North Texas, and a frequent book critic for the *Dallas Morning News*, the *Fort Worth Star Telegram*, and the *San Antonio Express-News*. He lives in Denton, Texas.